Lo

TOM CLANCY
with MARK GREANEY

PENGUIN BOOKS

PENGUIN BOOKS

Published by the Penguin Group
Penguin Books Ltd, 80 Strand, London WC2R ORL, England
Penguin Group (USA) Inc., 375 Hudson Street, New York, New York 10014, USA
Penguin Group (Canada), 90 Eglinton Avenue East, Suite 700, Toronto, Ontario, Canada M4P 2Y3
(a division of Pearson Penguin Canada Inc.)
Penguin Ireland, 25 St Stephen's Green, Dublin 2, Ireland
(a division of Penguin Books Ltd)
Penguin Group (Australia), 707 Collins Street, Melbourne, Victoria 3008, Australia
(a division of Pearson Australia Group Pty Ltd)
Penguin Books India Pvt Ltd, 11 Community Centre, Panchsheel Park, New Delhi – 110 017, India
Penguin Group (NZ), 67 Apollo Drive, Rosedale, Auckland 0632, New Zealand
(a division of Pearson New Zealand Ltd)
Penguin Books (South Africa) (Pty) Ltd, Block D, Rosebank Office Park, 181 Jan Smuts Avenue,
Parktown North, Gauteng 2193, South Africa

Penguin Books Ltd, Registered Offices: 80 Strand, London WC2R ORL, England

www.penguin.com

First published in the United States of America by G. P. Putnam's Sons 2011
First published in Great Britain by Michael Joseph 2011
Published in Penguin Books 2012
001

Copyright © Rubicon, Inc., 2011
All rights reserved

The moral right of the authors has been asserted

Typeset by Palimpsest Book Production Limited, Falkirk, Stirlingshire
Printed in Great Britain by Clays Ltd, St Ives plc

B-format ISBN: 978-0-241-96194-0
A-format ISBN: 978-0-718-15970-2

www.greenpenguin.co.uk

MIX
Paper from
responsible sources
FSC™ C018179

Penguin Books is committed to a sustainable
future for our business, our readers and our planet.
This book is made from Forest Stewardship
Council™ certified paper.

ALWAYS LEARNING   **PEARSON**

Locked On

I

The Russians call their Kamov-50 helicopter gunship Chernaya Akula—Black Shark. The name suits it, because it is sleek and fast, and it moves with cunning and agility, and, above all, it is a supremely efficient killer of its prey.

A pair of Black Sharks emerged from a predawn fog bank and shot through the moonless sky at two hundred knots, just ten meters above the hard earth of the valley floor. Together they raced through the dark in a tight, staggered formation with their outboard lights extinguished. They flew nap-of-the-earth, following a dry streambed through the valley, skirting thirty kilometers to the northwest of Argvani, the nearest major village here in western Dagestan.

The KA-50s' contra-rotating coaxial rotors chopped the thin mountain air. The unique twin-rotor design negated the need for a tail rotor, and this made these aircraft faster, as more of the engine's power could then be applied to propulsion, and it also made these aircraft less susceptible to ground fire, as it reduced by one the points on the big machine where a hit will cause a devastating malfunction.

This trait, along with other redundant systems—a self-sealing fuel tank, and an airframe built partially from composites, including Kevlar—makes the Black Shark an exceptionally hearty combat weapon, but as strong as the KA-50 is, it is equally deadly. The two helos streaking toward their target in Russia's North Caucasus had a full load-out of air-to-ground munitions: Each carried four hundred fifty 30-millimeter rounds for their underbelly cannon, forty 80-millimeter unguided finned rockets loaded into two outboard pods, and a dozen AT-16 guided air-to-ground missiles hanging off two outboard pylons.

These two KA-50s were Nochny (night) models, and they were comfortable in the black. As they closed on their objective, only the pilots' night-vision equipment, their ABRIS Moving Map Display, and their FLIR (Forward-Looking Infrared Radar) kept the helos from slamming into each other, the sheer rock walls on either side of the valley, or the undulating landscape below.

The lead pilot checked his time to target, then spoke into his headset's microphone. *"Semi minute."* Seven minutes.

"Ponial"—Got it—came the reply from the Black Shark behind him.

In the village that would burn in seven minutes, the roosters slept.

There, in a barn at the center of the cluster of buildings on the rocky hillside, Israpil Nabiyev lay on a wool blanket above a bed of straw, and he tried to sleep. He tucked his head into his coat, crossed his arms tightly, and wrapped them around the gear strapped to his chest. His thick beard insulated his cheeks, but the tip of his nose stung; his gloves kept his fingers warm, but a cold draft through the barn blew up his sleeves to his elbows.

Nabiyev was from the city, from Makhachkala on the shore of the Caspian Sea. He'd slept in his share of barns and caves and tents and mud trenches under the open sky, but he had been raised in a concrete apartment block with electricity and water and plumbing and television, and he missed those comforts right now. Still, he kept his complaints to himself. He knew this excursion was necessary. It was part of his job to make the rounds and visit his forces every few months, like it or not.

At least he wasn't suffering alone. Nabiyev never went *anywhere* alone. Five members of his security detail were bunked with him in the cold barn. Though it was pitch-black, he could hear their snores and he could smell their bodies and the gun oil from their Kalashnikovs. The other five men who'd accompanied him from Makhachkala would be outside on guard, along with half of the local force. Each man awake, his rifle in his lap, a pot of hot tea close by.

Israpil kept his own rifle within arm's reach, as it was his last line of defense. He carried the AK-74U, a cut-down-barrel variant of the venerable but potent Kalashnikov. As he rolled onto his side to turn away from the draft, he reached out and put a gloved hand on the plastic pistol grip and pulled the weapon closer. He fidgeted for another moment like this, then rolled onto his back. With his boots laced on his feet, his pistol belt around his waist, and his chest harness full of rifle magazines strapped to his upper torso, it was damn hard to get comfortable.

And it was not just the discomforts of the barn and his gear that kept him awake. No, it was the gnawing constant worry of attack.

Israpil knew well that he was a prime target of the Russians, because he knew what they were saying about him that *he* was the future of the resistance. The future of his people. Not just the future of Islamic Dagestan, but the future of an Islamic caliphate in the Caucasus.

Nabiyev was a top-priority target for Moscow, because he'd spent virtually his entire life at war with them. He'd been fighting since he was eleven. He'd killed his first

Russian in Nagorno-Karabakh in 1993 when he was only fifteen, and he'd killed many Russians since, in Grozny, and in Tbilisi, and in Tskhinvali, and in Makhachkala.

Now, not yet thirty-five years old, he served as the military operational commander of the Dagestani Islamic organization Jamaat Shariat, the "Islamic Law Community," and he commanded fighters from the Caspian Sea in the east to Chechnya and Georgia and Ossetia in the west, all fighting for the same goal: the expulsion of the invaders and the establishment of Sharia.

And, *inshallah*—God willing—soon Israpil Nabiyev would unite all the organizations of the Caucasus and see his dream fulfilled.

As the Russians said, he *was* the future of the resistance.

And his own people knew this, too, which made his hard life easier. The ten soldiers in his security force, along with thirteen militants of the local Argvani cell—each and every one of these men would proudly lay down his life for Israpil.

He flipped his body around again to shield it from the draft, moving the rifle with him as he tried to find some elusive comfort. He pulled the wool blanket over his shoulder and flicked the straw from his beard that came with it.

Oh, well, he thought to himself. He hoped none of his men would have to lay down his life before daybreak.

Israpil Nabiyev drifted to sleep in the darkness as a rooster crowed on the hillside just above the village.

The crowing of the rooster interrupted the transmission of the Russian lying in the weeds a few meters away from the big bird. He waited for a second and a third call from the rooster, and then he put his lips back to the radio

4

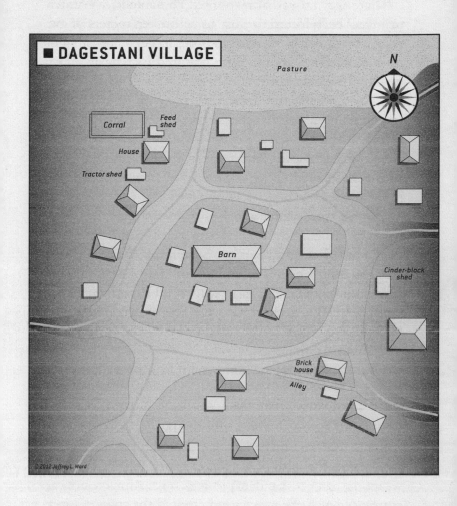

■ DAGESTANI VILLAGE

Pasture

N

Corral

Feed shed

House

Tractor shed

Barn

Cinder-block shed

Brick house

Alley

© 2012 Jeffrey L. Ward

attached to his chest harness. "Alpha team to overwatch. We have you in sight and will pass your location in one minute."

There was no verbal response. The sniper overwatch team had been forced to close to within ten meters of the edge of a cinder-block shed in order to get a line of sight on the objective, another one hundred meters on. They would not speak, not even whisper, so near to unfriendlies. The spotter just pressed his transmit button twice, broadcasting a pair of clicks as confirmation that he'd received Alpha's message in his earpiece.

Above the spotter, higher on the steep hillside, eight men heard the two clicks, and then they slowly approached in the black.

The eight men, along with the two-man sniper team, were troops from Russia's Federal'naya Sluzhba Bezopasnosti, their Federal Security Service. Specifically, this team was part of the Alpha Directorate of the FSB's Special Operations Center. The most elite of all Russian Spetsnaz units, the FSB's Alpha Group were experts in counterterror operations, hostage rescue, urban assault, and a vast array of additional deadly arts.

All the men in this unit were alpinists, as well, though they possessed more mountain training than they needed for this hit. The peaks behind them, toward the north, were much higher than the hills of this valley.

But it was the other training these men possessed that made them the ideal fit for the mission. Firearms, edged weapons, hand-to-hand, explosives. This Alpha team was composed of hard-core select killers. Silent movers, black operators.

Through the night the Russians had advanced slowly, all senses on alert despite the hardships their bodies were

6

forced to endure on the journey. The infiltration had been clean; in their six-hour insertion to their objective way-point they had smelled nothing but forest and had seen nothing but animals: cows sleeping upright or grazing unattended in meadows, foxes darting into and out of the foliage, even large horned ibex high on the rocks of sheer mountain passes.

Alpha Group were no strangers to Dagestan, but they had more experience operating in nearby Chechnya because, frankly, there were more terrorists to kill in Chechnya than in Dagestan, though Jamaat Shariat seemed to be doing its best to catch up to their Muslim brothers to the west. Chechnya was more mountains and forest, the major conflict zones of Dagestan more urban, but this location, tonight's Omega, or objective, split the difference. Wooded hills of rock all around a tight cluster of dwellings bifurcated by dirt roads, each road sporting a trench down the middle to drain the rainfall lower toward the river.

The soldiers had dropped their three-day packs a kilometer back, removing from their bodies everything save for tools of war. Now they moved with supreme stealth, low crawling through the pasture just above the village and then bounding in two-man teams through a corral. They passed their sniper team at the edge of the village and began darting between the structures: a feed shed, an outhouse, a single-family dwelling, and then a baked-brick and tin-roofed tractor shed. As they progressed, the men eyed every corner, every road, every black window, with their NODs—night observation devices.

They carried AK-105 rifles, hundreds of rounds of extra 5.45x39-millimeter cartridges in low-profile magazine chest rigs that allowed them to lie flat on the ground to hide from either a sentry's eyes or an enemy's gunfire.

Their green tunics and green vests of body armor were smeared with mud and covered with grass stains and wet with melted snow and the sweat of their exertion, even out here in the cold.

On their belts, holsters held .40-caliber pistols, the Russian Varjag model MP-445. A few also carried suppressed .22-caliber pistols to muzzle guard dogs with a hushed 45-grain hollow-point admonishment to the head.

They found their target's location, and they saw movement in front of the barn. Sentries. There would be others in nearby buildings; some would be awake, though their alertness would suffer at this time of the early morning.

The Russians made a wide arc around the target, cradling their rifles and crawling on their elbows for a minute before going to their hands and knees for two minutes more. A donkey stirred, a dog barked, a goat bleated, but nothing out of the ordinary for early morning in a farm village. Finally the eight soldiers spread around the back of the building, four groups of two, covering predetermined fields of fire with their Russian rifles, each weapon topped with an American EOTech holographic laser sight. The men peered intently at the red laser aiming reticle, or, more specifically, at the piece of window or door or alleyway that the red laser aiming reticle covered.

Then, and only then, did the team leader whisper into his radio: "In position."

If this had been a regular hit on a terrorist stronghold, Alpha would have arrived in big armored personnel carriers or helicopters, and airplanes would have rained rockets on the village while Alpha leapt from their APCs or rappelled to the ground from their transport helos.

But this was no regular hit. They'd been ordered to attempt to take their target alive.

FSB intelligence sources said the man they were after knew the names, locations, and affiliations of virtually all the jihadist leadership in Dagestan, Chechnya, and Ingushetia. If he was picked up and drained of his intelligence value, the FSB could deal a virtual death blow to the Islamic cause. To this end, the eight men who crouched in the dark twenty-five meters from the rear of the target building were a blocking force. The attackers were on their way, also on foot and moving along the valley from the west. The attackers would, if the real world bore any resemblance to the op-plan, lead the target into the trap set at the back of the barn.

The op-plan was hopeful, Alpha Group decided, but it was based on knowledge of militant tactics here in the Caucasus. When ambushed by a larger force, the leadership would run. It was not that the Dagestani and Chechens were cowards. No, courage they possessed in spades. But their leaders were precious to them. The foot soldiers would engage the attackers, manning outbuildings and sandbagged bunkers. From there a single man with a single weapon could hold off an entire raiding force for the time it took the leader and his close protection detail to flee into impenetrable mountains that they would likely know as well as they knew the contours of their lovers' bodies.

So the eight men of the Spetsnaz blocking force waited, controlled their breathing and the beating of their hearts, and prepared to capture one man.

In the administrative pouches of their ballistic plate carriers, each operator on the mission carried a beige laminated card with a photograph of the face of Israpil Nabiyev.

To be captured by these Russian Special Forces and

have your face match the photo of the man they sought would be an unenviable fate.

But to be captured by these Russian Special Forces and have your face *not* match the photo of the man they sought would be even worse, because these Russians needed only one man in this village alive.

2

The dogs were the first to react. A growl from a large Caucasian sheepdog started a chorus from other animals around the village. They had not alerted to the smell of the Russians, because the Spetsnaz men masked their scents with chemicals and silver-lined underwear that held in body odors, but the dogs sensed movement, and they began to bark in numbers that spared them from the .22 pistols.

The Dagestani sentries at the front of the barn looked around, a few waved flashlights in bored arcs, one yelled at the animals to shut up. But when the barking turned into a sustained chorus, when a few of the animals began howling, then the sentries stood, and rifles were brought to shoulders.

Only then did the thump of the rotors fill the valley.

Israpil had fallen asleep, but now he found himself up, standing before fully awake, moving before fully aware of what, exactly, had roused him.

"Russian choppers!" someone shouted, which was plain enough at this point, because Nabiyev could hear the thumping rotors across the valley and no one save for the Russians had any helicopters around here. Israpil knew they had seconds to flee, and he gave the order to do just that. The leader of his security force shouted into his radio, ordered the Argvani cell to grab their rocket-propelled grenade launchers and get into the open to engage the approaching aircraft, then he told the two drivers to bring their pickups right up to the front door of the barn.

Israpil was fully alert now. He thumbed the safety down on his short-barreled AK and moved toward the front of the barn with the weapon at his shoulder. He knew the sound of choppers would resonate in the valley for another minute before the Russians would actually arrive overhead. He'd spent the past two decades ducking Russian helos, and he was an expert on their abilities and shortcomings.

The first truck arrived at the front of the barn thirty seconds later. One of the guards outside opened the passenger door and then leapt up into the bed behind. Then two more men opened the front door to the barn, not twenty feet away.

Israpil was the third man out the door; he'd taken no more than two steps into the early-morning air when the supersonic cracks of small-arms fire erupted nearby. At first he thought it was one of his men shooting blindly into the dark, but a hot, wet slap of blood against his face dispelled him of that notion. One of his guards had been shot, his ripped chest spewing blood as he heaved and fell.

Israpil crouched and ran on, but more bursts of gunfire erupted, tearing through the metal and glass of the truck. The military commander of Jamaat Shariat saw muzzle flashes in the road next to a tin shack some twenty-five meters up the hill. The man standing in the truck bed fired a single shot of return fire before he tumbled off the side and down into the muddy ditch in the center of the road. The incoming gunfire continued, and Nabiyev recognized the reports as several Kalashnikovs and a single Russian PPM light machine gun. As he turned, he was showered with sparks from copper-jacketed bullets impacting the stone wall of the barn. He ducked lower and crashed into his protection detail as he shoved them back into the barn.

He and two others ran through the dark structure, shoved past a pair of donkeys tied on the western wall, making for a large window, but an explosion stopped them in their tracks. Nabiyev pulled away from his men, ran to the stone wall, and peered out through a wide crack that had been torturing him with a draft throughout the night. Above the village, hanging over the valley, two helicopter gunships arrived on station. Their silhouettes were just blacker than the black sky, until each fired another salvo of rockets from their pylons. Then the metal beasts were illuminated, the streaks of flame raced toward the village ahead of white plumes, and earthshaking explosions rocked a building a hundred meters to the west.

"Black Sharks!" he called out to the room.

"Back door!" one of his men yelled as he ran, and Nabiyev followed, although he now knew his position would be surrounded. No one would crawl for miles to hit this place, as he was now certain the Russians had done, only to forget to cut off his escape route. Still, there were no options; the next rocket salvo could hit this barn and martyr him and his men without allowing them the opportunity to take some infidels with them.

The Russians at the back of the barn stayed low and silent in their four groups of two, waiting patiently while the attack commenced up the hill and the Black Sharks arrived on station and began dispensing death through their rocket pods.

Alpha Group had positioned two of their men to secure their six-o'clock position, to keep an eye out for any mujahideen or armed civilians moving up the hill through the village, but the two-man team with that duty did not have line of sight on a small cinder-block shed just to the southeast of the easternmost pair of Spetsnaz operators. From a dark open window the muzzle of a bolt-action rifle inched out, aimed at the nearest Russian, and just as the back door of the barn opened, the bolt-action rifle barked. The Alpha Group man was hit in the steel plate on his back, and the round knocked him forward onto his chest. His partner spun toward the threat and opened up on the cinder-block shack, and the rebels escaping out the back of the barn had a moment's warning that they were stumbling into a trap. All five Dagestanis entered the open space behind the barn with their fingers on their triggers, Kalashnikov rounds spraying left and right, peppering everything ahead of them in the dark as they stumbled through the doorway.

One Spetsnaz officer took a chunk of copper—a hot, twisted fragment from a 7.62-millimeter ricochet off of a stone in front of him—directly into his throat, tearing through his Adam's apple and then severing his carotid artery. He fell backward, clutching his neck and writhing in his death throes. All pretense of a capture mission disappeared in that moment, and his men returned fire on the terrorists in the road as more mujahideen gunmen poured out of the doorway of the stone barn.

The leader of Nabiyev's security detail shielded him with his body when the Russians started shooting. The man was hit within a second of doing so, his torso riddled with 5.45-caliber rounds. More of Nabiyev's men fell around him, but the team kept up the fire as their leader desperately tried to get away. He dove to the side, rolled in the dirt away from the barn door, and then climbed back up to his feet while blasting the night with his AK-74U. He emptied his weapon while running parallel to the wall of the barn, then stumbled into a dark alleyway between two long tin storage huts. He had the sense he was alone now, but he did not slow his breakneck sprint to look around. He just kept running, amazed that he had not been hit in the same fusillade of bullets that had raked through his men. As he fled, he banged against both of the tin walls, and he stumbled again. His eyes were fixed on the opening twenty meters ahead; his hands struggled to pull a fresh magazine for his rifle from his chest rig. His rifle, its barrel blisteringly hot from his having just fired thirty rounds through it at full auto, steamed in the chilly morning.

Israpil lost his balance a third time as he seated the magazine and pulled back the Kalashnikov's charging handle; he fell all the way to his knees now, the rifle almost tumbling out of his gloved hands, but he caught it and regained his feet. He stopped at the edge of the tin storage shacks, looked around the corner, and saw no one in his path. The automatic gunfire behind him continued, and the sound of booming explosions from the helos' rockets impacting the hillside beat against the valley walls and bounced off them, each salvo assaulting his ears numerous times as the sound waves moved back and forth through the village.

The radio on the shoulder strap of his chest harness squawked as men shouted to one another all over the area. He ignored the communications and kept running.

He made his way into a burning baked-brick house lower on the hill. It had taken a Russian rocket through its roof, and the contents of the one-room home burned and smoldered. There would be bodies in here, but he did not slow to look around, he just continued on to an open back window, and once there, he leapt through it.

Israpil's trailing leg caught the window ledge, and he

tumbled onto his face outside. Again, he struggled to stand up; with all the adrenaline pumping through his body, the fact he'd tripped and fallen four times in the past thirty seconds did not even register.

Until he fell again.

Running on a straight stretch of dirt alleyway one hundred meters from the stone barn, his right leg gave out and he fell and tumbled, a complete forward roll, and he ended up on his back. It had not occurred to him that he'd been shot by the Russians at the barn. There was no pain. But when he tried again to climb to his feet, his gloved hand pushed on his leg and it felt slick. Looking down, he saw his blood flowing from a jagged hole in the threadbare cotton. He took a moment to stare at the blood, glistening from the firelight of a burning pickup truck just ahead. The wound was to the thigh, just above the knee, and the shimmering blood covered his camouflaged pants all the way down to his boot.

Somehow he made it back to his feet again, took a tentative step forward using his rifle as a crutch, and then found himself bathed in the brightest, hottest white light that he'd ever known. The beam came from the sky, a spotlight from a Black Shark two hundred meters ahead.

Israpil Nabiyev knew that if the KA-50 had a light trained on him, it also had a 30-millimeter cannon trained on him, and he knew that in seconds he would be *shahid*. A martyr.

This filled him with pride.

He exhaled, prepared to lift his rifle up to the big Black Shark, but then the butt of an AK-105 slammed into his skull from directly behind, and everything in Israpil Nabiyev's world went dark.

*

He awoke in pain. His head hurt, a dull ache deep in his brain as well as a sharp pain on the surface of his scalp. A tourniquet had been cinched tight high on his right leg; it stanched the blood flow from his wound. His arms were wrenched back behind him; his shoulders felt as if they would snap. Cold iron cuffs had been fastened on his wrists; shouting men pulled him this way and that as he was yanked to his feet and pressed against a stone wall.

A flashlight shone in his face, and he recoiled from the light.

"They all look alike," came a voice in Russian behind the light. "Line them up."

Using the flashlight's beam, he saw he was still in the village on the hill. In the distance, he heard continued, sporadic shooting. Mopping-up operations by the Russians.

Four other Jamaat Shariat survivors of the firefight were pushed up to the wall next to him. Israpil Nabiyev knew exactly what the Russians were doing. These Spetsnaz men had been ordered to take him alive, but with the dirt and perspiration and beards on their faces and the low predawn light, the Russians were having trouble identifying the man they were looking for. Israpil looked around at the others. Two were from his security detail; two more were Argvani cell members he did not know. They all wore their hair long and their black beards full, as did he.

The Russians stood the five men up, shoulder to shoulder, against the cold stone wall, and held them there with the muzzles of their rifles. A gloved hand grabbed the first Dagestani by the hair and pulled his head high. Another Alpha Group operator shined a flashlight on the mujahideen. A third held a laminated card next to the rebel's face. The photo of a bearded man looked back from the card.

"*Nyet,*" said someone in the group.

Without hesitation, the black barrel of a Varjag .40-caliber pistol appeared in the light, and the weapon snapped. With a flash and a crack that echoed in the alleyway, the bearded terrorist's head jerked back, and he dropped, leaving blood and bone on the wall behind him.

The laminated photo was held up to the second rebel. Again, the man's head was pulled taut to display his face. He squinted in the flashlight's white beam.

"*Nyet.*"

The automatic pistol appeared and shot him through the forehead.

The third bearded Dagestani was Israpil. A gloved hand pulled matted hair from his eyes and smeared dirt off his cheeks.

"*Ny*— . . . *Mozhet byt*"—Maybe—said the voice. Then, "I think so." A pause. "Israpil Nabiyev?"

Israpil did not answer.

"Yes . . . it is him." The flashlight lowered and then a rifle rose toward the two Jamaat Shariat rebels on Israpil's left.

Boom! Boom!

The men slammed back against the wall and then fell forward, down onto the mud at Israpil's feet.

Nabiyev stood alone against the wall for a moment, and then he was grabbed by the back of the neck and pulled toward a helicopter landing in a cow pasture lower in the valley.

The two Black Sharks hung in the air above, their cannons burping at irregular intervals now as they ripped buildings apart and killed humans and animals alike. They would do this for a few minutes more. They would not kill every last soul—that would take more time and effort than they wanted to expend. But they were doing their best to systematically destroy the village that had been hosting the leader of the Dagestani resistance.

Nabiyev was stripped to his underwear and carried down the hill, through the loud and violent rotor wash of an Mi-8 transport helicopter. The soldiers sat him on a bench and handcuffed him to the inner wall of the fuselage. He sat there sandwiched between two filthy Alpha Group men in black ski masks, and he looked out the open door. Outside, as dawn just began to lighten the smoke-filled air in the valley, Spetsnaz men lined up the bodies of Nabiyev's dead comrades, and they used digital cameras to photograph their faces. Then they used ink pads and paper to fingerprint his dead brothers-in-arms.

The Mi-8 lifted off.

The Spetsnaz operator on Nabiyev's right leaned in to his ear and shouted in Russian, "They said you were the future of your movement. You just became the past."

Israpil smiled, and the Spetsnaz sergeant saw this. He jabbed his rifle into the Muslim's ribs. "What's so funny?"

"I am thinking of everything my people will do to get me back."

"Maybe you are right. Maybe I should just kill you now."

Israpil smiled again. "Now I am thinking about everything my people would do in my memory. You cannot win, Russian soldier. You cannot win."

The Russian's blue irises glared through the eye ports of the ski mask for a long moment as the Mi-8 gained altitude. Finally he jabbed Israpil in the ribs again with his rifle and then leaned back against the fuselage with a shrug.

As the helicopter rose out of the valley and began heading north, the village below it burned.

3

Presidential candidate John Patrick Ryan stood alone in the men's locker room of a high school gymnasium in Carbondale, Illinois. His suit coat hung from a hanger on a rolling clothes rack next to him, but he was otherwise well dressed in a burgundy tie, a lightly starched cream-colored French-cuff shirt, and pressed charcoal dress pants.

He sipped bottled water and held a mobile phone to his ear.

There was a gentle, almost apologetic, knock on the door, and then it cracked open. A young woman wearing a microphone headset leaned in; just behind her Jack could see the left shoulder of his lead Secret Service agent, Andrea Price-O'Day. Others milled around farther down the hallway that led to the school's packed gymnasium, where a raucous crowd cheered and clapped, and brassy amplified music blared.

The young woman said, "We're ready whenever you are, Mr. President."

Jack smiled politely and nodded, "Be right there, Emily."

Emily's head withdrew and the door shut. Jack kept the phone to his ear, listening for his son's recorded voice.

"Hi, you have reached Jack Ryan Jr. You know what to do."

The beep followed.

Jack Sr. adopted a light and airy tone that belied his true mood. "Hey, sport. Just checking in. I talked to your mom and she said you've been busy and had to cancel your lunch date with her today. Hope everything is going okay." He paused, then picked back up. "I'm in Carbondale at the moment; we'll be heading to Chicago later tonight. I'll be there all day and then Mom will meet me in Cleveland tomorrow night for the debate on Wednesday. Okay . . . Just wanted to touch base with you. Call me or Mom when you can, okay? Bye." Ryan disconnected the call and tossed the phone onto a sofa that had been placed, along with the clothes rack and several other pieces of furniture, into the makeshift dressing room. Jack wouldn't dare put his phone back in his pocket, even on vibrate, lest he forget to take it out before walking onstage. If he did forget and someone called, he'd be in trouble. Those lapel microphones picked up damn near everything, and, undoubtedly, the press corps traveling with him would report to the world that he had uncontrollable gas and was therefore unfit to lead.

Jack looked into a full-length mirror positioned between two American flags, and he forced a smile. He would have been self-conscious doing this in front of others, but Cathy had been prodding him of late, telling him that he was losing his "Jack Ryan cool" when talking about the policies of his opponent, President Ed Kealty. He'd have to work on that before the debate, when he sat onstage with Kealty himself.

He was in a sour mood this evening, and he needed to shake it off before he hit the stage. He hadn't talked to his son, Jack Junior, in weeks—just a couple of short-and-sweet e-mails. This happened from time to time; Ryan Sr. knew he wasn't exactly the easiest person to get in touch with while out on the campaign trail. But his wife, Cathy, had mentioned just minutes before that Jack hadn't been able to get away from work to meet up with her in Baltimore that afternoon, and that worried him a little.

Though there was nothing unusual about parents wanting to stay in touch with their adult child, the presidential candidate and his wife had added reason for concern because they both knew what their son did for a living. Well, Jack Sr. thought to himself, *he* knew what his son did, more or less, and his wife knew . . . to an extent. Several months back, Sr. and Jr. had sat Cathy down with high hopes of explaining. They'd planned on laying out Jack Junior's occupation as an analyst and operative for an "off-the-books" spy agency formed by Sr. himself and helmed by former senator Gerry Hendley. The conversation had started off well enough, but the two men began equivocating under the powerful gaze of Dr. Cathy Ryan, and in the end they'd stammered out something about clandestine intelligence analysis that made it sound as if Jack Junior spent his days with his elbows propped on a desk reading computer files looking for ne'er-do-well financiers and money launderers, work that would expose him to no more danger than carpal tunnel syndrome and paper cuts.

If only that were the truth, Jack Sr. thought to himself as a fresh wash of stomach acid burned into his gut.

No, the conversation with his wife had not gone particularly well, Jack Sr. admitted to himself afterward. He'd broached the subject a couple of times since. He hoped he'd been able to peel back another layer of the onion for Cathy; just maybe she was beginning to get the idea that her son was involved in some real intelligence fieldwork, but again, Ryan Sr. had just made it sound like Ryan Jr. occasionally traveled to European capitals, dined with politicians and bureaucrats, and then wrote reports about their conversations on his laptop while sipping burgundy and watching CNN.

Oh, well, thought Jack. *What she doesn't know won't hurt her.*

And if she did know? *Jesus*. With Kyle and Katie still at home, she had enough on her plate without having to also worry about her twenty-six-year-old son, didn't she?

Jack Sr. told himself that worrying about Jack Junior's profession would be *his* burden, not Cathy's, and it was a burden that he had to shake off for the time being.

He had an election to win.

Ryan's mood brightened a little. Things were looking good for his campaign. The latest Pew poll had Ryan up by thirteen percent; Gallup was right there at plus eleven. The networks had done their own polling, and all three were slightly lower, probably due to some selection bias that his campaign manager, Arnold van Damm, and his people had not bothered to research yet because Ryan was so far ahead.

The electoral college race was tighter, Jack knew, but it always was. He and Arnie both felt he needed a good showing in the next debate to keep some momentum for the home stretch of the campaign, or at least until the last debate. Most races tighten up in the final month or so. Pollsters call it the Labor Day spread, as the narrowing in the polls usually begins around Labor Day and continues on until Election Day on the first Tuesday in November.

Statisticians and pundits differ on the reasons for this phenomenon. Was it that likely voters who had switched sides were now getting cold feet and returning to their original candidate? Could there be more independent thinking in the summer than there was in November, now closer to the time when answering a pollster's questions had actual consequences? Was it the near wall-to-wall news coverage on the frontrunner as Election Day approached that tended to highlight more gaffes for the leading candidate?

Ryan tended to agree with Arnie on the subject, as there were few people on earth who knew more about matters related to campaigns and elections than Arnie van Damm. Arnie explained it away as simple math. The candidate leading the race had more people polling in his favor than the candidate trailing. Therefore, if ten percent of both voters shifted allegiance in the last month of a race, the candidate with more initial voters would lose more votes.

Simple math, Ryan suspected, nothing more. But simple math would not keep the talking heads on television talking or the twenty-four/seven political blogs blogging, so theories and conspiracies were ginned up by America's bloviating class.

Ryan put down his water bottle, grabbed his coat and slipped it on, then headed for the door. He felt a little better, but anxiety about his son kept his stomach churning.

Hopefully, thought Ryan, Jack Junior was just out tonight enjoying himself, maybe on a date with someone special.

Yeah, Senior said to himself. *Surely that's all.*

Twenty-six-year-old Jack Ryan Jr. sensed movement on his right, and he spun away from it, twisted his body clear of the knife's blade as it made to plunge into his chest. As he continued his rotation he brought up his left forearm, knocked his attacker's hand away as he grabbed the man's wrist with his right hand. Then Ryan heaved his body forward, into his attacker's chest, and this sent the man tumbling backward toward the floor.

Jack immediately went for his gun, but the falling man took hold of Ryan's shirt and brought Ryan down with him. Jack Junior lost the space he'd created from his enemy that he needed to draw his pistol from his inside-the-waistband holster, and now, as they crashed to the floor together, he knew the opportunity was lost.

He'd just have to fight this battle hand to hand.

The attacker went for Jack's throat, fingernails digging into his skin, and again Jack had to knock away the threat with a violent arm sweep. The assailant flipped from a sitting position to his knees, and then hopped up again to his feet. Ryan was below him now, and vulnerable. With no other options, Jack went for his pistol, but he had to roll onto his left hip to free the weapon from its holster.

In the time it took to execute this move, his attacker had pulled his own gun from the small of his back, and he shot Ryan five times in the chest.

Pain stitched across Jack's body with the impact of the projectiles.

"Dammit!" he yelled.

Ryan was shouting at the pain, yes. But more than this, he was shouting with the frustration of losing the fight.

Again.

Ryan ripped the goggles off his eyes and sat up. A hand came down to assist him, and he took it, regained his feet, and reholstered his weapon—an Airsoft version of the Glock 19 that used compressed air to fire plastic projectiles that stung like hell but did not injure.

His "attacker" took off his own eye protection and then retrieved the rubber knife from the floor. "Sorry about the scratches, old boy," the man said, his Welsh accent obvious, even buried as it was behind his heavy breathing.

Jack wasn't paying attention. "Too slow!" he shouted at himself, his adrenaline from the hand-to-hand melee mixing with his frustration.

But the Welshman, in stark contrast to his American student, was calm, as if he'd just stood after sitting on a park bench feeding pigeons. "No worries. Go tend to your wounds and come back so I can tell you what you did wrong."

Ryan shook his head. "Tell me now." He was mad at himself; the cuts on his neck, as well as the scrapes and bruises all over his body, were the least of his concerns.

James Buck wiped a thin sheen of sweat from his brow and nodded. "All right. First, your assumption is off. There is nothing wrong with your reflexes, which is what you are talking about when you say you are too slow. Your speed of *action* is good. Better than good, actually. Your body can move as quick as you please, and your dexterity and agility and athleticism are quite impressive. But the trouble, lad, is your speed of thought. You are hesitant, unsure. You are thinking about your next move when you need to be full-tilt action. You are giving off subtle little clues with your thoughts, and you are broadcasting your next move in advance."

Ryan cocked his head, and sweat dripped from his face. He said, "Can you give me an example?"

"Yes. Look at this last engagement. Your body language did you in. Your hand twitched toward your hip twice during the fray. Your gun was well hidden in your waistband and under your shirt, but you revealed its existence by thinking about drawing it and then changing your mind. If your assailant didn't know you had a gun, he would have just fallen to the ground and climbed back up. But I already knew about the gun because you 'told' me about it with your actions. So when I started to fall back, I knew to pull you down with me so you wouldn't get the space you needed to draw. Make sense?"

Ryan sighed. It did make sense, though, in actuality, James Buck knew about the pistol under Ryan's T-shirt because James Buck had given it to Ryan before the exercise. Still, Jack conceded, an incredibly savvy enemy could possibly discern Ryan's thinking about making a play for a hidden weapon on his hip.

Shit, Ryan thought. His enemy would have to be almost psychic to pick up that tell. But that's why Ryan had been spending the vast majority of his nights and weekends with trainers hired by The Campus. To learn how to tackle the incredibly savvy enemies.

James Buck was ex-SAS and ex-Rainbow, a hand-to-hand and bladed-weapons expert, among other cruel specialties. He'd been hired by the director of The Campus, Gerry Hendley, to work with Ryan on his martial skills.

A year earlier, Ryan had told Gerry Hendley that he wanted more fieldwork to go along with his analytical role at The Campus. He'd gotten more fieldwork, almost more than he'd bargained for, and he'd done well, but he did not have the same level of training as the other operators in his organization.

He knew it and Hendley knew it, and they also knew their options for training were somewhat limited. The Campus did not officially exist, it did not belong to the US government, so any formal training by FBI, CIA, or the military was absolutely out of the question.

So Jack and Gerry and Sam Granger, The Campus's chief of operations, decided to seek other avenues of instruction. They went to the veterans in The Campus's stable of operators, John Clark and Domingo Chavez, and they sketched out a plan for young Ryan, a training regimen for him to undergo in his off-hours over the next year or more.

And all this hard work had paid off. Jack Junior was a

better operator for all the training he'd undergone, even if the training itself was humbling. Buck, and others like him, had been doing this all their adult lives, and their expertise showed. Ryan was improving, no question, but improving against men like James Buck did not mean defeating them, it merely meant "dying" less often and forcing Buck and the others to work harder in order to defeat him.

Buck must have seen the frustration on Ryan's face, because he patted him on the shoulder, a gesture of understanding. The Welshman could be vicious and cruel at times, but on other occasions he was fatherly, even friendly. Jack didn't know which of the two personalities was the "put-on," or if they were both necessary aspects of his training, a sort of carrot-and-stick approach. "Chin up, old boy," Buck said. "Heaps better than when you started. You've got the physical assets you need to handle yourself, and you've got the smarts to learn. We just have to keep working on you, continue to build on your technical proficiency and mind-set. You're already a sharper tack than ninety-nine percent of the blokes out there. But that one percent remaining are right bastards, so let's keep at it until we have you ready for them, all right?"

Jack nodded. Humility was not his strong suit, but learning and improving was. He was smart enough to know that James Buck was right, even though Jack wasn't crazy about the prospect of getting his ass kicked a few thousand more times in pursuit of excellence.

Jack put his eye protection back on. James Buck smacked the side of Ryan's head with his open hand playfully. "That's it, lad. You ready to go again?"

Jack nodded again, this time more emphatically. "Hell, yes."

4

Under the heat of the midday Egyptian sunshine, Cairo's Khan el-Khalili market overflowed with lunchtime diners and bargain shoppers. Food vendors grilled meat, and the heavy aroma wafted through the air; it mixed with the other smells as coffeehouses vented the scents of their brewed beans and the smoke from their hookah pipes out into the narrow winding alleyways that made up a warren of shops and tent stalls. The streets, alleys, and narrow covered passageways of the marketplace wrapped around the mosques and the stairways and sandstone walls of ancient buildings, and sprawled across a wide portion of the Old City.

This souk had begun its life in the fourteenth century as a caravanserai, an open courtyard that served as an inn for caravans passing through Cairo on the Silk Road. Now the ancient and the modern mixed together in a dizzying display in the Khan el-Khalili. Salespeople haggled in the middle of the narrow thoroughfares dressed in *salwar kameez* alongside other shopkeepers decked out in jeans and T-shirts. The thin tinny beats of Egyptian traditional music spilled out of cafés and coffeehouses and mixed with the techno music that blared from sales bays of stereo and computer vendors, creating a melody like that of a buzzing insect, save for the clay and goat-skinned drums and synthesized backbeats.

Vendors sold everything from handmade silver and copper wares and jewelry and rugs to flypaper, rubber sandals, and "I ♥ Egypt" T-shirts.

The crowd shifting through the alleys were young and old, black and white, Arab, Western, and Asian. A group of three Middle Eastern men strolled through the market, a portly silver-haired man in the center and two younger muscular men flanking him. Their pace was leisurely and relaxed. They did not stand out, but anyone in the market who paid attention to them for any length of time might well notice that their eyes shifted left and right more than those of the other shoppers. Occasionally, one of the younger men glanced back over his shoulder as they walked.

Just then, the man on the right turned quickly and checked the crowd in the alley behind. He took his time looking at the faces and hands and mannerisms of every-one in sight. After more than ten seconds, the muscular Middle Easterner finished his six-o'clock scan, turned back around, and picked up his pace so he could catch up with the others.

"Just three best buddies out for a lunchtime stroll." The transmission came through a small, nearly invisible earpiece secreted in the right ear of a man twenty-five meters behind the three Middle Easterners, a Western male in dirty blue jeans and a loose-fitting blue linen shirt who stood outside a restaurant, pretending to read the handwritten French menu posted by the door. He was American, thirtyish, with short dark hair and a scruffy beard. Upon hearing the radio transmission, he looked away from the menu, past the three men in front of him, and ahead into a dusty archway that led away from the souk. There, so deep in the cool shadows that he was only a dark form, a man leaned against a sandstone wall.

The young American brought the cuff of his blue linen shirt to his mouth as he swatted an imaginary fly from his face. He spoke into a small microphone secreted there.

"You said it. Goddamned pillars of the community. Nothing to see here."

The man skulking in the shadows pushed away from the wall, began strolling toward the alley and the three Middle Easterners, who were now just passing in front of him. As he walked he brought his hand to his face. In a second broadcast received in his earpiece, the American in the blue linen shirt heard, "Okay, Dom, I've got 'em. Shift one road over, overlap the target, and move up to the next choke point. I'll update you if he stops."

"He's all yours, Sam," Dominic Caruso said as he turned left, departing the alley via a side passageway that led up a staircase that emptied out on al-Badistand Road. Once he hit the larger street, Dom turned right and moved quickly through pedestrians and bicycles and motorized rickshaws as he maneuvered to get ahead of his target.

Dominic Caruso was young, fit, and relatively dark-complexioned. All these traits had served him in these past few days of surveillance here in Cairo. The latter, his skin and hair color, helped him blend in with a population that was predominately dark-haired and olive-toned. And the former, his fitness and relative youth, was helpful on this operation because the subject of his surveillance was what was known, in Dominic Caruso's line of work, as a hard target. Mustafa el Daboussi, the silver-haired fifty-eight-year-old man with the two musclemen serving as his bodyguards, was the focus of Dom's mission in Cairo, and Mustafa el Daboussi was a terrorist.

And, Dominic did not need to be reminded, terrorists did not often make it fifty-eight years on this earth by being oblivious to men following them. El Daboussi knew every countersurveillance trick in the book, he knew these streets like the back of his hand, and he had friends here in the government and the police and the intelligence agencies.

A hard target, indeed.

For Caruso's part, he wasn't exactly a debutant at this game himself. Dom had been tailing some scumbag or another for most of the past decade. He'd spent several years as a special agent in the FBI before being recruited into The Campus along with his twin brother, Brian. Brian had been killed the year before on a Campus black op in Libya. Dom had been there, he'd held his brother in his arms as he died, and then Dominic returned to The Campus, hell-bent on doing the hard, dangerous work that he believed in.

Dom stepped around a young man selling tea from a large jug hanging by a leather strap from his neck, and he picked up the pace, anxious to get to the next decision point for his target: a four-way intersection some hundred yards to the south.

Back in the alleyway, Caruso's partner, Sam Driscoll, followed the three men through the winding passageways, careful to keep his distance. Sam had decided that if he lost contact with his target, so be it; Dom Caruso was making his way forward to a choke point ahead. If el Daboussi disappeared between Sam's and Dom's positions they would look for him, but if they lost him today they would pick him up later, back at his rented house. It was better, it had been determined by the two Americans, to chance losing the target rather than to press their luck and run the risk of compromising themselves to their target or his protection detail.

El Daboussi stopped at a jewelry store; something had caught his eye in a dusty glass display case just inside the wide entrance. Sam continued forward a few yards and then stepped into the shadow of a canvas tent, under which young salesgirls sold chintzy plastic toys and other tourist kitsch. As he waited for his target to move on, he stepped deeper into the shade. He felt he blended well into the scenery, but a teenage girl in a chador saw him and approached with a smile. "Sir, you wanna sunglasses?"

Shit.

He just shook his head, and the girl got the message and moved on.

Sam Driscoll had the ability to intimidate with a glance. An ex-Ranger with multiple tours of duty in the sandbox and beyond, he'd been scooped up by The Campus after an introduction from Jack Ryan Sr. Driscoll had been chased from the military by Justice Department lawyers doing the bidding of a Kealty administration hungry for Sam's blood after a cross-border incursion into Pakistan left a few too many dead bad guys for Kealty's taste.

Driscoll would have been the first to agree that he'd violated those terrorist shitheads' civil rights by firing a .40-caliber hollow-point into each of their brainpans. But as far as he was concerned, he'd done his job, and no more than what was necessary for his mission.

Life's a bitch, and then you die.

Jack Sr.'s publicity of the Driscoll affair was enough to get the DOJ to drop the matter, but Ryan's recommendation along with John Clark's personal appeal to Gerry Hendley had gotten Sam hired into The Campus.

At thirty-eight, Sam Driscoll was several years older than Dom Caruso, his partner on this op, and even though Sam was in excellent physical condition, he wore his extra mileage on him, manifested in a graying beard, deep-set creases around his eyes, and a nagging old wound to his shoulder that he woke up to each and every morning. The injury had come in a firefight on the exfil during his Pakistan mission; a jihadist's AK round had shattered a rock in front of Driscoll's firing position, sending natural shrapnel into and through the Ranger's upper body.

The shoulder didn't bother him so much at the moment, the stiffness and soreness melted away with movement and exercise, and a couple hours of "foot follow" surveillance through Cairo's Old Town had given him plenty of both today.

And Driscoll was about to get some more exercise. He looked up and noticed el Daboussi was on the move again. Sam waited for a moment, and then stepped out into the alleyway to resume his tail of the silver-haired terrorist.

A minute later, Sam stopped again as his target entered a busy *kahwah,* a boisterous neighborhood coffeehouse ubiquitous in Cairo. Men sat in chairs around small tables that spilled out into the center of the alley; they played backgammon and chess and smoked hookah pipes and cigarettes while drinking thick Turkish coffee or fragrant green tea. El Daboussi and his men walked past these open-air tables and continued deep into the dark room.

Sam spoke softly into his cuff mike. "Dom, come back?"

"Yep," came the reply into Driscoll's earpiece.

"Subjects have stopped. They're in a coffeehouse on . . ." Sam scanned the walls and corners of the impenetrable market alleyway for a sign. Up and down the souk he saw stalls and canvas-covered kiosks but no signs referencing his exact location. Sam had had a better sense of direction humping through the mountains of Pakistan than he did right here in Cairo's Old Town. He chanced a surreptitious glance down to his map to get his bearings. "Okay, we just made a left off of Midan Hussein. I think we are still just north of al-Badistand. Say fifty meters from your location. Looks like our boy and his goons are going to sit and chat. How 'bout you come over here and we can split the coverage?"

"On the way."

While Sam waited for his backup, he wandered over to a chandelier shop and gazed appreciatively at a glass light fixture. In the reflection of a large crystal bauble he could see the front of the *kahwah* well enough to watch it in case his target left. But instead of anyone leaving, he saw three other men step into the *kahwah* from the opposite direction. Something about the look of the leader of this little pack gave him pause. Driscoll chanced a pass by the entrance, and he looked inside as if he was searching for a friend.

There, in the back against a stone wall, Mustafa el Daboussi and his men sat at a table right next to the new arrival and his men.

"Interesting," Sam said to himself as he wandered off a few yards away from the coffeehouse's entrance.

Dom arrived in the alleyway a minute later, shouldered up to Sam as both men picked through the wares of another tiny kiosk. Driscoll leaned over a table and pulled a pair of jeans out of a pile as if to look them over. He whispered to his partner. "Our boy is having a clandestine meet and greet with an unknown subject."

Dom did not react; he only turned to a cheap mannequin at the front of the stall and pretended to look at the tag on the vest the mannequin wore. While doing so, he looked past the plastic life-size figure and into the café across the street. Driscoll passed behind him closely. Dom whispered, "It's about damn time. We've been waiting for days."

"I hear you. Let's grab a table at the café across the way, maybe get some pictures of these jokers. We'll send them back to Rick and see if his geeks can ID them. The one in back looks like he's in charge."

A minute later, the two Americans sat in the shade under an umbrella in the open-air café that faced the *kahwah*. A waitress in a chador stepped up to the table. Dom took the lead with the ordering, much to the surprise of Sam Driscoll. *"Kahwaziyada,"* he said with a polite smile, and then motioned to himself and Sam.

The woman nodded and stepped away.

"Do I want to know what you just ordered us?"

"Two Turkish coffees with extra sugar."

Sam shrugged, stretched the tight scar tissue of his shoulder wound with a long, slow neck roll. "Sounds pretty good. I could use the caffeine."

The coffee came, and they sipped it. They did not look over at their target. If his security detail was any good, they would be evaluating the Westerners sitting across the alley, but probably only for the first couple of minutes. If Sam and Dom were careful to completely ignore them, then el Daboussi, his men, and the three other new arrivals would satisfy themselves that the Westerners were just a couple of tourists, sitting and waiting while their wives shopped the souk for rugs, and there was nothing to be concerned about.

Even though Sam and Dom were operational and in no small danger here spying on a terrorist, they enjoyed being outside, sipping coffee in the sunlight. For the past few days they'd gone out only at night, and then only in shifts. The rest of the time they'd operated from a studio apartment across from a posh walled residence rented by el Daboussi in the upscale Zamalek neighborhood. They had spent long days and nights peering through scopes, photographing visitors, and eating rice and lamb in quantities that caused both men to no longer be great fans of either rice or lamb.

But Sam and Dom, as well as their support team back at The Campus, both knew this work was important.

While Mustafa el Daboussi was Egyptian by birth, he'd been living in Pakistan and Yemen for the past fifteen years or so, working for the Umayyad Revolutionary Council. Now that the URC was in utter disarray due to the disappearance of their leader and a number of recent intelligence successes attributed to the CIA and other agencies, el Daboussi was back home, ostensibly working for the new government in some paper-pushing job in Alexandria.

But The Campus had learned there was more to this story. Jack Ryan Jr. had been going down the roster of known URC players, trying to find out where they were and what they were doing now, by using both classified and open-source intelligence. It was difficult work, but it had culminated with the discovery that MED, as Mustafa el Daboussi was known at The Campus, had been given a "no show" job by members of the Muslim Brotherhood who held the reins of power in parts of Egypt. Further investigation had indicated that MED had been placed in charge of setting up a pair of training camps near Egypt's border with Libya. According to classified CIA documents, ostensibly the plan was to have Egyptian intelligence train Libya's civilian militia into something of a real national defense force.

But some in the CIA, and *everyone* at The Campus, thought that was a lie. MED's history showed he had interest only in supporting terror against infidels; he didn't seem like a good fit to train a home guard in North Africa.

So when a coded e-mail from a MED associate's account was picked up by The Campus saying el Daboussi would spend a week in Cairo meeting with foreign contacts who would be helping him with his new "enterprise," Sam Granger, the chief of operations, immediately sent Sam Driscoll and Dominic Caruso over to get pictures of whoever came to see MED at his rented house, in hopes of getting a better idea of the real objective of these new camps.

While the Americans sat at their table and pretended to be nothing more than bored tourists, they talked about the Turkish coffee they were drinking. They agreed that it was incredibly good, even though they had identical stories about accidentally sucking down a mouthful of the bitter grounds that collected in the bottom of the cup the first time they tried it.

After their coffee was more than half put away, they returned to their operation. One at a time, they took turns glancing into the dim room across the alley. Just nonchalant little eye sweeps at first. After a minute of this, they recognized they were in the clear—none of the six men at the table gave them any unwanted attention.

Dom pulled his sunglasses case from his jeans and placed it on the table. He opened the top and then pinched the padding and fabric away from the inside of the lid. This revealed a tiny LCD screen, and the screen projected the image being captured by the twelve-megapixel camera secreted into the base of the case. Using his mobile phone, he transmitted a Bluetooth signal to the covert camera. With the signal he was able to increase the zoom on the camera until the LCD monitor displayed a perfectly framed image of the six men at the two tables. As el Daboussi and his two henchmen smoked *sheesha* and talked to the three men at the next table, Caruso took dozens of digital images through the surreptitious camera on the table by using the photo button on his mobile phone.

While Dom concentrated on his work, careful not to *look* like he was concentrating, Sam said, "Those new guys are military. The big guy in the middle, the one with his back to the wall, is a senior officer."

"How can you tell?"

"Because I was military, and I was *not* a senior officer."

"Right."

Driscoll continued. "Can't explain how I know, exactly, but he's at least a colonel, maybe even a general. I'd bet my life on it."

"He's not Egyptian, that's for sure," said Dom, as he slid the camera back into his pocket.

Driscoll did not move his head. Instead he studied the coarse, wet grounds in the bottom of his coffee cup. "He's Pakistani."

"That was my guess."

"We've got pictures, let's not push our luck," said Sam.

"Agreed," replied Dom. "I'm tired of watching other people eat lunch. Let's go find some food."

"Rice and lamb?" asked Sam morosely.

"Better. I saw a McDonald's by the metro."

"McLamb it is."

5

Jack Ryan Jr. pulled his Hummer into his designated parking space in the lot of Hendley Associates at 5:10 a.m. He struggled to climb out of the big vehicle. His muscles ached; cuts and bruises covered his arms and legs.

He limped through the back door of the building. He did not like coming in so early, especially considering how beat-up he was this morning. But he had important work that could not wait. At this moment there were four operatives in the field, and although he truly wished he were out there with them, Ryan knew it was his responsibility to provide them the best real-time intelligence he could in order to make their tough work, if not easier, at least not any harder than it needed to be.

He passed a security man at the reception desk in the lobby. As far as Jack was concerned, the guard was freakishly awake and alert at this rude hour.

"Morning, Mr. Ryan."

"Hey, Bill." Normally Ryan didn't come in until eight, and by then Bill, a retired Air Force Security Force master sergeant, had handed off his post to Ernie. Ryan had met Bill only a couple of times, but he seemed like he was born to do his job.

Jack Junior took the elevator up, shuffled through the dark hallway, dropped his leather messenger bag off in his cubicle, and headed for the kitchen. There he started a pot of coffee and then reached into the freezer and pulled out an ice pack that had been getting a lot of use of late.

Back at his desk while the coffee brewed, he lit up his computer and flipped on the lamp. Other than Jack, some IT guys who worked twenty-four/seven, a third-shift analytical/translation unit, and the security men on the first floor, the building would be dead for at least another hour. Jack sat, held the ice to his jaw, and put his head down on his desk.

"Shit," he mumbled.

Five minutes later, the coffeemaker dripped its last drop into the pot just as Ryan grabbed a mug from the cabinet; he poured steaming black liquid into it and hobbled back to his desk.

He wanted to go back home and lie down, but that was not an option. The after-hours training Ryan had been going through was kicking his ass, but he knew he wasn't in any real danger. His colleagues out in the field were the ones in peril, and it was his job to help them out.

And his tool to help them was his computer. More specifically, it was the data that the parabolic dishes on the roof and the antenna farm of Hendley Associates pulled out of the ether, the data the code breakers and a mainframe supercomputer decoded from the near constant haul of encrypted information. Jack's daily morning fishing expedition derived its fish from data traffic from CIA in Langley, from the National Security Agency at Fort Mead, from the National Counterterrorism Center at Liberty Crossing in McLean, from the FBI in D.C., and from a host of other agencies. Today he saw he had a particularly large pull to go through even this early in the morning. Much of it was traffic that came to Langley from friendly nations overseas, and this is what he'd arrived early to peruse.

Jack logged in to the NSA's Executive Intercept

Transcript first. The XITs, or "zits," would alert him to any big goings-on that he had missed since leaving work at six the previous afternoon. As his screen began filling with data, he took mental stock of what was going on today. The operational tempo, or OPTEMPO, here at The Campus had been going up precipitously in the past few weeks, so Jack found it harder and harder each morning to decide on a starting place for his day's duties.

The four Campus operatives out in the field were divided into two teams. Jack Junior's cousin Dominic Caruso was teamed with ex-Army Ranger Sam Driscoll. They were in Cairo, tailing a Muslim Brotherhood operative who, Jack and his fellow analysts at The Campus had reason to suspect, was doing his best to raise some hell. According to the CIA, the man had been setting up training camps in western Egypt and was purchasing weapons and ammunition from a source in the Egyptian Army. After that . . . Well, that was the problem. No one had been able to figure out what he was doing with the camps and the guns and the know-how he'd obtained working for the URC and other groups for the past two decades. All they knew was that he and his camps and his guns were in Egypt.

Jack sighed. Egypt, post-Mubarak. Pre-fucked-up free-fire zone?

The American media declared as fact that the changes in the Middle East would promote peace and tranquility, but Ryan, The Campus, and a lot of people in the know around the world thought it likely that the changes in the Middle East would usher in not moderation but rather extremism.

To many in the American media, people who thought such things were pessimists at best, and bigots at worst.

Ryan considered himself a realist, and for this reason he didn't run out into the street to praise the rapid change.

The extremists were out in force. With the disappearance of the Emir nearly a year earlier, all over the map the terrorists were shifting safe houses, allegiances, occupations, and even host nations.

One thing hadn't changed, though. Ground zero for the entire jihadist movement was still Pakistan. Thirty years ago, all the fledgling jihadists of the world flocked there to fight the Russians. Every male kid in the Islamic world past the age of puberty was offered a gun and an express ticket to paradise. Every boy younger than that was offered a place in a madrassa, a religious school that fed them and clothed them and gave them a community, but the madrassas set up in Pakistan taught only extremist beliefs and war-fighting skills. These skills were handy for the students, as these children were just being made ready to send into Afghanistan to fight the Russians, but the skill sets they'd learned, along with the madrassas' promotion of jihad, didn't leave them many options when the Russians left.

It was inevitable that when the Soviets quit Afghanistan, the hundreds of thousands of armed and angry jihadists in Pakistan would become an incredible thorn in the side of the government there. And it was equally inevitable that these armed and angry jihadists would push into the vacuum that was post-Soviet Afghanistan.

And thus began the story of the Taliban, which created the safe haven for Al-Qaeda, which brought Western coalition forces over a decade earlier.

Ryan sipped his coffee, tried to focus his thoughts back on his duties and away from the big geopolitical issues that governed all. When his dad made it back into the

White House, then his dad would have all that to worry about. Junior, on the other hand, had to deal with the comparatively tiny day-to-day ramifications of all those big problems. Small stuff, like ID'ing some mutt for Sam and Dom. They had e-mailed him another batch of pictures for him to look at. Pictures including some of the unknown Pakistani who had met with el Daboussi the day before.

Ryan forwarded that e-mail to Tony Wills, the analyst who worked in the cubicle next to Jack's. Tony would work on ID'ing the subject. For now, Jack knew he needed to concentrate on the other team in the field, John Clark and Domingo Chavez.

Ding and John were in Europe at the moment, in Frankfurt, and they were mulling over their options. They'd spent the last two days preparing a surveillance operation to monitor an Al-Qaeda banker who would be heading into Luxembourg for some meetings, but the man canceled his trip from Islamabad at the last minute. The men were all dressed up with no place to go, so Jack decided he'd spend some time this morning digging deeper into the background of the European bankers the URC man planned on meeting with, in the hopes of getting a fresh lead for his colleagues in Europe to check out before they packed up and came home.

For this reason, Jack had rolled in to work much earlier than usual. He did not want them to return with nothing to show for their trip; it was his responsibility to feed them the intel they needed to find the bad guys, and he'd spend the next few hours trying to find them some bad guys.

He scanned through the XITs and a proprietary software program created by Gavin Biery, The Campus's head of IT. Gavin's catcher program searched data strings following the wishes of the analysts here at The Campus. It allowed them to filter out much of the intelligence that was not relevant to their current projects, and for Jack this software had been a godsend.

Ryan opened a series of files with clicks of his mouse. While he did this, he marveled at the number of tidbits of intelligence that were coming on a one-way street from US allies these days.

It depressed him a little, not because he didn't want America's allies to share intel; rather, he was bothered because, these days, it was *not* a two-way street.

To most in the US intelligence community, it was an outrageous scandal that President Edward Kealty and his political appointees in top intelligence posts had spent the past four years degrading the US's abilities to unilaterally spy on other countries. Kealty and his people had instead shifted the focus of intelligence gathering, relying not on America's own robust spy services but instead relying on the intelligence services in foreign nations to provide information to the CIA. This was safer politically and diplomatically, Kealty correctly determined, although diminishing America's spy services was unsafe in every other respect. The administration had all but precluded nonofficial cover operators from working in allied nations, and CIA clandestine-services people functioning in overseas embassies found themselves hamstrung with even more rules and regs, which made the already difficult dance of their work nearly impossible.

The Kealty administration had promised more "openness" and "transparency" in the clandestine CIA. Jack Junior's father had written an op-ed in *The Washington Post* that suggested, in a manner that was still respectful to the office of the presidency, that Ed Kealty might want to look up the word *clandestine* in the dictionary.

Kealty's intel appointees had eschewed human intelligence, instead stressing signals intelligence and electronic intelligence. Spy satellites and drones were far, far safer from a diplomatic standpoint, so these technologies were implemented more than ever. Needless to say, longtime CIA HUMINT specialists complained, quite rightly saying that although drones do a spectacular job showing us the top of an enemy's head, they were inferior to human assets, who often could tell us what was *inside* the enemy's head. But these HUMINT proponents were seen by many as dinosaurs, and their arguments were ignored.

Oh, well, Ryan thought. *Dad will be in charge in a few months,* he was sure of it, and he hoped most or all of the damage done could be undone during his father's four-year term.

He pushed these thoughts out of his head so he could concentrate, and he took a long swig of quickly cooling coffee to help his still-sleepy mind focus. He kept clicking on the one-way overnight intelligence haul, paying special attention to Europe, as that was where Chavez and Clark were right now.

Wait. Here was something new. Ryan opened a file that sat in the inbox of an analyst at the CIA's OREA, the Office of Russian and European Analysis. Jack scanned it quickly, but something piqued his interest, so he went back and read it word for word. Apparently someone at DCRI, the French internal security arm, was letting a colleague at the CIA know that they'd gotten a tip that a "person of interest" would be arriving at Charles de Gaulle that afternoon. Not a big deal in itself, and certainly not something that would have been pushed into one of Jack's queries on its own, except for a name. The French intelligence source, not described in the message to the CIA but likely some form of SIGINT or HUMINT, gave them reason to suspect the POI, a man only known to the French as Omar 8, was a recruiter for the Umayyad Revolutionary Council. DCRI heard he would touch down at Charles de Gaulle Airport at 1:10 that afternoon on an Air France flight from Tunis, and then he would be picked up by local associates and taken to an apartment in Seine-Saint-Denis, not far from the airport.

It looked to Jack like the Frenchies did not know much about this Omar 8. They suspected he was URC, but he wasn't someone they were particularly interested in themselves. The CIA didn't know much about him, either—so little that the analyst at OREA had not even replied yet or forwarded the message to Paris Station.

Neither the CIA nor the DCRI had much information on this POI, but Jack Ryan Jr. knew all about Omar 8. Ryan had gotten his intelligence straight from the horse's mouth. Saif Rahman Yasin, aka the Emir, "gave up" Omar 8's identity the previous spring, while under interrogation by The Campus.

Jack thought about that for a second. Interrogation? No . . . It was torture. No sense calling it anything else. Still, in this case anyway, it had been effective. Effective enough to know Omar 8's real name was Hosni Iheb Rokki. Effective enough to know he was a thirty-three-year-old Tunisian, and effective enough to know he was not a recruiter for the URC. He was a lieutenant in their operational wing.

Jack immediately found it odd that this guy would be in France. Jack had read Rokki's file many times, as he had read the files of all the known players in all the major terrorist organizations. The guy was not known to ever leave

Yemen or Pakistan, except for rare trips home to Tunis. But here he was, flying into Paris under a known alias.

Weird.

Jack was excited by this nugget of intel. No, Hosni Rokki was no big fish in the world of international terror; these days, after the incredible degradation of the URC brought on by The Campus, there was only one URC operative who could be considered a serious player on an international level. That man's name was Abdul bin Mohammed al Qahtani, and he was the operational wing commander of the organization.

Ryan would give *anything* for a shot at al Qahtani.

Rokki was no al Qahtani, but, wandering around France, so far from his normal area of operations, he was certainly interesting.

On a whim, Jack clicked open a folder on his desktop that contained a subfolder on each and every terrorist, suspected terrorist, cutout, etc. This was not the database used by the intelligence community at large. Virtually all federal agencies used the TIDE, the Terrorist Identities Datamart Environment. Ryan had access to this massive file system, but he found it unwieldy and populated with way too many nobodies to be of any use to him. He referred to the TIDE when he was building his own folder, or Rogues Gallery, as he called it, but only for specific information on specific subjects. Most of the rest of the data for his Rogues Gallery was his own research, with odds and ends added on by his fellow analysts here at The Campus. It was a tremendous amount of work, but the effort itself had already paid dividends. As often as not, Jack found himself not needing to check his folder, because in the preparation of the files he had committed the vast majority of this information to memory, and he allowed himself to forget a tidbit of intel only once the man or woman had been confirmed dead by multiple reliable sources.

But since Rokki was not a rock star, Ryan did not remember all of the man's specs, so he clicked on Hosni Rokki's folder, took a look at the pictures of his face, scrolled down the data sheet, and confirmed what he already knew. As far as any Western intelligence agency was aware, Rokki had never been to Europe.

Jack then opened the folder of Abdul bin Mohammed al Qahtani. There was only one picture on file; it was a few years old, but the resolution was good. Jack didn't bother reading the data sheet on this guy, because Jack had written it himself. No Western intelligence agency had known anything about al Qahtani until after the capture and interrogation of the Emir. Once the man's name and occupation passed the Emir's lips, Ryan and the other analysts at The Campus went to work piecing together the history of the man. Jack himself took the lead on the project, and it was something he couldn't take much pride in, since the information they'd managed to compile after a year of work was so goddamned thin.

Al Qahtani had always been camera- and media-shy, but he became incredibly elusive after the disappearance of the Emir. Once they knew who he was, he seemed to just drop off the map. He'd stayed in the dark for the past year, until last week, that is, when fellow Campus analyst Tony Wills uncovered a coded posting on a jihadist website claiming al Qahtani had called for reprisals against European nations—namely, France—for passing laws outlawing the wearing of burkas and head scarves.

The Campus distributed that intel—covertly, of course—back out to the intelligence community at large.

Ryan connected the dots, such as they were. The head of URC ops wants to strike out at France, and within a week a junior achiever in the organization shows up in the country, apparently to meet with others.

Tenuous. Tenuous at best. Certainly not something that would normally make Ryan move operators to the area. Under normal circumstances, after this sighting he and his coworkers would just make a point of monitoring French intelligence feeds and CIA Paris Station traffic to see if anything else developed during Hosni Rokki's European vacation.

But Ryan knew Clark and Chavez were in Frankfurt, just a quick hop away. Further, they were geared up and ready to go for a surveillance op.

Should he send them to Paris to try to learn something from Rokki's movements or contacts? *Yes.* Hell, it was a no-brainer. A URC goon, out in the open? The Campus might as well find out what he was up to.

Jack grabbed his phone and pushed a two-digit code. It would be just after noon in Frankfurt.

While he waited for the connection to be made, Jack picked up his melting ice pack and held it to the back of his sore neck.

John Clark answered on the first ring. "Hey, John, it's Jack. Something popped up. It's not going to knock your socks off, but it looks semi-promising. How do you feel about taking a side trip to Paris?"

6

One hundred miles south of Denver, Colorado, on Highway 67, a 640-acre complex of buildings, towers, and fences sprawls across the flatlands in the shadows of the Rocky Mountains.

Its official name is the Florence Federal Correctional Complex, and its designation in the nomenclature of the Bureau of Prisons is United States Penitentiary Administrative Maximum, ADX Florence.

The Bureau of Prisons classifies its 114 prisons into five levels of security, and ADX Florence is alone at the top of this list. It is also in the *Guinness World Records* as the most secure prison in the world. It is America's tightest "supermax" prison, where the most dangerous, the most deadly, and the hardest-to-hold prisoners are locked away.

Among the security measures are laser trip wires, motion detectors, night-vision-capable cameras, automatic doors and fences, guard dogs, and armed guards. No one has ever escaped from ADX Florence. It is unlikely anyone has even escaped a cell at ADX Florence.

But as difficult as it is to get out of "the Alcatraz of the Rockies," it is perhaps equally hard to get in. There are fewer than 500 inmates at Florence, out of a total US federal prison population of more than 210,000. Most regular federal prisoners could more easily find acceptance to Harvard than Florence.

Ninety percent of ADX Florence's convicts are men who have been taken out of the population of other prisons because they pose a danger to others. The other ten percent are high-profile or special-risk inmates. They are housed, predominately, in general-population units that keep the inmates in solitary confinement for twenty-three hours a day but allow a level of nonphysical contact among the inmates and—via visits, mail, and phone calls—the outside world.

Ted Kaczynski, the Unabomber, is in the general-population D Unit, along with Oklahoma City conspirator Terry Nichols, and Olympic bomber Eric Robert Rudolph.

Mexican drug lord Francisco "El Titi" Arellano is housed at Florence in the general population as well, as is Lucchese mob family underboss Anthony "Gaspipe" Casso, and Robert Philip Hanssen, the FBI traitor who sold American secrets to the Soviet Union and then Russia for two decades.

The H Unit is more restrictive, more solitary, and here inmates face SAMs, Special Administrative Measures—Bureau of Prisons parlance for the rules for housing the especially difficult cases. In all of the federal prison system, there are fewer than sixty inmates under SAMs, and more than forty of them are terrorists. Richard Reid, the Shoe Bomber, spent many years in H until moving into D after good behavior and high-profile lawsuits. Omar Abdel-Rahman, "the Blind Sheikh," is in H Unit, as is Zacarias Moussaoui, "the twentieth hijacker." Ramzi Yousef, the leader of the cell that detonated the bomb in the World Trade Center in 1993, splits his time between H and even more restrictive quarters, depending on his shifting moods and behavior.

The men here are allowed just a one-hour visit to a one-man concrete recreation yard that looks like an empty swimming pool, and then only after undergoing a strip search and a walk in cuffs and leg irons while escorted by two guards.

One to hold the chains, the other to hold a baton.

Still, H Unit is not the highest-security wing. That is Z Unit, the "ultramax" disciplinary unit, where the bad boys go to think about their transgressions, should they violate any of their SAMs. Here there is no recreation and no visitors, and minimal contact with even the guards.

Remarkably, even Z Unit has a special section, where only the worst of the worst are sent. It is called Range 13, and at this moment only three prisoners are housed there.

Ramzi Yousef was put here for violations of his SAMs while in Z Unit, where he was staying due to violations of his SAMs in H Unit.

Tommy Silverstein, a sixty-year-old career inmate who was convicted of armed robbery in 1977, was put here long ago for killing two inmates and a prison guard at another maximum-security prison.

And a third prisoner, a male inmate who was brought here by masked FBI agents some months prior only after an existing Range 13 cell was specially sealed off from the rest of the ultramax subunit, making it even more restrictive. The new cell is known only to Range 13 personnel, and only two have seen the new resident's face. He is guarded not by BOP officers but by a special ad hoc unit from the FBI's Hostage Rescue Team, fully armed and armored paramilitary officers who observe their one prisoner through a glass partition twenty-four hours a day.

The HRT men know the inmate's true identity, but they do not speak it. They, and the few Range 13 personnel who are aware of this odd arrangement at all, refer to the man behind the glass only as Register Number 09341-000.

Prisoner 09341-000 does not have the twelve-inch black-and-white television allowed most other inmates. He is not allowed out of the room to go to the concrete rec yard.

Ever.

Most inmates are allowed one fifteen-minute phone call a week, provided they pay for it out of their own trust fund account, a prison banking system.

Prisoner 09341-000 has neither telephone privileges nor a trust fund account.

He has neither visitor nor mail privileges, either, nor access to the psychological or educational services afforded the other prisoners.

His room, his entire world, is eighty-four square feet, seven feet by twelve feet. The bed, the desk, and the immovable stool in front of the desk are poured concrete, and other than the toilet-sink combo designed to shut off automatically if intentionally plugged, there are no other furnishings in the cell.

A four-inch-wide window on the back wall of the cell has been bricked over so that the inmate inside has neither a view to the outside nor any natural light.

Prisoner 09341-000 is the most solitary prisoner in America, perhaps the world.

He is Saif Rahman Yasin, the Emir. The leader of the Umayyad Revolutionary Council, and the terrorist mastermind responsible for the deaths of hundreds in a series of attacks on America and other Western nations, and also the perpetrator of an attack on the West that easily could have killed one hundred times that number.

The Emir climbed up from his prayer rug after his morning *salat* and sat back on the thin mattress on his concrete bed. He checked the plain white calendar on his desk by his left elbow, and saw that today was Tuesday. The calendar had been given to him so that he could hand his laundry out through the electric-operated steel hatch for cleaning at the proper times. Tuesday, Yasin knew, was the day his wool blanket needed to go through the hatch to be cleaned. Dutifully he rolled it into a tight ball, walked past his steel one-piece toilet-and-sink unit, took another step that moved him past a shower that worked on a timer so that he would not be able to cover the drain and flood his cell.

One more step brought him to the window with the hatch. There, two men in black uniforms, black body armor, and black ski masks stared blankly through the Plexiglas back at him. On their chests, MP5 sub-guns hung at the ready.

They wore no badges or insignia at all.

Only their eyes were visible.

The Emir held their gazes, one after the other, for a long moment, his face not more than two feet from theirs, though both men were several inches taller. All three sets of eyes broadcast hatred and malevolence. One of the masked men must have said something on the other side of the soundproof glass, because two other masked and armed men sitting at a desk in the back of the viewing room turned their heads toward their prisoner, and one flipped a switch on a console. A loud beep rang out in the Emir's cell, and then the small access hatch opened below the window. The Emir ignored it, continued the staring contest with his guards. After a few seconds he heard another beep, and then the amplified voice of the man at the desk came from a speaker recessed in the ceiling above the Emir's bed.

The masked guard spoke English. "Put your blanket in the hatch."

The Emir did not move.

Again, "Put your blanket in the hatch."

Nothing from the prisoner.

"Last chance."

Now Yasin complied. He had made a small show of resistance, and here that was a victory. The men that had held him in those first weeks after his capture were long gone, and Yasin had been testing the fervency and resolve of his captors ever since. He nodded slowly, dropped his blanket into the hatch, and then the hatch shut. On the other side, one of the two guards close to the window retrieved it, opened it up and looked it over, and then walked toward the laundry basket. He walked past the basket and tossed the wool blanket into a plastic garbage can.

The man at the desk spoke into the microphone again: "You just lost your blanket, 09341. Keep testing us, asshole. We love this game, and we can play it each and every fuckin' day." The microphone switched off with a loud click, and the big guard returned to the glass to shoulder up next to his partner. Together they stood as still as stones, staring through the eyeholes in their masks at the man on the other side of the window.

The Emir turned away and returned to his concrete bed.

He would miss that blanket.

7

Melanie Kraft was having an exceptionally bad week. An intelligence reports officer with the Central Intelligence Agency, Melanie was only two years out of American University, where she received her B.A. in international studies, and her master's in American foreign policy. This, augmented with having spent five of her teenage years in Egypt as the daughter of an Air Force attaché, made her a nice fit for the CIA. She worked in the Directorate of Intelligence—more specifically in the Office of Middle East and North Africa Analysis. Principally an Egypt specialist, young Ms. Kraft was bright and eager, so she occasionally reached out a little from her daily duties to work on other projects.

It was this willingness to stick out her neck that now threatened to derail a career that was barely two years old.

Melanie was accustomed to winning. In language classes in Egypt, as a soccer star in high school and then during her undergrad years, and with perfect grades in school. Her hard work won her fawning appreciation from her professors and then exemplary performance reviews here at the Agency. But all her intellectual and professional success had come to a screeching halt one week ago today, when she leaned into her supervisor's office with a paper that she had put together on her own time.

It was titled "An Evaluation of Political Rhetoric by the Muslim Brotherhood in English and in Masri." She'd combed English and Egyptian Arabic (Masri) websites to chronicle the growing disconnect between Muslim Brotherhood public relations with the West and their domestic rhetoric. It was a hard-hitting but well-sourced document. She'd spent months of late nights and weekends creating and using phony profiles of Arab men to gain access to password-protected Islamist forums. She'd gained the trust of Egyptians in these "cyber coffee shops," and these men let her into the fold, discussed with her Muslim Brotherhood speeches at madrassas across Egypt, even told her of Mo-Bro diplomats going to other nations in the Muslim world to share information with known radicals.

She contrasted all she learned with the benevolent façade the Brotherhood was projecting to the West.

She finished her paper and handed it over to her immediate supervisor. He sent her in to Phyllis Stark, chief of her department. Phyllis read the title, nodded curtly, and then tossed the brief onto her desk.

This frustrated Melanie; she had expected some show of enthusiasm from her chief. As she'd walked back to her desk, she'd hoped, at least, that her hard work would get passed upstairs.

Two days later, she got her wish. Mrs. Stark *had* passed it on, someone *had* read it, and Melanie Kraft was called into a fourth-floor conference room. Her supervisor, her department chief, and a couple of suits from the seventh floor that she did not recognize were already there when she entered.

There was no pretense about the meeting at all. From the looks and gesticulations of the men at the conference table, Melanie Kraft knew she was in trouble even before she sat down.

"Miss Kraft, what is it you thought you would accomplish

with your moonlighting? What is it you want?" a seventh-floor political appointee named Petit asked her.

"Want?"

"Are you trying to get a new gig around here with your little term paper, or do you just want it to circulate around so that, if Ryan wins and brings in his own people, you will be the flavor of the month?"

"No." That had not occurred to her in the slightest. Theoretically, an administration change should have next to nothing to do with someone at her level in the Agency. "I just have been reading what we've been putting out on the Brotherhood, and I thought it could stand some countervailing data. There is open-source intelligence—you'll see in the brief I cited everything—that points to a much more ominous—"

"Miss Kraft. This isn't grad school. I'm not going to check your footnotes."

Melanie did not respond to that, but she didn't bother continuing her defense of her paper, either.

Petit continued, "You have overstepped your boundaries at a time when this agency is at its most polarized."

Kraft didn't think the Agency was polarized at all, unless the polarization was between the seventh-floor graybeards who stood to lose their jobs with a Kealty defeat and the seventh-floor graybeards who stood to move into better positions with a Ryan win. That world was far removed from her own, and she would have thought Petit could have seen that.

"Sir, it was not my intention to cause any rift here in the building. My focus was on the realities in Egypt, and the information that was—"

"Did you prepare this document while you were supposed to be working on your daily reports?"

"No, sir. I did this at home."

"We can open an investigation into you, to see if you used any classified resources to create—"

"One hundred percent of the information in that document is open-source. My fictitious Internet identities were not created from actual Agency legends. Honestly, there is nothing I have access to on a daily basis that would have been any help to me in preparing my paper."

"You have a strong opinion that the Brotherhood is nothing but a gang of terrorists."

"No, sir. That is not the conclusion of my paper. The conclusion of my paper is that the rhetoric in the English-speaking world runs counter to the Masri rhetoric put out by the same organization. I think we should just keep track of some of these websites."

"Do you?"

"Yes, sir."

"And you think we should do this because there has been an official finding of some sort, or you think we should do this because . . . because you just think we should do this."

She did not know how to answer.

"Young lady, the CIA is not a policy-making organization."

Melanie knew this, and the paper was not intended to steer US foreign policy toward Egypt in any direction, but instead to offer a dissenting view to conventional wisdom.

Petit continued, "Your job is to generate the intelligence product that you are asked to generate. You are not a Clandestine Services officer. You have stepped out of your lane, and you have done so in a way that looks very suspicious."

"Suspicious?"

Petit shrugged. He was a politician, and politicians

assumed everyone else thought only about politics as well. "Ryan is ahead in the polls. Melanie Kraft happens to—in her free time, no less—create her own covert operation, and thereby shoot off on a tangent that would serve the Ryan doctrine."

"I . . . I don't even know what the Ryan doctrine is. I am not interested in—"

"Thank you, Miss Kraft. That's all."

She'd walked back to her office humiliated but still too confused and angry to cry. But she cried that night back in her little apartment in Alexandria, and there she asked herself why she had done what she'd done.

She could see, even at her low level in the organization and with her limited view of the big picture, that the political appointees in the CIA were molding the intelligence product to suit the desires of the White House. Was her brief her own, small, bullheaded way to push back against that? In that moment of reflection the night of her fourth-floor meeting, she admitted that it probably was.

Melanie's father had been an Army colonel who instilled in her a sense of duty as well as a sense of individuality She grew up reading biographies of great men and women, mostly men and women in the military and government, and she recognized through her readings that no one rose to exceptional greatness exclusively by being "a good soldier." No, those few men and women who went against the establishment from time to time, only when necessary, were what ultimately made America great.

Melanie Kraft had no great ambition other than to stand out from the pack as a winner.

Now she was learning another phenomenon about standing out. Nails that stuck out often were hammered back into place.

Now she sat in her cubicle, sipping an iced coffee and looking at her screen. She'd been told the day before by her supervisor that her brief had been squashed, destroyed by Petit and others on the seventh floor. Phyllis Stark had angrily told her the deputy director of the CIA, Charles Alden himself, had read a quarter of it before he tossed it in the trash and asked why the hell the woman who wrote it still had a job. Her friends there at the Office of Middle East and North Africa Analysis felt for her, but they didn't want their own careers to be sidetracked by what they saw as an attempt by their colleague to leapfrog ahead of them by working on intelligence on her own time. So she became the office pariah.

Now she was, at twenty-five, thinking about leaving the Agency. Finding a job in sales somewhere that paid a bit more than her government salary, and getting the hell out of an organization that she loved but that clearly did not love her back at present.

Melanie's desk phone rang, and she saw it was an outside number.

She put down the iced coffee and picked up the receiver. "Melanie Kraft."

"Hi, Melanie. It's Mary Pat Foley at NCTC. Am I catching you at a bad time?"

Melanie almost spit her last swallow of coffee across her keyboard. Mary Pat Foley was a legend in the US intelligence community; it was impossible to exaggerate her reputation and the impact her career had had on foreign affairs or on women at the CIA.

Melanie had never met Mrs. Foley, though she'd seen her speak a dozen times or more, going back to her undergrad days at American. Most recently, Melanie had sat in on a seminar Mary Pat had given to CIA analysts about the work of the National Counterterrorism Center.

Melanie stammered out a reply: "Yes, ma'am."

"I *am* catching you at a bad time?"

"No, excuse me. You aren't catching me at a bad time." The young analyst kept her voice more professional than her emotions. "How can I help you today, Mrs. Foley?"

"I wanted to give you a call. I spent the morning reading your brief."

"Oh."

"Very interesting."

"Thank y— . . . How so?"

"What kind of response are you getting from the graybeards on the seventh floor?"

"Well," she said, as she frantically searched for the right words. "Honestly, I'd have to say there has been some pushback."

Mary Pat repeated the word slowly. "Pushback."

"Yes, ma'am. I did expect some reticence on the part of—"

"Can I take that to mean that you are getting your ass kicked over there?"

Melanie Kraft's mouth hung open for a moment. She finally closed it self-consciously, as if Mrs. Foley were sitting in her cube with her. Finally she stammered an answer. "I . . . I would say I have been taken to the woodshed over my work."

There was a brief pause. "Well, Ms. Kraft, I think your initiative was brilliant."

A return pause. Then, "Thank you."

"I have a team going over your report, your conclusions, your citations, looking for information relevant to the work we do here. In fact, I'm planning on making it required reading among my staff. Beyond the Egypt angle, it shows how someone can hit a problem from a different slant to shed new light on it. I encourage that from my people over here, so any real-world examples I can find are very helpful to me."

"I am very honored."

"Phyllis Stark is lucky to have you working for her."

"Thank you." Melanie realized she was just saying "Thank you" over and over, but she was so focused on not saying anything she would regret, it was all that came out.

"If you ever are looking for a change of pace, just come and talk to me. We are always on the hunt for analysts who aren't afraid to upset the apple cart by delivering the cold, hard truth."

Suddenly Melanie Kraft came up with something to say. "Would you be available this week sometime?"

Mary Pat laughed. "Oh, God. Is it that bad over there?"

"It's like I have leprosy, although I suppose if I had leprosy I'd at least receive get-well cards."

"Damn. Kealty's people over there are a disaster."

Melanie Kraft did not respond. She could riff on Foley's comment for an hour, but she held her tongue. That would not be professional, and she did actually consider herself to be apolitical.

Mary Pat said, "Okay. I'd love to meet you. You know where we are?"

"Yes, ma'am."

"Call my secretary. I'm pretty tied up through the week, but come have lunch with me early next week."

"Thank you," she said again.

Melanie hung up the phone and, for the first time in a week, she wanted to neither cry nor smash her fist through a wall.

8

John Clark and Domingo Chavez sat in their Ford mini-van and watched the apartment building through the rainy night. Both men held SIG Sauer handguns in their right hands, resting on their thighs. They kept the weapons low in the shadows but ready for quick use. In their left hands, Clark held thermal binoculars, Chavez a camera with a long-range lens. Crushed plastic coffee cups and gum wrappers filled a plastic bag on the floor below the passenger seat.

Though their weapons were drawn, they would do their best to avoid using them. Any shooting that might be necessary tonight would be defensive in nature, and the trouble wasn't likely to come from the terrorist assassin and his pals up the street in their safe house, which, in actuality, was a fourth-floor walk-up tenement flat. No, the immediate threat was the neighborhood itself. For the fifth time in the past four hours, a dozen-strong crowd of steely-eyed young men passed on the sidewalk next to their vehicle.

Chavez took a break from staring through the telephoto lens of his Canon at the lighted entryway of the apartment to watch the men pass. Both he and Clark kept their eyes on the group in their rearview mirror until they disappeared in the rainy night. When they were gone, Chavez rubbed his eyes and glanced around at his surroundings. "This sure isn't postcard Paris."

Clark smiled, reholstering his pistol in the shoulder rig

under his oiled canvas jacket. "We're a long way from the Louvre."

They were in the *banlieues*—the outer suburbs. The safe house was located in a housing project in the not inappropriately named Stains commune, in Seine-Saint-Denis, a *banlieue* of low-income residents, many of them poor immigrants from Morocco, Algeria, and Tunisia, North African nations from which France had imported millions of workers in the twentieth century.

There were housing projects all over Seine-Saint-Denis, but the two Americans had the misfortune tonight to find themselves on the outskirts of one of the roughest. Decrepit, graffiti-festooned concrete apartment buildings lined both sides of the street. Gangs of youth milled about the neighborhood. Cars blaring North African rap music drove by slowly, while rats scurried along the trash-strewn gutters next to the van and disappeared down the iron drains.

Earlier, during their afternoon and evening sitting in the minivan, the two Americans noticed that the neighborhood postman wore a helmet, lest items be thrown from the buildings onto his head just for kicks.

And they also noticed that they had not seen one police car in the neighborhood.

This part of town was too dangerous to patrol.

The Ford Galaxy Clark and Chavez sat in sported torn molding and a dented, rusted body, but its windows and windshield were intact and deeply tinted, all but obscuring the inside of the van. Most strangers in parked cars who sat for long on this street would have been harassed by the locals, but Clark had picked this vehicle out from a budget lot in Frankfurt because, he felt, it would give them the greatest chance for anonymity.

That said, it would take only one set of curious eyes to pick out this vehicle, to spend some time looking it up and down, and to realize that it was not from around here. Then the neighborhood heavies would surround it, smash the windows, and then loot and torch it. Chavez and Clark would race off before they let that happen, but they certainly did not want to give up their surveillance on the safe house two hundred meters up the street.

The Americans had positioned themselves on the avenue at the rear of the building, assuming that even with the bare minimum of tradecraft, the cell would, at least, know not to enter and exit the building on the other side, where there was a high-traffic boulevard and consequently many more eyes that could turn their way as they came and went.

Clark and Chavez knew that with one vehicle, there was no way to properly stake out their target location. Instead they decided they would just try to get pictures of whoever came and went, and to that end Chavez had a Canon EOS Mark II camera with a massive 600-millimeter super-telephoto lens that allowed him, with the attached monopod, to get incredibly detailed photographs of anyone who stepped into the lighted doorway at the back of the building in the distance.

Pictures would be helpful, but other than that, there was not much they could realistically accomplish here. A surveillance force of at least four vehicles and eight watchers would be needed to make any sort of respectable effort at covering all the access points of this target location, and a six-vehicle fleet, crewed with two men each, would be the bare-minimum protocol for mobile surveillance in an urban area like Paris when working with a target trained in countersurveillance, as Hosni Iheb Rokki certainly was.

Chavez and Clark had yet to see Hosni Rokki, but the odds looked good that he was, in fact, here. This was the address Ryan passed on from French internal security, and they had noticed a few young toughs milling around outside the apartment building like a security cordon, perhaps URC men but more likely a local gang hired by the target to act as a trip wire, should any police or other forces come snooping around.

And earlier in the evening, just after dark, Chavez had flipped his hoodie up over his short, dark hair, climbed out of the minivan, and performed a half-hour of foot reconnaissance. He'd made a wide, arcing circle of the apartment building, and strolled through a few parking lots, a playground that looked like it was used these days primarily by glue-sniffers and heroin users, and through the ground level of a four-story parking garage. He then made his way back to the black Ford Galaxy.

Immediately after Chavez climbed in, Clark had asked, "What's the word?"

"Same three or four guys downstairs at the back of the building. Four guys at the front entrance, too."

"Anything else?"

"Yep. We aren't the only ones interested in that apartment."

"No?"

"Beige Citroën four-door. This side of the road, in the parking lot on the other side of that building there on the left. Male driver. Female passenger. Both black, in their thirties."

"Surveillance," Clark said. Chavez wouldn't have mentioned them if they weren't.

"Yeah. They were subtle enough, but they have line of sight on Rokki's place, and we've got eyes on the entrance to that parking lot and didn't see the car arrive, which means they've been there since before we got here. So, yeah, they are definitely watchers. Who do you think they are?"

"DCRI would be my first guess. If I'm right about that, then there will be more cars around here; they probably have a surveillance box set up, but I doubt we're inside it. They are probably closer than we are because they won't all need to have eyes on the target. They would just tuck into the parking lots and stay in comms with each other. I'm glad the French are watching these guys, but I sure as hell wish they had some stronger measures on their plate. It would be nice for them to pick Rokki up, give him a shake, and see what falls out."

"Keep dreaming, John. Not the French. The CIA used to do a little of that, before Kealty put the kibosh on offending terrorists."

"Heads up, Ding," John said suddenly. A pair of young toughs walked by on the left from behind. Both men slowed and looked into the van. John and Ding were somewhat concealed behind the heavy tint, but they were by no means invisible. Clark stared back at the two young African immigrants for a long moment.

Then the men walked on.

Clark's steely-eyed gaze had won the encounter, but they were prepared if they had to actually talk to the locals. The two American spies never worked any operation without a plausible cover for action, a reason to be in a location other than the actual motive. Both men had worked under so many covers over the years, oftentimes preparing themselves on the fly, that they possessed the abilities of well-trained actors.

The cover for this op, should they be pulled out of the vehicle by police or internal security or even a well-armed neighborhood drug gang, was clever in both its simplicity and plausibility. Clark and Chavez were, if anyone demanded to know, American private investigators watching the flat of a woman who cleaned the home of a wealthy American living in the Latin Quarter. According to their story, their employer suspected the cleaning lady of stealing his valuables and then fencing them from her flat.

It would bear short-term scrutiny only, but nine times out of ten, that was enough.

One by one, the lights turned off on the fourth floor of the ramshackle building two hundred yards up the street. Clark looked through his binoculars through the rain.

"It's ten-thirty. Is it bedtime?" Clark asked Chavez.

"Maybe so."

Moments later, a Renault van passed Clark and Chavez's position; it slowed at the target building and then pulled to the front door and stopped.

"Maybe not," said Chavez now, and he readied his camera on the monopod, focused it on the area of light near the back door.

A minute later, a man exited the lobby of the building, walked directly to the light on the wall by the door, and unscrewed the bare bulb. The entire scene went dark.

"Son of a bitch," muttered Chavez.

Clark kept his eyes on his thermal binoculars, and they picked up the white-hot silhouette of the man who'd unscrewed the lightbulb as he walked down to the street and shook the hand of the driver of the Renault. He then spoke into a mobile phone, and soon four more ethereal silhouettes appeared from the back door of the dark building.

Chavez had given up on his camera for now, and instead he held a thermal monocular up to his eye. He saw the ghostly white figures exiting the building, and could tell they were four men, and he could see they pulled rolling bags and carried briefcases.

"Can you ID Rokki?" Chavez asked.

"Not positively through these thermal optics," said Clark. What he could discern, although just barely, was that the four men with the luggage all wore suits and ties.

The driver of the van and the man who'd unscrewed the lightbulb helped the four travelers get their bags into the back of the vehicle. The interior light came on as they opened the tailgate. It wasn't enough light for long-range camera work, but the two Americans were able to get a better look at the men and their luggage.

"Is that Louis Vuitton?" Chavez asked, his eyes peering through his camera's high-powered lens.

"I wouldn't know," admitted Clark.

"Patsy made me look at handbags for two hours in London once. I'm pretty sure that's the same design. Even Louis Vuitton handbags can run over a grand; can't imagine how much those big rolling suitcases go for."

The four men climbed efficiently into the van. They moved like a team as they found their seats and shut the door, extinguishing the lights.

"The tallest guy looks like he could be Hosni Rokki, but I can't be certain," Clark said.

"Whoever they are, they look like they're heading back to Charles de Gaulle."

"Maybe," said Clark. "But it seems odd Hosni would fly into town just to meet up with three guys, then fly right back out. I think something else is going on."

Chavez said, "This time of night there is no way we can tail them without being compromised. If these jokers are any good, they are going to spot us. It's a shame we don't have any more vehicles to split up the coverage."

Clark looked ahead to the entrance of the parking lot where Chavez had noticed the surveillance team during his recon. "Maybe we do. If the French have a fixed surveillance operation around the target, then I'm willing to bet they have a mobile surveillance operation ready to go. Maybe we can just piggyback on them."

"What do you mean?"

"I'm thinking we can stay back, away from the target, and do our best to pick out the vehicles following him. If we can manage to stay behind the DCRI backing car, we can follow the target without being spotted."

"So we tail the tail."

"Right. You up for it?"

Ding Chavez just nodded. "Sounds like fun."

The Renault van with the driver and the four men in suits turned around in the street and began heading back in Chavez and Clark's direction. The Americans sat patiently as the vehicle passed. They did not start their vehicle; instead they just packed up their gear and waited for the van to turn left some seventy-five yards behind them.

Both men knew what to expect next.

"Here we go," said Chavez calmly. "Let's see who's working the night shift at DCRI."

For a moment all was still on the dark street, until one by one the headlights of three vehicles lit up the night. An ancient four-door Toyota in the parking lot of the building ahead and to the right of Clark and Chavez's position, a black Subaru station wagon facing their position but on the other side of the street and a good hundred yards past Rokki's abandoned flat, and a white Citroën mini-truck that faced the apartment forty yards past Clark and Chavez. One after the next, all three vehicles pulled out into the street and turned down three different roads, all toward the south.

Seconds after this, the beige Citroën with the black couple pulled into view, made a left and then a right, and headed off in the direction of all the other cars.

When it was dark and quiet again, Clark still did not start the Ford; he drummed his fingers on the steering wheel for a moment.

Ding was confused by this at first, but then it dawned on him. "That looked pretty bush league for French intelligence. They wouldn't have all left together like that unless they were trying to draw out countersurveillance. There's one more out here somewhere."

"Yep," said Clark. "There is a trigger vehicle. Somebody who has eyes on this street right now." He paused. "Where would *you* be, Ding?"

"Easy. I like that parking garage that I walked through. If I could get in and out without too much fuss, I'd plant my trigger car on the second level so I could see the street and Rokki's building."

Just then, some thirty seconds after the last surveillance vehicle disappeared from the dark road, headlights lit up the second level of the parking garage, right where Ding and John were looking. It was a four-door sedan; neither of the Americans could see more than the hood and windshield and the glowing lights as the car backed up, turned around, and then headed down the ramp to the exit that led out to the boulevard.

John Clark started his engine and then pulled out into the street.

"Good call," Chavez said.

"Even a blind squirrel finds a nut from time to time."

"Roger that."

9

They caught up to the beige Citroën and stayed several car lengths behind it after determining it to be the backing car, the vehicle trailing behind the lead of the mobile surveillance unit. The Citroën would be in radio contact with the rest of the detail, and all the follow vehicles would move in and out of formation to change out the command vehicle, the name given to the vehicle directly tailing the target. Other cars and trucks would be racing ahead on side streets so they could naturally fill in the slots of the running box surveillance.

As they drove, the two Americans kept their eyes peeled, just in case there were more units in the French security detail around or behind them that they didn't ID at the target location.

For several blocks they suspected a brown bread truck was involved in the tail. It wove through traffic and seemed to mirror the movements of the beige Citroën, but John and Ding ultimately ruled it out when it pulled up to a large commercial bakery and parked in a loading bay.

They also had their eyes on a black Suzuki motorcycle, driven by a man in a black leather outfit and black helmet. Bikes were great for surveillance work on congested streets, and although there were other motorcycles on the road, they'd first noticed this Suzuki a few minutes after leaving the target location. They couldn't be sure, but both men decided they'd keep track of the black bike.

After no more than five minutes on the road, Chavez

and Clark had their answer to the question of whether or not the target was headed to Charles de Gaulle Airport when the chase car continued on south past the Autoroute du Nord.

"CDG is the other way," said Clark. "We're heading into town."

"You're doing pretty good for a blind squirrel."

Clark nodded, then noticed the Citroën sedan pulling ahead. "Looks like the backing car is rotating up."

Seconds later the white mini-truck appeared ahead of them from a side street. It was now the backing vehicle of the mobile fleet, so Clark and Chavez followed it.

The black Suzuki did not move around in the surveillance formation, it just stayed a bit ahead of John and Ding as it headed into Paris. This ruled it out as part of the DCRI unit.

A steady rain began to fall as the procession reached Paris proper, passing into the Eighteenth Arrondissement. They turned to the east once, then took another turn that led them due south. Clark flipped the Ford Galaxy's windshield wipers to their highest setting so he and Chavez could get the clearest look through the rainy night at the taillights of the car ahead. Within minutes the mini-truck increased its speed and disappeared into the night, but not before a black Honda four-door pulled out of the parking lot of a fast-food restaurant and headed in the same direction as Clark and Chavez.

"Must be the car from the parking garage," Chavez said.

Clark nodded appreciatively. "This detail is damn good. If we didn't know they were here, we'd never spot them."

"Yeah, but it's going to tighten up for them, and for us, as we get deeper into the city. Wish we had a clue where Rokki was heading."

Just then, as if on cue, the Honda four-door slowed behind a Mercedes that pulled out of a private garage below a luxury apartment building. John was in the left lane, and it was clear ahead of him except for the black Suzuki, so he calmly switched lanes to put himself a few cars directly behind the Honda, so he wouldn't have to pass him. But upon doing this, he noticed the black Suzuki had pulled into traffic behind the Honda as well. It was an obvious move to stay behind the DCRI backing vehicle.

Both men, their minds wired to pick up on tradecraft much more subtle than a maneuver like this, noticed the Suzuki's action. Chavez said, "Shit, that bike *is* with the follow team."

"And that guy isn't half as slick as his buddies," said Clark.

"You think he's spotted us?"

"No. He may be looking for guys behind Rokki to see if Rokki has countersurveillance vehicles, but we've got to be a quarter-mile back. We should be good."

They passed into the Ninth Arrondissement, and the backing car of the surveillance detail changed three times in quick succession. As Chavez had said, with more intersections and stop signs to cut down the distance between the follow team and the target, and more buildings and cars to obstruct the follow team's line of sight, the surveillance crew was having to work harder and harder to stay in position behind their target without being spotted. It seemed like all the chase vehicles were scrambling, with the exception of the Suzuki. He stayed just ahead of Clark and Chavez as if fixed behind the backing cars.

There are three types of countersurveillance: technical, passive, and active. Technical countersurveillance meant, normally, electronic means such as the target using radio scanners to listen for short-range radio traffic from a surveillance detail. It was the most rare form of countersurveillance, as encrypted digital radios were the norm these days, and picking up transmissions was nearly impossible without special equipment and a good deal of time.

Passive countersurveillance was the easiest to employ, as it required nothing more than the target's eyes and knowledge of what kinds of cars and methods would be used against them. The Renault target vehicle would be employing passive countersurveillance measures, as it was certainly full of men with their eyes peeled for a tail. But passive was also the easiest to defeat, because a large surveillance fleet could move their vehicles around in a pattern that meant no one vehicle would spend much time close enough to be spotted.

Active countersurveillance meant just that: performing some action to draw out any surveillance tail. If the Renault pulled to the side of the road quickly, any followers would have to either stop or drive on by, possibly compromising their mission. If the Renault started going down quiet side streets or alleys or driving through parking lots, any followers would have to reveal themselves to stay with the target.

But neither of these active measures was the worst-case scenario for a following force. No, the worst-case scenario was exactly what happened to the DCRI unit Clark and Chavez tailed right as they passed into the Eighth Arrondissement.

"Heads up!" Chavez shouted when he saw the DCRI's Subaru station wagon pull too quickly to the side of the road, and then turn down a narrow alley. There was no reason for the backing car to make such a maneuver unless he'd just gotten a warning on his radio that the target vehicle had made a U-turn and was now racing back toward the trailing cars in the surveillance detail.

It was a dramatic security sweep that was not uncommon for a team heading toward a covert mission, but the Renault had tricked the DCRI by not using any other active measures before their U-turn, thereby lulling the followers into thinking the target wouldn't try anything so extreme.

Clark and Chavez did not pull to the side of the road; there was no way they could manage that without compromising themselves to the DCRI team, if not to the target vehicle itself, whose headlights they now could see a hundred yards ahead.

"Just have to roll on by," Clark said, and he did just that, keeping to the same lane, the same speed. He didn't turn his head when the target vehicle passed; instead he just kept going, arriving at the Avenue Hoche and continuing southwest.

Chavez said, "Look who else kept going." The black Suzuki motorcycle continued on, still in front of Clark and Chavez. "He had plenty of time to pull off before Rokki made it back this far if he's got comms with the rest of the team."

Clark nodded. "Unless he's not with the French. He's with Rokki. He was watching for a tail."

"He's URC?"

"Looks like it."

"No way he missed the backing car pulling off."

"No way at all. DCRI are burned."

"Do you think DCRI will continue the follow?"

"They have at least five cars in the set, probably more. They'll pull in the one or two that the Renault didn't just

pass, and they'll try to tail him with that. We've got to figure Rokki and his guys are just about at their destination."

A minute later, Clark and Chavez sat at an intersection
on the wide Boulevard Champs-Élysées. They'd managed
to allow the Renault van to slip back in front of them
with the luck of a minor traffic accident that slowed the
flow on the boulevard and a couple of red lights that
stopped it cold. They avoided checking their rearview
mirrors to look for the DCRI; they knew two men in a
vehicle who kept checking their mirrors would likely be
spotted by trained surveillance professionals.

The Renault turned off the Champs-Élysées, made a
few more turns, and then found its way to the tree-lined
Avenue George V. As the target vehicle slowed in front
of them, Clark said, "Looks like we're here."

Chavez looked down to the GPS on his iPhone.

"Just up ahead on the right is the Four Seasons hotel."

Clark whistled. "Four Seasons? That's pretty swanky
for a lieutenant in the URC and his three buds."

"Isn't it, though?"

The Renault van did, in fact, pull over just a few car
lengths from the front of the luxurious hotel. Clark drove
by as one man climbed out of the van and opened his
umbrella, then began walking toward the entrance.

Clark made a right at the corner and then quickly pulled
to the sidewalk. "Go check it out."

"On it," Ding said as he slid out of the passenger seat
of the Galaxy minivan. He entered the hotel via an
employee entrance.

Clark circled the block, and when he returned, Chavez
was standing in the rain by the employee entrance. He
climbed back into the Galaxy. "One guy just checked in
to one suite. Reservation under the name Ibrahim. Two

nights. I didn't get the room number, but I heard the desk clerk call a porter and tell them to take them to their suite. The rest of the team is coming in right now. They have all the luggage we saw when they got in the van."

"Were you able to ID Rokki?"

"Sure did. That was him with the umbrella. He spoke French. Bad French, but that's the only kind I know."

Clark and Chavez drove off, west on the Avenue Pierre 1er de Serbie. Clark shook his head in wonder. "So a URC gunman picks up three mutts and a bunch of gear in the ghetto and moves them straight into a suite at the Four Seasons."

Chavez just shook his head. "A suite here must cost five grand a night. Can't believe the URC is billeted here unless—"

Clark was nodding; his reply was distant: "Unless it's part of an op."

Chavez sighed. "These guys are about to go loud."

"Within a day. The Seine-Saint-Denis safe house was a staging area. The Four Seasons *is* the mission. We don't have much time."

"Wish we had a better idea what their target was."

"They can hit anything in Paris from here. We can tail them till the moment they act, but that's too risky. Depending on what's in those bags, Hosni Rokki could be planning to assassinate a high-profile VIP staying at the Four Seasons, rake the US consulate with machine-gun fire, or blow up Notre Dame."

"We can tip off the French."

"Ding, if we had any idea who or what the target was, then we could alert the right people and have the target moved or the location shut down. But just telling the French cops that a group of shady bastards are in a particular suite at the Four Seasons? No . . . Think about it. They won't want an incident, they won't want to violate anyone's rights, so they'll make some gentle inquiries with the hotel—"

Ding finished the thought. "Meanwhile, these mutts run out with some det cord and Semtex and take out the Eiffel Tower and everyone in it."

"You got it. DCRI is tailing them already. We have to work under the assumption that that is all the heat this cell of tangos is going to get for now."

"So we take them down?"

Clark thought it over. "We haven't had an opportunity like this since the Emir. Ryan says Rokki isn't that big a deal by himself, but if he's here doing a job for al Qahtani, you can bet he knows more about al Qahtani than we do."

"You want to bag him?"

"It would be nice. We can stop his hit, kill the other guys in his cell, and then snag him for a little chat."

Chavez nodded. "I like it. Don't guess we have time to wait around."

"No time at all. I'll make the call. We're going to need some help to pull this off."

10

Jack Ryan Jr. held an ice pack to his face. He'd just taken an elbow to the upper lip. It was followed with a "Sorry, old boy" by James Buck, a not-quite-apology that did nothing to improve the mood in the spartan training room. Jack knew the "accidental" elbow had been delivered purposefully.

Buck was playing a one-man version of the good cop/ bad cop routine. This was some strategy to keep Jack Junior on his toes; Jack himself recognized this. And it worked. One minute Buck was telling Ryan how great he was doing; the next he was choking him out from behind.

Jesus, Jack thought. *This sucks.* But he realized how amazing this training was from a standpoint of imparting information and teaching his mind and body to react to unpredictable threats. He was smart enough to realize that someday, some *much* later date after the bruises healed, he would appreciate the hell out of James Buck and his split personality.

Buck's philosophy of teaching pushed mind-set as much as it stressed his tactics. "No such thing as a fair fight, lad. If one of the fighters is fighting 'fair,' then the fight won't last long. The dirtier bastard will always win."

Ryan began to find himself transforming under the weight of the ex-SAS man's "dirty" tactics. A few weeks back he'd grappled and thrown straight punches and hooks. Now as often as not, he used his opponent's clothing against him, twisted him in excruciating arm bars, and even jabbed at his Adam's apple.

Ryan's body was covered in bruises from head to toe, his joints had been twisted and wrenched, and scratches crisscrossed his face and torso.

He could not say he'd won more than a few of the hundred or so encounters he'd had against Buck, but he recognized his incredible improvement over the past month.

Ryan was mature enough and smart enough to recognize what was happening. Buck had nothing personal against him at all. He was just doing his job, and his job consisted of first breaking Ryan down.

And he was doing a hell of a job at that, Jack confessed.

"Again!" shouted Buck, and he began crossing the teak floor, approaching his student. Ryan quickly put the ice pack down on a table and prepared himself for another encounter.

Someone called from the dojo's office. "James? Phone call for Ryan."

Buck's eyes had narrowed in concentration for the impending attack. Upon hearing the distraction he stopped, turned toward the man in the office. "What did I bloody tell you about calls whilst we're in training?"

Jack's body tensed. His trainer was ten feet away; two quick steps and he'd be in arm's reach. Ryan thought about launching himself toward his trainer at this moment, when his eyes were diverted. It would be a dirty shot, but Buck encouraged just exactly that.

"It's Hendley," came the voice from the office.

The Welshman sighed. "Right. Off you go, Ryan," he said as he turned back to the young American.

Ryan's amped-up body relaxed. *Damn.* He could have totally waylaid Buck, and, from the look Buck was giving him now, the hand-to-hand and edged-weapons instructor knew it, too. His surprised eyes realized he'd come a half-second from getting his ass handed to him by his young student.

James Buck smiled appreciatively.

Ryan recovered, wiped a little blood from his nose with the back of his hand. He walked toward the office and the telephone, careful to hide the fact that Buck's last kick to the inside of his knee had left residual pain there, lest Buck see Jack's injury and exploit it in their next melee.

"Ryan."

"Jack, it's Gerry."

"Hi, Gerry."

"Situation in Paris. The Gulfstream is fueling up at BWI as we speak. There will be gear bags on board, a folder on the table with your documents, some credit cards and cash, and further instructions. Get there as quick as you can."

Ryan kept his face impassive, though he felt like a school kid who'd just been let out for summer vacation in February. "Right."

"Chavez will call you on the way and have you go through some equipment that he's ordered that will be on board."

"Got it." *Paris,* Jack thought. *How great is that?*

"And Jack?"

"Yeah, Gerry?"

"This one could get rough. You will *not* be going to provide analysis. Clark will use you as he sees fit."

Jack quickly admonished himself for thinking about beautiful girls and outdoor cafés. *Get your head in the game.*

"I understand," he said. He handed the phone to Buck. The Brit took it and listened. Jack thought the older man looked like a lion watching a gazelle escape.

"I'll be back," Ryan said as he turned toward the locker room.

"And I'll be waiting, boyo. Might want to get that dodgy knee sorted whilst you're on holiday, because my boot will be hunting for that weak spot upon your return."

"Great," Jack mumbled as he disappeared through the door.

Dom Caruso and Sam Driscoll sat on a pair of cots they'd stationed by the window of their studio apartment in Cairo's Zamalek neighborhood. They sipped Turkish coffee that Sam had made in a metal pot on the stove, and watched the property on an adjacent hillside a few blocks away.

Throughout the evening, el Daboussi had received only one visitor. Caruso had taken a few pictures of the car, an S-class Mercedes, and he'd caught the tag. He'd e-mailed the images to the analysts at The Campus, and they'd reported back in minutes that the vehicle was registered to a high-level Egyptian parliamentarian who, until just nine months ago, was a member of the Muslim Brotherhood living in exile in Saudi Arabia. Now he was back home and helping to run the country. This was all well and good, Dom thought, unless and until he began cavorting with a known former URC trainer with experience in the Al-Qaeda camps of Afghanistan, Pakistan, Yemen, and Somalia.

Shit, Caruso said to himself, and then, aloud, "Hey, Sam. I watch American TV. They say the Muslim Brotherhood only want democracy and equal rights for women. What gives with their midnight meetings with jihadists?" He was being facetious, of course.

"Yeah," said Sam, picking up on the false naiveté. "I thought the Mo-Bros were the good guys."

"Right," said Dom. "I saw some nutjob on MSNBC say that the Muslim Brotherhood used to be terrorists, but now they are as benign as the Salvation Army in the US Just another religious-based organization that only wants to do good."

Sam didn't say anything.

"No opinion?"

"I tuned you out when you said MSNBC."

Dom laughed.

Caruso's Thuraya Hughes satellite phone chirped, and he checked his watch as he answered it. "Yeah?"

"Dom, it's Gerry. We're going to have to pull you out. Clark and Chavez need some help in Paris right away."

Caruso was surprised. He knew Clark and Chavez were working an op in Europe, but last he'd heard, their target had jetted back to Islamabad.

"What about Sam?" Dom asked. Driscoll eyed him from the cot on the other side of the tiny darkened room.

"Sam, too. The situation in Paris is the kind that is going to need the type of help you and Driscoll can provide. Ryan is on the way there in the jet. He's got everything you will need."

Caruso hated to leave this op, the guy they'd seen in the market meeting with MED, the one Driscoll pegged for a Pakistani general, had not yet been ID'd. He'd love to hang around until the intel nerds at The Campus got a hit on the man's face. But despite his high hopes for this mission, he said nothing. If John Clark and Ding Chavez needed help, then, Dom knew, there was definitely something serious brewing over in Europe.

"We're on the way."

Jack Ryan Jr. sat in the principal's seat of a business jet that streaked at 547 nautical miles per hour through the thin air 47,000 feet above and 41 miles southeast of Gander, Newfoundland.

He was the only passenger of the aircraft. The three crew members—pilot, first officer, and flight attendant—had mostly kept to themselves in order to let Ryan read a thick binder that had been left for him on one of the leather cabin chairs.

While he read, he sipped a glass of California cabernet and picked absentmindedly at a sausage plate.

His laptop was open in front of him, as well, and he'd virtually held the handset of his seat's phone to his neck for most of the past hour, talking to Clark in Paris, and to various operations and intelligence men at The Campus in Maryland. He also spoke briefly with Driscoll, who, along with Caruso, was at that moment boarding a flight from Cairo to Paris.

Ryan would be finished with this part of his evening's work within a couple of hours, but he already knew he wouldn't be getting any sleep on this transatlantic flight. There was a large amount of gear on board that he'd have to go through while getting directions from Clark and Chavez on the phone in order to make sure everything was ready to go as soon as he touched down in France.

And once he got all that done, if it wasn't too late, he needed to call his mom and dad. He'd been so busy lately, he'd canceled a lunch with his mom and his brother and sister, Kyle and Katie, when Mom was home from the campaign.

Actually, he thought as he took a sip of cabernet, that day he had not really been too busy to get away for lunch. No, it was a big red cut on the bridge of his nose, courtesy of James Buck, that had caused him to call off the get-together at the last minute. Since then, though, it had been ten-hour days at the office and then three to four hours in the dojo before staggering home, into a bath filled with Epsom salts, chugging a few gulps of Budweiser, before crashing on the sofa in his Columbia, Maryland, apartment.

As the jet raced over the eastern shores of Newfoundland now, flying on a heading that would take it across the Atlantic and to the continent before dawn there, Ryan finished a twenty-minute cram session over a map of the Eighth Arrondissement neighborhood where the Four Seasons George V was located. The one-way alleyways and the large, wide boulevards and avenues would take days to memorize properly, but he had to do his best, to become as familiar as possible with the area before the team went to work there. He had been informed by Clark that he would be the "wheel man," the driver, though Clark also warned him that they were such a small force he would undoubtedly be called on for other things.

Perhaps even things that required the use of the Glock 23 .40-caliber pistol that had been left on the aircraft for him.

Jack reached for a printed layout of the Four Seasons hotel itself to study the floor plan of the building, but he turned away, took a moment to look up at the high-definition moving map monitor on the cabin wall to check his time of arrival. He saw he'd land in Paris at 5:22 a.m.

Jack sipped his wine and took a moment more to appreciate the beautifully appointed cabin. This jet was still new, and he had not yet gotten accustomed to sitting in it.

This was The Campus's newest toy, a Gulfstream G550 ultra-long-range corporate jet, and it filled a couple of extremely important needs for the fledgling off-the-books intelligence organization. Since the capture and interrogation of the Emir, the operational tempo of their work had gone through the roof as they'd turned into more of an intelligence gathering force and less of an assassination squad. The five operators, as well as the top brass and some of the analytical team, found themselves with increasing regularity heading all over the world to conduct surveillance on targets or to track leads or to perform other necessary tasks.

Commercial flights worked just fine ninety percent of the time, but on occasion Hendley and his chief of operations, Sam Granger, needed to move a man or men extremely quickly from the D.C./Baltimore metro area to some far-off point, usually so they could get eyes on a target who might be in place for only a short period of time. Commercial carriers flying from Washington Dulles, Ronald Reagan Washington National, and Baltimore Washington International airports had dozens of daily direct international flights, and hundreds more locations could be accessed from these airports with just a single connection, but occasionally the three to twelve added hours of time needed to get through airport security and customs, wait for delayed flights, make connections, and anything else that every commercial airline passenger is subject to just wasn't going to allow The Campus to accomplish its mission. So Gerry Hendley began looking for a private jet that would suit the needs of his organization. He established an ad hoc committee of in-house personnel to meet and decide on the exact requirements that would fit the bill. Money was not an object, though it was Hendley's job to grumble to the aircraft committee to keep it reasonable and to not spend one cent more than was required for them to find what they needed.

The group reported back to Gerry with their findings after several exhaustive weeks of research and meetings. The speed, size, and range they required could be accomplished by several ultra-long-range corporate jets made by Dassault, Bombardier Aerospace, Embraer, and Gulfstream Aerospace. Of these, it was determined the perfect aircraft for their needs would be the new Gulfstream 650.

It was not lost on Hendley that the 650 was also the most expensive aircraft of those in the running, but the statistics in its favor were convincing. Hendley began looking for a 650 but immediately realized the pickings were slim. The Campus wanted to keep the purchase of the jet as quiet and as low-key as possible, and sales of the new 650s were simply generating too much interest in the corporate aircraft community. He reconvened the committee, and they settled, if one could call choosing the second most luxurious and advanced aircraft in that class as *settling,* on the Gulfstream Aerospace G550, a model that was not yet ten years old and still very much top-of-the-line. Immediately, quiet feelers were sent out into the market by Hendley and other executives in The Campus.

It took nearly two months, but the right aircraft did come along. It was a seven-year-old G550 that had been owned previously by a Texas financier who'd been sent to prison for knowingly working with Mexico's Juárez Cartel. The government had liquidated the financier's assets, Gerry had gotten a call from a friend at DOJ who was involved in the auction, and Hendley was delighted to learn he could get the airplane at a price far lower than what the aircraft would have gone for at open sale.

The Campus then arranged the purchase via a shell company based in the Cayman Islands, and the aircraft was delivered to a fixed-base operator at a regional airport near Baltimore.

Once Gerry and his executives went out to see the plane in person for the first time, all agreed they'd gotten a hell of a deal on a hell of a jet.

With a 6,750-nautical-mile range, their G550 could fly anywhere on earth with only a single refueling stop, transporting as many as fourteen people in comfort as the aircraft's two Rolls-Royce engines propelled them at .85 mach.

Those in the cabin during long-haul flights had access to six leather seats that folded down to turn into beds, a pair of long couches aft of the chairs, and all manner of high-tech communications throughout. There were flat-screen satellite televisions, broadband multi-link coverage over North America, the Atlantic, and Europe, as well as two Honeywell radio systems and a Magnastar C2000 radiotelephone for those in the cabin.

There were even several features built into the craft to reduce jet lag of the passengers, a critical factor for Hendley, considering he might be rushing men into harm's way without any time whatsoever to acclimate themselves to their new surroundings. The large, high windows delivered much more natural light than regular commercial aircraft or even other high-end corporate jets on the market, and this helped to reduce the physiological effects of a long flight. Further, the Honeywell Avionics environmental systems refreshed one hundred percent of the oxygen every ninety seconds, reducing the risk of airborne bacteria that might slow his men during their missions. The environmental systems also held the pressurization inside the cabin three thousand feet below a commercial aircraft flying at the same altitude, and this reduced jet lag upon arrival, as well.

Hendley's friend at DOJ had mentioned something else in their conversations about the plane. The original owner, the crooked moneyman, had been flying to Mexico City in his jet, then stuffing bags of US currency into hidden compartments built throughout the craft by Colombian engineers, and then taking everything up, over the border, and into Houston. From there, the cash was distributed to low-level operatives in the Juárez Cartel, who took the cash, minus a small percentage, to Western Unions across the state of Texas. These Mexicans wired the money back down to accounts in Mexican banks, thereby laundering it. The Mexican banks in turn made wire transfers to anywhere in the world the *narcos* wanted it sent; purchasing drugs from South America, bribing government officials and police throughout the world, buying guns from militaries, and anointing themselves with the finest in luxuries.

Gerry had listened politely to this explanation of the money-laundering process although he understood the movement of world currency, both illegal and legal, better than all but a few. But what really got his attention was the existence of these secret stash compartments in his new jet. Once the aircraft was delivered to the fixed-base operator at BWI, a dozen employees of The Campus and a maintenance team at the FBO spent a day and a half looking for the secret hides.

They found several stashes of different sizes throughout the airplane. Although most people assume the cargo area of all jets is below the floor, on most smaller private aircraft like the Gulfstream G550, the cargo compartment is actually in the rear below the tail. Below the floor of the cabin was a large space that was partially taken up by wiring, but the Colombian engineers had created hidden compartments under the inspection panels in the floor that were large enough to hide as many as four small backpacks full of gear. Another vacant space was found in the lavatory, under the top panel that held the toilet seat. With sixty seconds and a screwdriver, one could remove the panel to reveal a large square empty space. The Colombians had added a small tube for waste to pass through, leaving a hide large enough for a single backpack, thankfully without affecting the function of the lav itself. Maintenance also found another ten smaller spaces hidden behind inspection panels and servicing access doors throughout the aircraft. Some of these hides would allow for the stowage of nothing more than a pistol; others were bigger, maybe the size of a submachine gun with a folded stock and a few extra magazines.

All in all, maintenance crew found nearly ten cubic feet of nearly perfect hiding places, enough to transport a fair amount of gear covertly wherever and whenever The Campus needed to move items surreptitiously. Pistols, rifles, explosives, surveillance equipment that would have sent foreign customs agents into seizures, documents, money. Anything that Gerry Hendley's men needed to do their work.

Hendley hired a flight crew of three, all ex-military and vetted for Campus operations. The lead pilot was from the Air Force, which would have surprised no one. The fact that she was female should not have surprised anyone, either. She was fifty-year-old Captain Helen Reid, a former B1-B pilot who had made the jump into corporate jets by taking a job with Gulfstream. She had been on the G650 project as a test pilot, but she didn't seem to mind "slumming" by flying the G550 instead. Her first officer was Chester Hicks, but everyone still called him by his call sign of "Country" because of his pronounced southern drawl. He was an ex-Marine Corps aviator from Kentucky who'd flown rotary and fixed-wing aircraft in the Corps. He spent the last six years of his career training young pilots at Naval Air Station, Corpus Christi, piloting B-12 Huron multi-engine aircraft, before retiring and going into business aviation. He'd flown G500s and G550s for a decade.

Hendley had surprised the five operators of The Campus back in June by taking them on their first ride in the G550. They'd driven to BWI, through the gate of an FBO called Greater Maryland Charter Aviation Services, which was run by a friend of Gerry Hendley's. Gerry's FBO-owning friend allowed Hendley's aircraft and his employees to avoid virtually all scrutiny.

On this first flight, the six men had boarded their new plane, and Gerry introduced everyone to Captain Reid and Country, and then Hendley introduced them to their flight attendant.

Adara Sherman was an attractive thirty-five-year-old with short white-blond hair and bright gray eyes that she kept behind serious glasses. She wore a blue uniform with no insignia, and she always kept her jacket on.

Sherman had spent nine years in the Navy, and she looked like she had not let her physical training slack in the least since leaving the service.

She was polite and professional as she showed the men around the cabin for a one-hour flight that would have them circling the area and then performing a touch-and-go in Manassas, before returning to BWI.

As Jack sipped his wine over the Atlantic, he thought back to that day, and it made him chuckle. During takeoff, while Adara Sherman was out of earshot, Gerry Hendley had addressed the three single men in the cabin. "We're going to play a word-association game, gentlemen. Our flight attendant is Adara Sherman. I want you to think of her as *General* Sherman, and think of yourselves as Atlanta. Got it?"

"Keep it businesslike," Sam had said with a slight smile. "You got it."

Caruso nodded obediently, but Jack spoke up. "You know me, Gerry."

"I do, and you are a good man. I also know what it's like being twenty-six years old. I'll just leave it there, okay."

"I understand. The flight attendant is a no-fly zone."

All the men had laughed, just as Adara unstrapped herself and returned to offer coffee to the passengers. Immediately Dom, Sam, and Jack Junior looked away from her, kept their eyes low, somewhat nervously. Clark, Chavez, and Hendley just chuckled.

Adara wasn't in on the joke, but she worked it out pretty quickly. The single men had been told that she was off-limits, and that was best for everyone. A minute later, she'd leaned across a table to grab a towel, and her jacket rose as her arms stretched. Jack and Dom both chanced quick glances—it had been coded into their DNA, after

95

all—and both men saw a small but serious-looking Smith and Wesson with a stainless-steel slide and a spare magazine tucked into a holster that disappeared into her skirt in the small of her back.

"She's packing," Caruso had said appreciatively when she returned to the forward galley.

Hendley just nodded. "She provides security for the aircraft. She has a couple of weapons to help her do that."

Jack smiled again thinking about Sherman and her weapons. He looked down to his watch and saw it was 10:30 p.m. on the East Coast. He grabbed the phone and called his mother's mobile.

"I was hoping to hear from you today," she said as she answered.

"Hey, Mom. Sorry it's so late."

Cathy Ryan laughed. "I don't have morning rounds tomorrow. I'm with Dad in Cleveland."

"Which means you'll still have to get up, get ready, and walk through a diner shaking hands at morning rush hour, right?"

Now she laughed out loud. "Something pretty close to that. We're going to a conveyer belt factory, but first breakfast with the media here at the hotel."

"Fun."

"I don't mind it. And don't tell him I told you, but I think your dad enjoys it more than he admits. Well, parts of it, anyway."

"I think you're right. How are Katie and Kyle?"

"Everybody's fine. They are back at home; Sally is watching them for a couple of days. You should go up if you can get away from work. I wish I could give the phone to your dad so you could say hi, but he's meeting with

Arnie in a conference room downstairs. Can you wait a few minutes?"

"Uh, no. I'll have to catch up to him later."

"Where are you?"

Jack exhaled slowly, then said, "Actually, I'm on a plane right now. Flying over the Atlantic."

That got a quick response. "Heading where?"

"Nowhere exciting. Just work."

"Do you know how many times your father has given me that exact response?"

"Probably because it was true most of the time. You have nothing to worry about."

"Are you sure?"

Jack Junior started to say "I promise" but refrained. He'd told himself he would not lie to his mother. Telling her she had nothing to worry about was damn close to an outright falsehood, but he sure wasn't going to tip the scales into the realm of deceit by promising anything. He had no idea what he was about to get into, other than the fact he'd be on a crew of five armed men who planned on killing three other armed men and capturing one more.

Cathy said, "I'm worried, Jack. I'm a mother, it's my job to worry."

"I'm fine." He changed subjects quickly. "So is Dad ready for the debate tomorrow night?"

He had no doubt that his mother would know what he was doing. His father had told him she would be able to see any "tricks" he tried to play on her from a mile away, and, so far, his dad had been right about that.

Still, she let it go. "I think so. He's got the facts and figures dead to rights. I just hope he can keep his hands to himself and not reach out and slap Ed Kealty. This is the debate where the two candidates sit right next to each

97

other at a table. It is supposed to be less formal, more like a friendly chat."

"I remember Dad talking about this one. Kealty didn't want to do this format at first, but since he's down in the polls, he changed his mind."

"Right. Arnie thinks this will be your father's best chance to show his warm-and-fuzzy side."

They both laughed at that.

Adara Sherman appeared over Jack with a small pitcher of water. Jack shook his head with a polite smile but made certain not to hold eye contact for too long, lest Gerry somehow find out about it later. She turned to head back to the forward galley, and he wanted to watch her walk away, but he knew this cabin was full of reflective surfaces, and he did not want to get caught checking her out, so he just looked down to his laptop.

"Okay, Mom. I'd better go. Get some beauty sleep for the presser in the morning."

"I'll do that. And you please be careful, okay?"

"I promise." That was a promise he felt he could keep. He had every intention of doing his best to avoid getting shot in the a.m.

Mother and son signed off, and Jack Junior returned to his work. He was racing to meet up with a dawn that itself was racing to meet up with him, and that left him so little time.

12

Captain Helen Reid banked onto final approach at Paris-Le Bourget Airport just after five in the morning, positioned the nose of the Gulfstream toward runway 25, just behind another executive jet, a Falcon 900EX. The Falcon touched down and then taxied onto the taxiway, and the G550 followed suit ninety seconds later.

Captain Reid brought the aircraft to a large yellow box on the ramp that was the designated customs area. Once there, the aircraft idled with its door sealed, as per customs requirements, and Jack Junior arranged his luggage on the seats for the customs inspector to look over. Adara had arranged for a customs officer to be waiting for the flight so that they could be cleared immediately, and within a few minutes there was a knock at the door. Adara opened the door and greeted an extremely sleepy-looking man. He boarded, shook hands with Jack and the crew, and made a perfunctory glance into one of Ryan's bags. All in all, he spent a grand total of two minutes on board doing this, as well as stamping passports and looking over the aircraft's registry information, before telling the captain that she was now free to park the aircraft at a nearby FBO.

The tired-looking customs official bid everyone on board *bienvenu, bonjour,* and *adieu,* and he stepped back down the steps and off into the darkness enveloping the ramp.

Five minutes later, Captain Reid and Country shut down the aircraft at the FBO, and Adara opened the cabin door once again. Dominic Caruso, himself a recent arrival to France, greeted Ms. Sherman on the other side of the door, and then he and Jack unloaded the four backpacks full of gear from the airplane and put them in the back of the Ford Galaxy.

The Gulfstream crew walked toward the lounge of the FBO to arrange for the jet to be refueled and for the oxygen stores to be replenished. They would then wait on the jet until it was time to leave France, whether that moment was to be in three hours or three days.

Dominic and Jack drove off the airport grounds in the Galaxy with no security check whatsoever of their gear or their documents.

When hauling contraband around the world, private aircraft was, indeed, the only way to fly.

At this time of the morning it was only a fifteen-minute drive from Paris-Le Bourget to the Paris safe house. Jack Junior himself had secured this apartment the day before, just after sending Ding and John from Frankfurt to Paris. At that time, he could not have imagined he'd be pulling up at the door himself just nineteen hours later.

The men parked the minivan in the street in front of the apartment. They began unloading the backpacks by themselves, but Driscoll and Chavez appeared at their sides in the dark, and all four men unloaded without speaking. Once the men were back inside the small, furnished flat, the bags were laid out on the floor, the door was shut, and only then was the overhead light turned on.

Under the illumination of a simple steel chandelier, John Clark handed Ryan a cup of coffee. Clark nodded with a crooked smile. "You look like shit, kid. Staff Sergeant Buck has been putting you through the ringer, hasn't he?"

"Yes. I've learned a lot," replied Jack as he accepted the hot caffeine.

"Excellent. There is a box of day-old croissants and some ham and cheese on a plastic tray in the fridge."

"I'm okay for now."

"You were wined and dined on the plane?"

"Perks of the job."

"Damn right. Okay, then let's get right to it." Clark addressed the room: "Everybody front and center." He stood in front of the television while the four others found seats in the modern living room.

Clark referred to a notebook as he talked. "We'll organize gear in a bit, but for now let's go over the op. The plan, in short, is this: I've got us the room right above Rokki's, and a room right next to his. We'll hit them hard and fast, and from multiple entry points, all while they're sipping their morning coffee."

"You got two rooms at the Four Seasons George V? Gerry is going to love *that* invoice," Ryan said with a chuckle.

Clark smiled himself. "He knows, and we aren't paying for it. The rooms were already booked for tonight, so Gavin Biery went into the hotel's reservation system and moved the existing reservations to other rooms. He made our reservations with a credit card number that we have, which is linked to a guy in Islamabad who moves money between Saudi fat cats and AQ accounts. It will be, according to Gavin, as if someone changed the reservations from one of the terminals at reception in the lobby. The Campus is clean on this operation, and the only vague trackbacks investigators will find after the fact will be the credit card, and that will lead them to an AQ player in the Middle East. When we hit the URC, it will look like some sort of lovers' quarrel between the two groups."

"Nice," said Dom appreciatively.

John smiled. "At the end of the day, gentlemen, we are professional troublemakers." That got a round of tired laughs from the room.

"Biery is also going to kill the security cameras at the Four Seasons as we come through the front door. He says it will look like the plug was pulled on the inside."

"Amazing," said Jack.

"Yes, he is, and he knows it."

Then Clark turned serious. "Ding and I will lay out exactly how this hit will go down in a minute, but first there is a significant complication we need to talk about."

The three men who had just arrived leaned forward or sat up straighter.

Chavez took over now, standing and facing the room. "DCRI, French internal security, has been tailing the guy they only know as Omar 8 since he arrived from Tunis yesterday. When he and his mates left their Seine-Saint-Denis safe house last night, the surveillance team tailed them here to central Paris, but they ran into some bad luck. Rokki and his guys had a mutt on a motorcycle pulling a surveillance detection sweep behind him, and we're ninety percent certain that motorcycle man spotted the backing car."

Jack winced. "So . . . French security is burned?"

"Looks that way, but French security doesn't seem to know it. They completed their tail to the Four Seasons, and now a DCRI static surveillance team is set up around the corner from Rokki's place in the Hôtel de Sers. They got a room with line of sight on Rokki's suite. I'm going to guess they needed to be that close because they are using a laser microphone system until they can get a better bug in place."

Sam looked down at a map of the Eighth Arrondissement. "Wow, DCRI are right on top of the action. Really close, in fact."

"Too close, we think," said Clark. "If they have line of sight on Rokki and Rokki knows he's being monitored . . . well, we have to proceed on the assumption the URC cell has spotted the French officers in their hotel room at the other hotel."

Sam asked, "What do we know about DCRI? Are they any good?"

Clark said, "*Damn* good. We liaised with them in Rainbow on multiple occasions. But they are like the investigators in our FBI. If you need detectives, surveillance men, man hunters anywhere in France, then that's who you call. But if you're sitting on top of an assassination team in the heart of Paris that looks like it's about to go loud . . . then surveillance time is over, and these guys are out of their depth. They usually aren't even armed."

Sam asked, "Any chance the URC will just bug out? Call off whatever they were planning and leave town?"

Jack Ryan answered this. "Under normal circumstances, yes. That's what we would expect them to do. But these are desperate times for the URC. We've seen them take some crazy chances since the disappearance of the Emir was acknowledged. Remember, we think Rokki is there because his boss, al Qahtani, is pissed off at the French government for policies he interprets as anti-Muslim. Rokki doesn't want to fail his boss, so if he's pegged the DCRI as just a hotel room full of surveillance guys with microphones and cameras, which is, in fact, the case . . . well, that just might not scare Rokki and his goons off."

"Have we figured out what Rokki's plan is?"

"No idea at all. All we can say with confidence is that it will be somewhere here in the area and it will go down today unless we do something to stop it."

Dom spoke up now. "You know me, I'm all for a good fight with these assholes, but why don't you just alert the local authorities that the URC is here and they are on to the men watching them? We can pay a kid twenty euros to go knock on the DCRI's door and tell them they've been burned."

Clark said, "Because the five of us have the best chance to stop Rokki, right here and right now. Plus, frankly, we need him alive and in our custody. This is our opportunity to get a line on Abdul bin Mohammed al Qahtani. Al Qahtani is the last real leader of the URC."

Everyone in the room nodded.

Clark continued, "Okay. Now on to the op plan. Guys, we've gone most of a year without drawing blood." He looked down to his watch. "In about three hours, that is going to change."

Ryan's heart was pumping a mile a minute. He looked around the hotel room and wondered what the other men were feeling. Dom seemed somewhat amped up, but not much. Driscoll, Chavez, and Clark looked like they could be sitting at a Starbucks, sipping a cup of coffee and doing the crossword puzzle of the Sunday *Times*.

Chavez spent the next twenty minutes laying out everyone's duties during the operation to come. He used his notebook with hand-scribbled maps. He and Caruso would enter the suite above Hosni Iheb Rokki's third-floor suite, and they would attach three long ropes to an anchor point, most likely the iron pipes leading to the toilet in the master bath. Dom and Ding would attach themselves to two of the ropes, and lead the other one out the balcony and then swing it down to Sam, who would be waiting in the room next to Rokki's.

Clark would enter the hotel after texting Gavin Biery in Maryland, giving him the order to disable the cameras. Then Clark would head quickly and calmly to the hallway outside Rokki's door. When all elements were ready, Sam Driscoll, attached to a nylon harness, would swing over to the bathroom window of the suite. If the bathroom was unoccupied, he would attempt entry there; if someone was using the bathroom, he would make his way along the wall to the bedroom balcony and enter there. He would be armed with a suppressed Glock 23, but his mission would be to take Hosni Iheb Rokki alive by administering a self-contained propellant-powered injector of anesthesia that would knock him out cold.

When Sam was in position hanging over the courtyard, Chavez and Caruso would rappel from their balcony down to the balcony of Rokki's living room, and they would use their suppressed MP7A1 short-barreled submachine guns to take down Hosni Rokki's confederates. John Clark would hit at the same time from the front door. He also had a CO_2 injector of anesthesia, along with a suppressed SIG Sauer pistol.

Ryan would serve as the wheel man down on the street, but he would also be tasked with watching out for any signs of police and, if any of the four tangos squirted out of the ambush, he might well be called on to go after them.

After Rokki's goons were down and Rokki was unconscious, they would put him in a large rolling bag and take him out the front door of the hotel. Ryan would pick them all up and return to the safe house. With luck, they would be wheels up at Paris–Le Bourget ninety minutes after Clark gave the men the go to execute the op.

Finally, when he finished, Clark stood back up and asked, "Any questions? Comments? Concerns?"

Jack was confused by something. "If DCRI are watching the suite, they are going to see every bit of this."

Chavez shook his head. "See? No, it's a corner unit, and they have line of sight on the southwest-side window, and we are hitting from the balconies over the courtyard on the north. Sam, Dom, and Ding will be shielded from view, but if the French are using a laser mike to get audio, they will damn well hear some noise. We will communicate with hand signals while in the suite."

Caruso shrugged, then spoke up: "A lot of moving parts on this one, Mr. C. Lots of stuff that can go wrong."

Clark nodded, a severe expression on his face. "Tell me about it, kid. It's the nature of the beast with this type of urban hit. Whacking the guys would be tough, but taking one of them alive makes the danger go up exponentially. Anything specific you don't like?"

Dom shook his head. "No. I like the plan. Let's do it."

Clark nodded. "All right. Rokki and his men have called for one pot of coffee and one pot of tea to be delivered to their suite at eight-thirty. We'll hit them at eight forty-five. We leave in one hour."

And with that, the meeting broke up so that each man could take a few minutes to organize his gear as per the op plan Chavez had just laid out. Sam and Ryan checked their .40-caliber Glock pistols and suppressors; Dom and Ding performed function checks on their submachine guns. They threaded their silencers on the barrels, nearly doubling the length of the weapons, but still they found them compact, lightweight, and well balanced.

They also checked their other equipment. Rappelling ropes, encrypted mobile phones with voice-activated Bluetooth headsets. Flash-bang grenades, smoke grenades, small shaped charges to breach doors or make doors, whatever the case may be.

They didn't plan on using smoke grenades or flash-bang grenades, and they had no plans to breach the walls of the Four Seasons. Chavez's laundry list of items that Ryan had brought with him from the States was designed for the mission in mind, but he'd also added a few other odds and ends in case everything went "tits up."

Clark went into the kitchen, pulled items from another bag that Ryan had brought from the States. After giving the team time with their gear, he called them over.

On the table his men saw he'd laid out what looked like five small spongy pieces of rubber.

"What are these?" Sam asked. He reached over and picked one of the "bags" up. It felt like a small wad of rubbery dried glue.

Clark lifted one himself. "We don't have time for a long tutorial, so I'll just demonstrate." With that, he turned away from the room, fumbled with the item for several seconds, and then leaned over. Driscoll looked to his colleagues seated around him for an idea of what was going on. They all just watched.

Clark stood back up, turned toward his men, and Sam Driscoll gasped audibly. John's face had completely changed features. His cheekbones were more pronounced, his nose seemed to have taken on a more angular profile, his square jaw had rounded out noticeably, and the deep creases around his mouth and eyes had filled in. After staring at him for several seconds, Sam could discern that the face did not look natural—it was somewhat alien, frankly—but if he were just passing him by in the street, he would neither notice anything amiss nor, and this was the important thing, be able to recognize John Clark.

"Jesus," Driscoll said, and the other men voiced their amazement as well.

"There is one of these for each of you. As you can hear, it doesn't alter your voice or your ability to speak at all. It just fills in shallow areas and restructures soft tissue on your face to make you unrecognizable. It is a tube; there are holes at both ends so your hair is not covered. Also, your ears are exposed, so we can use our Bluetooth headsets. Go ahead and try them on."

By now the rest of the men were putting on their masks like boys playing with new toys. They all found it difficult to orient the eyeholes and pull the tubes over their heads. As they worked and struggled, Clark continued talking. "These things aren't perfect. They are uncomfortable to wear and hard to put on, and as you can see, they make you look creepy, like you've either had way too much plastic surgery or you come from another planet. Primarily they are to foil facial-recognition software, to change our faces so we can't be recognized after the fact, and to confound any eyewitnesses to our actions." Clark looked around the room. He chuckled. "Jack, you still look like a million bucks. Ding? Amigo, I'm sorry to say this does nothing for you."

The men looked at one another and laughed, a light moment in what was sure to be an incredibly tense day. They then shouldered up to each other in front of a wall mirror.

Dom said, "They sure do the trick, but I'm going to need a lot of practice getting this thing on. If I have to do it on the fly for some reason, it's not going to be pretty."

Clark said, "The same goes for all of us. We'll keep these with us on the op just in case, but we'll have regular ski masks we can use if we need to throw something on quick. If we run into trouble and need to get out of there surreptitiously, then we'll go with these for the exfil. Also, it's very important to use sunglasses, too. Most facial-recognition algorithms use the distance between the eyes as a key identity measurement. Shades mess up their ability to determine identity more than anything else. In fact, when you leave this house, I want you wearing shades. You can put the masks on later if you need them."

13

At eight-thirty a.m. Ryan sat behind the wheel of the Ford Galaxy. He was alone in the vehicle now; he'd parked in a space on the Avenue George V across the wide boulevard from the Four Seasons hotel. He faced away from the hotel, but all three of his mirrors were positioned to cover the front entrance and the street and sidewalks approaching the entrance from either direction.

It was a bright and clear morning, and for this reason his dark sunglasses would not seem so out of place if he had to get out of the car. He also wore a light zip-up parka and his black ski mask high on his head like a knit watch cap so he could pull it over his eyes in moments if he had to.

The rest of the team had exited the vehicle five minutes earlier. Clark was on the street now, a block north of Ryan's location. He wore his sunglasses, a mobile phone earpiece, and a charcoal gray suit, and he carried a briefcase. He looked like any other late-middle-aged man heading to or from a breakfast meeting in the Eighth Arrondissement.

But he wasn't anyone else. His briefcase contained a lightweight camel-colored sport coat and a dark wig that he could change into in seconds. In his right rear pants pocket he carried his facial-distortion mask and a pair of wire-rimmed glasses. The tiny earpiece in his right ear was linked to an encrypted mobile phone in his right front pocket, and the system was set in a voice-activated mode that allowed him to transmit without pressing a button.

He also could, by pressing buttons on the front of the mobile phone, either speak to individual members of his team or broadcast on all channels simultaneously.

In the inside pocket of his jacket he carried a propellant-powered injector that contained enough ketamine to render an adult male unconscious in mere seconds.

And in a small leather holster secreted in the waistband of his charcoal gray slacks he carried a SIG Sauer P220 Compact SAS model .45-caliber pistol. The gun possessed a threaded barrel to allow for the addition of the suppressor that he carried in his left front pocket.

No, John Clark was not an ordinary man strolling the Eighth Arrondissement this morning.

Not by a long shot.

"Ding for John," Chavez's voice came through Clark's earpiece.

"Go, Ding."

"Dom and I are in the suite above Rokki's, no trouble getting in. We'll be ready in five mikes."

"Good."

"Sam for John."

"Go, Sam."

"I'm in position in the room next to the target. I'll hook up once Chavez swings the rope down."

"Roger."

"Jack for John."

"Go, Jack."

"All clear in front. Negative police on the sidewalk or patrol cars in the street. We're looking good."

"Okay."

Jack checked his mirrors again and made himself blow out a long, calming breath. He had done this sort of thing

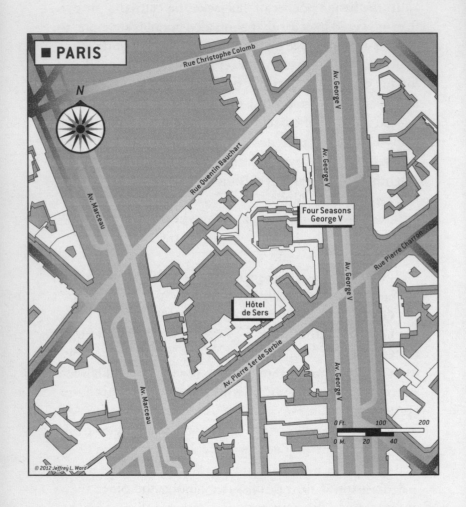

just enough to know that the next five minutes would feel like an eternity. He kept the back of his head on the headrest of his driver's seat, tried to appear relaxed, but he kept scanning his mirrors with eyes that moved a mile a minute. He knew the Galaxy's windows were tinted, so he wasn't terribly worried about being noticed, but he wanted to avoid any furtive movements that would telegraph his intentions, just on the off chance that someone was paying close attention to him.

A small white French Prefect Police patrol car passed by. Jack avoided the impulse to alert Clark; he knew the police would patrol around here as a matter of course, and although it made his heart pound even harder, he knew there was nothing to worry about.

The patrol drove on, followed the heavy morning traffic to the north. Ryan tracked the police car until it disappeared from view.

Jack looked to his left just as a big black Mercedes Sprinter van passed across from him, blocking his view of the front of the Four Seasons. The truck passed on a moment later, and then drove through the intersection of Avenue George V and Avenue Pierre 1er de Serbie. The truck pulled out of traffic and stopped alongside a hair salon on the corner, and Ryan turned away to check the opposite sidewalk. He could see John Clark on the far side of the street now, moving along with a large group of pedestrians as he headed toward the entrance to the Four Seasons.

Ryan listened to transmissions among the other men on his team as he kept scanning with his three mirrors, and then out the windows of the Galaxy. Clark announced that Gavin Biery had confirmed that the cameras in the hotel were down, and then, seconds later, Jack watched the older man disappear into the luxurious lobby of the hotel.

Ryan wished he was inside with the others, but he understood his role here. Someone had to drive; someone had to be on the lookout for both enemies and friendlies that could get in the way of this op.

But it was hard to know what, exactly, he was on the lookout for. Certainly any police arriving at the hotel. He and Clark had discussed the slim possibility that French police might come to make an arrest of Rokki at just exactly the wrong time. And also he had to keep an eye out for any obvious URC goons. Jack had memorized dozens and dozens of faces of terrorists from their photos in the Rogues Gallery he kept on his computer, though at this distance he'd be hard-pressed to ID any terrorist who didn't have a Kalashnikov in his hand and a bomb vest strapped to him.

Still, he knew his role was vital, even if it felt like he was just the bus driver for this op.

For the twentieth time in the past few minutes, Jack checked the driver's-side mirror for any police on the sidewalk approaching the hotel from the south. *Nope.* Then he repeated the drill with the passenger-side mirror; it had been adjusted to give him a look at the sidewalk on the far side of the intersection.

It, too, was clear of police.

"Three minutes," said Clark. "All units check in at ninety seconds."

Ryan started to turn his eyes back to the rearview. *Wait.* He turned back to the driver's-side mirror. A second later, he swiveled around and looked out the back window of the minivan.

The big black Mercedes truck that had passed him a

minute ago was still there by the hair salon, but its side door was open, and several men had climbed out.

Three, four . . . five guys, all dark-haired and all possessing dark complexions. One of them slid the door shut, and the van pulled away from the curb, made a quick U-turn during a break in the traffic, and turned left on the Avenue Pierre 1er de Serbie.

The five men on the pavement wore dark blue coveralls and carried small tool bags; they looked like they could be window washers or plumbers or some other type of laborer. Together they crossed the street at the intersection. At first Jack thought they were heading to the front door of the Four Seasons behind him, but instead, once they'd crossed the Avenue Pierre 1er de Serbie, they turned in the opposite direction. There, just out of Ryan's field of vision, was the employee entrance to the Four Seasons.

Jack knew he couldn't let a crew of unknown subjects enter the hotel without making sure they weren't up to anything nefarious. He leapt out of the minivan, raced around the side, and looked up the street. He just saw the back of the last man as he disappeared . . . not into the employee entrance of the Four Seasons but rather into the front entrance of the Hôtel de Sers.

This was the hotel where the French internal security surveillance team had set up shop to monitor Rokki's suite in the hotel next door.

"Ninety seconds," Clark said through the comms, and then the other operators began checking in.

"Sam is in position. I'll swing out over the courtyard at fifteen."

"Domingo and Dominic are in position."

Ryan began crossing the Avenue George V. He wanted

to see where the men in blue coveralls were heading. Something was off about them, their appearance, their purposeful strides, the actions of the driver of their vehicle.

Clark's voice came through his earpiece. "You with us, Ryan?"

"Uh . . . yes. Ryan is in position." He wasn't really, but he was not going to shut down the hit at the Four Seasons because he was checking out something at the hotel next door.

"Clark in position."

Ryan all but ran to the Hôtel de Sers through the throngs of pedestrians on the sidewalk. When he arrived he stepped through the doorway, looked into the dim lobby, and saw the five men waiting in a group by the reception desk, their tool bags over their shoulders. They were being handed some sort of badges, which they clipped onto their coveralls.

Shit, Ryan thought. Maybe they *were* okay. Just here to clean the windows?

"Forty-five seconds." Clark's clipped countdown came through his earpiece.

Ryan started to head back outside, but he stopped in mid-turn.

His leather shoes squeaked on the marble floor as he turned back around.

He looked again at the five men. Focused on one in particular.

His eyes widened. "Son of a bitch," he said softly to himself.

Slowly, Jack Ryan Jr. turned away again and headed through the door, back into the street. He grabbed his mobile from his jacket pocket, and he changed the transmit channel so his words would go only to Clark.

"Thirty seconds," Clark whispered on the open net. Right now he'd be in the hallway outside Rokki's room.

"John."

"Yeah?" Clark whispered to Ryan, alone now.

"Abdul al Qahtani is here."

There was a brief tense pause, before, "Here *where*?"

"Hôtel de Sers. He's with four other men in the lobby. They have bags and they are getting employee badges." Ryan looked across the street now. He saw the big Mercedes Sprinter double-parked thirty meters west of the hotel, the driver behind the wheel. "One more in a van outside."

"They're going after the DCRI unit?" Clark asked.

"I . . . I don't know," answered Ryan. He wanted to sit down and think about it, to analyze the situation like he was at his desk in the office. But he wasn't in his office, he was out in the field, and here he had no time to do anything more than act on nothing more substantial than his best guess. "Yes," he said now. *What else could they be doing?*

Clark did not hesitate. When Ryan received his next transmission, it was broadcast on all channels. John spoke quickly but calmly, the consummate professional, even under extreme stress. "All units abort. I need Dom and Ding to double-time it to the Hôtel de Sers around the corner. Ryan has eyes on al Qahtani himself with a possible wet team that are heading to the third floor, targeting the DCRI team in room 301. Grab whatever you can and get over there fast. Ryan has eyes on tangos."

"On it," said Chavez. "How many new mutts?"

"Ryan says five, plus a driver still in the vehicle up the street. I'm heading over now, my ETA is three minutes."

Chavez said, "We're gonna need four mikes. Five, tops."

"I know, Sam. Just make your way off the wall and sanitize both rooms. Get all the gear down to the van."

"Roger," Sam said. There was nothing he could do about it, but surely he felt as if he was letting his team down. After a heartbeat's pause, he said, "Good luck."

Chavez and Caruso carefully placed their rubber masks on their faces, reattached their earpieces, and then moved in a silent blur as they slung over their heads coils of ropes that hung down on one side of their bodies and then slung over their heads their Heckler & Koch MP7 rifles that hung down the other way. Over this gear each man threw on a rain parka; donned a messenger bag with extra ammo, a handgun, and smoke and frag grenades; and then rushed out of the room.

The bed in the room was covered with more equipment, and Driscoll's taut rope still led out onto and then over the balcony, but there was no time to worry about that now. They had mere moments to get down four flights of stairs, cross the street, and get back up four flights to the DCRI's suite on the third floor of the hotel.

They left the room, ran up the empty hallway, and then moved as quickly as possible down the stairs without raising suspicion.

Chavez said, "En route."

14

Ryan was back inside the Hôtel de Sers. The five terrorists had spoken to the manager, and now they were being led through an employee access door. Ryan passed close to them as he headed for the main stairwell. He took the stairs at an even pace until he rounded the first landing and was shielded from the lobby. Then he began sprinting to the third floor, which was, in the European system, four flights of stairs up from ground level.

As he climbed he spoke into his headset: "John . . . you want me to call the local cops?"

Clark's voice came right back; he sounded like he was in the lobby of the Four Seasons now. "There won't be time to get a SWAT team together, which means the first few beat cops that make the scene are going to get slaughtered, as well as any passersby if the fight dumps out into the lobby."

"Right," Ryan said as he passed the second floor in a sprint, heading to the third.

Ryan pulled his Glock from the waistband under his jacket as he arrived at the third floor. He screwed the silencer on the end of the barrel of his pistol and then cracked open the door from the stairwell to the hallway. The hall was dimly lit and narrower than he'd expected. He took a full step out to check the room number closest to him. 312.

Shit.

He whispered, "I have eyes on the hallway. The service elevator is directly ahead about one hundred feet. DCRI's room is all the way down the hall by the elevator. No sign of them. I'm going to alert DCRI."

"Negative, Ryan," said Clark. "You get caught out in that hallway and you're dead."

"I'll make it quick."

"Listen to me, Jack. You are *not* to engage al Qahtani and his men. Stay right where you are."

Ryan did not reply.

"Ryan, confirm my last transmission."

"John, DCRI doesn't carry weapons. I'm not going to just let al Qahtani kill everyone in that room."

Now Caruso's voice came over the net. From the sound of it, he was down on the sidewalk and walking quickly. He kept his voice low. "Listen to Clark, cuz. Five against one is not going to end well for you. Your Glock is going to feel like a squirt gun if those fucks come out of the elevator with assault rifles. Just stay in the stairwell and wait for the cavalry."

But in the stairwell, Ryan's nostrils flared as he readied himself for action. He couldn't just stand there and watch a massacre unfold before him.

The elevator chime clanged at the far end of the hall.

Inside room 301, six officers of the Direction Centrale du Renseignement Intérieur were positioned in two teams. Three men lounged on the two beds, reading the morning paper, drinking coffee, and smoking cigarettes. And three more stood or sat around a desk that had been moved in front of the open balcony doors, though it was back from the balcony a dozen feet or so. On the desk were two laptop computers and a Laser-3000 microphone listening device mounted on a tabletop tripod. The semi-conductor laser beam that emitted from the boxlike mechanism shot through a small opening in the sliding glass doors of the balcony, beamed across the open space between the two hotels, reflected off a panorama window of the corner suite at the Four Seasons next door, and then returned to the DCRI room at the Hôtel de Sers. Here, the ray was projected onto a receiver on the Laser-3000, and this interpreted the fluctuations in the beam caused by vibrations on the window and translated these fluctuations into recognizable speech.

This wasn't a perfect surveillance operation by any stretch of the imagination. Since the curtains were closed on Omar 8's window, they could not see into the suite, and they could pick up only faint voices intermittently. But the device did confirm that Omar 8 and his associates were still in there, and that was important. As soon as they left, one of the three-man DCRI teams would head over to the Four Seasons and plant several more effective bugs while the other monitored from this overwatch position.

In the meantime, they all drank coffee and smoked and complained about the American government. A few years ago, they would have received support for an op like this from the CIA. Omar 8 was allegedly URC; the United States was undeniably interested in URC operators, especially when they were moving through Western capitals with fighting-aged associates and a hundred pounds or so of baggage. Sure, the URC had made many threats against the French, one just the week before. But they had never attacked France, whereas they had attacked the United States multiple times, killing hundreds there and abroad. The damn American consulate was just a mile away—why weren't *les américains* here right now, providing intelligence and equipment and manpower for this operation?

Les américains, mumbled the DCRI detail as they monitored the corner suite next door. They all agreed they certainly weren't what they used to be.

The elevator door slid open on the third floor of the Hôtel de Sers. One hundred feet away, concealed by much of the stairwell door and dim lights behind him, Jack Ryan Jr. leveled his suppressed Glock at the movement.

A single housekeeper pushed a rolling cart full of towels and trash bins out of the service elevator and onto the floor. There was no one behind her. Jack lowered the pistol before she saw it, or even him, and he quietly shut the staircase door until only the tip of his shoe held it open.

He breathed a muted sigh of relief. The housekeeper had delayed the arrival of the terrorists, but only by a minute or so. They would be here soon enough. She and her cart continued up the hallway slowly, completely oblivious to any danger.

Just then, the sound of running up the stairs below Ryan caused him to turn. Before he had time to do much more than register that he was hearing the footfalls of two men, Chavez transmitted on the net. "We're coming to you, Ryan. Hold fire."

"Roger."

Clark transmitted next. "Ding, I'm in the main elevator. ETA sixty seconds. Can you and Dom make entry on 301's balcony via 401?"

Chavez and Dom ran past Ryan at a full sprint, their faces distorted and unrecognizable due to their rubber masks. Chavez spoke as he climbed: "I like it. We'll do a rush-job version of what we'd planned next door."

"You're gonna have to make it quick," Ryan said.

Clark replied, "Ryan. I need you down in the lobby."

Jack couldn't believe what he was hearing. "What?"

"You have to be ready to get the van and bring it around. Sam doesn't have the keys. You do. We can't wait around when this is over. Plus, we have a tango still on the street. If he comes in, I want you ready to stop him."

Ryan started to protest; he had to whisper because the maid was only a few feet away. She opened the door to a room after knocking, and disappeared inside. "John, you've got to be kidding. I've got eyes on the hall, I can cover—"

"Ryan, I'm not going to argue with you! Go down to the lobby!"

"Yes, sir," Jack said, and he spun away from the door and began heading down the stairs. "God damn it."

Ding Chavez got slightly ahead of Dominic as they sprinted up the fourth-floor hallway. Both men doffed their rain parkas and let them fall as they ran on, got their hands on their sub-guns, and unslung the ropes from their necks. When he arrived at the door to room 401, Chavez just shouldered right through it, smashing the bolt out of the doorjamb and sending the door flying in. He fell to the ground, and Caruso leapt over him with his HK trained toward movement on the bed.

A middle-aged couple were eating their room-service breakfast on their bed and watching television.

"What the bloody hell?" shouted the man in a thick English accent.

The woman screamed.

Caruso ignored the couple; instead, he just ran toward

the balcony and slid the door open. Chavez was back with him now; together they hurriedly dropped their ropes, took the metal carabiners fixed to one end of them, and then hooked the carabiners on the heavy iron railing of the balcony.

Right then Clark transmitted in a whisper. His voice sounded pleasant and happy, and he spoke in a British accent. "Got delayed a bit heading up, darling. I'll be there in half a minute. Feel free to start breakfast without me."

The men on the balcony knew they were on their own. Clark was still in the elevator. Obviously surrounded by civilians. They had no time to wait on him.

Dom and Ding climbed over the fourth-floor railing, holding onto their HK sub-guns with one hand and their ropes with the other. They turned to face the hotel room and noticed the English couple had already hustled out the front door, no doubt terrorized by what they had just witnessed.

With a quick look between them and a nod from Chavez, both he and Dom leaned back, away from the railing of the balcony. Five stories down was the Avenue Pierre 1er de Serbie; traffic rolled by without a care. The two Americans high above the traffic pushed off with their legs. They spent just over a second in the air before swinging down to the balcony below.

Directly in front of them now, behind the glare of the sun's reflection on balcony doors that were just slightly cracked open, they could see three of the six DCRI men in the room. One stood right on the other side of the glass, six feet from the Americans' noses; in his hand was a cup of coffee and a cigarette. Two more sat behind a table in the center of the room. Ahead and to the left of Chavez and Caruso were the bed and bathroom, wide of the balcony. And behind the desk with the surveillance equipment was a narrow entryway in front of the door.

Needless to say, the three Frenchmen reacted with shock to the armed men rappelling onto their balcony. Even more so when the two men released their ropes and brought the short butt stocks of their weapons to their shoulders.

Caruso and Chavez each took a step forward into a half-crouch firing stance. Chavez screamed, *"Dégagez!"*—Move!—just as, directly behind the wide-eyed Frenchmen, the door to their room flew open behind the shoulder of one of the Middle Eastern assassins.

15

John Clark had been forced to physically push two Chinese businessmen out of the elevator on the second floor. They had ignored him when he asked them to take another car, they'd yelled back at him angrily when he demanded they get out, and even when he resorted to pulling his pistol on them they just stared at it in confusion. Finally he shoved them out and pushed the close door button before continuing on up alone.

Now he was arriving at the third floor; his SIG pistol was out and ready, the silencer in place. He knew al Qahtani and his men would be in the hall by now, if they were not already in room 301, and he also knew his own arrival on the floor would be announced in advance with a ringing bell and a flash of light above the elevator doors.

Not exactly a covert dynamic entry.

When the doors opened, he leaned out and to the right with his pistol at eye level. Immediately he ducked back into the elevator. No sooner had he pulled his head out of the hallway when unsuppressed fully automatic machine-pistol fire tore into his elevator car. He flattened himself on the floor, then reached up with the tip of his silencer and pressed the door hold button, locking open the doors here in range of the enemies.

He'd seen the gunmen right as they kicked at the door to 301. They were carrying Škorpion machine pistols, a small weapon that fired a .32-caliber bullet at a rate of 850 rounds per minute. Only one man was looking back in

Clark's direction, but that tango had been ready to gun down whoever the hell exited the elevator. John had felt the overpressure of the supersonic rounds and they missed his face by inches, and now he was effectively pinned down inside the elevator.

Another burst of fire tore through the aluminum car as he pressed his face flat on the cold floor, the sound in the hallway like the ripping of paper into a microphone attached to the amp stacks of a heavy-metal band.

Al Qahtani and his men fired first; Ding heard the sound of automatic weapons fire just as he got his finger to the trigger of his HK. The Frenchmen in the hotel room reacted surprisingly quickly. The two men at the desk dove for the floor, and the man standing with the coffee and cigarette spun away from the gunmen on the balcony and ducked upon hearing the door smash and the gunfire behind him. Ding got a snap sight picture on an armed tango in the doorway and squeezed off a double-tap through the glass of the sliding balcony doors, hitting the chest of the first terrorist. The man spun 180 degrees, his Škorpion flew from his hands, whipped by the sling around his neck as he landed on his back.

The glass of the balcony door shattered with the impacts. Dominic Caruso fired a pair of double-taps at the threats across the room, then kicked a remaining crotch-high glass shard free from the doorframe as he stepped through it. The second terrorist through the door had sighted his machine pistol on the first DCRI operative, but Dom took him out with a double-tap to the forehead.

The man's skull exploded; blood drenched the wall of the entryway.

Both Dom and Ding had entered the room now; the

third assassin dove to the floor of the hallway, using the slumped bodies of his two dead compatriots for cover. The Frenchmen in the bedroom scrambled to get themselves out of the line of fire. They dove to the floor next to the bed or crawled into the bathroom. Not one of them had a firm grasp on what was happening right in front of them, but the two men who'd rappelled to the balcony had made it clear with their shouts and actions that they were there to help.

A long uncontrolled spray by the third gunman at the door emptied his Škorpion. He rolled onto his side to reload it, and his partners in the hall covered for him by firing into the room indiscriminately. Both Dom and Ding had advanced farther into the room to get out of the line of fire. Chavez shepherded the six Frenchmen into the bathroom; one of the men had been shot through the hand. With the bathroom door shut, Caruso lay on the floor in front of the bed, rolled out onto his right shoulder to get a narrow field of fire on the tangos. He fired short, controlled bursts from his HK, hitting one of the men in the hallway in both legs, dropping him into the entryway.

Dom then shot the wounded man in the face with his last bullet.

"Reloading!" he shouted to Chavez. Ding stepped over him, leaned around the corner toward the entryway, and fired 4.6-millimeter rounds at the opposing force. Three of his bullets tore through the face and throat of the terrorist on the floor of the entryway, sending the man tumbling backward and causing arterial blood to jet into the air like a sprinkler.

There was one more tango, but he was out in the hall. Chavez couldn't hit him unless the man stuck his head back into the doorway.

Dom had reloaded, and he covered the entryway while Chavez took a moment to put a fresh magazine into the grip of his weapon. As Chavez worked his HK's action to chamber another round, he spoke into his headset. "There's one out there with you, John."

"John?"

John Clark did not answer Chavez, careful not to make a sound as he peered around the open door of the elevator car. He looked down the hallway toward the source of all the gunfire. Still in a low crouch, he held his SIG Sauer pistol at the end of his extended arms at eye level.

Other than two dead bodies half in and half out of room 301, the hallway was empty. *Where the fuck did the last guy go?*

The door to the suite immediately on Clark's right opened, and an Asian man peered out. Clark swiveled his weapon toward the movement, but he recognized quickly this was no threat. He took his left hand off his pistol to motion for the guest to go back inside and shut the door, and the Asian man was all too happy to comply with this request.

But when John turned his attention back to the hall in front of him he did see movement, and it came from a doorway on the left, on the opposite side and just closer than the DCRI's room. The door was open, and a blond-haired woman stepped out slowly. The forearm of a man was wrapped tightly around her neck.

She came all the way into the hallway now, and she was not alone. Holding her from behind was Abdul bin Mohammed al Qahtani, operational commander of the Umayyad Revolutionary Council. He held a black Škorpion machine pistol in his right hand, and the tip of his barrel was pressed tight under the woman's chin.

The lady was in her fifties. Clark guessed she might have been Swedish, but he had no way to know for sure. She sobbed, and mascara dripped down her cheeks as she slammed her eyes shut.

Clark stepped out into the hallway fully now, keeping his weapon pointed at the threat ahead of him and his eyes on his target through his notch and post sights. Calmly he spoke softly into his earpiece microphone. "Stay in the room and get ready to leave. I'll be right there."

"Roger that," said Dominic.

The blond woman's eyes opened now, black tears drained down her cheeks. She blinked away the wetness and saw the armed man in the hallway, twenty feet ahead. Her eyes went wide and her pink face reddened even more.

For his part, al Qahtani looked a little more relaxed than his hostage, but not much. He shouted in Arabic, "Stay back or I will kill her." He took a single step backward, pulling the blonde with him.

"Of course," replied Clark in Arabic, surprising al Qahtani by speaking his native tongue. "I will stay back. What do you want?"

The Arab did not answer, he just stared at the figure with the distorted face in amazement. Who was this man? How did he get here? Was he with the others, the ones who'd just killed all his men and thwarted his operation?

"I'm listening," Clark said calmly. "I am listening to you, friend. Just tell me your demands, and please do not hurt the woman." He kept the weapon trained on the URC commander while he spoke.

Al Qahtani recovered a little more as he realized he retained some control over this situation. He pulled the blonde tighter to him with his forearm; by this action he literally pinned their faces together, cheek to cheek. He kept the machine pistol pressed tight under her chin. He did not know who this man was, but he spoke as if his main concern was the safety of the woman. Al Qahtani screamed, "I want everyone back! Out of my way!" He began pulling the blonde backward to the service elevator, the friction of the carpet against her high heels ripping the shoes from her feet. "I want all the police to leave the hotel, and the stairwell cleared, and a car brought to the entrance."

Clark nodded but kept his weapon steady. "Of course! Of course. This is no problem. Just don't hurt her. There is no need. I will get a car for you. But where will the car take you? Do you need a helicopter or a plane? We can arrange for you to go to the airport or the train station, or, if you like, you can go to—"

John Clark pressed the soft trigger of his SIG 220 and shot Abdul bin Mohammed al Qahtani through the right eye orbit, severing the man's medulla oblongata and knocking him backward into the service elevator.

The body hit the cold metal floor even before Clark's .45-caliber shell casing landed on the carpet of the hallway.

The Škorpion machine pistol clanged off the wall and landed at al Qahtani's feet.

The woman looked at Clark for a long moment before putting her hand out to the wall next to her. She took a single slow step forward.

Clark lowered his pistol, hurried to her, and caught her under her arms as she fainted. He lowered her onto the carpet gently and then turned to run back to room 301.

During all the action above, Jack Ryan had stood on the landing between the ground floor and the first floor. Below him, he could see a portion of the lobby, but he remained concealed from the hotel employees by the reception counter.

When the shooting started, people ran past him on their way down from the guest floors above. Some were screaming, some were calm, but all were hustling down to the lobby, or even out into the street.

Ryan just stood there on the landing, his hands empty.

He'd been listening to the few transmissions from his three teammates above him, and from this he had an understanding of what was going on. He had worked out that they had eliminated all the threats. He assumed Clark would send him to get the minivan with his next transmission.

But the next transmission did not come from Clark, it came from Driscoll. "Sam for Ryan, you copy me?"

"Ryan copies."

"I'm at the van."

"Okay, I'll come out."

"Listen up. The black Mercedes truck just pulled up at the corner. The driver is heading inside like he's got someplace to be."

Quickly Jack turned around toward the lobby. The stairwell was clear now, there were no more stragglers heading down past him. He backed up the stairs to the first floor and then trained his eyes on the landing turn from where he had just come. He pulled his Glock and shielded it between his right hip and the wall.

Clark's voice came over the net now. "Jack, that target is yours."

"Understood." He prepared for the man to appear on the staircase, but then a thought entered his amped-up brain. What if the guy ran straight into the guest elevator in the lobby? Or into the employee area, where he could take the employee elevator? *Shit.* Jack would miss him, and the tango would hit the team upstairs and catch them unprepared.

Jack began running down the stairs; he had to get eyes on the lobby so he could determine where the—

A large bearded man appeared from the lobby, running up the staircase hard and fast, and he crashed into Ryan. Both men lost their balance and tumbled. As Jack fell he felt his ribs brush against the grip of a pistol in the bearded man's hand, just as Ryan's own handgun slipped out of his fingertips.

Together the two men rolled out into the lobby.

Ryan recognized the other man as the driver of al Qahtani's Mercedes truck. The terrorist ended his fall on top of Jack, and he reached back to hit the American in the face, but Ryan shoved the palm of his hand hard into the bearded man's chin, and then flipped him off him to the marble floor.

Ryan started to go for his gun, he could see where it skidded after hitting the lobby floor, but instead al Qahtani's driver rolled quickly to his knees and then charged from a three-point stance. Ryan could not get out of the way of the attack, so he dropped backward toward the floor, reached out and grabbed the man's jacket, and spun him back to the ground.

The big man crashed to the ground, but he rolled up to his knees quickly, then turned and charged Ryan again. This time Jack leapt to his feet, sidestepped the attack, and slammed the palm of his right hand into the driver's head as he stumbled past him.

The URC terrorist fell to the floor, dazed by the blow to his skull.

Jack had the advantage now, and he leapt on the man, grabbed him by the hair, and slammed his head viciously into the marble tile floor, once, twice, and then a third time, when there was no resistance from the neck muscles of the terrorist and the skull cracked audibly, echoing in the empty lobby.

Ryan hesitated for just a moment, tried to catch his breath, then he gave up. Still on the verge of hyperventilation, he climbed off the dead terrorist and grabbed his pistol from the floor. He holstered it and then reached up to check for his earpiece. Miraculously it was still in place in his ear.

"This is Ryan. Tango down."

"Copy that. You okay?" It was Clark.

Ryan nodded to himself, held his breath for a second to catch his wind, and then said, "I'm bringing the van around. Two minutes."

Ryan crossed the wide floor, heading for the exit, but he was met by uniformed Prefect Police who poured through the doors with pistols in their hands. Jack stepped to the side, held his hands up, and then, feigning panic, he crouched like a terrified tourist. Outside in the street by the black Mercedes truck he saw several police cars. The vehicles were empty; their occupants had just passed him on their way to the stairs. After the police ran past him through the lobby, Ryan hurried out the door and spoke into his headset. "Guys, listen up. Eight cops heading up the main stairwell. You're going to have to find another exit."

"Okay." It was Clark's voice now. "I'm with Ding and Dom. We'll come up with something. Be ready to pick us up."

16

Ninety seconds later, Domingo Chavez fired bursts from his Heckler & Koch MP7 through the hinges of a locked metal door to the roof of the hotel. The three men stepped out into a bright sky, as all around them the sounds of sirens echoed off the buildings. They found themselves on a flat roof here, but in order to move away from the entrance to the hotel they were forced to head to the northwest, crossing two large early-modern-style apartment buildings. Here the roofs of the adjacent buildings were steep, with glazed brick masonry. The roofs were all of different heights and gradients, with only a few narrow walkways. The next building over was a full story taller than the one they were on, so they were forced to climb up narrow masonry steps to begin their escape from the police.

And the police were close behind. Chavez led the way, and he directed Dom and John to pull on their black ski masks. There was no sense now in even maintaining the semi-covert facial-distortion masks, so they might as well attempt to hide even the color of their skin.

As they ran, climbed, and skittered five and six floors above the streets of Paris, they heard shouting on the roof behind them at the Hôtel de Sers. From the tone of the yelling, they knew they'd been spotted.

Clark called back over his shoulder to Caruso, "Toss smoke to cover us."

Dom reached into the messenger bag on his back,

pulled a smoke grenade and yanked the pin from it. Bright red smoke spewed from one end, and Dom laid it down next to the vertical glass side of a sawtooth roof. He ran on. The smoke cloud fattened in the breeze on the roof, and it obstructed the Americans' retreat.

After sliding on their backsides down the steep side of a mansard roof that ended at a partition to the next building, they climbed over the low wall and found themselves looking down five stories into a beautiful garden courtyard surrounded by a stony Art Nouveau building full of luxury office space. Faces in the windows of the offices stared at the armed men in the ski masks. Some turned quickly and ran away; others just looked on, wide-eyed, as if they were watching a police drama on television.

Chavez, Clark, and Caruso continued on to the northwest. Within another thirty seconds they began to hear the persistent thump of a helicopter. They did not bother to stop and look for it. Whether it was a police helo or television station's traffic chopper, it did not matter. They had to get off the roof.

Finally they skittered to the end of the flat part of a two-angle mansard roof. Beyond that they found themselves looking down, five stories down, on to the Rue Quentin Bauchart, a two-lane street that signified the end of the block. There was no obvious way down, no well-anchored drainpipe, no easy way to descend the architectural flourish on the façade. Only a large bay window ten feet below them that jutted out of the steeply angled roof.

They were trapped. The shouts from behind grew in volume.

The three men knelt on the edge of the roof. The squawking of sirens back on the Avenue George V was unreal. There had to have been fifty emergency vehicles in the area now. There didn't seem to be a police presence directly below them on the street, yet anyway, as the Rue Quentin Bauchart was not really the back of the hotel itself, rather the Americans had managed to reach this position only by clawing their way over partitions between buildings and along small access walls that connected the buildings of the block together. Still, with so many vehicles and men it certainly would not take the French police much more time to branch out at ground level as well, and once that happened, this street would be locked down by the authorities.

"What's below us, Ding?" John asked, as Chavez had the best look over the edge.

"Looks residential. Could be civilians under the roof, there's no way to know."

Caruso and Clark knew what he meant. They did have small explosives in Dom's bag. They could blow a hole in the roof and climb down into the building, then use the stairs to get out. But they wouldn't blow the roof without knowing for certain that there wasn't an occupied apartment, a day care, or an old folks' home directly below them. And there was only one way they could find out.

Dom stood quickly. "I've got it. John, get back behind that chimney." Caruso took his HK from around his neck and unfastened the ballistic nylon sling attached to it. He took a moment to pull on the sling to bring it to its full length, and he wrapped his right hand several times around one end, then he gave the other end to Ding. Chavez took a firm hold, then grabbed the iron railing with his other hand. Clark moved back, and when Ding knelt down at the edge of the roof, Dom Caruso climbed over the side, slid down the steep roof, his shoes scuffing the masonry as Chavez lowered him. He did get just low enough to make it to the bay window. As he hung from his sling, the men still on the roof heard a cracking of window glass as Caruso used his rifle to shatter the pane. Ding struggled with the sling, it dug into his hand and wrist and forearm, but he held tight. After a few more crashes, he felt the sling move hard to the left. And then, suddenly, the weight left the strap.

Caruso was in the apartment below them. This was progress, but it didn't really help Clark or Chavez, as far as they were concerned. Caruso had not taken time to explain what he was doing, and this confused the two men on the roof for a moment, but within ten seconds of his disappearance from the side of the building, The Campus operators on the roof heard Dom in their earpieces.

"Okay, I'm in the attic. It's empty. Gonna use these charges to make you guys a hole. Ding, get over there with John and both of you keep your heads down."

Clark nodded appreciatively even as he looked back over his shoulder. He heard voices on the roof; the police had made their way through the smoke and were closing fast, likely while following a trail of broken masonry and cracked roofing tiles. They were still on the Art Nouveau building next door, but they would find their way here within a minute.

Seconds later a loud explosion blew smoke, roofing material, and wood into the air on the other side of the brick chimney. While the last of the bits of debris rained back down, Clark and Chavez ran across the roof to the fresh opening and looked in. As soon as the smoke cleared, they saw Caruso pushing a chest of drawers across a wooden attic floor below them. When he had it below the hole, Clark helped Domingo down on top of it. Chavez quickly turned back to help his partner down.

A crack from a pistol fifty feet behind Clark caused Chavez to duck instinctively as he took hold of Clark's arm. He felt a jolt go through the other man's body, and John Clark spun around, then fell into the hole in the roof. Chavez and Clark fell off of the chest of drawers and onto Dominic Caruso.

"Shit!" shouted Chavez. "Where you hit, John?"

Clark was already struggling to his feet. He winced in pain, raised a forearm to show that his dirty sport coat was covered in blood. "It's not bad. I'm fine," he said, but both Caruso and Chavez had been around firearms long enough to recognize Clark was in no position to know how badly he'd been hurt.

Even with this, Caruso had the presence of mind to worry about the cops above them on the roof. Quickly he reached into his backpack and pulled out a flash-bang grenade, he pulled the pin and lobbed it out into the direction of the men approaching. He thought it likely that French police officers would not recognize the device, at least not instantly, and they would have to entertain the possibility that they were being fired on by the fleeing gunmen.

The Americans needed to buy a few seconds' time to make their way downstairs, and the grenade did just that. It exploded next to the chimney with an earsplitting boom.

Clark led the way out of the attic, down a flight of stairs, and onto a circular staircase that spiraled down to ground level.

Chavez spoke tersely into his mike: "Jack, we're coming out, ground floor of an apartment building, about one hundred yards northwest of the Hôtel de Sers. Thirty seconds."

"Roger that. I'll be there. Sirens approaching from the

Avenue Marceau behind me, and George V is full of heat."

"Whatever," Chavez said as he and his two colleagues rushed down the stairs. That was a problem for sixty seconds from now; he couldn't worry about it just yet.

All three Americans flew out of the door of the apartment and onto the street. Jack and Sam were there in the maroon Galaxy with the side door open. The three fell inside just as the first police cars skidded around the corner and into the street from behind them. Driscoll helped Clark into a seat and immediately began assessing his bloody arm.

Even though the police were fifty yards back, Ryan didn't floor it; he had the presence of mind to drive normally as he headed toward Avenue George V. They passed a language school and a restaurant where the waiters were just setting up bistro tables on the pavement for the lunch service. Several men and women on the sidewalk stared at their minivan as they passed; perhaps they'd come outside to investigate the origin of the sirens, then heard or saw the ruckus on the roof and then the men pouring out of the apartment. But so far, no one on the street had raised an alarm.

Jack knew he couldn't drive onto Avenue George V in front of him; it was crawling with police and a roadblock had likely already been set up. Instead he drove slowly toward it, watched his rearview mirror until the police cars behind him began stopping on the street in front of the apartment, and only when he could wait no longer, he jacked the wheel to the left and turned into the one-way traffic pouring off of the Rue Magellan.

Certain that at least some of the parked police cars had seen him, he punched the accelerator now as he leaned toward the windshield to take in as much of the road in front of him as possible. The cars on the street shot toward him; he wove left and then right to avoid the oncoming traffic. Within seconds he made a right on the Rue de Bassano, found himself on a second street traveling in the wrong direction, but he kept going, faster and faster. A last-second reaction to avoid a taxi sent Ryan and the rest of the team up onto the narrow sidewalk; they scraped a pair of parked cars as they shot through passersby diving into doorways or out into the street to avoid the dented minivan. At an intersection Ryan avoided a group of employees standing in front of their Russian restaurant, and he pulled back onto the street, crashed through a neat line of bicycles for rent, then passed the Louis Vuitton flagship store as he pulled out onto the wide Champs-Élysées.

For the first time in a minute and a half he found himself driving in the same direction as traffic. Also, for the first time in several minutes, the men did not hear the shrill squawking of police sirens right behind them.

Jack reached up to wipe sweat from his forehead, but his rubber mask got in the way. His hairline was soaked with perspiration, so he slicked back his dark hair to get it out of his face.

"Where to now?" Ryan asked the men behind him.

Clark's voice was gravel, broadcasting to the vehicle the pain the ex-Navy SEAL was in at the moment, but his voice remained strong. "Safe house," he said. "We're going to need a new ride. Can't pull into the airport driving the most wanted vehicle in France."

"Roger that," said Ryan, and he punched a button on the GPS that would lead him to the safe house. "How are you feeling?"

"I'm okay," said Clark.

But Sam Driscoll had been checking Clark. He applied pressure to the wound as he leaned forward into the front seat. "Get there as fast as you can."

Adara Sherman stood inside the doorway of the Gulfstream with an HK UMP .45-caliber submachine gun held in one hand behind her back. She watched a four-door sedan pull to a stop on the tarmac, saw the five men climb out and approach. Four of them carried backpacks, but John Clark had his arm in a makeshift sling under his blue sport coat. Even from a distance she could see his face was ashen.

Quickly she'd scanned the airport grounds, determined the coast to be clear, then rushed back inside the aircraft to grab medical supplies.

On board she bandaged Clark quickly, knowing that a customs official would be on his way out to see them off. While she helped him get a clean jacket on, the other men changed into clean suits and ties that had been ready for them in the Gulfstream's coat closet, but only after stowing their clothing and gear in the stash compartment below an inspection panel in the floor.

Within minutes a female customs agent climbed aboard. She opened two of the businessmen's briefcases and glanced inside and then asked the bearded gentleman if he wouldn't mind opening his suitcase. This he did, but she didn't look past the socks and gym clothes. The older gentleman reclining on the couch in the back was not feeling well, so she did not disturb him other than to see that his face matched the passport handed to her by one of his younger employees.

The female customs official finally checked the pilot's paperwork, thanked everyone, and was seen out the door by the flight attendant. The door shut behind her, and within seconds the aircraft was taxiing out of the yellow customs square on the ramp.

Captain Reid and First Officer Hicks had the wheels up in five minutes. While they were still on their takeoff climb out of Paris airspace, Sherman had stopped the bleeding from Clark's arm. Before the aircraft reached ten thousand feet she had an IV line in the top of his hand and an antibiotics drip moving slowly into his bloodstream to stave off any infection.

As soon as Country turned off the seatbelt light in the cabin, Chavez rushed back to check on his friend. "How is he?" Chavez asked, a worried tone in his voice.

Sherman poured antiseptic into the wound now, examining the holes as the clear liquid cleaned the blood away. "He's lost a fair amount of blood, he needs to lie flat for the flight, but the round went through and through and he's moving his hand okay." She looked up at her patient. "You'll be fine, Mr. Clark."

John Clark smiled at her. With a weak voice he said, "I had a feeling Gerry didn't hire you to pass out peanuts."

Sherman laughed. "Naval corpsman, nine years."

"That's a tough job. You were deployed with the Marines?"

"Four years in the sandbox. I saw a lot of wounds worse than yours."

"I bet you did," John said with a nod of understanding.

Caruso had headed alone up to the galley. He returned, stood over everyone who was kneeling over Clark. In his hand was a crystal highball of Johnnie Walker Black Label scotch. He addressed Sherman. "What do you think, doc? Can I give him a dose of this?"

143

She looked Clark over and nodded. "In my professional opinion, Mr. C. looks like he needs a drink."

The Gulfstream flew over the English Channel, leaving French airspace just after eleven a.m. at a cruising altitude of thirty-six thousand feet.

17

Even though he looked every second of his sixty-nine years, Nigel Embling was no pushover. At six feet, four inches and two hundred fifty pounds, he retained considerable brawn to go with his fertile brain. Still, within one second of opening his eyes, he recognized his predicament and raised his hands to indicate he would put up no fight.

He'd awoken to guns in his face, flashlight beams in his eyes, and shouts in his ears. Though startled and worried, he did not panic. As a resident of Peshawar, Pakistan, he knew well that he lived in a city rife with crime, terrorism, and government and law enforcement thuggery, so even before he'd forced the cobwebs of sleep out of his mind he was already wondering which of these three he was waking up to this morning.

Clothes were thrown to him, and he struggled out of his nightshirt and into the ensemble offered by the gunmen, and then he was shoved to his staircase, down the stairs, and toward the front door.

Mahmood, Embling's young orphaned houseboy, knelt on the floor with his face against the wall. He'd made the mistake of rushing one of the armed men who'd kicked in the front door. For his bravery Mahmood received a boot in his chin and a rifle's butt in the back. He was then ordered to kneel and face the wall while Embling was collected from his bedroom and allowed to dress. In Urdu tinged with a phony Dutch accent, Embling shouted at the young gunners, admonishing them like children for their treatment of the boy. In the next breath, in soothing words, he told Mahmood to run along to a neighbor's to have his bruises and scrapes seen after, and he promised the terrified boy that there was nothing to be alarmed about and that he would return straightaway.

Once outside in the dark street, he had a better idea about what was going on. Two black SUVs of the same make and model common with Pakistan's Inter-Services Intelligence Directorate agents sat parked on the curb, and four more plain-clothed men stood in the street carrying big HK G3 rifles, a standard military-issue weapon of the Pakistani Defense Force.

Yes, Embling was certain now, he was being scooped up by the ISI, the national spy agency. It wasn't good news by any stretch. He knew enough about their modus operandi to recognize that a predawn rousting at gunpoint likely meant a basement cell and a bit of the rough stuff at the very least. But getting picked up by the Army-run intelligence organization was a damn sight better than being kidnapped by Tehrik-i-Taliban, the Haqqani network, Al-Qaeda, the URC, Lashkar-e-Omar, the Quetta Shura Taliban, the Nadeem Commando, or any one of the other terror outfits running around armed and angry on these dangerous streets of Peshawar.

Nigel Embling was a former member of British foreign intelligence, and he knew how to talk to other intelligence officers. That he might be forced to do so while getting his knuckles broken or his head dunked in a bucket of cold water hardly appealed to him, but he knew this was preferable to dealing with a room full of jihadists who would just quickly and messily hack his head from his neck with a dull sword.

The plain-clothed riflemen on either side of Embling in the backseat of the SUV said nothing as they drove through the empty streets of the city. Embling didn't bother to ask the men any questions. He knew he would have his only opportunity to get answers wherever it was he was going. These men were just the scoop crew. These men had been provided with a name and a picture and an address, and then they'd been sent out on this errand as if they'd been sent down to the corner market for tea and cakes. They would be here for their ability to squeeze triggers and put their boots into backsides . . . They wouldn't be sent along with the answer to any of Embling's questions.

So he kept quiet and concentrated on their route.

The ISI's main HQ in Peshawar is just off Khyber Road in Peshawar's western suburbs, which would have required the SUVs to turn left onto Grand Trunk, but instead they continued on, into the northern suburbs. Embling imagined he was being taken to one of the God-knows-how-many offsite branch locations. The ISI kept a number of safe houses, simple residential flats and commercial office space, all over the city, so that they could cause more unofficial mischief than they could during an official visit to the HQ. The senior Brit expat's suspicions were confirmed when they pulled up in front of a darkened office building, and two men with radios on their vests and Uzi submachine guns hanging from their shoulders stepped out from behind the glass door to greet the vehicles

Without a word, some six men walked Nigel Embling across the pavement, through the doorway, and then up a narrow staircase. He was led into a dark room—he fully expected it to be a cold and stark interrogation cell, but when someone flipped on the fluorescent lighting he saw it to be a well-used small office, complete with a desk and chairs, a desktop computer, a phone, and a wall full of Pakistani military banners, emblems, and even framed photos of cricket players from the Pakistani national team.

The armed men put Embling in the chair, unlocked his handcuffs, and then left the room.

Embling looked around, surprised to be left alone in this small but not uncomfortable office. Seconds later, a man entered from behind, stepped around Embling's chair, and slid behind the desk. He wore the tan uniform of the Pakistani Army, but his green pullover sweater covered any insignia that might have revealed information to the man sitting across from him. All Embling could discern was that the man was in his late thirties, with a short beard and mustache and a ruddy complexion. He wore narrow frameless glasses that were propped halfway down his angular nose.

"My name is Mohammed al Darkur. I am a major in the Inter-Services Intelligence Directorate."

Nigel opened his mouth to ask the major why he'd been dragged from his bed and driven across town for the introduction, but al Darkur spoke again.

"And you, Nigel Embling. *You* are a British spy."

Nigel laughed. "Kudos for getting right to the point, even if your information is incorrect. I am Dutch. True, my mother was from Scotland, which is technically part of the British Empire, although her family preferred to think of themselves as—"

"Your mother was from England, from Sussex," al Darkur interrupted. "Her name was Sally, and she died in 1988. Your father's name was Harold, and he was from London, and his death predated the death of your mother by nine years."

Embling's bushy eyebrows rose, but he did not speak.

"There is no use in lying. We know all about you. At different times in the past we have had you under surveillance, and we are quite aware of your affiliation with the British Secret Service."

Embling composed himself. Chuckled again. "You really are doing this all wrong, Major Darkur. I certainly won't tell you how to do your job, but this isn't much of an interrogation. I believe you need to take a few lessons from some of your colleagues. I've sat in a few ISI dungeons in my time here as a guest of your delightful nation; I've been suspected of this or that by your organization since you were in nappies, I'd wager. This is how you do it. First, you are supposed to start with a little deprivation, maybe some cold—"

"Does this look like an ISI dungeon?" asked al Darkur.

Embling looked around again. "No. In fact, your overlords might want to send you back for some remedial training; you can't even get the scary environment down. Doesn't the ISI have decorators who can help you create that perfect, claustrophobic 'modern horror' look?"

"Mr. Embling, this is not an interrogation room. This is my office."

Nigel looked the man over for several seconds. Shook his head slowly. "Then you really haven't a clue how to do your job, do you, Major al Darkur?"

The Pakistani major smiled, as if indulgent of the old man's taunts. "You were picked up this morning because another directorate in the ISI has asked that yourself, and other suspicious expatriates like you, be brought in for interrogation. After interrogation, I am ordered to begin the process of having you expelled from the country."

Wow, thought Embling. *What the bloody hell is going on?* "Not just me? All expatriates?"

"Many. Not all, but many."

"On what grounds would we be given the boot?"

"No grounds whatsoever. Well . . . I suppose I am to make up something."

Embling did not respond. He was still gobsmacked by this information, and more so by the frank way this man was delivering it.

Al Darkur continued, "There are elements in my organization, and in the Army as a whole, who have enacted a secret military intelligence order that is only to be used in times of high internal conflict or war, in order to lessen the risk of foreign spies or agents provocateurs in our country. We are always in times of high internal conflict here, this is nothing new. And we are not at war. Therefore, their legal grounds are shaky. Still, they *are* getting away with it. Our civilian government is not aware of the scope or the focus paid to this operation, and this gives me great pause." Al Darkur hesitated for a long moment. Twice he began to speak but stopped himself. Finally he said, "This new edict, and other things that have been going on in my organization over the last months, have given me reason to suspect some of my high-ranking colleagues of planning a coup against our civilian leadership."

Embling had no idea why this military officer, a stranger, would be telling him all this. Especially if he really did believe him to be a British spy.

"I hand-selected your case, Mr. Embling, I made sure that my men would pick you up and bring you to me."

"What on earth for?"

"Because I would like to offer my services to your nation. It is a difficult time in my country. And there are forces in my organization that are making it more difficult. I believe the United Kingdom can help those of us who . . . shall I say, do not want the type of change that many in the ISI are seeking."

Embling looked across the desk at the man for a long time. He then said, "If this is legitimate, then I must ask. Of all places, why are we doing this here?"

Al Darkur smiled a handsome smile now. He spoke in an attractive lilting cadence. "Mr. Embling. My office is the one environment in this country where I can be absolutely sure no one is listening in on our conversation. It is not that this room is not bugged, of course it is. But it is bugged for my benefit, and I can control the erase function on the recorder."

Embling smiled. He loved nothing more than clever practicality. "What division do you work for?"

"JIB."

"I'm sorry, I don't recognize the acronym."

"Yes you do, Mr. Embling. I can show you my file on your associations with other members of the ISI in the past."

The Brit shrugged. He decided to drop the pretense of ignorance. "Joint Intelligence Bureau," he said. "Very well."

"My duties take me into the FATA." The Federally Administered Tribal Areas, a sort of no-man's-land of territory along the border with Afghanistan and Iran, where the Taliban and other organizations provided the only real law. "I work with most of the government-sponsored militias there. The Khyber Rifles. The Chitral Scouts, the Kurram Militia."

"I see. And the department that is working to have me kicked out of the country?"

"The order has come through normal channels, but I believe this action is being initiated by General Riaz Rehan, the head of Joint Intelligence Miscellaneous

Division. JIM is responsible for foreign espionage operations."

Embling knew what JIM was responsible for, but he allowed al Darkur to tell him. The Englishman's fertile brain raced through the possibilities of this encounter. He did not want to admit to anything, but he damn well wanted more intelligence about the situation. "Major. I am at a loss here. I am not an English agent, but *were* I an English agent, I would hardly want to involve myself in the middle of the nasty infighting that goes on, as a matter of course, in the Pakistani intelligence community. If you have some quarrel with Joint Intelligence Miscellaneous, that's your problem, not Britain's."

"It *is* your problem, because your nation *has* picked sides, and they have chosen poorly. Joint Intelligence Miscellaneous, Rehan's directorate, has been given a great deal of support by the UK, as well as the Americans. They have charmed and fooled your politicians, and I can prove it. If you can provide me the back channel access to your leadership, then I will make my case, and your agency will learn a valuable lesson about trusting anyone in JIM."

"Major al Darkur, please remember. I never said I worked with British intelligence."

"No, you didn't. *I* said that."

"Indeed. I am an old man. Retired from the import/export field."

Al Darkur smiled. "Then I think you need to come out of retirement, maybe export some intelligence out of Pakistan that might be useful to your nation. You could import some assistance from MI6 that might be useful to my country. I assure you that your nation has never had an asset in Pakistani intelligence as well placed as myself, with as much incentive to work for our joint interests as myself."

"And what about me? If I am given the boot from Pakistan, I won't be much help."

"I can delay your departure for months. Today was just the initial interview. I will drag my feet through every phase of the process after this."

Embling nodded. "Major, I just have to ask. If you are so sure your organization is rife with informants for General Rehan, how is it you are able to trust all these men working for you?"

Al Darkur smiled again. "Before I was ISI I was in SSG, Special Services Group. These men are also SSG. Commandos from Zarrar Company, counterterrorism operators. My former unit."

"And they are loyal to you?"

Al Darkur shrugged. "They are loyal to the concept of not getting blown to bits by a roadside bomb. I share their allegiance to that concept myself."

"As do I, Major." Embling reached out and shook the major's hand. "So nice to find common ground with a new friend." It was a polite thing to say, but neither man in this room trusted the other so early in such a risky relationship.

Two hours later, Nigel Embling sat at home, drank tea at his desk, and drummed his fingers on a well-worn leather blotter.

His morning had been interesting, to say the least. From a dead sleep to a pitch from a highly placed intelligence asset. It was enough to make his head spin.

Houseboy Mahmood, sporting a nasty purple-and-red gash on his head, brought his employer a plate with slices

153

of *suji ka,* a coconut flour, yogurt, and semolina-based pastry. He'd brought it home from the neighbor's house when Embling was returned by the SUVs from ISI. Embling took a sweet cake and bit into it, but he remained lost in thought.

"Thanks, lad. Why don't you go play football with your mates this afternoon? You've had a long day already."

"Thank you, Mr. Nigel."

"Thank *you,* my young friend, for being brave this morning. You and your mates will inherit this country someday soon, and I should think they will need a good and brave man like you will turn out to be."

Mahmood did not understand what his employer was talking about, but he did understand that he had the afternoon free to kick the soccer ball in the street with his friends.

As his houseboy left him alone in his study, Embling ate his cakes and drank his tea, his mind filled with worry. Worry about the potential for him to be expelled, for the dangers of high-level infighting in the Pakistani Army's spy service, for the work that he would need to do to check out this Major al Darkur to see if he was, in fact, who he said he was, and not affiliated with any of the naughtier elements roaming around.

As worrisome as all this was, the chief concern of Embling's right now was supremely practical. It appeared, to him, as if he'd just recruited an agent to spy on behalf of a nation that he did not represent.

He'd had no direct working relationship with London for years, though a few of the graybeards working at Legoland, the nickname of London's SIS headquarters on the Thames, gave him a call from time to time to check up on this or that.

Once, the year before, they'd actually passed his name off to an American organization that he'd helped with a small matter here in Peshawar. The Yanks who'd arrived had been top-notch, some of the sharpest field operators he'd ever worked with. What were their names? Yes, John Clark and Ding Chavez.

As Embling finished the last of his mid-morning snack and wiped his fingers clean with a napkin, he decided he could, if this al Darkur chap checked out, run a very unusual version of the "false flag." He could operate al Darkur as an agent without Embling actually revealing to al Darkur that he had no one, officially speaking, to pass his intelligence up the chain to.

And then, when Embling had something important, something solid, Embling would find a customer for his product.

The big Englishman sipped the rest of his tea and smiled at the audacity of his new plan. It was ridiculous, really.

But why on earth not?

18

Jack Ryan Sr. stepped over to a full-length mirror on the wall between two sets of lockers. Tonight's presidential debate at Cleveland's Case Western Reserve University was being held in the Emerson Physical Education Center to accommodate the huge crowd. It was also known as the Veale Center, and Ryan had no trouble picturing this venue hosting a basketball game. Around him on the walls of the locker room that had been converted into a dressing room for the presidential candidate, big Spartan silhouettes looked back at him. The adjacent bathroom set aside for Ryan's needs had a dozen showers.

He'd needed none. He'd showered at the hotel.

Tonight's debate was the second of three scheduled between himself and Kealty, and this was the one of the three Jack had insisted on. Just one moderator asking questions of the two men, seated at a table. Almost like a friendly conversation. It was to be less formal, less stiff. Kealty had objected at first, saying it was also less presidential, but Jack had held firm, and the backroom dealing of Jack's campaign manager, Arnie van Damm, had won the day.

The theme of tonight's debate would be foreign affairs, and Jack knew he had Kealty beat on the subject. The polls said so, so Arnie agreed, too. But Jack was not relaxed. He looked into the mirror again and took another sip of water.

He liked these all-too-brief moments of solitude. Cathy

had just left the dressing room; right now she would be finding her seat in the front row. Her last words to him before leaving chimed in his ears as he looked at himself in the mirror.

"Good luck, Jack. And don't forget your happy face."

Along with Arnie and his speechwriter Callie Weston, Cathy had been his closest confidante on this campaign. She did not get into policy discussions very often, unless the subject of health care came up, but she had watched her husband closely during his hundreds of television appearances, and she gave him her opinions on how he conveyed himself to the public.

Cathy considered herself supremely qualified for the role. No one in the world knew Jack Ryan better than she did. She could look into his eyes or listen to the sound of his voice and know everything about his mood, his energy, even whether or not he'd snuck an afternoon cup of coffee that she did not permit when they were traveling together.

Normally Jack did great in front of a camera. He was natural, not stiff at all; he came off just like the man he was. A decent, intelligent guy who was, at the same time, strong-willed and motivated.

But occasionally Cathy saw things that she did not think helped him get his point across. Of particular concern to her was the fact that, in her opinion, whenever he talked about one of Kealty's policies or comments that he did not agree with—which was essentially everything that came out of Kealty's White House—Jack's face had a tendency to turn dark.

Cathy had recently sat in bed with her husband on one of the almost nonexistent nights that found him taking a quick break at home from the campaign trail. For nearly an hour she held the remote control for the flat-screen TV on the wall. That would have been hell enough for Jack Ryan, even if his mug was *not* on all the programs that she had recorded and flipped through. That was murderous for a guy who never liked seeing his face or hearing his voice on television. But Cathy was unrelenting; she used their TiVo, cycled from one press conference to the next, from lofty sit-down interviews with major network anchors all the way to impromptu exchanges with high school reporters while walking through shopping malls.

In each clip she showed him, every time a Kealty policy was brought up, Jack Ryan's face changed. It wasn't a sneer, and for that Jack felt he should get a damn medal, as incensed as he was by, literally, every last decision of importance by the Kealty administration. But Cathy was right, Jack could not deny it. Whenever an interviewer brought up a Kealty policy, Jack's eyes narrowed slightly, his jaw tightened just perceptibly, and often his head shook back and forth, just once, as if to say "No!"

Cathy had tracked back for a moment to show Jack at a barbecue in Fort Worth, with a paper plate of brisket and corn on the cob in one hand and an iced tea in the other. A C-SPAN camera crew following him picked up an exchange where a middle-aged woman mentioned Kealty's recent push for more regulation on the oil and gas industries.

While the woman relayed the hardships her family were enduring, Jack's jaw tightened and he shook his head. There was empathy relayed in his body language, but only after his initial recoil of anger. His first reaction, that first flash of rage, locked into a still frame when Cathy pressed the pause button, was unmistakable.

As they sat in bed together Jack Ryan tried to lighten

the moment. "I think I deserve partial credit on that one for not tossing up the baked beans I'd just eaten. I mean, we *were* talking about increasing red tape and bureaucracy on business in *this* economy."

Cathy smiled, shook her head. "Partial credit isn't going to get you the highest office in the land this time, Jack. You are winning, but you haven't won yet."

Jack nodded. Chastened. "I know. I'll work on it, I promise."

And now, in the locker room at Case Western Reserve, Jack worked on it. He tried out his happy face on the empty room, while thinking back to that poor woman's family unable to find work in an environment that stifled the entire industry in which she sought employment.

Chin up, a slight nod, eyes relaxed, no squinting.

Ugh, Jack thought. *Feels unnatural.*

He sighed. He realized, not for the first time, that if it feels unnatural, then that means Cathy was right, and he had been making faces ever since he'd thrown his hat into the ring.

He worried now that debating foreign policy in person with Ed Kealty would be a tremendous challenge to his self-control.

Jack spent one more moment practicing the happy face. Thought about Cathy watching this debate from the audience.

He smiled unnaturally at the mirror. Did it again A third time.

The fourth smile on his lips was real. He almost laughed. He couldn't help it. A grown man making faces into a mirror.

He snorted out a laugh now. Politics, when you drilled right down into it, was ultimately so goddamn ridiculous.

Jack Ryan Sr. shook his head and stepped to the door. One more long sigh, one more affirmation to himself that he could pull off the happy face, and then he turned the knob.

Outside in the hall, his people began moving. Andrea Price-O'Day stepped up to his shoulder. The rest of his security team formed in a diamond around him for the walk to the stage.

"Swordsman is moving," Price-O'Day said into her cuff mike.

19

Ed Kealty and Jack Ryan stepped out from opposite wings onto a stage awash in television lighting. There was polite applause from a crowd of students, media, and Clevelanders who'd managed to secure tickets. They met in the middle. Jack had a quick mental image of the men touching gloves, but instead they just shook hands. Ryan smiled and nodded, said "Mr. President," and Kealty himself nodded, reached behind Ryan and patted him on the back with his right hand as both men stepped forward to the round table.

Ryan knew that Ed Kealty wished he had a switchblade in that hand.

The two men sat at the small conference table. In front of them sat *CBS Evening News* anchor Joshua Ramirez, a young-looking fifty-year-old who wore his hair slicked back and stylish glasses that, with the glare of the stage lighting, created a distracting shine in Ryan's eyes. Jack liked Ramirez overall; he was smart and affable enough when the camera was off and professional enough when the camera was on. CBS had been no friend to Ryan's first presidency, and they certainly seemed to be continuing the pro-Kealty slant through this campaign, but Josh Ramirez was just a foot soldier in their army, a working stiff, and Ryan didn't blame him.

Ryan had been kicked around in the media long enough not to take it personally. Some of the things the media said and wrote about him, virtually accusing him of everything from stealing money from the elderly to taking lunches from school kids' mouths, were nothing if not incredibly personal.

Jack Ryan, you are a vile human being . . . nothing personal. Right.

Still, Ramirez wasn't as bad as some of the others. The general media's collusion in Kealty's reelection campaign was prevalent. A few weeks back, a guy at a Kealty Q&A in Denver had the temerity to ask the President of the United States when he thought gas prices would drop back down to where he could afford a road trip with his family. Kealty, in a moment that must have made his minders groan, shook his head at the question from the working stiff and suggested that the man see this as an opportunity to go out and buy a hybrid vehicle.

Not one of the major media outlets or wire services ran the quote. Ryan himself brought it up the next morning at an electric motor plant in Allegheny, Pennsylvania, making the obvious point, seemingly lost on Kealty, that a family having trouble filling their tank might have trouble purchasing a new car.

Five minutes after making the quip, as Jack climbed back into his SUV to leave the motor plant, Arnie van Damm just shook his head. "Jack, you just delivered a great line that no one but those people on that factory floor will ever hear."

Arnie was right. None of the big media outlets ran it. Van Damm promised Ryan he could not count on any "gotcha moments" by the mainstream media against Ed Kealty. No, all the "gotcha moments" would go against Jack Ryan.

Liberal bias in the media was a fact of nature. Like the rain and the cold, Ryan just dealt with it and moved on.

Ramirez opened the debate with an explanation about the rules, then a lighthearted story about arguments between his elementary school children, finishing by joking that he hoped the two men in front of him would "play nice." Ryan smiled as if the comment was not outrageously patronizing, and then the moderator began with the questions.

Ramirez's line of questions started out in Russia, moved to China, to Central America, and then to the United States' relationships with NATO and allies around the world. Both Ryan and Kealty addressed the CBS anchor directly with their answers, and they avoided any fireworks, even agreeing on a few topics here and there.

International terrorism was all but avoided until the second half of the ninety-minute debate. Ramirez turned to the subject by lobbing a softball to Kealty, a question about a recent drone hit on a compound in Yemen that had taken out an Al-Qaeda operative wanted for bombing a nightclub in Bali.

Kealty assured America that once reelected, he would continue his carrot-and-stick policy of high-level engagement with anyone, friend or foe, who would come to the negotiating table with America, while at the same time eliminating America's enemies when they refused to negotiate.

Ramirez turned to Ryan. "Your campaign has attempted to position you as the candidate who is the best choice in America's fight against those who would do us harm, but when you were President, there were fewer successful targeted killings of high-level terrorists than under President Kealty's first term. Are you willing to accept that you no longer can lay claim to the title of terrorist hunter?"

Ryan took a sip of water. To his left, he could sense

Kealty leaning in slightly, as if to make a show of listening to how Ryan would answer this one. Jack kept his attention on Joshua Ramirez as he spoke. "I would like to suggest that President Kealty's drone attacks, while unquestionably taking some of the terrorist leadership off the table, do little to fight a successful war in the long-term sense."

Kealty leaned back in his chair, waving the comment away as if it were preposterous.

"And why is that?" Ramirez asked.

"Because if I've learned one thing in my thirty-five years of public service, it is that good intelligence is the key to good decision-making. And when we go to the trouble to identify someone, some terrorist leader who has an absolute treasure trove of intelligence resources in his head, only as a last resort should we be blowing him to pieces. An unmanned aerial vehicle is an important asset, but it is only one asset. It is only one tool. And it is a tool, in my opinion, that we are overusing. We need to exploit the hard work that has been done by our military and intelligence people in identifying the target in the first place, and we need to do our best to exploit the target."

"Exploit it?" Ramirez asked. He really did not expect Ryan to question the uptick in UAV assassinations.

"Yes. Exploit. Instead of killing the man we're after, we need to try to learn what he knows, who he knows, where he's been, where he's headed, what he's planning, those sorts of things."

"And how will President Jack Ryan do that?"

"Our intelligence community and military should be allowed to, when possible, detain these people, or we should pressure the governments hosting these people to pick these men up in the field and turn them over to us. We need to give our forces, and the forces of our allies, our *true* allies, the resources and the political cover to do this. That is not happening under President Ed Kealty."

"And once we have them?" For the first time in tonight's debate, Kealty blurted in, directing his comment toward Ryan. "What do you suggest? Bamboo shoots up the fingernails?"

Joshua Ramirez lifted a finger off the desk in an extremely gentle wag, a feeble and ineffective means of admonishing Kealty to play by the agreed-upon rules of the debate.

Jack ignored Kealty himself but addressed the question: "Many people say we cannot derive intelligence from means other than torture. My experience knows that to be untrue. Sometimes it is difficult to encourage our enemies to be forthcoming; they are not only highly motivated but they are also very well aware that we will extend them privileges and rights they would never extend to any prisoner they hold. It doesn't matter how kindly and gently we handle their prisoners, they will kill and torture our people whenever they get them."

The CBS anchor said, "You speak about these 'means' that we have at our disposal to coax information from our enemies. But just how effective are they?"

"A very fair question, Josh. I can't go into the procedures that were in place when I was at the CIA or when I was President, but I promise you that our success rate getting intelligence from terrorists was much better than my opponent's tactic of blowing up people from an altitude of twenty thousand feet. Dead men tell no tales, as they say."

Ramirez turned halfway to Kealty before the President began his rebuttal. "Josh, my opponent would risk American lives unnecessarily by sending our kids in the military into harm's way in the most dangerous places in the world just for the chance to interrogate an enemy combatant. I assure you, interrogations under a Jack Ryan presidency will be beyond what is allowed in the Geneva Conventions."

It was Ryan's turn to rebut. He forgot his happy face, but he took care not to look at Kealty, instead keeping his focus on the annoying reflections in the glasses of Joshua Ramirez. "First, I consider our fighting men and women to be just that, men and women. Many of them are young, a heck of a lot younger than President Kealty and I, but I bristle at the description of them as kids. Second, the men and women who work in those elite units of the military and intelligence communities who are tasked with the admittedly difficult and dangerous job of capturing our enemies in the field are professionals, and they go into harm's way with regularity already. Often for the policies of my opponent, which, I believe, aren't getting us anywhere." Now he looked to Kealty with a polite nod. "You are absolutely right about that, Mr. President, that is a very, very difficult duty to give anyone"—then back to Ramirez—"but these men and women are the best in the world at this type of work. And to the last man, and the last woman, I truly believe that they know that their hard work saves American lives. They understand their duty, a duty they volunteer for, and a duty that they believe in. I have nothing but the most tremendous respect for our UAV crews." He paused. "I'm sorry, unmanned aerial vehicles. It is an incredible resource operated by incredible people. I just feel that at the strategic level, we should be doing a better job directing our assets to exploit our intelligence successes to the highest possible degree, and I do not believe we are doing that under Ed Kealty's administration."

Ramirez started to say something else, but Ryan continued, "Joshua, your network reported just the other day about the capture in Russia of the leader of one of the most deadly rebel groups in the Caucasus region by Russia's FSB. Now, I will surprise no one in your audience tonight when I say I am not a huge fan of a lot of Russia's recent decisions and policies." Ryan smiled when he said this, but his face was no less intense when he was smiling. "Especially when it comes to some of their reported treatment of their own people in the Caucasus. But by capturing this man, Israpil Nabiyev, instead of just killing him, they can potentially learn so much about his organization. This can be a game changer in the region." Jack Ryan paused, shrugged. "We could use a game changer or two in the Middle East, I think we can all admit that."

Many in the crowd clapped.

Ramirez turned back to Kealty. "Thirty seconds' rebuttal on this topic, Mr. President, and then we will need to move on."

Ed Kealty nodded, leaned back in his chair. "Here is something you don't hear too much, Josh. I actually agree with my opponent. We do need, as he put it, a game changer over there. I did not plan on revealing this tonight, but I just got the okay to do so from the Department of Justice. I am going to take this opportunity to announce the recent capture, by US federal law enforcement agencies working with my administration, of Mr. Saif Rahman Yasin, better known as the Emir."

Kealty waited for the gasps in the audience to subside. They did, eventually, and then he continued. "Yasin has killed dozens of Americans here at home, and he has killed hundreds of Americans and others around the world. He is now on US soil, in US custody, and I believe we will have a photograph made available to confirm this in the coming hours. I apologize for not bringing this to light before now, but, as you can imagine, there are a lot of security concerns involved, a lot of things to consider, so we have waited to—"

Thirty seconds was up, but Ed Kealty was just getting started.

"—bring this to the attention of the public. Now, Josh, I won't be able to comment on any of the details of Yasin's capture or his detainment or his whereabouts, this is all to keep the brave men and women involved in our operation safe, but I will say that I have spoken with the attorney general at length about the case, and we plan to bring Mr. Yasin to trial just as soon as is feasible. He will be indicted for the incidents he has been tied to here in the United States. In Colorado, in Utah, in Iowa, and in Virginia. Attorney General Brannigan will determine where the trial will take place, but clearly it will be in one of these locations."

Jack Ryan did not lose his cool; he even smiled slightly, nodded pleasantly. *Happy face, Jack,* he said to himself, over and over. He knew this day would come. He knew the Emir was in custody. At first he thought his capture had been kept secret for security reasons, as Ed Kealty just now claimed. But Arnie van Damm had insisted from the beginning that Kealty was keeping the Emir on ice until he could "play" him for full advantage in the campaign. At the time, many months earlier, before the Ryan–Kealty battle had even begun in earnest, Jack did not believe his campaign manager. He thought Arnie was just being even more cynical than usual.

But not anymore. Van Damm had point-blank predicted that Ed Kealty would dump the Emir out onto the table during one of the debates; he even said it would be number two or number three.

Jack wanted to turn his head right now and make eye contact with van Damm, and it took every bit of willpower to keep from doing so. But he knew that "look" would be capitalized on by the media outlets in Kealty's corner. The front page of *The New York Times* tomorrow would read "Ryan Looks for Cover."

Unless they'd already used that headline once before. It was so hard to remember.

So Ryan sat there; he'd turned toward President Kealty as if Jack were hearing this for the first time. He'd groaned inwardly at the claim that Ed's administration had had anything whatsoever to do with the capture of the most wanted man in the world. Ryan had no doubt that the offhanded inference Kealty had made was on purpose.

Ryan concentrated on his poker face while he thought about the capture of the Emir. What was it now, ten months since The Campus had taken him down in Nevada? What role his son played in Yasin's capture Ryan had no idea. Surely he was not in on the ground operation. No, that would have been Chavez, Clark certainly, even Jack's nephew Dominic. Jesus, the poor kid had to deal with all that just after the death of his own brother.

But Jack Sr. could not get his head around the fact that his son was involved in the capture of the Emir.

True, his oldest boy was changing, had changed. He'd grown into a man. That was to be expected, even though Jack Sr. did not like it one bit. But his role in the events of the capture of—

"Anything you would like to say to follow up, Mr. President?"

Ryan snapped out of it, chastised himself for letting his

mind wander at just the wrong time. Jack caught a sly smile on Josh Ramirez's face, but he knew the cameras had missed it. Every camera in the building was on Ryan. Hell, there was probably a shot halfway up his sinuses, they were so tightly focused on him right now. He wondered if he had a "deer in the headlights" look. The media would accuse him of it; this would be one hell of a gotcha moment unless he turned it around right now.

Happy face, Jack. "Well, this is certainly fantastic news. I would like to take this opportunity to extend my sincere and profound congratulations—"

Ed Kealty sat up straighter in his chair next to Ryan.

"—to the great men and women of our military, intelligence, and law enforcement organizations, and I would also like to thank any foreign nation or service involved in bringing this terrible human being to justice."

Kealty glowered at Ryan now; Jack could see it in Ramirez's glasses.

"This is a great day in America, but I also see this as an important crossroads for us. Because, as you all just heard, President Kealty and his administration plan to try the Emir in our federal court system, and I could not possibly disagree with this any more strongly. As much respect as I have for our system of laws, I think they should be reserved for our citizens and for those who have not made it their life's work to make war on the United States of America. Putting Yasin on the witness stand is not justice; it would be the highest order of injustice.

"This moment is a fork in the road in our war on terrorism. If President Kealty wins the election in November, for the next couple of years the Umayyad Revolutionary Council, all its supporters, and its affiliated organizations will have the opportunity to own the bully pulpit. The

Emir will use the courts to promote his brand of hate, he will use the courts to reveal the sources and methods of our intelligence services, and he will use the courts to create theater that will only draw attention to him and his cause. And you all, ladies and gentlemen taxpayers, you all will be footing the bill for millions or tens of millions of dollars of increased security in our federal courtrooms.

"If you think that is a good idea . . . if you think giving the Emir this opportunity is the right call . . . well, then I'm sorry to say this, but you'd better go ahead and vote for my opponent.

"But if you think that is a bad idea, if you think the Emir should get his day in court, but in a military court, where he will have more rights than any prisoner he or those like him ever had in their custody, but still not the same set of rights of every law-abiding, tax-paying American citizen, then I hope you will vote for me."

Ryan shrugged slightly, looked right at Josh Ramirez.

"Josh, I don't make many campaign promises. I get kicked around in a lot of newspapers and the news shows, including yours, for the fact I campaign on my record and on my character, but not on what I promise to do at some later date." Ryan smiled. "I just think most Americans are pretty smart, and they've seen enough campaign promises never come to fruition. It has always been my thinking that if I just show America who I am, what I stand for and believe in, and if I can show myself to be a guy that you can trust, then I'll get some folks to vote for me. If it is enough to win, great. But if it's not, well . . . America will pick who it thinks is best, and I'm okay with that.

"But I *am* going to make a campaign promise right here and now." He turned to the camera. "If you see fit to put me in the White House, the first thing I'll do, *literally* the first thing I do when I get back to 1600 Pennsylvania from the Capitol steps, is sit down at my desk and sign papers remanding Saif Yasin into military custody." He sighed. "You will never see his face on television or hear his voice on the radio, nor the voice of his attorney. His trial will be fair, he will have a robust defense, but it will be behind a wall. Some people may not agree with that, but I have six weeks before election day, and I hope you will extend me the courtesy of trying to convince you that this is the right move for the United States of America."

Many in the crowd applauded. Many did not.

The debate ended soon after, Kealty and Ryan shook hands for the cameras, then they kissed their wives at the front of the stage.

Jack leaned into Cathy's ear. "How did I do?"

Dr. Cathy Ryan kept a wide smile on her face as she whispered back, "I'm proud of you. You kept your happy face through all that." She kissed him again and then said with a grin, "I do love it when you listen to me."

20

Newport, Rhode Island, sits on the southern tip of Aquidneck Island, some thirty miles south of Providence. As well as being the home of Naval Station Newport and more surviving colonial buildings than any other city in the United States, it also retains a number of gargantuan nineteenth- and early-twentieth-century mansions built by many of America's wealthiest industrial and financial tycoons of that time period. John Jacob Astor IV, William and Cornelius Vanderbilt, Oliver Belmont, and Peter Widener of US Steel and American Tobacco, as well as others, all constructed palatial summer retreats on the island during the Gilded Age of the post-Reconstruction period.

Most of the billionaires are gone; their homes now owned by trusts or by family estates or by museums or foundations, but a few über-affluent individuals still called Newport home. And the most well-heeled resident on the island lived in a massive seaside estate on Bellevue Avenue, just three blocks from St. Mary's Cathedral, historically important as the location of the 1953 wedding of John F. Kennedy and Jacqueline Bouvier.

This homeowner's name was Paul Laska, he was seventy years old, he was currently number four on the *Forbes* list of wealthiest Americans, and he was of the opinion that a second presidential term of John Patrick Ryan would probably mean, within a couple of years, the end of the world.

Sitting alone in the library of his opulent mansion, Paul Laska watched Jack Ryan kiss his wife at the end of the debate. Then Laska stood, turned off the television, and walked alone to his bedroom. His pale, aged face flushed red with anger and his slumped shoulders reflected his sour mood.

He had hoped tonight's debate would be the moment when Ed Kealty's fortunes turned. Laska had hoped this, had all but expected this, because he knew something almost no one else in the world knew until thirty minutes ago.

The aging billionaire already knew that the Emir was in US custody. This nugget of information had kept his spirits up while Ryan's lead in the polls remained through the summer and into the early fall. He'd told himself that when Ed made the "big reveal" in the second presidential debate he would put to bed that tired adage about Jack Ryan that said he was the "tough on terror" candidate. Then, with a few weeks of heavy campaigning in key battleground states, Kealty would shoot ahead for the home stretch.

Now, as Laska took off his slippers and climbed into bed, he realized that his hopes had been fanciful.

Somehow Jack Ryan had still won the damned debate, even with the rabbit Kealty had pulled out of his hat.

"*Hovno!*" he shouted at the cold, dark house. It meant "shit" in Czech, and Paul Laska always fell back on his native tongue when cursing.

Paul Laska was born Pavel Laska in Brno, in the present-day Czech Republic. He grew up behind the iron curtain, but he'd not suffered particularly for this misfortune. His father had been a party member in good standing, which allowed young Pavel to go to good schools in Brno and then Prague, and then to university in Budapest and then Moscow.

After obtaining advanced degrees in mathematics, he returned to Czechoslovakia to follow his father into banking. A good communist, Laska had done well for himself in the Soviet satellite nation, but in 1968 he came out in support of the liberal reforms of First Party Secretary Alexander Dubček.

For a few short months in 1968, Laska and other Dubček supporters felt the reforms of the Czechoslovakian decentralization from Moscow. They were still communists but nationalized communists; their plan was to break away from the Soviets and apply Czech solutions to Czech problems. The Soviets didn't like that plan, needless to say, and KGB operatives flooded into Prague to break up the party.

Pavel Laska and a radical girlfriend were picked up with a dozen others at a protest and held for questioning by the KGB. Both were beaten; the girlfriend was sent to prison, but somehow Laska returned to work with the leadership of the uprising, and he stayed with them until one night in August when Warsaw Pact tanks rolled into Prague, and the fledgling rebellion was crushed on orders from Moscow.

Unlike most of the leadership, Laska was not killed or imprisoned. He returned to his bank, but soon emigrated to the United States, taking with him, as he'd told the story thousands of times, only the clothes on his back and a dream.

And by most anyone's standards his dream had been realized.

He moved to New York in 1969 to attend NYU. Upon graduation, he went into banking and finance. First he had a few good years, then he had a few great years, and by the early eighties he was one of the wealthiest men on Wall Street.

Though he bought properties including his homes in Rhode Island, Los Angeles, Aspen, and Manhattan, in the 1980s he and his wife used much of their money on their philanthropy, throwing their huge financial resources behind reformers in Eastern Europe in an attempt to enact the changes that had failed to materialize during the Prague Spring. After the fall of world communism, Paul started the Progressive Nations Institute to assist grass-roots change in oppressed countries around the world, and he funded development projects across the globe from clean-water initiatives in Central America to land mine eradication efforts in Laos.

In the late 1990s Laska turned his sights inward, toward his adopted nation. He'd long felt the America of the post-Cold War period to be no better than the Soviet Union of the Cold War days; to him the United States was an oppressive brute in world affairs and a bastion of racism and bigotry. Now that the Soviet Union was no more, he poured billions of dollars into causes to fight American evils as he perceived them and, along with spending enough effort engaging in the capitalistic shrine known as the New York Stock Exchange to benefit himself, Laska spent the rest of his time and money supporting the enemies of capitalism.

In 2000 he formed the Progressive Constitution Initiative, a liberal political action organization and law firm, and he staffed it with the best and the brightest radical lawyers from the ACLU, academia, and private practice. As well as taking on states and municipalities, the main function of the organization was to sue the

US government for what it considered to be overreaches of power. It also defended those prosecuted by the United States, and worked against any and all state or federal capital punishment cases, as well as many other causes célèbres.

Since the death of his wife seven years before, Laska had lived alone, save for a team of servants and a security detail, but his homes were rarely lonely places. He threw lavish parties attended by liberal politicians, activists, artists, and foreign movers and shakers. The Progressive Nations Institute was run out of midtown Manhattan, and the Progressive Constitution Initiative out of D.C., but ground zero for the overarching belief system of Paul Laska was his home in Newport. It was no joke when people claimed that more progressive punditry had been doled out on Paul Laska's pool deck than in most liberal think tanks.

But his influence did not stop at his organizations or his garden parties. His foundation also financed many left-wing websites and media outlets, and even a confidential online clearinghouse for liberal journalists to gather and pass on story ideas and agree on a cohesive progressive message. Paul funded, sometimes covertly, sometimes not, many radio and television networks across the country, always with a quid pro quo that he and his causes would be given positive press. More than once an organization had had its financial spigot shut off, either temporarily or permanently, because its reporting did not match the political beliefs of the man who financed the entire operation from behind the scenes.

He had contributed to the campaigns of Ed Kealty for fifteen years, and many political junkies gave Paul Laska much of the credit for Kealty's success. In interviews Paul shrugged at these claims, but in private he fumed. He did not deserve much of the credit for Kealty's success. No, he felt he deserved *all* of the credit. Laska thought Kealty to be a blow-dried dolt, but a dolt with the right ideas and just enough of the right connections, so Laska had thrown his extensive support behind the man years earlier.

It would be unfair to sum up the political beliefs of the billionaire immigrant into one headline, but the *New York Post* had done so recently after a Laska speech at a Kealty fund-raiser. In typical *Post* fashion, they filled the inches above the fold with "Laska to Ryan: You Suck!" Just hours after the paper came off the presses, Ryan was photographed mugging for the cameras, smiling and holding the newspaper in a "Dewey Defeats Truman" pose.

Laska, not to be outdone, was also shown holding the paper, but in typical humorless Laska style, he was not smiling. He held it up for the camera, his eyes framed by square glasses on a square head, and he stared expressionless at the lens.

Needless to say, this picture did not convey the lighthearted moment that Ryan's photo did.

It was true, Laska hated Jack Ryan, there was no other way to describe the feelings he had for the man. To Laska, Ryan was the perfect embodiment of everything evil and wrong with America. A former military officer, a former head of the dreaded CIA, a former operative himself whose evil deeds around the world had been swept under the rug and replaced with a legend that made him appear to the fools in flyover country like some sort of rugged and handsome paladin.

To Laska's way of thinking, Ryan was an evil man who had stumbled into incredible fortune. The plane crash at the Capitol just as he was awarded the vice presidency was evidence of a cruel God as far as Laska was concerned.

Paul had suffered through the first Ryan presidency, and he'd supported Ed Kealty in his campaign against Ryan's underling Robby Jackson. When Jackson had all but sewn up the victory and was assassinated, leaving Kealty to win the election by default, Laska began to have hope for God after all, though he never said such a thing anywhere other than on his pool deck.

Kealty had not been the savior the progressives had hoped he would be. Yes, he'd had some wins in Congress on issues dear to the hearts of those on the left, but on Laska's main concern, the American government's projection of power both at home and around the world, Kealty had proven to be not much better than his predecessor. He'd launched more missiles against countries with whom America was not at war than any president in history, and he'd made only cosmetic changes to federal laws against habeas corpus, illegal searches and seizures, wirctapping, and other issues Paul Laska cared about.

No, the Czech American was not satisfied with Ed Kealty, but he was a damn sight better than any Republican who would run against him, so Laska had begun investing heavily in Kealty's reelection as soon as he took office.

And this investment had been in danger ever since Ryan had put his hat in the ring. Things looked so bleak earlier in the summer, when Ryan came out strong after the Republican convention, that Laska had made it known to Kealty's campaign manager that he would be scaling back his fund-raising for the embattled Democratic incumbent.

He didn't come right out and say it, but the inference was clear. Ed was a lost cause.

This provoked an immediate response from Kealty and his people. The next morning, Laska was on his jet from Santa Barbara with a private dinner invitation to the White House. He was ushered in to "the people's house" quietly, no record of his visit was recorded, and Kealty sat down for a private dinner with the venerable liberal kingmaker.

"Paul, things may look bleak right now," the President said between sips of pinot noir, "but I have the mother of all trump cards."

"Another assassination is in the works?"

Kealty knew Laska did not possess a sense of humor, so this was, in fact, a serious question. "Jesus, Paul!" Kealty shook his head violently. "No! I had nothing to do with . . . I mean . . . Don't even . . ." Kealty paused, sighed, and then let it go. "The Emir is in my custody, and when the time is right, I will pull him out and shut off Jack Ryan's asinine claim that I am weak on terrorism."

Laska's bushy eyebrows rose. "How did you get him?"

"It doesn't matter how I got him. What matters is that I have him."

Paul nodded slowly and thoughtfully. "What are you going to do with the Emir?"

"I just told you. Late in the election—my campaign manager, Benton Thayer, says I should do it at the second or third debate—I am going to announce to the country that I—"

"No, Ed. I am talking about his trial. How will you proceed with holding him accountable for his alleged actions?"

"Oh." Kealty waved an arm in the air as he slid another luscious morsel of prime rib onto his silver fork. "Brannigan at Justice wants to try him in New York; I'll probably let him do that."

Laska nodded. "I think you should do just that. And you should send a message to the world."

Kealty cocked his head. "What message?"

"That America is, once again, the land of justice and peace. No kangaroo courts."

Kealty nodded slowly. "You want your foundation to defend him."

"It's the only way."

Kealty nodded, sipped his wine. He had something that Laska wanted. A high-profile case against the US government. "I can make that happen, Paul. I'll get heat from the right, but who gives a damn? Probably more ambivalence from the left than I would like, but nobody on our side of the aisle will squawk too much about it."

"Excellent," Laska said.

"Of course," Kealty said, his tone changed a little now that he was no longer sitting in front of Laska with his hat in hand, "you know what a Ryan victory would do to the trial. Your Progressive Constitution Initiative would have no role in a military tribunal at Gitmo."

"I understand."

"I can only make this happen if I win. And even with this big reveal I plan at the presidential debate, I will only win with your continued support. Can I count on you, Paul?"

"You give my people the Emir case, and you will have my continued backing."

Kealty grinned like the Cheshire cat. "Wonderful."

Paul Laska lay in bed and thought back to that conversation at the White House. Laska's PCI legal team had ironed out all the complicated secret details with the Department of Justice in the intervening months, and now that the news was out about his capture, Laska's people would begin preparing their defense of the Emir the next morning.

As Paul listened to the grandfather clock tick in the corner of his dark bedroom, all he could think about was how Ryan would undo it all when he became President of the United States.

When, not *if,* Laska said to himself.

Hovno. Fucking Ed Kealty. Kealty couldn't even win a debate where he had the best news the country has heard in a year.

Son of a bitch.

Paul Laska decided, at that very moment, that he would not spend one more goddamned dime on that loser Ed Kealty.

No, he would divert his funds, his power, into one thing.

The destruction of John Patrick Ryan, either before he took his inevitable seat in the Oval Office or during his administration.

21

One full day after the Paris operation, all The Campus operators, John Clark included, sat in the conference room on the ninth floor of Hendley Associates in West Odenton, Maryland. All five men were still tired and sore from the op, but they'd each had a chance to go home and sleep for a few hours before heading into the office for the after-action debriefing.

Clark had slept more than the others, but that was only because of the meds. On the aircraft, Adara Sherman had administered painkillers that knocked him out until touchdown, and then he'd been picked up by Gerry Hendley and Sam Granger themselves and driven to the private office of a surgeon Hendley had retained in Baltimore for just such an eventuality. In the end, Clark hadn't needed surgery, and the doctor was effusive in his praise of the work of the person or persons who'd given the injury its initial cleaning and bandaging.

He had no way of knowing the person who had treated the wounded man had worked on more than her share of gunshot wounds in Iraq and Afghanistan, and most of those GSWs were much more serious than the hole left by the 9-millimeter round that pinged off of Clark's ulna. Other than administering an X-ray that revealed a hairline fracture of the bone, then handing over a removable cast, a sling, and a course of antibiotics, Hendley's surgeon had little to do other than to remember to keep quiet about the entire matter.

Hendley and Granger then drove Clark home. Both John's wife, Sandy, a retired nurse, and his daughter, Patsy, a doctor herself, were there waiting for him. They checked his wound over, yet again, ignoring his protests that he was fine and the complaints about the seemingly constant pulling and changing of the medical tape holding his dressing. Finally John managed to crash a few hours before driving himself back to work for the morning after-action debriefing.

Gerry started the briefing by entering the room, pulling off his coat and draping it over the chair at the head of the table. He blew out a long sigh and said, "Gentlemen, I, for one, miss the days of poison pens."

The first several "wet" missions The Campus had undertaken, the operators had employed succinylcholine injector pens that were an efficient means for taking a life. A quick turn of the nub of the pen to reveal the syringe tip, then a stroll past the target, and finally a quick jab in the target's ass. The assassin had, in all but a couple of cases, just walked on unnoticed while the target himself continued on down the street, wondering what had just bit or stung him.

Until moments later, when the target succumbed to a sudden heart attack, and died there, his colleagues standing over him with no idea what was wrong, and no idea the man gasping for air had just been murdered before their eyes.

It was quick and it was clean, and that was Gerry's point. No one fought back against a heart attack. No one even pulled their guns or their knives, because no one realized they were under attack.

"Would that it always worked like that," Gerry said to the room.

Next each of the operators talked about what they did,

what they saw, what they thought about what they did and saw. They went around the room like this for most of the morning, and other than some self-criticisms over small things, the general consensus was that they had all done extremely well to react and respond to the drastic change in the operation at, literally, the last minute.

And they also all agreed that they had been damn lucky, John Clark's forearm not withstanding.

Campus head of operations Sam Granger had kept quiet through most of the discussion. He had not been on the scene, after all. After the five operators had finished, he stood up and addressed the table. "We've gone over what happened, but now it's time to talk about fallout. Comebacks. Because even though you guys saved the DCRI officers and took down a known terrorist leader and five of his confederates, that does not mean the FBI won't be fast-roping down on Hendley Associates if the word gets out that we were involved."

A smile from Dom and Sam Driscoll, the two most "go with the flow" operators in the unit. The other men were a little more serious about the implications. Granger said, "I've been monitoring the media reports of the incident, and there is speculation already that this is some sort of terrorist catfight that French security found themselves in the middle of. It is not being reported that DCRI was rescued from assassination by unknown armed individuals. As shitty as it was for you guys at the time that this was such a complicated takedown, it was even more confused from the side of the DCRI. They just saw men crashing into their room and shooting at each other. I can't imagine what they were thinking."

Sam motioned to Rick Bell, the chief of analysis at The Campus. "Fortunately, I don't have to. Rick has tasked his analysts downstairs to look into what French authorities know, or think they know, about what's going on."

Rick stood and addressed the boardroom. "DCRI and judicial police are both investigating this, but DCRI has not granted interviews of its people on the scene to the police investigators, so the judicial police aren't getting anywhere with their inquiry. DCRI does recognize there were two different sets of actors here, not a single cell that went berserk and shot it out with each other. They haven't gotten much further than that yet, but they are going to dig a lot deeper.

"That they will continue to investigate is the bad news, but it's nothing that we didn't expect. The good news is, as far as video evidence, you guys seem to be in the clear. There are a couple of distant grainy shots from street cameras. Jack crossing the Avenue George V on his way around the corner to the Hôtel de Sers, and one of John going in the front of the Four Seasons and then coming back out. Also Ding and Dom turning the corner with the gear under their jackets. But the best facial-recog software in the world doesn't have algorithms that can solve for the distortion masks and the sunglasses all you guys are wearing during the ops."

Rick sat back down, and Sam Granger again addressed the room: "That isn't to say some tourist with a cell phone cam didn't get a close-up shot of one of you. But if that happened, so far, it has not come out."

There were a few nods in the room, but no one spoke.

Rick said, "Okay. Now let's talk about what you guys helped prevent. According to intercepted communications from French security officials, al Qahtani and his men had over five hundred rounds of live ammo between them. There were no suppressors on their machine pistols. Those bastards were going to shoot their way in and then shoot their way out. You men saved six security officers, but you probably saved another twenty cops and civilians as well."

"What about Rokki?" Chavez asked.

"He's gone. One hundred sirens on the street saw to that."

Granger said, "I am of the opinion that Hosni Rokki and his men were just MacGuffins. They were not there to commit any sort of terrorist act. They were not there because they were pissed off about the burka ban. Instead, I think Rokki just came to town under orders of al Qahtani to draw out French security officers, so that al Qahtani and the real terror squad, who were already in place, could ID them and murder them."

"Damn it," said Ryan. "I led us into a buzz saw by sending John and Ding after Rokki in the first place."

Clark said, "I'm glad you did what you did. If we weren't on the scene, it would have been bad. Short term, you saved some innocent lives. Long term . . . hell, those DCRI surveillance operatives might just save the world someday. I'm glad they're still around to do it."

"Yeah," Ryan said with a shrug. That made sense.

Gerry Hendley turned back to Granger. "Conclusions, Sam?"

Sam Granger stood. "My conclusion is . . . you guys did well. But we can't let anything like this happen again. A running gun battle on the streets of a European capital? Cameras, witnesses, police, civilians in the way? This isn't what The Campus was set up to do. Jesus, this could have been a debacle."

Jack Ryan Jr. had been riding high for the past twenty-four hours. Other than Clark's injury, he felt like everything had gone perfectly, except for the fact Rokki and his men got away. Even John's busted arm was determined by everyone to be not terribly serious early on. But somehow Sam Granger had just put it all into perspective, and now Jack wasn't so sure how great he and his team were. Instead, he wondered how much of it could, in fact, be chalked up to luck. They'd raced along a razor's edge on that op, and they hadn't fallen. Luck exists, Jack realized. This time it was good. Next time, it might be bad.

The meeting broke for lunch, but Gerry Hendley asked Ryan to stay behind for a second. Chavez and Clark remained in the conference room, too.

Jack Junior thought he was about to be taken to the woodshed for arguing with Clark in the middle of the operation about leaving the impending fight and, instead, heading down to the lobby. He'd been expecting this ever since, and he was sure that if John hadn't been injured and sedated during the flight home, he'd have given Jack a stern talking-to on the plane.

But instead of a lecture about following orders during an operation, Gerry went in a different direction. "Jack, we are all impressed as hell with you for all the training you've been putting yourself through these past several months. That said, we are a small shop, and with the uptick in OPTEMPO, I can't risk having you miss a day of work right now. I'm going to pull you out of training for a bit."

"Gerry, I know that—"

Gerry held a hand out so that he could stop Ryan's argument, but Chavez jumped in.

"Gerry's right. If we were a bigger operation, we could keep men rotating in and out of training all the time. We all respect what you're doing, and I know it's helped you out a lot, but in Paris you showed that you are absolutely one of the team now, and every one of us needs you out there with us."

Chavez's opinion meant everything to Jack Junior, but still, he felt he needed more experience and, at only twenty-six years old, he didn't think it possible he could actually be injured during his training. "Guys, I appreciate it. I do. I just think—"

Now Clark spoke up: "You're going to get the rest of your training on the job."

Ryan stopped talking. Instead he nodded. "Okay."

As the four men left the conference room for their break, Ryan caught up to Clark in the hall. "Hey, John. You got a second?"

"Sure. What's up?"

"Mind if we go in your office?"

"Not if you get us some coffee first."

"I'll even stir in your sugar so you don't spill it over your desk doing it one-handed."

Five minutes later, both men sipped coffee in Clark's office. The older man sat with his injured arm out of its sling and propped up on his desk by the elbow of the cast.

Ryan said, "John. When you told me to go down to the lobby, I shouldn't have questioned that. I was wrong, and I'm sorry."

Clark nodded. "I've been around the block a few times, Jack. I know what I'm doing."

"Of course you do. I just thought—"

The older man interrupted. "Thinking is good. It was your thinking that put us in a position to help by sending us after Rokki, and your thinking when you saw the van with the suspicious guys sent us to the right location. Your thinking saved a lot of people's lives. I'm never going to tell you to stop thinking. But I *will* tell you when it is time to shut up and listen to orders. If everybody does what they *think* is right when the bullets are about to start flying, then we won't operate as a cohesive unit. Sometimes you may not like the order you are given, sometimes it might not make sense to you, but you have to do as you're told. If you had spent some time in the military, this would be automatic to you. But you haven't, so you're just going to have to trust me."

Ryan just nodded. "You are right. I just let my emotions get in the way. It won't happen again."

Clark just nodded. Smiled.

"What?" Jack asked.

"You and your dad."

"What about my dad?"

"The similarities. Stories I could tell you."

"Go ahead."

But the older man just shook his head. "'Need to know,' kid. 'Need to know.'"

Jack himself smiled now. "Somehow, someday, I'm going to get all those stories out of either you or my dad."

"Your best chance was on the Gulfstream coming back over the Atlantic. Miss Sherman had me pretty well loopy on pain meds."

Ryan smiled. "I missed my chance. Hope I get another chance that doesn't involve you getting shot."

"Me too, kid." Clark shook his head and chuckled. "I've been shot worse than this, but this is the first time I took a round from some cop just trying to do his job. It's hard to get good and mad at anybody but myself."

Clark's phone chirped on his desk. He picked it up. "Yeah? Sure, I'll send him down. Me too? Okay, be right there." Clark looked up at Ryan as he hung up the phone. "Tony Wills needs us at your desk."

22

Jack found Tony Wills sitting in his cube, which was next to Ryan's. With Tony sat Gavin Biery, the company IT chief. In Ryan's chair, his cousin Dom Caruso sat waiting for him. Sam Driscoll leaned against the partition of the cubicle. Sam Granger and Rick Bell, chiefs of ops and analysis, respectively, were also there and standing around.

"Is this a surprise party?" Ryan asked. Dom and Sam both shrugged. They didn't know why Tony had called them down, either.

But Wills had a pleased grin on his face. He called everyone over to his monitor. "So it took a while, mostly because the Paris op got in the way, but also because of the quality of the photos, but the facial-recog software finally came back with some hits on the guy that Sam and Dom saw meeting with Mustafa el Daboussi in Cairo the other day."

"Cool," said Dom. "Who is he?"

"Gavin," said Wills. "You have the con."

"Well"—Gavin Biery made his way through the scrum of men in the cubicle and sat down at Wills's chair—"the software has narrowed Cairo man down to two probables." He worked the keyboard for a moment and one of the pictures taken by Dom's covert camera in the caravanserai in Cairo appeared on one half of the twenty-two-inch monitor.

Gavin said, "Facial recog says there is a ninety-three percent chance that this guy is . . ." He clicked his mouse.

"This dude." A picture appeared next to Dom's photo of the man. It was a shot of a Pakistani passport for a man named Khalid Mir. The man wore glasses with round frames and had a trim beard, and he appeared to be several years younger than he looked in the Cairo photo.

Immediately Caruso said, "He's changed a lot, but I think that's the same guy."

"Yeah?" said Wills. "Well then, your boy is a Khalid Mir, aka Abu Kashmiri, a known operative for Lashkar-e-Taiba over in Pakistan. They are nasty, and Khalid Mir used to be one of their big shots."

"Used to be?"

Ryan answered before Wills, "One of Kealty's drone attacks supposedly took him out in Pakistan, about three years ago. That was about the same time LeT started branching out and sending its operatives against Western targets. Before that they had been almost exclusively a Kashmir-based terror group who struck India and only India."

Dom Caruso spun around and looked at Ryan. "No offense, Junior, but aren't you supposed to know all these guys on sight?"

Jack shrugged. "If this guy was LeT fighting against India, and he died three years ago, he wasn't exactly on my threat matrix for dangerous Western terrorists."

"Makes sense. Sorry."

"Not at all."

Granger looked at Driscoll now. "Sam? You aren't saying anything. Dom thinks this is the guy you saw in Cairo."

Dom answered for his partner: "Sam pegged the guy at the time as a military officer."

Driscoll nodded. "I was sure of it, but this photo does look like it could be the same guy."

Gavin Biery smiled. "You thought he was a military

officer, huh? Well the recog software says there is a ninety-six percent chance you are right." He made a few more clicks of his mouse. The photo of Khalid Mir's passport disappeared and was replaced by a grainy photo of a man in an olive green uniform crossing a street, carrying a briefcase and papers under his arm. This man looked older and fuller in the face than the passport photo of Khalid Mir.

Driscoll nodded forcefully. "*That* is the guy from Cairo."

"I'll be damned," muttered Sam Granger. "Who is he, Tony?"

"He is Brigadier General Riaz Rehan."

"General of what?"

"He's in the Pakistani Defense Force. He is also the current director of Joint Intelligence Miscellaneous of the ISI. A shadowy figure, even though he's a department head and a general. There are no known photos of the man other than this one."

"But wait," Clark said. "If this is Cairo guy, can Khalid Mir be Cairo guy, too?"

"Could be," said Biery, but he didn't clarify.

Tony Wills admonished him. "Gavin, we talked about this. No dramatics, please."

Biery shrugged. "Damn. We IT guys never get to have any fun. Okay, here's the thing: Both of these pictures, the ISI guy and the LeT guy, have been in the database the CIA uses for facial recognition for a long time, but they were never matched with one another."

"Why not?" asked Clark.

Gavin seemed glad to be asked this question. "Because facial-recognition algorithms aren't perfect. They do better when the faces being compared are photographed from the same angle with the same light values. By using facial metrics, that is to say the distance between key land-marks, like eyes and ears and such, the software determines a statistical probability that it is looking at the same face. If there are too many anomalies, either because the faces don't match very well or because the photographs are taken at different resolutions or one of the pictures is reg-istering some movement of the subject, then the match probability goes down precipitously. We can solve for these external discrepancies somewhat by using some-thing called the active appearance model, which removes the shape of the face and only uses the texture as a com-parison."

Dom Caruso said, "Sorry, Gavin, but we have to be back upstairs in ten minutes. Can you cut to the chase?"

"Dom, let's indulge him for another minute, okay?" asked John.

Dom nodded, and Biery addressed Clark directly now, as though the other men were not in the room. "Anyway, the picture of Khalid Mir on his passport and the picture of Riaz Rehan crossing the street in Peshawar are just too different for current facial-recognition software to connect, because there are too many variances in angle, lighting, type of equipment used for the photograph, and of course Rehan is wearing sunglasses, which is not as much of a problem as it used to be before a newer soft-ware design began being used, but it sure doesn't help. So these two pictures"—he drew his cursor back and forth between the two older pictures on the monitor—"do not match." Then he took the cursor over to the Cairo pic-ture taken three days earlier. "But both of these two pictures do match this picture, because it retains just enough of the characteristics of the other two. It's in the middle, so to speak."

Chavez asked, "So all three shots are definitely the same guy?"

Biery shrugged. "Definitely? No. We don't like to use that term when discussing mathematical probabilities."

"Okay, what is the probability?"

"It's about a ninety-one percent chance Cairo dude, general dude, and dead dude are all the same dude."

All eyebrows in the room raised high. Ryan spoke for the group: "Holy shit!"

"Holy shit indeed," said Wills. "We have just learned that a known terrorist for LeT is not only not dead but is now a department chief for Pakistani intelligence."

And Granger said, "And this department head for the ISI, who is, or was, an LeT operative, is now meeting with a known bad guy in Cairo."

"I hate to state the obvious," Dominic said, "but we need to learn more about this Rehan guy."

Granger looked at his watch. "Well, that was the most productive lunch break we've had in a while. Let's head back up to the conference room."

Back upstairs, Granger filled Hendley in on the developments. Immediately the discovery made by Tony Wills and Gavin Biery superseded the Paris operation as the main focus of the meeting.

"This is big," said Hendley, "but it's also all very preliminary. I don't want to jump the gun on this and leak intelligence to CIA or MI6 or anyone else that isn't one hundred percent solid. We need to know more about this general in the ISI."

Everyone agreed.

Hendley said, "How can we check this out?"

Ryan spoke first. "Mary Pat Foley. The National Counterterrorism Center knows as much about Lashkar as anyone. If we can find out more about Khalid Mir, before he became Riaz Rehan, maybe we can use that to link the two guys together."

Hendley nodded. "We haven't paid a visit on Mary Pat in a while. Jack, why don't you give her a call and take her to lunch? You can run on down to Liberty Crossing and show her the Mir-Rehan connection. I bet she'll find that very interesting."

"I'll give her a call today."

"Okay. Keep our sources and methods under your hat, though."

"Understood."

"And Jack? Whatever you do, don't mention that you just got back from Paris."

The conference room erupted in tired laughter.

23

Sixty-one-year-old Judith Cochrane's rental car came with in-dash GPS, but she did not set it for the forty-mile drive down from Colorado Springs. She knew the way to 5880 State Highway 67, as she had been here many times to visit her clients.

Her rented Chrysler pulled off South Robinson Avenue, and she stopped at the first gate of ADX Florence. The guards knew her by sight but still they looked over her documents and identification carefully before letting her pass.

It wasn't easy for an attorney to see a client at Florence; it was harder still for an attorney to see a client housed in H Unit, and a Range 13 client was nigh on impossible to meet with face-to-face. Cochrane and the Progressive Constitution Initiative were in the later stages of drafting a lawsuit to address this issue, but for now she had to play by the rules of supermax.

As one of the most regular visitors to ADX Florence, Judith had come prepared. She would carry a purse with nothing of value in it because she would have to leave it in a locker, and she would not bother entering with her laptop or cell phone, because these would be taken from her immediately if they were on her person. She knew to wear comfortable shoes because she would be walking from the administration unit to her prisoner's cell, a journey of hundreds of yards of hallways and covered outdoor walkways, and she made sure to dress in an especially conservative pantsuit so that the warden would not refuse her entry due to the preposterous accusation of provocative attire.

She also knew she'd be going through X-ray machines and full-body scanners, so she followed prison rules for visitors and wore a bra that was free of underwire.

She drove on past the guard shack, past a long, high wall. She looped around to the south and went through more remote gates, and as she drove slowly she encountered more guard towers, shotguns, assault rifles, German shepherds, and security cameras than she could possibly count. Finally she pulled into a large, half-empty parking lot outside the administration wing. Behind her, at the entrance to the lot, a row of bright yellow hydraulically operated spikes rose from slats in the concrete. She would not be leaving until the guard force here was ready for her to leave.

Judith Cochrane was met at her car door by a female guard, and together they walked through a series of secure doors and hallways in the administrative wing of the prison. There was no conversation between the two, and the guard did not offer to help the much older woman carry her briefcase or pull her laptop bag.

"Lovely morning," Judith Cochrane said as they marched down a clean white passageway.

The guard ignored her comment but continued to lead the way with professionalism.

Most guards at ADX Florence didn't think much of the attorneys who defended the prisoners incarcerated here.

Cochrane didn't care, she could schlep her own bags, and she'd long ago decided that she much preferred the company of the inmates of supermax prisons to the guard force, who were, as far as she was concerned, just uneducated thugs.

Her worldview was as bleak and cruel as it was simple. Prison guards were like soldiers who were like police who were like any federal agent who wielded a gun. They were the bad guys.

After graduating and passing the bar in California, Judith Cochrane was hired by the Center for Constitutional Rights, a legal advocacy group that focused on civil rights cases. After a few years of this she went into private practice, and she'd worked some high-profile cases, including serving as a junior lawyer on the legal team that defended Patty Hearst on bank robbery charges.

After that, she worked for the ACLU for a dozen years, and then Human Rights Watch for several more. When Paul Laska funded the development of the Progressive Constitution Initiative, he'd recruited her personally to join the well-bankrolled liberal judicial advocacy group. He didn't have to work too hard at getting her; Cochrane was thrilled to take a job that let her pick and choose her cases. Almost immediately after the start-up of the organization, the attacks of September 11, 2001, occurred, and to Judith Cochrane and her coworkers, that meant something truly terrible. She knew a witch hunt by the American government was on the horizon: Christians and Jews against Muslims.

For more than half a decade Cochrane was asked to appear on hundreds of television programs to talk about the evils of the US government. She did as many appearances as she could while still defending her clients.

But when Ed Kealty was elected President, Judith Cochrane suddenly found herself blacklisted. She was surprised that the networks didn't seem to care as much about civil rights when Kealty and his men ran the FBI, the CIA, and the Pentagon as they had during the Ryan years.

These days, with Kealty in the White House, Cochrane had as much time as she needed to work on her cases. She was unmarried with no children, and her work was her life. She had developed many close personal relationships with her clients. Relationships that could never lead to anything more than emotional closeness, as virtually all of her clients were separated from her by Plexiglas windows or iron bars.

She was also married, in the figurative sense, to her convictions, a lifelong love affair with her beliefs.

And it was these convictions that brought her here to supermax to meet with Saif Yasin.

She was led into the warden's office, where the warden shook her hand and introduced her to a large black man in a starched blue uniform. "This is the unit commander for H. He will take you to Range 13 and to the FBI detail in charge of your prisoner. We don't have actual custody of Prisoner 09341-000. We are essentially just the holding facility."

"I understand. Thank you," she said as she shook the uniformed man's hand. "We'll be seeing a lot of each other."

The unit commander replied professionally, "Ms. Cochrane, this is just a formality, but we have our rules. May I see your state bar card?"

She reached into her purse and handed it over. The unit commander looked it over and handed it back to her.

The warden said, "This prisoner will be handled differently. I assume you have a copy of his Special Administrative Measures, as well as the directives for your meetings with him?"

"I have both of those documents. As a matter of fact, I have a team of attorneys preparing our response to them."

"Your response?"

"Yes. We will be suing you shortly, but you must have known that already."

"Well . . . I—"

Cochrane smiled thinly. "Don't worry. For today, I promise to oblige your illegal SAMs."

The unit commander was taken aback, but the warden stepped in. He'd known Judith Cochrane long enough to remain unfazed, no matter what she said or accused him of. "We appreciate that. Originally we had planned to have you meet with him via 'video visiting,' like our other Special Housing Unit inmates, but the AG said you absolutely refused that arrangement."

"I did. This man is in a cage, I understand that. But I need to have some rapport with him if I am to do my job. I can't communicate with him on a television screen."

The unit commander said, "We will take you to his cell. You will communicate to the prisoner via a direct phone line. It is not monitored; this has been ordered by the attorney general himself."

"Very good."

"We have a desk for you outside his cell. There is a partition of bulletproof glass; this will serve as an attorney/client visiting booth, just like if you were meeting with one of your other clients in the visitation center."

She signed papers in the warden's office, putting her name to agreements that had been worked up by the Justice Department and the Bureau of Prisons regarding what she could and couldn't say to the prisoner, what he could and couldn't say to her. As far as she was concerned it was all bullshit, but she signed it so she could get started on the man's defense.

She'd worry about it later, and she'd violate her

agreement if it was in the best interest of her client. Hell, she'd sued the Bureau of Prisons many times before. She was not going to let them tell her how she would represent her client.

Together she and the unit commander left the administration building, walked under a covered walkway to another wing of the prison. She was ushered through more locked doors, and on the other side she walked through an X-ray scanner just like those at airport security. On the other side of the scanner a set of doors opened, and here she was met by two men in black body armor and black ski masks, with rifles.

"Oh, dear," she said. "Is all this really necessary?"

The unit commander stopped at the door. He said, "I have my responsibilities, and they end right here at the threshold of Range 13. You are now in the care of the FBI, who are operating the annex that houses your prisoner." The unit commander extended a polite hand, and she shook it without really looking at him. Then she turned away, ready to follow the federal officers.

The FBI escorted her inside, and here they put her purse in a locker on the wall of the stark white room, then walked her through a full-body scanner. On the other side of this she was handed a legal pad and a single soft-tip marking pen, and then led through two sets of security doors that were monitored by closed-circuit cameras. Once through these, she found herself in an anteroom outside the recently modified cell. In front of her were four more armed HRT men.

The lead FBI SWAT officer spoke with a thick Brooklyn accent: "You understand the rules, Ms. Cochrane. You sit in the chair at the desk and talk on the phone to your client. Your conversations will be private. We will be right outside that door, and we can watch you on CCTV, but there is no microphone in this room or in the prisoner's cell." He handed her a small button that looked like her garage door opener. "Panic button," he explained. "The prisoner couldn't get through that glass with a Gatling gun, so there's nothing to worry about, but if he does something that makes you feel uneasy, just press that button."

Cochrane nodded. She hated these smug men with their dehumanizing rules, their heinous weapons of hate, and their cowardly masks. Still, she was professional enough to feign kindness. "Wonderful. Thank you for your help. I'm sure I'll be just fine."

She turned away from the guard and looked around the room. She saw the window that looked into the cell, and she saw a wheeled desk had been put there, on this side, for her benefit. A telephone was on it. But she was not satisfied. "Officers, there should be a pass-through slot in the Plexiglas in case I need him to look at documents or sign something."

The HRT officer in charge shook his head. "Sorry, ma'am. There is a hatch for us to send his food and clothing through, but it is locked up for your visit. You'll have to talk to the warden about that for next time." And with that, the HRT men, all four of them, backed through the door and shut it with a loud clang.

Judith Cochrane stepped to the little desk by the glass and sat down, placed her pad in her lap with her pen, and only then did she look into the cell.

Saif Rahman Yasin sat on his concrete bed, facing the portal. He'd been reading from a Koran that he gently placed on the desk at the foot of the bed. When Cochrane looked to him, he took off his prison-issued eyeglasses and rubbed his eyes, and Judith immediately thought of a younger Omar Sharif. He stood and crossed the small cell toward her, sat down on a three-legged stool that had been placed next to a telephone on the floor. Judith noticed the red phone had no buttons or dials; it would connect him only with the receiver in her hand. Yasin lifted the telephone off the cradle and held it to his ear tentatively. He kept his face impassive, looked the woman in the eye, as if waiting for her to speak.

"Good morning, Mr. Yasin. My name is Judith Cochrane. I am told you speak excellent English, is my information correct?"

The prisoner said nothing, but Cochrane could tell he understood her. She'd worked almost exclusively with those whose native language was other than her own, and she had no trouble discerning either recognition or befuddlement. She continued, "I am an attorney for the Progressive Constitution Initiative. US Attorney General Michael Brannigan has decided that your case will be handled in US District Court for the Western District of Virginia. The AG's office will be preparing the prosecution against you, and my organization has been retained to provide you with your defense. Do you understand me so far?"

She waited a moment for a response, but the man known as Prisoner 09341-000 just stared back at her.

"We can expect this to be a lengthy process, certainly over a year in duration, likely closer to two years. Before that can even begin, there are several preliminary steps we need to—"

"I would like to speak with someone from Amnesty International about my illegal imprisonment."

Cochrane nodded sympathetically but said, "I am afraid I am not in a position to make that happen. I assure you that I *am* working in your interests, and the first order of business will be to assess the conditions of your confinement so that you are afforded proper care and treatment."

The Emir just repeated himself. "I would like to speak with someone from Amnesty International about my illegal imprisonment."

"Sir, you are lucky that you are speaking to anyone at all."

"I would like to speak with someone from Amnesty International about my—"

Cochrane sighed. "Mr. Yasin. I know your playbook. One of your manuals was picked up by American Special Forces soldiers in Kandahar a few years ago. It laid out, in minute detail, instructions for dealing with capture and captivity.

"I knew you would ask for a representative of Amnesty International. I am not with Amnesty International, true, but I am with an organization that will be much more beneficial to you in the long run."

Yasin stared at her for a long moment, holding the receiver to his ear. Then he spoke again, altering the script. "You have given that speech before."

"Indeed. I have represented many men and one or two women that the United States has labeled enemy combatants. Every last one of you has read that manual. You may be the first person I've spoken to who likely wrote some of the manual." She smiled when she said this.

Yasin did not respond.

Cochrane continued, "I understand how you must feel. Don't talk for now. Just listen to what I have to say. The President of the United States and the attorney general have personally spoken with the director of the Bureau of Prisons to stress how important it is that you have confidential conversations with your legal team."

"My . . . my *what?*"

"Your legal team. Myself, and other attorneys from PCI, that is the Progressive Constitution Initiative, who you will meet in the coming months."

The Emir did not speak.

"I'm sorry. Are you having trouble understanding me? Should I arrange for a translator?"

The Emir understood the woman perfectly. It wasn't the English language that was slowing down his portion of the conversation, it was, rather, his astonishment that the Americans were, after all this time, going to put him on trial. He stared at the fat woman with the short gray hair. She looked to him like a man, a very ugly man who dressed in women's clothing.

He smiled at her slowly. Saif Rahman Yasin had long known that it was only the fool's luck of geography that the United States of America had survived two-hundred-plus years on this earth. If these imbeciles had their nation lifted out of their hemisphere and dropped into the center of the Middle East, with their childlike acquiescence to those who would do them harm, they would not survive a single year.

"Miss, are you saying that there is no one listening to what we say?"

"No one, Mr. Yasin."

The Emir shook his head and grunted. "Preposterous."

"I assure you, you can speak freely with me."

"That would be insane."

"We have a Constitution that allows you some rights, Mr. Yasin. It's what makes my country great. Unfortunately, the climate in my country is against people of color, people of other races and religious beliefs. For this reason, you are not afforded all the benefits of our Constitution. But still . . . you get some. You have the right to confidential meetings with your legal counsel."

He saw now that she was telling the truth. And he fought back a smile.

Yes . . . that is what makes your country great. It is populated with fools like you.

"Very well," he said. "What would you like to talk about?"

"Today, only the conditions of your confinement. The warden and the FBI team in charge of your custody have shown me the Special Administrative Measures that you are under. They tell me that when you arrived here all your rules were explained to you."

The Emir said, "It was worse in the other places."

Cochrane raised a small wrinkled hand. "Okay, now is probably a good time to go through some of our ground rules. I can go into more detail when we actually begin working on your case, but for now I will just say that I am not allowed to record any detail of your capture or detainment before you arrived here at ADX Florence three months ago. In fact, I am required to inform you that you are not allowed to tell me about anything that happened before you were transferred into federal custody from"— she chose her next words carefully—"from where you came from before."

"I am not allowed?"

"I'm afraid not."

Yasin shook his head slowly, incredulously. "And what will my punishment be if I violate that arrangement?" He winked at the woman in front of him. "Will they put me in jail?"

Judith Cochrane laughed. Quickly she caught herself. "I can understand that this is a unique situation. The government is making this up as they go along. They are having some . . . growing pains in deciding how to handle your situation. They have a track record of trying so-called enemy combatants in federal court, though, and I can assure you my organization will hold the attorney general's office to high standards during your trial."

"ADX Florence? Is that what this place is called?"

"Yes. I'm sorry; I should have known that was not clear to you. You are in a federal prison in Colorado. Anyway . . . tell me about your treatment here."

He held her gaze as he said, "My treatment here is better than my treatment at the other places."

Cochrane gave another sympathetic nod, a gesture she'd made a million times in her long career of defending the indefensible. "I'm sorry, Mr. Yasin. That part of your ordeal will never be a part of our discussions."

"And why is that?"

"We had to agree to this condition in order to be allowed access to you. Your time in US custody is divided, and the dividing line is the moment you came here, the moment you entered the federal system. Everything before that, I assume, involved the US military and intelligence community, and that will not be part of your defense. If we force this issue at all, the Department of Justice will just remand you back to military custody and you will be sent to Guantánamo Bay, and God knows what will happen to you there."

The Emir thought this over for a few moments and then said, "Very well."

"Now, then. How often are you allowed to bathe?"

"To . . . bathe?" *What madness is this?* thought the Emir. If a woman asked him this in the Pakistani tribal regions where he'd spent much of the past few years, she would be flogged to death surrounded by a crowd of gleeful onlookers.

"Yes. I need to know about your hygiene. Whether or not your physical needs are being met. The bathroom facilities, are they acceptable to you?"

"In my culture, Judith Cochrane, it is not proper for a man to discuss this with a woman."

She nodded. "I understand. This is not comfortable for you. It is awkward for me. But I assure you, Mr. Yasin, I am working in your interests."

"There is no reason for you to be interested in my toilet habits. I want to know what you will do about my trial."

Cochrane smiled. "As I said, it is a slow process. Immediately we will petition for a writ of habeas corpus. This is a demand that you be taken before the judge, who will then determine if the prison system has the authority to hold you. The writ will be denied, it won't go anywhere, it never does, but it puts the system on notice that we will vigorously attend to your case."

"Miss Cochrane, if you were vigorous about defending me, you would listen to my explanation of how I was captured. It was wholly illegal."

"I told you. That is off-limits by agreement with the Justice Department."

"Why would they do that? Because they have something to hide?"

"Of course they have something to hide. There is no legal justification for the United States' kidnapping of you. I know that and you know that. But that is what happened." She sighed. "If I am going to represent you, you are going to have to trust me. Can you please do that for me?"

The Emir looked at her face. It was imploring, sincere,

earnest. Ridiculous. He would play along for now. "I would like a paper and pencil. I would like to make some sketches."

"Sketches? Why?"

"Just to pass the time."

She nodded, looked around the room. "I think I can persuade DOJ that that is a reasonable request. I will get to work on that as soon as I get back to my hotel."

"Thank you."

"You are welcome. Now . . . recreation. I would like to hear about what your recreation consists of. Would you care to talk about that?"

"I would prefer we talk about the torture I endured at the hands of American spies."

Cochrane folded her notebook with another long sigh. "I will be back in three days. Hopefully by then you will have something to sketch with and some paper; I should be able to manage that with a letter to the attorney general. In the meantime, think about what I've told you today. Think about our ground rules, but also please think about ways you can benefit from a trial. You need to consider this as an opportunity for you and your . . . your cause. You can, with my help, stick a finger in the eye of the American government. Wouldn't you like that?"

"And you have helped others stick their fingers in the eye of America?"

Cochrane smiled proudly. "Many times, Mr. Yasin. I told you I have a lot of experience in this."

"You told me you have a lot of clients in prison. That is not experience that I find particularly impressive in an attorney."

Now she spoke defensively. "Those clients are in prison, but they are not on death row. And they are not in a military stockade, unlike a lot of others. The supermax prison is not the worst fate."

"Martyrdom is preferred."

"Well, I won't help you with that. If you want to be dragged into a dark corner of this place and given a lethal injection, you manage that on your own. But I know men like you, Mr. Yasin. That's not what you want."

The Emir kept a faint smile on his lips, but it was just for show. In his head he was thinking, *No, Judith Cochrane. You do not know any man like me.*

But when he spoke he said, "I am sorry I have not been more pleasant. I have forgotten my manners in the many months since my last conversation with a kind soul."

The sixty-one-year-old American woman melted in front of him. She even leaned forward toward the glass partition, closing the distance between the two of them. "I will make things better for you, Saif Rahman Yasin. Just trust me. Let me get to work on the paper and pencil; perhaps I can arrange a little privacy for you, or a little more space. As I tell my clients, this will always be a prison, not paradise, but I will make it better."

"I understand that. Paradise awaits me; this is merely the waiting room. I would choose it to be more luxurious, but the suffering I endure now will only serve me in paradise."

"That's one way to look at it." Judith Cochrane smiled. "I'll see you in three days."

"Thank you, Ms. Cochrane." The Emir cocked his head and smiled. "I am sorry. How rude. Is it Mrs. or Miss?"

"I am unmarried," replied Judith, warmth filling her fleshy cheeks and jowls.

Yasin smiled. "I see."

24

Jack Ryan Jr. arrived at Liberty Crossing, the name given the campus of the National Counterterrorism Center, just after eleven a.m. He had a lunch date with Mary Pat Foley, but Mary Pat asked him to come early for a personal tour of the building.

At first Mary Pat had suggested she and Jack dine at the restaurant there at NCTC after the tour. But Junior had made clear that there would be a business component to the lunch, and for that reason he preferred they went someplace off-site and quiet where they could talk shop. Mary Pat Foley was the only person at Liberty Crossing who knew of the existence of The Campus, and Jack wanted to keep it that way.

Jack pulled to the front gate in his yellow H3; he showed his ID to a tough-looking guard who checked his name off a list of approved visitors on his computer. The guard waved the Hummer through, and Jack continued on to his meeting with the number-two NCTC executive.

She met him in the lobby, helped him get his credentials, and together they shot up an elevator to the operations center. This was Mary Pat's realm, and she made certain to spend a portion of each day walking among the analysts working here, making herself available to anyone who needed a moment of the deputy director's time.

The room was impressive; there were dozens of workstations facing several large wall displays. The huge open space amazed Ryan; he couldn't help but compare it to his own shop, which, although possessing state-of-the-art technology, did not look nearly as cool as the NCTC's setup. Still, Jack realized, he and his fellow analysts were privy to virtually every bit of intelligence that flashed across the monitors around him.

Mary Pat enjoyed the role of tour guide for young Ryan, as she explained that more than sixteen agencies worked together here at the National Counterterrorism Center, compiling, prioritizing, and analyzing data that came to it from intelligence sources across the US intelligence community as well as directly from foreign partners.

This op center, she explained, was up and running twenty-four/seven, and she was proud of its impressive feat of coordination in a bureaucracy such as the US federal government.

Mary Pat did not bother any of the analysts working at their desks as she and Jack wove through the busy operations center—if each person in the room had to stop what they were doing each time a VIP was ushered by, little important work would get done but she did direct Jack to a workstation near the hallway that led to her office. Here Jack noticed a gorgeous girl about his age with mid-length dark hair in a ponytail.

Mrs. Foley finished her spiel on the virtues of interagency cooperation with a shrug. "That's how it's supposed to work, anyway. We do pretty well, most of the time, but like anything else, we are only as good as the data we analyze. Better product means better conclusions."

Jack nodded. It was the same with him. He was looking forward to getting out of the building so he could share with Mary Pat the excellent product he had brought with him.

"Thanks for the tour."

"You bet. Let's go eat. But first, I'd like you to meet someone."

"Great," said Jack, and he caught himself hoping it was the good-looking girl busy at her desk right next to them.

"Melanie, do you have a second?"

To Ryan's pleasure, the girl with the chestnut hair stood and turned around. She wore a light blue button-down shirt and a navy knee-length pencil skirt. Jack saw a navy jacket over the back of her swivel chair. "Jack Ryan Jr., meet Melanie Kraft. She's my newest star here at the op center."

The two shook hands with smiles.

Melanie said, "Mary Pat, when I joined, you didn't tell me I would get to meet celebrities."

"Junior's not a celebrity. He's family."

Ryan groaned inwardly at being called Junior in front of this girl. Jack thought she was stunning; he had a hard time turning away from her bright, friendly eyes.

Melanie nodded and said, "You are taller than you look on TV."

Jack smiled. "I haven't been on TV in years. I've grown up a bit, I guess."

Mary Pat said, "Jack, I kidnapped Melanie from her desk at Langley."

"Thank goodness for that," Melanie said.

"You couldn't work for a better boss," Jack replied with a smile. "Or do more important work than NCTC."

"Thanks. Are you here because you are planning on following in your dad's footsteps in government service?"

Jack chuckled. "No, Mary Pat and I have a lunch date. I'm not here looking for work. I appreciate what you guys do, but I'm a money guy. A greedy capitalist, you might say."

"Nothing wrong with that, as long as you pay your taxes. My salary has to come from somewhere."

They all three laughed about that.

"Well, I'd better get back to work," Melanie said. "It was nice meeting you. Best of luck to your father next month. We're rooting for him."

"Thank you. I know he appreciates what you all do here."

Mary Pat had just shut the door on Ryan's Hummer, he had not even turned over the engine, when she turned to him and smiled. He smiled back. "Something on your mind, Mary Pat?"

"She's single."

Jack laughed. With a slight affectation in his voice, he said, "I have no idea what you are talking about."

Mary Pat Foley just smiled. "You'd like her, she's very smart. No, not smart. I think she's damn brilliant. Ed and I have already had her over to dinner, and Ed is smitten."

"Great," Jack said. He did not get embarrassed particularly easily, but he was starting to blush. He'd known Mary Pat since he'd been in diapers, and she had never once even asked him about his dating life, much less tried to set him up with someone.

"She's from Texas, if you didn't notice her drawl. Doesn't have too many friends around town. Lives in a little carriage-house apartment down in Alexandria."

"This is all interesting, Mary Pat, and she seems nice and all, but I actually had another reason for coming down. Something a little more important than my love life."

She chuckled. "I doubt it."

"Just wait."

They pulled into a strip-mall sushi bar on Old Dominion Drive. The little restaurant was as nondescript as any eatery in the city, stuck tight between a cleaner and a bagel shop, but Mary Pat promised the sashimi was as good as Ryan would ever eat this side of Osaka. As the first customers of the day they had their pick of tables, so Ryan chose a secluded booth in the back corner of the restaurant.

They chatted about their families for a while, ordered lunch, and then Ryan pulled the two photographs from his Tumi bag, placed them side by side.

"What am I looking at here, Junior?"

"The guy on the right is ISI. Head of Joint Intelligence Miscellaneous."

Foley nodded, and then said, "And that's also him on the left, younger and out of uniform."

Jack nodded. "LeT operative named Khalid Mir, aka—"

Mary Pat looked up at Jack with astonishment. "Abu Kashmiri?"

"That's right."

"I was wrong, Jack."

"About?"

"About your love life being more interesting than what you wanted to talk about. Kashmiri was killed three years ago."

"Or was he?" Ryan asked. "Rehan is Khalid Mir. And Khalid Mir is also known as Abu Kashmiri. If Rehan is alive, then, to paraphrase Mark Twain—"

Mary Pat said, "The rumors of his death have been greatly exaggerated."

"Exactly."

"I saw a digital image of a body, but it was after a particularly well placed Hellfire, so it could have been anybody.

That's one of the troubles with missile strikes. Unless you go in and get DNA yourself, then you never really know if you got the right person."

"I guess we don't have CSI Waziristan just standing by, ready to rush to every scene and swab for evidence."

Mary Pat laughed. "I am *so* stealing that line." She turned serious. "Jack, why don't I know about this Kashmiri-ISI connection already?"

Ryan shrugged. Gerry had directed him to keep detail of The Campus operations out of the conversation, so he couldn't tell her that Dom and Driscoll saw this guy in Cairo and their photo actually made the connection in the recog software.

"Jack?"

Ryan realized he was just sitting there

Mary Pat said, "Let me guess. Senator Hendley told you to show me the pictures but not to reveal your shop's sources or methods that discovered the connection."

"Sorry."

"No need to be sorry. That's the business we're in. I respect that. But you are here for some reason other than to just show me you've made this connection, right?"

"Yeah. This guy, Brigadier General Riaz Rehan. There was a sighting of him a few days ago in Cairo."

"And?"

"He was meeting with Mustafa el Daboussi."

Foley's eyebrows rose. "Well, that's not good. And it doesn't make a hell of a lot of sense. El Daboussi has a benefactor already; he's Muslim Brotherhood. He doesn't need the ISI. And the ISI has militant organizations doing their bidding right there, in Pakistan. Why would Rehan need to go to Cairo?"

Jack knew what Mary Pat Foley was thinking but not

saying. She wasn't going to come right out and mention el Daboussi's work on the training camps in western Libya. That was classified intelligence. It was also something The Campus had intercepted from CIA traffic to the NCTC, which is how Jack knew this in the first place.

"We don't know. We are surprised by it, too."

When the food came, they ate in silence for a moment while Mary Pat Foley multitasked, using her iPad to look at some sort of database. Jack assumed it was classified intelligence, but he did not ask. He felt a little uncomfortable knowing that he and his organization were, in a manner of speaking, spying on the NCTC and the work they did, but he did not dwell on it long. He needed only to look at this conversation here, where Jack and his colleagues had exploited intel derived from US intelligence community sources, improved on it with their own work, and now fed the new-and-improved product right back to them, free of charge.

The Campus had been doing this for much of the past year, and it was a good relationship, even if one of the members of the romance was not aware of the other.

Mary Pat looked back to Ryan. "Well, I now know why this General Rehan was not on my radar. He's not a beard."

"A beard?"

"An Islamist in the Pakistani Defense Force. You know they are split down the middle in the Army over there, the ones pushing for theocratic rule, and the ones who are still Muslim but want a nation ruled under a secular democracy. There have been two camps in Pakistan for the past sixty years. 'Beards' is the term we use for the theocratic government proponents in the PDF."

"So Rehan is a secularist?"

"The CIA thought he was, based on what little was

known about the man. Other than the name and the one photo, there is literally no bio for the guy, other than the fact he was promoted from colonel to brigadier general about a year back. Now that you have shown me that he is also Abu Kashmiri, I'm going to go out on a limb and say the CIA was wrong. Kashmiri was no secularist."

Jack sipped his Diet Coke. He wasn't sure how important this information was, but Mary Pat seemed energized by it.

"Jack, I am very glad to hear you guys have been working on this."

"Really? Why?"

"Because I was a little worried you were involved in that shootout in Paris the other day. Not you, personally, of course, but Chavez and Clark. I guess if your shop is working in Cairo, then you weren't operating in Paris at the same time."

Ryan just smiled. "Hey, I can't talk about what we are and are not involved in. Sources and methods, right?"

Mary Pat Foley cocked her head a little. Jack could tell she was trying to get a read on him right now.

Quickly he changed the subject. "So . . . Melanie is single, and she lives down in Alexandria, huh?"

25

Judith Cochrane took her seat at the little desk in front of the window into Saif Rahman Yasin's cell. He was still seated on his bed. He held a notepad and a pencil in his lap. Upon seeing his lawyer, he stepped up to the window and sat on his stool, bringing his pen and his pad with him.

With a smile and a nod, he lifted the receiver of the red phone on the floor.

Cochrane said, "Good morning."

"Thank you very much for arranging for me to get some paper and a pencil."

"That was nothing. It was a reasonable request."

"Still, for me it was very nice. I am grateful."

Cochrane said, "Your writ of habeas corpus was denied. We knew it would be, but it was a motion we had to go through."

"It is of no consequence. I did not expect them to let me walk away."

"Next, I am going to petition the courts to allow you to—"

"Do you have any ability, Miss Cochrane, to draw?"

She wasn't sure she heard him correctly. "To draw?"

"Yes."

"Well . . . no. Not really."

"I enjoy it very much. I studied art for a short period in England at university, and I have continued it as a pastime. Normally I draw architecture. It fascinates me very much the design of buildings all over the world."

Judith did not know where, if anywhere, this was going. "I can arrange perhaps some paper that is a better quality if you would like or—"

But Yasin shook his head. "This paper is fine. In my religion, it is a sin to photograph or draw the face of any living, walking thing." He held up the pencil in his hand as if to clarify the point. "*If* you are doing it for no reason. It is not a sin if you are doing it to remember a face for some important reason."

"I see," Cochrane said, but she didn't see the point in this conversation at all.

"I would like to show you some of my work, and then, perhaps, I can teach you a bit about art." The Emir reached into his notepad and pulled out four sheets that he had already torn from the pad. He held them up, one at a time, to the thick bulletproof glass. He said, "Judith Cochrane, if you would like to assist me with my case, if your organization has any interest in holding your nation accountable to its own laws, then you will need to copy these pictures. If you work slowly on the desk there with your pen, I can watch you and help you along. We can have an art class right here."

Judith Cochrane looked carefully at the drawings. They were sketches of four men. She did not recognize them, but she had no doubt that they were real people who would be recognized by anyone who knew them, so detailed and careful were the renditions.

"Who are they?" she asked, but she feared she knew the answer.

"These are the Americans who kidnapped me. I was walking down the street in Riyadh. They came from nowhere. The young one, this man with the dark hair, he shot me. The old man, this one, was the leader."

Cochrane knew the FBI men could see her through the closed-circuit camera behind her. If they were watching right now, and she was certain they were, then they would see the Emir showing her pages from his pad. There was no reason for that to raise any sort of red flag, but still she waited nervously to hear the door behind her open.

"We have been through this over and over. I can't discuss any of that with you."

"You are my lawyer, are you not?"

"I am, but—"

"Judith Cochrane, I have no interest in helping the United States government in a charade to convince the world I am guilty. If I cannot tell my own lawyer what has happened to me, then I—"

"We have rules we must obey."

"Rules imposed on you by your opponent. Clearly they are—what is the term you use in America?—stacking the deck."

"Let's talk about your nutrition."

"I am not going to talk about my nutrition. It is halal, it is permissible for a Muslim to eat. Other than that, I don't care about it."

Cochrane sighed, but she realized he was still holding up the pictures, and she realized she was still looking at them. Despite herself, she asked, "Are they CIA? Military? Did they tell you who they worked for?"

"They did not tell me. I assume they are in your Central Intelligence Agency, but I need you to find out."

"I can't find out."

"You can show people these pictures. There were others, but these four are the ones I remember the best. The old one who was the leader, the young one who shot me, the short foreign man with the tough eyes, and the young one with the short haircut. There was another man, a man with a beard, but I was not satisfied with my pictures of him.

"All the other people I came into contact with after these men, either I was wearing a hood, or they were wearing masks. I have not seen any faces since I saw these faces here. Until I saw yours." He held up the pictures again. "These men are fixed in my memory. I will never forget them."

Cochrane wanted his information. Damn the agreement she had with Justice.

"All right," she said. "Listen carefully. I am working on getting a pass-through slot opened up so that we can exchange documents. I won't be able to leave with anything, though, so maybe I can bring some tracing paper in my pocket or something. I can trace your drawings and then give them back to you."

The Emir said, "I will work on these some more, and I will add some written details below the pictures. Height, age, anything I can think of."

"Good. I don't know what I will do with this information, but there is someone I can ask."

"You are my only hope, Judith."

"Please, call me Judy."

"Judy. I like that."

Judy Cochrane looked at the four pieces of white paper again. She had no way of knowing that she was looking into the faces of Jack Ryan Jr., Dominic Caruso, Domingo Chavez, and John Clark.

Life at Hendley Associates was returning to normal after the Paris operation. Most employees in at eight. A quick meeting in the conference room at nine, and then everyone back to their desks for a day of investigations, analysis, fishing in the murky waters of the cyberworld to find the enemies of the state who lurked there.

The analysts sifted through their traffic feeds, applied pattern analysis and link analysis to the data, hoping to unlock some critical piece of information America's official intelligence communities had missed, or exploit some intelligence find by American intelligence in a way the overly bureaucratic agencies could not.

The field operatives spent their days testing equipment for the field, training, and sifting through the analysis to look for potential operations.

Two weeks after the Paris op, Gerry Hendley entered the conference room fifteen minutes late. His key operatives and analysts were already there, as well as Sam Granger, director of operations. All the men were sipping coffee and chatting when he arrived.

"Interesting new development. I just got a call out of the blue from Nigel Embling."

"Who?" asked Driscoll.

Chavez said, "Ex-MI6 guy in Peshawar, Pakistan."

Now Driscoll remembered. "Right. He helped you and John last year when you were tracking the Emir."

Clark said, "That's right. Mary Pat Foley tipped us off to him."

Hendley nodded. "But now he's coming straight to us and he's bringing an interesting lead. He's running a source in the ISI. A major who suspects a coup is in the works. He wants to help Western powers stop it."

"Shit," mumbled Caruso.

"And who do you think this major's best guess is as to who is behind this coup?"

The men at the table looked at one another. Finally Jack said, "Rehan?"

"You got it."

Chavez whistled. "And why did this major tell Embling about this? Obviously he knows Nigel is a spy?"

"Knows or suspects. Problem for Nigel is he's *not* a spy. Not anymore. MI6 isn't listening to him, and he is afraid the CIA is hamstrung by the politics of the Kealty administration."

"Welcome to our world," muttered Dom Caruso.

Gerry smiled but said, "So Nigel went back to Mary Pat and said, 'I want to talk to those guys I met with last year.'"

"When do we go?" asked Clark.

Gerry shook his head. "John, I want you to take another couple weeks off before you return to fieldwork."

Clark shrugged. "Hey, it's your call, obviously, but I'm good to go."

Chavez disagreed. "You are healing up nicely, but a GSW is nothing to mess with. Better you stay around here. A wound infection would take you off the active roster real quick like."

Clark said, "Guys, I'm too old to give you any macho shit about how I'm one hundred percent. It's stiff and sore. But I sure as hell am fit enough to fly over to Peshawar and drink some tea with Embling and his new friend."

But Sam Granger made it clear the matter was not up for debate. "I'm not sending you this time, John. I can use you around here. We have some new gadgets to test out. Some remote surveillance cameras came in last night, and I'd like your input."

Clark shrugged but nodded. Clark was subordinate to Granger, and like most every military veteran, he understood the need for a command structure, whether or not he agreed with the decision.

"This Embling guy. What does he know about The Campus?" Driscoll asked.

"Nothing, other than that we aren't 'official channels.' His mates at MI6 trust Mary Pat, and Mary Pat trusts us. Also John and Ding made a good impression on him last year."

Ding smiled. "We were on our best behavior."

The men laughed.

Granger said, "I'm going to send Sam this time. This is a one-man op; just go over and meet with this ISI major, get a feel for him and his story. Don't commit to anything, just see what he will offer up. In this business we don't trust anyone, but Embling is as solid as they come. He's also been in the game for pushing a half-century, so I've got to assume he knows how to ferret out disinformation. I like our chances here, and the more we can learn about Rehan, the better."

The meeting broke up soon after, but Hendley and Granger asked Driscoll to stay behind for a moment.

"You good with this?" Granger asked.

"Absolutely."

"Go on down to the support desk and draw your docs, cards, and cash." Granger shook Driscoll's hand and said, "Listen. I'm not going to tell you anything you don't know here, but Peshawar is a dangerous place, and getting more dangerous by the day. I want your head on a swivel twenty-four/seven, okay?"

No, Sam Granger *wasn't* telling Sam Driscoll anything he didn't know, but he appreciated the concern. "We're on the same page, boss. Last time I took a little vacation in Pakistan, the shit hit the fan. That's not something I'm looking to repeat this go-around."

Driscoll had gone over the border more than a year

earlier, and he'd come back with a serious wound to his shoulder and a series of letters to write to the parents of his men who did not make it back.

Granger nodded thoughtfully. "If there is a coup being planned by the ISI, too much digging around by an American is going to draw a lot of attention. Debrief Embling and his asset, and then come on back. Okay?"

"Sounds good to me," said Sam.

26

Brigadier General Riaz Rehan of the Joint Intelligence Miscellaneous Division of Pakistan's Inter-Services Intelligence Directorate cut an impressive figure in the back of his silver Mercedes sedan. A lean and healthy forty-six years old, Rehan was nearly six-two, and his round face was adorned with an impressive mustache and a trim beard. He wore his military uniform on most occasions when he was in Pakistan and he looked intimidating in it, but here in Dubai he looked no less powerful, dressed in his Western business suit and regimental tie.

Rehan's property here was a walled two-story luxury garden villa with four bedrooms and a large pool house. It sat at the end of a long curved road on Palm Jumeirah, one of five man-made archipelagos off the coast of Dubai.

Coastal property in Dubai used to be markedly scarcer, as nature blessed the Emirate with only thirty-seven miles of beaches, but the leader of Dubai did not see the geographical realities of his nation as geographical boundaries, so he began crafting his own changes to their coastline through the reclamation of land from the sea. When the five planned archipelagos were completed, more than five hundred fifty miles of coast would be added to the nation.

As General Rehan's luxury vehicle turned onto al Khisab, a residential road of stately homes that also, when viewed from high altitude, served as the top-left frond of a palm-tree-shaped man-made island, Rehan took a call on his mobile. The caller was his second-in-command, Colonel Saddiq Khan.

"Good morning, Colonel."

"Good morning, General. The old man from Dagestan is here now."

"Extend my apologies for the delay. I will be there in minutes. What is he like?"

"He is like my crazy old grandfather."

"How do you know he does not speak Urdu?"

Khan laughed. "He is in the main dining room. I am upstairs. But I doubt he speaks Urdu."

"Very well, Saddiq. I will meet with him and then send him on his way. I have too much to do to listen to an old man from the mountains of Russia yell at me."

Rehan hung up and looked at his watch. His Mercedes slowed on the small street to let a car from the protection detail that had been following it pass and rush ahead to the house.

Rehan always traveled abroad with a security detail one dozen strong. They were all ex-Special Services Group commandos, specially trained for bodyguard work by a South African firm. Still, even with this large entourage, Rehan found a way to move in a relatively low-profile manner. He ordered his men to not pack his car with bodies; instead his driver and his lead personal protection agent rode with him, just three men in his SUV. The other ten normally stayed with them in traffic, moving around them like spokes to a hub in their unmarked and un-armored sedans.

A general in the Pakistani Defense Force, even one seconded to the Directorate of Inter-Services Intelligence, would not normally operate from a safe house abroad, especially one with an address as opulent as Palm Jumeirah, Dubai, United Arab Emirates.

But there was nothing about the life or career of Riaz Rehan that could, in any conceivable way, be considered normal. He lived and worked at the property in Palm Island because he had wealthy benefactors in the Persian Gulf who had supported him since the 1980s, and he had these benefactors because, for thirty years, Riaz Rehan had been something of a wunderkind in the world of terrorist operations.

Rehan was born in Punjab, Pakistan, to a Kashmiri mother and an Afghan father. His father ran a midsized trucking concern in Pakistan, but he was also a devoted Islamist. In 1980, shortly after Russian Spetsnaz soldiers parachuted into Kabul and Russian ground troops rolled in to begin their occupation of Afghanistan, fourteen-year-old Riaz traveled with his father to Peshawar to help organize convoys to resupply the mujahideen fighting over the border. Rehan's father used his own resources and personality to assemble a convoy of light weapons, rice, and medicine for the Afghan rebels. He left his son behind in Peshawar and set off to return to the country of his birth with his load.

Within days, Rehan's father was dead, blown to bits during a Russian airstrike on his convoy in the Khyber Pass.

Young Riaz learned of his father's death, and then he went to work. He organized, assembled, and led the next shipment of weapons over the border himself on a donkey caravan that bypassed the highway of death that the Khyber Pass had become, instead heading north over the mountains of the Hindu Kush into Afghanistan. It was only the hubris of the young and his faith in Allah that sent him through the mountains in February, but his caravan arrived unscathed. And although it delivered nothing more than old British Army Lee-Enfield rifles and winter blankets for the mujahideen, ISI leadership soon learned of the bold actions of the young boy.

By his third trip over the mountains, the ISI was helping him with intelligence on Russian forces in his area and within months powerful and wealthy Wahhabi Arabs from oil-rich Gulf States were footing the bill for his shipments.

By the time he was sixteen, Riaz was leading huge convoys with Kalashnikov rifles and 7.62 ammunition over the border to the rebels, and by 1986, when the American CIA delivered the first lot of shoulder-fired Stinger missiles to Peshawar to the ISI, the ISI entrusted the twenty-year-old operative from Kashmir with getting the high-tech weapons over the border and into the hands of the missile crews who'd already been trained and were now just waiting for their launchers.

By the time the war ended, the ISI had Rehan pegged as a prime candidate to be a top-flight international operative, so they sent him to school in Saudi Arabia to improve his Arabic, and then to London to properly Westernize himself and study engineering. After London he joined the Pakistani Defense Force's officer corps, rose to the rank of captain, and then left the military to become an agent of, but not an employee of, the ISI.

Rehan was used by Pakistani intelligence for recruiting, organizing, and orchestrating the operations of the smaller terror groups active on Pakistani soil. He served as something of a liaison between ISI leadership and the criminal and ideological groups who fought against India, the West at large, and even Pakistan's own secular government.

Riaz Rehan was not a member of any of the jihadist organizations with whom he worked, not the Umayyad

Revolutionary Council, not Al-Qaeda, not Lashkar-e-Taiba, not Jaish-e-Mohammed. No, he was a freelancer, a contract employee, and he was the man who translated the general interests and goals of the Pakistani Islamist leadership into actions on the ground, in the trenches.

He worked with twenty-four different Islamist militant groups, all based in Pakistan. And to do this he adopted twenty-four different cover identities. To Lashkar-e-Taiba he was Abu Kashmiri, to Jaish-e-Mohammed he was Khalid Mir. He was, in effect, twenty-five people, including his given name, and this made him virtually impossible for Indian and Western intelligence agencies to track. His personal security was also helped along by the fact that he was neither fish nor fowl: not a member of a terror group, and not a member of the Pakistani intelligence services.

Terror cells acting under his patronage executed missions in Bali, Jakarta, Mumbai, New Delhi, Baghdad, Kabul, Tel Aviv, Tanzania, Mogadishu, Chittagong, and all over Pakistan itself.

In December 2007 in Rawalpindi, Riaz Rehan conducted his biggest operation, though no more than a handful of upper-level ISI and PDF generals knew about it. Rehan himself selected, trained, and handled the assassin of Pakistani prime minister Benazir Bhutto on behalf of the Ministry of Defense and the ISI. And in true cold, calculating Rehan fashion, he also selected the man who stood behind the gunman, the man who blew the assassin up, along with a sizable portion of the crowd, with a suicide vest, right after the prime minister had been shot, to ensure that these dead men would indeed tell no tales.

It was crucial to the leaders in Pakistani intelligence who used the jihadist groups and criminal gangs as proxy fighters that they keep their hands clean, and Rehan was the cutout who helped them do just that. For Rehan himself to stay clean as the cutout, they put great resources into his personal and operational security. Rehan's contacts in the Arab world, wealthy oil sheiks in Qatar and the UAE whom he had known since the war with Russia in Afghanistan, began to sponsor him to further insulate and protect him. He was bankrolled by these wealthy Wahhabis, and eventually, in 2010, he returned to the Pakistani Army at the rank of brigadier general simply because his powerful Arab friends demanded of the ISI that Rehan be given a senior operating role in the nation's intelligence structure. The Islamist generals put him in charge of Joint Intelligence Miscellaneous, a role normally given to a higher-ranking major general. This handed over to Rehan the responsibility for all international espionage assets and operations.

His benefactors in the UAE, those who knew him (or more precisely knew *of* him) since his days as a teenager humping mule trains over the mountains solidified their special relationship with Rehan by giving him access to a walled compound on Dubai's Palm Islands. This became, for all intents and purposes, his office. Yes, he had an office in Islamabad at the beautifully maintained headquarters of the Directorate of Inter-Services Intelligence in Aabpara, but as often as not he was in Dubai, away from those in the government of Pakistan who did not know he existed, or in the Army of Pakistan who did not support his goal for a caliphate.

And away from those few in the ISI who actively sought to bring him down.

General Rehan arrived at his compound a short time after his call with Colonel Khan, and a few minutes after that he sat across the table from Suleiman Murshidov, the venerable spiritual leader of Jamaat Shariat of Dagestan. The old man must have been eighty, Rehan thought, as he looked at eyes milky from cataracts and skin like beach sand blown into folds by the wind. He was of the mountains of the Caucasus, and Riaz assumed he had never been to Dubai, had never seen skyscrapers higher than the squat Soviet-era concrete monoliths in Makhachkala, and had never met with a person in power in a foreign intelligence organization.

A few of Rehan's officers and guards stood around the dining room, and the old man was in the company of four others, all younger, some much more so. They didn't look like security, more like sons and grandsons. They also appeared as if they were here under duress. Perspiration glistened on their foreheads, and they glanced around at the armed security walking the grounds and the house as if they might, at any moment, be taken prisoner by these dark-skinned men.

The Dagestani spiritual leader had asked for this meeting several days ago, and Rehan knew why. The general thought it was childish, really. Rehan had been traveling the world in the past few months, meeting with insurgent groups and international terror outfits in Egypt, Indonesia, Saudi Arabia, Iran, Chechnya, and Yemen.

But he had bypassed Dagestan. Jamaat Shariat, the main Dagestani Islamist group, took a backseat to the Chechens in the eyes of Rehan and his men. More so now that Jamaat Shariat had lost the commander of their armed wing, Israpil Nabiyev. But even before Nabiyev had been captured by the Russians, Riaz Rehan had not bothered to include the Dagestanis in his meetings. The Chechens worked with the Dagestanis, so he had met only with the Chechens.

And now, Rehan assumed, the Dagestanis were mad. Offended at the slight. They had sent their spiritual leader here to explain that they were still viable and only Jamaat Shariat spoke for Dagestan, blah, blah, blah.

Rehan looked at the old man across the table. The Pakistani general was sure he was about to be lectured by this holy man from the mountains.

Everyone in the room spoke Arabic. Rehan greeted the contingent from Dagestan, asked after their needs, and inquired about their journey.

With the niceties out of the way, Rehan was anxious to finish his morning meeting. "How may I be of service to you today?"

Murshidov said, "I am told by my friends in Chechnya that you are a man of God."

Rehan smiled. "I am a humble follower."

"My people have been dealt a painful blow with the capture of Israpil Nabiyev."

"I have seen this. I know he was a valiant commander of your troops." In truth, Rehan did not think much of the Dagestanis. He knew the Chechens better, had more respect for their abilities as fighters. Still, this Nabiyev fellow had impressed the Chechens. They said he was supposedly a cut above the other Dagestani fighters who'd been, by Rehan's way of thinking, little more than cannon fodder for the Russians.

Murshidov nodded, appreciative of the kind words. "He was my great hope for the future of my people. But without him, I believe now we must look outward for assistance."

Oh, so there is a pitch to be made today. Rehan was pleased. If this old man needed something, then maybe he wouldn't have to sit through a tongue-lashing. "I am at your service. How can I help you?"

"The Chechens say you will soon lead Pakistan."

Rehan's face remained impassive, but inside him his blood began to boil. He had sworn all the attendees at his meetings to secrecy. "That is premature. Right now, the situation is difficult for—"

But the old man kept talking, almost as if he were talking to himself and did not know Rehan was in the room with him. "You have told the Chechens you will gain control of nuclear weapons, and you have offered these weapons to the Chechens. They have refused you, because they are afraid that if they possessed nuclear weapons they would become a nuclear target themselves."

Rehan did not speak. The muscles in his face flexed under his trim beard. He glanced up at Khan and the other colonels in the room with him. He gave them a look that he knew would indicate to them that they would never work with those Chechen fools again if they could not keep a conversation like that to themselves.

Rehan almost stood and left the room. He was about to do just that, but Murshidov kept talking. The old man appeared to be nearly in a trance, unconcerned about the impropriety of the words that came from his mouth.

"I know that you wish to give the bombs to an organization outside of Pakistan. When you do this, when the world learns nuclear weapons have been stolen, then your weak civilian government will fall, and you will take power in a coup. My men, general, can take your bombs."

Now Rehan forced a laugh. "I do not have any bombs. And if I did have them, I would not need your men. I respect you, old man. I respect your sacrifice and your submission to Allah, and the wisdom you have gained just by virtue of being old. But you come here to my home and say things like this?"

"We have a need for the bombs. And we are not afraid."

Rehan stood now. Angry and tired of the old man from Russia. "What bombs? What bombs are you talking about? Yes, my country has nuclear weapons. This is common knowledge. They were designed and manufactured under the direction of A. Q. Khan, a Pakistani patriot and a good Muslim. But I am a general in the Army and a member of external intelligence. I cannot just back a truck up to a warehouse and ask the men there to load nuclear missiles into the bed of the truck. That is foolishness!"

Murshidov looked at Rehan through his cataract-clouded eyes. "Your plan has been explained to me in great detail. It is remarkable, and it can work. But you have failed in one respect. You made your offer to the wrong people. The others you invited into your scheme have refused you, and now you can do nothing. I am here to show you that Jamaat Shariat is the right path for you. We will help you, and you will help us."

Rehan looked to Khan. Khan shrugged. *What the hell.*

General Rehan sat back down on the sofa. "You think you know things that are not true, old man. But you make me curious. What will you and your poor mountain men do with nuclear bombs?"

Murshidov's glassy eyes seemed to clear suddenly. He smiled, exposing thin, brittle teeth. "I will tell you *exactly* what we will do with nuclear bombs."

Ninety minutes later, Rehan rushed toward the helipad behind his house and leapt into his Eurocopter EC135. The aircraft's rotors were already turning, their pitch increased as soon as the door was locked, and in seconds the helo lifted over the house, dipped a little as it headed out over the gulf, then banked toward the incredible skyline of Dubai.

Khan sat next to him in the back of the six-seat chopper. The colonel spoke into his headset, told his general that he had made the secure satellite connection with Islamabad, and Rehan need only speak into his microphone. "Listen to me, brother," Rehan said, nearly frantic with excitement. "I am leaving now for Volgograd." He listened. "Russia. Yes, Russia!"

The Eurocopter headed toward the skyscrapers of downtown Dubai. Just on the other side of these was Dubai International Airport. There, the crew of a Rockwell Sabreliner jet was scrambling to prepare their aircraft for immediate flight.

"I will know by tomorrow, but I think we are in position to begin Operation Saker. Yes. Get everyone ready to move at a moment's notice. I will come to Rawalpindi and brief the committee myself just as soon as I am finished." He listened to the other man for a moment, and then said, "One more thing. Last month I met a contingent of four Chechens in Grozny. I want you to draw up a plan to eliminate these four men, quickly and quietly. One of them talks too much. I am glad he did it in this instance, but I cannot have him talking to others. I want them all out of the way to make certain that we plug this leak before all the water passes through the dam."

Rehan nodded to his second-in-command, and Khan then disconnected the call.

"It is too much to wish for?" Rehan asked Khan.

"Allah is good, General."

Brigadier General Riaz Rehan smiled, and he willed his helicopter to fly faster, because he had no time to waste.

If all the polls in America were correct, then Jack Ryan would be President of the United States again soon, and once Ryan was back in the White House, Operation Saker would not stand a chance.

27

Charles Sumner Alden, deputy director of the Central Intelligence Agency, sat in the back of a Lincoln Town Car that rolled through the gates of the Newport, Rhode Island, estate of Paul Laska. The DD/CIA was dressed for dinner but hoped this evening would involve business as well as pleasure.

He'd been to Laska's Rhode Island home on several occasions. A lovely garden wedding for a Democratic Congressman, a fund-raiser for Ed Kealty's run against Robby Jackson, highbrow cookouts and pool parties, and a Christmas soirée a few years back. But when Laska called him and invited him for dinner tonight, the old man made it plain it was to be just the two of them.

This was a big deal, even to a political insider like Charles Sumner Alden.

Alden assumed—no, he *knew*—that he was going to be offered a position in one of Laska's think tanks, contingent on the obvious: that the Kealty administration would cease to exist on January 20 of next year.

The Lincoln drove through the beautiful garden and parked in a parking circle next to the house, overlooking the water. The perimeter of the grounds was patrolled by armed security, and every inch of the property was wired with cameras, security lighting, and motion sensors. Alden's driver and bodyguard were armed, of course, but no one expected trouble here worse than the DD/CIA potentially burning the roof of his mouth on the lobster bisque.

Alden and Laska were served drinks in the library by the staff, and then they dined on a windowed back terrace that sheltered them from the cold air but still gave them a great moonlight vista over Sheep Point Cove. The conversation never strayed from financial matters, politics, and social issues. Alden knew enough about Laska to realize there would be little in the way of lighthearted banter. But it was a good conversation between men who were in general agreement with each other, enhanced somewhat by a gentle dose of Charles Alden's ass-kissing of his presumed future employer.

After dinner they walked out back for a moment, sipping Cognac and discussing events in Hungary and Russia and Turkey and Latvia. Alden felt he was being tested on his knowledge and his views, and he did not mind. This was a job interview, or so he'd told himself.

They moved to the library. Alden commented on the man's great collection of leather-bound tomes, and as they sat across from each other on antique leather sofas, the CIA political appointee praised the magnificent home. Laska shrugged, explained to the younger man that this was his summer cottage, or at least that's what he called it in front of those with whom he did not keep up the façade of being a populist. He told Alden that he also owned a twenty-two-room penthouse apartment on New York's Upper West Side, a beach house on Santa Barbara that was the largest in the county and one of the largest oceanfront properties in California, as well as a lodge in Aspen, which was the site of an annual polit ical retreat that hosted four hundred.

Alden had been to the Aspen retreat, twice, but he did not want to embarrass his host by reminding him of this.

Laska refilled both men's snifters with another splash of impeccable Denis-Mounié Cognac from the 1930s. "Any idea why I've asked you here today, Charles?"

Alden smiled, cocked his head. "I'm hoping it's about a position, should President Kealty fail to win reelection."

Laska looked above the eyeglasses resting low on his nose. He smiled. "I'd be proud to have you come aboard. I can think of a couple of key spots right off the top of my head where we could use you."

"Great."

"But it is bad form to begin selling the parlor furniture while grandfather is still upstairs on his deathbed. Would you agree?"

Alden said nothing for a moment. "So . . . I am not here to discuss my options for next January?"

Laska shrugged. His cashmere sweater barely moved as his narrow shoulders went up and down inside it. "You will be taken care of in a post-Kealty America. Do not fear. But no, that is not why you are here."

Alden was at once both excited and confused. "Well, then. Why *have* you asked me here?"

Laska grabbed a leather-bound folder resting on the end table next to the sofa. He pulled out a sheaf of papers and placed them in his lap. "Judy Cochrane has been meeting with the Emir."

Alden's crossed legs uncrossed quickly, and he sat up straight. "Oh, okay. I need to be careful about that matter, as I am certain you understand. I can't give you any information regarding—"

"I am not asking you anything," Laska said, then smiled thinly. "*Yet.* Just listen."

Alden nodded stiffly.

"Mr. Yasin has agreed to allow the PCI to handle his

representation in the Western District of Virginia for the Charlottesville attack three years ago."

Alden said nothing.

"As part of our agreement with the Department of Justice, Judy and her team are not allowed to detail the capture of the Emir nor his imprisonment until the day he was delivered by the FBI to the Bureau of Prisons."

"I'm sorry, Paul, but you are already treading in waters that are too deep for me."

Laska kept talking as if Alden had not protested. "But the story he tells is quite incredible."

Alden indulged the old man, who, quite possibly, held the key to Alden's future. He explained, "The attorney general questioned me at length about any CIA involvement in the Emir's case. We had no participation whatsoever, and I communicated that to him. That is already more than I should say to someone without the proper clearance."

Laska shook his head, talked over the last part of Charles Alden's words. "He says he was attacked on the street in Riyadh by five men, shot when he resisted, then kidnapped, brought to a location in the United States, and tortured for a number of days, before being handed over to the FBI."

"Paul, I don't want to hear—"

"And then the FBI shipped him off to some other location for several months, a so-called black-site prison, before delivering him to Florence, Colorado."

Alden raised his eyebrows. "Frankly, Paul, this is starting to sound like a bad movie. Pure fantasy."

But Laska relayed the Emir's claims as fact. "He got a great look at four of the men who kidnapped and tortured him. And although the Emir is, if you believe the allegations against him, a terrorist, he is also quite an artist." Laska took four pages from the file in his lap and offered them to Alden.

The deputy director of the CIA did not reach out and take them.

"I'm sorry" was all he could say.

"You said they were not CIA. So you will not know these men. What is the harm?"

"Frankly, I am very disappointed that your true motivation for having me over this evening was nothing more than—"

"If you don't know them, Charles, just hand the pages back to me, and you will not spend the next several years testifying as the former head of Clandestine Services of the Central Intelligence Agency. The man at the helm when an illegal rendition was performed in an allied nation against the direct orders of the President of the United States."

Alden emitted a long sigh. In truth, he didn't know what many of the CIA's foot soldiers looked like, as he rarely left the seventh floor at Langley. Did Laska think the Agency's paramilitary men just hung out at a water cooler on the top floor, covered in grease paint and battle gear, waiting for their next mission? Certainly, Alden told himself, he would not be able to recognize a drawing of any field man in the Special Activities Division, the CIA's paramilitary arm and the operators who would have had the training to make this happen. After talking to AG Brannigan about the Emir's capture a year earlier he'd gotten the impression the DOJ thought the Emir had been picked up by some Middle Eastern intelligence agency for some personal beef and then snuck into the United States and dumped at the FBI's door in order to curry favor at some later date. It was a mystery, yes, but it wasn't anything Alden had to worry about.

He decided he'd take a look at the drawings, shake his head, and hand them back. If that was all it took to secure a position in a Laska foundation after his time in the CIA ended, then so be it.

He shrugged. "I'll indulge you and look at the pictures. But I won't discuss this matter with you any further."

Laska smiled. His square face widened. "It's a deal."

Alden took the pages, crossed his legs, and looked up at Laska. The CIA political appointee retained a slightly annoyed appearance while doing this.

Laska said, "What you have there are photocopies of some tracings Judy made of the Emir's original drawings. The quality is not perfect, but I think they get the point across as to what the men look like."

This first picture, just as he expected, was a detailed but not particularly lifelike sketch of a man's face, a face Charles Alden did not recognize. The man was young, white, and his hair was shaded in with a pencil, presumably to indicate that it was black or dark brown. He wore some sort of bandage on his chin. Below the picture were some handwritten notes. "Kidnapper 1. American, 25 to 30 years old. 183cm. This man shot me on the street. He was wounded slightly on the face, hence the bandage."

It was a decent drawing of a good-looking guy in his twenties, but otherwise Alden did not find the photo remarkable.

Charles shook his head no for Laska's benefit and moved on.

Drawing number two was of another young man. He wore his hair shorter than the first man, and it was dark. He was nondescript in every other way. The text under the drawing said: "Kidnapper 2. 28 to 35 years old. Shorter than #1."

Still, Alden didn't know the man.

Another shake of the head, and on to the next drawing.

Alden's eyes widened, and then narrowed, and he immediately worried that his host might have seen the change in his expression. This drawing was of an older man, much older than the others. Quickly he scanned down to the notes Saif Yasin had written about Kidnapper 3: "Maybe sixty years old. Healthy. Thin. Very strong and angry. Cold eyes. Speaks fair Gulf Arabic."

Oh my God, Alden thought to himself, but he was careful to betray no more emotion to Paul Laska. His eyes flicked back up to the picture. Short hair lightly shaded as if to indicate that it was gray. Deep-chiseled features. Years etched into his skin. A square jaw.

Could it be? A sixty-year-old who was still out on the sharp edge? There were a few, but it certainly narrowed it down. One man did stand out, however, and he bore a more than passing resemblance to the drawing.

Alden thought he recognized this man, but he was not certain.

Until he turned to the next page.

A rendering of a Hispanic male, mid-forties, with short hair. The caption below his name said he was "Kidnapper 4: short but very powerful."

God fucking damn it! Alden screamed it internally. *John Clark and his partner. The Mexican guy from Rainbow? What was his name? Carlos Dominguez? No . . . that's not it.*

Alden did not try to hide his amazement now. He let the other pages fall to the floor of the library, and he held each photocopy in a hand. Clark in the left, the Hispanic fellow in the right.

These two men had sat in Alden's office a year earlier. He'd sent them packing, cashiered them from the Central Intelligence Agency.

And now there was credible evidence linking them with a kidnapping operation that had infiltrated Saudi Arabia and captured the most wanted man in the world. Who the hell could they be working for? JSOC? No, the military has its own units to do that sort of thing. DIA, NSA? No way, this wasn't their type of mission.

"You know these men? They are CIA?" Laska asked. His voice sounded so hopeful.

Alden looked away from the images, up to the old man on the other leather sofa. Laska held a brandy snifter as he leaned forward with excitement.

Alden took a moment to compose himself. He softly asked, "What can you do with this information?"

"My options are limited, as are yours. But you can order an internal investigation against the men, use other evidence to bring this to light."

"They aren't CIA."

Laska cocked his square head and his bushy eyebrows rose. "But . . . clearly you recognize them."

"I do. They left the Agency a year ago. I . . . I don't know what they are supposed to be doing now, but they are long gone from the CIA. Suffice it to say, wherever they are working, they were acting sub rosa when they went terrorist hunting."

"Who are they?"

"John Clark is the white guy. The other . . . I can't remember his name. It might be Dominguez. Something Hispanic, anyway. Puerto Rican, Mexican, something like that."

Laska sipped his Cognac. "Well, it is clear that if they

are not working for the CIA, then they are working for someone. And they had no authority whatsoever to detain Saif Yasin."

Alden realized Laska did not understand the scope of this. The man was just trying to get that shit the Emir out of prison. "There's more going on here than that. John Clark didn't just work for Jack Ryan at the CIA. He was Ryan's driver and Ryan's close friend. I imagine he still is. They worked black ops together before Ryan rose through the ranks. Their history goes back thirty years. That was one of the reasons I shit-canned the old bastard instead of letting him hang around as a trainer for a few years."

Laska sat up straight. He even grinned a little, a rare occurrence. "Interesting."

"Clark has a lot of blood on his hands. He was everything that was wrong with CIA operations. I don't know many of the details, but I do know one thing."

"What is that, Charles?"

"I know that President Ryan himself gave Clark the Medal of Honor for actions in Vietnam, then he pardoned him for his killings in the CIA."

"A secret presidential pardon?"

"Yes."

Alden was still shaking his head in amazement at this revelation, but slowly he regained control. Suddenly his job with a Laska foundation was forgotten. He all but berated the older man with his tone. "I don't know what ground rules DOJ has given your organization, but I find it very hard to believe the attorneys would be allowed to pass this information to you. You aren't a lawyer yourself, nor are you part of the legal team."

"That is all very true. I am more a figurehead. But nevertheless, I have this information."

"You know that I can't do a damn thing about this, Paul. I can't walk into my office tomorrow morning and start asking questions about what happened to Clark and Dominguez without people wanting to know why. You and I both could get in a lot of trouble passing around this information because of the nature of the source. You have implicated me in a felony."

With that, Alden picked his snifter off the table and drained it into his mouth. Laska took the old bottle and poured him a hefty refill.

Laska then smiled. "You don't need to tell anyone about this. But this information needs to come out somehow. These men need to be captured and held accountable." Laska thought for a few seconds. "The problem with this information is the source, the way it was derived. What if I changed the source?"

"What do you mean?"

"Can you get me more information on Clark's career with the CIA? I'm not talking about this. The Emir incident. I'm talking about everything he's done that's in the record."

Alden nodded. "I remember that Admiral James Greer had a dossier on him. That goes way back; I could dig a little more on my own to see if there are details since then. I know that he ran Rainbow in the UK for several years."

"Men in Black," Laska said with disdain, using the nick name for the secret NATO anti-terror outfit.

"Yeah. But why do you want this information?"

"I think it could help Ed."

Alden looked at Laska for a long time. He knew there wasn't a damn thing that could help Ed Kealty, and he knew Paul Laska was smart enough to know that, too.

No, there was some game going on in Laska's head.

Alden didn't challenge the old Czech. "I'll see what I can do."

"Just get me what you can, and I'll take this off your hands, Charles. You have been most helpful, and I will not forget that come January."

28

The skyline of a city as large and as developed as Volgograd, Russia, should have been visible for many, many miles in all directions. But as Georgi Safronov raced southeast on the M6 Highway, only a dozen or so miles until he hit the city limits, the view in front of him was low rolling pastureland that disappeared quickly into thick gray fog, and it gave no hint of the huge industrial metropolis that lay just ahead. It was ten in the morning, and he'd been driving all night along the Caspian Highway, but even after eight hours behind the wheel the forty-six-year-old continued to push his BMW Z4 coupe, desperate to arrive at his destination as soon as possible. The man who'd asked him to drive five hundred seventy miles today would not have summoned him to this meeting without good reason, and Georgi fought sleep and hunger so that he would not have to keep the old man waiting.

The wealthy Russian was middle-aged, but other than a tinge of gray in his red hair, he did not look it. Most Russian men drank, and this tended to age their faces prematurely, but Georgi had not touched vodka or wine or beer for years; his only peccadillo of consumption was the sugary sweet tea of which the Russians are fond. He was not athletic at all, but he was thin, and his hair was a bit long for a man his age. A flop of it fell across his forehead, just above his eyes, which is why he positioned his BMW's heater vents to blow it back while he drove.

He had no instructions to go into Volgograd proper, and that was a shame, because Safronov rather liked the city. Volgograd had once been Stalingrad, and that made it interesting to him. In the Second World War, Stalingrad was the site of perhaps the most incredible resistance against a powerful invading force in the history of warfare.

And Georgi Safronov had personal interest in the phenomenon of resistance, although he kept this interest to himself.

His eyes flashed down to the GPS map on the center console of the well-appointed coupe. The airport was off to his south now; he'd leave the M6 in minutes, and then follow the preprogrammed route to the safe house just off the airport property.

He knew he had to take care to avoid drawing attention. He'd come alone, having left his bodyguards behind in Moscow, telling them only that he had personal business to attend to. His protection force was not Russian, they were Finns, and they were whoremongers, so Georgi used their imaginations against them by hinting that his secret appointment today involved a woman.

After the meeting, Safronov thought he might continue on into Volgograd proper and find a hotel. He could walk the streets alone and think of the battle of Stalingrad, and it would give him strength.

But he was getting ahead of himself. Maybe the man who had invited him here today, Suleiman Murshidov, would want him to leave the safe house immediately and get on a plane and return with him to Makhachkala.

Murshidov would tell Georgi what to do, and Georgi would listen.

Georgi Safronov was not his real name in the sense that his real parents did not call him Georgi, and *they* were not called Safronov. But as long as he could remember this had been his name, and as long as he could remember everyone around him told him he was Russian.

But in his heart, he was certain that he had always known his name and his heritage to be lies.

In truth, Georgi Safronov was born Magomed Sagikov in Derben, Dagestan, in 1966, back when it was just a far-flung and obedient mountainous coastal region of the Soviet Union. His birth parents were mountain peasants, but they moved to Makhachkala on the Caspian Sea soon after his birth. There, young Magomed's mother and father died within a year from disease, and their child was placed in an orphanage. A young Russian Navy captain from Moscow named Mikhail Safronov and his wife, Marina, chose the child out of a roomful of offerings, because Magomed's mixed Azar-Lezgian heritage made him more attractive to Mrs. Safronova than the other children of his age who were full-blooded Azars.

They named their new baby boy Georgi.

Captain Safronov was stationed in Dagestan with the Caspian flotilla, but he was soon promoted to the Black Sea fleet and sent to Sevastopol, and then to Leningrad to the Marshal Grechko Naval Academy. Over the next fifteen years Georgi grew up in Sevastopol (where his father rejoined the Black Sea fleet) and then Moscow (where his father served in the office of the commander in chief).

Safronov's mother and father never deceived him about the fact he had been adopted, but they told him he'd come from an orphanage in Moscow. Never did they mention his true roots, nor the fact that his parents had been Muslim.

Young Safronov was a brilliant child, but he was small, weak, and uncoordinated to the extent that he was hopeless in sports. In spite of this, or likely because of this, he excelled in his schoolwork. As a very young boy he developed a fascination with his country's cosmonauts. This developed into a childhood fascination with missiles, satellites, and aerospace. Upon graduation from school, he was accepted into the Felix Dzerzhinsky Military Rocket Forces Academy.

After graduation he spent five years as an officer in the Soviet Strategic Rocket Forces, then returned to university at the Moscow Institute of Physics and Technology.

At the age of thirty he went into the private sector. He was hired as a project manager by Kosmos Space Flight Corporation, a fledgling rocket motor and space launch company. Georgi was instrumental in his company's purchase of Soviet-era intercontinental ballistic missiles, and he led a project to reengineer the ICBMs, turning them into space delivery vehicles. His military-like leadership, his bold ideas, his technological know-how, and his political savvy combined to make KSFC, by the late 1990s, the principal contractor of Russian space delivery operations.

In 1999 Mikhail Safronov, Georgi's father, was visiting his son's fine home in Moscow. It was shortly after the first Russian invasion of Dagestan, and the retired naval officer made a series of disparaging remarks about the Dagestani Muslims. When Georgi asked his father what he knew of Dagestanis, or Muslims, for that matter, Mikhail inadvertently mentioned that he had once been stationed in Makhachkala.

Georgi wondered why neither his father nor his mother had ever mentioned his deployment in Dagestan. A few weeks later, he called some influential friends in the Navy, and they dug into the records to provide the son with his father's dates of service in the Caspian fleet.

As soon as Safronov went to Makhachkala, he found the orphanage, and got them to reveal that he was, in fact, born to Muslim Dagestani parents.

Georgi Safronov knew then what he would later say he'd always known. That he was not like every other Russian that he'd grown up with.

He was Muslim.

Initially this did not have a great effect on his life. His company was so successful—especially after American space shuttle missions were put on an extended hold because of the *Columbia* disaster in February 2003—that Safronov's life was his work. Kosmos Space Flight Corporation was perfectly positioned at the time to take over the American shuttle contracts. At age thirty-six, Georgi had just taken over as president of the company, and his talent, dedication, connections in the Russian Air Force, along with his powerful personality, helped his company take full advantage of this opportunity.

Initially the Russian government had had no financial interest in the company, and it had been successfully privatized. But when Safronov turned it into, literally speaking, a rocket-powered money-making machine, the Russian president and his cronies began initiating governmental measures to take over the company. But Safronov met with his new adversaries in person, and made them a counteroffer. He would give up thirty-eight percent of his business, the men in the meeting could do with it what they wished, and Safronov would retain the rest. And he would continue to work for its success, 365 days a year.

But, Georgi had told the men at the meeting, if the Russian government wanted to make it a state-owned enterprise, just like in the olden days, then they could expect olden-days results. Safronov would sit at his desk and stare at the wall, or they could push him out and replace him with some old apparatchik who could pretend to be a capitalist but who, if a century of history was any basis for evidence, would fuck up the business inside of a year.

The Russian president and his men were flustered. Their attempt at extortion had been parried with some confounding form of ... what, reverse extortion? The government blinked, Safronov retained sixty-two percent ownership, and KSFC flourished.

A year later Kosmos was presented with the Order of Lenin on behalf of an appreciative country, and Safronov himself received the Hero of the Russian Federation.

With his personal fortune passing one hundred million dollars he invested in blue-chip Russian companies, and he did so with a shrewd eye toward the connections of the owners. He understood the lubricant of success in his adopted country; businessmen who stuck their necks out only kept them if they were friends with the Kremlin. It became very easy for an insider to discern who was held in favor by the ex-KGB men who now ruled in Moscow, and Safronov hedged all his bets so that, as long as the current leader and his men were in power, he would do well.

And this tactic had been working for him. His personal wealth was estimated at more than one billion dollars, which, even though it did not put him on the *Forbes* list, should have afforded him everything he wanted.

But in truth, his wealth meant nothing to him at all.

Because it was impossible for him to forget that his name was not really Georgi and he was not really Russian.

Everything changed for Georgi Safronov on his forty-second birthday. He had been driving his new 2008 Lamborghini Reventón from Moscow to one of his dachas in the countryside. He brought his vehicle's speed-ometer to within twenty miles of top speed, hitting roughly two hundred miles per hour on a straight road.

Whether it was oil or water or just a simple drift of his rear tires, Georgi never knew. But for some reason he felt a slight fishtail, he lost control, and he was certain it was over. In the one-half second from his first realization that he was merely a passenger in the runaway vehicle until the Lambor-ghini's bright silver hood in front of the windscreen pointed off the road, Georgi's life did not so much flash in front of his eyes; rather, it was the life he had not lived that he saw replayed before him. It was the cause he'd turned his back on. It was the revolution that he had taken no part in. It was his potential that he had not realized.

The Lamborghini flipped, the neck of the twenty one year-old ballerina sitting next to Safronov snapped with the first impact with the snowy field—for years after, Georgi was certain he'd heard the pop amid the cacoph-ony of exploding metal and fiberglass.

The space entrepreneur spent months in the hospital with his Russian Koran; he kept it hidden inside the jack-ets of technical manuals. His faith deepened, his sense of place in this world and the next solidified, and he told himself that his life would take on a new direction.

He would give it all up to be *shahid*. To martyr himself for the cause into which he was born and for which he drew each and every breath. He understood that the Lam-borghinis and jets and power and women were not paradise, as intoxicating as they were for his admittedly human flesh. He knew that there was no real future in his human form. No, his future, his everlasting future, would be in the afterlife, and he sought this out.

Not that he would sell his body cheaply to his cause.

No, Georgi recognized that he had become perhaps the greatest asset in the cause of an Islamic Republic in the Caucasus. He was a mole in the world of the enemy.

When he recovered, he relocated covertly to a simple farmhouse in Dagestan. He lived in complete austerity, a far cry from the life he'd led before his accident. He sought out Suleiman Murshidov, the spiritual leader of Jamaat Shariat, the Dagestani resistance group. Murshidov was suspicious at first, but the old man was surprisingly cunning and intelligent, and in time he began to recognize the tool, the weapon, that was Georgi Safronov.

Georgi offered all of his money to the cause, but the spiritual leader turned down the offer. In fact, he forbade Safronov from any philanthropy toward Dagestan or the Caucasus. The old man from the mountains somehow had the foresight to see that Georgi was his "inside man" in the Russian corridors of power, and he would not allow anything to threaten that. Not new schools, not new hospitals, not any benefit for his cause whatsoever.

On the contrary, Murshidov instructed Safronov to return to Moscow and support the hard-line stance against the republics. For many years Georgi had been sickened to sit with his adopted father's friends and discuss the stamping out of insurgencies in the Caucasus. But these were his orders. He lived within the belly of the beast.

Until that day when Murshidov called for his return, his help, and *inshallah*—God willing—his martyrdom.

Safronov did as he was told. He returned briefly and in secret once each year to meet with Suleiman, and in one of these meetings he'd asked to be introduced to the famous warrior, Israpil Nabiyev. The old spiritual leader forbade this meeting, and this angered Safronov greatly.

But Georgi knew now that his leader had been correct all

along. If Nabiyev knew about Safronov, even a hint that there was a man high in the ranks of Russia's private space service, then Safronov would now be dead or in prison.

Safronov now knew that his own vanity had been in control when he'd insisted that Suleiman introduce him to Nabiyev last year in Makhachkala. And it had been the hand of Allah himself, working through Suleiman, when Suleiman had refused to make the introduction.

So Safronov stayed away from Jamaat Shariat. It was just as well, too, because his company's fortunes had continued to rise through the years, and he found himself extremely busy in Moscow. KSFC benefited with the sunset of the US Space Shuttle program. KSFC contracts increased even more as it became one of the major players in space delivery. Yes, there were other launch vehicles, run by other companies, launching satellites and supplies and men. The Soyuz, the Proton, the Rokot, to name three. But Safronov and his Dnepr-1 vehicle were expanding operations at a faster pace than the others. In 2011, Safronov's firm successfully launched more than twenty rockets from their three launch platforms at the Baikonur Cosmodrome in the flat grassy steppes of Kazakhstan, and 2012 contracts were on pace to outperform even that.

He was a busy man, to be sure, but he was not too busy to drop everything and head south on the Caspian Highway when the message came from Murshidov, Abu Dagestani—Father of Dagestan.

Georgi Safronov looked down at his Rolex and was happy to find he would arrive at the meeting exactly on time. He was a rocket scientist, after all. He abhorred imprecision.

29

Jamaat Shariat used the farmhouse just west of Volgograd from time to time when they had business north of their area of influence. The property was close to the airport but secluded from the hustle and bustle of the city itself, so they did not need more than a few sentries patrolling the dirt roads and a carload of Dagestani gunmen up near the turnoff to the highway to keep those meeting or overnighting inside the property secure from Russian police or internal security forces.

Georgi Safronov made it through the light cordon of security with a pat-down and a check of his identification, then he was led inside the dimly lit farmhouse. Women in the kitchen averted their eyes when he greeted them, but the sentries brought him into the great room of the house, where he was met by his spiritual leader, Suleiman Murshidov, the one he called Abu Dagestani.

A low table was adorned with a lace tablecloth. The women placed a bowl of grapes, a bowl of individually wrapped candies, and a two-liter bottle of Fanta orange soda in front of the men, and then they disappeared.

Safronov beamed with pride, just as he always did when in the presence of the spiritual leader of the organization fighting for the rights and the future of Georgi's own people. He knew he would not have been asked to come here, in this way, if it were not of the utmost importance. The capture of Israpil Nabiyev the previous month— Russian authorities had not said they had taken the man alive, but survivors of the attack on the Dagestani village had seen him carried off in a helicopter—must have something to do with why he was being called here.

The Russian space entrepreneur expected that Suleiman Murshidov was going to ask him for money. Perhaps a large sum to try to effect the release of Israpil. Georgi was excited at the prospect of playing, for the first time, a tangible role in the struggle of his people.

The old man sat on the floor on the other side of the table. Behind him, two of his sons sat on chairs, but they were removed from this conversation by the width of the room. Murshidov had spent the past few minutes asking about Georgi's journey, about his work, and telling the Russian/Dagestani about events in the Caucasus. Safronov felt much more love for this old man than he did for his own father, the man who betrayed him, who took him from his people, who tried to turn him into something he was not. Abu Dagestani, in contrast, had given him back his identity.

The old bearded man said, "My son, son of Dagestan, Allah supports our resistance against Moscow."

"I know this to be true, Abu Dagestani."

"I have learned of an opportunity that, with your help, can do more for our cause than anything that has ever happened in all the days before. More than the war, more than brother Israpil was able to accomplish with all his troops."

"Just tell me what you need. You know I have begged you to let me do something, to play some role in our struggle."

"Do you remember what you told me when you were here last year?"

Safronov thought back. He had said many, many things, all ideas he had that would allow him to aid the cause of

Jamaat Shariat. Georgi stayed up nights working on schemes to promote the cause, and during his annual visits to Makhachkala he offered up his best ideas to Murshidov. He did not know which of these plans his leader was referring to. "I . . . Which thing, Father of Dagestan?"

A thin crease of a smile spread across the old man's lips. "You told me that you were a powerful man. That you controlled the rockets that went off into space. That you could redirect your rockets to hit Moscow."

Safronov beamed with excitement at the same moment his mind filled with worry and consternation. He had told the old man about his many ideas for retribution against the Russians with whom he lived and worked. Changing the path of one of his space delivery vehicles so that it would not reach orbit but instead send its payload into a crowded population center was, by far, the most fanciful of his boasts to Murshidov. There were a hundred or more problems with that plan of his, but yes, it was not beyond the realm of possibilities.

Safronov knew now was not the time to show doubt. "Yes! I swear I can do it. Just give me the word and I will force the Russians to either return our military leader or suffer for this crime."

Murshidov began to speak, but Safronov, amped with excitement, said, "I need to say that such a strike would be best used against an oil refinery, even if it is outside of a city. The capsule itself is not explosive, so although it would hit at a high rate of speed, it will need to hit something flammable or explosive to do the greatest amount of damage." Georgi worried the old man would be disappointed in this; he'd probably neglected to give a realistic explanation of just what a kinetic missile could accomplish when he'd made his boast the year before.

But Murshidov posed a question: "Would your weapons be more powerful if they were tipped with nuclear bombs?"

Safronov's head cocked. He stammered briefly. "Well . . . yes. Of course. But that is not possible, and even without them they still can be powerful conventional weapons. I promise you that if I target fuel storage or—"

"Why is it not possible?"

"Because I *have* no bombs, Father."

"If you did, would you still proceed? Or is your heart made heavy by the thought of the deaths of hundreds of thousands of your adopted countrymen?"

Safronov's chin rose. This was a test. A hypothetical. "If I had bombs, I would act with even *more* passion. There is no equivocation in my heart."

"There is a man here that I want you to meet. A foreigner."

Safronov had seen no foreigner. Was this a hypothetical, too? "What man?"

"I will let him tell you who he is. Talk to him. I trust him. He comes highly respected from our brothers in Chechnya."

"Of course, Abu Dagestani. I will speak with him."

Suleiman Murshidov motioned to one of his sons, who beckoned Safronov to follow him. Georgi stood, confused by what was happening, but he followed the man into the hall and up the staircase, and then into a large bedroom. Here three men in casual clothing stood with assault rifles hanging over their shoulders. They were not Dagestanis; not Arabs, either. One man was very tall, and he was Georgi's age; the other two were younger.

"*As salaam aleikum,*" the older man said. So they spoke Arabic, anyway.

"*Wa aleikum as salaam,*" Safronov replied.

"Lift your arms in the air, please."

"I am sorry?"

"Please, friend."

Safronov did so, unsure. The two young men approached him and frisked him thoroughly but with no obvious intentions of disrespect.

Once this was complete, the older man bade Safronov to sit on a worn sofa against the wall. Both men sat down, and glasses of orange soda were placed on a table in front of them.

"Mr. Safronov, you may call me General Ijaz. I am a general in the Pakistani Defense Force."

Georgi shook the man's hand. *Pakistan? Interesting.* Slowly Suleiman Murshidov's words downstairs began to bear some context.

Rehan asked, "You are Dagestani? And a faithful Muslim?"

"I am both of these things, General."

"Suleiman promised me you were just exactly the man I need to speak to."

"I hope I can be of service."

"You are in charge of Russian space operations?"

Safronov started to shake his head. That was a gross oversimplification of his role as president and main shareholder of Kosmos Space Flight Corporation. But he stopped himself. Now was no time to equivocate, though he did explain further. "That is almost true, General Ijaz. I am president of the company that owns and operates one of Russia's best space launch vehicles."

"What do you deliver into space?"

"We deliver satellites into orbits, primarily. We made twenty-one successful launches last year, and expect twenty-four next year."

"You have access to the missiles to launch the vehicles?"

Safronov nodded, proud of himself and the company he had grown over the past fifteen years. "Our principal space delivery vehicle is the Dnepr-1 Space Launch System. It is a converted RM-36."

Rehan just stared at the Russian. He did not like to admit that he did not know a fact. He would wait silently until this little man explained himself.

"The RM-36, General, is an intercontinental ballistic missile. Russia . . . I should say the Soviet Union, used this to deliver nuclear missiles. It was only in the 1990s when my company reconfigured the system into a civilian space rocket."

Rehan nodded thoughtfully, feigning only mild interest when, in fact, this was an incredible piece of news.

"What can be put inside of this missile, Mr. Safronov?"

Georgi smiled knowingly. He understood from Murshidov's questions what was happening here. He also understood it was his job to sell this idea to this stern-faced Pakistani in front of him.

"General, we can put in it whatever you have for us that will fit inside the payload envelope."

"The devices I am considering are 3.83 meters by .46 meters."

"And the weight?"

"Just over one thousand kilograms."

The Russian nodded happily. "It can be done."

"Excellent."

"Are you prepared to tell me what this device is?"

The man Safronov knew as General Ijaz just looked him in the eye. "Nuclear bombs. Twenty-kiloton yield."

"Bombs? Not the warheads of a missile?"

"No. These are air-dropped bombs. Is that a problem?"

"I know very little about bombs, more about Russian missile warheads from my time in the military. But I do know the bombs can be removed from their cases to make them smaller and lighter. This will not affect the yield of the blast. We will need to do this to put them in payload containers for our missiles."

"I see," Rehan said. "Tell me this. Your missiles . . . where can they go?"

Now Safronov took on a guarded expression. He started to speak but stopped himself. Stammered a bit.

Rehan said, "I am only curious, friend. If I decide to give these devices to your organization, then they are yours to do with as you wish." Rehan smiled more broadly. "Although I'd prefer you did not target Islamabad."

Safronov relaxed a little. For a moment he worried this operation was to be some sort of job for the Pakistanis. Safronov would not do this for money. He would only do this for his cause.

"General Ijaz, my missiles will go anywhere I tell them to go. But there will be no debate. One of them will land in Red Square."

Rehan nodded. "Excellent," he said. "Finally Moscow will beg at your feet for mercy. You and your people can have what you have long desired. An Islamic caliphate in the Caucasus."

The thin Russian with the boyish flop of hair on his forehead smiled, the rings of his eyes reddened and moistened, and the two men embraced there in the cold attic room.

As Riaz Rehan hugged the smaller man, the Pakistani general himself smiled. He had been marshaling zealots and criminals since he was a fourteen-year-old boy, and he was very, very good at it.

After the emotional embrace, Rehan returned to the business at hand. "Mr. Safronov. You may, in the coming days, hear faint rumors of strangers asking questions of you, your history, your background, your education, your faith."

"Why is this?"

"First and foremost, I will have to look into you very carefully."

"General Ijaz, I understand completely. You and your security service may look into me all you wish, but please do not take too long, sir. There is a scheduled launch at the end of the year. Three Dnepr-1 rockets carrying three satellites for United States, British, and Japanese companies will be launched on three consecutive days."

"I see," said Rehan. "And you will be there?"

"I had already planned on it." Safronov smiled. "But you give me additional incentive."

The two men went over details for the rest of the afternoon, and then into the evening. They prayed together. By the time he returned to the Volgograd airport, Rehan was ready to hand the bombs over to the energetic Dagestani partisan.

But first he had to acquire the bombs, and for this he had a plan, yes. But he also had much work still to do. Operation Saker, a plan that he had been working on for years and thinking about for well over a decade, needed to begin as soon as he returned to Pakistan.

30

Jack Ryan Jr. breathed out a long, slow breath, and with it a small measure of his anxiety.

He dialed the number. With each ring, half of him hoped there would be no answer on the other end. His blood pressure was up, and his palms perspired slightly.

He'd gotten the phone number from Mary Pat Foley. He'd written several e-mails to her over the last few days, but each one he'd deleted before hitting that irrevocable send key. Finally, on perhaps his fourth or fifth try, he'd written Mary Pat a succinct but friendly message thanking her for the tour around the office the other day, and, oh, by the way, he was wondering if she would pass on Melanie Kraft's phone number.

He groaned when he read his message, he felt more than a little foolish, but he sucked it up and hit send.

Twenty minutes later a friendly message came back from Mary Pat. Mary Pat said she had enjoyed running out for sushi, and she had found their conversation exceedingly interesting. She hoped to be able to add to the conversation soon. And at the end, following a simple "Here you go," Jack saw the area code 703, Alexandria, Virginia, preceding a seven-digit number.

"Yes!" he shouted at his desk.

Behind him, Tony Wills spun around, waited for an explanation.

"Sorry," said Jack.

But this was all yesterday. Jack's initial excitement had

turned to butterflies, and he was doing his best to fight them as Melanie's phone continued ringing.

Shit, Jack thought to himself. It wasn't exactly a gun battle in central Paris he was facing here at the moment. Why the nerves?

A click indicated that someone had answered. *Shit. Okay, Jack. Play cool.*

"Melanie Kraft."

"Hi, Melanie. This is Jack Ryan."

A brief pause. "It is an honor, Mr. President."

"No . . . Not . . . It's Jack Junior. We met the other day."

"I'm just kidding. Hi, Jack."

"Oh. Hey, you got me. How are you?"

"I'm great. Yourself?"

The pace of the conversation slowed. "I'm fine."

"Good."

Jack did not speak.

"Can I help you with something?"

"Uh." *Snap out of it, Jack.* "Yes. Actually, a little bird told me you live down in Alexandria."

"Does that little bird happen to serve as associate director at the National Counterterrorism Center?"

"As a matter of fact, she does."

"Thought so."

Jack could hear a smile in Melanie's voice, and he could immediately tell everything was going to be okay.

"Anyway, that got me thinking . . . There's a restaurant down there on King Street, Vermillion. It has the best strip loin I've ever tasted. I was wondering if I could take you to dinner there on Saturday."

"That sounds great. Will it be just you, or will your Secret Service detail be coming with us?"

"I don't have protection."

"Okay, just checking."

She was teasing him, and he liked it. He said, "That doesn't mean I won't have my dad's detail check you out thoroughly before our date."

She laughed. "Bring it on. It can't be any worse than going through the TS-SCI process." She was referring to the CIA vetting process that took months and involved interviews with everyone from neighbors to elementary school teachers.

"I'll pick you up at seven?"

"Seven's fine. We can actually walk from my place."

"Great. See you then."

"Looking forward to it," Melanie said.

Jack hung up the phone, stood, and smiled at Wills. Tony stood and high-fived his young coworker.

Paul Laska stood on the long balcony of the Royal Suite of the Mandarin Oriental Hotel in London, and he looked out over Hyde Park below.

It was a cool morning in October, but certainly no cooler than it would be back in Newport. Paul had come alone, with only his personal assistant Stuart, his secretary Carmela, his dietitian Luc, and a pair of Czech-born security officers who traveled with him wherever he went.

That's what passed for "alone" in the life of a high-profile billionaire.

The other man on the balcony really had come alone. Yes, there was a time, years before, when Oleg Kovalenko would have been flanked by guards everywhere he went. He had been KGB, after all. A case officer in several Soviet satellites in the sixties and seventies. Not a particularly high-riser in the KGB, but he'd retired as *rezident,* the KGB's equivalent to a CIA station chief, even though he was only *rezident* of Denmark.

After retirement, Oleg Kovalenko returned home to Russia to live a quiet life in Moscow. He'd rarely traveled out of the country since, but an insistent phone call the day before put him on a jet to London, and now here he sat, feet up on a chaise longue, his thick, soft body tired from the travel, but enjoying the first of what he hoped would be many excellent mimosas.

Laska watched the morning Knightsbridge commuters file below him and waited for the old Russian to break the ice.

It did not take long. Kovalenko had always hated uncomfortable silence.

"It is good to see you again, Pavel Ivanovich," Kovalenko said.

Laska's only reply was a quiet sardonic smile that was delivered toward the park in front of him, and not to the big man on his right.

The heavy Russian continued, "I was surprised that you wanted to meet like this. It is not so public here, really, but others could be watching."

Now Laska turned to the man on the chaise longue. "Others are watching *me,* Oleg. But no one is watching you. No one cares about an old Russian pensioner, even if you once wielded some power. Your delusions of grandeur are quite childish, actually."

Kovalenko smiled, sipped his morning drink. If he was offended by the insult, he made no show of it.

"So, how can I help you? This is, I am guessing, about our good old times together? You feel the need to settle something from our past?"

Laska shrugged. "I left the past behind. If you haven't done that yet yourself, you are an old fool."

"Ha. That is not how it worked for we Russians. The past left *us* behind. We were more than willing to remain there." He shrugged, drained his mimosa and immediately began looking around for a fresh one. "*Tempus fugit,* as they say."

"I need a favor from you," Laska said.

Kovalenko stopped searching for a drink. Instead he looked to the Czech billionaire, then he climbed out of the chaise and stood with his hands on his wide hips. "What could I possibly have that you need, Pavel?"

"It's Paul, not Pavel. It has not been Pavel for forty years."

"Forty years. Yes. You turned your back on us a long time ago."

"I never turned my back on you, Oleg. I was never *with* you in the first place. I was never a devotee."

Kovalenko smiled. He understood completely, but he pressed. "Then why did you help us so eagerly?"

"I was eager to get out of there. That's all. You know that."

"You turned your back on us, just as you turned your back on your own people. Some would suggest you have turned yet again, turning away from the capitalism that made you in the West. Now you support everything that is not capitalism. You are quite a dancer for an old man. Just the same as when you were young."

Laska thought back to when he was young, in Prague. He thought back to his friends in the movement, his initial support of Alexander Dubček. Laska also thought about his girlfriend, Ilonka, and their plans to get married after the revolution.

But then he thought of his arrest by the secret police,

the visit to his cell by a big, powerful, and dominant KGB officer named Oleg. The beating, the threats of imprisonment, and the promise of an exit visa if the young banker only informed on a few of his fellow rabble-rousers in the movement.

Pavel Laska had agreed. He saw it as an opportunity to go to the West, to New York City, to trade on the New York Stock Exchange, and to make a great deal of money. Kovalenko turned him with this enticement, and Laska had helped turn the tide against the Prague Spring.

And inside of two years the traitor was in New York.

Paul Laska shook Pavel Laska out of his mind. Ancient history. "Oleg, I am not here to see you. I need something else."

"I am going to let you pick up the check for my lovely room downstairs, I am going to let you reimburse me for my flight, I am going to drink your Champagne, and I am going to let you speak."

"Your son, Valentin, is SVR. High-ranking, higher than you ever made it in the KGB."

"Apples to oranges. Very different times. A very different industry."

"You don't seem surprised that I know about Valentin."

"Not at all. Everything can be bought. Information as well. And you have the money to buy everything."

"I also know that he is assistant *rezident* in the UK."

Oleg shrugged. "You would think that he'd call on his old father when he learned that I was here. But no. Too busy." Kovalenko smiled a little. "I remember the life, though, and I was too busy for *my* father."

"I want to meet Valentin. Tonight. It must be in complete secrecy. He is to tell no one of our appointment."

273

Oleg shrugged. "If I can't get him to see me, his dear father, how can I persuade him to see you?"

Laska just looked at the old man, the KGB officer who beat him in Prague in 1968, and he delivered his own blow. "Apples to oranges, Oleg Petrovich. He will see me."

31

General Riaz Rehan launched the opening volley of his Operation Saker with a phone call over a voice-over-Internet line with a man in India.

The man had many aliases, but forever more he would be known as Abdul Ibrahim. He was thirty-one, thin and tall, with a narrow face and deep-set eyes. He was also the operational chief for Lashkar-e-Taiba in southern India, and October 15 would be the last day of his life.

His orders had come in a phone call from Majid just three nights earlier. He'd met Majid several times before at a training camp in Muzaffarabad, Pakistan, and he knew the man to be a high-ranking member of the Pakistani Army and a commander in the ISI. The fact that Ibrahim did not know that Majid's real name was Riaz Rehan was unimportant, as unimportant as the fact that the four other men who would go on this mission did not know the other aliases of Abdul Ibrahim.

Ibrahim and his cell had been operating in the Karnataka region of India for some time. They were no sleepers; they'd bombed a railroad exchange, four electrical power stations, and a water treatment facility, and they'd shot a policeman and firebombed cars in front of a television station. For LeT it was small-time stuff, but Abdul Ibrahim had been ordered by Majid to perform harassing operations against the population in a manner that would not put his cell into too much jeopardy. He'd long assumed he was being kept safe and in place for a major operation, and when Majid called him on his voice-over Internet line three days prior, it had been the proudest moment of Abdul Ibrahim's life.

Following orders received in the phone call, Abdul Ibrahim had picked his five best operators, and they all met at their safe house in Mysore. Ibrahim appointed one of the men his successor as chief of operations. The young man was shocked to be told he would be in charge of Lashkar-e-Taiba ops in southern India in two-days' time. The other four men felt lucky to be told they would be going with Abdul on a martyrdom operation in Bangalore.

They took the best weapons from the cache: four grenades, ten homemade pipe bombs, and a pistol and rifle for each of the five men. This along with nearly two thousand rounds of combined ammunition they packed into backpacks and suitcases along with a change of clothing. Within hours they were on a train to the northeast, and they arrived in Bangalore early in the morning of their second-to-last day.

A local man with Pakistani roots met them, took them to his home, and handed them the keys to three motorcycles.

Riaz Rehan himself had picked the target. Bangalore is often referred to as the Silicon Valley of India. With a population of six million, it possesses many of the largest technology companies in the huge nation, many located in Electronics City, a 330-acre industrial park in the western suburbs of Bangalore—more precisely in Doddathogur and Agrahara, former villages that had been swallowed up with the explosion of both population and progress here.

Rehan felt that Abdul Ibrahim and his four men would be slaughtered relatively quickly if they attacked this target. Electronics City had good security for a nongovernmental installation. But still, any success at all by Abdul Ibrahim and his men would send a symbolic message. Electronics City was a major outsourcing hub of India and the operations run from offices there involved hundreds of companies, large and small, around the world. Blowing up people and property here would affect, to one degree or another, many of the Fortune 500 companies, and this would ensure that the attack would have a huge amount of play in the Western media. Rehan reasoned that a single death here by the southern India cell of LeT would carry the value of twenty deaths of peasants in a Kashmiri village. He intended for Abdul Ibrahim's act in Bangalore to create a thunderclap of terror that would reverberate across the globe and frighten the West, ensuring that India would not be able to downplay such an attack.

More attacks would follow, and with each attack the conflict between India and Pakistan would worsen.

Riaz Rehan understood all this because he was a Westernized jihadist, an army general, and an intelligence chief. All these titles attributed to just one man gave him another, more ominous identity—Riaz Rehan, aka Majid, was, above all, a master terrorist.

When Abdul Ibrahim and his four men arrived in Bangalore and fueled up their motorbikes, they immediately began reconnaissance on their target, because they had no time to waste. They found that the industrial park was covered with heavily armed security, both private guards and police. Further, the Central Industrial Security Force, the Indian paramilitary force in charge of government industrial installations, airports, and nuclear site security, was now working under contract for certain well-heeled private businesses in Electronics City. The CISF had even established checkpoints at the entrance to the industrial park. Ibrahim was certain he and his men would not be able to breach any of the major buildings themselves. He was dejected, but nevertheless he decided to spend much of the time until the attack driving around the perimeter of Electronics City, searching for a way in.

He did not find a way in, but on the final morning, just hours before his planned attack, he decided to pass by his target one last time in daylight. He traveled alone on his motorcycle along the Hosur Main Road, took the huge, modern Bangalore Elevated Tollway, a ten-kilometer fly-over that ran between Madiwala and Electronics City, and he immediately found himself surrounded by dozens of buses packed with workers heading to their jobs from Bangalore proper.

Instantly he saw his mission before him. Abdul Ibrahim returned to the safe house in the city and told his men that the plans had changed.

They did not attack that night as he'd promised Majid. He knew his handler would be furious with him for disobeying a direct order, but he obeyed his other order and made no contact with his handler, nor any other LeT asset. Instead he destroyed his mobile phone, prayed, and went to sleep.

He and his men awoke at six a.m. They prayed again, drank tea in silence, and then climbed aboard the three motorcycles.

They arrived at the flyover at eight a.m. Abdul rode his own bike two hundred meters behind the second motorcycle, which itself was two hundred meters behind the first. He carried the pipe bombs and grenades in his backpack slung on his chest to where he could reach into the bag and pull them out while he drove.

The first bike pulled alongside an articulated bus with

fifty passengers inside. As the driver of the motorcycle advanced slowly along the long, two-sectioned vehicle, the rider pulled an AK-47 from a bag in his lap, its wire stock folded to shorten its length. The gunman calmly and carefully lined his sights up on the side of the bus driver's head, and he pressed the trigger. With a short pop and a burst of gray smoke, the bus driver's window shattered and the man tumbled out of his seat, and the huge bus careened sharply to the right and then jackknifed. It hit several other cars as it skidded at speed, then it slammed into the concrete wall of the flyover, striking more cars that had pulled quickly off the road in an attempt to get out of the way.

Some in the bus died in the crash, but most were merely wounded after having been thrown from their seats. The first motorcycle moved on, leaving the wounded bus behind as it continued up the road, attacking more vehicles in its path.

But the second motorcycle, also carrying a driver and a gunman, passed by the crash thirty seconds later. The rear rider's AK barked, and his seventy-five-round drum spun, releasing its supersonic bullets through the barrel. The rounds tore into the bus and into the wounded, killing the men and women as they tried in vain to scramble free of the wreckage, and killing those in other vehicles who had pulled over to help.

This second bike, too, rolled on, leaving the carnage behind as the rear gunner reloaded and prepared to attack the next scene of horror up the flyover.

But Abdul Ibrahim arrived at the articulated bus and the wreckage around it just moments later. He pulled up in the middle of the slaughter, just like dozens of other cars, vans, and motorcycles had done. The thin Lashkar-e-Taiba operative took a pipe bomb from his satchel, lit it with a lighter, and rolled it under a small Volkswagen bus that was parked in the jam, and then he drove away quickly.

Seconds later the VW exploded, the hot metal and shattered glass tore through the traffic jam, and fire ignited leaking gas from the articulated bus. Men and women burned alive across the two southbound lanes of the flyover as the Lashkar cell continued on, a rolling three-stage attack along the raised toll road.

They continued on like this for several kilometers; the first two bikes poured automatic weapons fire into moving busses, the vehicles stopped suddenly, careened left or right, many crashed into cars and trucks. Ibrahim cruised slowly and calmly through the wreckage left behind by his comrades, pulled to a stop next to one bus after another, smiled grimly at the screams and moans from inside the wreckage, and tossed in grenades and pipe bombs.

Twenty-four-year-old Kiron Yadava was driving himself to work that morning because he had missed his carpool. A *jawan* (enlisted soldier) with the Central Industrial Security Force, he worked the day shift as a patrolling constable at Electronics City, an easy job after two years of service deployed in a paramilitary unit. Normally he packed into a van with six of his mates at a bus stop in front of the Meenakshi Temple for the ride across town to work, but today he was running late and, consequently, traveling alone.

He had just paid his toll to get on the flyover, and he pushed the accelerator on his tiny two-seater Tata nearly down to the floorboard to climb the ramp to the restricted access road that traveled to Electronics City. As he drove he listened to a CD in his stereo, the riffs of Bombay

Bassment were jacked up full volume, and he rapped along with the MC at the top of his lungs.

The track ended as Kiron merged into the thick traffic, and the next song had just begun, a thumping electronic reggae-infused dance beat. When the young man heard a low *whump whump* that seemed to defy the rhythm, he looked at his stereo. But when he heard it again, louder than the music coming through his speakers, he looked into his rearview mirror, and he saw black smoke rising from a dozen sources on the flyover behind him. The nearest plume was just a hundred yards back, and he saw a flaming minibus in the far right-hand lane.

Constable Yadava saw the motorcycle a moment later. Just forty meters away, two men rode a yellow Suzuki. The rear rider held a Kalashnikov, and he fired it from the hip at a four-door sedan that then sideswiped a bus as it swerved to escape the hot lead.

Yadava could not believe the images in his rearview mirror. The motorcycle streaked closer and closer to his tiny car, but Constable Yadava just kept driving, as if he were watching an action show on television.

The Suzuki bike passed by his car. The rider was hooking a fresh mag into his AK, and he even made eye contact with Yadava in his tiny two-seater, before the pair of terrorists wove in front of other cars and out of view.

The CISF *jawan* heard more shooting behind him now, and finally he reacted to the action. The Tata pulled off the road on the left, just ahead of another car that had done the same. Yadava climbed out, then reached back in, grabbing his work bag. After unzipping the bag he reached in, his fingers felt past his plastic lunch container and his sweater, and they wrapped around the Heckler & Koch MP5 submachine gun that he carried while on duty. He grabbed his weapon as close rifle fire and incessant honking of horns assaulted his ears.

With the gun and his single reserve magazine of thirty rounds of ammo, Yadava sprinted into traffic, searching for a target. Men on motorcycles and men and women in private cars raced by. Everyone on the flyover knew they were under assault, but there was nowhere to turn off until the next off ramp more than a kilometer farther on. Vehicles hit one another as they fought to get out of the way of the slaughter, and Yadava, operating on one part training to three parts adrenaline, just ran out into the midst of all this madness.

Fifty meters back, he saw a yellow Mazda SUV slam hard into the waist-high protective barrier on the edge of the road. It hit with such speed that it then flipped over the side and spun through the air, almost as if in slow motion, before it hurtled some forty feet down toward the heavy traffic on the service road below the flyover.

A motorcycle approached Yadava. It was nearly identical to the one that had passed him a minute before, and the man behind the driver held a rifle with a large drum magazine.

The driver saw the uniformed CISF constable with the black sub-gun standing in the traffic, but he could not warn his gunner, so as Yadava raised his MP5 to fire, the biker slid his Suzuki onto the ground. He rolled off of it, and then slid with his partner.

Yadava raised his ring sight over the man with the Kalashnikov and he fired. Now his training in the paramilitaries was put to good use. His shots tore up the road and then the man, blood fountained from the terrorist's *salwar kameez*. The man in the street dropped his AK and then stilled, and Yadava moved his sights to the driver.

The CISF warned their *jawan*s that Pakistani terrorists, as this man certainly was, often wore suicide vests that they would detonate if they faced capture, and the CISF therefore instructed their men to offer no quarter to a terrorist operative when caught in the act.

Young Kiron Yadava did not weigh the pros and cons of shooting an unarmed man. As long as the Islamist lived on this earth he was a danger to India, the country the constable had sworn to protect to his dying breath.

Kiron Yadava emptied his weapon into the man lying in the street.

As he reloaded his MP5, he turned to begin running after the other bike, but he heard the detonation of a hand grenade in the heavy traffic behind him. He knew instantly there was a third motorcycle still behind him. It would be approaching in moments, and it was up to him to stop the attack.

Abdul Ibrahim fired his Makarov pistol into the chest of the driver of a passenger van. The driver slumped to the floor, his foot came off the brake, and this caused the big vehicle to rear-end a Fiat with a dead husband and wife in the front seat. In the back three rows of the van, eight Europeans in business suits recovered from the crash and then cowered at the sight of the terrorist climbing off his bike, and then, with an incredible expression of peace on his face, pulling a pipe bomb out of a bag hanging from his chest.

Ibrahim looked down to his lighter, careful to put the flame on the tip of the short wick of his bomb, lest he martyr himself accidentally. He lit his wick, replaced the lighter in his pocket, and then reached back to toss the bomb under the van.

Just then he heard the rat-a-tat of a submachine gun

firing up the street. He turned to look at the source of the fire, he knew his men carried heavier rifles. He saw the Indian CISF man, saw the flash of fire from his weapon, and then felt his body buckle and spasm with the impact of the bullets. He was hit twice in the pelvis and groin, and he fell to the ground, on top of his improvised explosive device.

Abdul Ibrahim shrieked *"Allahu Akbar!"* just before his pipe bomb detonated into his chest, blowing him to bits.

Constable Kiron Yadava came upon the bullet-riddled bodies of the final two men in the terror cell a few minutes later. The pair had tried to run their Suzuki motorcycle through a hasty CISF roadblock just before the last off ramp before Electronics City. The eight constables stood over the dead men, but Yadava screamed at them. He told them to stop admiring their handiwork and to help him tend to the two dozen or so scenes of bloodshed all the way down the southbound lane of the ten-kilometer stretch of the Bangalore Elevated Tollway.

Together these men, followed soon by hundreds of other first responders, spent the entire day treating survivors of the massacre.

Riaz Rehan was in his office at ISI headquarters in the Aabpara district of Islamabad when his television reported a huge traffic accident in Bangalore. It meant nothing to him at first, but when the size of the carnage was relayed by the news anchor, Rehan stopped his other work and sat in rapt attention at his desk, watching the television. Within minutes there was confirmation that there had been a gun battle and within minutes more terrorists were being blamed for a massacre.

Rehan had awoken furious with the LeT cell for not executing the night before, but now he was ecstatic. He could not believe these reports out of Bangalore. He had hoped for a casualty count of twenty with at least ten dead, perhaps some news footage of a burning guard post or a crater next to a building. Instead his five-man-strong cell, with only five rifles and a few small explosives, had managed to massacre sixty-one people and injure an incredible one hundred forty-four.

Rehan beamed with pride and made a mental note that when he became president of Pakistan he would have a statue built in honor of Abdul Ibrahim, but he also realized the attack had actually done more damage than he wanted. LeT would be targeted with renewed vigor by not only the Indians but also the Americans. The pressure on Pakistan's government to root out LeT would be twice what he'd expected. Rehan knew that the US/Pakistani Intelligence Fusion Center would be working overtime now and shifting their workload toward LeT.

Rehan did not panic. Instead he reached out to his LeT contacts and told them he would take over as project manager for the next operation, and it would need to be moved up on the calendar. Forces opposed to LeT in his government, forces who were allied with the United States, would begin rounding up the usual suspects after this attack, and Rehan knew that every day before phase two of his plan to bring Pakistan and India to the brink of war would increase the chance that Operation Saker would be somehow compromised.

32

Valentin Kovalenko was nothing like his father. Where Oleg had been big and fat, thirty-five-year-old Valentin looked like a gym rat. He was thin but muscular; he wore a beautiful tailored suit that Laska had no doubt cost more than the car Oleg drove back in Moscow. Laska knew enough about luxury items to recognize that Valentin's fashionable Moss Lipow eyeglasses cost more than three thousand dollars.

Another stark departure from the demeanor of his father, especially the version of his father that Laska remembered from Prague, was that Valentin seemed quite friendly. Upon his arrival in Laska's suite just after ten p.m., he'd complimented the Czech on his tireless philanthropy and support for the causes of the downtrodden, then he'd taken a chair by the fireplace after politely turning down the offer of a snifter of brandy.

When both men were settled in front of the fire, Valentin said, "My father says he knows you from your days in Prague. That is all he has said, and I have made it a point to not ask him for any more information than that." His English was spoken with a noticeable British accent.

Laska shrugged. Valentin was being polite, and it might even be true, but if Laska's plan was to go forward, there was not a chance in the world that Valentin Kovalenko would not look into the past of the famous Czech. And there was no chance he would not find out about Laska's duties as a mole. There was no point in hiding it. "I worked for your father. Whether or not you know that yet, you will soon enough. I was an informant, and your father was my handler."

Valentin smiled a little. "My father impresses me sometimes. Ten thousand bottles of vodka down the hatch and the old man still can keep secrets. That is bloody impressive."

"He can," agreed Laska. "He did not tell me anything about you. My other sources in the East, via my Progressive Nations Institute, were the ones who told me about your position in SVR."

Valentin nodded. "In my father's day we'd send men and women to the gulag for revealing that information. Now I will just send an e-mail to internal state security mentioning the leak and they will file the e mail away and do nothing."

The two men watched the fireplace in the huge suite for a moment. Finally Paul said, "I have an opportunity that I think will interest your government greatly. I would like to suggest an operation to you. If your agency agrees, I will only work with you. No one else."

"Does it involve the United Kingdom?"

"It involves the United States."

"I'm sorry, Mr. Laska, but that is not my area of operations, and I am very busy here."

"Yes, being assistant *rezident*. But my proposal will make you *rezident* in your pick of nations. What I am offering is that important."

Valentin smiled. An affectation of amusement, but Laska could see a glint in the boy's eyes that reminded him of his father in his younger years.

Valentin Kovalenko asked, "What is it you are proposing, Mr. Laska?"

"Nothing less than the destruction of the American President, Jack Ryan."

Valentin's head rose. "You've given up hope for your friend Edward Kealty?"

"Completely. Ryan will be elected. But I have hope that he will not set foot in the Oval Office to begin his second term."

"That is a great hope you have there. Give *me* reason to share this hope."

"I have a privately acquired file . . . a dossier, if you will, on a man named John Clark. I am sure you know who he is."

Valentin cocked his head, and Laska tried but could not read into the gesture. The Russian said, "I might know that name."

"You are just like your father. Not trusting."

"I am like most all Russians in that regard, Mr. Laska."

Paul Laska nodded in recognition of the truth of the comment. In reply he said, "This exercise will not require your trust. John Clark is a close confidant of Jack Ryan. They have worked together, and they are friends."

"Okay. Please continue. What does the file say?"

"Clark was a CIA assassin. He did the bidding of Jack Ryan. Ryan signed a pardon for this. Do you know what a pardon is?"

"I do."

"But I think Clark has done other things. Things that, if brought out into the light of day, will implicate Ryan directly."

"What things?"

"You need to get your service's file on Clark and put it with my file on Clark."

"If we had such a document already, that is to say, a file

on this John Clark that had incriminating evidence, do you not think we would have exploited it by now? During the first Ryan presidency, perhaps?"

Laska waved away the comment. "Very quickly and quietly your service should reinterview anyone, anywhere, with knowledge of the man or his operations. Make one large dossier, with every truth, half-truth, and innuendo."

"And then?"

"And then I want you to give it to the Kealty campaign."

"Why?"

"Because I cannot let it be known who my source of this information is. The file must come from someone else. Someone out of the USA. I want your people to dress it up with what you have to disguise the source."

"Innuendoes do not convict men in your adopted country, Mr. Laska."

"They can destroy a political career. And more than that, it is what Clark is doing right now that must be revealed. I have reason to believe that he is operating for some extra-judicial organization. Committing crimes around the world. And he would not be out committing these crimes if not for the full pardon given him by John Patrick Ryan. We get enough on Clark to Kealty, Kealty will force the Justice Department to investigate Clark. Kealty will do it for his own selfish reasons, no question. But it doesn't matter. What matters is that the investigation will find a house of horrors."

Valentin Kovalenko looked into the fire. Paul Laska watched him. Watched the firelight flicker off of the lenses of his Moss Lipow glasses.

"This sounds like an easy operation for my side. A quick thumbing through of a dusty old file, a quick investigation using men from some third-party group as a cutout, not SVR or FSB. More cutouts to pass the results on to someone in Kealty's campaign. We will not be over-exposed. But I do not know that there is much chance for success of the operation."

"I can't believe your country has any interest in a strong Ryan administration."

Kovalenko had done little to tip his hand at any point in this conversation, but to Laska's last comment he shook his head slowly, staring the older man in the eye. "None whatsoever, Mr. Laska. But . . . will there be enough to bring him down through Clark?"

"In time to save Ed Kealty? No. Perhaps not even in time to prevent his inauguration. But Richard Nixon's Watergate took many months to germinate into something so big and bountiful that it resulted in his resignation."

"Very true."

"And what I know about the actions of John Clark makes the events of Watergate look like some sort of fraternity prank."

Kovalenko nodded. A thin smile crossed his lips. "Perhaps, Mr. Laska, I will take one small snifter of brandy as we chat further."

33

On a frigid October night in Makhachkala, Dagestan, fifty-five fighters of Jamaat Shariat met in a low-ceilinged basement with Suleiman Murshidov, the elderly spiritual leader of their organization. The men were aged between seventeen and forty-seven, and together they possessed hundreds of years of experience in urban warfare.

These men had been handpicked by operational commanders, and five of their number were cell leaders themselves. It had been explained to them that they would be sent to a foreign base for training, and then they would embark on an operation that would change the course of history.

To a man they thought their operation would involve a hostage situation, likely in Moscow, with their ultimate goal being the repatriation of their commander, Israpil Nabiyev.

They were only half right.

None of these grizzled fighters knew the clean-shaven man with Murshidov and his sons. To them he looked like a politician, not a rebel, so when Abu Dagestani explained that he would be their leader for their operation, they were stunned.

Georgi Safronov spoke passionately to the fifty-five men in the basement; he explained that their ultimate goal would be revealed to them in due time, but for now they would all be flying in a cargo plane to Quetta, Pakistan, from where they would venture northward to a camp.

There, he explained, they would undergo three weeks of intense training by the best Muslim fighters in the world, men with more operational experience in the past decade than even their brothers in nearby Chechnya.

All fifty-five men were pleased to learn this, but it was hard for them to look at Safronov as their leader.

Suleiman Murshidov saw this, and he'd expected it, so he spoke again to the group, promised them all that Georgi was Dagestani, and his plan and his sacrifice would do more for the North Caucasus in the next two months than Jamaat Shariat could do without him in the next fifty years.

After a final prayer, the fifty-five men loaded into minibuses and headed toward the airport.

Georgi Safronov wanted to travel with them, but this was deemed too dangerous by General Ijaz, his Pakistani partner in this endeavor. No, Safronov would fly commercial to Peshawar, under documents made by Pakistani intelligence, and there he would be picked up by Ijaz and his men and flown directly to the camp near Miran Shah.

At the camp, Georgi was expected to train with the other men. He would not be as skilled with a weapon, as physically fit, or as battle-hardened in his heart. But he would learn, he would strengthen, and he would toughen.

He hoped he would earn the respect of the men who'd lived their adult lives resisting the Russians in and around Makhachkala. No, they would never look at him like they did Israpil Nabiyev. But they would obey Abu Dagestani and follow Safronov's orders. And if he could learn the martial skills in Pakistan that would be necessary during their struggles ahead, Safronov thought that perhaps they would see him as a true commander, not just a sympathizer of their cause with a plan.

*

Jack Ryan Jr. parked his yellow Hummer in front of Melanie Kraft's address a few minutes after seven. She lived on Princess Street in Alexandria, right up the road from the boyhood home of Robert E. Lee, near the former home of George and Martha Washington, on a portion of the street that was still paved with pre-Revolutionary War cobblestones. Ryan looked around at the beautiful old homes, surprised that a government employee in her mid-twenties could afford to live here.

He found her door and understood. Melanie lived at the address of a beautiful brick Georgian home, yes, but she lived in a carriage house in the back through the garden. They were still pretty nice digs, but he saw from the outside that her place was just larger than a one-car garage.

She invited him in, and he confirmed that the apartment was, indeed, tiny, but she kept it neat.

"I love your place."

Melanie smiled. "Thank you. I love it, too. I'd never be able to afford it without help."

"Help?"

"An old professor of mine from AU is married to a real estate guy; they own the home. It was built in 1794. She rents the carriage house to me for about what I'd pay for a regular apartment around here. It's tiny, but it's all I need."

Jack glanced over at a card table in the corner. On top of it sat a MacBook Pro and a massive stack of books, notebooks, and loose printed pages. Some of the books, Ryan noticed, were printed in Arabic script.

"Is that NCTC south?" he asked with a smile.

She chuckled, but quickly grabbed her coat and her purse and headed for the door. "Shall we?"

Jack figured that was it for the grand tour, but other

than the bathroom, he could see it all from where he stood, anyway. He followed her out the door and into the cool evening.

It was a ten-minute stroll to King Street, and they chatted about the old buildings as they walked. There were a lot of other people out, walking to and from dinner at this hour on a Saturday night.

They stepped into the restaurant and were led to a romantic table for two overlooking the street. As they settled in with their menus, Jack asked, "Have you been here before?"

"Honestly, no. I hate to admit it, but I don't eat out much. Twenty-five-cent wing night at Murphy's is a big time splurge for me."

"Nothing wrong with wings."

Jack ordered a bottle of pinot noir, and they perused the menu while they chatted.

"So you were at Georgetown." Melanie said it as a statement.

Ryan smiled. "Do you know that because Mary Pat told you, because you Googled me, or because you are in the CIA and you know everything?"

She blushed slightly. "I was at AU. I saw you a few times at things around town. You were a year ahead of me, I think. You were hard to miss with that big Secret Service guy around you all the time."

"Mike Brennan. He was a second dad to me. Great guy, but he scared off a lot of people. He's my excuse for having a boring social life in college."

"Good excuse. I'm sure being a celebrity has its drawbacks."

"I'm not a celebrity. Nobody recognizes me. My parents had money, but I sure as hell wasn't raised with a silver spoon in my mouth. I had a summer job through high school and college, I even worked construction for a while."

Melanie said, "I was just talking about the trappings associated with being famous. I wasn't suggesting you don't deserve to be successful."

"Sorry," said Jack. "I've had to defend myself more than once on that front."

"I understand. You want to be accepted for your own talents, not for who your parents are."

"You are very perceptive," Jack said.

"I'm an analyst." She smiled. "I analyze."

"Maybe we should both analyze the menus before the waiter comes back."

Melanie's smile widened. "Uh-oh. Somebody is trying to change the subject."

"Damn right." They both laughed now.

The wine came, Jack tasted it, and the waiter poured for them both.

"To Mary Pat."

"To Mary Pat." They clinked their wineglasses and smiled at each other.

"So," Jack asked, "tell me about the CIA?"

"What do you want to know?"

"More than you can tell me." He thought for a moment. "Have you spent any time overseas?"

"You mean with the Agency?"

"Yes."

"I have."

"Where?" He caught himself. "Sorry. You can't tell me where, can you?"

"Sorry," she said with a shrug. Jack saw that although she'd lived the life of an intelligence analyst for only a couple of years, she was comfortable with secrets.

"Do you speak a foreign language?"

"Yes."

Jack started to ask her if that was classified, too, but she filled him in.

"Level-three Masri—Egyptian Arabic—level-two French, level-one Spanish. Nothing to write home about."

"How many levels are there?"

"Sorry, Jack. I don't get out much." She laughed at herself. "I don't have many conversations with people outside government service. It's called the ILR scale. Interagency Language Roundtable. There are five levels of proficiency. Level three means, basically, that I have normal rate of speech function in the language, but I make small mistakes that don't affect the comprehension of a listener native in the language I am speaking."

"And level one?"

"It means I'm sloppy." She laughed again. "What can I say? I learned Arabic living in Cairo, and I learned Spanish in college. Nothing quite like needing to speak a language to get fed to promote the learning of it."

"Cairo?"

"Yes. Dad was an Air Force attaché; we spent five years in Egypt when I was in high school, and two more in Pakistan."

"How was that?"

"I loved it. It was tough moving around as a kid, but I wouldn't trade it for the world. Plus I learned Arabic, which has proven very helpful."

Jack nodded. "I guess in your line of work it is." He liked this girl. She did not put on airs at all, she neither tried to be overly sexy or a know-it-all. She was obviously highly intelligent, but she was self-deprecating about it at the same time.

And she was very sexy, and it was all natural.

He did notice, more than once, that she seemed to direct the focus of the conversation back on him.

"So," she said with a playful smile. "I'm going to go out on a limb and guess you don't live in a four-hundred-square-foot carriage house subsidized by your ex-professor."

"I've got an apartment in Columbia. It's near work. And near my parents in Baltimore. What about your family?"

The waiter brought their salads, and Melanie began talking about the restaurant. Jack wondered if she just possessed one of those minds that had a tendency to branch off into different subjects during conversations, or if she was trying to avoid the subject of her family. He couldn't tell which it was, but he let it go.

They meandered back to the subject of Jack's work. He explained his work at Hendley Associates in the most boring general terms imaginable, not entirely lies, but his explanation was rife with holes and secrets.

"So," she asked. "When your dad becomes President again, you will have a Secret Service detail following you around wherever you go. Is that going to cause problems around your office?"

You have no idea, Jack thought to himself. He smiled. "Nothing I'm not used to. I became great friends with guys on my detail."

"Still. Didn't it get stifling?"

Jack wanted to put on a cool face, but he stopped himself. She was asking him an honest question. She deserved a straight answer. "Actually, yes. It was tough. I'm not looking forward to that. If my dad becomes President, I'll talk to him and my mom. I live a pretty low-profile life. I am going to refuse protection."

"Is that safe?"

"Yeah, sure. I'm not worried." He smiled over his wineglass. "Don't they teach you CIA folks how to kill a man with a spoon?"

"Something like that."

"Great. You can watch my back."

"You couldn't afford me," she said with a laugh.

Dinner was excellent; the conversation was fun and it flowed except for when Jack tried to probe Melanie once again about her family. She stayed as tight-lipped about her family as she did about the CIA.

They strolled home together after ten; the streets had thinned of foot traffic, and a cold wind blew in from the Potomac.

Jack walked her up the drive toward the door of her tiny apartment.

"I had fun," Melanie said.

"Me, too. Can we do it again soon?"

"Of course." They got to the door. "Listen, Jack. I'd better get this out of the way. I don't kiss on the first date."

Ryan smiled. "Neither do I." He extended a hand, which she took slowly, careful to keep the astonishment and embarrassment off her face.

"Have a great night. You'll be hearing from me."

"I hope so."

Nigel Embling's house was in the center of Peshawar, not far from the massive and ancient Bala Hisar Fort, which, with its ninety-foot ramparted walls, commands the high ground of the city and lands around it.

The city bustled with activity, but Embling's home was quiet and clean, an idyllic oasis of plants and flowers, the sound of tinkling fountains in the courtyard, and the smell of old books and furniture polish in the very British study on the second floor.

Embling sat next to Driscoll at a wide table in his study. Across from them, thirty-five-year-old Major Mohammed al Darkur wore Western civilian clothing, a pair of brown slacks with a black button-down shirt. Al Darkur had come alone to Embling's to meet a man he assumed was an officer in the CIA. He'd done his best to establish the bona fides of the man he had been introduced to as "Sam," but Driscoll had deflected his questions about other CIA officers that al Darkur had run into while working with the ISI.

This worked to Driscoll's benefit. The CIA was, as far as al Darkur was concerned, too supportive of elements in Pakistani intelligence. Elements that al Darkur knew were actively working against them. He found the CIA and America by extension to be naive and too ready to put its trust in those who paid lip service to the shared values between the two organizations.

The fact that Sam appeared to be working outside the lines of American intelligence already entrenched in Pakistan, and the fact that Sam seemed to hold suspicions against al Darkur himself, only increased the Pakistani major's opinion of the man.

Embling said, "I've done my best to look into this Rehan fellow. He's a bloody mystery."

Sam agreed. "We are trying on our end, as well. He's done a great job of covering his tracks in his career. It looks like he just materialized as a high-level PDF officer working for the ISI."

"Not easy to do in the PDF. That lot loves their ceremony, always getting photographed and awarded this or that trinket for one thing or another. They learned pomp and circumstance from we English, and I can say with just a wee bit of pride that we show military off like no other."

"But no pictures of Rehan?"

"A few, but years and years ago, when he was a young officer. Otherwise he's a bloody shadow."

"But not anymore. What has changed?"

"That's what Mohammed and I are trying to find out."

Al Darkur said, "The only reason I can think is that he is being groomed for something. Lieutenant general, head of the ISI, perhaps even head of the PDF someday. I believe he is working on a coup, but certainly he is too unknown to take the reins of government himself. He seems to have spent his entire career as a spy, which is not common for military officers. Most serving in ISI are just sent there for a few years. They are not professional spies but professional soldiers. I myself was a commando with the Seventh Battalion, Special Services Group, before coming to ISI. But Riaz Rehan seems to be the exact opposite. He spent a few odd years as a lieutenant and captain in the regular PDF, in the Azad Kashmir Regiment, but since then he seems to have had some role with Inter-Services Intelligence, although they have kept that quite secret, even from the rest of the ISI."

"Is he a beard?" asked Driscoll, referring to an Islamist within their ranks.

"Only by association do I know that to be true. His benefactors at the head of the Army and intelligence services are most definitely Islamists, though Rehan never turns up at any mosque, or on any list of attendees of the secret meetings the beards are always having. I've had prisoners of the hostile jihadist groups in my custody, and I've asked them, quite aggressively, I must admit, if they knew Rehan from JIM. I am convinced none of them do."

Driscoll sighed. "So. What is the next step?"

Now al Darkur brightened a little. "I have two pieces of information, one of which your people can help me with."

"Great."

"First, my sources have discovered that General Rehan, in addition to his office at our headquarters in Islamabad, is also working out of a safe house in Dubai."

Driscoll cocked his head. "Dubai?"

"Yes. It is the financial hub of the Middle East, and his department most likely does banking for its foreign operations there, but that in itself would be no reason for him to work there. I think he and his cadre of upper-level employees go there to plot against Pakistan itself."

"Interesting."

"In my position in the Joint Intelligence Bureau I do not have the reach or assets to investigate him outside of our borders. I thought maybe your organization, with its near infinite reach, might like to see what he is doing in Dubai."

"I'll pass it up the chain of command, but I am reasonably sure they will want to look into this safe house of his."

"Excellent."

"And the other piece of information?"

"This other avenue I will be able to look into with my own assets. There is an operation I have recently learned about that involves Rehan's department and the Haqqani network. You are, I am certain, familiar with Haqqani?"

Driscoll nodded. "Jalaluddin Haqqani. His forces run large patches of the borderland of Pakistan and Afghanistan. He's tied with the Taliban, runs a network many thousands strong, and has killed hundreds of our soldiers in Afghanistan, as well as hundreds more locals in bombings, rocket and mortar attacks, kidnappings for ransom, et cetera, et cetera."

Al Darkur nodded. "Jalaluddin is an old man, so his son, Siraj, is leading the organization now, but otherwise you have it right. I have a prisoner in custody, a courier in the Haqqani network, who I captured in Peshawar after he met with an ISI lieutenant who is a known supporter of the Islamists. He has told my interrogators that the ISI is working with Haqqani network fighters at a camp of theirs near Miran Shah."

"Working on what?"

"This courier does not know, but he does know they are expecting a foreign force there at the camp, and the ISI and Haqqani men will train these outsiders."

"URC? Al-Qaeda?"

"He does not know. I, however, intend to find out who they are and what they are doing."

"How will you do that?"

"I will go myself, the day after tomorrow, and I will watch the road to the camp. We have a base in Miran Shah, of course, but Haqqani's people know about it. They lob in an occasional mortar shell, but otherwise they go on about their business. But we also have some safe houses around town, mostly to the south. Siraj Haqqani's forces know of some of them, so we do not use them anymore, but my agents have secured a location on the Boya–Miran Shah road, and this happens to be near where the prisoner says this training camp is located."

"Great. When do we leave?"

"*We*, Sam?" asked al Darkur with raised eyebrows.

Embling broke in. "Don't be daft, lad."

Sam shrugged. "I'd like to see this for myself. No offense. I'll tell my office about Dubai, but I'm here. Might as well come along with you, if you'll have me."

"It will not be safe. It is Miran Shah; there are no Americans there, I can promise you that. I will be heading down with a handpicked crew of Zarrar Special Service commandos, men I trust implicitly. If you come, I can promise you that myself and my men will be in as much danger as you, so you will benefit from our desire for self-protection."

This made Driscoll smile. "Works for me."

Embling didn't like it at all, but Sam had made up his mind.

Twenty minutes later, Driscoll sat on the cool rooftop veranda of Embling's house, drinking tea with one hand and holding a satellite phone with the other. The device, like all Hendley Associates sat phones, was equipped with a chip that held an NSA type-1 encryption package that made it secure. Only the person on the other end of the line would be able to hear Driscoll.

Sam Granger answered on the other end.

"Sam, it's Sam here."

"What's the word?"

"The ISI contact seems solid. Not going to promise anything, but we may have a lead on Rehan and his activities." Driscoll told Granger about the Dubai safe house.

"That is incredible, if true."

"Might be worth sending the guys over," Sam Driscoll suggested.

"You don't want to go yourself?" asked Granger, somewhat surprised.

"I'm going with the major and a team of his SSG guys to North Waziristan for a little SR."

"SR?"

"Strategic reconnaissance."

"In Haqqani territory?"

"Roger that. But I'll be with friendlies. Should be okay."

There was a pause in the connection. "Sam, you are the one whose neck is on the line, and I know you're not reckless. But still . . . you will be in the belly of the beast, so to speak, will you not?"

"I will be as safe as the SSG men around me. They seem like they have their heads screwed on straight. Plus, we need to know what the ISI is up to at this camp. Any proof of Rehan or his people there is going to be critically important if we need to leak this guy to the intelligence community at a later date. I'm going to do my best to get pictures and shoot them back to you."

Granger said, "I don't know if Hendley will like this."

"Let's ask forgiveness instead of permission."

"Like I said, it's your neck."

"Roger that. I'll be in touch when I get back to Pesh. Don't stress if you don't hear from me for a while, it may be a week or two."

"I understand. Good luck."

The city of Miran Shah is the capital of North Waziristan, which lies within the Federally Administered Tribal Areas of western Pakistan, not far from the Afghan border. The area is not under the control of the Pakistani government in Islamabad, though there is a small and often harassed Pakistani Defense Force base here.

The town and the region, including areas reaching far past the irrelevant Afghan border to the west, are under the control of the Haqqani network, a massive insurgent group that is closely allied with the Taliban.

Jalaluddin Haqqani fought the Russians in Afghanistan in the 1980s and became a warlord of increasing power and scope. His sons followed in their father's footsteps, and they had a hand in virtually every aspect of life here in North Waziristan that was not snuffed out by American unmanned aerial vehicles that patrolled the sky above, waiting to be cleared hot for a missile launch.

Their international reach, their dozens of covert insurgent camps, and their close ties with the Pakistani intelligence service made the Haqqani family a natural partner of Riaz Rehan throughout the years. He had used their territory and facilities to train fighters and operatives for missions in India and Afghanistan, and he had reached out to them again recently, asking for their assistance in training a large cell of foreign fighters for a mission.

The Haqqani leadership accepted the request of Joint Intelligence Miscellaneous to send the men, and Rehan himself came along to oversee the initial phases of the training.

Though he had no military or insurgent training whatsoever, Russian rocket entrepreneur Georgi Safronov was the leader of the unit of Jamaat Shariat forces who arrived at the Haqqani camp near Boya, west of Miran Shah, in the third week of October. With him was the man he knew as General Ijaz, as well as his unit of fifty-five Dagestani rebels. The huge force of foreigners was outfitted by the Haqqani forces and billeted in a large cave complex dug into the walls of a hillside.

Much of the training itself took place inside the man-made caves and under corrugated tin roofs painted to look like dirt and farmland so as not to attract the attention of US drones, but some team tactics training did take place in fields and on hillsides. The UAVs were not invisible; specially trained spotters were posted to keep an eye out for America's "eyes in the sky." But the UAVs were stealthy enough that Rehan himself ordered the Haqqani network to place absolute priority, not on the quality of the training of the foreigners, but on maintaining the security of the operation.

Rehan did not really care if the Dagestani insurgents had the talents necessary to take over and hold a space launch facility in Kazakhstan. No, he was instead interested only in their ability to succeed in a mission here in Pakistan that they would need to undertake to gain control of the two nuclear weapons. If they lost half their number while executing this mission, it was of no great concern to Rehan.

His only concern was that the world learned that nuclear bombs had been stolen out from under the Pakistanis' noses by foreign terrorists. He felt certain that this would lead to the disintegration of the Pakistani government within days or weeks.

The Haqqani network took Rehan's order to ramp up security seriously. They sent spies into the villages and neighborhoods between Miran Shah and Boya, keeping an eye out for anyone interested in the movement of men and material. Little happened in North Waziristan without Haqqani knowing about it, but now there was virtually nothing that could avoid detection by the powerful force.

The Pashtun fighters found the Dagestani fighters to be quite good with their weapons and extremely motivated individuals. But they lacked unit cohesion and this was something that Haqqani's people had developed by necessity in the decade they had been fighting coalition forces over the border.

The only member of the unit who did not know how

to handle a gun, or handle himself in any physical sense, was their leader. Safronov had adopted the nom de guerre Magomed Dagestani, Mohammed the Dagestani, but although he now possessed a name that conveyed his intent, he lacked any martial abilities to back it up. But he was smart and motivated to learn, so slowly the Taliban in the cave complex taught him how to use handguns and rifles and grenade launchers and knives, and by the end of the first week he had come a long way.

Rehan was in and out of the camp, splitting time between his home in Dubai, his office in Islamabad, and the cave complex. All the while, Rehan encouraged the Dagestanis to stay motivated for the hard work ahead and Safronov to stay strong and committed to the action.

34

The third and final presidential debate was held in Los Angeles, at the Edwin W. Pauley Pavilion on the campus of UCLA. It was a more formal affair than the last encounter; this time the two men would be at lecterns in front of a panel of questioners, reporters from the big media outlets as well as one of the wire services.

It was an open forum; there was no particular theme to the event, with the idea that the biggest issues in the last three weeks of the campaign would naturally be discussed. In theory, this would lead to a few topics that would get passionate attention from the candidates, but in actuality, other than a few questions on economic bailouts of foreign nations, China's massive increase of military expenditures, and rising gas prices, one topic was at the forefront.

The President's decision to try Saif Yasin in the federal system got the lion's share of attention, as well as candidate Jack Ryan's vocal opposition to this.

With the subject of the Emir naturally came the subject of Pakistan. The Islamabad government had spent the past decade taking billions of dollars annually from the United States while simultaneously working at cross-purposes with American military and intelligence efforts, and the safe haven that western Pakistan had become had given much aid and comfort to the organizations that committed terrorist atrocities around the world. Kealty's plan to influence Pakistan to rehabilitate and provide real support for US interests was, essentially, to double down. While he threatened to cut off aid to Islamabad unless the situation improved, covert funding and support for the ISI and PDF actually increased as the White House tried to buy off commanders and departments that held influence over strategy.

Ryan's plan, like most of his ideas when compared to Kealty's, stood in stark contrast. When asked by the AP reporter on the panel what he would do to the funding levels of the Pakistani intelligence and military services, he replied, succinctly, "Cut it. Cut it and use some of that money to support our great friends and allies in the region, India."

He'd been saying this on the campaign trail for some time, and he'd been taking a beating for it in the media. The American press spun his support for India over Pakistan as stirring up an old conflict by putting US strength behind one power over another, despite Ryan's retort that Pakistan supports terrorism against the United States while India does not.

"Of course we want to put our strength behind our friends and pull support for our enemies. Pakistan does not have to be our enemy," he said into the cameras at the Pauley Pavilion, "but that has been their choice. When I return to Washington, I will turn off that spigot of support until Islamabad shows us that they can control their urges and combat Islamic terrorism in India and the West."

The CBS Washington correspondent was next, and she asked Ryan how he could possibly punish the entire nation of Pakistan for the actions of a few rogue agents in the ISI.

Ryan nodded slowly before replying. "The ISI does

not have rogue agents. It is a rogue *agency*. My opponent says individual men or individual units are the problem. I disagree. The rogue elements of the ISI, frankly, are the ones who are on our side. The ISI and the Army are our enemy, save for a limited number of men, a limited number of units, who are our friends. We need to find these rogues and do what we can to support them in ways other than just sending billions of dollars unchecked into the coffers of the Pakistani government. That is a welfare check for the supporters of terror, and that, ladies and gentlemen, is a decade-long strategy that has not produced the desired results."

Kealty's rebuttal was short. "President Ryan supported Pakistan to the tune of several billion dollars when he was President."

To which Jack, speaking out of turn but speaking nonetheless, said, "And I was wrong about that. We all were, and I hate to admit it, but I will *not* stick with a failed policy just to hide the fact I made a mistake."

The journalists on the panel sat and stared at Ryan. A presidential candidate admitting a mistake was alien to them.

The next questioner was from CNN, and she asked both candidates about the trial of the Emir. Kealty repeated his support for the process, and he challenged Ryan to tell him why, exactly, he felt the Department of Justice would not be able to aggressively prosecute Mr. Yasin.

Ryan looked into the camera with raised eyebrows. "President Kealty, I accept your challenge. We have brought several terrorists to trial in the federal system over the past twenty years. Some of those prosecutions were more successful than others. Many of the cases in which the attorney general failed to get a conviction involved defendants who were represented by a powerful legal team who, in the opinion of many legal scholars, bent the rules in the defense of their clients. Now, the American system of justice could not survive without a vigorous defense, but many of these defense attorneys crossed the line.

"This happened on my watch, so I was very close to the work of my AG, and I saw what these defense attorneys did, and I was sickened by it.

"The Emir will not have many of these defense attorneys, and you may think that is a good thing, ladies and gentlemen, but it is not, because nine of these attorneys who advocated for the terrorists who killed thousands of Americans at home and on the battlefields are now working for the Justice Department. If these people, all unabashed advocates of the terrorists, are part of the government's prosecution, and the terrorists' own lawyers are unabashed advocates of the terrorists, who is there to be an advocate of the American people?"

Kealty's nostrils flared on rebuttal. "Well, Mr. Ryan. You keep calling these defendants 'terrorists.' They are alleged terrorists until they are convicted. I don't know if any of these men are guilty, and neither do you."

Ryan replied, again turning the moderated debate into an unmoderated conversation, "One of the men who was defended by people who are now representing the United States in the Justice Department's case against the Emir said from the witness box, he screamed it, actually, and this was the quote from the trial transcript. 'I hope the jihad will continue and strike the heart of America and all kinds of weapons of mass destruction will be used.' Can we not take this man at his word that he is an enemy of our nation? A terrorist?"

Kealty waved it away and replied. The moderator had lost all control. "You aren't a lawyer, Jack. Sometimes people say things that are intemperate; that does not make them guilty of the crime for which they are being tried."

"'Intemperate'? Screaming that you hope America is destroyed is 'intemperate,' Mr. President? That's right, you *are* a lawyer."

The crowd laughed.

Jack put his hand up quickly. "Nothing against attorneys. Some of my best friends are lawyers. But even they tell the most biting lawyer jokes."

More laughs.

Ryan continued, "Now, ladies and gentlemen, you will be forgiven for not knowing about this terrorist, his outburst, and the fact that nine of his defense attorneys now work in the Kealty administration. You will be forgiven because there was very little mention of this in the media at the time.

"But it troubles me, Mr. President, that nine members of your administration worked on the defense of terrorists. Now they are in positions of influence in our government, where they bring the same warped sensibilities to their jobs which, ultimately, is the national security of the United States. And then, when the military commissions are suggested, you and your people say these defendants can only get a fair trial in federal court. I think most Americans would be bothered by this"—he looked to the panel of journalists sitting before him—"if they only knew about it."

Jack also wanted to wink at Arnie van Damm, who, right now, would be reaching for the Maalox. Arnie had told Jack over and over not to antagonize the press, because it didn't look presidential.

Screw how it looks, Jack decided. *They have it coming.*

"President Kealty's attorney general made the comment recently—again, it wasn't reported by the mainstream press, for some reason—that the FBI put Capone in prison for tax evasion, and maybe we should look into similar means to prosecute the terrorists we captured on the battlefield, because their capture was clearly not in the rule of law. Do you agree with this, President Kealty? Do you or your Justice Department know how many captured terrorists filed US income tax forms last year?"

Kealty did his best to control his rage, but his face reddened under his makeup. He replied, "My opponent believes there is one type of justice for 'us,' and another type of justice for 'them'."

"If by 'them,' you are saying Al-Qaeda, or the Umayyad Revolutionary Council, or any one of a number of groups that mean to destroy us . . . then yes, that is what I believe. They deserve their day in court, a chance to defend themselves, but they do not deserve each and every right afforded the citizens of the United States."

Mohammed al Darkur, Sam Driscoll, three ISI captains, and a dozen Zarrar commandos flew out of PAF Base Peshawar at four a.m. in a Pakistani Air Force Y-12 turbo-prop transport aircraft. The pilot took them to the southeast, over the mountains of Khyber and Kurram Agencies, and finally into North Waziristan.

They landed on Miran Shah's one useful runway and were immediately shuffled by local forces into an armored personnel carrier for the ride through the dark town to the military fort.

Within seconds of entering the main gate of the base, al Darkur, Driscoll, the three captains, and two sections of soldiers piled into four heavy-duty delivery trucks with canvas-covered beds, and they rolled straight out of the rear gate of the compound. If any Haqqani network spies were watching the comings and goings of the PDF forces in town, this would throw them off the scent. There would be spies near the fort, and the ISI had developed certain countermeasures to lose any surveillance they picked up before heading out to one of their safe houses.

The four delivery trucks rolled back through town at dawn, passed the airport to the west, and separated onto different roads. Each truck pulled into a different small walled compound in a different part of the city, and the men inside the vehicles climbed out and then climbed aboard new trucks. Spotters on the roofs of the compounds watched to see if their visitors had picked up any tails and, when they deemed the streets clear of Haqqani watchers, radioed down an all clear to the new trucks. The gates were reopened by men stationed in advance at the safe house, and the new, cleansed trucks departed.

The four vehicles drove individually through the early-morning traffic toward the south, and then each vehicle, spaced five minutes or so apart, headed out of Miran Shah. Driscoll found himself in the back of the third truck; he'd been cloaked with a shawl to cover his Western features, but he peeked out of it and saw armed men walking the streets, riding on motorcycles, and peering out of walled compounds. These were exclusively Haqqani's fighters; there were thousands, and even though the PDF had a tiny outpost here and the ISI maintained a few safe houses, Miran Shah was Haqqani's town.

As they drove farther south, leaving the town and entering cultivated fields, Sam thought he could hear automatic weapons fire behind him. He motioned to one of the soldiers in the truck with him, trying to find out if the man knew of the source of the fire. But the young soldier just shrugged as if to say, "Yeah? Somebody is shooting, so what?"

Driscoll's truck turned west on the Boya–Miran Shah road, and it headed along steep cliffs, made twists and turns, and climbed with a rumble in the engine that let the American operator know that the vehicle was straining under the effort. Finally, just after seven in the morning, the truck turned off the road, climbed a steep rocky path that led to a compound on a flat table on a steep hillside, and then pulled through the open front gate.

Two of the other trucks were already there, parked in a two-car garage facing the main gate. Al Darkur, two captains, and one of the two squads of security got together in the dusty courtyard and began speaking animatedly in Urdu. Driscoll had no idea what the problem was until Mohammed himself stepped over to him. "The other truck did not make it. They were hit in the center of town. One of my captains has been shot in the wrist, and a soldier was hit in the stomach. They made it back to the base, but they do not think the soldier will survive."

"I'm sorry."

Al Darkur patted Driscoll on the shoulder. "We made it though. Congratulations. Before I was only going to let you sit and watch while we did the work. But now I need you to help."

"Just tell me what you need."

"We will set up surveillance on the road. The camp is just three kilometers farther west, and everyone who goes there from the airport or the city of Miran Shah must pass on the road below us."

The six soldiers joined with six men who were already

there at the compound and formed into a low-profile security cordon, while al Darkur, Driscoll, and the two ISI captains used a window in a second-story hallway as an observation point. They set up a pair of long-range cameras and pulled mattresses off beds in other rooms so that they could keep up the surveillance with minimal breaks.

Al Darkur had one of his captains bring a large trunk into the hallway, and he set it down near Driscoll's mattress.

"Mr. Sam," al Darkur said in his singsong Pakistani accent. "Am I correct in assuming you had a military career before the CIA?"

"I was in the Army, yes."

"Special Forces, perhaps?"

"Perhaps."

Al Darkur smiled. "Even though you are my guest, I would feel better if you outfitted yourself in the gear my captain has here for you."

Driscoll looked in the trunk and found an American M4 rifle with a 3.5-power Trijicon ACOG scope, an Original Special Operations Equipment chest harness with Kevlar and steel armor and eight extra magazines for the rifle, a helmet, and a utility belt with a Glock 9-millimeter pistol and extra magazines.

He looked up at the major with a wink. "I would feel better, too." Driscoll suited up. It felt good to carry what was essentially the same rig he used in the Rangers. Once outfitted with the fighting gear, he looked up to al Darkur and gave him the thumbs-up.

Al Darkur said, "Now we drink tea, and we wait."

35

The Sunday after the debate, Benton Thayer walked alone through the parking lot of the Chevy Chase Club, one of the oldest and finest country clubs in the greater D.C. area. Even though it was not yet noon and he was decked out for a day at the links in Hollas large plaid pants and knits and a purposefully clashing Ian Poulter tartan flat cap, Benton had just left the rest of his foursome after only nine holes. With the last debate out of the way, he'd taken the first half of his Sunday off for some time outside on this crisp fall day, but he needed to get back to the city and back to work. As President Edward Kealty's campaign manager, he would have to wait until after November 6 for some R&R.

And as Benton headed for his white Lexus SUV he told himself he'd likely have a lot of free time after November 6. Not just because the election would be over, but because his man would lose, which meant his govern-ment-sector prospects in D.C. would be zilch, and his private-sector opportunities around here would be tinged by his failure to retain the Oval Office for his boss.

No self-respecting campaign manager throws in the towel publicly with three weeks until election day, and Thayer had five radio spots and nine television interviews planned for Monday, when he would confidently declare just the opposite of what he knew to be true, but the forty-three-year-old walking alone in the parking lot was no idiot. Short of Jack Ryan being caught with his pants around his ankles outside a day care, the writing was on the wall, and the election was over.

Still, he considered himself a good soldier, and there were the media appearances in the morning that he needed to prepare for, so he was off to work.

As he climbed into his Lexus, he noticed a small manila envelope tucked under his windshield wiper. He leaned out, grabbed the package, and sat back in the car. Thinking that someone who belonged to the club must have left this for him—the grounds were fenced and guarded, after all—he tore into the bag without a thought.

Inside there was no note, no indication of who had left the package. But what he did find was a small thumb drive.

If he had been anywhere else, at the mall, in his driveway, returning to his car from his office at campaign headquarters, Benton Thayer would have taken an unknown and unsolicited package like this and tossed it in the street.

But this was different. He decided to give it a look when he got to work.

Two hours later, Thayer had switched into khakis, an open-collared dress shirt, a wrinkle-free navy blue blazer, and loafers, no socks, and he sat at his desk in his office. The thumb drive had been forgotten for a bit, but he held it now, turned it back and forth, looking for any clue as to who had passed it. After another moment's hesitation, he sat up and began to connect the drive to his laptop, but he stopped himself, hesitating again. He worried about the mysterious drive containing a virus that could either damage his machine or somehow steal the data from it.

Seconds later, Thayer stepped into the large open loft that served as the "war room" of the Washington campaign office. Around him, dozens of men and women manned computers, phones, printers, and fax machines. A buzz of activity fueled by a long row of coffee urns on cloth-covered tables against the wall to his left. There, at the closest table, a college-aged girl was filling her eco-friendly travel mug with hot coffee.

Thayer didn't know the girl; he didn't bother to learn the names of more than the top five percent of his staff. "You," he said with a point of his finger.

The young lady jolted when she realized he was talking to her. Coffee splashed out of her mug. "Yes, sir?" she replied nervously.

"You have a laptop?"

She nodded. "At my desk."

"Get it. Bring it in here." He disappeared back into his office, and the college girl scurried to do as she was told. The third of the room that was in earshot of the exchange stopped working and stared, watched the girl grab her Mac and rush back toward Thayer's office as if they were regarding a condemned criminal on the way to the gallows.

Benton Thayer did not ask the girl her name or what she did. Instead he instructed her to put the thumb drive into her MacBook Pro and open the folder. She did this with slightly quivering fingers that were still sticky with spilled sugary coffee. As the single folder opened, revealing several files, Thayer told her to wait outside.

The young lady was all too happy to oblige.

Satisfied now that his own machine would not be damaged by a corrupt thumb drive, Benton Thayer began going through the files that had been surreptitiously delivered to him.

There was no explanation, no electronic version of a

cover sheet. But the file was titled "John Clark." Thayer knew a couple of guys named John Clark, it was a common name, but when he opened the file and saw a series of photos, he realized he did not know this man.

Then he began clicking through pages and pages of data on the man. A dossier of sorts. A personal history. US Navy. SEAL team. Military Assistance Command, Vietnam—Studies and Observations Group. Thayer had no idea what that was, but it sounded shady as hell to him.

Then CIA. Special Activities Division.

Targeted killings. Sanctioned denied operations.

Thayer shrugged. *Okay, this guy is a spook, and a spooky spook, but why should I care?*

Then specific operations were laid out. He thumbed through them quickly. He could tell these were not CIA documents, but they seemed to contain detailed information about Clark's Agency career.

It was a complicated mess of information. Information that might be interesting to someone. Human Rights Watch? Amnesty International? But Benton Thayer? He was growing bored looking through it. He carried on an internal dialogue with the mysterious person who delivered him this thumb drive. *Jesus. Like I give a shit. Get to the point.*

Then he stopped. *Huh? Is this the point?*

Photos with Clark and a younger John Patrick Ryan. Details of their relationship, spanning a quarter-century.

So the guy is old, and he's ex-CIA. Ryan is old and ex-CIA. They knew each other? That's all you've got, mystery man?

And then, after a rundown of John Clark's years in Rainbow, a single document that seemed to be out of place. An allegation of a murder Clark committed in Germany, thirty years ago.

Why isn't this in its place in the timeline? Thayer read it carefully. From all the information present, he got the impression that this intel was coming from a source outside of the United States.

He flipped to the next page.

A document detailing a presidential pardon given in secret to Clark for assassinations carried out at the CIA.

"So . . ." Thayer muttered to himself. "CIA chief Ryan orders Clark to kill people, then President Ryan papers over the crimes after the fact."

"Holy shit!"

Thayer picked up the phone, pushed a pair of buttons. "It's Thayer. I need to see him tonight, just as soon as he gets out of Marine One and back into the White House."

36

Traffic on the Boya–Miran Shah road had been light throughout the day, and it turned near nonexistent at night. Some transport vehicles, Taliban on motorcycles, and a few brightly colored buses with small mirrors hanging from the sides like Christmas ornaments. But the men in the observation post saw nothing that seemed at all out of the ordinary. Mohammed al Darkur said that his prisoner had mentioned that ISI officers were coming into the area via aircraft, which meant they had to land at Miran Shah, and they had to travel this road to get to the camp.

But in the first thirty-six hours of the surveillance, Driscoll and the others had come up empty.

Still, al Darkur photographed each and every vehicle that passed. He had no way to be certain some high-ranking ISI officer, even General Riaz Rehan himself, would not dress himself up like a goat herder to make his way to the Haqqani training camps, so after each vehicle passed their position, al Darkur and his men reviewed the high-res images.

But so far they had seen no indication that the ISI, or even some foreign force, for that matter, was operating in the area.

Just after midnight, Driscoll was manning a night-vision camera on a tripod facing down to the road while the other three men lay on their cots in the hallway behind

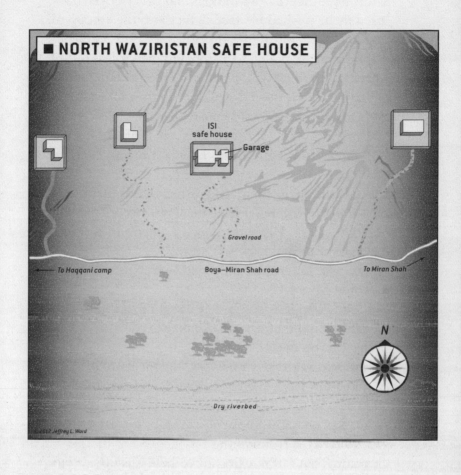

■ NORTH WAZIRISTAN SAFE HOUSE

ISI
safe house

Garage

Gravel road

To Haqqani camp

Boya–Miran Shah road

To Miran Shah

N

Dry riverbed

©2012 Jeffrey L. Ward

him. A jingle bus had passed a minute ago; the dust it kicked up still hung in the air above the Miran Shah–Boya highway.

Sam rubbed his eyes for a moment, and then looked back. Instantly he pushed his face tighter into the eyecup of the optic. There, on the road below him, four darkened pickup trucks had pulled to a stop and men rolled out of the back of the beds. They carried rifles, their clothing was black, and they moved stealthily up the rocky hillside, directly toward the ISI safe house.

"We're getting hit!" shouted Driscoll. Mohammed was at his side with his radio in his hand a moment later. He used his binoculars, saw the dozen or so men down a hundred yards below them, and turned to one of his captains. "Contact the base. Tell them we need a priority exfiltration, now!" His subordinate headed for his radio, and al Darkur turned back to Driscoll.

"If we take the trucks, they will destroy us with those RPGs on the road."

But Sam was not listening—he was thinking. "Mohammed. Why would they assault like that?"

"What do you mean?"

"They have to know we are watching the road. Why did they go to the road, the low ground, and not the high ground behind us?"

Al Darkur thought about it but only for a moment. "We are already surrounded."

"Exactly. That's a blocking force below us; the attack will come from—"

An explosion rocked the rear wall of the compound. It was thirty yards from where al Darkur and Driscoll stood in the hallway, but still it knocked them to the ground.

The ISI major began shouting commands into his

radio and he climbed back to his feet. Sam grabbed his M4 and ran toward the stairs, took them three at a time as he rushed to meet the enemy who would be trying to breach the rear wall.

Sam hit the ground floor and kept running for the back of the building. He passed two 7th Commando men in a room on his left. They trained the lights of their weapons out a ground-floor window, blanketing the eastern portion of the compound with white light, desperate to find targets. Driscoll continued toward the exit to the rear grounds, and hoped like hell the sentries posted at the back gate were still in the fight, keeping Haqqani's men pinned down in the surrounding brush and hills.

Chattering gunfire came from the front of the safe house as the enemy moved through the rocks up the hill toward the front entrance.

As Sam ran full speed toward the open rear door, preparing to shoot across the pitch-black grounds toward the gate, al Darkur came over the speaker of Sam's walkie-talkie. He spoke English now. "Sam! Our rear wall sentries are not checking in. The enemy must already be inside the compound!"

Driscoll's momentum took him through the doorway as he processed this information. He'd not made it five paces out into the night when bright flashes of light flickered from the gate twenty meters ahead, and booming Kalashnikov fire echoed off the outer walls of the house. Driscoll stumbled in the dust, turned, and retreated back to the doorway in a crouch.

The doorframe tore to splinters from the Haqqani fighters' rounds, but Sam managed to get back inside and up the hall without taking a bullet. Al Darkur met him there; he was still shouting into his walkie-talkie. Both men leaned back around the corner and fired a few rounds out into the dark night. Neither thought he could quell the attack with a couple of bursts of an assault rifle, but they did hold out hopes of making some impression on anyone who thought they could just rush in the open back door and make their way up the hall unimpeded.

Al Darkur shouted into Sam's ear after firing a few more bursts in the narrow hallway. "I've called for a helicopter from the base in Miran Shah, but the quick reaction force will not be ready for fifteen minutes."

"Not quick enough," said Sam as he dropped to his knees, leaned around the corner, and shot out the lights of the hall.

"It will be thirty minutes or more before they arrive."

Driscoll released the empty magazine from the magazine well of his rifle, then replaced it with a fully charged mag from his chest rig. Incoming gunfire from all sides had picked up now, and shouts over the comms, even though Driscoll could not understand the words, gave the impression that the building itself was about to be overrun.

"From the sound of it, we don't have anything like thirty minutes. How many men do you have left?"

Al Darkur got back on the walkie-talkie to find out while Driscoll went prone at the corner of the hall, then slowly rolled out on his right shoulder, putting him low in the hallway toward the back door, with his weapon's barrel scanning for threats. He could not see a thing in the dark, so he actuated his weapon light on the side rail of the M4. Instantly two hundred lumens of bright white light filled the hallway, illuminating two Haqqani fighters making their way silently toward Sam's position. They were blinded by the beam, but they raised their weapons anyway.

Driscoll pulled the trigger on his M4 rifle, swept a dozen rounds of automatic fire back and forth across the two men. They died before either of them got a shot off.

More sparkles of gunfire from the dark night outside forced Sam back around the corner, where he reloaded again.

"I have six men alive," Mohammed said.

Sam nodded as he reloaded. "All right. Any chance we can make it to the trucks in the garage on the east side?"

"We have to try, but the road will be covered with Haqqani's men."

"Who needs a road?"

Driscoll grabbed a fragmentation grenade from his chest harness, pulled the pin, and then flung it under-handed up the hallway like a tiny bowling ball. Mohammed al Darkur and Sam Driscoll took off toward the men fighting at the east window as the explosion tore through the doorway.

Two minutes later, a group of eight Haqqani fighters attacking from below had made it through the gate and up the drive on the southeast side of the compound. They'd left four of their number behind, one dead, felled by a shot through the stomach from a second-floor window of the enemy safe house, and three more wounded: one by gunfire and two by a hand grenade tossed down the hill by a sentry at the gate who had himself been shot dead one second later.

But now the eight survivors were within twenty meters of the garage. The door was open and it was dark inside, so the men approached quietly and slowly while their comrades fired into the building on the other sides. If they could make it into the building from the door here in the garage they could, by staying low to avoid fire from their own forces, comb through the structure and destroy any remaining forces there.

As the men came to within ten yards of the garage entrance, their leader was just able to make out two large trucks parked inside. His night vision had been all but ruined by his firing several magazines from his Kalashnikov, so as he moved forward now he had to squint to hunt for a door inside.

All eight men passed the two trucks, found the door giving them access to the building, and they went inside in a line, crouching and listening for threats.

As soon as the eight Haqqani men disappeared from the garage, Sam Driscoll, Mohammed al Darkur, two ISI officers, and four Zarrar commandos quietly climbed out from under the truck farthest from the door. A driver, al Darkur, and three others climbed in the front of the vehicle, while Sam and two others remained at the back of the garage. Once Sam heard the driver quietly release the hand brake, he and two men pushed the truck from behind with all their might. The nose of the vehicle was already oriented downhill, so once they had pushed the truck out of the garage it began to pick up speed quickly. Sam and the two men gave one more firm shove, then leapt into the back of the covered bed.

The driver did not turn over the engine, nor did he turn on the headlights. The only sound made by the dark vehicle was the crunching on the rocky driveway as it moved faster and faster down the hill. The driver had only a very faint light from the overcast sky to guide him toward the front gate, and if he missed it a few feet right or left, the truck would plow into the wall and they would then have to fire the engine, letting everyone still on the hillside or on the road below know exactly where they were.

But the driver made it through the gate, the truck rolled faster now, and the driver had to force the wheels to turn left and right by using all of his upper-body strength. It was still one hundred yards of steep winding gravel to the road below, and the pathway twisted and turned all the way down.

They made it out of the compound itself, which was where the majority of the enemy guns had concentrated by now, but someone on the hillside either heard or saw the truck when it was only twenty yards outside the gate. A shout, then a series of shouts, and then finally erupting gunfire put an end to the stealthy part of Sam Driscoll's plan. He shouted from the back of the vehicle to the driver, told him to forget about trying to stay on the gravel road, now it was all about getting away from the guns as fast as possible, no matter where the truck ended up or what condition it was in when it got there. The driver went off road, used his big heavy truck's momentum to propel him and his passengers down through the dark.

There were Haqqani men on all sides of the hurtling object, but most of them were unable to fire without hitting their fellow militants. A few men did fire, and Sam's position in the back of the truck was raked with 7.62 rounds. One man with him was shot through the head, another took two rounds in his left bicep and left shoulder, and Sam took a round high on his protective steel SAPI (Small Arms Protective Insert) plate in his chest rig vest. The impact knocked him over, down to the floor, just as the huge covered truck slammed hard on a large boulder and went airborne several feet. The nearly decapitated

Zarrar soldier's body rolled with Sam in the rear of the vehicle. The truck continued, careening down the hillside, it bounced again and again, and the driver had to focus all of his faculties on keeping the truck pointed downhill so that it would not veer sideways and flip.

They were only twenty yards or so to the road when Mohammed saw more Haqqani network fighters step out of the darkness and open fire on the hurtling truck. One man held an RPG.

There was no way to engage him from the middle of the cab of the truck; it would have been impossible even if they weren't being battered and jolted in all directions from the roll down the rocky hillside, but as it was there was no point even attempting to point a gun at the man.

Instead he shouted into the back, "Sam! RPG, right side, twenty meters!"

"Got it!"

Mohammed al Darkur could not see the American behind him, so he had no way of knowing that Driscoll hefted his M4, stood in the covered bed, and held on to a roll bar. As the vehicle hit the main road and swerved hard to the left to avoid a parked Haqqani pickup, Sam swung outside of the rear of the vehicle, one-handed his rifle up the road, and dumped a full thirty-round magazine at any and all movement he saw out in the dark. A rocket-propelled grenade ignited and streaked in his direction, but the glowing warhead shot harmlessly high up in the night sky.

Machine-gun fire from the other side of the road clanged against the metal parts of the big truck as it turned toward the east and headed back to Miran Shah. Sam tried to get back inside the truck to make himself as small a target as possible. His feet slipped, and he found himself hanging onto the roll bar, holding the canvas wall of the truck. He let go of his rifle to take the bar with both hands, and his weapon hung from its sling around his neck. While he fought to get his boots back in the vehicle, the one surviving commando in the back with him fired his M4 up the hillside from where they had just come. Return fire from the enemy flickered like fireflies off the rocky hill.

Just then, in the cab of the vehicle, a long stream of 7.62-millimeter tracer rounds tore through the windshield, shattering the glass from the major's left to his right. Burning bullets slammed into the chest plate of the ISI captain on al Darkur's left, then clanged off of the steel on his own body armor, and then finally raked across the neck of the driver. The man did not die instantly, though. With a gurgle and a hiss of air, he grabbed his neck wound and writhed in pain. The big truck immediately veered to the right with these movements, and ran off the road, bouncing down the hill again toward the dry riverbed below.

Sam had gotten both feet just inside the truck bed when the vehicle jacked to the right and went airborne before once again starting a violent high-speed descent. The movement spun Sam sideways, threw him hard against the side of the vehicle, and then he lost his grip on the metal bar.

The American fell off the truck just twenty yards or so from the road, and the big vehicle continued on down the hill.

37

Mohammed al Darkur did his best to control the hurtling truck by reaching over the dead driver and grabbing the steering wheel. It was easier said than done, as Mohammed's helmet had come off and now each and every bump the tires rolled over below him sent his head straight up into the metal ceiling of the cab. He felt blood dripping down his face, but he could not wipe it away before it filled his eyes because he needed both hands on the steering wheel.

Finally they leveled out at the bottom of the dry riverbed. He'd even managed to turn the wheel enough to keep them out of the majority of the limestone rocks that had collected there through thousands of rainy seasons. He could still hear gunfire in the distance, but he took the time to get a foot over on the brake and then wait for his captain to leave the left side of the truck and, while under fire from above, climb in on the right, pushing the dead man into the middle seat. The captain took the wheel now and al Darkur scooted to the left window, found his rifle on the floorboard of the truck, and fired at the flashes of light up on the hill as the truck raced off to the east.

Al Darkur was keenly aware that he did not hear any of the men in the back of the truck shooting. He worried about his men and he worried about the American who he had promised to protect with his life, but there would be no going back. They had to make it to the base on their own, and only then could they do anything to help the wounded or anyone left behind.

Sam awoke slowly. His body was rolled in a heap and lying next to a small boulder. He did not feel any immediate pain, but he'd been around long enough to know that he was most definitely injured. The tumble out of a truck moving at that speed would have hurt him, whether or not the adrenaline pumping through his bloodstream right now would mask it.

He remained still where he lay, and he watched the big truck continue off down the hillside. Men above him on the road fired down on it; they had not yet seen Driscoll, and he hoped he could lie here in the dark for now, wait for the Haqqani men to leave, and then sit up and assess his injuries.

Above him on the road, the gunfire died down as the truck raced away and disappeared up the dry riverbed. He heard men climb into trucks and drive off, and he heard other men, Haqqani fighters most likely, moaning in pain. He had no idea how many survivors were on the hill above him, but he had no doubts that the area up around the compound, higher on the hill from the road, would still have able-bodied enemy shooters.

Driscoll's hands moved over his body now; he felt blood on his arms and on his face, but he was able to move without pain. He then lifted his legs slowly, one at a time, and found them operational. He reached out into the dry dirt and brush, searching with his fingertips for his rifle, but the weapon had come off his body when he fell off the truck. His pistol was still on his hip, however. He knew this because the weapon was digging into his lower ribs.

Once reasonably certain that he was ambulatory, he looked around him in the dark. A low copse of trees lay fifty yards farther down the hill to the west, and he thought he might try to low crawl there to find cover before daylight.

Just then, from the road above, a flashlight's beam illuminated the trees. Another beam tracked to the east, to Driscoll's left. The lights searched the hillside haphazardly, searching perhaps for anyone who'd fallen from the escaping truck.

Sam did not move; there wasn't much he could do but hope the beam didn't settle on him as he lay there. If nothing else, he wanted his hand on the grip of his Glock 17 pistol, but even accomplishing that small feat would involve more movement than he was prepared to make.

The lights passed over him, and then stopped on a point on the hill to his left and another twenty yards on. Men on the road began shouting now, there was no question but that they had seen something.

Shit, thought Sam. If the Haqqani shooters started heading down the hill, he would have no choice but to—

And then, movement right where the flashlight beams had settled. A lone SSG commando, the man who had been in the back of the truck with Driscoll when it ran off the road, stood up and opened fire with his M16. He must have been tossed out as well, but he'd now been spotted, he knew it, and he had no choice but to go loud. Driscoll saw that the man was wounded; blood covered his clothing and gear and shone in the white light beams centered on him.

Sam could have stayed right where he was, but he did not even consider it. He rolled up to his knees, drew his Glock pistol, and opened fire on the men above. By doing this he knew he was risking the chance that the Zarrar soldier would shoot him in the back in surprise at the sudden movement and noise, but he decided to put his trust in the training and instincts of the commando and concentrate on killing as many of the Haqqani forces as possible.

With his pistol, he dropped both of the men holding flashlights, hitting one in the thigh and the other center mass. Others on the road dove for cover, giving Driscoll a second to turn toward his colleague in the SSG. "Head for those trees, ten yards at a time!" he shouted, and the young soldier looked back over his shoulder, found the copse halfway down the hill, and then turned and ran back ten yards. While he did this, Sam fired a few pistol shots up the hill, then when the SSG man laid down suppressive fire, Driscoll leapt to his feet and began running down toward the trees himself.

They moved in a leapfrog fashion—bounding ten yards, then providing supporting fire for the other, as they hurried for the relative cover of the trees below them. More than once either Sam or the SSG sergeant fell during his descent, slowing the process and giving the men above a near stationary target at which to shoot.

They made it to within twenty yards of the trees when the slide of Driscoll's Glock locked open after firing the last round. The Zarrar commando was bounding past him at just that instant. Sam pulled his last full pistol mag from his belt and slammed it into the gun's grip, and then dropped the slide, chambering a round.

Next to him he heard the soldier grunt loudly, then the man pitched forward and tumbled to the ground. The American fired seven rounds up toward the road, then spun and ran to help his wounded comrade. He dropped to the ground next to the commando's still form, and he found the back of the soldier's head completely sheared away by a well-placed AK round.

The man had died instantly.

"Fuck!" Sam shouted in frustration and anguish, but he could not stay here. The sparks kicked up by impacting jacketed bullets in the rocks around him encouraged him to move his ass. Driscoll grabbed the rifle off the dead man and then crawled, rolled, and slid the rest of the way to the trees.

The Haqqani network fighters wasted no time in targeting the woods where Driscoll had sought cover. Kalashnikov rounds tore into the trunks and limbs of the mulberry and fir and sent leaves and needles raining down like heavy mountain snowfall. This forced Sam to drop down onto his belly and crawl as fast as possible to the other side of the little copse. It was only thirty yards across and thirty yards deep, so he knew he could not hide out here for long.

Sam found a spot behind a thick tree trunk and he took a moment to check his body for injuries. He was slick with blood; certainly he'd caught shrapnel from kicked-up rocks on the hillside and cuts from head to toe falling out of the truck and rolling down to his current cover.

He also checked his gear, or what was left of it.

The rifle he had confiscated from the dead soldier was an older M16. A good gun with a nice long barrel, great for hitting targets at distance, though he would have preferred his scoped M4 lost up on the hillside. His three remaining M4 mags in his chest rig would work in the M16, and for this he was grateful. He reloaded his new rifle with an old magazine, and then he moved to another position, this one right at the southern edge of the grove.

Here he thought over his options. He could surrender, he could run, or he could fight.

He did not consider surrender for a moment, which left two options, run or fight.

Driscoll was a brave man, but he was a pragmatist. He had no problem hauling ass if that was his best option for survival at this point. He peered out of the woods and checked to see if there was any escape route possible.

A grenade, possibly fired from an RPG launcher, exploded thirty yards behind him.

Fuck.

He peered out across the valley now; a sliver of moon shone through a break in the clouds, casting a faint glow across the dry limestone riverbed that ran off to the east and west. The rock field was fifty yards wide at the floor of the valley, and anyone leaving the grove where he had sought cover would be exposed to the guns above him on the road for several minutes before he could find more cover.

No way Sam was going to slip away into the night. He couldn't run down to the riverbank and try to run away. It would be suicide.

Driscoll decided then and there that he wasn't going to go out with a bullet in the back. These trees would be his Alamo. He would face his enemy and fight them, make as many of them pay as he could before their sheer number did him in. Slowly, and with some reluctance, he hefted his M16, stood, and headed back up through the woods.

He'd not made it ten yards before chattering AK fire sent more leaves on top of him. He dropped down on his knees and fired blindly through the cover, dumped half a magazine downrange to put any heads down, then he regained his feet and ran up, charging toward the enemy.

A group of six Haqqani men had made it halfway down the hillside from the road. They'd been sent down by their leaders to search for the soldier who would certainly be hiding under a rock in the trees. Sam knew he surprised them by breaking out of the trees in front of them, his rifle on his shoulder and flames and smoke spewing from it. As they returned fire, along with a firing line of men on the road above, Driscoll dropped onto his heaving chest, sighted on the flashes of their Kalashnikovs, and fired three-round bursts until his magazine ran dry. He knew he'd taken out at least two of the men, and four remained, so he rolled onto his hip, pulled a mag out of his chest harness, and began reloading his gun.

Just then he saw a larger flash of light up on the roadside. Instantly he recognized the wide flash of an RPG taking flight, and in another instant he realized the missile was going to hit right where he lay.

With no time to think, he vaulted to his boots, turned, and leapt back toward the trees.

The grenade hit the ground just behind him, exploded in fire and light, and blew American operative Sam Driscoll end over end, sending hot sharp shrapnel into his body and tossing him into the woods like a discarded rag doll.

There he lay facedown and motionless while the Haqqani descended on his position.

38

President Ed Kealty had spent virtually all of the past two weeks on the campaign trail. There were five swing states that Benton Thayer felt could go either way, so Kealty canvassed them in Air Force One. This morning he went to a church in Grand Rapids, Michigan, and then headed to a wind-turbine plant for lunch and a quick tour. He then flew to Youngstown, Ohio, for a rally before shooting east for a dinnertime black-tie affair in Richmond, Virginia.

It was after ten-thirty in the evening when Kealty climbed out of Marine One on the White House's back lawn. On the short chopper flight over from Andrews Air Force Base he'd been informed by his chief of staff, Wesley McMullen, that Benton Thayer needed to meet with him in the Oval Office. Thayer had also asked that Mike Brannigan be there. This was odd, the campaign manager requesting the attorney general be present at a meeting, but Wes had everyone assembled and waiting on the President.

Kealty shot straight into the office without going to the residence first. He still wore his tuxedo, having not changed out of it during the twenty-minute flight from Richmond.

"Can we make this quick, guys? It's been a long day."

Thayer sat on one of the two sofas, Wes McMullen sat next to him, and Brannigan sat across, next to Kealty.

The campaign manager got right down to it. "Mr.

President. Something came into my possession today. A computer drive. It was left on my car at my club, I have no idea who gave it to me, or why I was chosen."

"What is on it?"

"It is a dossier on a retired Navy SEAL and CIA paramilitary operations officer named John Clark. He is a recipient of the Medal of Honor."

"I'm bored already, Benton."

"You won't be bored for long, Mr. President. Clark is a close personal friend of Jack Ryan's; they worked together on certain operations. Certain black-ops-type missions."

Kealty leaned forward. "Go on."

"Someone has plopped a computer drive into our laps that contains evidence of criminal wrongdoing by this Mr. Clark. Assassinations for the CIA."

Kealty nodded. "Assassinations?"

"As well as wiretaps, breaking and entering, et cetera, et cetera."

"This file comes from someone at the CIA?"

"It doesn't look like it. The drive does have information from CIA sources, that's for damn sure. There must be a leak over there. But this information looks like it might be coming from China, or Russia, or even a friendly government that doesn't want Ryan back in the saddle over here."

Kealty nodded. Looked at Brannigan. The AG was hearing about this for the first time. He had a look on his face like he knew he had a long night ahead of him checking all this out.

Thayer continued, "But all this stuff Ryan's buddy Clark did—every murder, every breaking and entering, every illegal wiretap, it is all inadmissible in court."

"And why is that?"

"Because several years ago President Ryan gave him a full pardon for each and every act he did while working for the CIA."

Kealty smiled as he stood up slowly. "He didn't."

"He did. Some in the Justice Department know about it, but not many."

Kealty turned to Mike Brannigan. "Mike. Tell me you didn't know."

"I had no idea, sir. It must have been sealed. Whoever has given us this information, if it is true, must have gotten the information illegally through—"

"Can he do it?" Kealty asked. "Was that legal, just waving a wand over a CIA black operator to say, 'no harm, no foul'?"

Brannigan did speak up with some authority now. "A presidential pardon can clean your slate for most any federal crime. Civil, state, and local charges aren't affected, although I assume with a CIA operator, that wouldn't be a factor."

Kealty's chest heaved with excitement, but then he deflated. "Okay. So . . . if Ryan gave this meathead a pardon, sure, we could leak it, if we did it carefully. That will be embarrassing for Ryan, but we won't be able to get to Clark. And without Clark in hand, up on charges, it won't be anything other than one-day news. You know how Ryan is. He'll wrap himself up in the flag and salute the camera and say, 'I did what I had to do to keep your kids safe,' or some bullshit like that."

Thayer shook his head. "Ryan pardoned him for his actions with the CIA. But there is one murder in the file that, apparently, did not happen as part of his CIA duties." Thayer looked down to the pages in his lap. "He supposedly killed an East German named Schuman, 1981, in

Berlin. The file I have doesn't have a word on it. I checked other avenues, as well. As far as the CIA is concerned, even internally, this never happened."

Kealty connected the dots. "So if he is off the hook for killings while working his CIA job, and this murder was not a CIA job . . ."

Thayer said, "Then the full pardon is irrelevant."

Kealty looked to Brannigan. "Is that enough to pick him up on?"

Mike Brannigan looked stunned. "Mr. President. I am only just hearing about this. I really need to get together with my staff, some key people at FBI, and look over any information you have on Clark. I can tell you DOJ is going to need to know that this information would be admissible in court before they will go any further. I mean, who the hell is this source?"

Kealty looked at the attorney general. "If you can corroborate information in Benton's file through CIA or other sources, then you won't need Benton's file anymore. The source becomes a nonissue. It's just a nudge in the right direction."

"Mr. President, I—"

"And Mike, I *know* you will do the right thing."

Wes McMullen, the chief of staff, had been silent throughout the conversation, but now he leaned in. "Isn't there a law that says we can't out a CIA agent?"

There were shrugs around the room, then all heads turned to Brannigan again. "I believe that is for active employees. If we know, and I mean one hundred percent *know*, that this guy is out of the intelligence services, then he's fair game."

Kealty looked relieved by this, but McMullen still had reservations.

"I'm worried this is going to look like sort of a lame Hail Mary. Like us digging up some thirty-year-old murder to try to pin tangentially on Jack Ryan here with just a few days until the election. I mean, really?"

Kealty said, "It's not a Hail Mary. The information was dumped in our laps. I will stress this, and I will ask the question: If this was handed to us and we did nothing, how would that look? We came into this term promising to right the wrongs of the Ryan years, and boys and girls, I am still the President of the United States."

Wes McMullen tried another approach to put this toothpaste back in the tube. "Clark has a Congressional Medal of Honor. They don't just hand those out in a box of Cracker Jack, sir."

"So? Big fucking deal! We throw in a line about how while we honor his military service we cannot condone acts of murder, blah, blah, blah! I'll mention that I am the goddamn commander in chief, for Christ sakes! Stop fighting me on this, Wes! I'm going forward. Mike, I need cover to do so."

Brannigan gave an unsure nod. "If we can get some bit of corroboration from the CIA, anything, really, then I'll be able to, at least, bring the man in for questioning."

Kealty nodded. "I'll talk to Kilborn at the CIA and tell him Justice Department investigators want to talk to everyone who worked with this John Clark."

Thayer said, "If we can get this to stick to Clark, it will affect Ryan, as it pushes the narrative that he acts above the law."

Kealty was standing and pacing now over by his desk. "Fuck, yes, this will affect Ryan! This needs to come out in the next twenty-four hours so that I can use it on my last swing through the Rust Belt. I can ask the crowd if a

President Ryan would just whack the president of Mexico the next time he doesn't get his way on a trade issue. It speaks to his past, it speaks to his present insofar as he is supposedly so strong on foreign affairs, but are you really strong on foreign affairs if you have to resort to sending out your goon squad to kill others, and then cover it up with a secret pardon?" Kealty was nearly breathless, but he thought of something else and spun in his patent-leather shoes to the three men on the sofas. "And it speaks to the future of this country if we allow a man who works with and cavorts with a bloodthirsty killer like this John Clark to take over the Oval Office."

Kealty looked to his chief of staff. "Wes, I'm going to need that line. Write that down and hang on to it."

"Of course."

"Okay, gentlemen. Anything else?"

Thayer said, "Clark has a partner. He was mentioned several times in the file. He is tight with Ryan, as well."

"Does *this* guy have a full pardon?"

"I don't know."

"Okay, let's get to work on him, too." He saw a look of reticence in Thayer's eyes. "No? Why not?"

"Domingo Chavez is the guy's name. He's Mexican-American."

"Shit," Kealty said, thinking it over. "There goes fucking Arizona and New Mexico. Won't affect Texas. I didn't have a prayer there." He gasped. "California?"

Thayer shook his head. "You could carpet-bomb Mexico City with B-52s and you won't lose California to Jack fucking Ryan. Still . . . you will lose a shitload of Hispanic votes, all over the country, if the FBI goes after a guy named Chavez."

"Okay." The political wheels in Kealty's head turned.

"Bury the Mexico angle on the Ryan story. Let's go after Clark and Clark alone."

Everyone agreed.

"All right. Mike, you go to Kilborn for access to CIA personnel, but Wes, I want you to get Deputy Director Alden over here tomorrow first thing. I want to see if he knows anything about John Clark. Alden is a suck-up. He'll play ball with me in a way Kilborn won't."

39

Melanie Kraft did not mind working late in the operations center of the National Counterterrorism Center. Her work consumed her, especially after she'd been handed a project by her boss, Mary Pat Foley, the week before.

Mary Pat had tasked her with learning everything she could about a brigadier general in Pakistan's ISI named Riaz Rehan. A curious tip to CIA from a one-time-use overseas e-mail address implicated the general as a former operative in both Lashkar-e-Taiba and Jaish-e-Mohammed. This was interesting, but NCTC needed to know what Rehan was up to now.

Melanie had worked the question from several different angles, and she'd struck out several times a day in the past week. But she'd been working the Rehan question all day, and she felt like she had something to show for it.

It was after midnight when she thought she had enough to go to the assistant director, and she knew Mary Pat was still in her office. She tapped on the office door, softly and somewhat reluctantly.

"Come in."

Melanie entered, and Mary Pat's tired eyes widened. "Dear Lord, girl, if you look that tired at your age, I must look like the walking dead."

"I'm sorry to bother you. I know better than to troubleshoot theories with the boss, but my brain is fried and there isn't anyone else to bounce this off of."

"I'm glad you popped in. Want to go grab a coffee?"

A minute later they were down in the cafeteria, spinning stirrer sticks in hot coffee. Mary Pat said, "Whatever you have has got to be more stimulating than what I'm working on. DHS is asking me to help with a report for Congress. I'd rather be doing something substantive, but you kids get to do all the fun stuff."

"I'm working on Rehan and his department at ISI."

"Joint Intel Miscellaneous, right?" Mary Pat asked.

"Yes. A misleading name for the division that runs all Pakistan's foreign spies and liaises with all the terrorists around the world."

"A lot of sneaky people work in government around the world," Foley said. "It's not below them to hide something nefarious behind bureaucratic-speak."

Melanie nodded. "From what I can tell of Rehan's organization, his department's operational tempo has been through the roof in the past month."

"Impress me with what you've found out."

"The general himself is such a cipher, I decided to dig into his organization a little more, maybe find something that can lead to an understanding of what they are doing."

"What did you find?"

"A thirty-year-old Pakistani was arrested two months ago in New York; he got in a fight buying a knockoff watch in Chinatown. In his possession NYPD found twelve thousand dollars, and thirteen prepaid Visa cards totaling thirty-seven grand, and a debit card for a checking account in Dubai. Apparently this guy was withdrawing cash with his debit card and then going to bodegas and drugstores and using the cash to buy the prepaid cards. A couple here, a couple there, so as not to attract attention."

"Interesting," Mary Pat said as she sipped her milky coffee.

"He was deported immediately, without much of an investigation, but I've been looking into the guy, and I think he was JIM."

"Why?"

"A, he fits the mold. Heavy Islamic family ties to the FATA, he served in a traditionally Islamist unit in the PDF, and then left that unit, going into reserve duty. That's common for ISI employees."

"B?" Mary Pat asked, not exactly sold on the circumstantial nature of Melanie's inference.

"B, the Dubai account. It's registered to a shell corporation in Abu Dhabi that we've tied to contributions to Islamist players in the past."

"A slush fund?"

"Right. The shell corporation has some transactions in Islamabad, and the bank itself has been used by different groups. Lashkar men in Delhi, Haqqani men in Kabul, Jamaat-ul-Mujahideen in Chittagong."

"Is there another shoe still to drop here?"

"I am hoping you will tell me." Melanie hesitated, then said, "Riaz Rehan, we have determined, was the man known as Khalid Mir. Mir is a Lashkar-e-Taiba operative."

"Right."

"Well, Lashkar men working in India on missions that have been linked to Khalid Mir have been known to use prepaid Visa cards bought with cash in New York."

Mary Pat nodded. "I think I remember reading that in the past."

"And Riaz Rehan was also known as Abu Kashmiri, a known high-level operative for Jaish-e-Mohammed."

"Yes?"

"Well, a three-man Jaish-e-Mohammed cell that was killed after an ambush in Kabul was found to be using prepaid Visas purchased in New York."

Mary Pat shook her head. "Melanie, lots of terrorist organizations have been using these prepaid cards in the past years. It is the easiest way to move money without leaving a financial trail. And we've picked up other shady Middle Eastern characters in New York with loads of cash on trips to buy prepaid cards, presumably to pass them out to others to create an untraceable conduit of operating funds."

"That's my point exactly. The other people who have been picked up and deported. What if they were working for Rehan, as well?"

"The ones we were able to tie down had no known association with JIM."

"Neither did Khalid Mir or Abu Kashmiri. I am just saying, if Rehan uses this MO, then the same method of operation might mean the same man is behind it. I am starting to think Rehan has more identities than the ones we know about."

Mary Pat Foley looked at Melanie Kraft a long time before speaking, as if she was trying to decide if she should. Finally she said, "For the past fifteen years there have been rumors. Just little whispers here and there that there was one unknown operative, a freelancer, who was behind all of the lower-level attacks."

Melanie asked, "What do you mean *all* of them?"

"Lots. An incredible amount. Some of our forensic guys over at Langley would point to little pieces of tradecraft that were used across all the operations. Everyone started using Dubai accounts around the same time. Everybody started using steganography around the same time. Everybody started using prepaid phone cards around the same time. Internet phones as well."

Melanie continued to look incredulous. "Playing the devil's advocate, it's not uncommon at all to find similar tradecraft in operations from unconnected groups. They learn from each other's ops, they pass field manuals around Pakistan, they get advice from ISI. Plus, when they do evolve individually, it is at a similar pace, using technology that they can get their hands on. It just stands to reason that, for example, all the groups started using long-distance phone cards around the time they became popular, or thumb drives when they became cheap enough. I don't buy this ghost story."

"You're right to be skeptical. It was an exciting theory that explained things the easy way, without any more work than saying, 'Forrest Gump probably did it.'"

Melanie laughed. "His code name was Forrest Gump?"

"Unofficial, he never got an official designation. But he was a character who showed up everywhere something happened. The name seemed to fit. And remember, some of these groups I am talking about had nothing to do with one another. But some at the Agency were convinced there was one common thread running through them all. One coordinator of operations. Like they were all managed, or advised, at least, by the same individual."

"Are you saying Riaz Rehan might be Forrest Gump?"

Mary Pat shrugged. Drained the rest of her coffee. "A couple months ago he was just another low-level general running an office in the ISI. Since then we've learned a lot about him, and it's all bad. Keep digging."

"Yes, ma'am," said Melanie, and she stood to return to her desk.

"But not tonight. Get out of here. Go home and get some sleep. Or better yet, call Junior. Have him take you to a very late dinner."

Melanie smiled, looked down at the floor.

"He called today. We're getting together tomorrow."

Mary Pat Foley smiled.

40

John Clark was new to trout fishing, and he recognized he had a lot to learn about it. On a couple of occasions he'd managed to catch a few rainbow and brown trout in his neighbor's creek, though the streams and brooks on his own farm had so far yielded him nothing but frustration. His neighbor had told him there was good trout to be caught on Clark's own property, but another local contradicted that, explaining that what were called trout in the little streams like those on Clark's farm were actually just creek chubs, a member of the minnow family that grew up to a foot in length and could be feisty enough when on the line to fool amateur anglers into thinking they were battling a trout.

John figured he'd get a book on fishing and read it when he had the time, but for this afternoon he just stood out here alone in his waders in his neighbor's creek, whipped his line back and forth, dumped the fly in a slow-moving pool, and then repeated that process, over and over and over.

It looked a lot like fly-fishing, except for the fact that he hadn't caught a damn thing.

John gave up for the afternoon and pulled his line in an hour before dark. Though he hadn't managed to fool any fish into biting his fly, it had been a good day nonetheless. His gunshot wound had all but healed, he'd gotten a few hours of fresh air and solitude, and, before his afternoon of relaxation, he'd put a first coat of paint on the master bedroom of the farmhouse. One more coat this coming weekend and he'd bring Sandy out so he could get a thumbs-up from her to begin painting the living room.

On top of that, he'd neither been shot again nor found it necessary to kill anyone or run for his life.

Yeah, a good day.

John packed up his fishing gear, looked up to a gray sky, and wondered if this was what retirement felt like.

He lifted his tackle box and his fly rod and shook off the thought like he shook off the cold breeze rolling down from Catoctin Mountain to the west. It was a good half-hour's slog through the woods back to his farmhouse. He started the hike to the east by climbing the stones out of the creek up to an overgrown trail.

John's farm was in Frederick County, west of Emmitsburg and within a mile of the Pennsylvania state line. He and Sandy had been looking for rural property since they'd returned from the UK, and when a Navy buddy who'd retired to a small dairy farm up here to make cheese with his wife told John about a "For Sale" sign in front of a simple farmhouse on fifty acres, John and Sandy came up for a look.

The price was right because the house needed some work, and Sandy loved the old house and the countryside, so they'd signed the contracts late last spring.

Since then John had been too busy at The Campus to do much more than drive up during a rare free day off to work on the house and to do a little maintenance and fishing. Sandy came up with him now and again, together they'd visited Gettysburg just a few miles up the road, and they hoped to get away soon for a weekend trip to Amish Country in nearby Lancaster County.

And when they retired, they planned to move up here full-time.

Or when Sandy retired, Clark reminded himself as he pushed his way up a thick copse of evergreen brush that covered the hill leading away from the tiny stream.

John had bought the property for their golden years, but he had no illusions that he would be one to just fade off into the sunset. That he would live long enough to retire and make cheese until his body slowly crapped out on him from age.

No. John Clark figured it would all end for him a lot more suddenly than that.

The bullet through his arm was about the fiftieth close call of Clark's life. Six inches inside its flight path and that 9-millimeter round would have gone right into a lung, and he'd have choked to death in his own blood before Ding and Dom could have carried him down to street level. Another four inches to the left and it would have pierced his heart and he would not have even made it out of the attic. A couple of feet higher and the round would have nailed the back of his head, and he would have fallen dead like Abdul bin Mohammed al Qahtani had dropped in the elevator of the Hôtel de Sers.

John was certain that, sooner or later—and John was running out of "later"—he'd die on a mission.

When he was young, really young, he'd been a Navy SEAL in Vietnam working in MACV-SOG, the Military Assistance Command, Vietnam—Studies and Observations Group. Clark, along with others in SOG, had lived within a hairsbreadth of death for years. He'd had many close shaves. Bullets that whizzed by his face, explosions that sent lethal shrapnel into men within arm's reach, helicopters that lifted five hundred feet into the air before deciding that they did not feel like flying anymore that day. Back then these brushes with death just pumped him full of adrenaline. Made him so fucking ecstatic to be alive that he, like many others of his age and in his profession, began to live for the drug called danger.

John ducked under the low limb of a young poplar as he walked, careful to keep his fly rod from snagging on the branches. He smiled a little, thinking about being twenty-two. So long ago.

The bullet that nearly dropped him dead on the Paris rooftop didn't exactly fill him with the same giddy thrills he'd felt as a young SEAL in 'Nam. Nor did it fill him with dread and fear. No, John wasn't going soft in his old age. More like fatalistic. The bullet in France and the farmhouse in Maryland had a lot in common.

They both told John that, one way or another, there *is* an end to this crazy ride.

John climbed over a split-rail section of the fence at the southwest corner of his property. Once on his own land, he hiked through a small wood of loblolly pine where the slope of a hill led down into a tiny valley where a shallow creek wound from north to south near the fence line.

He looked down at his watch and saw it was four-fifteen. He didn't have any cell phone coverage out here, so for the three hours that he'd been out for his impromptu fishing trip he'd been "off the grid." He wondered how many messages he'd have back on the landline at the house, and he thought back again to his past, fondly remembering a time before mobile phones, when he didn't feel guilty for a walk in the damn woods.

Being alone here in the wilds of Maryland made him think of being alone in the bush in Southeast Asia. Yeah, it was a long time ago, but not so long if you'd been there, and Clark had damn well been there. The plants were different in the jungle, obviously, but the feel was the same.

He'd always liked being out in nature; he'd sure gotten away from that in the last several years. Maybe once the OPTEMPO at The Campus died down to a reasonable level, then he could spend a little more time out here in his woods.

He'd love to take his grandson fishing someday—kids still liked stuff like that, didn't they?

He stepped into his creek, felt his way forward through the knee-deep water, and found himself especially thankful that he'd worn his waders this afternoon. The water was ice-cold, spring-fed, and deeper than usual. The current wasn't as fast-moving as it often was, which is why he crossed here as opposed to a hundred yards or so upstream, where large flat stones protruded just an inch or so out of the water across the width of the creek to make a natural, if slippery, bridge. But today Clark had no problem crossing right through the center of the stream, and even wading through a deeper pool created by a limestone depression, he found the water not more than waist deep.

John moved through the deepest part of the creek, stepped through a weed bed that sprang out of the limestone, and then he stopped.

He noticed something shining in the water, reflecting the setting sun's rays like steel.

What is that?

There, surrounding a clump of grass poking out of the knee-deep water, was a shiny pinkish film. As the water flowed downstream, the pink film trailed in the direction of the current, individual globules broke away from the rest of the form and floated on.

Unlike many Vietnam veterans, Clark did not have flashbacks, per se. He'd done so much in the intervening

356

forty years since 'Nam that his years in that country weren't any more traumatic than many of his later experiences. But right now, while looking at this viscous substance clinging to the grass, he thought back to Laos in 1970. There, with a team of Montagnard guerrillas, he had been crossing a stream not much deeper than this one, under a primeval rainforest. He'd noticed black film trailing downstream by their crossing point, and upon inspection he and the others determined it to be two-stroke engine oil. They then turned upstream, and found a spur of the Ho Chi Minh Trail that led them behind a group of North Vietnamese Army regulars who'd lost a scooter in the heavy current while trying to cross the stream. They'd fished out the bike, but not before its oil leaked out into the water, ultimately giving them away.

Clark and his team of Montagnard guerrillas had wiped out the enemy from behind.

Looking at the oil in the creek in front of him, he couldn't help but think back to Laos. He reached out and put his fingers into the thin film of pink, then brought them to his nose.

The unmistakable smell of gun oil filled his nostrils. He even thought he could determine the make. Yes, it was Break-Free CLP, his own favorite brand.

Immediately Clark turned his head to look upstream.

Hunters. He couldn't see them, but he had little doubt they had passed on the natural footbridge a hundred yards north sometime in the past half-hour or so.

There were white-tailed deer and turkey all over his property, and at this time of the evening the deer would be in abundance. But it wasn't deer season, and Clark's fence line was damn well posted. Whoever was on his property was breaking a multitude of laws.

Clark walked on, crossed the rest of the stream, and then picked up the trail that led through the woods to the open fields around his house. His walk through the forest seemed even more like Southeast Asia, now that he knew he was not alone out here in the bush.

It occurred to Clark that he'd have to break out of the woods right in front of open pastureland in order to get to his house. If there were hunters there, especially the kind of hunters who trespassed and killed game out of season, then, John recognized, it was not beyond the realm of possibilities that he could get shot a second time this month.

And this time it wouldn't be from a 9-millimeter pistol. It would be from a shotgun or a deer rifle.

Christ, Clark thought. He reached into his waders, pulled out the SIG pistol that he kept with him at all times, and pointed it to the dirt trail at his feet in order to fire a round to indicate his presence.

But he stopped himself before pressing the trigger.

No. He wasn't sure why, but he did not want to alert anyone to his presence. He wasn't worried about a group of turkey hunters intentionally turning their weapons on him, of course not. But he didn't know these guys, what their intentions were, or how much Jack Daniel's they'd been sipping on their little afternoon hunting sortie, so he decided to track them instead.

He headed off the trail he'd been traveling on, so that he could get behind where he thought they would have traveled through the woods. It took him a while to find their tracks. He blamed the low, dappled light here under the trees. Finally he saw evidence of two men where they crossed a smaller trail.

After a few dozen yards he detected the pattern of their

travel, and he found it odd. Whether they were turkey hunters or deer hunters, moving off the trail here didn't make much sense. Their quarry would be out in the open rolling fields closer to the farmhouse. Why were they moving covertly here, still fifty yards from the edge of the tree line?

He lost their tracks a few yards on when the dusk and the canopy of evergreen above blocked out all but the faintest traces of usable light.

Clark put his fishing tackle down, climbed out of his waders, lowered to his knees, and moved slowly up to the edge of the wood line. He was careful to keep himself low to the ground and shielded by a large hemlock spruce.

When he reached the edge of the pasture, he looked out over the low grasses, fully expecting to see bright orange–clad figures to the east.

But there was nothing.

He scanned over by his farmhouse, a good hundred yards to the north, but he didn't see anyone there, either.

But he did see a group of whitetail, eight in number, nibbling on grasses in the field between his position and the farmhouse. They were small females and young fawns, nothing a hunter would be interested in.

Quickly Clark's brain began computing all the data he'd taken in. The amount of time for the Break-Free oil to drift down from the natural crossing in the creek to where he found it passing his fording point. The amount of time the deer would stay clear of the field, had the hunters crossed here.

It didn't take long for him to realize that the hunters were here, in the woods with him.

Where?

John Clark was not a hunter, not of animals, anyway, so

he defaulted again to his Vietnam experience. A knoll rose out of the southern portion of the pasture ahead on his right. This is where a sniper would logically set his hide to get optimal coverage of the area. Maybe a hunter would do the same—

Yes. There, fifty yards away from where Clark lay, a flash of light where the sunset just over the mountain glinted off glass.

Then he saw the men. They were not hunters, this he could tell from here. They wore ghillie suits, head-to-toe camouflage of tied strands of green and brown fabric to simulate leaves and dry grasses. The two men looked like a pair of leaf piles behind a partially camoed rifle and a spotting scope.

And their lenses were trained on the farmhouse.

"What the fuck?" Clark whispered to himself.

One of the men was wet, this Clark could plainly see. It didn't take a brilliant investigator to put together what happened. These spotters had moved through the bush, crossed the creek a hundred yards or so north of where Clark crossed, and the man in the soaked camo had slipped on the flat rocks, dunked himself and his .308 rifle. Gun oil from his weapon would keep it from rusting, but that gun oil had given away the presence of the team to their target.

But why am I their target?

Clark thought he could backtrack over to his neighbor's house. It would take at least a half-hour, but there he could call the authorities, get some Frederick County Sheriff's Department deputies here to deal with the two snipers. But that would draw way too much attention to John Clark himself, inviting questions as to why a pair of military-trained men with a high-power rifle were on his property.

Or he could take care of this himself. Yes, it was the only way. He planned his route back into the trees, then south, behind the knoll, and then he planned his attack on the two men from behind.

But he didn't get very far. In the distance he saw big black vehicles, five of them, heading up the road toward his house. They moved fast, without announcing their presence with their headlights, and Clark just lay there and watched them with fascination.

From a hundred yards away he watched the big SUVs park around his property, front and back. Only then were they close enough for him to see that men in black body armor stood on the running boards, held on to railings on the roofs, and clutched M4 assault rifles with their other hands.

He couldn't actually read the white writing on the back of their uniforms and body armor, but he recognized the equipment and the tactics of the men using that equipment.

Clark closed his eyes and put his forehead down in the cool leaves. He knew who was smashing the front and back doors of his farmhouse.

This was an FBI SWAT team.

John lay there motionless and watched the FBI shatter his back door with a battering ram, then charge inside in a tactical train of men.

Within seconds their team leader announced they were clear, and men stepped back outside.

"Son of a bitch," John said softly as he backed up, returning to the concealment of the woods. Here he shed his waders and tucked them under a collection of leaves and pine needles. He didn't bother to take too much time on this project; he'd made no attempt to hide his tracks as he walked here through the woods, and he was about to make tracks in the other direction. When the FBI made it over here to the tree line, they'd see evidence that someone had wandered up on their raid, and then left the area.

After hiding the waders, Clark turned, stood, and began running back up the trail, looking to create some distance between himself and the men after him. He needed to find out what this was all about before he decided what the hell he would do about it.

As he ran, more than just about anything, he wished his mobile phone worked right now. He had a sinking suspicion he'd missed an important call or two while out fishing.

41

The press conference was hastily called for the end of the workday at the Robert F. Kennedy Department of Justice Building on Pennsylvania Avenue, just off the mall in D.C. There weren't many journalists around the DOJ building at that late hour, but when the news services learned the attorney general himself would be making an announcement, reporters shot over from the nearby Capitol building and assembled in a conference room not far from AG Michael Brannigan's office.

At five thirty-five, more than a half-hour late, Brannigan and a pair of his senior staff shuffled into the room. The journalists waited with growing interest in what he had to say.

The first indication that something remarkable was going on was when the attorney general stood at the lectern without speaking for a moment. He looked off to his subordinates a couple of times. Reporters following his eyes saw men on mobile phones in the corner, speaking softly and hurriedly into them. After several seconds of this, of Brannigan watching his men, obviously hoping for something from them, one of the assistant AGs looked up at his boss and shook his head no.

Brannigan nodded, showed no outward disappointment, and finally addressed the reporters in attendance. "Thank you for coming. This afternoon I am announcing that a federal arrest warrant has been issued for one John A. Clark, an American and former employee of the Central

Intelligence Agency. Mr. Clark is wanted for questioning for a series of cold-case murders spanning several decades, as well as implication in ongoing criminal activity."

The journalists jotted down the name and looked at one another. Brannigan's office had been making threats about going after CIA officers for actions in the field, but nothing much had happened. Was this the beginning, here at the end of Kealty's first term, of the pogrom against the CIA that many had said was long overdue?

None of them knew anything about Clark or any case about a CIA spook named Clark, so there were not even any questions as the AG paused.

Brannigan had been warned about this, and instructed by the White House to let slip the next line. "Mr. Clark, you may know, is a longtime friend, a confidant, and a former bodyguard of President Jack Ryan, both during Mr. Ryan's tenure in the CIA as well as after. We understand this is a politically charged case, but it is a case we cannot overlook due to the serious allegations against Mr. Clark."

Now the press began to scramble. Websites were opened on smart phones, questions of clarification were shouted out. A woman from NBC asked when the next update on the case would be given, presumably so she could have time to figure out just what the hell was going on.

Brannigan said, "I expect we'll have something for you within a few hours. As of this moment Clark is a fugitive from justice, but our dragnet should bring him in shortly."

Brannigan left the conference room, and the reporters followed him out with their phones to their ears. The TV media would have something on the case by the six-o'clock news. Print had a little more time to get some facts together.

*

Jack Junior arrived at Melanie's house at six o'clock. They had planned on a more formal evening in D.C., but both were tired after a long day at work, so they decided to just get together for a quick and casual dinner instead. When Melanie opened the door to her place, she looked beautiful, but she apologized to Ryan, asked for just a couple more minutes to get ready.

Ryan sat on a love seat, looking around the room to occupy himself. He noticed a collection of books and papers stacked on the little desk in the corner next to Melanie's laptop. Books on Pakistan, on Egypt, printouts full of maps, pictures, and text.

"Still bringing your work home with you, I see?" Jack asked with a smile.

"No. That's just some research I'm doing on my own."

"Mary Pat isn't giving you enough to do?"

Melanie laughed. "That's not it at all. I just like poking around in open source in my free time. There's nothing there that is in any way classified. Just out there for any-one."

"If it's not classified, can I take a look at it?"

"Why? Are you interested in terrorism?"

"I'm interested in you."

Melanie laughed, grabbed her coat, and said, "I'm ready when you are."

Jack cocked his head slightly, wondered what she had cooking over there by her laptop, but he climbed off the couch and followed the beautiful brunette out the door.

Fifteen minutes later, Jack and Melanie sat at the bar at Murphy's, an Irish pub on King Street, not far from her place. They were halfway into their first beer, and a big basket of Old Bay wings had just been delivered, when the bartender switched to a news channel. The two twenty-somethings ignored it for the most part while they chatted, but Ryan glanced up occasionally. He was hoping to see some new poll numbers for his dad that would allow his parents to breathe a little more easily, so he looked over Melanie's shoulder at the screen from time to time.

Melanie was talking about a cat she had in high school, when Ryan stole a check of the news.

His eyes widened, his mouth dropped open, and he said, "Oh, fuck, no!"

Melanie stopped talking. "Excuse me?"

Ryan leapt at the remote to the TV, yanked it off the bar, and turned up the volume. The television showed an image of Ryan's colleague John Clark. The report then switched to Michael Brannigan's news conference at DOJ, where Jack caught the AG's vague description of the charges and the political implications of the case.

Melanie looked at Ryan while he watched this. "You know him?"

"He is a friend of my dad's."

"I'm sorry."

"A legend at the CIA."

"Really?"

Ryan nodded distractedly. "He was on the other end. Operations."

"Case officer?"

"SAD."

Melanie nodded. She understood. "Do you think he—"

"Hell, no!" Ryan said, then controlled himself. "No. The guy has a damn Congressional Medal of Honor."

"Sorry."

Jack turned his head away from the TV, back to Melanie. "I'm sorry. I'm reacting to what Kealty is doing. Not you."

"I get it."

"He's got a wife. Kids. He's a grandfather. Jesus . . . You don't tear down a man like that without knowing what you are talking about."

Melanie nodded. "Can your dad protect him? When he gets back in the White House?"

"I hope so. I guess Kealty is doing this to prevent my dad from getting back in the White House."

"It's too transparent. It won't work . . ." Melanie said, but her voice trailed off at the end.

"Unless?"

"Unless . . . well, you say this Clark doesn't have any skeletons in his closet that weren't put there by his work in the CIA."

And that was it, exactly. Jack couldn't say it to Melanie, of course, but he knew a detailed investigation into John Clark just might uncover The Campus. Might that be the goal of this? Might some news have come out about what Clark had been up to for the past year or more? Something about the Paris operation, or even the Emir case?

Shit, Jack thought. This investigation, whether or not they have anything substantive on Clark, could bring about the destruction of The Campus.

The report ended, and he turned to Melanie. "I'm really sorry, but I need to call it a night."

"I understand," she said, but Ryan could see in her eyes that she did not. *Where was he going to go? What could he possibly do to help John Clark?*

42

Jack Ryan Sr. ate his hamburger before going onstage at the rally at the Tempe Mission Palms Hotel. He'd planned on just taking a few polite bites, this was a late lunch for him, and he had another event to attend in less than two hours, a Veterans of Foreign Wars dinner, also here in Tempe. But the burger was so damned good he devoured it while chatting with his supporters.

He took the stage at two thirty-five local time. The crowd was lively and ecstatic with the poll numbers. The polls had tightened since Kealty announced the capture of the man who had killed so many Americans a few years earlier, but Ryan was still ahead and beyond the margin of error.

When the music stopped, Jack leaned into the microphone slightly and said, "Good evening. Thank you. I appreciate it." The crowd loved him; it was taking them longer than usual to quiet down.

Finally he was able to thank his supporters for showing up this afternoon, and then warn them against letting down their guard too quickly. The election was still two weeks away, and he needed support now more than ever. He'd given this same speech for the past two or three days, and he'd give it for two or three more.

As Ryan addressed his supporters, he looked over the crowd. Off to the right he caught a glimpse of the back of Arnie van Damm as he walked out of the hall with his phone to his ear. Jack could tell Arnie was excited about something, but he couldn't tell if it was something good or something bad.

Van Damm disappeared behind a mountain of balloons just before exiting the hall.

Ryan began closing his speech; there were several applause lines that he delivered, each requiring a good thirty seconds or so before he could continue his remarks. He still had a couple more to go when van Damm appeared, directly below Ryan. He had a grave look on his face; it was hidden from view of the cameras, but he made a "Wrap it up" motion by swinging a finger in a circle.

Jack did just that, and fought for his happy face while he wondered what was going on.

Van Damm's expression left no doubt. Bad news was coming.

Normally Ryan would exit through the hall at the end of a rally, and he'd take several minutes to shake hands and pose for pictures as he moved through his supporters, but van Damm ushered him off stage right. The crowd cheered and the music blared as he headed off the stage, and he took the time to give one last big wave to everyone before heading out of view of the hall.

In the hallway, Andrea Price-O'Day shouldered up to him; van Damm led the way toward a side exit.

"What is it?" Jack shouted to him.

"Not yet, Jack," Arnie said as they walked briskly off the wings. The hallway was full of media and friends and supporters, and they moved through them quickly. Ryan's well-practiced smile was gone now; he rushed to catch up to his campaign manager.

"God damn it, Arnie. Is it my family?"

"No! God, no, Jack! Sorry." Arnie motioned for Jack to continue following.

"Okay." Ryan relaxed a little. It was politics, that's all.

They opened a side door and hurried out into a parking lot. Ryan's SUVs were parked in a row just ahead. More Secret Service met up with them, and van Damm led the way to the waiting vehicles.

And they almost made it. Within twenty feet of Ryan's SUV, a single reporter with a videographer in tow cut them off. Her microphone had the station ID of a local CBS affiliate.

With no preamble, she pushed the microphone between two big Secret Service men and into Ryan's face. "Mr. President, what is your reaction to the attorney general's announcement of the murder investigation into your bodyguard?"

Ryan pulled up short. That the reporter had screwed up the facts only made the expression on Jack's face appear more confused. He turned to his lead Secret Service agent, Andrea Price-O'Day, who was talking into her cuff mike to the drivers of the motorcade and therefore had not been listening to the question. *Andrea's been charged with murder?* "What?" Ryan asked.

"John Clark, your former bodyguard. Are you aware he is a fugitive from justice? Can you tell us the last time you spoke with him and the nature of your conversation?"

Ryan turned to van Damm, who also fought off a deer-in-the-headlights look. Arnie reached out and took Jack's arm, tried to lead him on to the vehicles.

Quickly Ryan recovered just enough to turn back to the reporter. "I'll have a statement on this in a short while."

More questions came, as the eager young reporter sensed that Ryan had no idea what the hell she was talking about. But Ryan said nothing else; he just hustled into the SUV behind his campaign manager.

Twenty seconds later, the SUV with Ryan, van Damm, and Price-O'Day pulled out as the door shut.

"What the fuck was that?" Jack asked.

Van Damm had his phone out already. "Just got a heads-up from D.C. Brannigan called a surprise press conference right before the six-o'clock news and said Clark was being picked up on a murder rap. I found out from FBI he managed to escape the SWAT team that went to arrest him."

"What murder?" Jack almost shouted.

"Something about his actions in the CIA. I am working on getting a copy of the arrest order from DOJ. I should have it in an hour."

"This is politics! I gave the man a full pardon for his work at CIA, just to prevent something like this from happening." Ryan was yelling inside the car, the veins in his neck exposed.

"It *is* politics. Kealty's going after him to get to you. We need to treat this with kid gloves, Jack. We'll go back to the hotel, kibitz for a while, and make a statement that is careful—"

"I'm going to get in front of the cameras right now and tell America what kind of a man Ed Kealty is picking on. This is bullshit!"

"Jack, we don't know the details. If Clark has done something other than what you pardoned him for, it is going to look extremely bad."

"I know what Clark has done. Hell, I ordered him to do some of it." Ryan thought for a moment. "What about Chavez?"

"He wasn't mentioned at Brannigan's press conference."

"I need to check on John's wife."

"Clark needs to turn himself in."

Jack shook his head. "No, Arnie. Trust me, he does not."

"Why not?"

"Because John is involved in something that needs to stay quiet. Let's just leave it at that. I will not go out on record with a call for Clark to come forward."

Arnie started to protest, but Ryan raised his hand.

"You don't have to like it, but you do have to drop it right now. Trust me, Clark needs to stay low until this blows over."

"*If* it blows over," Arnie said.

43

General Riaz Rehan entered the baked-brick hut with two of Haqqani's men. They stood on either side of him holding flashlights, and they shined their beams on a figure slumped on the floor in the corner of the room. It was a man, both of his legs were crudely bandaged, and he lay on the floor on his left shoulder, facing the wall.

The Haqqani operatives wore black turbans and long beards, but Rehan was in a simple *salwar kameez* and a short prayer cap. His beard was short and trim, contrasting dramatically with the two long-haired Pashtuns.

Rehan looked over the prisoner. The man's matted and soiled hair was more than half gray, but this was not an old man. He was healthy, or he had been so before he'd been blown ten feet by a rocket-propelled grenade.

Rehan stood over the man for several seconds, but the man did not look toward the light. Finally one of the Pashtun gunmen walked over and kicked the man on a bandaged leg. He stirred, turned to the light, tried to shield his eyes from it with his hands, then just sat up with his eyes closed.

The wrists of the infidel were shackled to an eyebolt on the poured-concrete floor, and his feet were bare.

"Open your eyes." General Rehan said it in English. The Pakistani general motioned for the two guards to lower their flashlight beams a little, and when they did so, the bearded Westerner's eyes slowly opened. Rehan saw the man's left eye was blood red, perhaps from some blow to his nose or eye but likely due to a concussion from the

RPG blast that, Rehan had been told, caused the prisoner's other injuries.

"So . . . you speak English, yes?" Rehan asked.

The man did not answer at first, but after a moment he shrugged, then nodded.

The general squatted down, close to his prisoner. "Who are you?"

No response from the prisoner.

"What is your name?"

Still nothing.

"It hardly matters. My sources tell me you are a guest in Pakistan of Major Mohammed al Darkur of the Joint Intelligence Bureau. You came here in order to spy on what Major al Darkur erroneously thinks is a joint ISI–Haqqani network facility."

The wounded man did not respond. It was difficult to tell in the low light, but his pupils were still somewhat dilated from his concussion.

"I would very much like to understand why you are here, in Miran Shah, right now. Is there something special you are hoping to find, or was it just fate that has your journey into the Federally Administered Tribal Areas coincide with my visit here? Major al Darkur has been meddlesome to my efforts of late."

The gray-haired man just stared at him.

"You, friend, are a very boring conversationalist."

"Been called worse."

"Ah. Now you talk. Shall we have a polite discussion, man-to-man, or shall I have my associates pry the next words past your tongue?"

"Do what you have to do, I'm going to catch a nap." And with that the American lay back on his side, his chains jangling on the concrete floor as he positioned himself.

Rehan shook his head in frustration. "Your country should have stayed out of Pakistan, just like the British should have stayed away. But you inject yourselves, your culture, your military, your sin, into all cracks on the globe. You are an infection that spreads insidiously."

Rehan started to say something else, but he stopped himself. Instead he just waved an angry hand at the prostrate wounded man and turned to one of the Haqqani operatives.

The American did not speak any Urdu, the native tongue of General Rehan. Nor did he speak much Pashto, the native tongue of the Haqqani network officer standing next to General Rehan. But Sam spoke English, so Rehan clearly intended for the prisoner to understand his command when he relayed it in English.

"See what he knows. If he tells you willingly, execute him humanely. If he wastes your time, make him regret doing so."

"Yes, General," replied the black-turbaned man.

Rehan turned and ducked his head as he exited the baked-brick cell.

From his position on the floor, Driscoll watched him leave. When he was alone in the room, Sam said, "You may not remember me, but I remember you, asshole."

44

John Clark stepped off the bus in Arlington, Virginia, at five-fifty a.m. He kept the hood of his jacket over his head as he walked up North Pershing into a neighborhood that was still asleep. His target was in the 600 block of North Fillmore, but he would not go there directly; instead he continued on Pershing, ducked up the drive of a darkened two-story clapboard home, and followed the property line to the back fence. There he climbed over, dropped down into the dark, and followed this fence line until he made his way to the carport across the street from his target.

He kept his eyes on the two-story whitewashed home on a zero-lot property in front of him, crouched next to a garbage can with a violent cracking in his knees, and waited.

It was cold this morning, below forty, and a wet breeze blew in from the northwest. Clark was tired, he'd been moving from place to place all night: a coffee shop in Frederick, a train station in Gaithersburg, a bus stop in Rockville, and then transfers to busses in Falls Church and Tysons Corner. He could have traveled on a more direct route, but he did not want to arrive too early. A man walking through the streets early on a workday was less noticeable than a man strolling through a residential neighborhood in the middle of the night.

Especially when there were trained watchers about.

From Clark's vantage point, here between a Saab four-door and a garbage can full of what John had determined to be soiled diapers, he could not see a surveillance crew monitoring the whitewashed wood home across tiny North Fillmore, but he imagined they were there. They would have determined there was a chance he'd come here to see the man who lived here, so they would have put one car with a two-person crew somewhere in a driveway on the street. The homeowner would have come out to see what the hell the car was doing there, but the watchers would have flashed their FBI creds, and that would have been the end of that conversation.

He waited twenty-two minutes before a light came on in an upstairs window. A few more minutes and a downstairs light flicked on.

Clark waited some more. While doing so he repositioned himself, put his butt down on the edge of the carport to allow the blood to flow back into his legs.

He'd just adjusted to his new position when the front door of the home opened, a man in a windbreaker stepped out, stretched for a moment on the fence, and started up the street in a slow jog.

Clark stood slowly in the dark and retraced his steps through the two backyards.

John Clark made certain no one was following James Hardesty, CIA archivist, before he began jogging behind him. There were a few more men and women out for their predawn, pre-workday exercise now, so Clark fit in to the residential color. Or he would as long as the only illumination came from streetlights. John wore a black vinyl hooded jacket that wouldn't raise any eyebrows on a jogger, but his belted khaki chinos and his Vasque boots weren't typical attire for the other runners around here.

He overtook Hardesty on South Washington Boulevard,

just as he passed Towers Park on the right. The CIA man glanced back for an instant as he heard the jogger behind him, he moved to the edge of the curb to let the faster man pass, but instead the man spoke. "Jim, it's John Clark. Keep running. Let's go up in the trees here and have a quick chat."

Without a word, both men ran up the little incline and stepped into an empty playground. There was just faint light in the sky, enough to see faces close. They stopped by a swing set.

"How's it going, John?"

"I guess you could say I've been better."

"You don't need that gun on your hip."

Clark didn't know if the weapon was printing under his jacket or if Hardesty had just assumed. "I don't need it for *you*, maybe. Whether or not I need it has yet to be determined."

Neither man was out of breath; the jog had lasted less than a half-mile.

Hardesty said, "When I heard you were on the run, I thought you might come looking for me."

Clark replied, "The FBI probably had the same suspicions."

A nod. "Yep. A two-man SSG team a half-block up the street. They showed up before Brannigan went on the news." The Special Surveillance Group was a unit of non-agent FBI employees who served as the Bureau's army of watchers.

"Figured."

"I doubt they'll come looking for me for a half-hour or so. I'm all yours."

"I won't keep you. I'm just trying to get a handle on what's going on."

"DOJ has a hard-on for you, big-time. That's pretty

much all I know. But I want you to know this. Whatever they got on you, John, they didn't get anything from me that wasn't in your file."

Clark did not even know that Hardesty had been questioned. "The FBI interviewed you?"

Hardesty nodded. "Two senior special agents grilled me at a hotel in McLean yesterday morning. I saw some younger special agents in another meeting room interviewing other guys from the building. Pretty much everyone who was around when you were in SAD was questioned about you. I guess I warranted the first-string agents because Alden told them you and I go way back."

"What did they ask?"

"All kinds of stuff. They had your file already. Guess those pricks Kilborn and Alden saw something in there that they didn't like, so they started some sort of DOJ investigation."

Clark just shook his head. "No. What could be in my CIA record that would warrant the CIA going out of shop like that? Even if they thought they had me on some bullshit treason charge, they'd bring me in themselves before they breathed a word of it to DOJ."

Hardesty shook his head. "Not if they had something on you that wasn't part of your CIA duties. Those fucks would sell you down the river because you are friends with Ryan."

Shit, thought Clark. What if this wasn't about The Campus? What if this was about the election? "What did they ask?"

Hardesty shook his head but stopped it in mid-shake. "Wait. I am the archivist. I know, or at least I have seen, virtually everything in the virtual record. But there was one thing they asked me about that threw me for a loop."

"What's that?"

"I know all your SAD exploits don't make it into the files, but normally there is a grain of something in the files that can link up to what you were actually working on. Meaning I might not have a clue what a paramilitary operations officer did in Nigeria, but I can tell you if he was in Africa on a particular date. Malaria shots, commercial air travel, per diems that correspond to the location, that sort of thing."

"Right."

"But the two feds asked me about your activities in Berlin in March 1981. I went through the files. . . ." Hardesty shook his head. "Nothing. Nothing at all about you being anywhere near Germany at that time."

John Clark did not have to think back. He remembered instantly. He gave away nothing, just asked, "Did they believe you?"

James shook his head. "Hell, no. Apparently Alden had told them to watch out for me because you and I have some history. So the feds pressed me. They asked me about a hit you did on a Stasi operative named Schuman. I told them the truth. I've never heard of any Schuman, and I didn't know a damn thing about you in Berlin in 'eighty-one."

Clark just nodded, his poker face remaining intact. The dawn filled out some of the features of Hardesty's face. The question John wanted to ask hung in the air for a moment, then Hardesty answered it unbidden.

"I did not say one *damn* word about Hendley Associates." Hardesty was one of the few at CIA who knew of the existence of The Campus. In fact, Jim Hardesty was the one who suggested Chavez and Clark go meet with Gerry Hendley in the first place.

Clark stared into the man's eyes. It was too dark to get a read on him, but, Clark decided, Jim Hardesty wouldn't lie to him. After a few seconds he said, "Thank you."

James just shrugged. "I'll take that to my grave. Look, John, whatever happened in Germany, this isn't going to be about you. You're just a pawn. Kealty wants to push Ryan into a corner on the issue of black ops. He's using you, guilt by association or whatever you want to call it. But the way he's having the FBI rummage through your past ops, pulling them out, and waving them around in the air, stuff that ought to just be left right the fuck where it is—I mean, he's digging up old bones at Langley, and *nobody* needs that."

John just looked at him.

"You know and I know they don't have anything on you substantive. No sense in you making the situation any worse."

"Say what you want to say, Jim."

"I am not worried about your indictment. You are a tough guy." He sighed. "I'm worried you are going to get killed."

John said nothing.

"It makes no sense to run from this. When Ryan gets elected, this whole thing will dry up. Maybe, just *maybe*, you do a dozen months in a Club Fed somewhere. You can handle that."

"You want me to turn myself in?"

Hardesty sighed. "You running like this isn't good for you, it isn't good for American black ops, and it isn't good for your family."

Clark nodded now, looked at his watch. "Maybe I'll do that."

"It's best."

"You'd better get on home now before SSG calls it in."
The men shook hands. "Think about what I said."

"I will." Clark turned away from Hardesty, stepped into the trees lining the playground, and headed for the bus stop.

He had a plan now, a direction.

He wasn't going to turn himself in.

No, he was going to Germany.

45

Clark sat in the back of a CVS pharmacy in the Sandtown neighborhood of West Baltimore. It was a blighted part of the city, rife with crime and decay, but it was also a good place for Clark to lie low.

Seated around him were locals, most old and sickly, waiting for their prescriptions to be filled. John himself kept his coat bunched up around his neck and his knit cap pulled down over his ears—it made him look like he was fighting a bad cold, but it also served to cover his facial features in case anyone around was looking for him.

Clark knew Baltimore; he'd walked these streets as a young man. Back then, he had been forced to disguise himself as a homeless person while he tracked the drug gang who had raped and then murdered his girlfriend, Pam. He'd killed a lot of people here in Baltimore, a lot of people who deserved to die.

That was around the time when he'd joined the Agency. Admiral Jim Greer had helped him cover up his exploits here in Baltimore so that he could work with the Special Activities Division. It was also the time when he'd met Sandy O'Toole, who later became Sandy Clark, his wife.

He wondered where Sandy was right now, but he would not call. He knew she would be under surveillance, and he also knew Ding would be taking care of her.

Right now, he needed to concentrate on his plan.

John knew that, as soon as the FBI missed him up in Emmitsburg, there would be a BOLO, a "Be on the lookout" order, broadcast among law enforcement agencies of the area, ensuring that everyone from traffic cops to organized-crime detectives would have his picture and his description and an order to pick him up if they saw him. In addition to this, Clark had no doubt the FBI was using its huge resources to hunt him down.

He felt somewhat secure right now, in this place, with this semi-disguise and this low-profile action, but he knew he wouldn't last long before he was spotted.

Though he sat with others in the pharmacy, he wasn't getting a prescription filled himself. Instead he was watching the mirrors high at the back of the store, looking for anyone following him.

For ten minutes he watched and waited.

But he saw nothing.

Next he bought a throwaway phone at the pharmacy and wandered the store while he took it out of its packaging and turned it on. He then thumbed a two-line text message to Domingo Chavez. He had no way of knowing if Ding was under surveillance himself, or exactly how far this had all spread, so he'd avoided Ding and The Campus since finding out the FBI was looking for him the previous evening. But he and Chavez had established codes between the two of them, should a situation arise where one could not be certain the other was clean.

A group of loud and rough-looking African-American teenagers entered Clark's aisle and immediately went silent. They gave him a long look, sizing him up like predators sizing up prey. Clark had been fumbling with his new phone, but he stopped what he was doing, stared back at the six youths just to let them know he was aware of their presence and their interest in him. This was more than enough to get the young toughs to move on to easier pickings, and John focused again on his work.

John received a text message. 9 p.m. BWI OK?

John nodded at the phone, then tapped back. OK.

Three minutes later he walked north on Stricker Street, removing the battery from the phone as he did so. He tossed his empty coffee cup, the phone, and the battery, in a drain culvert, and continued walking.

Seconds before nine o'clock that evening, Domingo Chavez stood on the dark ramp in front of Maryland Charter Aviation Services. A cold rain fell on him, wetting the brim of his ball cap and causing a steady drip in front of his eyes. His windbreaker shielded him from the wet, but not the cold.

Fifty yards off his left shoulder, the Hendley Associates Gulfstream G550 sat parked and ready, though at present it had filed no flight plan. Captain Reid and First Officer Hicks sat in the cockpit, and Adara Sherman readied the cabin, though they had no idea where they might be heading.

Ding looked at his Luminox watch. The tritium gas–filled tubes glowed in the dark here, just outside the residual lighting emitted by the aircraft fifty yards away.

Nine o'clock on the nose.

Just then a figure appeared out of the darkness. Clark wore a black hooded coat and carried no luggage at all. He looked like he could be an airport ground employee.

"Ding," he said with a curt nod.

"How you holding up, John?"

"I'm okay."

"Long day?"

"Nothing I haven't been through a hundred times before. Doesn't usually happen in my own country, though."

"This is fucking bullshit."

"No argument here. Any news?"

Chavez shrugged. "Just a little. The White House is using you to get to Ryan. No idea if they know about The Campus or that you have been working at Hendley Associates since retirement from the Agency. The indictment has been sealed, and no one is talking. If the existence of The Campus is known, or suspected, Kealty's people are tight-lipped about it. They are going about this like it's some cold-case file that just got a shake, and your name fell out."

"How 'bout the family?"

"Sandy is fine. We are all fine. I'll watch out for them, and if someone comes for me, the Ryans will take over. Everyone sends their love and support."

Clark nodded, sighed out a burst of steam that shone in lights from the auxiliary power unit.

Ding motioned to the Gulfstream. "And Hendley sent this. He wants you to go into hiding."

"I'm not going into hiding."

Chavez nodded thoughtfully. "You're going to need some help, then."

"No, Ding. I need to do this alone. I want you with The Campus. There is too much going on right now. I'll figure out who is behind this on my own."

"I understand you want to keep the shop insulated, but let me come with you. Cathy Ryan will make sure Sandy is okay while we're gone. We make a hell of a team, and you are going to need me to watch your back."

Clark shook his head. "Appreciate it, but The Campus needs you more than I do. The OPTEMPO is too high for both of us to be gone. I'll check in on back channels if I need a hand."

Chavez didn't like it. He wanted to be there for his friend. But he said, "Roger, John. The 550 will take you wherever you want to go."

"You have a clean passport on board for me?"

Now Ding smiled. "I do. Multiples. But I have something else on board in case you need to make a serious covert penetration, to enter an area without leaving any paper trail whatsoever."

Clark understood. "Does Captain Reid know about that?"

"She does, and she will comply. Miss Sherman will get you set up."

"Guess I'd better get going, then."

"Good luck, John. I don't want you to forget. Anytime. Anyplace. You say the word and I appear on your shoulder. You got that?"

"I got it, and I appreciate it." The men shook hands, and then they embraced. Seconds later, John Clark headed to the Gulfstream while Domingo Chavez watched him walk off in the rain.

The Hendley Associates Gulfstream flew to Bangor, Maine. This was not its final destination, but it served as a temporary staging area, a place to refuel and to wait until the next afternoon, when they would leave the country for Europe. John Clark did not leave the aircraft, though the crew did check into a local hotel to spend the balance of the evening and the next morning.

Their original flight plan showed them heading to Geneva, but they would amend that in flight. The departure customs check at Bangor was a breeze, even though Clark's face had been on the news for the past twenty-four hours. His false mustache and toupee along with his thick-lens costume eyeglasses made him unrecognizable as the man on television.

At five p.m. on Wednesday, the G550 took off on runway 33, banked to the northeast, and began the long flight over the Atlantic.

Clark had spent the day researching his target on a laptop on board the plane. He checked maps, train timetables, weather, yellow pages, white pages, and a never-ending list of German federal, state, and municipal government employee databases. He was looking for a man, a man who might very well be dead, but a man who would be crucial in helping him uncover information about those targeting him.

The sixty-four-year-old former Navy SEAL slept a few hours while in flight, until his eyes opened to the sight of the short blond hair and gentle smile of Adara Sherman looking over him.

"Mr. Clark? It's time, sir."

He sat up and looked out the window, saw nothing but clouds below them and a moon above.

"What's the weather like?"

"Cloud cover above eight thousand feet. Temperature in the thirties on the deck."

Clark smiled. "Long underwear, then."

Sherman smiled back. "Most definitely. Can I bring you a cup of coffee?"

"That would be great."

She turned for the galley, and Clark recognized for the first time how worried she was about what they were about to do.

Fifteen minutes later, Captain Helen Reid came over the cabin intercom. "We are at nine thousand feet. Beginning depressurization now."

Almost immediately Clark could feel pain in his ears and sinus cavity as the cabin depressurized. Clark had already dressed, but Adara Sherman put on her heavy double-breasted wool coat while sitting on the sofa next to him. She was careful to button all the buttons and to cinch the waist belt, and then secure it with a double knot. It was a fashionable coat by DKNY, but it looked a bit odd lashed down on her body like this.

While she slipped her hands into her gloves she asked, "How long since you've jumped out of a plane, Mr. Clark?"

"I've been jumping out of planes since before you were born."

"How long have you been avoiding answering difficult questions?"

Clark laughed. "About as long as I've been jumping. I'll admit it. I haven't done this in some time. I suppose it's like falling off a log."

Worry lines rimmed Sherman's eyes behind her glasses. "It's like falling off a log that is traveling at one hundred twenty miles an hour, seven thousand feet above the ground."

"I guess you're right."

"Would you like to go over the procedure again?"

"No. I've got it. I appreciate your attention to detail."

"How is the arm?"

"It's not on my top-ten list of problems, so I guess it's fine."

"Good luck, sir. I speak for the crew when I say we hope you will call us anytime you need us."

"Thank you, Miss Sherman, but I can't expose anyone else to what I have to do. I hope to see you again when this is over, but I won't be using the plane during my operation."

"I understand."

Captain Reid came over the PA. "Five minutes, Mr. Clark."

John stood with difficulty. Strapped to his chest was a small canvas bag. It carried a wallet with cash, a money belt, two false sets of documents, a phone with a charger, a suppressed .45-caliber SIG pistol, four magazines of hollow-point ammunition, and a utility knife.

And strapped to his back was an MC-4 Ram Air parachute system.

First Officer Chester "Country" Hicks stepped out of the cockpit, shook John's hand, and together Hicks, Clark, and Adara moved to the rear of the cabin. There, Sherman raised the small internal baggage door, creating cabin access to the baggage compartment. Sherman and Hicks buckled themselves into wide canvas straps attached to the cabin chairs and then they crawled, one at a time, into the tiny baggage hold. They had moved all the luggage into the cabin and lashed it to chairs earlier in the flight, so they had enough room to maneuver while on their knees.

Adara moved to the right side of the external baggage door, Hicks took the left side. Clark remained in the cabin of the aircraft, as the space was tight enough with two bodies in the cargo hold. He just dropped to his knees and waited.

A minute later, First Officer Hicks glanced at his watch. He nodded to Sherman, and then the two of them pulled on the external baggage door from the inside. The hatch itself was only thirty-six by thirty-eight inches, but it was very difficult to open. The external door was flush with the fuselage, just below the left engine, and the airflow over the skin of the aircraft created a vacuum suction that the two crew members in the cargo compartment had to defeat with brute force. Finally they got the door pulled in, a squeal as cold night wind rushed into the compartment. Once the door was inside, they slid it up like a tiny garage door, and this opened the thirty-six-by-thirty-eight-inch port to the outside.

The port-side jet engine was just feet away, and this created a raging noise that they had to scream over to be heard.

Captain Reid had dropped them below the cloud cover as they approached their destination airport, Tegel in Berlin. The earth below was black, with only a sprinkling of lights here and there. The hamlet of Kremmen, north-west of Berlin, would be the closest concentration of development, but Clark and Reid had chosen a drop zone west of there, because it contained a large number of flat open fields rimmed by a forest that would be virtually empty on an early Thursday morning.

Clark kept his eyes on Hicks in the luggage compartment in front of him. When the first officer looked up from his watch and pointed to Clark, John began counting backward from twenty. "Twenty, one thousand. Nineteen, one thousand. Eighteen, one thousand . . ."

He turned around, got on his hands and knees, and backed into the baggage hold. At "Ten, one thousand," he could feel Adara and Chester's hands holding the straps of his parachute rig, and he could tell the toes of his boots were just outside the aircraft. Captain Reid would have slowed to one hundred twenty knots or so, but still the jet noise and the pressure of the wind on his legs were intense.

At "Five, one thousand"—Clark had to shout it so the others could hear—Hicks let go of Clark's harness, and Sherman did the same, but she followed it with a quick squeeze on his shoulder.

At "Three, one thousand" he backed farther out into the dark, cold wind. It was tough doing this backward, but headfirst would have been dangerous, and feet-first, scooting out on his butt or back, would have increased the chances that his chute rig would catch on something inside the aircraft.

"One, one thousand. Go!" Clark pushed his body out of the aircraft; immediately he felt his right side slam against the threshold of the external baggage door, bruising his ribs. But he fell away and free of the Gulfstream as it raced off in the night toward the lights of Berlin in the distance, leaving behind John Clark as he turned end over end, spinning downward toward fields of winter wheat some seven thousand feet below.

46

The oval table in the conference room on the ninth floor of Hendley Associates was ringed with stern-faced men that Thursday morning. Sam Driscoll's and John Clark's seats were empty, but Domingo, Dominic, and Jack faced Gerry Hendley and Sam Granger. Rick Bell, Campus chief of analysis, begged off the meeting because he was focusing his energies on analyzing CIA and FBI traffic regarding the Clark investigation.

Gerry assented to Bell's request, as it was in everyone's best interest that they got some sort of heads-up in the event black trucks full of FBI tactical officers were on their way to the front door of their building.

For the past two days, Hendley Associates had been open for business, but the operators and much of the intelligence-analysis staff had been instructed to stay home. Instead the company functioned as a perfectly aboveboard trading and arbitrage shop, in case any of the intelligence the government was using in its sealed indictment on Clark also included information tipping off investigators about the real reasons behind Hendley Associates.

When no one came knocking on Tuesday or on Wednesday, Hendley, Bell, and Granger made the decision to bring their men in to work on Thursday. They had a very active and important investigation under way, with Sam Driscoll already out in the field, and plans to send the other operatives to Dubai to set up covert surveillance on Rehan's property there.

The first question of the morning was whether or not they could continue on with their investigation, or if they wanted to just pull up stakes, lie low for a while, and somehow try to support Clark.

Dominic Caruso took a long sip of coffee and said, "We need to be here, in the States, and ready to move to support Clark. Do we even know where he is?"

Granger said, "The Gulfstream dropped him off just outside of Berlin. They will be back at BWI this evening, and can fly you out to Dubai, via Amsterdam, tomorrow night."

Ryan said, "Look, I understand the Dubai surveillance is important. But in light of recent events . . . Shit. We can't just leave John alone on this."

Domingo shook his head. "He doesn't need us. He doesn't want us around. He's going to try and wiggle out of this mess on his own while we work our op. Don't lose sight of what we're working on, Jack. This is damn important."

"I know."

"Look, John may be a bit long in the tooth, but he's also the most BTDT operator on the planet."

"BTDT?"

"Been there, done that. Trust me, John Clark can handle himself. And if he needs support in the field he will contact us. Look. You know I'd die for that man, but I also do what he tells me, especially at a time like this. I'm staying out of his way, going on with my job, and you are, too. Okay, '*mano*?"

Jack didn't like it. He couldn't understand how Ding could be so relaxed after everything that had happened. Still, he understood that Chavez had earned the right to call the shots on something involving John Clark. The two had been partners for twenty years, and Chavez was Clark's son-in-law, as well.

"Okay, Ding."

"Good. Now, we've got today and tomorrow to get ready for our operation in Dubai, so that's what we'll do. Cool?"

Caruso and Ryan were struggling with what they took as something of an abandonment of their mentor, but they could not argue with Chavez's logic. Clark could always send for them. Even in Dubai.

It would be hard for the men to concentrate on the Rehan op, especially not knowing what might be still to come on the DOJ's Clark investigation, but they had a job to do, so they got down to it.

The Oval Office of the President of the United States was not the actual command center for the FBI's operation to capture John Terrence Kelley, aka John Clark, but one could be forgiven for having that impression. Throughout Tuesday and into Wednesday, Ed Kealty saw a steady stream of repeat visits from Benton Thayer, Charles Alden, Mike Brannigan, Wes McMullen, and others focused on bringing in Clark.

But by Wednesday afternoon the FBI had decided their elusive bird had flown the coop. Kealty ordered Brannigan, Alden, and Thayer all into his office at the same time. By the President's way of thinking, he needed to turn up the heat on his own people. To that end, he subjected the group sitting on the couches to a ten-minute tongue-lashing that ended with a question delivered in a tenor just short of a scream.

"How the hell does one man slip away like that?"

Charles Alden said, "With respect, sir. That is what he does."

Kealty replied, "Ryan could be helping him run. Alden, go back to CIA and dig deeper. If you can find a tighter connection to Ryan and Clark, then we can implicate Ryan in Clark's flight."

Alden said, "I am told that some of what Jack Ryan did, and much of what John Clark did, was never committed to paper."

"Bullshit," Kealty said. "You're being lied to by your own people. Make examples of a couple of the key people, and the others will open up."

"Tried that already, sir. These guys, the old guard, would rather hit the bricks than talk about John Clark."

"Fucking spooks," Ed Kealty said, waving away Alden's comment as he looked at Brannigan for a long moment. Finally the President pointed at his AG. "Listen to me, Mike. I want John Clark on the Ten Most Wanted list by the end of the day."

"Mr. President, there are a lot of concerns about that. Someone else, some terrorist or murderer or other dangerous man, will have to come off the list, and that is problematic as far as—"

"John Clark is a murdering dangerous man. I want him on there."

Wes spoke up: "I worry about how this is going to look to—"

"I don't give a good goddamn how it looks! I want this man caught! If he is a fugitive from justice, and if he has left the country, then we need to turn up the heat in any and all possible ways."

Brannigan asked, as respectfully as possible, "Who shall I remove, sir? Which one of the top ten will come off to put Clark on?"

"Your problem, Mike. Not mine."

Benton Thayer said, "Mike, sometimes there is a number eleven, isn't there? Like when they don't want to take anyone off but feel someone else needs to go on?"

The attorney general admitted, reluctantly, that Thayer was correct.

The meeting broke up minutes later, but DDO Charles Alden asked Kealty directly if he could stay behind to talk to him for just a moment. He also asked that Thayer remain in the Oval Office.

This was a breach of protocol for a meeting with the chief executive. Wes McMullen, the President's chief of staff, should have been approached by Alden if he wanted more time with the President. Wes was standing right there, he had been ignored, and he was determined to nip this in the bud.

"Guys, the President has a one-thirty Rose Garden stand-up with a —"

"Wes," Kealty said. "It's okay. Just give us a few minutes."

McMullen was as suspicious as he was frustrated, but he did as his boss told him and left the room, closing the door behind him.

Kealty sat on the couch with Alden and Thayer facing him. By looking at both men, he recognized immediately that his campaign manager did not know what was about to be discussed.

"What is it, Charles?"

Alden drummed his fingers on his knees while he carefully chose his words. "Mr. President, some information has come into my possession that makes me believe there is credible evidence that this Clark character was involved in the capture of the Emir."

Thayer and Kealty both sat there with their mouths

slightly open. Softly Kealty said, "What the hell are you talking about? What evidence, and why am I just hearing about this?"

"To insulate you, Mr. President. I think it's best that I don't say anything else."

But Kealty shook his head. "Justice says the Emir was likely dumped on us by a foreign intelligence agency. Do we believe now that Clark is spying for another country?"

Alden shook his head. "That is not Clark. I've read every scrap of paper that's ever been written about the son of a bitch. Not in a million years would he work for a foreign power."

Thayer leaned in closer. "Then what the fuck *is* he?"

"He is . . . he must be . . . working for someone here. Someone waving the flag. But *not* CIA. Definitely *not* CIA."

"What are you *not* saying?"

"The FBI did not get any wind of what Clark was working on from the CIA. But within the FBI itself . . . There are faint rumors about an off-the-books organization stocked with certain analytical and operational capabilities. Like a private spy shop. The FBI has suspicions that some in their house know about it, but getting any concrete evidence is like nailing Jell-O to the wall."

Edward Kealty literally gasped. "You are talking about a shadow government? Some sort of sub rosa American enterprise?"

"Nothing else makes a damn bit of sense," Alden said.

Benton Thayer was slower than the other two; he had no experience with either the military or intelligence communities, and hadn't thought much about how they were organized. But he did understand one aspect. "The Emir will know if Clark captured him. We get the Emir to ID him, and then Clark is fucking toast. And if Clark goes down, then Jack Ryan goes down with him."

Kealty was still gobsmacked by this new information. But he retained the presence of mind to say, "The Emir is under lock and key, with DOJ restrictions on the intel he can provide."

Thayer just shook his head. "You are the President of the United States. Just tell Brannigan to loosen the reins on the PCI. We can get everything we need."

Kealty, the consummate political animal, thought of a new angle to his problem. "But the Emir is the most unsympathetic witness we could possibly have on our side in this. So what if he IDs Clark? Then Clark comes off looking like a hero for capturing the man. Think about it! Does it bother us that there may be some sort of off-the-books spy shop out there? Fuck, yes! But is the tenth district of Ohio, or the third district of Florida, or any one of the other battleground states, going to support the trial of the guy who caught the Emir? I don't see it."

Alden shrugged. "We don't care if Clark goes to prison for this. But if we can implicate Ryan . . . If Clark is involved, maybe Ryan is involved, as well. Think about it. Who else would Clark work for on something as shady as an off-the-books intelligence house?"

Kealty said, "We will need Clark in hand to answer that question. We can offer him limited immunity, or even total immunity, to dump this on Jack Ryan."

Alden nodded. "I like it."

But Kealty then said, "But without Clark, we are dead in the water."

Alden looked to Thayer now. "May I have one minute alone with the President?"

Thayer just nodded without checking with Kealty himself.

He felt incredibly out of his depth, and he had a suspicion something was about to happen that he would not want to be involved in. So he rose from the couch and headed straight out of the office, closing the door behind him.

"Chuck?" Ed Kealty leaned forward, almost whispered.

"Mr. President. Just between you and me . . . I can get John Clark."

"We need him alive."

"I understand."

Kealty started to speak, his mouth opened to utter the word *how*, but he stopped himself. Instead he just said, "Just between you and me, Chuck . . . do it."

Alden rose, and the two men shook hands with hard looks between them.

Nothing else was said before the deputy director of the CIA left the Oval Office.

47

Deputy Director of the Central Intelligence Agency Charles Alden reached Paul Laska just after midnight. The old man was home in his bed, but he'd given Alden a number that would allow him to be contacted, no matter the hour.

"Hello?"

"Paul. It's Charles."

"I did not expect to hear from you. You told me you wouldn't get involved past what you've already done."

"It's too late for that. Kealty has pulled me in."

"You can refuse him, you know. He won't be President for much longer."

Alden thought this over for a moment. Then he said, "It's in everyone's interest that we capture John Clark. We have to find out who he's working with. How he managed to catch the Emir. Who the other people are in his group."

"I understand Mr. Clark has left the United States, and the CIA is working on this overseas."

"Your network of intelligence assets rivals my own, Paul."

A slight chuckle from the old man in his bed. "What can I do for you?"

"I am worried that despite my wishes and intentions, my colleagues at the Central Intelligence Agency will be disinclined to put the full might of their powers into the hunt for John Clark. The rank and file reveres the man. I've got everyone hunting for him, but these are hunters who are just going through the motions. And I . . . I mean, Kealty is on one hell of a time constraint."

After a long pause Laska said, "You would like my help in bringing in outsiders to do the work that needs to be done."

"That is it exactly."

"I know someone who can help us."

"I thought you might."

"Fabrice Bertrand-Morel."

The pause was brief now. Charles Sumner Alden said, "He owns an investigation concern in France, I believe?"

"Correct. He runs the largest international private detective firm there is, with offices all over the world. If Clark has left the US, then Fabrice Bertrand-Morel's men will ferret him out."

"He sounds like he will be a suitable choice," Alden said.

Laska replied, "It's six a.m. in France. If I call him now, I will reach him on his morning walk. I will arrange a late dinner for us this evening over there."

"Excellent."

"Good night, Charles."

"Paul . . . We need him alive. We understand that, right?"

"Good Lord. Why would you even entertain the thought that I might—"

"Because I know Bertrand-Morel has hunted men down and killed them in the past."

"I have heard the allegations, but nothing has ever gone past the inquiry stage."

"Well, that is because he has been helpful to the nations where his crimes have been committed."

Laska did not speak to this, so Alden rendered an explanation for his knowledge of this man and his company.

"I'm with the CIA. We know all about the work of

Fabrice Bertrand-Morel. He has a reputation as capable but unscrupulous. And his men have a reputation around the CIA as cutthroats. Now . . . please understand. I need absolute clarity between you and me that neither President Kealty nor anyone working with *or* for him is advocating that Mr. Clark be murdered."

"We have an accord. Good night, Charles," Laska said.

Sam Driscoll found himself surprised and quite confused to see the sunrise. His guards did not communicate with him at all, so he never knew why Haqqani's people did not follow General Rehan's order to interrogate him and then stand him up against the wall and shoot him.

Luck is real and, once in a while, it is even good. Driscoll would never know, but the day before his capture in the FATA, twenty-five miles north of his location in Miran Shah, three senior Haqqani network chiefs were picked up at a roadblock in Gorbaz, a small Afghani town just south of the Haqqani stronghold of Khost. For a few weeks Haqqani and his men thought NATO forces were holding the men, and Siraj Haqqani himself, after learning of the fortuitous capture by his men of a Western spy, sent orders countermanding Rehan's wishes. The American would be held in trade for his men, and he was not to be harmed.

It was not for another two months that the bodies of the three Haqqani network chiefs were found wrapped in burlap floor coverings and dumped in a garbage heap north of Khost. They were victims of a rival Taliban affiliate group. NATO had nothing to do with their capture or murder.

But this bought Driscoll a little time.

In the early morning after Rehan's visit, Driscoll's

chains were freed from the eyebolt in the floor and he was pulled to his feet. He wobbled on his injured legs. His head was covered in a traditional *patu* shawl, presumably to make him invisible to UAVs, and he was shuffled out of his cold cell, pushed into the dawn's light, and helped up into the back of a Toyota Hilux truck.

He was driven north, out of the compound by the Bannu Road bridge, up Bannu, and deeper into the city of Miran Shah. He heard truck engines and horns honking, at intersections he could hear men on foot as they walked the narrow streets, even so early in the morning.

They cleared the town minutes later. Sam knew this by the increase in speed, and the lack of noises from other vehicles.

They drove for almost two hours; as far as Driscoll could tell he was not in a convoy at all, just sitting in the back of a single pickup truck that cruised through open territory, seemingly without a care in the world. The men in the back with him—he had identified three distinct voices but felt sure there were more—laughed and joked with one another.

They didn't seem to worry about American drones or Pakistani Defense Force ground troops.

No, this was Haqqani territory; the men around Sam in the truck were in charge here.

Finally they rolled up the North Waziristan road into the town of Aziz Khel, and pulled into a large gated compound. Sam was hauled from the truck as it stopped and then frog-walked into a building. Here his head covering was removed and he found himself in a dark hallway. He was led down the hall; he passed rooms full of women in burkas who did their best to stay in the shadows, and he passed long-bearded armed Haqqani network gunmen at the top of a stone staircase that led down into a base-ment level.

He stumbled more than once. The shrapnel wounds in his thighs and calves had caused muscle injuries that made walking uncoordinated as well as painful, and with the metal chains on his wrists he could not reach out to bal-ance himself.

As he passed the locals here, he was somewhat sur-prised to see there was little interest in him from those around the compound. Either this place got a lot of pris-oners or they were just disciplined enough to not make a show of someone new in their midst.

Down in the basement he had his answer. He entered a room at the end of a stone hall, then passed a long row of small iron-bar-fronted cells on his left. Looking into the dim cages, he counted seven prisoners. One was Western, a young man who did not speak as Driscoll passed. Two more were Asian; they lay on rope cots and stared blankly back at him.

The rest of the prisoners were Afghans or Pakistanis. One of these men, a burly older man with a long gray beard, lay on the floor of his cell on his back. His eyes were half open and glassy. It was apparent even in the low light that his life would be leaving his body soon unless he received medical care.

Driscoll's new home was the last cell on the left. It was dark and cold, but there was a rope cot that would keep him off the concrete floor, and the guards removed his chains. As the iron bars clanged shut behind him, he stepped over the waste bucket and eased his sore body onto the cot.

For a former Army Ranger accustomed to living an austere life, these digs weren't the worst he'd ever seen.

They were a damn sight better than where he'd just come from, and the fact that it looked like he might be here for a while, while it was certainly not his first choice, caused his spirits to improve markedly from where they had been a day before.

But more than anything involving his own predicament, Sam Driscoll thought about his mission. He just had to find some way to get the word back to The Campus that General Rehan was working with Haqqani network agents on something that he very much wanted to keep shrouded in secrecy.

48

Paul Laska would have very much liked to visit this beautiful nineteenth-century French estate in the summer. The swimming pool was exquisite, the beach below was private and pristine, and there was outdoor seating all over the back of the huge walled property, ideal natural nooks in the gardens and grounds set for relaxing or dining or enjoying a cocktail as the sun set.

But it was late October now, and though it was still quite lovely here, out in the back garden, with afternoon temperatures hovering in the lower sixties and evenings dipping down into the upper forties, there was not much in the way of outdoor recreation to be had for a seventy-year-old man. The pool and the Mediterranean were both frigid.

And in any case, Laska did not have time for frivolity. He was on a mission.

Saint-Aygulf was a developed seaside town, without all the clutter and crowds of Saint-Tropez, just to the south on the southern tip of the Bay of Saint Tropez. But it was as beautiful as its more famous neighbor; in fact, the exquisite villa, the hills behind it, and the water in front of it were, to put it mildly, paradise.

The property was not his own; it belonged instead to an A-list Hollywood actor who split his time between the West Coast of the United States and the southern coast of France. A call from a Laska aide to the actor's people had secured the villa for the week, though Paul expected to be here less than a day.

It was well after nine p.m. when a burly Frenchman in his mid-fifties entered the back patio through the sliding glass doors from the library. He wore a blue blazer with a collar open to reveal his thick neck. He'd come up from Cannes, and he moved like a man who had someplace to be.

Laska stood from his chair by the infinity pool when the man approached.

"How wonderful to see you again, Paul."

"Likewise, Fabrice. You are looking healthy and tan."

"And you are looking like you are working too hard over there in America. I always tell you, 'Come to the south of France, you will live forever.'"

"May I fix you a cognac before dinner?"

"Merci."

Laska stepped over to a rolling cart near his table by the pool. As the two men discussed the beautiful villa and the beautiful girlfriend of the actor who owned it, the Czech billionaire poured cognac into a pair of brandy snifters and passed one to his guest. Fabrice Bertrand-Morel took the snifter, sipped, and nodded in appreciation.

Laska motioned for the Frenchman to take a seat at the table.

"You are always the gentleman, my dear Paul."

Laska nodded with a smile as he warmed the cup of the snifter with his hand.

Then Bertrand-Morel finished the thought: "Which makes me wonder why you allow your bodyguards to search me for a wire. It was a little too intimate."

The older man shrugged. "Israelis," he said, as if that somehow explained the frisking that had just taken place inside the house.

Bertrand-Morel let it go. He held his snifter over the

open flame of a tea-light candle on the table to warm it. "So, Paul. I enjoy seeing you in person, even if it comes with demands to lift my shirt and to loosen my belt. It has been so very long. But I am wondering, what could possibly be so *très* important that we would need to meet like this?"

"Perhaps the matter can wait until after dinner?"

"Let me hear it now. If it is important enough, then dinner can wait."

Laska smiled. "Fabrice, I know you as a man who can assist in the most delicate of affairs."

"I am at your service, as always."

"I imagine you know of the John Clark matter that is on the news in the United States?" Laska inflected the statement as a question, but he had little doubt that the French investigator knew all about the matter.

"*Oui, l'affaire Clark.* Jack Ryan's personal assassin, or so say the French papers."

"It is every bit as grave a scandal as that. I need you, and your operatives, to find Mr. Clark."

Fabrice Bertrand-Morel's eyebrows rose slightly and he sipped his drink. "I can see how I could be asked to get involved with the hunt for this man, as my people are all over the world and very well connected. But what I do not understand, at all, is why I am being asked to do this by you. What is your involvement?"

Laska looked out at the bay. "I am a concerned citizen."

Bertrand Morel chuckled; his large frame shifted up and down in his chair as he did so. "I'm sorry, Paul. I need to know more than that to agree to this operation."

Now the Czech-American turned his head to his guest. "All right, Fabrice. I am a concerned citizen who will see that your organization is paid whatever you wish to capture Mr. Clark and return him to the United States."

"We can do this, although I understand the CIA is working the same mission at present. I worry there is the potential for stepping on one another's toes."

"The CIA does not want to catch the man. They will not get in the way of a motivated detective like yourself."

"Are you doing this to help Edward Kealty?"

The older man nodded as he sipped his cognac.

"Now I see why President Kealty's people did not come to me about this." The Frenchman nodded. "Am I to assume he has information that would be embarrassing to candidate Ryan?"

"The existence of John Clark is embarrassing to candidate Ryan. But without him captured, without the footage on the news of him being dragged into a police station, President Kealty looks impotent and the man remains a compelling mystery. We do not need him as a mystery. We need him as a prisoner. A criminal."

"'We,' Paul?"

"I am speaking as an American and a lover of the rule of law."

"Yes, of course you are, *mon ami*. I will begin work immediately on finding your Mr. Clark. I assume you will be footing the bill? Not the American taxpayer?"

"You will give me the figures personally, and I will have my foundation reimburse you. No invoice."

"*Pas de problème.* Your credit is always good."

49

The wealth and connections of Gerry Hendley came in handy at times like these. Across four hundred meters of water from the Dubai safe house of Riaz Rehan in Palm Jumeirah sat the five-star Kempinski Hotel & Residences, and here a three-bedroom water bungalow was owned by an English friend of Gerry's who worked in the oil and gas business. Hendley told the man he needed to borrow his place, and the American financial manager offered an extraordinary sum for the property, paid out on a per-week basis. It would have been too perfect for the home to be empty at that moment. Instead the "friend of Gerry's" was there with his wife and young daughter. But the oil and gas man was only too happy to pack up his family and move over to the opulent Burj Al Arab, an exquisite "six-star" hotel in the shape of a sail that jutted out into the Persian Gulf.

All on Gerry Hendley's dime, of course.

The oil and gas man left his home just in time. The Gulfstream G550 landed at Dubai International Airport, cleared customs, and then parked in a great sea of corporate jets billeted at an FBO there on the ramp.

As Ryan, Caruso, and Chavez began unloading their gear from the baggage compartment, Captain Reid and First Officer Hicks stood glassy-eyed on the hot tarmac—not from exhaustion after the long flight but in amazement at what they figured to be something in the neighborhood of five billion dollars' worth of machinery parked around them.

Luxury jets and high-tech helicopters were lined up tip to tail, and Hicks and Reid both planned to get a closer look at each and every one.

The three operators had plans themselves to get a closer look at one of the craft. A Bell JetRanger owned by the Kempinski was waiting to ferry them and their baggage directly to their residence.

Twenty minutes after deplaning from the Gulfstream, Dom, Ding, and Jack were back in the air, lifting into the glorious morning sunshine. They flew low along Dubai Creek at first, the wide waterway that separated Old Dubai and its congested streets and low sprawling stone structures from the skyscrapers of New Dubai along the coast.

Soon they headed out over the water, flying over the five-kilometer-wide Palm Island itself, developed roads built up over the water in the shape of a tree trunk and fifteen palm fronds, all these surrounded by a crescent-shaped island that served as a breakwater.

On this breakwater sat the Kempinski Hotel & Residences, and here the helicopter landed.

The three Campus operators were led to their property, a luxurious bungalow alongside a placid lagoon. Four hundred yards away, Rehan's safe house sat on the end of one of the palm fronds. They would be able to see it from here with the Leupold binoculars they brought with them, though they planned on getting a much closer look once night fell.

At two-thirty in the morning Ryan, Chavez, and Caruso sat in a rubber boat halfway between the Kempinski Hotel & Residences and the "palm frond" upon which Rehan's safe house sat, and they watched the dark compound through their night optics. They were happy to determine that, other than the small permanent security force—a man at the front guardhouse and a couple of foot sentries on patrol—the grounds outside the main house seemed to be uninhabited. There would be cameras and motion detectors and perhaps even acoustic monitoring equipment, but Chavez, Caruso, and Ryan were prepared for this, so tonight they would execute the most dangerous portion of their operation.

They were much less concerned about equipment that could give them away and much more concerned about men who could shoot them.

They had rented the boat and the scuba gear from a PADI dive shop not far from their bungalow. All three men had significant scuba experience, though Domingo reminded them all that John Clark had more dives under his belt in one six-month period as a SEAL than Chavez, Ryan, and Caruso had in their combined lives. Still, the water was calm, and they were not planning on going very deep or staying under very long.

The small rubber boat was not optimal for the operation; neither was the scuba equipment they wore. But this was the equipment available to them, so when Ryan complained that their gear could be better, Chavez just reminded him that they would all have to "adapt and overcome."

If they had needed to make a true covert underwater entry on the compound itself, they would have preferred to use rebreathing equipment, regulators that did not emit bubbles but instead reprocessed the exhaled gas with fresh oxygen. Rebreathers were crucial for covert scuba work, but even though the basic open-circuit gear they had rented from the recreational dive shop would give off bubbles galore when they swam underwater, they did not plan on arriving close enough to the compound to attract attention before coming out of the water.

They dropped anchor and slipped into the water silently. Ryan handed weighted and watertight boxes over the side to the other two men before he climbed out of the rubber boat and attached his swim fins to his feet. Soon all three men, each with a box in his hand, swam down to a depth of ten feet and checked their dive computers, found the direction to their target, and lined their bodies up on the lubber line of their compasses. They headed out with Chavez in the lead.

Ryan brought up the rear. His pounding heart created an odd techno-style cadence when coupled with the hissing noise of his breathing through his regulator's valve. The warm black water cocooned him as he progressed, giving him the sense of being totally alone. Only the slight rhythmic pressures of his cousin Dominic's swim fins kicking ten feet or so ahead of him reminded him that his colleagues were with him, and he was comforted by this knowledge.

Finally, after he was underwater for ten minutes, Jack's forehead bumped gently into Dominic's tank. Dom and Ding had stopped; they were on a sandy terrace on the incline that led out of the water up to the narrow strip of beach by Al Khisab Road. The depth on the terrace was just eight feet, and here Chavez used a faint red flashlight to show the other two where they should deposit their scuba gear. The men took off their equipment, strapped it together, and lashed it to a large rock, and then they each took one more long breath on their regulators. This done, the three men walked out of the water, dressed head to toe in black neoprene and carrying the watertight boxes with them.

Ten minutes after leaving the ocean behind, Dom, Ding, and Jack had moved onto a darkened property four lots down from Rehan's estate. This home was neither walled nor patrolled, so they took a chance there were no motion detectors installed, either. Behind a large pool house, the Americans began setting up the equipment they'd pulled from the watertight cases. It took a good fifteen minutes of preparations, each man working on his own project, but shortly after three a.m. Chavez gave a silent thumbs-up and Ryan sat down with his back to the pool house wall. He placed a set of video glasses over his eyes, and he lifted a shoebox-sized remote control module out of a box.

From now until the deployment of the surveillance equipment was complete, Jack Ryan Jr. was in charge of this mission.

With a well-practiced flick of a switch on the controller in his hands, Ryan's glasses projected the image transmitted from the infrared camera hanging from a rotating turret on the bottom of a miniature radio-controlled helicopter that sat on a foldout plastic landing pad a few feet away. The over-under propellers of the tiny aircraft were only fourteen inches in diameter, and the device looked not much different from a high-end toy.

But this was no toy, as evidenced by the sound it made when Jack engaged the engine. Its motor generated only thirty percent of the noise of a regular RC helo of this size, and the device also carried a payload from an operator-releasable locking mechanism on its belly.

The German company that manufactured the micro-helo sold it as a remote viewing and transporting device for the nuclear and biological waste industries, giving an operator standoff capability to view unsafe areas and deliver remote cameras and testing equipment. As The

Campus had moved from an assassination team to more of an intelligence-gathering shop in the past year, they had been on the lookout for new technologies that could serve as force multipliers in their endeavors. They had only five field operators, after all, so they did what they could to leverage their efforts with high-tech solutions.

Jack had a total of five payloads to deploy tonight with his microhelo, so he did not waste a moment before lifting his aircraft into the night sky.

When Ryan had his tiny craft hovering fifty feet above its landing pad, his deft fingers moved to a toggle switch on the right side of his controller. Using this, he tilted down the camera on the turret below the nose, and with ninety degrees of tilt he was looking down on himself and his two colleagues tucked tightly into the darkest portion of yard behind the pool house. He then called out softly to Dom, "Set waypoint alpha."

Caruso sat next to him with a laptop computer opened and displaying the transmission from the tiny chopper's camera. With a click of a button, Dom created a waypoint in the memory of the microhelo so that when called back to "alpha," the craft's GPS and autopilot would fly it directly back to a position over its base.

After tapping the requisite keys of his computer, Dom said, "Alpha set."

Jack then climbed the aircraft to a height of two hundred feet. Once this altitude was attained, he flew over the three properties between his location and Rehan's estate, flying with a slightly downward tilt to the turret cam so that he could monitor the sky in front of him as well.

When he had positioned his helo and its payload directly over the flat portion of the roof of the estate, he called out to Dom, "Set bravo."

A moment later, the reply: "Waypoint bravo set."

Jack's target was the large air-conditioning vent on the roof of the building, but he did not descend immediately. Instead he used the turret cam, switched to thermal infrared, and began looking for Rehan's guard force. He had no great worry about the device being seen in the darkness above the roof, but he was instead concerned about noise. Because although the microhelo's engine was indeed quiet, it was definitely not silent, especially when operating over a darkened property on a dead-end street in the middle of the night. Ryan needed to make absolutely certain there were no guards on the roof or patrolling alongside the gardens at the northeastern part of the building.

There were some other limitations to the technology, as well, which Jack had to keep in mind, for the device's light weight made it susceptible to sea breezes coming in from the gulf. Even with the stability-control internal gyroscope, Jack had to take care that a breeze that pulled him off course did not disorient him and send him into a wall or a palm tree. He could combat this by trying to gain altitude or calling for Dom to send the helo back up to waypoint bravo, but he knew he would not have much time to make that decision once he got down closer to the ground.

He scanned slowly; with his video glasses all he saw through his own eyes was what was picked up by the tiny camera two hundred feet over the ground and one hundred fifty yards away. Both he and Dom were involved in what they were doing, so it was Chavez's job to serve as team security. He had no laptop to monitor, no goggles obstructing his vision. Instead he knelt by the pool house, using the infrared scope on his suppressed HK MP7 submachine gun, scanning for threats.

Through his goggles Jack made out the heat register of the man at the front gate, and a second man, standing outside the guardhouse chatting with him. Scanning back to the building he found a third signature, a sentry strolling lazily all the way over by the tennis court/helicopter pad. Ryan determined all three to be well out of earshot of his microhelo.

He finally allowed himself a second to wipe a thick sheen of sweat from his brow before it dripped into his eyes. Everything—their entire mission, their biggest chance to obtain actionable intelligence on General Riaz Rehan—depended on his fingertips and his decision-making in the next few minutes.

"I'm going in," he said softly, and he gently touched the Y-axis joystick on the controller, bringing his buzzing craft down to 150 feet, then 100 feet, then 50 feet. "Set waypoint Charlie," he whispered.

"Charlie set."

Quickly he panned the camera back to the front guardhouse, then back to the helipad. He saw the three perimeter guards; they were right where they needed to be for him to continue on with his mission. He scanned the roof again, and it was clear.

A breeze from the ocean sent his craft rocking to the left. He combated the motion with a countermotion on the X-axis joystick of the controller. Jack did not feel the breeze on his body by the pool house, but at fifty feet it had come very close to sending his helo tumbling off course. He had a backup microhelo in one of the watertight cases, but setting it up for use would waste precious time. They had decided that if they lost a helo on the insertion, they would use the second craft to attempt to recover the first, as they did not want to leave a radio-controlled helicopter with a high-tech camera and a transmitter on the grounds of their target, lest the security force there be tipped off to the surveillance mission against them.

Caruso leaned in to his cousin's ear. "It's okay, Jack. Just try again. Take your time."

More sweat dripped into Ryan's eyes now. This wasn't like back on the roof or in the parking lot of Hendley Associates. This was the field, the real world, and it bore no resemblance to his training.

Jack let the sweat drip freely now as he concentrated on landing his remote aircraft.

He touched down gently next to an air-conditioning vent on the roof. Immediately he shut down the helo, then put down the controller, and lifted a second controller from the grass, finding it only by feeling around for a moment with his hands. This device was a one-handed module, not one-third the size of the remote control for the microhelo. On this second handheld unit he pushed a single button, and now his video glasses projected a new image over his eyes. It was a low-light camera image that showed one of the struts over the microhelo's landing skids, and behind it, the narrow slats of the ventilation shaft.

This second camera was fixed to a four-inch-long, two-inch-wide, one-inch-tall robot that had been attached to the bottom of the helo by a magnet. On command from Ryan's controller it released its magnetic hold, and when Ryan powered it up, two rows of tiny legs extended like a centipede, and it lifted off the roof.

The legs were the propulsion system of this ground-traveling bug-bot, and Ryan tested the device by ordering it forward and backward, then panning the 108 op video camera in all directions. Once satisfied that the robot was working nominally, he powered it down, then switched back to the helo controller. He ordered the microhelo to hit its three waypoints and return to its helipad.

Five minutes later he was flying a second bug-bot to Rehan's roof, landing it near the first. The wind had picked up a little between flights, so the second sortie took almost twice as long as the first.

"Ready for number three," Jack whispered when the helicopter was back on its pad.

Chavez loaded the bug-bot on the aircraft. "Microhelo is ready to launch payload three."

"How are we on time, Ding?" Ryan asked.

After a moment's hesitation, Chavez said, "Fair. Don't rush, but don't fuck around, either."

"Roger that," Jack said, and he switched his video glasses back over to the camera in the swivel turret under the microhelo's nose.

After the third and fourth bug-bots were delivered to the air vent over the attic of the target building, Jack brought the helo back to waypoint alpha, two hundred feet above his head, in preparation for a landing. Chavez was ready with the fifth payload and fresh battery for the chopper, as they had determined it could not fly for more than an hour on a single charge.

"Okay," Jack said. "I'm bringing it down."

Just then a breeze caught the helicopter, pushing it inland. Jack had dealt with a half-dozen such incidents in the past forty-five minutes, so he did not panic. Instead he brought the chopper back out over the water, it took a second for it to right itself, and he thought he had control. But it drifted again, and then a third time as he started his descent.

"Damn it," he whispered. "I think I'm losing her."

Caruso was watching the feed in his monitor. "Just bring her down a little faster."

"Okay," Jack said. At one hundred fifty feet the craft jolted forward, and Ryan had to pull it back. "I'm losing the GPS hold. Could be losing battery."

Caruso said, "Ding, can you see it?"

Chavez looked into the night sky above. "Negative."

"Keep looking, you may have to catch it."

But it was too late. Jack saw his video feed turn away from the water and the lights of the Kempinski Hotel as the microhelo began to spin slowly, and its descent speed increased sharply.

"Shit!" he said, a little too loudly considering their covert position. "It's dead. It's dropping."

"I don't see shit," Chavez said. He was walking around with his eyes in the sky. How fast is it coming down?"

Just then the helicopter slammed into the grass ten feet from its launch pad. It exploded into a dozen fragments.

Jack took off his goggles. "Son of a bitch. Set up the reserve helo."

But Chavez was already moving toward the wreckage. "Negative. We'll go with the four bots we have in place. That's going to have to do it. We don't have time to send another bird up."

"Roger that," said Jack, secretly relieved. He was exhausted with the stress of flying the tiny aircraft into the target location, and he looked forward to getting back across the water, where Caruso would be in charge of operating the bug-bots in the air vents.

50

It was approaching five a.m. when the three men got back to their bungalow. Jack was beyond exhausted. While Domingo and Dominic set up the remote equipment for the bug-bots, Ryan dropped onto the couch, still wet from his swim. Dom laughed; he'd been through every bit of the physical exertion that his cousin had endured, but the mental strain of launching, flying, and landing had all been on Jack Junior.

Now it was Caruso's turn to drive.

Dominic had studied the architectural plans from the developers of several of the Palm Jumeirah properties in order to find the best entry points for their bug-bots. The attic vents were deemed the best bet, and as the former FBI agent drove his first little bug-shaped robot into the vent, he was happy to find no post-construction metal grating or wire mesh in his way.

The tiny legs on the robot could be magnetized for moving up and down metal surfaces, just like in the duct-work of the air-conditioning system, so he had no problem moving on both the X and Y axes as he progressed deeper into Rehan's safe house.

The video quality was amazingly good, though the fluc-tuating transmission speeds at times caused a degradation in the quality. Dom and the other operators at The Cam-pus had also tested a thermal infrared camera, similar to but superior to the one in the nose turret of the micro-helo's thermal cam, but ultimately they decided that that feature would not be necessary for the indoor work they had planned here in Dubai, plus the infrared cams drew more battery power and this would be detrimental to their mission, so they were not attached to the ground drones.

After twenty minutes of operation, he had his first bot in position at the ground a/c return duct in the master bedroom. Dom adjusted the tilt of the camera and checked to make certain that nothing was obstructing the pan. Then he set the white balance and focused.

The laptop in the bungalow displayed a near-perfect color image of the room, and even though there was nothing to hear at the moment, the rush of air through the vent convinced him the audio was working nominally.

Dominic Caruso repeated this process twice more over the course of the next hour. The second bug-bot he placed in a duct overlooking the great room. The camera afforded only a narrow view of the sofa area and the entry hall—by no means a perfect shot of every corner of the room— but Caruso felt sure the microphone was positioned well to record anything that was said in the room below.

The third bug-bot started normally and moved a few inches, but stopped within a foot of the entrance to the ventilation system. Dom and Jack spent a few minutes troubleshooting the problem, but finally they gave up, unable to tell if there was some hardware damage to the transmitter or if a software glitch was creating the problem. They declared the device dead, and Caruso moved on to the last robot. This one he placed in a second-floor office area without any problems.

By seven a.m. the operation was complete and Dominic powered down all the cameras. The surveillance equipment, the cameras and the microphones, were passive systems, meaning they did not operate all the time—

instead they had to be turned on remotely. This saved battery power greatly, but it also would be incredibly beneficial for an operation that was expected to last a week or more.

Caruso called Granger in Maryland, and Granger confirmed that they had been able to pick up feeds from three of the cameras and audio from three of the mikes, just as Dom, Jack, and Ding could from the bungalow. The feed needed to be sent to The Campus instantly as, it was assumed, much of the audio they would pick up would be in Rehan's native tongue, and Rick Bell had an Urdu-speaking analyst at the ready twenty-four/seven.

Caruso asked Granger if there was any news about Clark, but John had not checked in. Sam Granger also said that Sam Driscoll had not checked back in yet, either, but they had no reason to suspect anything was amiss.

When Chavez hung up with Granger, he flopped on the couch next to Ryan. Both men were worn out.

At first Jack Jr. was dejected with the success of the mission. "All that work and just three out of five cams and mikes are online? Are you serious? For all we know Rehan likes to sit at the kitchen table when he works. If that's the case, we're fucked, because we won't hear a damn thing that isn't in the office, the great room, or the master bedroom."

But Domingo calmed his junior colleague. "Don't ever forget, 'mano, the real world isn't like the movies. As far as I'm concerned three out of five is a home run. We are in. Doesn't matter if it's one camera or one hundred cameras. We are fucking in! We'll get the goods, trust me."

Chavez insisted the other two celebrate with him by ordering a massive breakfast. Ryan begged off at first, said he needed to catch some sleep, but once the Moët champagne, huge omelets, and flaky pastries arrived, Ryan got his second wind and he indulged with the other two.

After breakfast, they cleaned their scuba gear.

And then they slept.

51

It took Clark several days to locate his target in Germany. The man he sought was Manfred Kromm, and Kromm had proven to be an exceedingly challenging person to find. He was not undercover, nor was he taking active measures to ensure he remained hidden. No, Manfred Kromm was difficult to locate because he was a nobody.

Thirty years ago he had played a role in East German intelligence. He and his partner had done something illegal, and Clark had been brought in to sort it out. Now the man was in his seventies, and he was no longer in Berlin, no longer a government employee, and no longer someone who anyone cared about.

Clark knew he was still alive because the questions the FBI asked Hardesty could have been triggered only by Manfred Kromm. Yes, it was possible Kromm could have written down his version of events years ago and passed away in the interim, but Clark did not suppose that was a document Kromm would have written willingly, and he did not suppose there was any reason that information should come to light right now, unless Kromm had only recently told his story.

Kromm now lived in Cologne, Germany, in the state of North Rhine–Westphalia, on the Rhine River. Clark had found his man finally after going to his last known address, a two-story building in the Haselhorst section of Berlin, and then pretending to be a long-lost relative. A woman there knew Kromm had moved to Cologne, and she knew he wore a brace on his leg due to nerve damage from his diabetes. Clark took this information and headed to Cologne, where he spent three full and very long days posing as an employee of a medical equipment company from the United States. He printed up business cards and invoices and phony e-mail exchanges, and he took them to nearly every end-user supplier of medical devices in town. He claimed to have a customized ankle-and-foot orthotic ordered by a man named Kromm, and requested help finding the man's current address.

Some shops turned him away with a shrug, but most efficiently checked their databases, and one had a listing for a man named Manfred Kromm, age seventy-four, address Thieboldgasse thirteen, flat 3A, who was sent monthly supplies of insulin test strips and syringes.

And just like that, John Clark had found his man.

Clark found the home of his target in the Altstadt of Cologne. Number thirteen Thieboldgasse was a four-story white stucco apartment building that was a carbon copy of the fifty or more that ran down both sides of the road, accented here and there with a single tree out front. The near-identical properties had tiny grass lawns bisected by fifteen-foot walkways up to the single glass doors to their lobbies.

For an hour John strolled the neighborhood in an afternoon rain shower that allowed him to use an umbrella and wear the collar of his raincoat high above his ears and thereby mask his face. He determined possible escape routes in case his meeting did not go well, found his way to the bus stop and to the *Strassenbahn*, and from the streetcar he kept an eye out for cops or postmen or any others who could be a bother if they passed up the street at the wrong time. These were rental buildings, and there was enough foot traffic in and out of them that he did not worry about drawing attention from passersby, and after the hour of peripheral surveillance he focused his attention on building number thirteen.

The building was not old in the European sense; very little in Cologne could be considered old, as the city had been altogether flattened during the Second World War. Spending several minutes across the street staring at number thirteen Thieboldgasse through the rainfall, Clark found the building to be as featureless and colorless and charmless as the Cold War itself.

Back then, during a Cold War that was never cold enough for men on the sharp edge like John Clark, Clark had come to Germany on a special operation. He was CIA/SAD at the time, the Special Activities Division.

He was pulled out of a training evolution in North Carolina with members of the Army's newly minted tier-one unit, Delta Force, and he was put on a CIA 35A Learjet and flown to Europe. After a stop at Mildenhall AFB in Suffolk, England, to refuel, Clark was back in the air.

No one told him where they were taking him or what he'd be doing when he got there.

Clark landed at Tempelhof in Berlin, and was whisked to a safe house within pistol shot of the Berlin Wall.

There he met an old friend named Gene Lilly. They'd worked together in 'Nam, and now Lilly was the chief of the CIA's Berlin Station. Lilly told Clark he was needed for a simple bag-drop operation over the border, but Clark smelled the bullshit in the story. He knew they didn't need an SAD hard asset for a bag drop. He relayed his doubt to his superior, and then Gene Lilly broke down in tears.

Gene said he'd been caught in a honey trap by a hooker

working with a couple of Stasi foot soldiers who'd gone rogue to make some extra cash. They had extorted from him all of his life's savings, and he needed John to hand over the satchel full of cash and pick up a folder full of negatives. Clark did not ask what was on the negatives— he was damn certain he did not want to know.

Lilly made it clear to Clark that there was no one else in the Agency he trusted, and the thirty-three-year-old SAD asset agreed to help out his old friend.

Minutes later John was handed a satchel full of deutschmarks and taken to the U-Bahn, then he shuffled into a train half full of locals.

The exchange between Clark and the Stasi extorters was to be in a surreal location, unique to Berlin and the Cold War. The West German subway system had a few underground rail lines that, rather inconveniently, ventured under East Berlin. Before the partition of the city this was of no consequence, but after the Berlin Wall was erected in 1961, the lines that rolled under the wall were no longer allowed to stop at the stations on the other side. The East Germans boarded or barred the doors at street level, in some cases they even built apartment complexes over their access, and they wiped any references to the subway stations from East German rail maps. Down below, these dark, vacant, and labyrinthine halls became known as *Geisterbahnhöfe*—ghost stations.

A few minutes past midnight, John Clark dropped out of the back of the last car of the U8 train that rolled under the Mitte district of East Berlin. As the train clicked and clacked its way up the tunnel, the American pulled out a flashlight, adjusted the satchel over his shoulder, and walked on. In minutes he'd found his way to the Weinmeisterstrasse U-Bahn ghost station, and here he waited on the darkened concrete platform, listening to the sounds of rats below him and bats above him.

Within minutes a flashlight's beam appeared in a stairwell. A single man appeared behind it, shined his light on Clark, and told him to open the satchel. Clark did as he was told, and then the man lowered a package to the dusty concrete and slid it over to the American.

Clark picked up the package, checked it to make certain they were the negatives, and then he left the satchel.

It could have, it *should* have, ended right there.

But the Stasi crooks were greedy, and they wanted their negatives back for another round of blackmail.

John Clark turned and began heading toward the edge of the platform, but he heard a noise on the opposite platform, across the rails. He shined his light over there in time to see a man with a handgun leveled at him. Clark dove and rolled onto the filthy concrete floor as a pistol shot cracked and echoed around the maze of tunnels and open halls.

The American CIA officer came out of his roll onto his feet with a Colt .45-caliber 1911 model pistol in his hands. He fired twice across the tracks, hit the shooter both times in the chest, and the man dropped where he stood.

Clark then shifted to the man with the money satchel. The Stasi agent had retreated back up the stairwell. Clark took a shot but missed low just before the man disappeared from view. He considered going after the man, it was the natural tendency of a direct-action expert like Clark, as he could not be certain the surviving Stasi man would not turn the tables and come after him. But just then the next train through the ghost station approached, and Clark was forced to quickly duck behind a concrete column. The bright lights of the train cast long shadows on the dusty platform. Clark slid to the tiled floor and chanced a look toward where the East German had disappeared. He saw nothing in the moving lights, and he knew that if he missed this train, he'd have to wait here another ten minutes for the next one.

Clark timed his leap onto the rear car perfectly; he caught onto a handhold by the back door and then moved around behind the car. He rode back there through the dark for several minutes, until he was in West Berlin, where he melted into the light station traffic.

Thirty minutes later he was on a streetcar full of West Germans heading home after working the night shift, and thirty minutes after that he was handing the negatives off to Gene Lilly.

He flew out of Germany on a commercial flight the next day, certain that nothing that had happened would ever go into the archives of the CIA or the East German Staatssicherheitsdienst.

Standing there in the cold rain in Cologne, he shook off the memory and looked around. The Germany of today bore little resemblance to the divided nation of thirty years ago, and Clark reminded himself that today's problems needed his undivided attention.

At four p.m. the day's light was leaving the gray sky, and a light came on in the tiny lobby of number thirteen Thieboldgasse. Inside he could see an elderly woman leashing her dog at the foot of a stairwell. Quickly Clark crossed the street, hitched his collar higher up around his neck, and arrived at the side of the building just as the woman exited the front door, her eyes already on the street ahead. As the door closed behind her, John Clark moved up the wall through the grass and stepped in silently.

He was already halfway up the staircase with his SIG Sauer pistol in his hand by the time the door latch clicked behind him.

Manfred Kromm reacted to the knock at his door with a groan. He knew it would be Herta from across the hall, he knew she would have locked herself out yet again while walking that little gray bitch poodle of hers, and he knew he would have to pick her lock like he'd done dozens of times before.

He'd never told her where he learned to pick locks. Nor had she asked.

That she locked herself out purposely so that he would pay attention to her only annoyed him further. He could not be bothered with the old woman. She was a pest of the highest order, only slightly less annoying than her yapping *Hündchen* Fifi. Still, Manfred Kromm did not let on that he knew her weekly lockouts were a ruse. He was a loner and a social hermit, he would no more insinuate to people that they were interested in him than he would sprout wings and fly, so he smiled outwardly, groaned inwardly, and unlocked the old bitch's *gottverdammt* door each time she knocked.

He climbed up from his chair, shuffled to the door, and lifted his picks off of the table in the entryway of his flat. The aged German put his hand on his door latch to step into the hall. Only the old force of habit made him look through the peephole. He went through the motions of glancing into the hallway, had begun to remove his eye after looking so he could open the door, but then his eye widened in surprise and it rushed back to the tiny lens in the door. There, on the other side, he saw a man in a raincoat.

And in the man's hand a stainless-steel automatic pistol with a suppressor attached was pointed directly at Manfred Kromm's door.

The man spoke in English, loud enough to be heard through the woodwork. "Unless your door is ballistic steel, or you can move faster than a bullet, you'd better let me in."

"Wer is denn da?" Who the hell is it? Kromm croaked. He spoke English, he'd understood the man with the gun, but he had not used the language himself in many years. The right words would not pass his lips.

"Someone from your past."

And then Kromm knew. He knew exactly who this man was.

And he knew he was about to die.

He opened the door.

"I know your face. It's older. But I remember you," Kromm said. As instructed by Clark, he had moved to his chair in front of the television. His hands were on his knees, kneading the swollen joints slowly.

Clark stood above him, his weapon still pointing at the German.

"Are you alone?" Clark asked the question but searched the tiny flat without waiting for a response.

Manfred Kromm nodded. *"Selbsverständlich."* Of course.

Clark kept looking around, keeping the SIG pointed at the old man's chest. He said, "Keep perfectly still. I've had a lot of coffee today, you don't want to see how jumpy I am."

"I will not move," the old German said. Then he

433

shrugged. "That gun in your hand is the only weapon in this flat."

Clark checked over the rest of the tiny apartment. It did not take long. It could not have been four hundred square feet, including the bathroom and the kitchen. He found a door to a fire escape in the kitchen, but nothing whatsoever as far as luxuries. "What, thirty-five years in the Stasi, and this is all you get?"

Now the German in the chair smiled a little. "From the comments of your government regarding you, Herr Clark, it does not look like your organization has rewarded your efforts much more than my organization has rewarded mine."

Clark cracked a sour grin himself as he used his legs to push a small table flush against the front door. It might slow someone coming in from the hall for a moment, but not much more than that. Clark stood next to the door, kept the SIG trained on the burly man sitting uncomfortably on the recliner.

"You have been telling tales."

"I have said nothing."

"I don't believe you. And that is a problem." Clark kept his weapon trained as he moved sideways along the front wall of the room into the corner. On the adjoining wall sat a tall antique china cabinet. He pushed it toward the open doorway to the tiny kitchen, in order to block the entrance to the flat from the rear fire escape. Inside, dishes rocked and a few tipped over as the big wooden piece came to rest, covering the doorway. Now the only entrance to the room was the bedroom behind Manfred.

"Tell *me* what you told *them*. Everything."

"Mr. Clark, I have no idea what you—"

"Thirty years ago, three people went into the *Geisterbahn-*

434

hof. Two of those people came out alive. You were working for the Stasi, as was your partner, but you two fellows were not playing by Stasi rules, which means you extorted that money for yourself. I was ordered to let you two walk away, but your partner, Lukas Schuman, tried to kill me after you got the money.

"I killed Lukas Schuman, and you got away, and I *know* you did not run back to Markus Wolf and tell him about how your illegal moonlighting job turned ugly. You would have kept your mouth shut to everyone so you didn't have to turn over the cash."

Kromm did not speak, but only squeezed his hands into his knees as if he were kneading fat *Brötchen* before putting them in the oven.

Clark said, "And I was under orders to keep the affair out of the official record of my agency. The only person, other than you, me, and poor dead Lukas Schuman, who knew about what happened in the ghost station that night was my superior, and he died fifteen years ago without breathing a word of it to anyone."

"I don't have the money anymore. I spent it," Kromm said.

Clark sighed as if disappointed with the German's comment. "Right, Manfred, I came back thirty years later to retrieve a messenger bag full of worthless deutschmarks."

"Then what do you want?"

"I want to know who you talked to."

Kromm nodded. He said, "I think this is an American movie cliché, but it is the truth. If I tell you, they will kill me."

"Who, Manfred?"

"I did not go to them. They came to me. I had no interest in digging up the buried bones of our mutual past."

Clark lifted the pistol and looked down its tritium sights.

"Who, Manfred? Who did you tell about 'eighty-one?"

"Obtshak!" Manfred blurted it out in panic.

Clark's head cocked to the side. He lowered the weapon. "Who is Obtshak?"

"Obtshak is not a who! It's a what! It's an Estonian criminal organization. A foreign office of the Russian mob, so to speak."

John did not hide his confusion. "And they asked you about *me*? By name?"

"*Nein,* they weren't asking in the regular sense. They hit me. They broke a bottle of beer, put the broken bottle up to my throat, and *then* they asked me."

"And you told them about Berlin."

"*Natürlich!*" Of course. "Kill me for it if you must, but why should I protect you?"

Something occurred to Clark. "How did you know they were Obtshak?"

Kromm shrugged. "They were Estonian. They spoke Estonian. If someone is a thug and they are Estonian, then I presume them to be in Obtshak."

"And they came here?"

"To my house? *Nein.* They had me meet them at a warehouse in Deutz. They told me there was money for me. Security work."

"Security work? Don't bullshit me, Kromm. No one is going to hire you to do security work."

The German's hands rose quickly as he began to argue, but the barrel of Clark's SIG was trained again on Kromm's chest in the space of a heartbeat. Kromm lowered his hands.

"I have done some . . . some work for members of the Eastern European immigrant community in the past."

"What? Like forgery?"

Kromm shook his head. He was too proud to keep quiet. "Locks. Lock picking."

"Cars?"

Now the old German smiled. "Cars? No. Car *lots.* Dealerships. It helps to add to my tiny pension. Anyway, I knew some Estonians. I knew the man who asked me to go to the warehouse, otherwise I would never have agreed to go."

Clark reached into the pocket of his raincoat, pulled out a notepad and a pen, and tossed it to the old man. "I want his name, his address, any other names you know, Estonians working in Obtshak."

Kromm deflated in his chair. "They will kill me."

"Leave. Leave right now. Trust me, whoever questioned you about me is long gone. *That's* who I'm after. The men who set it up are just the local thugs. Get out of Cologne and they won't pester you."

Kromm did not move. He only looked up at Clark.

"I will kill you, right here, right now, if you do not do as I say."

Kromm slowly began to write, but then he looked up, past the gun barrel, as if he had something to say.

"Write or talk," Clark said, "but do it now or I put a bullet in one of those sore knees of yours."

The German pensioner said, "After they took me, I spent a day in the hospital. I told the doctor I was mugged. And then I came home, angry and determined to retaliate against the men. The leader, the man who asked the questions, he was not a local. I could tell this because he spoke no German. Only Estonian and Russian."

"Keep talking."

"I have a friend still in Moscow, he knows his way around."

"Around the Mafia, you mean?"

Kromm shrugged. "He is an entrepreneur. Anyway, I called him up and asked him for information on Obtshak. I did not tell him the real reason. I am certain he assumed I had business. I described the man who interrogated me. Fifty years old, but with hair dyed like he was a twenty-year-old singer in a punk-rock band."

"And your friend gave you a name?"

"He did."

"And what did you do?"

Kromm shrugged. He looked at the floor in humiliation. "What *could* I do? I was drunk when I thought I could get revenge. I sobered up."

"Give me the man's name."

"If I do that, if I tell you about the man in Tallinn who came here and ordered the others to beat me, will you bypass the men here in Cologne? Maybe if you go directly to Tallinn they will not know that I informed."

"That suits me just fine, Manfred."

"*Sehr gut,*" said Kromm, and he gave Clark a name as the last of the afternoon's light left the sky outside.

52

Unlike the government agencies searching for international fugitive John Clark, Fabrice Bertrand-Morel Investigations billed by the man-hour, so they used a lot of men working a lot of hours.

And it was only this intense canvassing of choke points across Europe that helped them locate their quarry. Bertrand-Morel had concentrated his hunt in Europe because Alden had, through Laska, passed the Frenchman a copy of the dossier on the ex–CIA man. FBM decided Clark's recent work in Europe with NATO's Rainbow organization would mean he would have sympathetic contacts on the continent.

So a single FBM man had been placed in each of sixty-four train stations across Europe, working fourteen-hour shifts, passing out fliers and showing photos of Clark to station employees. They had turned up nothing in days of waiting and watching. But finally a man working a pretzel stand at the Cologne Hauptbahnhof had caught a glimpse of a figure in a crowd passing by. He looked at the photo on the small card he'd been handed three days earlier by a bald Frenchman, and then he quickly dialed the number on the back of the card.

The Frenchman had offered him a large reward, paid in cash.

Twenty minutes later the first FBM man arrived at the Cologne Hauptbahnhof to interview the pretzel salesman. The middle-aged man was clearheaded and convincing; he was certain John Clark had passed him heading for the front entrance of the Hauptbahnhof.

Soon three more FBM men, the entire force within an hour's drive, were in the station working on a plan of action. They had little to go on save for the report that their man had entered the city; they could not very well just spread out, sending four men out into the fourth-largest metropolis in Germany.

So they left a man at the station while the other three checked the nearby hotels and guesthouses.

It was the agent at the station who got the hit. Just after nine on the cold and rainy evening, forty-year-old Lyonnais private detective and employee of Fabrice Bertrand-Morel Investigations Luc Patin stood just at the entrance smoking a cigarette, his eyes occasionally drifting up to the incredible Cologne Cathedral just to the left of the train station, but his main focus remained on the foot traffic that streamed past him toward the tracks behind. There, in a large group of pedestrians, a man who bore a reasonable resemblance to his target shuffled by with the collar of his raincoat up high.

Luc Patin said softly, *"Bonsoir, mon ami."* He reached into his pocket and retrieved his mobile phone.

Domingo Chavez had set up a more low-tech monitoring operation for Rehan's Dubai safe house than that of the two younger operators with their robot cameras and microphones. One of the three bedrooms in the bungalow looked out over the lagoon, into the waterway between the crescent-shaped breakwater upon which the Kempinski sat and the palm-frond-shaped peninsula where Rehan's safe house was located. The distance between the two locations was easily four hundred meters, but that was not too far away for Chavez to employ a toy he'd brought along on the flight in from the States.

He set up the variable-power Zeiss Victory FL spotting scope on its tripod, and he placed the tripod on a desk in the bedroom in front of the window. From his chair at the desk he could see the very back of Rehan's walled-in compound, and several second-floor windows. The blinds had remained closed as had the back gate, but he hoped that the property might open up a little bit when it was actually being lived in by Rehan and an entourage from Islamabad.

When he realized that he had a fair line of sight on the compound, he also got another idea. If Rehan was truly as dangerous as their investigations were leading them to believe, might The Campus not decide, sooner rather than later, to take him out? And if they did make the call for the operators to assassinate the general, would it not be much easier to do it right here, with a long-range rifle and good optics, as opposed to having to find some other opportunity to get close to the man, either here in Dubai or, God forbid, in Islamabad?

Chavez determined he could make the shot on General Rehan if the man stepped out onto his second-floor balcony or even appeared in an upper-floor window of the safe house, and he ran his thoughts by Ryan and Caruso. Both men supported the idea of being ready for a termination order from Hendley and Granger, so Chavez called Sam Granger and asked to have some equipment flown in so that he would be ready, in the event something during their surveillance led to the green light to drop Rehan.

The Gulfstream would be flying in the equipment in two days' time, which meant Ding would have a gun ready to make the shot well before he expected his potential target to arrive in the city.

Clark saw the watcher just after nine p.m. He had just finished his second dry-cleaning run of the evening before returning to the station; he hadn't seen anyone following him at any point in his visit to Cologne, but when he stood in line at a kiosk to buy a couchette ticket to Berlin, a gentle sweep of his head in all directions revealed a single man watching him from thirty-five yards away. A second glance several seconds later confirmed it.

He'd been spotted.

John stepped out of the line at the kiosk. This would be conspicuous but a hell of a lot better than waiting around for the watcher's backup to arrive. He strolled through the station toward the northern exit, and seconds later he realized that two new men had joined the hunt.

They were on him before he was out of the station and he knew it, because he'd been spotting tails since before these three goons were born. Two men with short beards and dark hair, the same approximate age, the same build, the same general style of raincoat. They were entering the station as he was exiting two minutes earlier, and now they were walking thirty yards behind and slightly to the right as John turned in front of the cathedral.

A wet sleet fell on them all as Clark headed south.

John did not get overly excited by having acquired a tail. He was not going to let a little surveillance shake him up. He could lose these men in the darkness and foot traffic of the city and then be on his way again in no time. He turned left at the southern edge of the cathedral and headed for the western bank of the Rhine River. After passing a section of road with worn stones laid by the Romans, he tried to catch a glimpse of the men behind him in the glass of the Dorint Hotel. The two men were there, together, not more than twenty-five yards back. He wondered if the third man was trying to get ahead of him now.

Clark turned south, walked along Mauthgasse, full of restaurants with tables spilling away from building façades toward the river's edge, and with diners laughing and mingling with one another under heated canopies. He was as concerned about his status as an internationally sought criminal as he was afraid of the men tailing him. The locals and tourists were a definite danger. He assumed his face had been on the news in Europe as well as the States, though he himself had not watched any television in the past week. With an abundance of caution and a desire to avoid running into a do-gooding waiter with a black belt, he adjusted his watch cap lower on his forehead and made a turn up a quiet street.

John walked down the middle of the cobblestoned alleyway as it rose and turned to the left. His tail followed, still twenty-five yards back and on his right. He found himself in the Heumarkt, another open area full of people walking under umbrellas and electric lights, and he turned back to the north. All along he scanned reflections, judging the disposition of the men behind him whenever he could get a glimpse of them. He was beginning to think that maybe these guys were not waiting on backup before arresting him, though they had made no move to close their distance just yet.

He strolled through the Alter Markt, still heading north and parallel to the Rhine a few blocks away on his right. A quick glance in a traffic mirror on a blind street corner showed him that one of his followers had dropped out of the hunt, but the other had closed even more. This man was not fifteen yards behind him now. Picking his way through the pedestrians, John began to worry. There were two men who could right now be moving into position ahead of him, ready to try to snag him at the very next corner. He liked his chances in any one-on-one encounter, but the proximity of civilians and cops could easily allow any situation to grow unmanageable.

Clark picked up his pace, found himself passing a beer museum and a covered courtyard full of singing Germans, and he turned again to the right, moving now along the bank of the river. He thought about stopping, turning, and confronting the man who had closed to within thirty feet; there was no way this guy was going to take Clark in on his own, but any altercation in front of a crowd would just about ensure that someone would notice him, recognize him, and call for the police. The man behind him was threatening suddenly with his overt proximity, his unknown intentions, and his power to draw unwanted attention to the American fugitive.

John turned right again at Fischmarkt, away from the crowds and into a dimly lit alley.

There was a quick left in front of it. Also dark and quiet. The sign said "Auf dem Rothenberg" and John picked up the pace as he made the turn.

The second man, the one who had dropped off surveillance, stood in front of him in the dark. A pistol was low in his right hand. "Monsieur Clark, please come quietly so that you do not get hurt."

John stopped, twenty feet from the man with the gun. He heard the man behind him stop in the alley, as well.

The American nodded, took one step forward, then spun on his shoes and ran through the back door of a pizza parlor, leaving his pursuers in the alleyway.

John was not fast. Speed, he knew, was a young man's game. But he leveraged his years in the field with each and every footfall, looking to make a quick turn here, to duck into a shadow there. He moved straight through the kitchen of the Croatian-run pizza restaurant, knocking pans and cans and cooks into the path of the men who were entering the back door behind him. He darted into the narrow dining room, pushed past the customers lined up to order their pies, knocking several of them down to the floor in order to slow the men in pursuit.

In the street in front of the pizza shop he did not turn either left or right. Instead he crossed the street in a sprint and ran into the open door of a post–World War Two apartment building. He was not sure if the chasers had seen him enter, but he ran up the stairs in the entryway, taking the steps three at a time, wheezing and grunting with the effort.

The building was four stories tall, and it was connected to other buildings on either side. Clark thought about going all the way to the roof and trying to put space between himself and those chasing him by moving along the tops of the other buildings, just like he and his mates had done in Paris. But when he got to the third floor, he heard noise above, a large group in the stairwell on the fourth floor, heading his way. They sounded like they may have been just a group of young people on their way to a night on the town or a party; by their high voices and laughter they did not sound like a snatch team from the FBI. But Clark was alone now, and he did not want to rush into a group of people who could ID him or tell the men on his tail which way he was heading.

Clark left the stairwell, ran up a hallway, and saw a window at the far end. Outside, under dim electric lights, he could see a fire escape. He charged to the window, half exhausted and nearly out of breath, and pulled it open.

In seconds he was back out in the rain. The fire escape rattled and creaked with his movements, but it seemed like it would hold for his descent of the flights to the alleyway. He had just turned away from the window, grabbed the railing to head to the first set of rickety stairs down, when a man appeared coming up. Clark hadn't heard him climbing with all the noise Clark himself had made coming out of the window onto the fire escape.

"No!" John exclaimed as the man, the same man he had seen watching him in the train station at the ticket kiosk, drew a silver automatic pistol and tried to level it at his prey. But the men were too close to each other on the steep and wet iron steps, and Clark kicked the gun out of the lower man's hand. The weapon flew over the side of the fire escape and the man slipped back, down two steps to the landing just a few feet below Clark.

The two men stared at each other silently for a second. John had his gun on his hip, but he did not go for it. He was not going to shoot an FBI agent or a French detective or a CIA officer or a German cop. Whoever this man was, Clark had no plans to kill him.

But when the man reached inside his raincoat, Clark launched down toward him. He had to close the distance before another weapon came out.

Luc Patin spooked when Clark knocked his weapon away. He reached for a knife he kept in a scabbard on a neck chain under his shirt. He tore the blade free and slashed through the air at the American.

John saw the motion, brought his arm up and knocked away the blow, but took a slashing cut to the back of his hand. He cried out in pain, then he fired out his right hand, palm up and out, and he connected under the chin of the French private detective.

Luc Patin's head snapped back with the punch to the jaw, and he reeled backward and then slipped, his hips hitting the low railing behind him hard, and he tumbled backward off the fire escape. His feet flew into the air as he fell. Clark leapt forward to catch his attacker by his coat, but the rain shower and the slick blood on his left hand caused him to lose hold as soon as he grabbed it, and the Frenchman fell three stories down to the cobblestones.

His head hit with a sound like a baseball bat striking a melon.

Fuck, thought Clark, he had not meant to kill him, but he would have to worry about that later. Now he stumbled off the fire escape at the second floor by forcing open a thick wooden door to a kitchen apartment. He found a roll of paper towels, wrapped his hand in them as he stepped back into the hallway, and then raced downstairs and back out onto the street.

Three minutes later, he walked past the entrance to a subway, and then he hurried back to it. As he headed down the stairs he chanced a glance behind. He saw two pursuers, men in raincoats running together through the rain across an intersection twenty-five meters behind. A Peugeot swerved and honked in their wake. It did not appear to Clark that the men had spotted him, but it did appear that they'd gotten word that their colleague was dead.

John bought a ticket and rushed to the platform of the next train. He held his breath to keep from hyperventilating. *Play cool, stay calm.* He stood near the edge by the track, waiting with a dozen others for the next train.

John could not believe his luck. Somehow he had managed to make it down the steps without being seen by his pursuers, and as he struggled to fill his aching lungs with oxygen, he checked again to make sure he had not been followed. *No.* He could get on a train to anywhere and then make his way to safety.

Well, relative safety.

He felt the cool breeze from the tunnel on his left indicating the impending arrival of the train. He stepped to the edge of the platform so he could be the first one through the doors. A final check to the stairs on his left. Clear. He absentmindedly looked over his right shoulder as the train came out of the tunnel on his left.

They were there. Two men. New guys, but definitely from the same crew. They approached him with hard faces.

He knew he had made it easy for them. On the edge of the track, they needed only a little shove and he would be gone. If they weren't planning on killing him before, he had little doubt that the death of their colleague would change their mission, no matter their original orders.

He turned away from them and faced the tracks. The train was fifty feet away and closing fast, from his left to his right. John leapt off the edge of the platform, down the four feet to the tracks.

The others on the platform screamed in shock.

John crossed the rails right in front of the speeding U-Bahn. A black chain-link fence separated the eastbound line from the westbound, and he had to get over this before the train passed. He leapt onto the fence, pulled himself up with a bloody hand and an arm still aching from a month-old gunshot wound, then he kicked his legs over the fence as the train behind him screeched and wailed. The first car struck his right foot and his heel felt like it had been smacked with a ball bat, and Clark spun off the top of the fence, falling to his hands and knees next to the other track. Like a deer in the head-lights, he looked up to face another train, farther away but barreling down on him from the west. He could hear screams from the platform next to him. He rose and leapt forward, posting on his injured ankle to do so, and made it to the edge of the platform without touching any of the track's rails. He tried to heave himself up on the con-crete before the train came, but the muscles in his arms faltered. He dropped back down, his body spent.

Clark turned and looked at the train that would kill him.

"Achtung!"

Two young men in soccer jerseys came to his rescue. They knelt at the edge of the platform and scrambled to grab his collar and yank him up and over the edge. They were big and young and a hell of a lot stronger than Clark; his worn-out arms tried to help, but they just hung by his sides.

Three seconds later, the train filled the space his body had just vacated.

John lay on his back on the cold concrete, both hands holding his aching ankle.

The men shouted and slapped him roughly on his shoulder. John picked up the word for "old man." One of them laughed, and he helped Clark up, patted him again on the shoulder.

An old woman pointed her umbrella angrily at his face as she chastised him.

Someone else called him an *Arschloch*. Asshole.

John struggled to put weight on his injured foot, then

nodded with a smile at the men who had saved him, and he tottered into the train that had almost crushed him. Inside, he collapsed on a bench. No one else on the platform followed. The train moved, and he looked through the window toward the eastbound platform. His two pursuers were still there.

Watching him escape from their grasp.

53

The White House press corps assembled in the briefing room quickly. An announcement was made that the President would be making a short statement.

Within five minutes, a blink of an eye for those accustomed to waiting on Kealty, the President stepped into the briefing room and up to the microphone. "I have just spoken with officials of both the State Department and the Justice Department. I am told that, well, with a reasonable degree of certainty, that the fugitive John Clark has been implicated in the murder last night at around ten p.m. local time in Cologne, Germany, of a French businessman. I don't have all the details on this just yet; I am sure Attorney General Brannigan's office will have more on this as it develops. This event underscores how important it is that we get this individual into custody. I took a bit of heat from many of my political opponents, many in the Ryan camp, who accused me of only going after Mr. Clark because of the Ryan pardons and his relationship with Jack Ryan.

"Well . . . now you see that this is not politics at all. This is life and death. I am sorry that my vindication for the decision I made concerning John Clark has come at such a high cost.

"Mr. Clark has fled the United States, but I want to assure everyone, including our friends in Germany and all over the world, that we will not rest until Mr. Clark is back in US custody. We will continue to work with our able partners in Germany, in Europe, wherever he goes, and we will find him, no matter what rock he chooses to hide under."

A reporter from MSNBC shouted over his colleagues, "Mr. President, are you at all worried that there is a time limit on this manhunt? In other words, that if you do not win next week and you fail to catch Clark before your term ends, President Ryan will end the manhunt?"

Kealty had begun stepping away from the microphone, but he returned to it now. "Megan, I am going to win the election on Tuesday. That said, whatever support Jack Ryan has, he has not been entrusted by the American people to determine the guilt or innocence of individuals. He tried that before when he gave this murderer a pardon, and . . . well . . . look where we are now. That is a job for our Department of Justice, our courts. Mr. Clark is a killer, a murderer. I can only imagine what there is still to learn about Clark's history. His crimes." Kealty's face reddened slightly. "So to you all in the media, I would like to say that if Jack Ryan tries to sweep this man's past and present crimes under the rug . . . well, you are the fourth estate. You have a responsibility to keep that from happening."

Kealty turned away from the press and left the briefing room without taking another question.

One hour later, Jack Ryan Sr. made his own statement in the driveway of his home in Baltimore. His wife, Cathy, stood by his side. "I don't have any of the details of the specifics of the charges against John Clark. I don't know what happened in Cologne, and I certainly do not know if Mr. Clark was involved, but I have known John Clark long enough to know that if he did, in fact, kill Mr. Patin, then Mr. Patin posed a real threat to John Clark."

A reporter for CNN asked, "Are you saying Luc Patin deserved to die?"

"I am saying John Clark does not make mistakes. Now, if President Kealty wants to go after a Medal of Honor winner, put him on the FBI's Ten Most Wanted list, well, I can't stop him from doing that. But I can promise everyone that John deserves more than this country could ever give him as repayment for his services. And he certainly does not deserve the treatment he's getting from this president."

The CNN reporter interjected, "It sounds like you are saying your friend is above the law."

"No, I'm not saying that. He is not above the law. But he is above this political theater disguised as law. This is disgusting. My wife has quite correctly admonished me in the past for getting a look on my face like I've just bitten a lemon when Ed Kealty is mentioned. I've tried to hide it as best I can. But right now, I want everyone to see how repulsed I am by what is going on relative to John Clark."

As soon as Ryan reentered the house through the kitchen, Arnie van Damm turned to face him. "Jesus, Jack!"

"What I said was true, Arnie."

"I believe you. I do. But how is that going to play?"

"I don't give a shit how it plays. I'm not going to mince words on this. We've got an American hero out there being hunted down like a dog. I am not going to pretend like there is anything else going on."

"But—"

Ryan snapped back, "But nothing! Now, next topic. What's next on the day's agenda?"

Arnie van Damm looked at his boss for a long time. Finally he nodded. "Why don't we take the afternoon off, Jack? Me and my people will let you and Cathy and the kids have the house to yourself. Rent a movie. Eat a pizza. You deserve it. You've been working your ass off."

Jack calmed himself down. He shook his head. "You've been working harder than me. Sorry I jumped on you."

"Lots of stress in a normal campaign. This is not a normal campaign."

"No, it's not. I'm fine. Let's get back to work."

"Whatever you say, Jack."

54

Gerry Hendley lived alone. Since the death of his wife and children in a car accident, he had wrapped himself in his work, continuing on as a senator before leaving public service, and then taking over as the head of the most private spook shop in the world.

His work at Hendley Associates, on the white side as well as the black side, kept him occupied a good sixty hours a week, and even at home he watched the overseas markets on FBN and Bloomberg to keep his edge for the white side of his work, and he read *Global Security* and *Foreign Affairs* and *Jane's* and *The Economist* to keep up with happenings that might affect his job overseeing black ops.

Gerry had trouble sleeping, understandable due to the intense pressures of his occupation as well as the loss he had experienced in his life: most important, the loss of his family, though the death of Brian Caruso the year before and the current situation with John Clark also took a personal toll on Hendley.

Hendley coveted sleep, it was a scarce and precious commodity, so when his phone rang in the middle of the night, it filled him with anger even before his wondering about the news to come filled him with dread.

It was three-twenty a.m. when his phone rang, rousing him from his rest.

"Yeah?" He answered in a gruff and annoyed tone.

"Good morning, sir. Nigel Embling calling from Pakistan."

"Good morning."

"I'm afraid there is a problem."

"I'm listening." Hendley sat up in bed. Now the anger disappeared and the woe appeared.

"I have just learned that your man Sam is missing near Miran Shah."

Now Gerry was up and walking toward his office, heading for his desk and his computer. "What do you mean, missing?"

"The unit of soldiers he was with was attacked by Haqqani network fighters several days ago. There were heavy losses on both sides, I am told. Sam and others were making their escape in a vehicle; my contact, Major al Darkur, was in the front. Your man was in the back. It is possible he fell out of the vehicle on the way to safety."

On the surface that sounded, to Gerry Hendley, like utter bullshit. His first inclination was to think the ISI officer Embling had put up as reliable had double-crossed his man in the field. But he did not have enough data to make that charge just yet, and he certainly needed Embling's help more than ever now, so he was careful to avoid lashing out with any accusations.

He'd been a senator just long enough to know how to talk out of both sides of his mouth.

"I understand. So there is no word on whether he is dead or alive?"

"My man went back to the location of the skirmish with three helicopters full of troops. The Haqqani folks had left their fallen where they lay, and several of al Darkur's men were there, as well. Sam's body was not there. The major thinks it is likely he's been taken by the enemy."

Hendley gritted his teeth. He felt that death in battle might well have been an end preferable to Driscoll than whatever the Taliban had in store for him. "What do you suggest I do on my end?"

Embling hesitated, then said, "I know very well how this looks. It looks like the major has not been truthful to us. But I've been at this long enough to know when I'm being played. I trust this young man. He has promised me that he is working to find the location of your man, and he has promised to keep me apprised of the situation several times a day. I ask you to allow me to relay this information to you as I receive it. Perhaps between the three of us we can come up with something."

Gerry did not see that he had any options. Still, he said, "I want my men to meet this major."

"I understand," replied Embling.

"They are in Dubai at the moment."

"Then we will both come to them. Until we find out how the operation in Miran Shah was compromised, I don't think it is a good idea to send anyone else here."

"I agree. You make arrangements, and I'll notify my men."

Hendley hung up, then called Sam Granger. "Sam? Gerry. We've lost another operator. I want all senior staff in the office in one hour."

Riaz Rehan's second attack on India came two weeks after the first.

While his Bangalore attack was bloody, it could be quickly and easily attributed to a single Lashkar-e-Taiba cell. And while LeT was undoubtedly a Pakistani terrorist organization and virtually everyone in the know realized it was, to one degree or another, backed by "the beards" of Pakistan's ISI, the Bangalore massacre did not scream "massive international conspiracy."

And that had been by Rehan's careful design. To start with a big event that opened the eyes of everyone but did not put too much direct focus on his organization. It had worked, arguably it had worked too well, but Rehan had not yet noticed any detrimental effects of the massive body count, such as wholesale arrests of his LeT operatives.

No, everything was moving according to his plan, and now it was time to begin phase two of that plan.

The attackers came by air, land, and sea. By air, four Lashkar operatives traveling under forged Indian passports landed at the airport in Delhi, and then met up with a four-man sleeper cell that had been there for more than a year, waiting to be activated by their ISI handlers in Pakistan.

By land, seven men successfully crossed the border overland into Jammu, and made their way to Jammu city itself, taking residence in a boardinghouse full of Muslim workers.

And by sea, four rigid-hulled inflatable boats landed at two different locations on the Indian coast. Two craft in Goa on India's west coast and two in Chennai in the east. Each boat carried eight terrorists and their equipment, meaning sixteen armed men for each location.

This put a total of forty-seven men in four different locations across the width of India, and all forty-seven men had mobile phones with store-bought encryption systems that would slow down India's intelligence and military response to the attacks themselves, though Rehan had no doubt the transmissions would eventually be decoded.

In Goa the sixteen men split into eight groups, and each group attacked a different beachside restaurant on

Baga and Candolim beaches with hand grenades and Kalashnikov rifles. Before police could kill all of the attackers, 149 diners and restaurant workers were dead.

In Jammu, a city of more than four hundred thousand, the seven men who'd crossed overland from Pakistan broke into two teams. At eight p.m. the teams blew open the emergency exits at movie houses on opposite sides of the city, and then the men, three in one location and four in the other, ran through the broken doors, stood in front of the movie screens, and opened fire on the huge Friday-night theater crowds.

Forty-three Indians lost their lives at one theater, twenty-nine at the other. Between the two locations, more than two hundred people were injured.

In the massive coastal city of Chennai, the sixteen terrorists attacked an international cricket tournament. Security for the tournament had been beefed up after the Bangalore attack, and this undoubtedly saved hundreds of lives. The sixteen terrorists were wiped out after killing twenty-two civilians and police and injuring just under sixty.

In Delhi the eight-man cell entered the Sheraton New Delhi Hotel in the Saket District Centre, killed the security guards in the lobby, and then split into two groups. Four used the stairs to begin going floor to floor, room to room, to shoot anyone they encountered. The other four burst into a banquet hall and sprayed automatic fire on a wedding reception.

Eighty-three innocents were killed before the eight LeT operatives were hunted down by the Rapid Action Force of the Indian Central Reserve Police Force.

The project manager of the entire assault had been Riaz Rehan; he and his top men worked out of a safe house in Karachi, used voice-over Internet phones attached to encrypted computers in order to stay in touch with the teams of men to help them maximize the lethality of their actions. Three times during the evening, Rehan, known to the terrorists in India as Mansoor, prayed with individual cell members before the men stormed into the guns of police. He had explained to all forty-seven Lashkar men that the entire operation, the entire future of Pakistan, hinged on them not being taken alive.

All forty-seven did as they were told.

Riaz Rehan had deliberately crafted this operation so that it would appear incredibly intricate and over the heads of the leadership of Lashkar, as he wanted the Indians to see evidence of a Pakistani conspiracy against them. This worked as he knew it would, and by daylight on October 30 the Indian government had ordered its military at full alert. Indian prime minister Priyanka Pandiyan and Pakistani president Haroon Zahid both spent the morning huddled with their military leaders and cabinet ministers, and by noon Pakistan had heightened the readiness of its own military in case India took advantage of the confusion of the attacks to reach over the border in retaliation.

Riaz Rehan could not have been more pleased with how events unfolded, because Operation Saker had required such a response to go forward.

Once the India attacks were complete, Rehan and his officers and staff headed to Dubai to avoid the scrutiny of the factions of the non-Islamists in the ISI.

55

The United Arab Emirates was a nation based on commerce and capitalism, but it also possessed a black core of powerful Islamists, men of a darker age. Where these two phenomena met, where ancient religious barbarity and cold hard cash intertwined, was the world of the benefactors of Riaz Rehan.

These men also possessed influence in all facets of the government, spies in the corridors of power, informants in every bastion of life in the Emirates. If Rehan sought information about anyone or anything in the UAE, it was his for the asking.

Which is how he learned that Major Mohammed al Darkur and a British expatriate traveling under a Dutch passport would be landing at Dubai International Airport at 9:36 p.m.

Rehan and his contingent of security and plain-clothed ISI officers were due to arrive in Dubai early the following morning, so the Pakistani general assumed al Darkur and the English spy were in town to get information on him. Clearly al Darkur's operation in Miran Shah, an op that coincided with his training of the Jamaat Shariat troops at the Haqqani camp, indicated that the young major was investigating Rehan. There was no reason he would show up here, now, unless it involved some further interest in the JIM Directorate.

Riaz Rehan was not worried about the major's investigation into him. On the contrary, he saw it as incredibly good fortune that the man and his associate had come to Dubai.

Because while confronting the meddlesome major and his foreign ally in Pakistan could have been problematic for the low-profile ISI general, here in Dubai, Riaz Rehan could, quite literally, get away with murder.

Embling and al Darkur took a private car to their apartment at the incredible Burj Khalifa, the tallest building in the world. They were in town to meet with members of The Campus, but for security reasons Gerry Hendley had forbade his operators from giving either Embling or his suspicious ISI informant any information about where they were staying while in Dubai, so al Darkur himself had made arrangements for accommodations. The massive needle-like skyscraper with 163 inhabitable floors (and a forty-three-story spire topping that) was a quick and easy place for them to find quarters. Embling and al Darkur shared a two-bedroom flat on the 108th floor.

Mohammed did not trust most of the ISI any more than did Gerry Hendley. He had used a personal credit card and handled details of the trip on a computer at an Internet café in Peshawar, lest his own organization get wind of his travel plans.

Once settled in at their flat, Embling called a number Hendley had given him. It connected him to the satellite phone of one of the two Campus operators he had met the year before in Peshawar, the forty-something-year-old Mexican-American who went by the name Domingo.

They made arrangements to meet at Embling's place at the Burj Khalifa as soon as possible.

*

At the same moment Rehan and company's Pakistan International Airlines flight from Islamabad landed at Dubai International Airport, Jack Ryan, Dom Caruso, and Domingo Chavez stood in an elevator in the Burj Khalifa. The elevators at the world's tallest building are, not coincidentally, the world's fastest, and they jetted the three Americans higher into the gargantuan tower at over forty-five miles an hour. They were let into the apartment and found themselves in a large open room with a sunken sitting area in front of floor-to-ceiling views of the Persian Gulf from an altitude nearly that of the top of the Empire State Building.

Nigel Embling stood in the modern living room full of dark wood and metal and glass, in front of the incredible panoramic view. He was a big Englishman with thin snow-white hair and a bushy beard. He wore a slightly rumpled blazer over an open-neck button-down shirt and brown slacks.

"My dear friend Domingo," said Embling with an air of sympathy. "Before we get into the other disaster that has befallen your organization, I must tell you how sorry I am to hear about this affair involving John Clark."

Chavez shrugged. "Me, too. It will get straightened out."

"I'm certain of it."

"Just don't believe everything you hear," Ding added.

Embling waved his hand. "I haven't heard one bloody thing that doesn't sound like just another day at the office for a man in Mr. Clark's profession. I may be old and soft, but I haven't forgotten the way of the world."

Chavez just nodded and said, "May I present my associates? Jack and Dominic."

"Mr. Embling," Jack said as he shook the older man's hand.

Of course the Englishman recognized the son of the former and presumed future President of the United States, but he gave off no hint of his making the connection.

He then walked the three Americans over to the only other inhabitant of the apartment, a physically fit cinnamon-skinned Pakistani in shirtsleeves and black jeans.

They were surprised to learn this was the ISI major. "Mohammed al Darkur, at your service." The attractive man held out a hand to Chavez, but Chavez did not extend his own.

All three of the Campus operators held this man personally responsible for the loss of their friend. While Hendley had been careful not to tip his hat to Embling that he had his suspicions, Domingo Chavez was not about to play nice to the son of a bitch who likely got his colleague killed in the wilds of Pakistan's lawless tribal region.

"Tell me, Major al Darkur, why I shouldn't bash your head against the wall?"

Al Darkur was taken aback, but Embling interjected, "Domingo, please understand. You have little reason to trust him, but I hope you have somewhat more reason to trust me. I have made it my mission in the past months to check the major out, and he is one of the good guys, I assure you."

Dom Caruso addressed the older Englishman: "Well, I don't know you, and I definitely don't know this asshole, but I know what the ISI has been doing for the past thirty years, so I'm not going to trust this bastard until we get our man back."

Ryan did not get a chance to echo the sentiment before the Pakistani replied, "I completely understand your point of view, gentlemen. I have come today to ask you to give

464

me just a few days to work with my contacts in the region. If Mr. Sam is being held by the Haqqani network, I will pull every string I can to either get him released or else get an operation launched to rescue him."

"You were with him when he was taken?" asked Chavez.

"I was, indeed. He fought very bravely."

"I heard it was a hell of a fight."

"Many killed on both sides," al Darkur admitted.

"Can't help but notice that you look none the worse for wear."

"I'm sorry?"

"Where are you hit? Bullet wounds? Shrapnel?"

Mohammed al Darkur reddened as his eyes lowered. "It was a chaotic situation. I was not injured seriously, but men on my left and right died."

Chavez snorted. "Listen, Major. I don't trust you, my organization doesn't trust you, but we *do* trust Mr. Embling. We think it's possible that you have managed to charm him somehow, but don't think your trip here is going to charm us. We will respond favorably to results, not promises. If you and your colleagues can find our man, we want that information immediately."

"And you shall have it, I promise. I have people working on that, just as I have men looking into the Haqqani–ISI connection."

"Again. Results are what impress me."

"Understood. I do have one question, though."

"What's that?"

"I understand you are in Dubai to monitor General Rehan. Is the rest of your team monitoring him now?"

There was no "rest of" Chavez's team, but he did not say this. Instead he replied, "Trust me, when he comes to Dubai, we will be on him."

Now Mohammed al Darkur's eyebrows rose. "My information is that he arrived in Dubai this morning. I assumed I would help you translate any conversations he has at his safe house."

Chavez looked to Caruso and Ryan. Their passive monitoring devices were dormant in the air ducts of the Rehan compound. If their target was here in Dubai, then they needed to return to the Kempinski and begin the surveillance.

Ding nodded slowly. "We have translators. My team will know it as soon as Rehan gets to his place."

Al Darkur seemed satisfied by this, and soon Chavez left the apartment with Caruso and Ryan.

In front of the elevators, Jack said, "If Rehan is here, we could already have missed something important."

Chavez said, "Yeah. You guys hustle back to the bungalow and get on it. I need to head over to the airport and meet the plane to pick up the equipment, but first I'm going to get Embling away from the major and debrief him thoroughly. I'll see you guys back at the place in a few hours."

Chavez spent three hours in discussions in the 108th-floor flat. The first hour was exclusively in a room with Nigel Embling. The British expat spent the vast majority of that time going over everything he had learned about Mohammed al Darkur in the past month and a half. Embling's other contacts within the PDF had convinced him that neither the 7th Battalion of the Special Services Group, called the Zarrar commandos, with whom al Darkur was aligned, nor the Joint Intelligence Bureau, to which al Darkur had been assigned in the ISI, was overrun or heavily influenced by Islamist radicals, as were many sectors of the PDF. Further, al Darkur's own actions leading an SSG unit against terrorist groups in the Swat Valley and Chitral had won him commendations that would have made him a target of the "beards" in the PDF.

Last, Embling assured Ding Chavez that he himself had been in the room when Sam Driscoll insisted on going along on the Miran Shah operation. Major al Darkur had been against the American's participation, and had only reluctantly allowed him to go.

It took the full hour, but finally Chavez was convinced. He spent two more hours talking to al Darkur about the operation on which Sam disappeared, and he quizzed him on his staff and the contacts he claimed to be shaking down to get information on the missing American's whereabouts. Finally, sometime around noon, Chavez left the men in their apartment and headed to the airport to pick up the sniper rifle and other gear sent in on the Gulfstream.

Ryan and Caruso returned to their bungalow at the Kempinski Hotel & Residences and activated their passive surveillance equipment across the water, and all three cameras came to life. There was definite activity in the house, though at first none of their cameras revealed Rehan to be present. While they waited and watched the feeds from the cameras and listened to various men speaking Urdu stroll through the entry hall and great room, they called Rick Bell. It was just past two a.m. in Maryland, but Rick promised that he, a technical analyst, and an Urdu-speaking translator would be on station at Hendley Associates within forty-five minutes. Ryan and Caruso recorded all received image and audio captures until then, and they fed them on for analysis.

It was after eleven a.m. Dubai time, some two hours after Dom and Jack arrived back at the bungalow, when a flurry of excitement appeared to take over the guard force in the house. Men tightened their ties and took up positions in the corners of the rooms, more men appeared through the front door carrying luggage, and finally a big man with a trim beard came through the front door. One by one he greeted all the guards standing there with a kiss on the cheek and a handshake, and then he and another man, who seemed to be a high-level officer, entered the great room. The men were deep in conversation.

Caruso said, "The big guy is Rehan. Looks about the same as he did in Cairo back in September."

"I'll e-mail Bell and let him know you have confirmed Rehan."

"I should have shot that fucker back then."

Ryan thought that over. His concerns about Sam in Waziristan and Clark in Europe were eating him up, and he knew it was even worse for his cousin. A year earlier, Dominic's twin brother had been killed in a Campus operation in Libya. The thought of losing two more operators must have weighed extra-heavy on Caruso.

"We're going to get Sam back, Dom."

Dominic nodded distractedly as he watched the feed.

"And Clark will either fix his own situation, or he'll hang out until my dad takes office, and Dad will look after him."

"There's going to be a lot of pressure on your dad not to get involved."

Jack sniffed. "Dad would take a bullet in the chest for John Clark. A few bleeding-heart congressmen aren't going to stop him."

Dom chuckled, and they discussed it no further.

Soon Dominic called Ryan over from where he had been sitting in the bedroom, peering through the spotting scope at Rehan's safe house. "Hey. Looks like everyone is heading back out."

"Busy fucker, isn't he?" Ryan said as he hustled back in to watch on the monitor.

Rehan had taken off the suit coat he was wearing, and now he was clad in a simple white shirt and black suit pants. He and the man who was beginning to look like his second-in-command were standing back in the hall with a group of about eight men, most of the guard force that had come with them from Pakistan, as well as a couple of faces Ryan recognized as being regulars at the house.

The audio was good, Dominic and Ryan could hear every word, but neither man spoke Urdu, so they would have to wait for the translator in West Odenton, Maryland, to translate the conversation in order to put some context to the scene.

Seconds later, Rehan and an entourage left through the front door.

"Show's over for now, I guess," said Dom. "I'm going to make a sandwich."

Twenty minutes after Domingo Chavez left Embling and al Darkur's flat, there was a knock at the door. The Pakistani major was on the phone with his staff in Peshawar, so Embling went to answer it. He knew there was security in the building that would not allow anyone off on this floor of private residences who did not have permission from one of the occupants, so he was not concerned about his security. As he looked through the peephole he saw a waiter in a white tuxedo jacket holding a wine bucket full of ice and a bottle of champagne.

"May I help you?" he asked through the door. Then he mumbled to himself, "By taking that lovely bottle of Dom Pérignon off your hands?"

"Compliments of property management, sir. Welcome to Dubai."

Embling smiled, opened the door, and then he saw the other men rushing up the hallway. He made to slam the door shut, but the waiter had flung his wine bucket aside, drawn a Steyr automatic pistol, and leveled it at Nigel Embling's forehead.

Embling did not move.

From around the side of the doorway, hidden from sight from the peephole, General Riaz Rehan of Joint Intelligence Miscellaneous appeared. He carried a small automatic pistol himself.

"Indeed, Englishman," he said. "Welcome to Dubai."

Nine other men burst into the apartment, past Nigel, with handguns held high.

56

Caruso had finished his sandwich, and he and Ryan were in the process of powering down the bug-bot surveillance devices in order to save battery power. They would wait until evening to fire them up again, hoping that Rehan would be back by then.

The sat phone on the table rang, and Caruso answered it.

"Yeah?"

"Dom? It's Bell."

"What's up, Rick?"

"We've got a problem. When we got into the office, we started at the beginning of your transmission of the audio, so we've been about fifteen minutes behind on the translations."

"Not a problem. Rehan took off a little while ago so we are powering down the—"

"There *is* a problem. We just translated what he said before he walked out the door."

Domingo Chavez was stuck in traffic just a quarter-mile from the exit to the airport. On his way back from picking up his sniper rifle and ammo from the Hendley Associates Gulfstream, he got caught behind a bad traffic accident on the Business Bay Bridge, and now he sat in the BMW, very glad at the moment that the air conditioner was saving him from the brutal heat, because it looked like he'd be going nowhere soon.

In front of him, some three miles away, he could see

the Burj Khalifa reach up into the sky. On the other side of that, all the way over at the coast, was Palm Jumeirah, his destination.

Just then his mobile rang. "Go for Ding," he said.

It was Ryan, his voice rushed and intense. "Rehan knows Embling and al Darkur are at Burj Khalifa! He's headed there now with a crew of goons."

"Shit! Call Nigel."

"I did. No answer. Tried the landline to his place, too. Nobody picked up."

"Son of a bitch!" Chavez said. "Get over there as fast as possible. I'm stuck in gridlock."

"We're moving, but it will be twenty minutes, at least."

"Just haul ass, kid! They are our only link to Sam! We can't lose them!"

"I know!"

In the BMW just west of Business Bay Bridge, Domingo Chavez slammed his hands into the steering wheel in frustration. "Dammit!"

Both Mohammed al Darkur and Nigel Embling had been secured with plastic restraints, their hands behind their backs, their ankles zip-tied together. Rehan had ordered his men to stand the men up against the floor-to-ceiling windows in the sunken living room with their backs against the glass. General Rehan sat in front of them on the long couch, his legs crossed and his arms back over the cushions. He was a man in his element, comfortable here with prisoners at his mercy.

Rehan's men—Colonel Khan and an eight-strong security force—stood around the room. Another sentry remained outside in the hallway. They each carried a pistol of their own choosing—Steyrs and SIGs and CZs were represented in the force, and Rehan and Khan both carried Berettas in shoulder holsters.

If Nigel Embling still harbored any faint shred of doubt as to the trustworthiness of ISI Major Mohammed al Darkur, that doubt was dispelled. Rehan's men bashed al Darkur's face into the glass window multiple times, and the thirty-five-year-old Pakistani shrieked curses at his elder countryman.

Nigel did not need forty years of in-country experience in Pakistan to recognize that these two Pakistanis did not care for each other.

Al Darkur shouted at Rehan. He spoke in English. "What did you do with the American in Miran Shah?"

The calm general smiled and answered in English. "I met with the man personally. He did not have much to say. I ordered him tortured for information about your plans. I suppose your future plans are not as important to me now as they were when I gave that order, seeing how you now have no future."

Al Darkur kept his chin high. "Others are on to you. We know you are working with the coup organizers, we know you have trained a foreign force at the Haqqani camp near Miran Shah. Others will come behind me and they will stop you, *inshallah!*"

"Ha," Rehan laughed. "*Inshallah?* If Allah wills it? Let's see if Allah wills you to succeed, or if he wills me to succeed." Rehan looked to his two guards standing near the prisoners by the window. "It is stuffy in this pretentious apartment. Open a window."

The two guards drew their pistols, turned as one, and fired over and over into a ten-by-ten-foot pane of the thick floor-to-ceiling window glass against which the two prisoners stood. It did not shatter immediately, but as the

473

number of holes increased in the pane, from five to ten to twenty, white fissures spread between the bullet holes. The men reloaded their handguns while the cracking and popping of the glass continued, growing in volume until the massive glass square shattered outward, sending razor-sharp shards falling 108 stories down.

Warm wind blew into the luxury apartment, some pebble-sized flecks of glass with it, and Rehan and his men had to shield their eyes while the dust settled. The whine of the airflow up the side of the building rushing into the open panel in the window forced Rehan to stand up from the couch and come nearer to his prisoners to be heard.

He looked at Major al Darkur for a moment before turning to Nigel Embling, propped against the window glass, hands and legs bound, next to the huge opening to the bright sky. "I've looked into your background. You are from another century, Embling. The expatriate spy of a colonial power that has somehow missed the message that it no longer has any colonies. You are a pathetic man. You and the other infidels of the West have so long raped the children of Allah that you can no longer understand that your time has passed. But now, old fool, *now* the caliphate has returned! Can you not see it, Embling? Can you not see how the destruction of British colonialism has so perfectly set the stage for my ascendance to power?"

Embling shouted at the big Pakistani standing just feet from his face, and spittle flew from his mouth. "Your ascendance to power? Your lot are the ones destroying Pakistan! It is good men like the major here who will lead your country back from the abyss, not monsters like you!"

Riaz Rehan just waved a hand in the air. "Fly home, Englishman." And with that he gave a curt nod to two ISI security men standing near Nigel Embling. They stepped forward, yanked the big man off balance by his shoulders, and pulled him backward toward the open window.

He screamed in horror as they pushed him over the edge, then let him go, and he fell backward, away from the building, tumbling out, head over feet through the hot desert wind, dropping 108 floors toward concrete and steel below.

Major Mohammed al Darkur screamed at Rehan. *"Kuttay ka bacha!"* Son of a dog! Though bound hand and foot, he pushed forward off the glass, tried to lunge at the big general. Two security men grabbed him before he fell forward into the apartment, and they wrestled with him, finally pulling him backward toward the ten-by-ten-foot hole in the floor-to-ceiling glass.

Rehan's men looked up to their general for guidance.

General Rehan just nodded with a slight smile. "Send him to join his English friend."

Al Darkur cursed and shouted and tried to kick. He shook one of his arms away from the man dragging him to the edge, but another gunman holstered his weapon and rushed forward. Together three men now fought the major on the ground in the flecks and chips of broken window glass.

It took a moment, but they gained control of al Darkur. The others in the room stood around laughing as the ISI officer fought with only the movements of his torso.

Al Darkur screamed at Rehan. *"Mather chot!"* Motherfucker!

The three guards dragged Major al Darkur across the floor, pulled him closer to the edge. Mohammed stopped his fight now. The wind racing from the desert floor, up 108 stories of hot glass and metal, blew the cinnamon-skinned Pakistani's black hair into his eyes, and he shut them, squinted tight, and began to pray.

The three gunmen took him under his shoulders, lifted him up, and grabbed him by his belt as well. As one they heaved his body back, ready to launch him forward toward the sun.

But they did not move forward as one. The security officer holding al Darkur's left shoulder lurched away from the window and spun around; he dropped the major and, in so doing, caused the other two to lose their grip.

Before anyone in the room could react, a second man at the window's ledge moved away from the bound major. This man fell backward into the apartment, rocked back on his heels, and tumbled down into the sunken seating area by the sofa.

Rehan turned to look at the man, to see what the hell he was doing, but instead his eyes looked past his guard and toward the cream-colored leather sofa that was now covered in a crimson splatter of blood.

Rehan looked back out the window. In the distance he saw a black speck in the sky a few hundred feet over the Burj Al Arab hotel in the distance. A helicopter? One second later, just as the last man holding al Darkur let go of the major and grabbed his bloody leg while falling to the floor, General Riaz Rehan shouted to the room.

"Sniper!"

Colonel Khan leapt over the sofa and tackled Rehan to the tile just as a hot rifle round raced past the general's forehead.

57

"Get me closer, Hicks!" Domingo Chavez shouted into the boom mike of the headset as he slammed a second five-round magazine into the magazine well of his HK PSG-1 sniper rifle. He'd missed with his last two shots, he was certain, and only by getting closer could he nail Rehan and his men, as they were now running and crawling and scrambling for cover.

"Roger that," Hicks said in a calm Kentucky drawl, and the Bell JetRanger raced nearer to the massive spire-like structure.

Even with the broken windowpane in al Darkur and Embling's place, Chavez would never have been able to identify the location of their apartment had he not also been able to catch a glimpse through his twelve-power scope of something tumbling out of the side of the building, spiraling down toward the ground.

It was a man, Ding knew this instinctively, though he could not take the time to try to identify who was plunging before him to their death. Instead Chavez had to range his weapon for five hundred meters and do his best to line a target up in his mil-dot crosshairs.

Even though Chavez had not spent much range time working on sniper craft in the past year, he still felt comfortable making a five-hundred-meter shot under the right conditions. But the helicopter's vibrations, the downwash of the rotors, the upward movements of the air currents along the skyscraper, all had to be solved in order to make a precision hit.

So Chavez did not go for precision. He did his best to calculate everything he could to the best of his ability, and then he lined up for a gut shot. Center mass on his targets. A man's stomach was not the perfect location for a sniper shot. No, perfect would have been the brainpan. But targeting the upper stomach gave him the greatest margin of error, and he knew there would be some errors in his targeting, considering everything he had to deal with.

He fired from the backseat of the chopper, propping his weapon in the open window. This would absolutely destroy the carefully tuned barrel harmonics of his rifle, but again, getting closer would fix everything.

"Closer, brother!"

"You worry about your gadget. Let me worry about mine," replied Hicks.

To say the call from Chavez to the aircraft twenty minutes earlier had come as a surprise to Chester Hicks was putting it mildly. He had been going through some paperwork with Adara Sherman when his mobile rang.

"Hello?"

"Country, I'm on my way back! I need you to scare me up a helicopter in ten minutes! Can you do that?"

"You bet. There is a charter service right here at the FBO. Where should I tell them you are heading?"

"I need you to fly it, and we will likely be heading into combat."

"You're kidding, right?"

"This is life-and-death shit, 'mano."

A quick pause. "Then get your ass back here. I'll grab us an aircraft."

Hicks had been all action after that. He and Adara Sherman jogged across the tarmac to a dormant JetRanger that belonged to a resort hotel twenty miles up the coast. There were many newer and fancier helos on the tarmac, but Hicks had flown the JetRanger, he'd trained on Bell helos, and Hicks figured the most important factor on this hasty mission ahead of him would be the skill of the pilot, and not the most advanced technology. After looking the craft over for just a few seconds, he sent Sherman to the FBO to collect the keys by any means necessary. He removed the tie-downs and checked the fuel and the oil while she was gone, and even before he sat behind the cyclic, Sherman was back, tossing him the keys.

"Do I want to know what you did?"

"Nobody home. I probably could have snagged some sheik's Boeing wide-body if I wanted it."

Chavez arrived five minutes later, and they were in the air as soon as he strapped in.

While Chavez loaded his sniper rifle, Hicks asked over the intercom, "Where are we going?"

"The tallest building in the world, doubt you could miss it."

"Roger that." He turned the nose of the JetRanger toward the Burj Khalifa and increased his rate of climb and his ground speed.

Rehan and Khan crawled across the tile floor of the apartment toward the door to the hallway. The colonel kept his body positioned between the shooter in the helicopter and his general as they scrambled, until another protection officer slid over next to them both and then covered General Rehan.

Just as Rehan entered the hallway and rolled out of the

line of fire from the helicopter outside, one of his security men grabbed him by the collar and pushed him forward to the elevator. This guard was nearly as big as Rehan himself, a hulking six-foot-three-inch-tall bruiser in a black suit and carrying a big HK pistol. He banged on the down button with his fist, turned to make sure Rehan and Khan were still with him, and then turned back as the doors slid open.

Ryan and Caruso were surprised by the size of the armed Pakistani who appeared right in front of them in the hallway, but they were ready for trouble. Both men held their pistols high. They dropped to their knees as one as the ISI security man's eyes widened. The Pakistani lifted his own gun up into action, but both Campus operators fired into the broad chest of their target at no more than six feet.

The guard did not fall away from them, instead he lunged forward, into the elevator car. Both men fired a second and then a third time, stitching 9-millimeter rounds across his upper torso, but the ISI officer crashed into Jack Junior, pinned him in the corner, and headbutted the American with all the strength remaining in his body. He fired his HK pistol, but his arm had drooped low and the round went through Ryan's pants, just above the knee, somehow missing his leg.

More ISI men in the hallway fired into the elevator now. Ryan was pinned by the dead man, but Caruso had dropped low to the floor and was engaging targets. He caught a half glimpse of General Rehan running away, up the hall in the opposite direction of Embling's apartment, but he had to focus on the men shooting at him and Jack. He shot another of the general's security detail, hitting the man in the lower abdomen, and with another three-round volley he chased the remaining men out of his line of fire, sending them up the hallway, where they disappeared into the stairwell near Embling's flat.

Rehan had already headed into the stairwell, presumably to another floor to take an elevator down.

"Get this big motherfucker off me!" Ryan shouted.

Dom helped roll the dead man over, and immediately he saw blood on Jack's face. "Are you hit?"

Jack ignored the crack he had taken to his right eye and instead reached down to his leg. He'd felt a round brush him there as it passed a fraction of an inch from his knee. He found the hole in his pants, reached inside it, and felt around for blood. When his fingers came back clean he said, "I'm good. Let's go!" And they took off toward Embling's apartment, afraid of what they might find.

Inside, Dominic and Jack ran to al Darkur. The Pakistani major was having no luck trying to cut his cuffs off with a small piece of glass. Caruso pulled out a folding knife and made short work of the plastic restraints, and he and Ryan helped Mohammed up to his feet.

"Where is Embling?" Ryan had to shout it over the ringing in his ears after the gunfire in the hallway.

Al Darkur shook his head. "Rehan killed him."

That sank in for just a moment before Caruso grabbed al Darkur by the arm and said, "You are coming with us."

"Of course."

Dom waved to the chopper, and Hicks peeled his borrowed helo away, heading off with Chavez in the backseat.

Alarms sounded in the hallway here on the 108th floor, but the elevators were still in service. Mohammed, Jack, and Dom had no doubt there would be police in the elevators by now, but no one could have ascended more than a couple dozen floors of stairs since the shooting started, so all three ran to the stairwell and began heading down. They descended eighteen flights in three minutes of frantic running and leaping. Once down to the ninetieth floor they boarded an elevator with a few Middle Eastern businessmen who were slow to evacuate, complaining they had not smelled smoke and doubted there was any real fire. But al Darkur's bruised face, Ryan's bloody eye and nose, and the sopping sweat on the faces of all three of the men shocked the Middle Easterners.

When one of the men lifted his camera phone to take a photo of al Darkur, Dom Caruso snatched the device from the man's hand. Another made to shove Dom back, but Ryan drew his pistol and waved the men back against the wall.

As the elevator dropped at forty-five miles an hour, the Pakistani major and the two American operatives pulled the phones from all three men, stomped on them with their heels, and then stopped the carriage on the tenth floor. Here they ordered the men off, and then hit the button for the lower of two basement parking garages.

Fifteen minutes later, they walked out of the parking exit and into the sunlight. There the three men melted in with the crowd; they passed police and firefighters and other first responders rushing into the building, and headed out into the hot afternoon streets to find a taxi.

While Jack, Dom, and al Darkur raced to the airport, Chavez had Hicks drop him off in a parking lot near the beach. Hicks returned alone to the airport, and Ding took a taxi back to the Kempinski to break down all the surveillance equipment in the bungalow.

Their operation against Rehan here in Dubai was compromised, and that was putting it mildly. There would be no way the three men could go back to the bungalow and wait for Rehan to return; the heat would be turned up too high after the massive shootout. There would be bodies on the evening news in a city that did not have much in the way of crime, and the comings and goings of all foreigners would face tighter scrutiny. Ding had instructed Hicks to call Captain Reid and have the Gulfstream ready to go asap, but Chavez wouldn't be on it himself. He'd need a few hours to clean up all traces of their activities at the Kempinski, and he'd just have to find another way out of the country after that.

Hicks landed the chopper right where he'd picked it up, then met Sherman at the bottom of the stairs to the Gulfstream. She'd given the man working the desk at the FBO ten thousand euros when he'd come looking for the missing helicopter, and she felt reasonably certain he'd keep his mouth shut until they were wheels-up.

Once Jack, Dom, and Mohammed arrived in their taxi, they boarded the plane, and Helen Reid called the tower to let them know they were ready to execute their flight plan.

Their customs departure had been taken care of by Ms. Sherman, with the help of another ten thousand euros.

They flew Mohammed al Darkur to Istanbul. He would make his own way back to Peshawar. They all agreed it would be dangerous for him to return to his home country. If Rehan was willing to take a step as big as his Dubai attack, there was no question he would work to have al Darkur killed as soon as the major returned. But Mohammed assured the Americans he knew a place where he could lie low, away from the elements of the ISI that were plotting against the civilian leadership. He also promised them he would find where Sam Driscoll was being kept and report back as soon as possible.

58

Four days after returning from Dubai, Jack Ryan Jr. had an appointment that he could not cancel. It was November 6, Election Day, and Jack headed up to Baltimore in the late morning to be with his family.

Jack Ryan Sr. headed down to his local polling place in the morning with Cathy, surrounded by reporters. After that he returned home to spend the day with his family, with plans to head down to the Marriott Waterfront to give his acceptance speech that evening.

Or his concession speech, depending on the results in a few key battleground states.

The Clark controversy had hurt him, there was no denying this. Every show from *60 Minutes* to *Entertainment Tonight* had found an angle on the story, and every talking head on the news had something to say about it. Ryan took the high road throughout the last few weeks of his campaign, he'd made his statements regarding his friend, and he'd done his best to frame the story as a political attack on him, Jack Ryan, and not honest justice.

This worked with his base, and it swayed some undecided. But the unanswered questions as to the actual relationship between Jack Ryan and the mysterious man on the run from the government tipped many undecided toward Edward Kealty. The media framed the Ryan–Clark relationship as if the latter were the personal assassin for the former.

And whatever one could say about President Kealty,

there was certainly no chance he possessed *that* particular skeleton in his closet.

When Jack Junior arrived at his parents' house in the early afternoon, he drove through the security cordon, and a few members of the press took a picture of the yellow Hummer with Jack behind the wheel, but his windows were tinted and he wore aviator sunglasses.

When he came in through the kitchen he saw his dad standing there, alone in his shirtsleeves.

The two men embraced, and then Senior took a step back. "What's with the shades?"

Jack Junior took off his sunglasses, revealing bruising around his right eye. It was faint but still gray, and it was plain that it had been much worse.

In addition to the bruised skin, blood vessels in his eye had broken, and much of the eye was bright red.

Ryan Sr. looked at his son's face for a moment and then said, "Quick, before your mom comes downstairs. Into the study."

A minute later, the two men stood in the study with the door closed. Senior kept his voice down. "Jesus, Jack, what the hell happened to you?"

"I'd rather not say."

"I don't give a damn. What do all the parts of your body I *can't* see look like?"

Jack smiled. Sometimes his dad said things that showed him that the old man understood. "Not too bad. It's getting better."

"This happened in the field?"

"Yeah. I need to just leave it at that. Not for me. For you. You're about to be the President, after all."

Jack Ryan Sr. sighed slowly, leaned forward, and looked into his son's eyeball. "Your mother is going to throw a—"

"I'll keep my shades on."

Senior looked at Junior. "Son. I couldn't have pulled that trick over on Mom thirty years ago. It sure as hell won't work now."

"What should I do?"

Senior thought it over. "You'll show her. She's an ophthalmic surgeon, for crying out loud. I want her to check you out. Tell her you don't want to talk about it. She won't like it, not one bit, but you are not lying to your mother. We can keep details from her, but we aren't lying."

"Okay," the son said.

"It's a slippery slope, but we just have to do what's right."

"Yeah."

Dr. Cathy Ryan came into the study a minute later, and within seconds she had led her son by the arm into the bathroom. Here Cathy had Junior sit at the vanity while she held his eye open and checked it carefully with a penlight.

"What happened?" Her voice was clipped and professional. The eye was his mom's area of expertise, and she would, or at least Jack hoped she would, view an injury here more professionally and dispassionately than she would had he hurt something else.

"I got hit with something."

Dr. Ryan did not stop examining her patient to say, "No shit, Sherlock. What did you get hit with?"

Her husband was correct—Cathy did not like her questions about the origins of the injury being deflected.

Jack Junior responded guardedly, "I guess you could say I bumped heads with a guy."

"Any vision issues? Headaches?"

"At first, yes. Bled a little from that cut on the nose. But not anymore."

"Well, he got you right in your orbit. This is a nasty subcutaneous hematoma. How long ago?"

"Five days, give or take."

Cathy let go of his eye and stepped back. "You should have come right over. The trauma necessary to cause this amount of hemorrhaging on the eye and the tissue around it could have easily detached your retina."

Jack wanted to say something clever, but he caught a look from his dad. Now was not the time to be cute. "Okay. If it happens again, I will—"

"Why would it happen again?"

Junior shrugged. "It won't. Thanks for checking it out." He started to get up from the chair.

"Sit back down. I can't do anything for the subcutaneous hematoma, but I can mask that bruising on your nose and orbit."

"How?"

"I'm going to get some makeup to cover that up."

Junior groaned. "It's not that bad, Mom."

"It's bad enough. You are going to have your picture taken tonight, like it or not, and I am sure you don't want that image of you going out to the world."

Senior agreed. "Son, half the newspapers will go to press with a headline about how I smacked you when I learned you voted for Kealty."

Jack Junior laughed at the thought. He knew there was no point arguing. "Okay. Dad wears makeup every time he goes on TV, I guess it won't kill me."

The election returns began coming in during the early evening. The family and some of the key staff sat in the living room of a suite at the Marriott Waterfront, although Ryan Sr. spent much of the evening standing in the kitchen, talking to his kids or his senior staff, preferring to hear reports shouted in from the living room to actually watching all the play-by-play and pontificating himself.

By nine p.m., a tight race turned for the GOP when Ohio and Michigan both went his way. Florida took until nearly ten, but by the close of polling stations on the West Coast, the matter was decided.

John Patrick Ryan Sr. won with fifty-two percent of the vote, tighter than the margin he'd carried into the last month of the campaign, and most news organizations claimed this had to do with two things: the Kealty administration's capture of the Emir, and Jack Ryan's murky association with a man wanted for multiple murders.

It said little for Kealty that Ryan had managed to overcome both of these events to defeat him.

Jack Ryan stood on a stage at the Marriott Waterfront with his wife and children. Balloons fell, music played. When he spoke to the adoring crowd, he thanked his family first and foremost, and the American people for giving him the opportunity to represent them for a second four-year term.

His speech was upbeat, heartfelt, and even funny in places. But soon enough he came around to the two central issues of the election's home stretch. He called on President Kealty to halt his administration's pursuit of federal charges against Saif Yasin. Ryan said it would be a waste of resources, as he would order the Emir into military custody as soon as he took office.

He then asked President Kealty to reveal details of the sealed indictment to his transition team. He did not use the phrase "Put up or shut up," but that was the implication.

The President-elect reiterated his support for Clark and

the men and women in the military and intelligence communities.

As soon as they left the stage, Jack Junior called Melanie. He'd seen her once since his return from Dubai. He'd told her he'd been on a business trip to Switzerland, where he'd banged his eye and the bridge of his nose against a tree branch when he and his coworkers tried their hand at snowboarding.

He missed her tonight, and wished she could be with him right now, here amid all the excitement and celebration. But they both knew that if she showed up on the arm of the son of the former and next President of the United States, it would invite a lot of scrutiny. Melanie had not even met Jack Junior's parents yet, and this hardly seemed like the venue for that.

But Jack found a sofa in one of the suites the Ryan campaign had reserved for the evening, and he sat and chatted with Melanie until the rest of the family was ready to head back home.

59

The offices of Kosmos Space Flight Corporation in Moscow are on Sergey Makeev Street in Krasnaya Presnya, in a modern steel-and-glass structure that overlooks the eighteenth-century Vagankovo cemetery. Here Georgi Safronov worked long hours, diligently managing his personnel, his corporation's logistical resources, and his own intellectual faculties, to prepare for the launch of three Dnepr-1 rockets the following month.

Aleksandr Verbov, KSFC's Director of Launch Operations, was an affable heavyset man. He was a few years older than Georgi, loyal and hardworking. The two men had been friends since the eighties. Normally Verbov dealt with the day-to-day preparations of upcoming space launches without any help from the president of his company in the minutiae of this complicated endeavor. But Georgi had all but seconded Verbov for the much publicized upcoming triple launch. Aleksandr understood that the triple launch was dear to his president's heart, and he also knew that Safronov was as technically adept as anyone in the company. Georgi had held the director of launch ops job himself once before, when Verbov was a senior engineer.

If Georgi wanted to push the launch button himself on the three rockets—hell, if he wanted to work on the pad in the snow to mate the Space Head Modules to the launch vehicles in their silos—well, as far as Alex Verbov was concerned, that was his right.

But Alex was growing suspicious about one aspect of his boss's focus.

The two men met daily in Georgi's office. Here they had worked together on nearly every facet of the launch since Safronov returned from his vacation. Verbov had commented repeatedly on his boss's lean physique after three and a half weeks at a dude ranch somewhere in the western United States. Georgi looked fitter, even if his arms and hands were covered with old cuts and bruises. Cattle roping, Georgi had confided in Aleksandr, was incredibly tough work.

Verbov had asked to see a picture of his boss in a Stetson and chaps, but Georgi had demurred.

This day, like every other, they sat at Georgi's desk and sipped tea. Both men had high-end laptops open, and they worked both together and independently as they dealt with one aspect or another of the upcoming launches.

Alex said, "Georgi Mikhailovich, I have the last of the confirmations that the tracking stations will be online on the required dates. Two southern launches, one northern launch."

Georgi did not look up from his laptop. "Very good."

"We also received the updated spacecraft transit electrical link schematic, so we can troubleshoot any problems with the interface of the American satellite."

"Okay."

Alex cocked his head to the side. He hesitated for more than half a minute before he said, "I need to ask you a question."

"What is it?"

"The truth is, Georgi . . . Well, I am beginning to have some suspicions."

Georgi Safronov's eyes left his laptop and locked on the heavy man across the desk. "Suspicions?"

Alex Verbov shuffled in his chair. "It's just that . . . you don't seem as interested in the actual spacecraft and the orbit of the SC as you do in the launch itself. Am I correct in this?"

Safronov closed his computer and leaned forward. "Why do you say that?"

"It just seems this way. Is there something bothering you about the launch vehicles for these flights?"

"No, Alex Petrovich. Of course not. What are you getting at?"

"Honestly, my friend, I am somewhat suspicious that you are less than pleased with my recent work. Specifically, regarding the LVs."

Georgi relaxed slightly. "I am very happy with your work. You are the finest launch director in the business. I am lucky to have you working on the Dnepr system and not the Protons or Soyuz craft."

"Thank you. But why are you so disinterested in the spaceflight?"

Safronov smiled. "I confess that I know I could leave this all in your hands. I just prefer working on the launch. The technology for this has not changed so much in the past fifteen years. The satellites and communications and tracking systems have been updated since my time in your job. I have not been keeping up with as much of my technical reading as I should. I am afraid I would not do as good a job as you, and my laziness might show in poor results."

Alex breathed a dramatic sigh and followed it with a belly laugh. "I have been so worried, Georgi. Of course you could handle the newer technology! Probably better than me. If you like I could take you through some of the new steps to—"

Alex watched Safronov open his laptop again. In seconds he was back at work. While typing furiously he said, "I will leave that part to you while I do what I do best. Perhaps after the triple launch I will have time for tutoring."

Verbov nodded. Happy that his suspicions had proved totally unfounded. In seconds he himself was back to work, and he did not think of the matter again.

60

Judith Cochrane watched Saif Yasin get up from his concrete bed and make his way toward the Plexiglas wall. A small writing table and a chair had been placed on his side of the glass, and here his phone sat, along with his notepad and pens. On the table next to his concrete bed a tall stack of American law books and other papers were arranged so that he could help the PCI prepare his defense.

The Justice Department had been loosening the strict rules it had set up for the Emir's defense. It seemed like every day Judy got an e-mail or a call from someone at DOJ allowing her or her client access to more information, to more contact with the outside world, to more resources, in order for the PCI to put on a respectable defense. As soon as the path was cleared for Yasin to move to a federal cell in Virginia, then Judy would petition the court for even more access to classified material she and Saif would need to prove that he had been captured illegally and should therefore be allowed to go free.

Paul Laska had confided in Judy weeks ago that he'd learned from the CIA that the men who took the Emir off the streets of Riyadh were ex–CIA men, working in no official capacity with the US government. This complicated things for both sides of the federal case, but Judy was doing her best to leverage this information to her advantage. Laska had said that Ryan himself had some association with the criminals who kidnapped her client, so Judy was planning on threatening the new administration, promising to bring this relationship into the light to embarrass the President of the United States.

She felt she had Ryan dead to rights, and this would make him want to sweep the Emir back under the rug by fulfilling his campaign promise to turn the man back over to a military tribunal.

But she had a plan to stop that.

"Good morning, Judy. You look wonderful today," Yasin said as he sat. His smile was attractive, but Judith saw a hint of melancholy in it.

"Thank you. Before we start, I know you might be feeling down today"

"Because Jack Ryan will be the next President? Yes, I admit it is distressing news. How can your country allow this criminal back into power?"

Judith Cochrane shook her head. "I have no idea. I do not have a single friend or coworker who voted for him, I can promise you that."

"And yet still he wins?"

Judy shrugged. "Large portions of my country, I am sad to say, are in the hands of racists, warmongers, and ignorant fools."

"Yes. This must be true, as there seems to be no justice for an innocent man in America," said the Emir, with a hint of sadness.

"Do not say that. We will find justice for you. I came today to tell you that Ryan's victory is actually a good thing for your case."

The Emir cocked his head. "How so?"

"Because Ryan's friend, John Clark, was one of the men who kidnapped you. Right now the man is a fugitive from justice, but once Kealty's people capture him, he will be offered immunity to tell everything he knows about who he was working for when you were captured. Jack Ryan will be implicated."

"How do you know this?"

"Because it is possible Ryan was directly involved. And even if he was not directly involved or aware of your kidnapping, we will use back channels to threaten him. To tell him that, if you are sent to military custody, we will have no other course of action but to try your case in the media, and we will use the fact Ryan gave a secret pardon as evidence Ryan himself wanted John Clark to be free to kill and kidnap innocents. Ryan might win in the court of law, but in the court of public opinion, with the vast majority of the world media on our side, it will be as if President Jack Ryan himself shot you and kidnapped you. He and his administration will have no choice but to acquiesce to our demands."

"And what are our demands?"

"Minimum security. A reasonable sentence. Something that has you behind bars for the length of his administration, but no longer."

The Emir smiled. "For someone so pleasant and attractive, you are certainly a very shrewd individual."

Judy Cochrane blushed. "I am just getting started, Saif. Mark my words. You will win your case or we will destroy President Ryan in the process."

Now the Emir's grin showed no evidence of his earlier melancholy. "Is it too much to hope that both of these things happen?"

Judy herself grinned. "No. Not too much to hope at all."

It had been ten days since Clark found Manfred Kromm in Cologne. The wanted American had spent the majority of that time in Warsaw, Poland. Clark had no operational reason to go to Warsaw, but his visit became operationally prudent when it became clear his body would need some recovery time after the evening fleeing the men chasing him in Germany. His right ankle had become swollen and purple, the cut on his hand needed time to heal, and every joint in his body ached. His muscles were exhausted, his low back went from a dull ache the morning after the activity to complete spasms on the morning of day two.

Warsaw was not just a town on his way from Germany to Estonia. It was a much-needed pit stop.

Clark used a phony ID to rent a one-star en-suite room at a no name hotel in the city center. He filled the porcelain bathtub with Epsom salts and water nearly hot enough to boil a lobster, and he lowered every bit of his body in it, save for two extremities. His right foot, which was wrapped tight with a bag of ice and compression bandages, and his right hand, which held his SIG Sauer P220 .45-caliber pistol.

The hot bath and over-the-counter anti-inflammatories slowly helped him tackle his spasmed muscles.

In addition to his bumps and bruises, Clark also found himself sick with an incredible sinus infection. Running through the icy rain had seen to that. Again, he used over-the-counter meds to fight this, along with a steady supply of tissues.

Hot baths, downing pills, blowing his nose. Clark repeated this process over and over for almost a week before he felt, not like a young man, but at least like a new man.

Now he was in Tallinn, Estonia, walking past the Viru Gate, the entrance to the cobblestoned Old Town. He'd grown a decent beard in the past two weeks, and he'd changed his dress from the look of a late-middle-aged businessman to the look of a rugged world-weary fisherman. He wore a black watch cap low over his head, a black sweater under a blue waxed-cotton raincoat, and leather boots that kept the mobility in his still sore right ankle to a minimum.

It was a Thursday evening, and the November air was frigid, so there were few pedestrians on the streets. As he headed up the narrow medieval Saint Catherine's Passage, Clark walked alone, feeling also the self-imposed isolation of the past few weeks. When he was younger, much younger, Clark moved in the black as a singleton asset for weeks at a time without noticing a shred of loneliness. He was not inhuman, but he was able to compartmentalize his life so that when he was operational, his mind remained on the operation. But now he thought of family and friends and colleagues. Not so much as to turn around and head back to them but certainly more than he would have liked.

It was weird, Clark thought to himself as he headed closer to his target. More than Sandy, more than Patsy, the one person he wanted to talk to right now was Ding.

It was crazy that his diminutive son-in-law was at the forefront of his thoughts, and he would have laughed at the realization of it if everything going on around him weren't so damn serious at the moment. But after a moment of introspection, it made sense. Sandy had been there with him, through thick and thin. But not like Chavez. Domingo and John had been in tight spots together more often than either man would be able to count.

But as much as he would have liked to, he did not entertain the thought of checking in with a quick phone call.

He had walked by enough public phones—yes, they were still around here and there—that it would have been damn easy to make a quick call.

But no. Not yet. Not until it was absolutely necessary.

No, he was operating in the black, not in the gray. He could not reach out to those who would be the most imperiled by contact from him. He did not doubt for one second that Ding would be taking care of his wife, his daughter, and his grandkids, beyond the reach of photographers and reporters and long-dormant assassins, and any other asshole who would make trouble for the family of the ex–CIA operative.

Even though Ding wasn't here, standing shoulder to shoulder with him, John Clark knew Chavez still had his back.

And that would have to do for now.

Ardo Ruul was the Estonian mobster who had sent the heavies to interview Manfred Kromm. The Russians had a note in a file from 1981 that the KGB had heard rumblings that a CIA heavy named Clark had come to Berlin the day Stasi agent Lukas Schuman was shot dead in a ghost station under East Berlin. The KGB interviewed Schuman's partner, Kromm, and Kromm had admitted nothing. But the loose end was still there, in the Russian's file on John Clark, thirty years later.

So Valentin Kovalenko contacted Ardo Ruul. The Estonian gangster had worked in his nation's intelligence service in his twenties, and now that he was out of government and operating on his own, he did odd jobs for the SVR here and there. Kovalenko asked Ruul to send men to find this Kromm character, if he was still alive, and get to the bottom of the story. Ruul's people found

Kromm in Cologne, Ruul and his men had the old German lock picker come to a meet, and soon Kromm was telling the story that he had never told a soul, even identifying John Clark from a photo.

It wasn't a big deal for Ruul. The Estonian passed the intel on to Valentin Kovalenko, then went home to Tallinn after a long weekend in Germany with his girlfriend, and now he sat in his regular seat in his regular nightclub, watching the lights flash and too few Western tourists bounce up and down on the dance floor.

Ruul owned Klub Hypnotek, a stylish lounge and techno dance room on Vana Turg in Tallinn's Old Town. He came in most nights around eleven, and rarely strayed far from his throne, a corner wrap-around sofa flanked by two armed bodyguards, unless it was to head up to his office alone to count receipts or surf the Internet.

Around midnight he felt nature's call, and he took a circular staircase up to his second-floor lair, waved his bodyguard back downstairs, and stepped into the tiny private bathroom attached to his office.

He pissed, flushed, zipped, turned around, and found himself facing the barrel of a handgun.

"What the fuck?" He said it in Estonian.

"Do you recognize me?" These words were English.

Ruul just stared at the silencer.

"I asked you a question."

"Lower gun please so I can see you," Ruul said with a quake in his voice.

John Clark lowered the pistol to the man's heart. "How 'bout now?"

"Yes. You are American John Clark that everyone in your country looks for."

"I am surprised you did not expect me." Clark glanced

quickly back to the door to the circular stairs. "You *didn't* expect me, did you?"

Ruul shrugged. "Why would I expect you?"

"It's all over the news I was in Cologne. That didn't tip you off that I was looking for Kromm?"

"Kromm is dead."

This Clark did not know. "You killed him?"

Ruul shook his head in a way that made Clark believe him. "They told me he die before you spoke to him."

"Who told you that?"

"People who scare me more than you, American."

"Then you do not know me." Clark thumbed the hammer back on his .45.

Ruul's eyebrows rose, but he asked, "Are we standing in bathroom much longer?"

Clark backed up, letting the man into his office, but Clark's gun remained trained on Ruul's chest. Ruul kept his hands up slightly, though he ran them through his spiky blond hair as he looked toward the window to the fire escape. "You came in through my window? It's two stories up? You need to find rocking chair, old man. You behave like child."

"If *they* told you I got nothing from Kromm, they probably did that because they are using you as bait. My guess is *they* have been watching you, waiting for me to show up."

Ruul had not thought of this. John saw a sense of hope in the man's eyes, as if he expected someone to come to his rescue.

"And if they killed Kromm, they won't have any problem killing you."

Now John saw *this* realization register in the Estonian mobster's eyes. Still, he did not break easily.

"So . . . Who sent you to Kromm?"

"*Kepi oma ema,* old man," Ruul said.

"That sounded like some sort of a curse. Was that a curse?"

"It means . . . 'Fuck your mother.'"

"Very nice." Clark raised his weapon back to the Estonian's forehead.

"If you shoot me, you have no chance. I have ten armed men in building. One bang from your gun and they come kill you. And if you are right about more men coming, then you should think about your own . . ." He stopped talking and watched Clark holster the pistol.

The older American stepped forward, took Ardo Ruul by his arm, spun him around, and shoved him hard against the wall.

"I'm going to do something that will hurt. You will want to scream bloody murder, but I promise you, if you make a sound, I will do it to your other arm."

"What? No!"

Clark bent Ruul's left arm back violently, then drove his elbow into the back of the Estonian's hyperextended elbow.

Ardo Ruul started a shriek, but Clark took him by his hair and slammed his face into the wall.

Close in his ear, John said, "Another pound of pressure and your joint snaps. You can still save it if you don't scream."

"I . . . I tell you who sent me for Manfred Kromm." Ruul said with a gasp, and Clark let up the pressure. "A Russian fuck, Kovalenko is name. He is FSB or SVR, I do not know which. He sent me to see what Kromm knows about you in Berlin."

"Why?"

Ardo's knees went slack and he slid down the side of

the wall. Clark helped him to the floor. There the man sat, his face pale, his eyes wide with pain as he held his elbow.

"*Why*, Ruul?"

"He did not say me why."

"How do I find him?"

"How do I know? His name Kovalenko. He is Russian agent. He pay me money. This is all I know."

From downstairs at Klub Hypnotek, the crack of a gunshot, then screams from women and men.

Clark stood quickly and headed toward the window.

"Where you going?"

Clark raised the windowpane and looked outside, then turned back to the Estonian gangster. "Before they kill you, remember to tell them I am coming after Kovalenko."

Ardo Ruul pulled himself up to his feet with his one good arm and the corner of his desk. "Don't leave, American! We fight them together!"

Clark climbed out onto the fire escape. "Those guys downstairs are your concern. I've got my own problems." And with that he disappeared into the cold darkness.

Both men, American and Estonian, were roughly the same age. They were within an inch of the same height. Not more than ten pounds separated them in their weight. They both wore their salt-and-pepper hair short; both men had lean faces lined with age and hardened by life.

There the similarities ended. The Estonian was a drunk, a bum, prone on the cold concrete with his head propped against the wall and a see-through plastic crate holding his life's possessions.

Clark was the same build, the same age. But not the same man.

He'd been standing here in the dark under the train tracks,

watching the bum. He regarded the man a moment more, with only a brief hint of sadness. He did not waste much energy feeling sorry for the guy, but that was not because John Clark was coldhearted. No, it was because John Clark was on the job. He had no time for sentimentality.

He walked over, knelt down, and said in Russian, "Fifty euros for your clothes." He was offering the destitute man seventy bucks in local currency.

The Estonian blinked over jaundiced and bloodshot eyes. *"Vabandust?"* Excuse me?

"Okay, friend. You drive a hard bargain." Clark said it again. "You take my clothes. I give you one hundred euros." If the homeless drunk was confused for a moment, soon it became clear. It also became clear that this was no offer.

It was a demand.

Five minutes later, Clark strolled into the main rail station in Old Town Tallinn, staggering like a bum from shadow to shadow, looking for the next train to Moscow.

61

Jack Ryan Jr. spent the morning in his cubicle at Hendley Associates reading through reports generated by Melanie Kraft at the National Counterterrorism Center. Melanie's analysis dealt with the recent spate of attacks in India, and speculated that all the disparate cells involved had been run by the same operational commander.

Ryan did feel some shame that he was, figuratively speaking, looking at the work over the shoulder of the girl he was dating, but this shame was offset by the knowledge that he had a crucial job to do. Rehan's escalation of violence, both in North Waziristan and in Dubai, indicated to everyone at The Campus that he was a dangerous and desperate man. Now, looking at Melanie's analysis that indicated similarities in the recent terrorist carnage across India, Ryan could imagine that PDF Brigadier General Riaz Rehan, the director of foreign espionage in the ISI, could well be this character Melanie referred to as Forrest Gump in an e-mail to Mary Pat Foley.

Jack so wished he could take her to lunch right now and fill her in, fill in the blanks missing in her analysis, and pull from the raw intel that she possessed what might answer some of the questions he and The Campus had about their principal targets.

But telling Melanie about his work at The Campus was verboten.

His phone rang, and he reached for it without taking his eyes from the screen. "Ryan?"

"Hey, kid. Need a favor." It was Clark.

"John? Holy shit! Are you okay?"

"I'm holding together, but just. I could use your quick help."

"You got it."

"I need you to look into a Russian spook named Kovalenko."

"Russian? Okay. Is he FSB, SVR, or military intelligence?"

Clark said, "Unknown. I remember a Kovalenko in the KGB, back in the eighties, but that guy would be long out of the game by now. This Kovalenko could be a relative, or the name could just be a coincidence."

"All right. What do you need to know about him?" Ryan was scribbling furiously as he talked.

"I need to know where he is. I mean *physically* where he is."

"Got it." Ryan also thought, but did not say, that if Clark wanted to find this Kovalenko, it was probably because Clark wanted to put his hands around the man's throat. *This Russian dude is a dead man.*

John added, "And anything else you can get me on the guy. I'm flying blind at this point, so anything at all."

"I'll assemble a team to go through CIA data, as well as open source, and we'll pull out every last thing we can on him. Is he behind this smear on you?"

"He's got something to do with it—whether or not he's the nucleus of it remains to be seen."

"You going to call me back?"

"Three hours?"

"Sounds good. Sit tight."

*

A minute and a half after Clark's call, Ryan had a conference call going with a dozen employees around Hendley Associates, including Gerry Hendley, Rick Bell, Sam Granger, and others. Bell organized a team to dig into this Russian spook, and everyone immediately went to work.

It did not take long for them to realize that Clark was right about the family connection; the Kovalenko he was looking for was the son of the Kovalenko Clark remembered from the KGB. Oleg, the father, was retired though still alive, and Valentin, the son, was now the SVR assistant *rezident* in London.

At only thirty-five years old, assistant *rezident* in London was a pretty high-level job, all agreed, but no one could figure out how he could possibly be connected to any operation that the Russians could be running against John Clark.

Next the analysts began searching through CIA traffic looking for information on Valentin Kovalenko. These analysts did not normally spend their days tracking Russian diplomats, and they found it rather refreshing. Kovalenko was not holed up in a Waziristan cave like many of The Campus's targets. The CIA had information, the vast majority obtained through the United Kingdom's Security Service, also known as MI5, about his London apartment, where he shopped, even where his daughter went to school.

It soon became obvious to the analysts that MI5 did not follow Kovalenko on a day-to-day basis. They did show that he had traveled from Heathrow to Domodedovo Airport in Moscow for two weeks in October, but since then he had been back in London.

Ryan began to wonder about Valentin's father, Oleg Kovalenko. Clark had said that he knew of the man, though it didn't sound like John harbored any suspicions that the old man himself might be involved in his current predicament. Still, Jack saw a lot of brilliant analysts all digging into Valentin. He decided there was no sense in his duplicating their efforts, so instead he figured, what the hell, he'd work the Oleg angle.

For the next half-hour he read from the archives of the CIA about the KGB spy, specifically his exploits in Czechoslovakia, in East Germany, in Beirut, and in Denmark. Jack Junior had been in the game for only a few years, but to him the man did not seem to have had a particularly remarkable career, at least as compared with some other personal histories of Russian spies that he had read.

After digging through the man's past, Jack put his name into a Homeland Security database that would tell of any international travel he might have made to Western countries.

A single trip popped up. The elder Kovalenko had flown on Virgin Atlantic to London in early October.

"To see his son, perhaps?" Jack wondered.

If it was a family reunion, it was a damn short one. Just thirty hours in country.

The short trip was curious to Jack. He strummed his fingers on the desk for a moment, and then called Gavin Biery.

"Hey, it's Jack. If I give you the name of a foreign national, and I give you the dates he was in the UK, could you find his credit cards and get me a list of transactions he made while he was there so I can use that to try and track his movements?"

Jack heard Biery whistle on the other end of the line. "Shit."

Biery said. "Maybe."

"How long will it take?"

"Couple of days, at least."

Ryan sighed. "Never mind."

Biery started to laugh. Ryan thought, *What a fucking weirdo.*

But only until Gavin said, "Just messing with you, Jack. I can have that for you inside of ten minutes. E-mail me the guy's name and anything else you have on him and I'll jump on it."

"Umm. Okay."

Ten minutes later, Ryan's phone rang. He answered with, "What did you find out?"

Gavin Biery, mercifully, recognized the urgency in Ryan's voice. "Here's the deal. He was in London, no question. But he didn't pay for a hotel or a car or anything like that. Just a few gifts, and an incidental or two."

Ryan sighed in frustration. "So it sounds like someone else paid for his trip."

"He bought his own plane ticket, put it on a card. But once he was in London he was on someone else's dime."

"Okay . . . Guess that won't do me any good."

"What were you hoping to find?"

"I don't know. Just fishing. I hoped this trip had something to do with the Clark situation. I guess I thought if I could track him for the thirty hours he was in town I could get an idea—"

"I know where he stayed."

"You do?"

"He bought a box of cigars in the gift shop of the Mandarin Oriental at seven fifty-six in the evening, then he bought a box of Cadbury chocolates in the gift shop there at eight twenty-two the next morning. Unless he was just really in love with that gift shop, it sounds like he bedded down there for the night."

Jack thought this over. "Can you get a look at all the rooms that night?"

"Yeah, I checked. No Valentin Kovalenko."

"Oleg Kovalenko?"

"Nope."

"So someone else, not his son, paid his way. Can we get a list of every credit card that held a room for that night?"

"Sure. I can pull that out. Call you back in five?"

Ryan said, "I'll be at your desk in three."

Ryan showed up at Biery's desk with his own laptop, which he opened as he plopped into a chair next to the computer guru. Biery handed Ryan a printout, so Ryan and Gavin both could scan through the list of names of those registered at the hotel. Ryan didn't know what he was looking for, exactly, which made delegating half of the search to Gavin practically impossible. Other than the name "Kovalenko," which Biery had already said was not here, or the highly unlikely discovery of the name "Edward Kealty," he didn't really know what would pique his interest.

He wished like hell he could be sitting with Melanie right now. She would find a name, a pattern, *something*.

And then, from out of the blue, Jack got an idea in his head. "Vodka!" he shouted.

Gavin smiled. "Dude, it's ten-fifteen in the morning. Unless you've got some Bloody Mary mix—"

Ryan wasn't listening. "Russian diplomats who visit the UN in New York are always getting in trouble for drinking all the vodka in their minibars."

"Says who?"

"I don't know, I've heard it before. Might be an urban legend, but look at this guy." He pulled up a photo of

Valentin Kovalenko on his laptop. "You can't tell me he wasn't tipping back the Stoli."

"He's got that big red nose, but what does that have to do with his trip to London?"

"Check for a room with minibar charges, or a bar tab charged to the room."

Biery ran another report on his computer, and as he was doing so he said, "Or room service. Specifically, a liquor tab."

"Exactly," agreed Ryan.

Gavin began going through the itemized credit card charges of the subset of rooms that had ordered room service or charged bar items to their room. He found a few possibles, then a few more. Finally he settled on one charge in particular. "Okay, here we go. Here is a room paid for by an American Express Centurion card under the name of Carmela Zimmern."

"Okay. So?"

"So it looks like Ms. Zimmern, in her one evening at the Mandarin Oriental, enjoyed two servings of beluga caviar, four bottles of Finlandia vodka, and three porno movies."

Ryan looked at the digital receipt on Gavin's laptop. When he saw the three "in-room entertainment" charges, he was confused.

"How do you know they were pornos?"

"Look, they all ran at the same time. I guess Oleg wanted to channel-flip through the chatty parts."

"Oh," Ryan said, still putting this together. He started scrolling through the names on his sheet again. "Wait a second. Carmela Zimmern also booked the Royal Suite the same night. That's nearly six grand. So Kovalenko was in the other room? He was there to see her, maybe?"

"Sounds plausible."

Shit, thought Jack. *Who is this Carmela Zimmern?*

They Googled the name and found nothing. Well, not nothing, there were several Carmela Zimmerns. One was a fourteen-year-old girl in Kentucky who played lacrosse and another was a thirty-five-year-old mother of four in Vancouver who loved to crochet. They looked them over, one at a time, but there was certainly no one that looked like they'd be spending lavishly on five-star hotels or entertaining Russian spies in the UK.

"I'll find the address on her card," Biery said, and he began clicking his keyboard.

While he did this, Jack Ryan Jr. hunched over his laptop, reading through anything he could find on Carmela Zimmerns in social media, on random websites, anywhere in open source. Within a minute of beginning his search, he said, "Holy shit."

"What?"

"This one works for Paul Laska."

"*The* Paul Laska?"

"Yep. Carmela Zimmern, forty-six years old, lives in Newport, Rhode Island, works for the Progressive Nations Institute."

Gavin finished his check of the AmEx card. "That's our girl. Address in Newport."

"Interesting. Laska's PNI is based in New York."

"Right, but Laska *himself* is in Newport."

"So she works directly with the old bastard."

"Looks that way."

When Clark phoned back the call came through the speakerphone in the ninth-floor conference room. All the principals were there, some still poring over the information Ryan and Biery had just dug up.

"John, it's Ryan. I've got everyone here with me."

"Hey guys." Everyone in the room quickly called out to Clark one at a time.

Clark hesitated before speaking. "Where's Driscoll?"

Hendley took this. "He's in Pakistan."

"Still?"

"He's a POW. Haqqani has him."

"Fuck. God damn it."

Gerry interjected, "Look, we have a viable lead on getting him out of there. There is hope."

"Embling? Is he your lead?"

"Nigel Embling is dead, John. Killed by Riaz Rehan." Hendley said it softly.

"What the hell is going on?" Clark asked.

"It's complicated," Gerry said, putting it extremely mildly. "But we're working on that end. Let's concentrate on your situation for now. How are you?"

Clark sounded tired and angry and frustrated, all at the same time. "I'll be better when this gets worked out. Any word on Kovalenko?"

Hendley looked at Jack Junior and nodded.

"Yes. Valentin Kovalenko, age thirty-five. He is SVR's assistant *rezident* in London."

"And he's in Moscow?"

"No. He was there, in October, but only for a couple of weeks."

"Shit," said Clark, and Ryan got the impression from this reaction that Clark was in Moscow.

"There's more, John."

"Go."

"Kovalenko's father, Oleg. Like you said, he was KGB."

"Yesterday's news, Jack. He's got to be eighty."

"He's nearly that, but listen for a second. This guy never goes anywhere outside of Russia. I mean not as far back as Homeland Security's records go. But in October he flies to London."

"To see his kid?"

"To see Paul Laska, apparently."

There was a long pause. "*The* Paul Laska?"

"Yep," said Ryan. "This is preliminary, but we think it is possible that they knew each other in Czechoslovakia."

"Okay," Clark said it with a confused tone. "Go on."

"Right after Oleg's visit to London, Valentin races over to Moscow for two weeks. He gets back to London, and a few days later, the indictment on you drops out of the sky."

Clark filled in what he knew. "When he was in Moscow, Valentin sent a crew of thugs out to get intel on me from sources in my file with the KGB."

"Weird," said Caruso, who'd been silent until now. "If he is SVR, why didn't he send his own people?"

Clark answered this quickly. "He wanted to use cutouts to insulate him and his service from this."

"So Valentin knows about you through Laska?" asked Ryan.

"Looks like it."

Ryan was confused. "And Laska knows about you . . . how?"

Sam Granger answered this. "Paul Laska runs the Progressive Constitution Initiative, the group that is defending the Emir. Somehow the Emir fingered Clark, and Laska is orchestrating this all with Russia because he can't let on that the Emir is passing intel to him."

Hendley ran his fingers through his gray hair. "The

Emir may have described Clark to his lawyers. They, somehow, got a picture of you from CIA."

"So Paul Laska and his people are using the Russians, running their version of a false-flag operation," said Clark.

"But why would the Russians go along with this?" asked Chavez.

"To hobble the Ryan presidency, or maybe even kill it outright."

"We have to go after Laska," said Caruso.

"Hell, no," Hendley said. "We don't operate inside America against Americans, even misguided sons of bitches like him."

A mild argument broke out in the room, with Caruso and Ryan on one side, and the rest of the men on the other. Chavez stayed out of it for the most part.

Clark stopped the argument. "Listen, I understand and respect that. I will try to get more information on my end that we can use, and then I will report back."

"Thank you," said Gerry Hendley.

"There *is* another situation."

"What's that?"

"A crew coming after me. Not Russians. Not Americans. French. One of them died in Cologne. I didn't kill him, exactly, but he's just as dead. Don't guess his buddies are going to listen to my side of it."

The men in the conference room looked at one another for a moment. They had all heard the news about the death of the Frenchman, supposedly at the hands of John Clark. But if Luc Patin was part of a team *after* Clark, that meant there was another force involved in all this. Finally Rick Bell said, "We'll try to find out who they are. Maybe we can look into the dead guy a lot closer than the international media has, try and find out who he was working for."

515

Clark said, "I appreciate it. It wouldn't hurt to know what I'm dealing with on that front. Okay. Got to go. You guys focus on getting Sam back."

"Will do," said Chavez. "Watch yourself, John."

When Clark hung up, Dominic turned to Domingo. "Ding, you've known Mr. C the longest. He sounded tired, didn't he?"

Chavez just nodded.

"How much longer can he go on? The guy's what? Sixty-three, sixty-four? Shit. He's more than twice my age and I'm feeling the effects of everything I've been through the past few weeks."

Chavez just shook his head as he looked off into the distance. "No point in speculating how long his body can hold up to the day-to-day wear and tear."

"Why not?"

"Because if you do what John does, sooner or later, you're going to go out quick. One of the bullets that have been whizzing past his head for damn near a half-century is going to have his name on it. And I'm not talking about that little scratch he got in Paris."

Caruso nodded. "I guess we all have an expiration date on us, doing what we do."

"Yep. We roll the dice every time we go out."

The meeting was breaking up, but the conference room was still full when a call light on the phone console in the center of the table blinked again. Hendley himself picked it up. "Yeah? Good, put him through." Hendley looked to the men standing around. "It's al Darkur."

He punched the conference button to put the call through the speakers. "Hello, Mohammed. You are speaking to Gerry, and the others are listening in."

"Good."

"Tell me you have good news."

"Yes. We have found your man. He is still in North Waziristan, in a walled compound in the town of Aziz Khel."

Chavez leaned over the desk. "What are you going to do about it?"

"I have planned a raid on the compound. At this point I have not asked for approval because I do not want the information to leak out to the men holding him. But I expect the rescue attempt will launch within three days' time."

Chavez asked, "How did you happen to find out about this compound?"

"The ISI has known about the compound—it is used as a prison for kidnap victims of Siraj Haqqani. But the ISI did not have anyone of value held there, so there was no reason to risk tipping our hand about the existence of our intelligence asset that provided the information. I persuaded someone to tell me."

Chavez nodded. "How many gomers you think are there?"

Al Darkur paused on the other end. "How many what?"

"Sorry. How many of Haqqani's people? How much opposition at the compound."

A longer pause. "Maybe you would prefer to not know the answer to that question."

Chavez shook his head. "I'd rather have bad news than no news. Something I learned from a friend of mine."

"I think your friend is very wise. I am sorry that the news is bad. We expect there will be no less than fifty Haqqani fighters billeted within one hundred meters of where Sam is being held."

Ding looked at Jack and Dom. Both men just nodded to him. "Mohammed. We'd like to come over as soon as possible."

"Excellent. You men proved your talents in Dubai. I could use you again."

After the phone conversation with the ISI major, the three Campus operators sat back down at the table. They were joined, again, by Hendley and Granger.

It was clear that Jack, Dom, and Ding wanted to go to Pakistan, and they wanted to be involved in the raid on the compound where, according to the ISI, Sam Driscoll was being held captive by the Haqqani network.

Hendley did not want to send them, but as they pled their case he realized he could not deny them the chance to rescue their friend.

Gerry Hendley had lost his wife and three kids in a car crash, he'd lost Brian Caruso the year before in a Campus mission that he approved, and these facts were not lost on the other men in the room.

Gerry wanted Sam back as much as or more than anyone else on the team.

He said, "Men. Right now, like it or not, Clark is on his own. We will support him here, in any way we can, if he checks in with us and requests more help.

"This opportunity to go after Sam." Hendley just shook his head. "It sounds like a shit sandwich. It sounds really dicey. But I will never be able to live with myself if I don't allow you guys the chance to go after him. It is up to the three of you."

Chavez said, "We'll go to Pesh and talk to al Darkur. I trust him. If he says the men who are leading the raid are on the up-and-up . . . well . . . that's about all we can ask for, isn't it?"

Hendley agreed to let them go, but he was under no illusions they were just going to feel the situation out. He could tell by the looks in their eyes that these three men would be heading into battle, and he wondered if he could live with himself if they did not come back.

62

General Riaz Rehan sent a message to all of the organizations under his control. Not to the leadership of the organizations but to dozens of individual cells. The active units in the field were the men Rehan trusted to do their duty to his cause, and he took the time to spend the day in communication via e-mail, Skype, and sat phone, ordering them all into action.

India was the target. D-Day was now.

Attacks began within hours. Along the border between the countries, deep in the Indian interior, even Indian embassies and consulates in Bangladesh and other countries were attacked.

To those asking "Why now?" the answers varied. Many in the world press blamed President-elect Jack Ryan for his verbal attacks on the weak Pakistani government, but those in the know could tell the coordination necessary for these actions meant the plans had been in place for some time, long before Ryan promised he would back India if Pakistan did not end its support for terrorism.

Most people also knew that there was no reason to ask "Why now?" because although the scale of the conflict had increased in the past month, the conflict itself had been going on for decades.

The operation that Riaz Rehan had put into action in the past months, beginning with the attack on the Electronics City tollway in Bangalore, had come to him in a dream many years before, in May of 1999. At that time,

India and Pakistan were in the midst of a brief border skirmish that became known as the Kargil War. Pakistani forces crossed the Line of Control between the two nations, small battles raged, and artillery shells crashed down inside the borders of both countries.

Rehan was there on the border at the time, organizing militant groups in Kashmir. He had heard a rumor, later proven true, that Pakistan had begun readying some of its nuclear arsenal. The Pakistanis had possessed nuclear weapons for more than a decade by this point, although their first test of an atomic weapon had just taken place the year before. They had nearly one hundred warheads and air-to-ground bombs, all kept disassembled but ready for quick assembly and deployment in case of national emergency.

That night, sleeping in a mountain redoubt straddling the Line of Control, Rehan dreamt nuclear weapons were brought to his hut by a large saker falcon. The saker ordered Rehan to detonate warheads on both sides of the border in order to create an all-out nuclear war between the two nations. He set off the weapons along the border, the war escalated to the cities, and out of the ashes of the radioactive fires Rehan himself emerged as caliph, the leader of the new caliphate of Pakistan.

Since the night of the dream, he had thought of the falcon and the caliphate each and every day. He did not see his dream as the ruminations of a manipulative mind pulling data out of the real world and spinning it subconsciously into fantasy. No, he saw his dream as a message from Allah—operational orders, just like he would obtain directives from his ISI handlers, and just like he would relay his orders on to the cells under his control.

Now, thirteen years later, he was ready to put his plan

into practice. Operation Saker he called it, in honor of the falcon who came to him in the dream.

Over time he had seen it become necessary to change the operation somewhat. He realized India, with many, many more nuclear devices than Pakistan and better delivery capabilities, would destroy Pakistan if a true nuclear war broke out. Plus, Rehan realized, India was not preventing Pakistan from becoming a true theocracy. No, Pakistan itself was the impediment—or more precisely, the Pakistani secularists.

So he decided instead to use the theft of nuclear devices to topple the weak civilian leadership of his country. The citizenry would accept military rule, they had done so many times before, but not if it turned out the ISI or the PDF had stolen the nukes themselves to effect the change in leadership. So Rehan devised a plan to hand off the nukes to some Islamic militant group outside Pakistan, to throw off the scent that the entire operation was an inside job.

Once the government fell Rehan would take control and he would purge the military of secularists, and he would unleash his force of militant groups on secularists within the citizenry.

And Rehan would become caliph. Who better than he, after all? He had become, through years of following the orders of others, a one-man conduit between all the Islamic organizations fighting on behalf of the Islamists in the military. Without Rehan, the ISI could not control Lashkar-e-Taiba, they would not have the support of Al-Qaeda that they enjoyed, they would not have the other twenty or so groups doing their bidding, and they certainly would not possess the money and support that they received from Rehan's personal benefactors in the Gulf States.

General Rehan was not known in his country at large, he was very much the opposite of a household name, but his return to the PDF and his ascension to department director in the ISI had given him the status he needed to lead a coup against the secular government in charge when the time was right. He would have the support of the Islamists in the Army, because Rehan had the support of the twenty-four largest mujahideen groups in the country. The ISI's success depended on this large unco-ordinated but quite powerful proxy force, and the ISI/PDF leadership had created in their man Rehan something of a necessary link between themselves and their crucial civilian army.

Rehan was no longer just the cutout. Rehan had, by his work, his intelligence, and his guile, made himself a secret king, and Operation Saker was his route to his throne.

63

Domingo Chavez, Dominic Caruso, and Jack Ryan Jr. stepped out of the AS332 Super Puma helicopter and into a freezing cold predawn. Though none of the three men had a clue just where they were as far as a point on a map, they all knew from conversations over the satellite phone with Major al Darkur that they were being transported to an off-limits military base in the Khyber Agency run by the Pakistani Defense Force's Special Service Group. In fact they were in Cherat, some thirty-five miles from Peshawar, in a compound resting at 4,500 feet.

This commando camp would be the staging ground for the SSG hit into North Waziristan.

The American men were led by stone-faced hardened soldiers to a shack near a parade ground on a flat stretch of dirt surrounded by lush hills. Here they were offered hot tea and shown racks of gear, woodland-camouflage uniforms in brown and black over green, and black combat boots.

The men changed out of their civilian dress. Ryan had not worn a uniform since high school baseball; it felt strange and somewhat disingenuous to dress like a soldier.

The Americans were not given the maroon berets worn by the rest of the SSG men in the compound, but otherwise their dress looked identical to the others in the camp.

When all three men were decked out in the same kit, another helicopter landed on the helipad. Soon Major al

Darkur, himself dressed in identical combat fatigues, stepped into the shack. The men all shook hands.

The major said, "We have all day to go over the mission. We will attack tonight."

The Americans nodded as one.

"Is there anything at all that you need?"

Chavez answered for the group: "We're going to need some guns."

The major smiled grimly. "Yes, I believe you will."

At eight a.m. the three Campus operatives stood on the base's rifle range, test-firing their weapons. Dom and Jack were outfitted with the Fabrique Nationale P-90 automatic rifle, a space-age-looking weapon that was excellent for close-quarters combat due to a bull-pup design, which shortened the length of the barrel that extended past the body of the user. This helped an operator move through doorways without telegraphing his movements in advance with a protruding barrel.

The gun also fired a potent but light 5.7-millimeter x 28-millimeter round from a hearty fifty-round magazine.

Chavez opted for a Steyr AUG in 5.45-millimeter. It had a longer barrel than the P-90, which made it more accurate at distance, as well as a 3.5x power scope. The Steyr might not have been as good as the P-90 for close-in operations, but Chavez was first and foremost a sniper, and he felt the weapon was a fair trade-off.

Chavez worked with the two younger men on their rifles, had them practice magazine changes while standing, kneeling, and lying prone, and firing the guns on semiauto and full auto while stationary and on the move.

They also trained with three different types of grenades they would bring in on the op. Small Belgian mini-frag grenades, M84 stun grenades that delivered an incredible flash and bang after a two-second delay, and a 9-banger stun/distraction device that gave off nine less powerful explosions in rapid succession.

During a break in the action to reload their mags, Major al Darkur appeared on the far side of the large outdoor range carrying an M4 rifle and a metal can of ammunition. Chavez had his two less experienced partners continue while he stepped over to the dark-skinned Pakistani.

"What are you doing?" Ding asked.

"I am test-firing my rifle."

"Why?"

"Because I am going with you." The major placed Oakley protective glasses over his eyes. "Mr. Sam was my responsibility, and I failed. I will accept responsibility for getting him back."

Chavez nodded. "I'm sorry I doubted you before."

Al Darkur shrugged. "I do not blame you. You were frustrated about losing your friend. If the situation had been reversed, I would have felt the same outrage."

Ding put a gloved hand out, and Mohammed shook it.

Al Darkur asked, "Your men. How are they?"

"They are good, but they don't have much experience. Still, if your commandos occupy the forces at the perimeter, and the three of us move as a team through the compound, then I think we will be okay."

"Not three of you. Four of us. I will go inside the compound with you."

Now Chavez's eyebrows rose. "Major, if you are bluffing, you are shit out of luck, because I am not going to turn you down."

Mohammed flipped the safety off his rifle and fired five

quick shots downrange, each bullet banging against its target, a small iron plate that gave off a satisfying clang. "It is no bluff. I got Nigel and Sam into this. I cannot help Nigel, but perhaps I can help Sam."

"You are welcome on my team," said Chavez, immediately impressed with the Pakistani man's shooting.

"And when you have your man back," al Darkur continued, "I hope your organization will continue its interest in General Rehan. You seem to take him as a serious threat, as do I."

"We do, indeed," admitted Chavez.

The afternoon in Cherat was spent in a briefing by the Zarrar commandos, the unit that would head into North Waziristan with the Americans. The briefing was led primarily by a captain who explained what everyone should do, and what everyone should see, up until the moment when the Americans went inside the main building, where intelligence reports had indicated the prisoners were being kept.

The SSG captain used a marking board and an authoritative voice. "The helo carrying the Americans will land directly in front of the gate, and the three Americans will depart and then breach the gate. We cannot land in the courtyard inside due to electrical wires. Our four helicopters will then go to points above the four walls of the camp and circle there, and we will provide covering fire for the entry team. This should occupy enemy forces in the building outside of the camp as well as those in the courtyard or those in windows. But it will do nothing for the entry team once they are inside the buildings themselves. We have no intelligence as to what the inside of the camp looks like, nor do we know where the prisoners are being held. Unfortunately, the Haqqani network captives at our disposal have not been into the main building itself, only to the barracks on the eastern side."

Caruso asked, "Any idea as to numbers of opposition?"

The captain nodded. "Roughly forty to fifty men in the barracks, but again, our intention is to keep those men in their buildings so they cannot come into the main building behind you. There are another ten guards outside at any one time."

"And inside the main building?"

"Unknown. Completely unknown."

"Awesome," muttered Caruso.

The captain handed each of the Americans a small LED device called a Phoenix. Ding was very familiar with the beacon. It was an infrared strobe that could be seen at night by the helicopter crews and, theoretically at least, reduce the chance that Chavez and his mates would fall victim to fratricide during the attack.

"I need your men wearing these at all times."

"You got it," said Chavez.

Al Darkur and his American associates were also warned to stay away from any windows while they were in the building, as the Puma helicopters would be full of marksmen targeting movement there. The blinking strobes would be impossible to see from all angles, especially through doorways and windows.

After the briefing, Mohammed asked Chavez what he thought about the operation. The American chose his words carefully. "It's a little thin, to tell you the truth. They are going to take some casualties."

Mohammed nodded. "They are accustomed to that. Would you like to make some suggestions to make it better?"

"Would they listen?"

"No."

Ding shrugged. "I'm just a passenger on this bus. We all are."

Al Darkur nodded and said, "They will take us along so that we can go after Sam, but please remember, they will not enter the compound. The four of us will be on our own."

"I understand, and I appreciate you shouldering the danger with us."

The men were told to rest for a few hours before rallying at the helicopters at midnight. Chavez drilled his two younger partners for a couple more hours, and then all three men cleaned and lubed their weapons, before returning to a small hootch near the barracks to lie down on cots. But no one could sleep. They were just hours away from imminent danger.

Chavez had spent the entire day getting the two cousins as ready as he possibly could for the action they were about to undertake. He doubted it was enough. *Shit,* Ding thought, this operation needed a full Rainbow squadron, but that wasn't possible. He told the cousins something Clark had told him, way back when, on missions where they were poorly equipped.

"You've got to dance with the one that brought you."

If the Zarrar commandos were as tight as their reputation, they'd have a shot at this.

And if not? Well, if not, then the conference table at Hendley Associates was about to have three more empty chairs.

Sitting in the hooch, Ding caught Ryan's eyes drifting away, like the kid was daydreaming. Caruso seemed a bit overwhelmed by what was ahead as well. Ding said,

"Guys, listen carefully. Keep your head in the game. You've never ever done anything even remotely like what you are about to do. We're going to be up against, easily, fifty enemy."

Caruso smiled grimly. "Nothing like a target-rich environment."

Chavez grunted. "Yeah? Tell that to General Custer."

Dominic nodded. "Point taken."

The sat phone on Chavez's hip rang just then, so he stepped outside to take the call.

While Chavez was outside, Ryan thought about what he had just said. No, he'd never done anything like this. Dom, sitting next to him and reloading his pistol, had not either. The only guys on this force who were ready for a mission like this were Chavez, who would be, thank God, leading the way; Driscoll, who was somewhere at their target location, shackled in a cell maybe; and Clark, who was on the run from his own government, as well as others.

Shit.

Chavez leaned back into the door, behind him the lights from the helicopters shone and the noises of men assembling gear nearby rattled like a distant train. "Ryan. Phone."

Jack climbed off the cot and headed outside. "Who is it?"

"It's the President-elect."

Damn. This was hardly the time for a familial chat, but Jack realized that he truly wanted to hear his father's voice to help calm his nerves.

He answered with a joke. "Hey, Dad, are you the Prez yet?"

But Jack Ryan Sr. made it clear instantly that he was not in a playful mood. "I had Arnie contact Gerry Hendley.

He says you are overseas in Pakistan. I just need to know that you are safe."

"I'm fine."

"Where are you?"

"I can't talk about—"

"Damn it, Jack, what's going on? Are you in danger?"

Junior sighed. "We are working with some friends over here."

"You have to choose your friends carefully in Pakistan."

"I know that. These guys are risking everything to help us."

Ryan Sr. did not respond.

"Dad, when you get in office, are you going to help Clark?"

"When I get back to Washington, I'll move mountains to get his indictment overturned. But for now he is on the lam, and there is not a damn thing I can do about it."

"Okay."

"Do I hear helicopters in the background?"

"Yes."

"Is something going on?"

He knew he could have lied right now, but he did not. It was his father, after all. "Yes, something *is* going on, something much bigger than a couple weeks ago, and I'm in the middle of it. I don't know how it's going to play out."

A long pained pause on the other end of the line. Finally Ryan Sr. said, "Can I help?"

"Right this minute, no. But you definitely *can* help."

"Just say the word, son. Anything I can do."

"When you get into office, do whatever you can to help the CIA. If you can get them as strong as they were when you were President last time, then I'll be a lot better off. We all will."

"Trust me, son. Nothing is more important. Once I get—"

Chavez and Caruso stepped out of the hooch with greasepaint on their faces and their bodies laden with gear. "Dad . . . I need to go."

"Jack? Please be safe."

"Sorry, but I can't be safe *and* be here. And my job is here. You've done things . . . you know how it is."

"I do."

"Look. If something happens to me. Tell Mom . . . just . . . just try to make her understand."

Jack Junior heard nothing on the other end, but he sensed his father, stoic though he was, was in agony with the knowledge that his son was in imminent danger, and there was not a damn thing he could do to help him. The younger Ryan hated himself for putting his father in this position, but he knew he did not have time to undo the damage he had just caused by making him worry.

"Got to run. I'm sorry. I'll call when I can." *If I can,* he thought, but he did not say it.

And with that, Jack disconnected the phone and handed it back to Chavez, then stepped back into the little hut to grab his weapon.

64

The four Puma helicopters crossed into North Waziristan just after three a.m. The fat choppers flew low and close together to mask their approach, using roads through the mountains and deep river valleys to direct them toward their target of the town of Aziz Khel.

Ryan fought nausea as he sat on the floor of the helo, looking out at the dark landscape outside. He actually got to the point where he wanted to vomit all over himself to rid himself of any food or water in his stomach so that he might recover before go time. But he did not throw up, he just sat there, pinned tightly between Mohammed al Darkur on his right and Dom on his left. Chavez faced them, and five more Zarrar commandos sat with them in the chopper, along with a door-gunner manning a 7.62-millimeter machine gun and a loadmaster who rode up front near the two pilots.

The other choppers would be loaded up much the same.

Chavez shouted over the engines' roar, "Dom and Jack. I want you two guys on my back the whole time we're inside the walls. Keep your weapons at the high and ready. We move as a unit."

Ryan had never experienced terror like this in his entire life. Everyone for fifty miles in every direction, save for the men in the four choppers, would kill him if they saw him.

Al Darkur had been wearing a headset to communicate with the flight crew, but he pulled it off and replaced it with his helmet. He then leaned over to Chavez and yelled, "It is almost time. They will circle for ten minutes! No more! Then they leave us."

"Got it," Ding answered back.

Ryan leaned forward into Chavez's black-greased face. "Is ten minutes enough time?"

The diminutive Mexican-American shrugged. "If we get bogged down in the building, we're dead. The whole place, inside and out, is crawling with Haqqani's forces. Every second we are in there is a second some gomer has to draw a bead on us. If we aren't out in ten minutes, we ain't coming out, *'mano.*"

Ryan nodded, leaned away, and looked back out the window toward the undulating black hills below.

The chopper lurched up dramatically, and Jack spewed vomit against the glass.

Sam Driscoll had no idea if it was day or night. Usually he could make a guess as to the time of day going by the guard rotation or whether or not his meal was just bread (morning), or bread with a small tin of watery broth (night). After weeks in captivity he and the two men still held with him had begun to think that the guards had switched the meals up to confuse them.

A Reuters reporter from Australia was in the cell next to him. His name was Allen Lyle, and he was young, not over thirty, but he was sick with some sort of stomach virus. He had not been able to keep anything down for the past few days. In the furthest cell, the one closest to the door to the hallway, an Afghani politician was held. He'd been here only a few days, and he was getting occasional beatings from the guards, but he was in otherwise good health.

Sam's legs had healed for the most part in the past

month, but he had a significant limp and he could tell he had not avoided infection altogether. He felt weak and sick and he perspired through the night, and he'd lost a great deal of weight and muscle tone lying on his rope cot.

He made himself stand and hobble over to the bars so that he could check on the young guy from Reuters. For the first week or so the man badgered him relentlessly, asking him who he worked for and what he was doing when he was captured by the Taliban. But Driscoll never answered the guy's questions, and the Reuters man finally gave up. Now it looked like the Reuters man might give up on his life within a few days.

"Hey!" Sam shouted. "Lyle! Wake up!"

The reporter stirred. His eyes opened to half-mast. "Is that a helicopter?"

Fucking delirious, Sam thought. *Poor bastard.*

Wait. Sam heard it now, too. It was faint, but it *was* a chopper. The Afghan by the door stood and looked back to Sam for some confirmation as to what he was hearing.

The three jailers outside the cell heard it, too. They looked at one another, then stood and peered down the dark hallway, shouting to a guard somewhere out of Driscoll's sight.

One of the men made a joke, and the three laughed.

The Afghani politician looked to Driscoll and said, "They say it is President Kealty coming to look for you and the reporter."

Sam sighed. It wasn't the first time they'd heard Pakistani Army choppers overhead. They always faded after a couple of seconds. Driscoll turned to go sit back down.

And then . . . *Boom!*

A low crack erupted somewhere above him. Sam turned back to the hall.

Machine-gun fire came soon after. And then another explosion.

"Everybody get down on the floor!" Driscoll shouted to the other prisoners. If this was a rescue attempt by the PDF, and if there was any shooting down here, even out in the hall, then there would be ricocheted rounds banging all around this stone-walled basement, and friendly fire would hurt just as bad as enemy fire.

Sam started to look for some measure of cover himself, but one of the jailers came to his cell. The man's eyes were wide with fear and determination. Sam got the impression this fucker was going to use him as a human shield if the PDF made it down into the basement.

They'd been off the helicopter for nearly two minutes, and Jack Ryan had not yet seen the enemy. First they dropped into a knee-deep trash pit some one hundred yards from the target. Jack could not understand why the pilot had dumped them so far from their target until, upon running closer to the compound, they saw several rows of electricity poles and wires crisscrossing the open ground in front of the main gate.

Then, while Chavez set the water-tamped breaching charge at the perimeter gate, Jack, Dom, and Mohammed watched his six. They dropped to their knees and scanned the dark rooftops and gates of a cluster of walled compounds on the other side of a rocky plain, and they kept their eyes on the corners of the wall of the Haqqani compound to the north and south. Above them the big Puma choppers circled, occasionally emitting jackhammer bursts from door guns or staccato cracks from Zarrar commandos firing their small arms into the compound. A twenty-millimeter cannon fired from one of the fat birds sent explosive rounds into the hillside beyond the compound in order to let the forty Taliban supposedly in the barracks know that they needed to stay right where they were.

Finally, over the hellacious sounds from above, Jack heard, "Fire in the hole!" and he found cover by pressing himself against the fourteen-foot-high baked-brick wall. Just seconds after this came the boom of the breaching charge, blowing the black oak and iron gates of the compound in like tossed toothpicks.

And then just like that, they were inside the walls, running for the main building, thirty yards ahead. Ryan saw the long low barracks some forty yards off his right shoulder, and just as he looked tracer rounds kicked up sparks near the dark structure from machine guns fired from above.

Jack was tight on Dom's heels and Mohammed was just behind Jack, all the men running behind Chavez, who led the way with his AUG at his shoulder.

Jack was surprised when Chavez fired his rifle ahead. Ryan looked to see where the bullets were impacting and saw they were tearing up a small building or garage to the left of the main house. From there a bright light flashed and a rocket-propelled grenade launched into the sky but it seemed to have been poorly aimed.

Ding fired again and again, Ryan got his P-90 up to send some rounds downrange himself, but the team arrived at the wall of the main house before he even found a target in the night.

They scooted down the wall, closer to the front door, Ding still in the lead. Chavez nodded to Caruso, who quickly raced across the closed door and pressed up against the wall on the other side. Chavez nodded to Ryan, who started to pull a stun grenade from a pouch hanging on his right thigh. But as he reached for it he saw a second and a third RPG flying through the air, launched from the grounds behind the main building. Both grenades looked like they were perfectly aimed at a Puma that flew nearest to the barracks buildings.

And they were. The first RPG streaked right by the pilot's windscreen, and the second slammed into the tail just aft of the two engines. Ryan stood fascinated, watching as the tail exploded and the aircraft spun away to the right, turned nose down, and disappeared behind a plume of black smoke.

The crash came outside the wall, lower on the rocky plain.

Immediately one of the three remaining helicopters veered out of its tight circular pattern around the Haqqani compound and flew off toward the crash.

"Shit!" said Chavez. "We're losing our cover. Let's go!"

65

Dom kicked open the front door of the house, and Ryan tossed his stun grenade into the entry hall, staying just to the left of the doorway and out of the line of fire from inside the building.

Boom!

All four men rushed in; Dom and Ryan went to the right and Ding and Mohammed shifted to the left alongside the wall. They used flashlights mounted onto their weapons to illuminate a dark open room. Almost instantly Dominic saw movement through a doorway on the right. He shifted his light's beam, it flashed off the metal of a rifle, and Caruso fired a ten-round string of fire into the doorway.

A bullet-riddled bearded man fell out into the room by a wooden table, his Kalashnikov tumbled out of his hands.

Behind them in the courtyard, small-arms fire crackled. These were not guns fired from circling Pumas. No, these were AKs from the compound's guard force. The fire picked up, and it became clear that the men in the barracks had broken out; they were either targeting the choppers or heading toward the main building. Perhaps both.

Chavez, Caruso, Ryan, and al Darkur moved in a tactical train down a low hallway, clearing a few rooms on the left and right as they moved, using the same "wall-flood" tactics they had used to breach the first room. They'd hit a doorway, enter fast with guns high and lights on, the first and third men moving up the wall to the left of the entrance and the second and fourth men going right.

After the third empty room they came back into the hallway, and Mohammed al Darkur cut down two men trying to enter the front doorway. After that he dropped to his kneepads, keeping his gun trained on the door where men from the barracks would enter.

"Keep going! I'll keep them back!"

Chavez turned and led the way, with Ryan and Caruso right on his heels.

They made a turn, Ding shot at a gunman retreating up a staircase on his left, then knelt to reload his gun. There was another stone staircase on the right, heading down into a basement enshrouded in darkness.

Outside, large RPG explosions were mixing with small-arms fire.

Domingo turned back to the others, now shouting over the sound of al Darkur's cracking rifle. "We don't have any time! I'll check upstairs, you guys go down! Meet back here, but watch out for blue-on-blue fire!"

With that Chavez hustled up the stairs and out of view.

Caruso took a tentative lead down into the basement, shining his light ahead of him. He'd gotten no more than halfway down the uneven stone steps when a rifle up ahead boomed, and the steps and walls sparked around him as copper-jacketed ammo struck and bounced.

Caruso backpedaled up the stairs but crashed into Ryan. Both men fell and tumbled forward, sliding down the stairs on their gear packs before coming to rest in the dark hallway.

The gunman ahead continued firing. Ryan found himself on top of Caruso, pinning his cousin down, so he rose to his knees, aimed perfunctorily on the flashes ahead, and dumped twenty rounds from his weapon at the threat.

Then, through the ringing in his ears, he heard the clinking of his own hot brass bouncing against the stone before it came to rest all around him. Then he heard a heavier metal thud as a rifle fell to the floor ahead. He shined his light and saw a Taliban slumped against the wall at a turn in the basement hall.

"You okay, Dom?"

"Get off of me."

"Sorry." Ryan climbed off and stood up. Dom stood up, as well, and then covered ahead while Jack reloaded his P-90.

"Let's move."

They made it to the corner and then looked around. Up ahead was a single room at the end of the hall. Inside it was dark, but not for long.

AK fire from two rifles rang out, sending showers of sparks all the way up the hall toward the two Americans as the bullets pinged off the stone wall.

Dom and Jack tucked their heads back.

"I'm thinking that looks like it could be the jail."

"Yeah," agreed Ryan.

Apparently there were only two jailers, but they had good cover at the far end of the hallway. Plus they held a second advantage: Jack and Dom had no idea what was on the other side of the doorway. For all they knew, if they fired up the baked-brick hallway and into the room, their rounds might bounce around inside and hit the man they had come to save.

"Should we go get Chavez and come back?" asked Ryan.

"No time. We've got to get in there."

Together they thought for a moment. Suddenly Jack

said, "I've got an idea. I take a nine-banger, I throw it short, just outside the doorway. As soon as the first bang goes off, we run."

"Into the nine-banger?" Caruso asked incredulously.

"Fuck, yes! We shield our eyes. They'll have to pull their heads in the room while it's going off. When we get half-way up the hall you roll a flash-bang through the doorway, and that should stun them until we get in. We'll have to time it right, but that should keep them occupied."

Dom nodded. "I don't have anything better. But leave your rifle. Pistols only. We'll move better, and we don't want to hit Sam coming through the door."

The two young men slipped out of their rifle slings, and then pulled grenades from their chest pouches. Ryan drew his pistol and pulled the pin on his grenade.

Dom moved next to him at the edge of the corner. He patted his cousin on the shoulder and said, "No retreat. We start moving on their position, we can't stop and turn back around. The only chance is to keep going."

"Got it," Jack said, and he slung the grenade around the dark corner with a side-arm toss.

After just a couple of echoing metal-on-stone clanks, the first explosion and flash rocked the hall and the men at the far end of it. Dom moved ahead of Jack, sprinted into the forty-foot-long line of fire of the enemies' guns, and he rolled his flash-bang far into the room like a bowling ball, right through the flashes and smoke of Jack's nine-banger.

Together Caruso and Ryan ran forward with their eyes turned away from the bursts of fire.

The two jailers had tucked their heads back inside the small room to shield them from what they thought was an undertossed diversion. But by the time the last of the nine-banger's pops finished and they readied to turn back to resume firing up the hallway, a small canister bounced into the room between them.

They both stared at the flash-bang as it went off, pounding their brains inside their skulls and dilating their blinded eyes.

Jack entered the room first at a run, but he'd caught enough of the effects of Dom's flash-bang to disorient him. He ran right past the two men who'd fallen to the floor on either side of the doorway, and he crashed into the metal bars of the first cell before he was able to stop on his own.

"Fuck!" he shouted, half blinded and all deaf, at least for the next few seconds.

But Dominic came in behind him; Jack's body had shielded him from much of the light and some of the sound, so the ex–FBI agent still had his wits about him.

He shot both of the disoriented Haqqani fighters where they knelt on the floor, putting a bullet into the back of each man's head.

"In here!" It was Sam. His cell door was only a few feet from Ryan, but he could barely hear him.

Ryan shined his light on the cells in the room. A Pashtun man was crouched against the wall of the first cell, a sick-looking white-skinned blond man lay on the floor of the second cell.

Ryan now shined his light into the corner. In the last cell, Sam Driscoll sat astride a dead Haqqani fighter, the man's twisted neck in the American's hands.

Caruso found the overhead light and flipped it on. He stared at Sam, as well.

"You okay?"

Sam looked away from the man he had just killed with

his bare hands, the jailer who had planned to use him as a human shield, and he looked up at his two colleagues. "You boys playing army?"

66

Sam and Dom led the way back up the stairs while Jack and the Afghan carried the incapacitated Reuters reporter. It was a tough climb back to the ground floor, but once they were there, things became even more precarious. Chavez had cleared the upstairs, but now he and al Darkur were in the hallway near the stairs, firing toward the front of the building at enemy fighters positioned there.

The Pakistani major had been hit in the left shoulder and his rifle had been damaged by another round, but he continued to fire his pistol up the hall with his right hand.

Chavez saw that he had six people behind him now, and one was being carried. He nodded to himself and patted al Darkur on the shoulder. "Let's find a way out of here before the enemy starts firing RPGs!"

They headed toward the back of the building, a limping Sam Driscoll in the lead with a salvaged AK. Now Chavez brought up the rear and fired constantly to keep heads down in the rooms and hallways near the front of the house.

The hallway came to a T and Driscoll went right, with the rest of the procession following behind. Sam came upon a large room at the back of the house, but the windows had been bricked up and there was no door.

"No good!" he shouted. "Try the other direction!"

Chavez led now. He was surprised that the enemy fire up this stretch of hallway had lessened noticeably. With Ryan and Caruso firing down the base of the T, Chavez and al Darkur darted across, and then ran into a long narrow kitchen. There was no exit here, but a small side door looked promising. Chavez opened the door, desperate to find a window or a door or even a staircase back upstairs.

The doorway led to a dark room roughly fifteen feet across and thirty feet deep. It seemed to be some sort of repair shop, but Ding didn't focus on the room itself; instead he shined his rifle's light quickly along the walls, searching for any other exit. Seeing nothing, he started to turn away to try to go back and fight with the others. But he stopped when something caught his eye in the low light.

He'd ignored the wooden tables and shelves in the room when looking for a way out, but now he focused on them, or more specifically, what was on them.

Containers of car parts and electrical components. Batteries. Cell phones. Wires. Small drums of gunpowder. Steel pressure plates and a blue fifty-five-gallon drum full of what Ding immediately assumed was nitric acid.

On the floor were mortar shells, partially disassembled.

Ding realized he'd stumbled onto a bomb factory. The improvised explosive devices created here would be smuggled over the border into Afghanistan.

This explained why the Haqqani fighters hadn't fired a rocket toward Chavez and his team here in the back of the house. If anything in this room detonated, the entire compound would be obliterated, the Haqqani men included.

"Mohammed?" Ding shouted, and al Darkur peered into the room.

Immediately he nodded. "Bombs."

"I know what they are. Can we use them?"

Mohammed nodded with a crooked smile. "I know something about bombs."

*

Ryan and Caruso were both down to their last magazine. They fired individual rounds from the top of the T down to the base. They knew they'd taken out a lot of the Haqqani members with rifle fire, but there seemed to be an unlimited supply of armed assholes remaining.

One of the Puma helicopters was flying in circles behind the compound. This Jack could tell from occasional automatic fire from his six-o'clock high, coming from outside the building. He could not actually hear the helo—with the gunfire in the narrow hallways his ears were trashed, so nothing less than small-arms fire up close or heavy machine guns at distance registered.

Chavez appeared just behind the two men, sliding a fresh magazine around and into their chest rigs. While he did this he shouted, "There is a bomb factory in the back!"

"Oh, shit," said Ryan, realizing that he and his mates were, essentially, exchanging fire while sitting on top of a powder keg.

"Al Darkur is wiring an IED to blow the back wall. If he gets it right it should make us a hole in the back of the building. When it's time to go, just turn and run up the hallway. I'll cover your egress!"

Jack didn't ask what would happen if Mohammed did *not* get it "right."

Ding next said, "Do *not* head out back until you toss your LZ beacons. The door gunner in the Puma has been rocking his MG for the past ten minutes. Don't count on him to spot the IR strobe on your back. He'll turn you into ground beef. Use your LZ marker as a second way to alert them that friendlies are coming out."

The two young men nodded.

"Sam and the Afghan will drag the wounded man, you

guys just keep up the covering fire for them until the chopper lands and they get on board."

"Got it!" Dom said, and Ryan nodded.

Both Ryan and Caruso kept up the controlled fire, just enough to let the enemy know that, if they ventured up the hall toward the T, then they were going to pay a heavy price. They still took some fire, but it came from AKs that were just held around the corner and sprayed by their handlers, and the rounds banged along the walls, floors, and ceiling.

Twice al Darkur and Chavez passed behind them as they took IED material out of the bomb factory on Jack and Dom's right and carried it to the other end of the hallway on their left.

Within a minute, Chavez was back behind them. He screamed into their ears, "Get down!"

Both men dove to the stone floor of the hallway and covered their heads. Within a few seconds, an incredible boom from behind them pounded up the hallway with a concussive force that made Jack think the building would fall on top of them. Cracked mortar, stone, and dust did fall from the ceiling, raining down on all the men in the hallway.

Caruso was first to his feet. He ran up the hallway with Ryan close behind, passing the wounded Reuters man being dragged by his shoulders by Driscoll and the Afghani prisoner.

Jack caught up to him as they entered the room with the bricked-over windows. Their weapon lights were useless with the dust in the air. They just continued on toward the far wall until, finally, they could see open sky. Immediately Dominic threw the flashing landing-zone signal into the rear of the compound. The beacon would, in theory, alert the gunmen in the circling choppers that friendlies were in that area so they should not fire.

As Dominic stepped into the rear courtyard he worried he would take a blast from the door gun of the chopper, but fortunately the Zarrar commandos had good fire discipline. The American crouched behind a small stack of truck tires and covered the north side of the compound, while his cousin went prone beside a large pile of rubble left by al Darkur's bomb blast, covering the south side.

One of the SSG choppers had used its 20-millimeter cannon to take out the poles holding up the electric wires in the back of the property, so the helo landed near Major al Darkur, the prisoners, and the American operatives. Within seconds everyone was aboard and the helo lifted back into the air and immediately began racing for safety.

Inside the helicopter, all seven men who'd made it on board lay on the metal decking, arms and legs atop one another. Jack Ryan found himself near the bottom of the pile, but he was too exhausted to move, even to push the thick leg of the Afghani politician off his face.

It took another twenty minutes of nap-of-the-earth flying before the lights in the cabin of the helo came on and the pilot announced, through Mohammed al Darkur and his intercom-linked headphones, that they were out of danger. The men sat up, water bottles were passed around, and al Darkur's shoulder was attended to by the loadmaster of the aircraft, while one of the Zarrar commandos started an IV into the arm of the Australian Reuters correspondent.

The normally dry and stoic Sam Driscoll hugged each member of his extraction team, then he rolled into the corner and fell asleep with a water bottle tucked to his chest.

Chavez leaned over into Jack's ear to yell over the engine noise, "Looks like you had a pretty close shave back there."

Jack followed Ding's eyes to the canvas magazine rack on his chest. A jagged hole was torn through one of the pouches. He pulled out a metal and plastic P-90 mag, and found a bullet hole all the way through it. Fingering his way into the hole in his chest rig he fished out a twisted and sharp 7.62 round that had slammed into his ceramic breastplate.

In all the action, Jack had no idea he'd taken a hit right to the chest.

"Fuck me," he said as he held the bullet up and looked at it.

Chavez just laughed and squeezed the younger man's arm. "Not your time, *'mano.*"

"I guess not," Jack said, and he wanted to call his mom and dad, and he wanted to call Melanie. But he had to put both those communications on hold, because he suddenly felt the nausea return.

67

Riaz Rehan had men on the inside of each and every major institution in his nation. One of these institutions was the Pakistani nuclear ordnance industry. He, through his own network of cutouts, was in contact with nuclear scientists, engineers, and weapons manufacturers. Through them he learned that in Wah Cantonment, near Islamabad, was the storage location of many of his nation's nuclear devices. Several air delivery bombs, essentially US Mark 84 conventional bomb cases packed with five-to-twenty-kiloton-yield nuclear devices, were kept at the Kamra Air Weapon Complex inside the massive Pakistan Ordnance Factories there at Wah. The nuclear bombs were disassembled, but kept at something known as "screwdriver ready" status. This meant they could be assembled for deployment in hours if and when the head of state called for them to be made ready.

And, Rehan had learned from one of his high-ranking associates in the Ministry of Defense the previous morning, the President of Pakistan had made the call.

So the first portion of Operation Saker had already succeeded. In order to ensure that the weapons were assembled and deployed to their battle stations, General Rehan needed to bring his nation to the brink of war. That done, he monitored his contacts in the government and nuclear weapons branches of the military, and waited like a coiled snake in the grass to make his next move.

The Pakistanis had long boasted that their nuclear

weapons were protected by a three-tier national command authority security procedure. This was true, but ultimately it did not mean much. All one needed was the knowledge of the weakest link in the security of the device after its assembly, and some way to exploit this weakest link.

The general's agents at Pakistan Ordnance Factories told him that around nine p.m. two twenty-kiloton bombs would leave the Kamra Air Weapon Complex by truck, and then they would be delivered to a special train in nearby Taxila. At first Rehan considered attacking the truck convoy. A truck is easier to disable than a train, after all. But there were too many variables for which Rehan could not control so close to the large military presence there in Wah and Taxila.

So he began looking at the rail route. The bombs would be delivered by a heavily guarded freight train to the air force base at Sargodha, some two hundred miles of rail travel away.

A simple glance at a map was all it took to pinpoint the weakest link on the route. Just five kilometers south of the town of Phularwan, on a flat stretch of farmland bisected by the railroad, a cluster of abandoned mills and grain warehouses sat alongside wheat fields that ran right up to the tracks. Here a force could hide, ready to attack a train approaching from the north. Once they had achieved their objective the force could then load itself and the two ten-foot-long, one-ton bombs onto trucks, and access the modern M2 Highway, the Lahore–Islamabad road, where they could go north or south and disappear into either massive metropolis inside of ninety minutes.

In the first week of December, a cold steady rain fell, beating on the tin roofs of the grain shacks that lay just four hundred yards from the edge of the rail line.

General Riaz Rehan, his second-in-command Colonel Khan, and Georgi Safronov lay on prayer mats in the dark, tucked in a shed behind a rusted-out tractor that hopefully would afford them protection from stray gunfire when the attack commenced.

Rehan was awaiting a radio call from a spotter in Chabba Purana, a village just southeast of Phularwan. The fifty-five Jamaat Shariat gunmen, the students from the Haqqani camp in Miran Shah, were spread out in the field on the west side of the tracks. They were positioned one man every three yards, and every fourth man held a rocket-propelled grenade launcher, and the rest wielded Kalashnikovs.

The Dagestanis, led by ex–ISI officers handpicked by General Rehan because of their paramilitary experience, were positioned fifty meters or so away from the track, and a ten-meter-long stretch of rail had been removed just moments before. The speeding train would come off the rails right there in front of Jamaat Shariat, it would grind into the dirt, and then the North Caucasus fighters would quickly go to work killing every last living thing in each and every car.

Rehan had forbidden smoking ever since the six big truckloads of men arrived earlier in the evening. Even though there was no one around for several kilometers in each direction, he also forbade speaking other than in a whisper, and all but essential radio communication.

Now his radio crackled to life. It was on an encrypted channel, but still the message was in code. "Ali, before you go to bed the hens must be fed. They will be hungry."

Rehan patted the nervous Russian space entrepreneur crouched in the shed with him, then leaned into his ear. "That is my man up the tracks. The train is coming."

Safronov turned to Rehan and looked to him. Even in the low light of a rainy night, the man's face looked pale. There was no reason for Safronov to even be here for this attack. Rehan had argued against it, telling the Russian that he was too precious to the overall mission. But Safronov had insisted. He demanded to be with his brothers each step of the way on this operation. Though he had left the training early in North Waziristan, that was only because, at that point, he was working twenty-hour days in Moscow organizing the three rocket launches in Baikonur, and ensuring that only his handpicked scientists and staff would be there with him when the time was right.

But there was no way he would have missed tonight's fireworks, Rehan's dominant personality be damned.

Rehan had finally acquiesced to letting Georgi come along for the op, but he held his ground on having him take no part in the attack itself. He even demanded that the man wear a chest plate and remain in the shed until they loaded everything on the trucks, and Rehan had put Colonel Khan himself in charge of making sure the Dagestani remained safe.

There were a few other men nearby, as well, who would not be part of the gunplay because they played a bigger role in the op. The cold, calculating general knew that selling the fantasy that a band of mountain men from Dagestan could pull off such an incredible operation in Pakistan would be difficult if not impossible. Many in the know would immediately place blame on the Islamists in the ISI for helping them. To deflect this blame, Rehan had set up one of the organizations with whom he'd been working for more than a decade. The Muslim United Liberation Tigers of Assam, an Islamic militant group in

India, had been penetrated by agents from India's National Investigation Agency a year prior. When Rehan learned of MULTA's infiltration he did not get angry, and he did not immediately cut ties with them. No, he saw this as an opportunity. He took men from MULTA who were insulated from the NIA penetration, and he brought them into his fold. He told them they would be part of an incredible operation in Pakistan that would involve stealing a nuclear weapon, returning with it to India, and detonating it in New Delhi. The men would be martyrs.

It was all a lie. He documented their movements as he documented Indian intelligence's infiltration of their organization, saving evidence that he could use later to cover the tracks of the ISI in the theft of the bombs. He had plans for the four MULTA men here tonight, but it had nothing to do with them leaving these fields with the bombs.

These men would take the fall for the theft of the weapons, and by association the Indian government would have to explain their involvement with the group.

In furtherance of this ruse, Rehan and his men planned the attack with an appearance of sloppiness. A group of Islamic fighters from India being duped by Indian intelligence into working with Dagestani partisans in Pakistan would not possess any semblance of military precision, and for this reason the plan involved mayhem and chaos to achieve its objective.

Rehan heard a radio call from the unit farthest to the north. They reported the lights of the train in the distance.

The mayhem and chaos would begin within moments.

Rehan's plan never would have worked if the Pakistani government put as much effort into securing its nukes from terrorists as it did securing them from their neighbor to the east. The bomb train could have been longer, full of an entire battalion of troops, it could have had helicopter gunship escorts for the entire route, and the Pakistani Defense Force could have stationed quick-reaction troops along the tracks in advance of the train's leaving Kamra on its way to Sargodha Air Force Base.

But all these high-profile measures that would virtually eliminate the chance that a terrorist group could over-power the train and take the weapons would also telegraph to Indian satellites, drones, and spies that the nukes were under deployment.

And the Pakistani Defense Force would not let that happen.

Therefore, the security plan for the train relied on supreme stealth, and an onboard force of one company of troops, just more than one hundred armed men. If stealth failed and terrorists hit the train, one hundred men would, under virtually all circumstances, be sufficient to repel an attack.

But Rehan was prepared for one hundred men, and they would not stand a chance.

The lights of the train appeared in the flat distance, just a kilometer away now. Rehan could hear Safronov's heavy breathing over the pattering of the rain on the tin roof. In Arabic the general said, "Relax, my friend. Just lie here and watch. Tonight Jamaat Shariat will take a first important step in securing a Dagestani homeland for your people."

The Pakistani's voice was full of confidence and fake admiration for the fools out there in the grass. Inwardly he was hoping they wouldn't fuck it up. Out there with Jamaat Shariat were a dozen of his own men, also ready with small arms and radios to organize the attack. He had no idea how well the Haqqani trainers had prepared these fifty-five mountain men, but he knew he was seconds away from finding out.

The train itself appeared in the rain, screaming forward in the night behind its white light. It was not long, only a dozen cars. Rehan's contacts at Kamra Air Weapon Complex had no way of knowing which car the devices would be loaded into, and he had no one at Taxila railroad station to confirm this either. Obviously it would not be in the engine, and common sense said it would not be the rear car, as the security detail would logically post a portion of the force at the back in case of attack from the rear. So Jamaat Shariat had been ordered to fire their RPGs only at the engine and the last car, or at any large clusters of dismounted troops only when they were well away from the train. The RPGs could not set off a nuclear explosion even if they hit the bombs themselves, but they could very easily damage the weapons or set the rail car containing them on fire and make it difficult to extract the two big bombs.

Again, Rehan worried. If this did not work, his plan to take control of the nation was dead.

The conductor of the deployment train must have seen the missing portion of track ahead; he slammed on his brakes, and they squealed and screeched. Georgi Safronov tensed perceptibly behind the rusty tractor with General Rehan and Colonel Khan. Rehan started to calm him with gentle words, but suddenly a Kalashnikov rifle opened up, firing fully automatic, while the train was still moving.

Another AK joined the chorus, the sound barely perceptible over the incredible noise of the brakes of the locomotive.

Still, Rehan was furious. Jamaat Shariat had jumped the gun.

Rehan shouted into his radio at his men in the field,

"They were not to fire until the train derailed! Shut those bastards up, even if you have to shoot them in the head!"

But just as he finished his transmission, the heavy engine skidded off the track. Behind it, like a slowly collapsing accordion, the other cars turned both in and out. The train came to a slow, labored stop in the rain. Small fires ignited in the braking system.

Rehan started to countermand his last order, he pressed the transmit button on his walkie-talkie, but instead he held the device in front of Safronov's face. Softly the general said, "Give your men the order to attack."

The terrified Russian millionaire's white face filled with color in an instant of animalistic pride, and he shouted so loud into the microphone of the walkie-talkie that Rehan was certain his call would come out distorted on the radios of his gunmen.

"Attack!" he screamed in Russian.

Instantly the field ahead of the men in the shed flickered with the lights of launching RPGs. A couple streaked over the train, arcing off into the night, and one detonated against the second-to-last car on the tracks, but four more rocket-propelled grenades hit their mark on the engine, turning it into a fireball of twisted metal. Two more grenades slammed into the rear car, killing or maiming everyone stationed there.

The AK chatter from the field was incredible—loud and angry and sustained. Return fire from the train cars took a long time to begin. No doubt the hard braking and the derailment knocked the men around inside like beans shaken in a can, and they were in no position to fight in those first seconds. But finally large cracks of semi-automatic .308 fire from big HK G3 battle rifles began answering the Kalashnikovs in the wheat field.

More RPGs detonated against the train, mostly at the front and the rear, but some of the Dagestani forces controlling the launchers seemed, to General Riaz Rehan's way of thinking, to have extremely poor fire discipline. He heard shouts in the walkie-talkies, in Urdu and Arabic and Russian, and from across the dark rain-swept field, he watched the soldiers on the deployment train die.

These soldiers were not bad men. Many would be good Muslims. Many would support Rehan's cause. But in order for Operation Saker to succeed, some men would need to be martyred.

Rehan would pray for them, but he would not grieve for them.

Rehan used night-vision binoculars to watch the action from the shed. A group of ten or so PDF soldiers managed to make it out of the train; they attacked into the ambush in a disciplined fashion that made the general proud to be associated with such men. But the ambush line was too wide, the force in the wheat field too numerous, and the men were slaughtered within seconds.

The entire firefight lasted just over three and a half minutes. When the ISI officers in the field called a cease-fire, they sent teams of Jamaat Shariat fighters into each car, one at a time, so that there was no blue-on-blue shooting between the cars.

This took five more minutes, and resulted in what Rehan could tell just by listening was the execution of the wounded or the surrendering.

Finally a radio transmission came over Rehan's walkie-talkie. In Urdu, one of his captains said, "Bring the trucks!"

Immediately two large black dump trucks pulled out from behind the warehouses and drove up a wet road through the wheat field. A third vehicle, a yellow crane truck, followed behind.

It took only seven minutes to offload the bombs from the train onto the trucks. Four minutes after this and the first of the trucks full of Dagestanis had hit the Islamabad–Lahore road and turned to the north.

As Rehan and Safronov climbed into one of the vehicles, a long salvo of gunfire rang out from one of the abandoned warehouses. The weapons doing the firing were PDF G3 battle rifles, but Rehan was not worried. He had ordered his men to pick up weapons from the train's security force, and then use these weapons on the four MULTA men who, up until the moment the ISI shot them dead, thought that they would be returning to India with these weapons.

The ISI had Dagestanis carry the bodies into the field and dump them.

Jamaat Shariat lost thirteen men in the ambush. Seven died outright, and the others, men injured too badly to survive the trek ahead of them, were shot where they lay. All the bodies were loaded on trucks.

The first of the PDF response to the train attack arrived just twelve minutes after the last of Rehan's trucks left the wheat field. By then the two bombs were nearly fifteen kilometers closer to the impenetrable metropolis of Islamabad.

68

Since returning from Pakistan weeks earlier, Jack had seen Melanie almost every day. Usually he would leave work a little early to head down to Alexandria. They would walk from her apartment to dinner unless it was snowing or raining, in which case they'd take the Hummer. He'd stay the night, getting up the next morning at five to beat the traffic for the thirty-mile drive back to Columbia.

She'd mentioned something about wanting to see where he lived, so Saturday afternoon he picked her up and took her back up to Columbia for the night. They dined on Indian at Akbar, then they stopped in for a drink at Union Jack's.

After a beer and some conversation, they went back to Jack's apartment.

Jack had had girls over to his place before, although he was by no means a playboy. Normally, if he thought he might have company over later in the evening, he just gave his apartment a once over while grabbing his keys and heading out the door to go out, but for this date he had cleaned thoroughly. Mopping his hardwood floor, changing the sheets on the bed, scrubbing his bathroom from top to bottom. He'd play like he always kept the place so spic-and-span, but he was reasonably certain Ms. Kraft would be sharp enough to figure out that was not the case.

He liked this girl. A lot. He'd known that from the start, had felt the kindling of something on their early dates.

He'd missed her when he was in Dubai, and when he was in Pakistan he wanted nothing more than to hold her, to talk to her, to get some sort of validation from her that he was doing the right thing for the right reasons and that everything was going to work out.

Shit, Jack thought. *Am I going soft?*

He wondered if it had anything to do with the fact that two bullets had come within inches of ending his life in the past three weeks. Was that what was behind the feelings he was developing for this girl? He hoped that was not the case. She did not deserve someone falling for her as a result of some personal issue or a near-death experience. No, she warranted the head-over-heels feeling without any artificial additives.

His apartment was pricey and full of nice furniture and modern, open spaces. It was very much a bachelor pad. When Jack excused himself to go to the bathroom, Melanie snuck a peek into his refrigerator, and she found exactly what she expected. Not much but wine, beer, Gatorade, and days-old takeout boxes. She also gave his freezer a quick scan, she did work for a spy agency, after all, and found it filled with ice bags, many of which had melted and then refrozen.

She then opened a couple of cupboards in his kitchen by the freezer. Ace bandages, anti-inflammatories, Band-Aids, antibiotic ointment.

She remarked on this when he came back to the room.

"Any more bumps and bruises on the slopes?"

"What? No. Why do you ask?"

"Just wondering. I saw the emergency aid station you have set up."

Jack's eyebrows rose. "You've been snooping?"

"Just a little. It's a girl thing."

"Right. Actually I was taking a mixed martial arts class in Baltimore. It was great, but when I started traveling a lot for work I had to quit." Ryan looked around the room. "What do you think of my place?" he asked.

"It's beautiful. It lacks a woman's touch, but I suppose if it had a woman's touch, I'd have to wonder about that."

"That's true."

"Still. This place is so nice. It makes me wonder what you think about that little dump I've been making you stay over at."

"I like your place. It suits you."

Melanie cocked her head. "Because it's cheap?"

"No. That's not what I mean. I just mean, it's feminine and it still is full of books on terrorism and CIA manuals. It's kick-ass. Like you."

Melanie had adopted a defensive posture. But she relaxed. "I'm really sorry. I'm just feeling a bit over-whelmed by your money and your family ties, basically because I come from the other side of the tracks, I guess. My family never had any money. Four kids didn't leave much of my dad's military pay left over for nice things."

"I understand," Jack said.

"You probably don't. But that's my problem, not yours."

Ryan walked over to Melanie and put his arms around her. "That's in your past."

She shook her head and pulled away. "No. It's not."

"Student loans?" Ryan asked, and then immediately regretted it. "I'm sorry, it's none of my business, I just——"

Melanie smiled a little. "It's okay. Just no fun to talk about. Just be thankful for your family."

Now Jack was the one to go on the defensive. "Look, I understand that I was born into money, but my dad made me work. I'm not riding the family name to the bank."

"Of course you aren't. I totally respect that about you. I'm not talking about money." She thought that over for a second. "Maybe for the first time I'm not talking about money. I'm talking about your family. I see how you talk about them. How you respect them."

Jack had learned to not press her about her own upbringing. Each time he had tried she had withdrawn from the conversation or changed the subject. For a moment he thought she would finally go into her family life on her own. But she did not.

"So," she said, and he could tell that the subject had just been changed. "Does this place have a bathroom?"

At that moment her mobile phone chirped in her purse on Jack's kitchen counter. She reached for it and looked at the number.

"It's Mary Pat," she said in surprise, wondering why her boss would call at ten o'clock on a Saturday night.

"Maybe you are getting a raise," Jack joked, and Melanie laughed.

"Hi, Mary Pat." Melanie's smile faded from her face. "Okay. Okay. Oh . . . shit."

When Melanie turned away from him, Jack sensed trouble. But he sensed more trouble ten seconds later when his own mobile rang in his pocket. "Ryan."

"It's Granger. How quick can you be at the office?"

Jack turned away and walked into his bedroom. "What's up? Is it Clark?"

"No. It's trouble. I need everyone in immediately."

"Okay."

He hung up the phone and found Melanie in his room behind him. "I'm so sorry, Jack, but I have to go in to the office."

"What's going on?"

"You know I can't answer that. I hate that you'll have to drive me all the way to McLean, but it is an emergency."

Shit. Think, Jack. "Tell you what. That was my office that just called. They want me to come in for a bit, somebody's worried about how we're positioned for the Asian markets opening on Monday. Can I have you drop me at work and then you just take my truck?"

Ryan saw it in her eyes instantly. She knew he was lying. She covered; she did not press. It was likely she was more worried about whatever bad news Jack had yet to learn than she was that her boyfriend was a lying bastard.

"Sure. That will work."

A minute later, they headed for the door.

They drove mostly in silence to Hendley Associates.

After Melanie dropped Jack off at his offices, she drove off into the night, and Ryan stepped in the back door.

Dom Caruso was already there, downstairs in the lobby, talking to the security men on staff.

Ryan walked up to him. "What's going on?"

Dom walked up to his cousin and leaned into his ear. "Worst-case scenario, cuz."

Ryan's eyes widened. He knew what that meant. "Islamic bomb?"

Caruso nodded. "Internal CIA traffic says a Pakistani armaments train got hit last night local time. *Two* twenty-kiloton nukes got lifted, and are now in the hands of an unknown force."

"Oh my God."

69

The two twenty-kiloton nuclear bombs stolen from the Pakistani Air Force found themselves, just days later, in the skies over Pakistan. Rehan and his men had the bombs packed and crated into twelve-by-five-by-five-foot containers that were labeled "Textile Manufacturing, Ltd." They were then placed on an Antonov An-26 cargo plane operated by Vision Air, a Pakistani charter airline.

Their intermediate destination was Dushanbe, the capital of Tajikistan.

As much as General Rehan would like to send the Dagestanis on their way, to get them out of his country and somewhere where they could publicize what they had done and threaten the world with their bombs and their missiles, he knew Georgi Safronov was smarter than all the other cell members and insurgency leaders and even any of the government operatives he had worked with in his career. Georgi knew as much about nuclear weapons as Rehan did, and the general knew he needed to put one hundred percent of his efforts behind an authentic preparation of Safronov's operation.

To do that he would need two things: a private and secure place, outside Pakistan, to arm the bombs and fit the bombs into the Dnepr-1 payload containers, and someone with the technical know-how to do this.

Bilateral trade had increased precipitously between Tajikistan and Pakistan in the past four years, so travel from Pakistan to Dushanbe was commonplace. Dushanbe was also almost directly between Pakistan and the ultimate destination of the weapons, the Baikonur Cosmodrome.

The An-26 flew out of Lahore with its two cargo crates and its twelve passengers: Rehan, Safronov, Khan, seven of Rehan's personal security, and two Pakistani nuclear munitions experts. The Jamaat Shariat forces traveled out of the country via a second Vision Air charter that would take them to Dushanbe, as well.

Rehan's JIM Directorate had already spread bribes around Tajik customs and airport officials; there would be no impediments to either aircraft's offloading its cargo and crew once on the ground. A Tajik with the Dushanbe city government who had a long history as a paid informant and foreign agent of the ISI would be waiting on touchdown with trucks and drivers and more crated cargo that had recently arrived from Moscow.

The Campus worked twenty-four/seven looking for the nuclear bombs. The CIA had picked up ISI chatter within hours of the hijacking, and Langley and the National Counterterrorism Center at Liberty Crossing spent the intervening days looking into ISI involvement.

NCTC had more information on Riaz Rehan, some of it courtesy of The Campus and much of it thanks to the work of Melanie Kraft, so Jack Ryan and his fellow analysts found themselves virtually looking over the shoulder of Kraft for much of the time. It made Ryan feel creepy, but if there was anything actionable that Melanie found in her research, The Campus was in a position to act immediately.

Tony Wills had been working with Ryan; more than once he had looked at Melanie Kraft's research and commented, "Your girlfriend is smarter than you are, Ryan."

Jack thought Wills was half right. She was smarter than he was, true, but he wasn't sure she was his girlfriend.

The Pakistanis did an admirable job hiding the loss of the two nuclear devices from their own public and from the world's press for forty-eight hours. During this time they scrambled to find the culprits and locate the bombs, but the Pakistani Federal Investigation Agency came up empty. There was an immediate fear that it had been an inside job, and there was a related fear that the ISI was involved. But the ISI and the PDF were infinitely more powerful than the FIA, so these fears were not effectively explored as part of the investigation.

But when the news finally got out that there had been a massive terrorist act within Pakistan on a rail line, the Pakistani press put together, through their sources in the government, that nuclear devices had been on board the train. When it was confirmed, within hours, that the two devices, type and yield unspecified, had been hijacked by parties unknown, it came with a very public and very specific promise from the highest corridors of power in the military, civilian government, and the Pakistan Atomic Energy Commission that the theft of the weapons was of no great consequence. It was explained that the devices were equipped with fail-safe arming codes that one would need to render the devices active.

All the parties who said this publicly firmly believed what they were saying, and it was true, although one of the parties did leave out a critical morsel of information that was highly relevant.

The director of the Pakistan Atomic Energy Commission did not tell his peers in the government and military, and he did not tell the public at large, that two of his top weaponization physicists, two men able to bypass the arming codes and reconfigure the detonation systems, had gone missing at the exact moment the bombs were lost.

The next morning the two crates claiming to be property of Textile Manufacturing, Ltd, sat on a dusty concrete floor in the center of a warehouse at a school bus fleet maintenance yard on Kurban Rakhimov, in the northern part of Dushanbe. General Rehan and Georgi Safronov both were very happy with the choice of facility for this portion of the mission. The property was massive and fenced and gated on all sides, blocking the view from the tree-lined streets of the more than fifty foreign men working and patrolling the grounds inside. Dozens of trucks and school buses sat in various states of operational condition, which made the Dagestani and Pakistani trucks invisible, even from the air. And the large maintenance building was large enough for several busses, which made it more than large enough for the huge bombs. Further, there was a large array of hoists and rolling stands to lift and move the massive school bus engines that were scattered around the facility.

Of the people present, the only ones doing anything more than standing around were the two scientists who worked for PAEC, Pakistan's Atomic Energy Commission. They were missing back in Pakistan, and the few people who knew about their disappearance but did not know the men themselves suspected they had been kidnapped by a terrorist force. But those who knew them and knew of the missing nukes did not think for a moment that anyone was forcing them to do anything. That they were Islamic radicals was widely known among their peers. On this matter some had been accepting, and some had been uncomfortable yet quiet.

Both of these groups of people suspected these men were involved.

The two scientists, Dr. Nishtar and Dr. Noon, were united in their belief that Pakistan's nuclear weapons were not the property of the civilian government, nor were they fabricated and stockpiled, at great cost and at great risk they would hasten to add, only to be used as some sort of hypothetical deterrent. An invisible chess piece.

No. Pakistan's nuclear weapons belonged to the Ummah, the community of Muslims, and they could and *should* be used for the good of all believers.

And the two scientists believed in Riaz Rehan, and they trusted that now was the right time because he said that now was the right time.

The dour foreign men from the Caucasus all around them in the school bus maintenance facility were of the faithful, even if they were not Pakistani Muslims. Drs. Noon and Nishtar did not understand all of what was going on, but they were quite clear on their mission. They were to arm the weapons, they were to oversee the loading of the weapons into the rocket payload containers, and then they were to return to Pakistan with the ISI general, where they would remain in hiding until Rehan told them it was safe to come out in public and take their bow as heroes of the state.

Noon and Nishtar had been working for more than three hours in the cold warehouse, taking moments to warm their hands over a coal brick stove that had been lit in the corner so that their fingers would remain pliant for the intricate work of removing the nuclear devices from their MK84 bomb casings, necessary for them to fit in the payload containers. A group of Rehan's personal security force stood by, ready to help with engine hoists and rolling racks. Safronov offered up Jamaat Shariat men for this work but Rehan refused, told him to keep his gunmen inside the perimeter gates but ready for any threat from the outside. Once the bombs left Dushanbe, Rehan explained, they would be Safronov's, but for now Rehan retained possession and his people would handle them.

As Noon and Nishtar checked some data on a laptop on a table next to the first payload container, Rehan and Safronov stepped up behind them. The general reached out and put his thick hands on the two men's backs. They continued to work. "Doctors, how is your progress?"

Dr. Nishtar answered while he peered into the container, looking at the configuration of the warhead. "Minutes more for this one, and then we begin on the second weapon. We have bypassed the launch code mechanisms, and we have installed the radio altimeter fuses."

"Show us."

Noon pointed out a device bolted to the side of the bomb. It looked like a metal briefcase, and it contained several mechanical parts wired together, as well as a computer keypad and an LED readout. He said, "There is a radio altimeter that is already set. When the devices reach an altitude of sixty thousand feet it will arm the weapon, and when it descends to one thousand feet it will detonate. There is a backup barometer on the detonator, as well as a manual override for a timed detonation, which you will not need for a warhead launch. Also, we will rig a tamper trigger on the door of the payload container, so that if anyone tries to open it to remove the weapon, the nuclear bomb will detonate."

Georgi smiled and nodded, appreciative of the men's work on behalf of the Dagestani cause. "And you will do the same for the other device?"

"Of course."

"Excellent," Rehan said as his hands patted the men on their shoulders. "Carry on."

Safronov left the warehouse minutes later, but Rehan lagged behind. He returned to the two nuclear scientists and said, "I have one small request for you both."

"Anything, General," said Dr. Noon.

Ninety minutes later, General Rehan embraced Georgi Safronov outside the maintenance garage, and he shook the hand of each one of the Dagestani fighters. He called them brave brothers, and he promised them that if they should be martyred he would name streets in his country in their honor.

Then Rehan, Khan, the PAEC officials, and Rehan's protection detail departed through the front gates of the bus farm in four vehicles, removing with them every trace of their work, and leaving behind the Dagestani fighters and the two Dnepr-1 payload containers.

Minutes after that, the Dagestanis themselves departed, the gifts from Pakistan loaded carefully into their tractor-trailers for the long drive to the north.

John Clark spent an entire morning on a stakeout on a tiny park bench in Pushkin Square, central Moscow. Two inches of fresh snowfall surrounded him, but the sky was clear and bright. He took full tactical advantage of the temperatures by wearing a heavy coat with a thick fur hood. He imagined that if his own wife sat next to him on this park bench she would have no idea as to his identity.

And that was coming in handy at the moment. Two muscular Frenchmen were also in the park, also looking at the same location Clark had come to stake out. He'd spotted them and a pair of their colleagues the day before. The others were stationed in a van up on Uspenskiy Pereulok, a van that they'd kept running throughout the day and night. Clark had noticed the steaming exhaust on one of his "lazy eight" strolls through the neighborhood, just one of dozens of anomalies his fertile tactical mind had seen in the streets surrounding his target's house. The other anomalies he had, after checking them out, eliminated as potential tip-offs to watchers, but the two Frenchmen in the park, and the van that ran all day long in its parking spot, meant the men after him were using his target as bait.

It did not work for them in Tallinn, but here in Moscow, they would be determined not to fail again.

Clark used peripheral vision to watch the front door of the apartment of Oleg Kovalenko. The old Russian spy had not left his home at all the day before, but that had not surprised John Clark much. A pensioner his age would not want to stroll the icy streets of Moscow unless it was necessary; there were likely tens of thousands of elderly shut-ins filling tiny apartments throughout the frozen city this weekend.

The day before he'd bought a mobile phone with prepaid credits in a shopping center. He'd found Kovalenko's phone number in the phone book, and he'd considered just calling the man and asking him for a minute of his time somewhere safe. But Clark had no way of knowing if the ex–KGB officer's phone had been bugged by the French, so he discarded that plan.

Instead he had spent most of the day looking for a way into the Russian's apartment that would not tip off the Frenchmen. He got an idea around two in the afternoon, when an old woman in a purple cap pushed an old metal rolling cart out of the front entrance of the building and headed west through the square. He followed her into a market, where she bought several staples. In the checkout line Clark stood next to her, used his rusty Russian to strike up a friendly conversation. He was apologetic about his language abilities, explaining he was an American newspaper reporter in town working on a story about how "real" Muscovites deal with harsh winters.

Clark offered to pay for her groceries if she would sit down with him for a quick interview.

Svetlana Gasanova was thrilled with the opportunity for company with a handsome young foreigner, and she insisted on taking him back to her flat—she lived right up the street, after all—and making him a cup of tea.

The watchers in the park were not looking for a couple entering the apartment, and Clark was bundled up in his coat and hood to the point where they could not have identified him without standing six inches from his nose. He even carried a bag of groceries to give the impression he belonged in the building.

John Clark spent a half-hour chatting with the old pensioner. His Russian was strained every minute of his time in her flat, but he smiled a lot and nodded a lot, and he drank the jam-sweetened tea she made for him while she talked about the gas company, her landlord, and her bursitis.

Finally, after four p.m., the woman seemed to grow tired. He thanked her for her hospitality, took down her address, and promised to send her a copy of the newspaper. She led him to the door of her flat and he promised to return for a visit on his next trip into Moscow.

He headed to the stairwell, tossed the woman's address in an ashtray, and went upstairs instead of down.

Clark did not knock at Oleg Kovalenko's door. He had noticed when he entered Ms. Gasanova's flat that the heavy oaken doors in this old building were secured with large, easy-to-defeat pin tumbler locks. John had created lock picks days earlier by buying a small set of dental instruments at a pawnshop here in Moscow and then bending them to approximate lock picks he had used in the past in Russia.

From a pouch in his coat pocket he retrieved his home-made facsimiles of a half-diamond pick, a rake pick, and a tension wrench.

Checking up and down the wooden-floored hallway to make certain no one was around, he put the picks in his mouth, then manipulated the tension wrench inside the keyhole, turning it counterclockwise slightly and holding the tension on the wrench with his right pinky finger. Then, with his left hand, he took the rake pick from his mouth and slid it above the tension wrench, inside the keyhole. Using both hands while maintaining the pressure on his pinky finger he slid the pick in and out over the spring-loaded pins, pushing them down into place.

After he'd defeated all but two of the pins, he replaced the rake pick in his mouth, then took the half-diamond pick, slid it into place in the lock, and slowly manipulated the last two pins, pushing them down from back to front.

With a satisfying click that he hoped had not made much noise inside the flat, the tension wrench turned on the open cylinder and the bolt opened on the door.

Quickly John placed everything back in his pocket and drew his pistol.

He pushed open the door and slid into the kitchen of the tiny flat. Past this he found himself looking into a darkened and tiny living room. A couch, a tiny coffee table, a television set, an eating table with several liquor bottles on it. Big Oleg Kovalenko sat in a chair at the window looking outside through dirty blinds, his back to the room.

In English Clark said, "How much time before they know I'm here?"

Kovalenko started, stood from the chair, and turned around. His hands were empty, otherwise Clark would have pumped a .45-caliber round into his fat belly.

The big Russian grabbed at his chest, his heart pounding after he was startled, but soon he sat back down. "I do not know. Did they see you enter?"

"No."

"Then do not worry. You have more than enough time to kill me."

Clark lowered the pistol and looked around. This place wasn't even as nice as Manfred Kromm's little flat. *Shit*, the American thought. So little thanks for all our years of service to our countries. This old Russian spy, the old East German spy Kromm, and John Clark, himself an old American spy.

Three fucking peas in a pod.

"I'm not going to kill you." Clark nodded toward the empty vodka bottles. "You don't look like you need any help."

Kovalenko thought this over. "Then you want information?"

Now Clark shrugged. "I know you met Paul Laska in London. I know your son, Valentin, is involved as well."

"Valentin follows orders from his leaders, as do you. As did I. He has nothing personal against you."

"Who are those guys out there in the park?"

Kovalenko said, "They were sent by Laska, I think, in

order to capture you. They work for the French detective Fabrice Bertrand-Morel. My son is back in London, his part in this affair was political, and it was benign, he had nothing to do with men chasing after you." The old Russian nodded toward the gun low in Clark's right hand. "I would be surprised if my boy has ever touched a gun." He chuckled. "He is so fucking civilized."

"So are you in contact with the men in the street?"

"In contact? No. They came here. They told me about you. Told me you would come here, but they would protect me. I knew nothing of you before yesterday. I only set up the meeting between Valentin and Pavel. Sorry . . . Paul. I was not told what was discussed."

"Laska worked for the KGB in Czechoslovakia." Clark said it as a statement.

Kovalenko did not deny it. He only said, "Pavel Laska has been an enemy of every state he has ever lived in."

But John did not render judgment on Laska. The American ex–CIA man knew that the ruthless KGB could have destroyed the spirit of a young Paul Laska, turned him into something not of his own choosing.

The Cold War was littered with broken men.

Oleg said, "I am going to make myself a drink if you promise you won't shoot me in the back." Clark waved him toward his bottles and the big Russian lumbered over to the table. "Would you like something?"

"No."

Kovalenko said, "So what have you learned from me? Nothing. Go back home. You will have a new president in a few weeks. He will protect you."

Clark did not say it, but he wasn't looking for protection from Jack Ryan. Quite the opposite. He needed to protect Ryan from exposure to *him*, to The Campus.

Kovalenko stood at his table and poured himself a tall straight vodka into a water glass. He walked back over to the chair with the bottle and the glass in his hands.

"I want to talk to your son."

"I can call his office at the embassy in London. But I doubt he'd call me back." Kovalenko swigged half the glass and put the bottle down on the windowsill, rattling the blinds in the process. "You would have better luck calling him yourself."

The Russian seemed, to Clark, like he was telling the truth. He did not have much of a relationship with his son, and his son definitely was not here. Could Clark get to him in London, somehow?

He'd have to try. Coming to Moscow to bleed Oleg Kovalenko for information had been a dry hole.

Clark slipped his gun in his pocket. "I'll leave you with your vodka. If you do talk to your boy, tell him I would like a word. Just a friendly conversation. He'll be hearing from me."

The American turned to leave through the kitchen, but the Russian pensioner called after him. "Sure you won't join me for a drink? It will warm you from the cold."

"*Nyet*," John said as he reached the door.

"Maybe we could talk about old times."

Clark's hand stopped on the door latch. He turned, walked back into the living room.

Oleg cracked a little smile. "I do not get many visitors. I can't be choosy, can I?"

Clark's eyes sharpened as he scanned the room quickly. "What?"

His eyes stopped scanning, locked onto the vodka bottle on the windowsill. It pressed against the blinds, closing them.

A signal to the men in the park. "Son of a bitch!" Clark shouted, and he shot back through the kitchen, out the door, and up the hallway.

He heard noises in the stairwell, the chirping of a walkie-talkie and the slapping, echoing footfalls of two men. John ran to the top of the stairs and grabbed a heavy, round metal ashtray/garbage can that had been positioned there. He laid the cylinder on its side at the edge of the top stair, waited until the sounds of the men told him they were just around the corner below, and then he kicked the metal can. He just caught a glimpse of the first man turning at the landing; he wore a heavy black coat and carried a small black pistol and a radio. John drew his pistol and adopted a combat stance at the top of the stairs.

The metal garbage can picked up speed as it bounced down the stairs. As the men turned onto the flight just below Clark, the can bounced head high and banged into them, sending both men crashing to the tile floor. One man dropped his pistol, but the other retained his weapon and tried to aim it up the stairwell at the man standing above them.

John fired a single round. The .45-caliber bullet burned a red crease into the man's left cheek.

"Drop it!" Clark shouted in English.

The man on the tiled floor below did as he was told. Along with his partner he raised his hands into the air as he lay there.

Even with the silencer on his SIG Sauer .45 the echo of Clark's pistol in the stairwell was painfully loud, and he had no doubt residents would be on the phone to the police in seconds. He descended to the landing and stepped between the two men, keeping his pistol trained on them all the while. He liberated them of their guns and their walkie-talkies and their mobile phones. One of the men cursed Clark in French, but he kept his hands in the air while doing so, and John ignored him. John did not say another word to the men before continuing down the stairs.

He exited the back door of the apartment building a minute later, and here he dumped the men's equipment in a trash can.

He thought, for a fleeting hopeful moment, that he was in the clear, but a white panel truck passed by on the opposite side of the road, and then it slammed on its brakes. Four men leapt out, there were eight lanes of afternoon traffic between John and the four, but they began running through the cars, heading right for him.

John broke into a run. His original objective had been the Pushkinskaya Metro station. But the men were on his heels, not fifty yards back, and they were a lot faster than he. The underground station would slow his escape—he would never make it on a train before they caught him. He ran across busy Tverskaya Street, eight lanes of traffic that *he* had to negotiate like a violent dance.

On the other side of the street he chanced a glance behind him. The four men were joined by two more in the street. The six hunters were only twenty-five yards back now.

They were going to catch him, it was quickly becoming apparent. There were too many men, they were too well trained, too well coordinated, and, he had to admit, they were too motherfucking young and fit for him to outrun them all across Moscow.

He could not get away from them, but he could, with a little cunning and guile, "game" his capture.

John picked up the pace now, trying to put a little space

between himself and the six behind. As he did so, he pulled the prepaid phone he'd purchased the day before from his coat pocket.

The phone had an "auto answer" key that set the device to pick up automatically any incoming call after two rings. He enabled this feature with a few taps of his thumb, and then he turned down a side street that ran perpendicular to Pushkin Square. It was little more than an alley, but Clark saw what he was looking for. A municipal garbage truck rolled slowly in the opposite direction after just loading up with refuse from a dumpster outside the McDonald's. John took his phone, looked down at the number on the screen, and then hurled it into the back of the truck just as it made a left behind the McDonald's.

Then Clark turned into the doors of the restaurant as the men chasing him turned the corner behind.

John shot through the door, ran past smiling employees asking if they could help him, and pushed through a crowd that pushed him back.

He tried to escape through a side entrance but a black sedan screeched to a halt there, and two men in black sunglasses and heavy coats emerged from the backseat.

Clark ducked back into the restaurant and then headed toward the kitchen.

This Pushkin Square McDonald's was the largest McDonald's in the world. It could serve nine hundred customers simultaneously, and Clark got the impression they were having a busy afternoon rush. Finally he managed to make his way through the crowd and into the kitchen.

In an office beyond, Clark lifted the phone and dialed the number he'd just memorized. "Come on! Come on!"

After two rings, he heard a click and knew the call had been put through.

At that moment the six armed hunters appeared in the doorway to the office.

Clark spoke loudly into the phone: "Fabrice Bertrand-Morel, Paul Laska, and Valentin Kovalenko of the SVR." He said it again as the men closed on him, then he hung up the phone.

The biggest man of the crew lifted his handgun high over his head, then brought it down hard onto the bridge of John Clark's nose.

And then everything went black.

Clark awoke tied to a chair in a dark room without windows. His face hurt, his nose hurt, and his nostrils seemed to be full of bloody gauze.

He spit blood on the floor.

There was only one reason he was still alive. His phone call had confused them. Now these men, their boss, and their employer would all be scrambling to figure out whom he had communicated with. If they killed him now, after he'd passed the information on, it would do them no good.

Now they might beat him to get him to reveal his contact, but at least they would not put a bullet in his brain.

Not yet, anyway.

70

The Baikonur Cosmodrome, located north of the Syr Darya River in the steppes of the former Soviet satellite state of Kazakhstan, is both the oldest and the largest spaceport on earth. The entire grounds of the facility are roughly a circle some fifty miles in diameter, containing dozens of buildings, launch pads, hardened silos, processing facilities, tracking stations, launch control buildings, roads, an airfield, and a train station. The nearby town of Baikonur has its own airport and another rail station is nearby in Tyuratam.

The first rocket launch pad was built here in the 1950s at the start of the Cold War, and from here in Baikonur, Yuri Gagarin launched to become the first man in space. The commercial space industry would not exist for another thirty years, but today Baikonur is Russia's main hub of private commercial space operations. They rent the property out from Kazakhstan, paying not in dollars or rubles or euros, but in military equipment.

Georgi Safronov had been walking the halls, standing on the pads, driving trucks across the steppes here for nearly twenty years. He was the face of the new Russia when it came to outer space, not unlike Gagarin himself representing Russia's space operations a half-century earlier.

On his first day back at Baikonur, the day before the planned launching of the first of three Dnepr rockets in quick succession, forty-five-year-old Georgi Safronov sat in his temporary office in the LCC, the launch control center, situated some five miles west of the three launch silos devoted to Dnepr launches at Baikonur. The Dnepr area, though it encompassed dozens of square miles of territory, was actually quite small when compared with the launch facilities for the Soyuz, Proton, and Rokot systems in other parts of the Cosmodrome.

Georgi looked out his second-floor window at a light snowfall that obscured his view of the launch sites in the distance. Somewhere out there three silos already contained hundred-foot-tall headless rockets, but soon they would have their heads, and those three frozen concrete holes out there would become the most important and most feared place on earth.

A knock on the door to his office pulled his eyes away from the snowy vista.

Aleksandr Verbov, Safronov's director of launch operations, leaned in the doorway. "Sorry, Georgi, the Americans from Intelsat are here. Since I can't take them to the control room, I told them I would see if you were busy."

"I would love to meet my American customers."

Safronov stood as six Americans entered the small office. He smiled graciously, shaking their hands and speaking to them one at a time. They were here to monitor the launch of their communications satellite, but in fact their payload container containing their equipment would be switched out for a container presently sitting under guard in a train car a few miles from the Cosmodrome.

As he shook hands and exchanged pleasantries, he knew that these five men and one woman would be dead very soon. They were infidels, and their death was inconsequential, but he could not help thinking nevertheless that the woman was quite pretty.

Georgi damned his weakness. He knew his flesh would be rewarded in the afterlife. He told himself this and he smiled into the attractive communications executive's eyes and moved on to the next American, a short, fat, bearded man with a Ph.D. in something irrelevant.

Soon the Americans were out of his office and he returned to his desk, knowing the process would be repeated by the Japanese customers and the British clients. The LCC was officially off-limits to foreigners, but Safronov had allowed the representatives from his customers' companies some access to the second-floor offices.

Throughout the day he took full command of the preparations of the rockets. There were other people who could handle this, Georgi was president of the company after all, but Safronov explained away his personal attention by saying this was the first Dnepr multi-launch in history, with a trio of launches during a planned window of only thirty-six hours, and he wanted to make sure everything went according to plan. This could, he argued, help them attract more clients in the future if multiple companies needed their equipment launched in a specific time window. The Dnepr rockets did have the ability to take more than one satellite into space at a time, with all equipment loaded into the same Space Head Module, but this was only helpful if the customers all wanted the same orbit. The three-launch schedule for the next two days would send satellites to the south and to the north.

Or so everyone thought.

No one really raised an eyebrow at Safronov's hands-on approach, as Georgi was a hands-on leader as well as an expert on the Dnepr system.

But no one knew that his expertise would rely on work he had done over a decade earlier.

When the R-36 ballistic missile left service in the end of the 1980s, 308 missiles remained in the Soviet Union's inventory.

Safronov's company began refitting them for space launch operations under contract from the Russian government in the late nineties, but at the time the US Space Shuttle Program was in full gear, and America had plans for more space vehicles on the horizon.

Safronov worried that his company could not make the Dnepr system profitable with commercial space launches alone, so he concocted other plans for their use.

One of the ideas Safronov put forth and explored for years was the idea that a Dnepr-1 rocket could be used as a maritime lifesaving device. He postulated that if, say, a ship was sinking off the coast of Antarctica, a launch of a rocket in Kazakhstan could send a pod carrying three thousand pounds up to twelve thousand miles away in under an hour, with an accuracy of under two kilometers. Other payloads could be sent to other parts of the globe in emergency situations, an admittedly expensive but unparalleled airmail service of sorts.

He knew it sounded fanciful, so he spent months with teams of scientists working out the telemetry physics of his idea, and he had developed computer models.

Ultimately his plans went nowhere, especially after US shuttle launches ceased and then only restarted slowly after the loss of the Space Shuttle Challenger.

But a few months earlier, as soon as he returned from his meeting with General Ijaz, Safronov dusted off his old computer discs and put a team together to rework the mechanics of sending Dnepr vehicles into high atmosphere instead of low orbit, and then dropping them down to a particular location, parachuting a pod to earth.

His team thought it was hypothetical, but they did their job, and Safronov had the computer models and executable commands secretly loaded into the software now in use at the LCC.

He took a quick call from Assembly and Integration: the three satellites were now out of the clean room and had been placed in the payload containers and fitted into the Space Head Modules, the nose of the actual spacecraft that would, as far as the owners of the satellites knew, put their equipment into earth orbit. These spacecraft would now be taken out to the silos in transporter-erectors, large cranc-trucks that would mate them to the launch vehicles, the huge three-stage rockets that already waited in their silos. It was a several-hours-long process that would not end until late in the evening, and much of the staff would be out of the LCC to oversee or just spectate at the launch sites.

This would give Georgi time to coordinate with his men down in Baikonur, to prepare for the attack.

Everything was going according to plan so far, but Safronov expected nothing else, since every single action that he had taken was nothing less than Allah's will.

The Frenchmen working for Fabrice Bertrand-Morel might have been good detectives, good hunters of human prey, but as far as John Clark was concerned they were awful interrogators. For the past two days he'd been punched, kicked, slapped, denied food and water, and even denied a bathroom break.

That was torture?

Yes, the American's jaw was swollen and sore, and he'd

lost two crowns. And yes, he'd been forced to piss on himself and he was sure he'd lost enough weight in two days to ensure that, if he ever got up to leave this place, he'd need to make a beeline to a clothing store to get some clothes that would not fall off him. But no, these guys did not have the first idea of how to get someone to talk.

John had gotten no sense from the men that they were under any time constraints from their boss. It had been the same six men he'd been with since the beginning, they'd stuck him in some rented house, likely not far from Moscow, and they thought they could knock him around for a couple of days to get him to reveal his contacts and his affiliations. He was asked about Jack Ryan a lot. Jack Ryan Sr., that is. He was asked about his current job. And he was asked about the Emir. He got the impression that the men asking the questions did not know enough of the context of the information that was being sought to be any good at their questioning. Someone—Laska or FBM or Valentin Kovalenko—had sent them questions to ask, so that's what they did.

Ask question. Get no answer. Punish. Repeat.

Clark wasn't having any fun, but he could continue like this for a week or more before they really started to annoy him.

He'd been through worse. Hell, SEAL training was much, much worse than this shit.

One of the Frenchmen, the one John thought of as the nicest of the bunch, stepped into the room. He wore a black track suit now; the men had gone out and bought new clothes for the interrogation after Clark's sweat and blood and spit had made it onto their suits.

He sat on the bed; Clark was tied in his chair. "Mr.

Clark. Time is running out for you. Tell me about the Emir, Monsieur Yasin. You were working with Jacques Ryan to find him, with some of your old friends from the CIA, perhaps? *Oui?* You see, we know much about you and the organization with whom you work, but we just need a little bit more of the information. You give us this, it is no big thing to you, and then you go home."

Clark rolled his eyes.

"I don't want my friends to hit you again. There is no use in this. You talk, yes?"

"No." Clark said it through a sore jaw that he was sure was about to get a little more sore.

The Frenchman shrugged. "I call my friends. They will hurt you, Mr. Clark."

"As long as they don't talk as much as you."

Georgi Safronov liked to think that he had thought through every last detail of his plan. On the morning of the realization of his plot, the forty-three remaining Jamaat Shariat forces positioned nearby had already broken off into their small units, using tactics learned training with the very capable Haqqani network in Waziristan.

But there were two sides to any military engagement, and Safronov had not neglected to study his adversary, the site security force.

Security for Baikonur used to be the responsibility of the Russian Army, but they pulled out years earlier and, since that time, the protection of the nearly two-thousand-square-mile area was the job of a private company from Tashkent.

The men drove around in trucks, patrolling the grounds, and they had a couple of men positioned at the front gates, and they had a large barracks building full of men, but the fence line at Baikonur was low and poor in most areas and non-existent in others.

It was not a secure environment.

And although the land appeared at a distance to be nothing but wide-open range, Safronov knew that the steppes were crisscrossed with dry streams and natural depressions that could be exploited. He also knew that a local Muslim insurgent force, Hizb ut-Tahrir, had tried to enter the spaceport in the past, but they were so weak and poorly trained they had only bolstered the delusion of the hired Kazakh guard force that they were ready for an attack.

An attack was coming, Georgi knew, and he would see how ready they were.

Safronov himself had befriended the leader of the guards. The man made regular visits to the Dnepr LCC when a launch was imminent, and Georgi had called the man the evening before to ask him to come by early because Kosmos Space Flight Corporation, Georgi's company, had sent a token of appreciation from Moscow for all the fine work he was doing.

The director of security was thrilled, and he said he would arrive at Mr. Safronov's office at eight-thirty a.m.

It was now seven forty-five, and Safronov paced his office.

He worried his human form would not be able to do what must be done now, and it made him shake. His brain told him what must be done, but he was not certain he could see it through.

His phone rang, and he was glad for the interruption.

"Yes?"

"Hi, Georgi."

"Hello, Aleksandr."

"Do you have a moment?"

"I'm a little busy going over the numbers for the second launch. I won't have much time after the first launch this afternoon."

"Yes. But I need to speak with you about this afternoon's launch. I have some concerns."

Dammit! Not now! thought Georgi. He did not need to spend his morning dealing with a technical matter involving a satellite that would travel no farther than the distance his men dropped it next to the silo when they replaced it with their own Space Head Module.

Still, he needed to appear as if everything was normal for as long as possible.

"Come in."

"I am at Flight Data Processing. I can be there in fifteen minutes. Twenty if there is too much ice on the road."

"Well, hurry up, Aleksandr."

It took Director of Launch Operations Aleksandr Verbov the full twenty minutes to arrive at his president's office at the LCC. He entered without knocking, stamping his feet and pulling off his heavy coat and hat. "Fucking cold morning, Georgi," he said with a grin.

"What do you need?" Safronov was running out of time. He had to get his friend out of here in a hurry.

"I'm sorry to say it, but we need to cancel today's flight."

"What? Why?"

"Telemetry is having issues with some software. They want to troubleshoot for a while, then power down and reset. Some of our data collection and processing systems will be affected for a few hours. But the next window to launch all three vehicles in quick succession, as we planned, will be in three days' time. I recommend we cancel the launch sequence, power down the power pressure generators, offload the fuel from all three LVs, and put the SCs in temporary storage configuration. We will have a delay, but will still set the record for a narrow launch window, which ultimately is our goal."

"No!" Safronov said. "The launch sequence continues. I want 109 ready to go at noon."

Verbov was completely taken aback. This was a response unlike any he'd ever gotten from Safronov, even when the news was bad. "I do not understand, Georgi Mikhailovich. Did you not just hear me? Without proper telemetry readings European mission control would never allow the spacecraft to continue their flight. They will abort the launch. You know that."

Safronov looked at his friend for a long moment. "I want it to launch. I want all missiles ready in their silos."

Verbov smiled as he cocked his head. He chuckled. "Missiles?"

"LVs. You know what I mean. Nothing to worry about, Aleksandr. It will all be clear soon."

"What is going on?"

Safronov's hands trembled, he clutched the fabric of his pant legs. Over and over he whispered to himself a mantra given to him by Suleiman Murshidov. "One second of jihad equals one hundred years of prayer. One second of jihad equals one hundred years of prayer. One second of jihad equals one hundred years of prayer."

"Did you say something?"

"Leave me."

Aleksandr Verbov turned away slowly, headed out into the hallway. He'd gotten just ten feet or so from his boss's door when Safronov called to him from his office.

"I'm joking, Alex! Everything is fine. We can delay the launch if telemetry says we must."

Verbov shook his head with a snorted chuckle, something between confusion and mirth, then he returned to the office. He was through the doorway before he noticed the pistol in Safronov's hand. He gave an incredulous smile, like he did not believe the weapon was real. "Georgi Mikhailovich . . . what do you think you are—"

Safronov fired a single round from the suppressed Makarov auto pistol. It entered Aleksandr's solar plexus, passed through a lung, shattered a rib as it tore out his back. Alex did not fall, he'd winced with the noise of the gunshot, hesitated a moment before looking down at the bloodstain growing on his brown coveralls.

Georgi thought it took Aleksandr a long time to die. Neither man said a word, they only looked at each other with similar stares of bewilderment. Then Alex reached back, found the vinyl chair by the door, and sat down in it roughly.

Another few seconds and his eyes closed, his head sagged to the side, and a long final breath blew from his damaged lung.

It took Georgi several more seconds to control his own breathing. But he did so, and he placed the pistol on the desk next to him.

He pulled the dead man, still in his chair, into the closet in his office. He had made space for one man, the director of security, but now he would need to make more room for the Kazakh when he came in just minutes.

Safronov dumped Verbov's body out of the chair and onto the floor of the closet, pushed the dead man's feet inside, and then shut the door. Hurriedly he grabbed a roll of toilet paper in his bathroom and wiped up the drips of blood on the floor of his office.

Ten minutes later the director of security was dead as

well, flat on the floor of Safronov's office. He was a big man, and he still wore his coat and his heavy boots. Georgi stared at the body, the hangdog expression on the dead man's face, and he wanted to retch. But he did not retch, he focused himself, and he dialed his mobile with a trembling hand.

When the call was answered on the other end, he said, "*Allahu Akbar.* It is time."

71

Without their leader, the Kazakh security force did not stand a chance.

The Jamaat Shariat terrorists hit the main gate in force at 8:54 a.m. in a driving snow. They killed four guards posted there and destroyed three trucks full of reinforcements with RPGs before the Kazakhs fired a single shot.

The snowfall slowed as the six Dagestani vehicles— four pickup trucks carrying six men each, and two semi trailers, each one carrying a payload container, one with six men and one with seven—separated at a crossroads near the launch control center. A pickup of six men went to the processing facility, to take control of the sixteen foreigners who worked for the three companies with satellites here at Baikonur. The two semis headed for the three launch pads, along with one of the pickups leading the way. Another six-man unit remained at the turnoff from the main road to the Dnepr. They climbed out of their vehicles and into a low concrete bunker that was once a guard post for Russian military forces but now lay half buried in the snowy grasses of the steppes. Here they positioned RPG launchers and scoped rifles and scanned the roads, ready to take out any vehicle from a distance.

The remaining two six-man teams both drove to the LCC, and here they did meet stiff resistance. There were a dozen security men present, and they killed five of the twelve attackers before finding themselves overrun.

Several guards dropped their guns and raised their hands, but the Dagestanis killed the Kazakhs where they surrendered.

The Kazakhs' response to the attack was horribly uncoordinated after the disappearance of their leader. Their nearby barracks did not mount a counterattack for twenty-five minutes, and as soon as they took the first incoming RPG round, missing the first truck as it approached the turnoff, they turned back to rethink their strategy.

In the LCC, the civilians hunkered down on the second floor while the attack outside raged. When the sound of execution-style killing ceased, when all the huddled Russian space launch engineers sat sobbing and praying and cursing, Georgi Safronov alone walked down the stairs. His friends and employees called out to him, but he ignored them, and he opened the door.

Jamaat Shariat forces took the LCC without firing another shot.

Everyone was ordered into the control room, and Georgi made an announcement.

"Do as I say, and you will live. Refuse an order once and you will die."

The men, his men, looked up to him in wide-eyed astonishment. One gunman, one of three posted by the emergency exit, raised his rifle into the air. *"Allahu Akbar!"*

The chorus was joined by everyone in the room.

Georgi Safronov beamed. He was in charge now.

The first people outside the Cosmodrome to learn of the attack at Baikonur were in Darmstadt, Germany, at the European Space Operations Center, the facility that was set to direct the satellites once in orbit. They were in the middle of a live preflight on-camera linkup with launch control, so they saw the LCC employees run for their lives. They also saw everyone return, with armed terrorists walking in behind them, and then the president of Kosmos Space Flight Corporation, Georgi Safronov, entering last.

Safronov wore an AK-47 around his neck and was dressed head to toe in winter camouflage.

The first thing he did upon entering the room was cut the feed to the ESOC.

The launch control room of the Dnepr launch control center would not impress anyone accustomed to movies and television programs of the US Kennedy Space Center, a massive amphitheater with gargantuan displays on the walls, and dozens of scientists, engineers, and astronauts working at flat-panel displays.

Dnepr rockets were launched and controlled from a room that looked something like a lecture hall in a community college; there was seating for thirty at long tables of control panels and computers. Everyone faced two large but by no means massive display panels on the front walls, one showing telemetry information and the other a live shot of the closed silo lid at site 109, containing the first of three Dneprs set to lift off in the next forty hours.

Snow swirled around the site, and eight armed men in rifles and white and gray camo uniforms had taken up positions on the low towers and cranes across the pad, their eyes scanning the snowy steppes.

Safronov had spent the last hour speaking by phone and walkie-talkie to the technical director of the processing facility, explaining exactly what was to be done at each launch site. When the man protested, when he refused to carry out Safronov's wishes, Georgi ordered one of the technical director's staff shot. After the death of his colleague, the technical director had given Georgi no more problems.

"Cut the feed at 109," Georgi ordered, and the screen in front of the men at launch control went blank.

He did not want the men in the room with him knowing which silos had the bombs, and which rocket contained the remaining satellite.

Now Safronov was about to explain everything to the staff here at the LCC.

"Where is Aleksandr?" asked Maxim Ezhov, Kosmos's assistant launch director, the first man brave enough to speak.

"I killed him, Maxim. I did not want to, but my mission required it."

Everyone just stared at him as he explained the situation.

"We are putting new payloads into the SHC's. This will be done at the launch sites. My men are overseeing this now, and the technical director of the processing facility is leading his men. Once he says it is complete, I will go out to the launch silos and check his work. If he has done what I asked him to do, he and his entire staff will be free to go."

The launch team stared at the president of Kosmos Space Flight Corporation.

"You do not believe me, do you?"

Some of the men just shook their heads no.

"I anticipated this. Gentlemen, you have known me for many years. Am I an evil man?"

"No," one of them said, a hopeful note in his voice.

"Of course not. Am I a pragmatic, efficient, intelligent man?"

Nods all around.

"Thank you. I want to show you that I will give you what you want, if you give me what I want." Georgi lifted his radio. "Let everyone Russian and Kazakh remaining at the processing facility go free. They may take their personal vehicles, of course. I am sorry but the busses will have to remain. There are many more people here who will require transport from the facility when this is all over." He listened to his subordinate acknowledge the order, and then said, "And please, ask them all to call the switchboard here when they are out of the spaceport to tell their friends here at the LCC that it was no trick. I have no desire to hurt anyone else. The men here at the Cosmodrome are my friends."

The launch control facility personnel relaxed in front of him. Georgi was feeling magnanimous. "You see? Do what I ask and you will live to see your families."

"What will we be doing?" asked Ezhov, now the de facto leader of the hostages in launch control.

"You will do what you came here to do. You will prepare to launch three rockets."

No one asked what was happening, though some had their suspicions about what was going to be loaded on their space vehicles.

Safronov was just as he said, an efficient and pragmatic man. He allowed the staff at the processing facility to go free because he did not need them any longer, and he needed his troops guarding the staff at processing to move to the launch silos to protect them from Spetsnaz. And he also knew this show of goodwill would make it more likely the launch control personnel would follow orders.

When he did not need the controllers any longer, however, he would have no incentive to let them live. He would kill them all as part of his statement to the infidels in Moscow.

The ESOC in Darmstadt reported the attack to its counterparts in Moscow, among others, and Moscow notified the Kremlin. After an hour of discussions over the phone, a direct link with the Kremlin was established. Safronov found himself standing in launch control with a headset on, conversing with Vladimir Gamov, the director of the Russian Federal Space Agency, who was at the Kremlin in a hastily organized crisis center. The two men had known each other for as long as Safronov could remember.

"What is going on over there, Georgi Mikhailovich?"

Safronov answered, "You can begin by calling me Magomed Dagestani." Mohammed the Dagestani.

In the background on the other end of the line Safronov heard someone mumble *"Sukin si."* Son of a bitch. This made him smile. Right now it would be sinking into everyone in the Kremlin that three Dnepr rockets were under control of North Caucasus separatists.

"Why, Georgi?"

"Are you too stupid to see? To understand?"

"Help me understand."

"Because I am not Russian. I am a Dagestani."

"That is not true! I have known your father since we were at Saint Petersburg. Since you were a child!"

"But you met my father after I was adopted from Dagestani parents. Muslims! My life has been a lie. And it is a lie that I will rectify now!"

There was a long pause. Men mumbled in the background. The director went in a different direction with the conversation. "We understand you have seventy hostages."

600

"That is not correct. I have released eleven men already, and I will release another fifteen as soon as they return from the silos, which should be within a half-hour at most."

"At the silos? What are you doing to the rockets?"

"I am threatening to launch them against Russian targets."

"They are *space* vehicles. How will you—"

"Before they were space vehicles they were R-36s. Intercontinental ballistic missiles. I have returned them to their former glory."

"The R-36 carried nuclear weapons. Not satellites, Safronov."

Georgi paused for a long moment. "That is correct. I should have been more accurate in my words. I have returned two of these specimens to their former glory. The third rocket does not have a warhead, but it is a powerful kinetic missile nonetheless."

"What are you saying?"

"I am saying I have two twenty-kiloton nuclear bombs, loaded into the Space Head Modules of two of the three Dnepr-1 delivery vehicles in my possession. The missiles are in their launch silos, and I am in launch control. The weapons, I call them weapons because they are no longer mere rockets, are targeting population centers of Russia."

"These nuclear weapons you speak of . . ."

"Yes. They are the missing bombs from Pakistan. My mujahideen fighters and I took them."

"Our understanding from the Pakistanis is that the weapons cannot detonate in their current state. You are bluffing. If you even have the bombs, you cannot use them."

Safronov had expected this. The Russians were so

dismissive of his people, after all. He would have been stunned if it were any different.

"In five minutes I will send an e-mail to you directly, and the subdirectors of your agency, that is to say, men more intelligent than you. In the file you will see the decoding sequence we used to render the bombs viable warheads. Share it with your nuclear experts. They will attest to its accuracy. In the file you will also see digital photographs of the altimeter fuses we stole from the Wah Cantonment armaments factory. Share them with your munitions experts. And in the file you will also see several possible trajectory plots for the Dnepr rockets, in case you do not believe I can return the payloads to earth wherever I want. Show that to your rocket engineers. They will spend the rest of the day with their calculators, but they will see."

Safronov did not know if the Russians believed him. He expected more questioning, but instead, the director of the Russian Federal Space Agency just said, "Your demands?"

"I want proof that the hero of the Dagestani revolution, Israpil Nabiyev, is alive. You give me this, and I release several more hostages. When you release Commander Nabiyev, and he is delivered here, I will release everyone else here except for a skeleton crew of technicians. When you remove all Russian forces from the Caucasus, I will take one of the nuclear-tipped Dneprs offline. And when myself, Commander Nabiyev, and my men have safely left the area, I will relinquish control of the other weapon. This situation that you find yourself in can be behind you in a matter of a few short days."

"I will need to discuss this with—"

"You may discuss this with whoever you want. But

remember this. I have sixteen foreign prisoners here. Six are from the United States, five are from Great Britain, and five are from Japan. I will begin executing the prisoners unless I speak with Nabiyev by nine o'clock tomorrow morning. And I will release the missiles unless Russia has quit the Caucasus in seventy-two hours. *Dobry den."* Good afternoon.

72

In the beautiful library of Paul Laska's Newport, Rhode Island, home, the aged billionaire cradled the handset of his telephone at his desk, and he listened to the low ticking of the Bristol mahogany grandfather clock in the hallway.

Time ticking away.

It had been five days since Fabrice Bertrand-Morel had reported that Clark had found Kovalenko and learned of Laska's involvement in the dossier passed to the Kealty administration. In those five days Bertrand-Morel had called every twelve hours with the same story. The grizzled spy had not talked about his contacts, had not revealed whom he told or what he told them. Each time Laska added more questions for the French to ask the man, more things that, if only revealed, could create some sort of leverage for Laska in case the news of his conspiring with the Russians made it into the wrong hands.

It was no longer about defending the Emir, and no longer about destroying Jack Ryan, though Paul hoped for that even now. No, at this point the Czech immigrant was concerned for his own survival. Things had not gone according to plan, the FBI had fucked up the arrest of Clark, and the FBM had fucked up the capture of Clark since he had already learned about Laska and passed that info on.

And now, Paul Laska decided, it was time to end this game. He lifted the phone from the receiver and dialed a number written on the blotter in front of him. He'd had the number since the beginning and he had doubted he would ever need to use it, but now it was unavoidable.

Four rings, and then a mobile phone in London was answered.

"Yes?"

"Good evening, Valentin. This is Paul."

"Hello, Paul. My sources tell me there is a problem."

"Your sources include your father, I assume."

"Yes."

"Then yes, there is a problem. Your father spoke to Clark."

"Clark should not have made it to Moscow. Your mistake, not mine."

"Fair, Valentin. I'll accept that. But let's deal with the world as it is, not as we would like it to be."

There was a long pause. "Why did you call?"

"We have Clark, we are holding him in Moscow, trying to find out just what our exposure is on this."

"That sounds prudent."

"Yes, well, the men working for us are not interrogators. They have fists, yes, but I am thinking you would have some expertise that would be very helpful."

"You think I torture people?"

"I don't know if you do or not, though I can imagine it is in your DNA. Many people talked after a few hours in a basement with your father."

"I am sorry, Paul, but my organization needs to limit its exposure in this enterprise. Your side has lost. The developing situation in Kazakhstan is occupying the concerns of everyone in my nation right now. The excitement about bringing down Jack Ryan has passed."

Laska fumed. "You cannot just walk away from this, Valentin. The operation is not complete."

"It is for us, Paul."

"Don't be a fool. You are in as deep as I am. Clark gave your name to his contact."

"My name is, unfortunately, a matter of record in the CIA. He can say what he wants."

Now Laska could hide his fury no longer. "Perhaps, but if I make one telephone call to *The Guardian,* you will be the most recognizable Russian agent in Britain."

"You are threatening to out me as SVR?"

Laska did not hesitate. "You as SVR, and your father as KGB. I'm sure there are still some angry people in the satellites that would love to know who was responsible for the death of their loved ones."

"You are playing a dangerous game, Mr. Laska. I am willing to forget about this conversation. But do not test me. My resources are—"

"Nothing like my resources! I want you to take custody of Clark, then I want you to find out who he is working for, what his present connection to Ryan is, and then you make him disappear so he cannot speak about what he has learned in the past month."

"Or what?"

"Or I make phone calls in the United States and in Europe, revealing what you've been up to."

"That is a poor bluff. You can't reveal your involvement. You have broken laws in your country. I have broken no laws in mine."

"In the past forty years, I've broken laws that you cannot imagine, my young friend. And yet I continue. I will survive this. You will not."

Kovalenko did not reply.

Laska said, "Make him talk. Cut off all the loose ends. Clean this up and we can all move on."

BAIKONUR COSMODROME

N

Proton LCC

Yubileinaya Airfield

SHM and SC
processing facility

Dnepr
silo launchers

104

103

Yuzhnaya Hotel

Soyuz launch pad

106, 109

Living area

Dnepr LCC

Dyurmentyube

Syr Darya

Krayniy Airfield

Sputnik Hotel

Tyuratam

Baikonur

0 Miles   5   10

0 Kilometers   10

Kovalenko started to say something, to grudgingly agree to look into the matter personally, but to make clear that he would not commit to any particular measure.

But Laska hung up the phone. The old man knew Valentin Kovalenko would follow orders.

Georgi knew from the very beginning that the FSB's Alpha Group would attempt to retake control of the facility. His fertile mind could have guessed as much even if he had not witnessed a mock FSB raid to retake the Soyuz facility from a terrorist organization, just three years prior.

He had no reason to be involved in the Soyuz operation, but he had been in Baikonur at the time on other business, and he was invited by facility officials to witness the exercise. He'd watched it all with incredulous fascination: the helicopters and the overland movement of the camo-clad forces, the concussion grenades and the rappelling from the roof of the building.

He'd talked to some Soyuz engineers after the drill and had learned more about the Russian contingency plan in the unlikely event terrorists ever took control of the complex.

Safronov knew there was also a chance Moscow would simply decide to fight fire with fire, and nuke the entire Cosmodrome in order to save Moscow. Fortunately for his plan, the Dnepr launch site at Baikonur was the original launch site of the R-36, and was therefore built to withstand a nuclear attack. Sites 104, 103, and 109 contained hardened silos from which the missiles launched, and the launch control facility was built with thick reinforced concrete walls and blast-proof steel doors.

*

At six p.m. on the first day, eight hours after the facility was overtaken by Dagestani terrorists, a pair of Russian FSB Alpha Group Mi-17 helicopters landed on the far side of the Proton rocket facilities, twenty-five kilometers from the Dnepr LCC. Twenty-four operators, three teams of eight, climbed out, each man laden with sixty pounds of gear and covered in white winter camouflage.

Within minutes they were heading east.

Shortly after eight o'clock in the evening, an Antonov An-124 transport aircraft landed at Yubileinaya Airfield northwest of the Baikonur Dnepr facility. The An-124 was the largest cargo aircraft on earth, and the Russian military needed every inch of the cabin space and cargo hold for the ninety-six Spetsnaz assault troops and all their gear, including four assault vehicles.

Four more Mi-17 helicopters arrived an hour later along with a refueling aircraft.

The twenty-four men in the white camo had been traversing the Baikonur steppes throughout the evening, first in heavy four-wheelers handed over by the Kazakhs, but as they got closer they left the vehicles behind and marched through the snow-covered grassland in the dark.

By two a.m. they were in position, waiting for a go code from their leadership.

Safronov had spent a busy afternoon giving orders to his gunmen, as well as the launch control engineers. After loading the nuclear devices into the Space Head Modules, he'd released the rest of the processing team. This decision, and his decision to have the foreign hostages brought to the LCC, allowed him to consolidate his men.

He had four Jamaat Shariat men at the crossroads

bunker, four at silo 109, ten each at silos 103 and 104, and fifteen at the LCC. He ordered his men to sleep in shifts, but he knew even those men sleeping would do so with one eye open.

He expected the attack to come in the middle of the night but did not know if it would be this evening or the next. He knew that, before the attack itself, he would be contacted by the Russians in order to occupy his attention at that critical moment.

So when he was awoken by a ring and a flashing light on the comms control board to which his headset was attached, his heart began to pound. Sitting on the floor against the wall with his AK in his lap, he leapt to his feet.

Before he answered the call he reached for his radio. He broadcast to all of his Dagestani brethren, "They are coming! Be ready!" and then he screamed at all the prisoners in the launch control room, most of whom were sleeping on the floor. "Everyone to your positions! I want 109 ready to launch in five minutes or I start shooting! Onboard telemetry up! Separation systems armed! LV pyro armed!"

"Yes, sir!" replied several of the launch control directors as they executed the commands, their hands trembling.

Bleary-eyed men in rumpled clothing scrambled to their seats as Dagestani gunmen waved rifles at them.

While this was going on, Georgi Safronov grabbed his headset and placed it to his ear. In a sleepy voice that he found hard to fake with the adrenaline in his bloodstream he said, "Yes? What is it?"

The twenty-four men who had spent the last eight hours humping overland hit the LCC on three sides, corresponding to the main entrance, the rear entrance, and an equipment loading bay.

Each entryway was protected by three Dagestani rebels, and they had warning from their leader that the attack was coming. The men at the front entrance started firing into the night as soon as the call came, a mistake that benefited them greatly, as it gave the Alpha Group men, still just at the far edge of the snow-covered parking lot, the false impression that they had been spotted. All eight men took cover behind cars and fired back at the open doorway, effectively pinning down both forces.

The rear door was breached by the second Russian team, they tossed flash-bangs through the doorway before entering, but they found themselves facing a long narrow corridor of reinforced concrete walls. At the far end of the corridor three terrorists, men wholly unaffected by the blasts, fired AKs at the men in the white camo. Even though much of the automatic fire came from Jamaat Shariat men simply reaching around a blind corner with their guns and holding the triggers down, the wayward bullets banged off the walls, the floor, and even the ceiling. The ricochets pulverized the attacking force.

Two men went down within seconds, two more fell when they tried to pull their mates out of the hall. The four remaining Alpha Group men pulled back, outside the building, and began hurling hand grenades up the hall.

By then, however, the three terrorists had pulled back through an inner iron door, where they waited safely while the grenades exploded.

This entrance had turned into a stalemate for both parties, much like the front door.

The Alpha men at the loading dock had better luck. They managed to take out all three of the Dagestanis with the loss of only one of their own. They pushed into the downstairs lobby, but there they triggered a booby-trapped door. The projectile from an RPG had been rigged into an improvised exploding device, another lesson from the Haqqani network, and the ensuing devastation killed three Russians and injured three more.

One of the Mi-17 helos from Yubileinaya Airfield arrived over the roof of the LCC, and men fast-roped to the concrete. Then they headed for the door in a tight stack. This door had been rigged to blow as well, but the Russians anticipated this, and stood clear of the doorway after the breach.

But while the IED did not kill the men on the roof, it slowed them down, and gave the men on the first and second floors time to respond to the sound of a helicopter above.

The stairwell to the roof exit became a third stalemate area at the LCC. Four Jamaat Shariat men had good cover on the second-floor landing behind an iron doorway and a blast-proof wall, and the eight Alpha Group men had the high ground above. Grenades bounced down the stairs only to explode harmlessly on the landing, and AK rounds sliced the air through the stairwell only to miss their targets tucked around the sides of the doorframe.

Within a minute of the start of the assault, Russian helos attacked the three launch silos. Sites 103 and 104 each had ten defenders, and they were well spread out and under good hardened cover. Site 109 had only four men guarding it, and it was also the first to be reached by the helos. The Mi-17 fired 12.7-millimeter machine guns, raking the site, but the fire was ineffective because the gunner did not have the thermal optics that would have allowed him to easily pick out his targets at the frozen location.

The helo at site 109 lowered to just above the earth, and twenty operators fast-roped to the concrete pad. These well-trained killers had better luck finding and engaging the enemy throughout the site than the Mi-17 had.

Site 109 was cleared in under a minute, as there were only four Jamaat Shariat mujahideen there. As the chatter of gunfire continued from the other sites, each nearly a mile distant over the steppes, the Alpha Group men at site 109 raced toward the silo, frantic to carry out the next phase of their mission in time.

The soldiers could not disable the nuclear weapon; they wouldn't even be able to get to it inside the Space Head Module without wasting considerable time. But they had been instructed on how to take the Dnepr offline from here at the launch site, to cut its umbilical cord to the LCC, so to speak, so they rushed forward at a breakneck pace.

The men used lights on their helmets and their rifles as they peered into the deep silo; the only part of the 110-foot-long rocket visible was a large green conical fairing with the white letters KSFC. Below this was the Space Head Module, and below this were the three rocket stages. The men used their lights to identify a massive iron lid a few feet from the open silo; it looked like a giant manhole cover. They got the hatch open, and two of the men began descending down a metal ladder, racing for the support equipment level, a catwalk just a dozen feet down where they would find a second ladder, which would take them down another level. Here they could gain access to the three-stage launch vehicle itself and disable the communication linkage that wired the launch vehicle to ground control.

As they ran across the catwalk and started down the second ladder, the two men knew they had little time.

"Are we ready?" Safronov shouted to the two men at the launch control board. When they did not answer, he screamed at them, *"Are we ready?"*

The redheaded man on the left just nodded curtly. The blond on the right said, softly, "Yes, Georgi. Launch sequence complete."

"Launch 109!" The two launch keys were already in their locks.

"Georgi, please! I cannot! Please do not—"

Safronov pulled his Makarov and shot the blond man twice in the back. He fell to the floor writhing in pain, screaming in panic.

Georgi turned to the launch engineer seated next to the dying man. "Can you do it, or will I do it myself?"

The Russian man reached over, placed his hand on one of the keys at the top of his control board, and then closed his eyes.

He turned the key. Then, looking up at the pistol in his face, he quickly turned the second key.

Above him, Georgi Safronov said, "Swords into plowshares, and now back into swords."

Safronov pressed the button.

At site 109, the two Alpha Group operators tasked with decoupling the communications linkage had just left the ladder, and they ran up the small hallway toward the base of the Dnepr-1, frantic to take the LV offline before the madman at launch control blasted the rocket into the stratosphere.

They did not make it.

A loud metallic click below their feet on the catwalk was the last input their brains ever registered.

A power pressure generator below the rocket contained a black powder charge held at pressure, and this ignited below their feet, creating a mass of gases that expanded instantly, firing the 110-foot-tall rocket out of the silo like the cork from a popgun. The two men were incinerated in the blink of an eye as the missile pushed out of the silo and the hot expanding gases pushed out across the tunnel toward small exhaust vents.

The rocket itself rose quickly, but it slowed as the gases that propelled it out of its silo dissipated. With the bottom of the lowest stage of the launch vehicle just sixty feet above the frozen launch silo, the huge craft hung in midair for a moment.

The eight Spetsnaz operators stood below it, staring at the bottom of a space rocket that was about to launch just over their heads.

One of the men mumbled, *"Der'mo."* Shit.

With a pop like a champagne cork, explosives pushed the protective cap off the bottom of the first stage, exposing the rocket exhaust system.

Then the first stage ignited, scorching the earth and all those on it below with flaming rocket fuel.

All eight men died within two seconds of one another.

The Mi-17 helicopter had been hovering at one hundred feet. The pilot yanked the controls hard, saving the lives of himself and his crew, but the helicopter itself was too low for such a maneuver. He crashed in the snow, a survivable crash, though the copilot broke both of his arms and the men in back suffered various injuries.

The Dnepr-1 rocket rose into the night sky, moving faster with each second, smoke and steam and flame behind it on the launch pad and in the air. A screech filled the air and a thumping vibration shook the ground for miles in all directions.

The 260-ton machine achieved a speed of 560 miles an hour in less than thirty seconds.

As it rose, all Russian forces abandoned their attack on the Baikonur Cosmodrome.

73

Safronov had programmed the flight telemetry himself using data derived from the working group he'd assembled a few months back. The group had no idea they were working on a nuclear attack, their understanding was that they were to reinvestigate the plan to send rescue boats and other emergency aid via rocket launch. The LV had instructions loaded onto its onboard software that controlled pitch and yaw and burn time, all to direct it toward its destination.

It was the ultimate "Fire and forget" weapon.

The first stage of the launch vehicle separated and fell back to earth, landing in central Kazakhstan just eight minutes after launch.

Moscow was tracking the trajectory, and everyone in the know realized within a few short minutes that their former R-36 missile was on course to Moscow itself.

But there was no running away. No leaving the city. The weapon would hit in under fifteen minutes.

High above central Russia, the second-stage powered flight ended, and after the second stage separated, it crashed onto a farm road near the town of Shatsk on the Shacha River. The third stage then flipped in flight and began traveling backward, and within minutes the fairing jettisoned back to earth. Soon the third-stage rockets extinguished and a protective shield released and fell. This released the Space Head Module from the upper platform stack where the payload container was attached, and this piece, a green cylinder with a payload container holding the device, began returning to earth, a ten-foot-by-ten-foot object weighing in excess of two tons.

The payload dropped in an arc, the heavier atmosphere affected the trajectory somewhat, but Georgi and his scientists had solved for a great number of variables, and the device pushed through the friction at terminal velocity.

The men and women in Moscow who knew of the launch held their children or prayed or cried or hoped or cursed everything Dagestani. They knew there was nothing else they could do.

At 3:29 a.m., while the vast majority of the huge ice-covered city was asleep, a low boom echoed across the southeastern district of Moscow. Nearby residents were shaken from their beds a second later when a larger explosion erupted, windows blew from buildings, and a rumbling vibration rolled across the entire city like a small earthquake.

Those in the city center could see the glow to the south. It rose higher into the air like a sunrise out of the predawn, reflecting off ice crystals on the rooftops of the metropolis.

At the Kremlin's crisis center they could see the rising fire, a savage inferno just miles away. Men screamed and cried as they braced for what was still to come.

But nothing came.

It took minutes to be certain, but eventually they had reports from the area of the impact. Something had fallen from the sky into the Gazprom Neft Moscow Refinery, a 200,000-barrel-per-day facility southeast of the city center.

It had struck the gas oil vacuum distillation tanks and created a massive explosion that killed more than a dozen people at the refinery instantly, and more died during the ensuing fire.

But it clearly was *not* a nuclear device.

Clark woke to the sound of a low boom in the distance.

He had a crick in his neck from sleeping sitting up. That his sore cervical joints were the most annoying sensation of the moment was telling. After several days of "rough stuff," he would have thought that he would be hurting more from the—

Oh, yeah. There it was. The pain in his jaw and his nose and the dull throb in his head. It took a minute for the mind to accept the assaults to the nerves, but his mind was processing everything nicely now, and the pain receptors were working overtime.

After the boom he heard nothing else from outside. He thought that maybe an electrical transformer shorted out somewhere, but he could not be sure.

He spit more blood, and a molar loosened. He'd bit the inside of his cheek somewhere along the way, as well, and his mouth was swollen on both sides.

He was growing tired of this.

The door opened again. He looked up to see which of the Frenchies were coming for a chat, but he did not recognize the two men who entered.

No, the *four* men, as two more came through the door now.

Moving with speed and a distressing efficiency the four young men cut Clark's bindings and ordered him to his feet in Russian.

Clark stood on shaky legs.

Two more men appeared in the doorway. They carried Varjag pistols in their right hands; they held them low but menacing. Their clothes were civilian, but their thick dark jackets and utility pants made them look, to a trained eye like Clark's, as if they were part of some sort of special unit of military, police, or intelligence officers.

"Come with us," one of them said, and they walked him through a large house, right past the French detectives, and into a van.

On the surface, Clark realized, perhaps he should have been glad. But it just didn't smell to him like a rescue operation.

No, this had an "Out of the frying pan, into the fire" feel.

They blindfolded him and drove for an hour. No one spoke to Clark, nor did the men in the van speak to one another.

When they stopped he was led out of the vehicle, still under his own power. The air was freezing cold, and he felt thick snowflakes on his beard and lips.

Into another building, this with the smell and feel of a warehouse, and he was placed on a chair. Once again, his hands and legs were tied. The blindfold came off and he squinted into a bright light for a moment, before finally opening his eyes.

Three men stood before him, just in the shadows outside the light above. Two wore blue jeans and track-suit tops, their heads shaved and their wide flat Slavic faces cold and unfeeling.

The third man wore pressed slacks and a black ski jacket that looked to Clark like it might have cost several hundred dollars.

A table nearby, just out of the direct light, contained a pile of tools, stainless-steel surgical instruments, tape, wire, and other items John could not make out.

Dread filled the American and tightness entered his stomach.

This wasn't going to be like playing punching bag for a group of French detectives. No, this looked like it was about to get ugly.

Clark also heard noises farther away in the warehouse. Armed guards, it sounded like, from the occasional shuffling of feet and the rattling of rifles on slings.

The man in the ski jacket stepped forward, under the light. He spoke excellent English. "My father says you are looking for me."

"Valentin." John said it in surprise. From the little he knew about the young man, he did not take him for someone that would make a house call to what, by all indications, seemed to be a torture facility. "I said that I wanted to talk to you." Clark looked at the table and the square-jawed men. "This is not exactly what I had in mind."

The thirty-five-year-old Russian just shrugged. "You and I are both here under duress, Mr. Clark. If I had a choice in the matter I would be anywhere else, but you are causing problems for my government and they have selected me to meet with you to resolve the problem. The Kremlin has given me free rein to deal with you."

"Sounds like a job for your father."

Valentin smiled mirthlessly. "This is not his job, nor his problem. I need to know everything about your current employer. I need to know who you spoke with in Moscow. We found the telephone that you called, but it had been dumped in a landfill, so we learned nothing."

Clark breathed a hidden sigh of relief.

Valentin continued, "The information I need can be extracted from you in many ways. Many humane ways.

But time is short, so if you resist we will have to seek other avenues. Less humane avenues, shall we say?"

Clark sized the young man up instantly. Kovalenko was uncomfortable in this role. He'd likely been in his element creating a political scandal for the incoming US President by leaking info from Laska, but standing here with tough guys in a frozen Moscow warehouse, getting ready to cut a prisoner to get him to talk ... This was not his realm.

Clark could not reveal the existence of The Campus to the Russians. He could have held out indefinitely with the French, at least until he died from beating, but Russians had other means. They allegedly possessed a drug, known as SP-117, that was a cut above other truth serums.

Clark knew nothing about the drug other than what he had read in open source. Russia as a threat had been off the ex–CIA operative's radar for a while.

But why was the drug not here? Why were there only torture devices and tough-looking guys present? Where was the medical facility, the doctors, the FSB psychologists who would normally do this sort of thing?

Clark understood.

John looked at Valentin. "I get it. You are working for Paul Laska. I have a feeling he has something on you, personal or professional I do not know, that is making you do this."

Valentin shook his head no, but he asked, "Why do you suggest this?"

"Because this is not your world. That you are here in person tells me you could not get FSB support. You are SVR, foreign intelligence. FSB has the interrogators here in Moscow that could do this, but where is the FSB? Why have you brought me into a fucking warehouse? You don't have a government facility for this sort of work? No, Valentin, your own ass is on the line, so you are breaking rules. You've scrounged up a couple of ex–Spetsnaz guys here, am I right? But they don't know how to do a proper interrogation. They will bash my fucking skull in before I talk."

Valentin was not accustomed to being outsmarted; Clark could see this in his eyes. "You have been at this since before I was born, old man. You are a dinosaur like my father. But unlike my father, you still retain a little spark in you. I am sorry to say that I will be the one to extinguish that spark. Right now."

Clark said nothing. The kid did not have state backing for what he was about to do, but he was no less motivated to do it.

Not good.

"Who are you working for, Mr. Clark?"

"Fuck you, sonny."

Kovalenko's face seemed to grow slightly pale. He looked to Clark as though he was not feeling well.

"Very well. You force my hand. Shall we begin?" He said a few unintelligible words to his two men, and they stepped over to the instruments on the table. While the thought of doctors in white lab coats was disconcerting to Clark in an interrogation environment, the concept of big men in track suits applying surgical instruments to his body was something beyond horrifying.

Kovalenko said, "Mr. Clark. I have degrees in economics and political science. I have studied at Oxford. I have a wife and a beautiful little girl. What is about to happen has nothing to do with me, with my world. Quite frankly, just the thought of what I am about to do to you makes me want to retch." He paused, then smiled a little. "I wish I had my father here for this. He would know exactly how to ratchet up the pain. But I will try my own methods. I will not begin with something benign, I can see that the men of Fabrice Bertrand-Morel Investigations have already failed with that tactic. No . . . tonight we will begin by devastating your body. After this you will be out of your mind with pain and distress, but you will see how incredibly prepared I am to inflict the ultimate damage upon you, and you will not want to see where I go with phase two of my interrogation."

What the fuck? thought Clark. This kid did not play by the rules. The men stepped behind Clark, they had blades in their hands. One grabbed the American by his head, the other took hold of his right hand.

Valentin Kovalenko knelt over John, looked him closely in the eyes, and said, "I have read your dossier multiple times. I know you are right-handed, and I know that gun hand of yours has served you well, ever since your nation's silly little war in Vietnam. Tell me who you contacted in Moscow, tell me who you work for, or I will have my associate here cut off your right hand. It is as simple as that."

Clark grimaced as the man on his right touched the skin on his wrist with a large cleaver. John's heart pounded against his rib cage.

Clark said, "I know you are just trying to clean up this mess that Laska made, Valentin. Just help me bring down Laska, and you won't need to worry about him."

"Last chance for your hand," the Russian said, and John saw that the young man's own heart was pounding. The pale white skin on his face was covered with a fresh sheen of sweat.

"We are both professionals. You do not want to do this."

"*You* do not want to make me."

Clark began taking short, rapid breaths of air. It was inevitable, what was about to happen. He needed to control his heart's reaction to it.

Valentin saw Clark resigned to his fate. A vein throbbed in the center of the Russian's forehead. Kovalenko turned away.

The cleaver rose off Clark's wrist. Hung in the air a foot above it.

"This is disgusting," Kovalenko said. "Please, Mr. Clark. Do not make me watch this."

Clark had no humorous retort to this. Every nerve in his body was on edge, every muscle tightened for the impending swing of the cleaver against his wrist.

Kovalenko looked back toward the American. "Really? You really will allow your body to be disfigured, your fucking hand to be severed, just to keep the information you have secret? Are you *that* fucking committed to some foolish cause? Are you *that* beholden to your masters? What sort of automaton are you? What kind of robot allows himself to be chopped to bits for some foolish sense of valor?"

Clark squinted his eyes shut. He'd readied himself as much as possible for the inevitable.

After thirty seconds, Clark opened his eyes back up. Valentin stared at him in disbelief. "They do not make men like you anymore, Mr. Clark."

Still, Clark said nothing.

Kovalenko sighed. "No. I cannot do it. I don't have the stomach to see his hand chopped off and lying on the floor."

Clark was surprised; he began to relax, just a little. But Valentin turned back to him, looking up to the man with the big sharp tool. "Put that down."

The man next to Clark heaved his chest. A little disappointed, maybe? He put down the cleaver.

Kovalenko now said, "Pick up the hammer. Break every bone in his hand. One at a time."

The Spetsnaz man quickly grabbed a stainless-steel surgical hammer that rested on the table next to the cutting instruments. With no warning whatsoever he slammed the hammer onto John's outstretched hand, shattering his index finger. He pounded a second and then a third time, while Clark shouted in agony.

Kovalenko turned away, jabbed his fingers into his ears, and walked to the far wall of the warehouse.

The fourth finger cracked just above the knuckle, and the pinky shattered in three places.

A final, vicious pounding of the back of Clark's hand threatened to send him into shock.

Clark gritted his teeth; his eyes were shut and tears dripped out from the sides. His face was a dark shade of crimson. He took short bursts of air, fast replenishments of oxygen, to keep from going into shock.

John Clark continued to cry out, slamming his head back hard against the stomach of the man behind him. He yelled, "You motherfucker!"

A minute later, Kovalenko was back over him. Clark could barely see the young man through the tears and sweat in his eyes and the poor focus of his dilated pupils.

Valentin winced as he glanced at the shattered hand. It was already swelling, black and blue, and two of the fingers were twisted perversely.

"Cover that!" he shouted at one of his men. A towel was tossed over the damaged appendage.

Kovalenko shielded his ears from the worst of the cries of agony, but he shouted, as if angry at the man in the chair for forcing him to do this, "You are a fool, old man! Your sense of honor will bring you nothing but pain here! I have all the time I need for you!"

Even through his agony, John Clark could tell Valentin Kovalenko was on the verge of nausea.

"Talk, old fool! Talk!"

Clark did not talk. Not then, not in the next hour. Kovalenko was growing more and more frustrated by the minute. He'd ordered Clark's head held under a bucket of water, and he'd had his men pound the American's rib cage, breaking a bone and bruising him so badly he could barely breathe.

John did his best to disassociate himself from what was going on with his body. He thought of his family, his parents, long since dead. He thought of friends and colleagues. He thought of his new farm in Maryland, and he hoped that, even though he would never see it again, his grandkids would grow up loving the place.

Clark passed out two hours after the torture began.

74

The light indicating an incoming call from the crisis center had been blinking now for more than ten minutes.

Safronov watched the news from Moscow on one of the main monitors, the other men at launch control, unwilling participants, sat in rapt attention.

Georgi had hoped for a bigger spectacle. He knew launch site 109 contained the Dnepr loaded with the satellite and not one of the nukes, but he had targeted the central fuel storage containers at the Moscow Oil Refinery, which should have created a much larger explosion and fire. The payload had missed its target only by a quarter-kilometer, however, and Safronov felt he had gotten his point across.

After watching the news a few seconds more he finally lifted the headset off the control panel, put it on, and accepted the call. *"Da."*

"You are speaking with President Rychcov."

Safronov responded in a cheery voice. "Good morning. You may not remember me, but we met at the Bolshoi last year. How is the weather in Moscow?"

There was a long pause before the president's reply, delivered curtly but with a slight tone of anxiety. "Your attack was unnecessary. We understand you have the technical capabilities to do that which you threaten. We know you have the nuclear weapons."

"That was punishment for your attack on this facility. If you attack again . . . well, President, I have no more kinetic missiles. The other two Dneprs at my disposal are nuclear-tipped."

"There is nothing for you to prove. We only need to negotiate, you in a position of power, me . . . in a position of weakness."

Safronov shouted into his headset, "This is not a negotiation! I have demanded something! I have not entered into negotiations! When will I be allowed to speak with Commander Nabiyev?"

The president of Russia replied wearily. "I have allowed this. We will call you back a little later this morning and you will be able to speak with the prisoner. In the meantime, I have ordered all security forces back."

"Very good. We are prepared for another fight with your men, and I do not believe you are prepared to lose five million Muscovites."

This was not how Ed Kealty planned on spending the time left in his term, but at nine p.m. Washington, D.C., time, he and members of his cabinet met in the Oval Office.

CIA Director Scott Kilborn was there, along with Alden, the deputy director. Wes McMullen, Kealty's young chief of staff, was in attendance, as were the secretary of defense, the secretary of state, the director of national intelligence, the chairman of the Joint Chiefs of Staff, and the national security adviser.

Kilborn gave a detailed briefing on the situation in Kazakhstan, including what the CIA knew about the attempted retaking of the Dnepr launch facilities by Russian Special Forces. Then the NSA briefed the President on the Baikonur launch and the fire at the oil refinery in Moscow.

While they were all together President Rychcov called, Kealty spoke with him through a translator for about ten minutes, while Wes McMullen listened in, taking notes. The call was amicable but Kealty explained he would need to talk some things over with his advisers before committing to Rychcov's requests.

When he hung up the phone, his polite demeanor evaporated. "Fucking Rychcov is asking us to send SEAL Team 6 or Delta Force! Who the hell does he think he is, requesting specific military units?"

Wes McMullen sat by his phone with his notepad in his lap. "Sir, I think he just knows who our tier-one antiterror assets are. Nothing malicious in his request."

The President said, "He wants political cover in case this all ends badly. He wants to tell his people that he trusted America and Ed Kealty promised him a happy resolution, but that we screwed up."

The men in the room were Kealty's people, for now, anyway. But to a man and to a woman they realized that their president was looking for a way out of this. A couple of them recognized he'd always been this way.

Scott Kilborn said, "Mr. President. I respectfully disagree. He wants to prevent two twenty-kiloton bombs from taking out Moscow or Saint Petersburg. That could kill . . ." Kilborn looked to the chairman of the Joint Chiefs. "What do your experts say?"

"Each weapon will kill in excess of one million in the initial blast and fallout. Another two million–plus within a week from burns and disruption of the infrastructure and electrical grid. God knows how many more down the road. Seven to ten million deaths are likely."

Kealty groaned; he leaned forward at his desk and put his head in his hands.

"Options?"

The secretary of state said, "I think we send them over. We can green-light or red-light any action later."

Kealty shook his head. "I don't want them to commit to anything. I don't want them walking into this hornets' nest and then having to act immediately. The Russians couldn't pull it off, and they've practiced there before. Who's to say we could do any better? Give me something else. Come on, people!"

Alden said, "Advisers."

"Advisers? What do you mean?"

"If we send a couple of JSOC people over there as advisers to their Spetsnaz, we can offer help, covertly, but not use our men in the attack."

Kealty loved the idea, everyone could immediately tell.

The chairman, an Army general with spec ops experience in the Rangers, said, "Mr. President. This is a very fluid event. If we don't have JSOC operators over there ready to act on a moment's notice, well, we might as well not send anyone at all."

Kealty sat at his desk, thinking it over. He looked to the secretary of defense. "Any chance they will launch a missile at us?"

SecDef held up his hands. "They are not threatening us. The Dagestani militants' problems are with Russia. I do not see the US as a target."

Kealty nodded, then beat on the desk. "No! I am not walking out the door of the Oval Office with this, this shit, being my legacy." Kealty stood. "Tell President Rychcov that we will send advisers. That's it!"

Wes McMullen said, "Remember, sir, there are six Americans at the facility."

"Whose safety I hold Rychcov personally responsible

for. Tell our advisers that any mission they help with needs to come up with a way to get our citizens out alive."

SecDef said, "Sir, with due respect—"

But Kealty stood and headed for the door. "Good night, ladies and gentlemen."

Melanie called Jack at one-thirty in the afternoon. "Hey. Really sorry, but it is nuts here today—can I get a rain check for dinner tonight?"

"Okay. Or if you want, I could bring some Chinese over late. We don't have to go out. I'd love to see you."

"That sounds awesome, but I don't know when or if I'm going to get out of here tonight. You can imagine. There is a lot going on these days."

"Yeah. I can imagine. All right, hang in there, okay?"

"Okay. Thanks, Jack." Melanie hung up the phone. She hated canceling plans with Ryan, but there would be more work to do than she would possibly get done this evening anyhow. The data to go through about Rehan's travel in—

The phone on her desk rang. "Melanie Kraft?"

Ninety seconds later, Melanie leaned into Mary Pat's office. "I need to run out for just a second. Maybe a half-hour. Can I pick up anything for you?"

Foley just shook her head. She started to say something, but her phone chirped.

Kraft walked out to the bus stop in front of her building and took the next bus toward Tysons Corner, but she got out at the Old Meadow stop. She walked alone into Scott's Run Community Park, made her way to some park benches overlooking a snow-and-ice-covered vista. Bare trees blew in a frigid wind, and she pulled her coat tighter around her.

She sat down.

The first man approached a minute later. He was big and black; he wore a long gray raincoat over his dark suit, but it was open as if he were impervious to the chill.

He was a security man, and he looked her over and then spoke into a cuff mike.

Behind her in the parking lot she heard a car pull up, but she did not turn around. She just kept looking at the swaying trees.

The security man turned away, walked up the path, and then stood there, watching the road.

Deputy Director of the CIA Charles Sumner Alden appeared from behind and he sat down next to her. He did not make eye contact. Instead he looked out over a snow-covered baseball diamond. "I am racking my brain here, Miss Kraft, trying to think how I may have possibly been more clear in my instructions to you. And I just can't think of a way. I was certain we had an understanding. But today you tell Junior that you don't have time to meet him tonight? Trust me, young lady. You *do* have time."

Melanie gritted her teeth. "Really, sir? You are bugging the phone of an analyst at NCTC? Are you that desperate?"

"Yes. Frankly, we are."

"About what?"

"About Jack Junior."

Melanie sighed cold vapor.

Alden changed his voice a bit, less smarmy and more fatherly. "I thought I was clear about what I needed."

"I've done what you've asked."

"I've asked you to produce results. Have dinner with him tonight. Find out what he knows about Clark, about his dad's relationship with Clark."

"Yes, sir," she said.

Now Alden was even more fatherly than before. "You wanted to help us. Has something changed?"

"Of course not. You told me you had heard Clark worked with Ryan. You wanted me to find evidence of Jack's work at Hendley Associates."

"And?" he asked.

"And you are the DD/CIA. Of course it is my job to follow orders."

"Jack Junior is tighter with Clark than he is letting on. We know this. We have guys at the Agency who can tie Clark and Chavez to Hendley Associates, your boyfriend's employer. And if Clark and Chavez work at Hendley, you can be goddamned sure more goes on there than arbitrage and trading. I want to know what Jack knows, and I want to know it now."

"Yes, sir," Melanie said again.

"Look. You have a bright future. I may be leaving my post soon, but the CIA is not about the political appointees. It's about the rank and file. The career men and women in the Agency know what you are doing, and they appreciate your hard work. We can't allow criminal actions in the name of national security. You know that. So dig deeper." He paused. "Don't do it for me. Do it for them." Then he sighed. "Do it for your country."

Melanie nodded distantly.

Alden stood, turned, and looked down at the twenty-five-year-old analyst. "Jack wants to see you tonight. Make it happen." He walked off through the snow, and his security man moved with him back toward the parking lot.

Melanie walked back to the bus stop, and she pulled her phone from her purse. She dialed Jack's number.

"Hello?"

"Hey, Jack."

"Hey."

"Look, I'm sorry about before. Just stressed from work."

"Believe me, I get it."

"To tell you the truth, I do need to get out of here for a bit. How 'bout you come over tonight? I'll make dinner, we can hang out and watch a movie."

The pause was long, and only broken when Ryan cleared his throat.

"Something wrong?"

"No. I wish I could, Melanie, but something came up."

"In the past thirty minutes?"

"Yeah. I've got to go out of town. I'm on the way to the airport right now, in fact."

"To the airport," she repeated, incredulously.

"Yeah, just a quick flight back over to Switzerland. My boss wants me to meet some bankers, take them to dinner, get them to spill secrets, I guess. Should just take a couple of days."

Melanie did not respond.

"I'm sorry. Dinner and a movie sounds great. Can we do it when I get back?"

"Sure, Jack," she said.

Melanie climbed off the bus ten minutes later and headed back to the operations center. As soon as she got out of the elevator she saw Mary Pat at her desk, leaving her a note. Mary Pat saw her approaching and motioned for her to head into her office.

Melanie was nervous. Did she know about the meeting with Alden? Did she know the deputy director of the CIA was using her to spy on Mary Pat's friend, Jack Ryan Jr., to see what his professional association with John Clark was?

"What's up?" she asked Mrs. Foley.

"Big happening while you were gone."

"Really?" Melanie swallowed nervously.

"A CIA asset in Lahore has positively identified Riaz Rehan. He arrived at the airport with his security detail and his second in command."

Melanie thought of Ryan's rapid travel plans. "Really. When did this happen?"

Foley said, "Within the past hour."

In an instant, Melanie knew. She did not know how he found out, because she was certain he was not CIA. But somehow Ryan had been tipped off and, for some reason, Jack Ryan Jr. was on his way to Lahore.

75

The on-site temporary command center for all Russian security forces for the Baikonur situation had been set up in the Sputnik Hotel in the town of Baikonur, well to the south of the Cosmodrome. Here Russian military and intelligence personnel, Federal Space Agency officials, Baikonur management, and other parties had set up camps both outside in heated tents and trailers and inside in the rooms, the restaurant, and the conference facilities. Even the Luna Disco off the main lobby had been taken over by a team of Army nuclear experts brought in from Strategic Rocket Forces.

At four p.m. local time a General Lars Gummesson stepped into the conference room, leading two younger men. The combat fatigues of all three were generic, without any marking or insignia. They sat down at a long table across from Russian politicians and diplomats and military leaders.

Gummesson was the leader of Rainbow, a secret international force of counterterror paramilitaries, chosen from the best tier one military units on earth. He and his men had been requested by the Russian and Kazakh governments within an hour of the failure of the Alpha commandos, and he was returning to the command center to deliver his report on the situation and Rainbow's readiness to engage.

"Gentlemen. My team leaders and I have spent the last four hours going over an operation plan to retake the

Dnepr launch control center and the two launch silos. Taking the lessons learned by last night's mission by the Russian Army into account, as well as our own capabilities at present, I regret to say that, although we feel confident that if we marshal all of our efforts on the LCC we have an eighty percent chance of success of retaking the building and rescuing the majority of the hostages there, it *is* a heavily fortified bunker and Mr. Safronov is entrenched there, he is highly skilled, and very motivated. We therefore feel there is a fifty-percent chance that he and the men there will have time to launch one vehicle, and a twenty-percent chance they will be able to launch both."

The Russian ambassador to Kazakhstan looked at General Gummesson for a long moment. In highly accented English he said, "So. That is it? All your men with guns, and you say it is fifty-fifty whether or not Moscow is destroyed?"

"I am afraid so. Our training funds have been cut in the past year or so, and the men rotating into service with us have not had the coordinated experience that Rainbow used to offer, back when we were called on more often. I am afraid our readiness has suffered."

"This is not simply an aversion to risk on your part, General Gummesson?"

The Swedish military officer showed no annoyance at the implication. "We have looked at the situation, and it is grim. We have no idea how many men Safronov has remaining with him. Interviews with men from the processing facility who were let go yesterday morning suggest the number could be over fifty. Presumably some were killed in last night's Spetsnaz attack, but we have no way of knowing how many there are remaining. I will not send my men into the unknown like this, no matter the stakes. My force and I will be returning to Britain immediately. Gentlemen, good afternoon, and good luck."

Gummesson stood, turned to leave, but a Spetsnaz colonel at the far end of the table stood quickly. "Excuse me, General Gummesson." This man's accent was even thicker than the ambassador's. "Could I ask you to remain here in Baikonur? At least for a few hours?"

"For what purpose, Colonel?"

"I will speak with you about it privately."

"Very well."

Clark had been given time alone to "think." His shattered hand remained under a dirty towel, but the pain from the swelling and soft tissue damage, and from broken bones in his hand and ribs that moved every time John tried to find a more comfortable position, was sheer and utter agony.

Sweat poured off of John's face and down his neck, even in the meat-locker cold of the warehouse, his shirt was soggy from the perspiration and this gave him chills.

His mind had gone numb, though his body had not. He wanted relief from the pain, but more than this he wanted relief from the worry that this stupid kid might actually break him if the barbarity continued.

Clark knew he could have lied, could have made up false relationships, told a complicated story that would take days to confirm. But he worried that any obfuscation on his part could be detected with fact-checking or a little legwork on the part of Kovalenko's people. And if he was caught in a lie, if he delayed for too long, then perhaps Valentin would come back with some SP-117, the truth serum that, according to some reports, was light-years ahead of the unreliable sodium pentothal of the past.

No, Clark told himself, as much misery as he was in

right now, he would take his lumps in the hope that his brutal torturers went a bit too far and killed him.

Better that than fucking with his mind and turning him into a one-man wrecking crew for The Campus and President Jack Ryan.

"Time is short, everyone back to work!" Kovalenko shouted as he reappeared in the light hanging above Clark's head. Valentin leaned in close and smiled, reinvigorated, apparently, from the smell of his breath, by strong coffee and a Russian cigarette. "How are you feeling?"

"I'm fine. How are *you* holding up?" Clark said dryly.

"Any desire to talk and stop the pain from continuing? We have some wonderful medicine we can give you to make it go away. And we will drop you off at a local hospital. Wouldn't that be nice?"

"Valentin," Clark said, "whatever you do to me, my people will find out. And whatever you do to me, they will do to you. Just keep that in mind."

Kovalenko just stared at the American. "Just tell me who they are, and there will be nothing more for me to do."

Clark looked away.

Kovalenko nodded. "I swear I wish my father was here now. The old ways were best for this, I am certain. Anyway, John, you have lost a hand already, but I am just getting started. You will leave here a crippled old man. I am about to destroy you."

He waited for John to ask how, but John just sat there.

"I will have my friends here shove a scalpel into your eyes, one at a time."

Clark stared Kovalenko down. "And my people will do the same to you. Are you prepared for that?"

"*Who* are your people? *Who?*"

John said nothing.

A big Slav grabbed John's head from behind and held it perfectly still. Clark's eyes watered, tears dripped down his face, and he blinked rapidly. "Fuck you!" he screamed through a jaw held tight with a meaty hand, and the head-lock tightened.

The other Spetsnaz goon stepped in front of John. A stainless-steel scalpel in his hand glinted in the light from above.

Valentin stepped back, turned away so that he could not see. "Mr. Clark. This . . . right now . . . is your very last chance."

Clark could tell by the resignation in the young man's voice. He would not back down.

"Fuck you!" was all that came out of the American's mouth. He took a deep breath and held it.

Kovalenko shrugged dramatically. While facing toward the wall he said, *"Votki emu v glaz."*

Clark understood. Put it in his eye.

Through the fish-eye effect of the water in his eyes, Clark saw the scalpel come closer to his face as the man knelt in front of him. Beyond that, he saw Kovalenko step away. He thought the Russian just had no stomach for what was about to happen, but in another instant John realized Valentin was reacting to a noise outside.

The sounds of a helicopter echoed through the warehouse. The thumping came fast and frantic, as if the aircraft was falling straight down out of the sky. It landed outside; Clark could see the lights shining through the walls, creating wicked shadows that wiped back and forth over everyone. The man with the scalpel stood up quickly and turned around. Over the incredible noise, noise that told John there was more than one helicopter in the mix—the other one likely hovering just feet above the tin roof—Valentin Kovalenko yelled orders to his security men around the perimeter. Clark caught a glimpse in the sweeping lights of the SVR assistant *rezident*. He looked like a panicked, cornered animal.

The helicopter above began circling slowly.

Shouting voices now. Barking orders and yelled threats. John tucked his head into his neck, there was nothing else he could do strapped to the chair, but it felt right to do something. His hand hurt like a motherfucker, so the new activity in the building gave him something to think about, at the very least.

Red laser lights appeared like fireflies shooting across the surfaces of the floors, the table, the men standing around, and John Clark himself. In the cold dusty air John could see the needle-thin lines of the red lasers as they swept around. He was then bathed in white light, and he shut his eyes tightly.

When he opened them he realized the overhead hanging light fixtures, two stories above him on the ceiling of the warehouse, had been turned on, and the big room was awash in light now.

Valentin Kovalenko was the smallest figure in the building. In front of him, facing him, black-clad gunmen with HK MP5 submachine guns.

These were Spetsnaz troops, and they were led by a man in civilian dress. Kovalenko and his men—there were eight in total, John could now see—all raised their hands.

Who the fuck was this new clown? Clark wondered. Out of the frying pan, then into the fire, but *now* what? Could it get any fucking worse?

Valentin and his crew were led out of the warehouse with just a few gruff comments from the man in street clothes, who then left the warehouse with several, but not all, of the paramilitaries. The helicopter took off a minute later.

The chopper that had been hovering above peeled away.

Behind the Spetsnaz soldiers remaining in the room a lean man in his late fifties walked into the cold cellar. The man had a short crew cut, narrow wire-rimmed glasses, and bright intelligent eyes on his deeply creased face. He looked like he ran five miles before breakfast every morning.

John Clark felt like he could be looking at a mirror image of himself, only in a Russian suit.

Except it wasn't a mirror. Clark knew the man in front of him.

The man stood over the American and he ordered one of the men to cut away Clark's bindings. While doing so the older man said, "Mr. Clark. My name is Stanislav Biryukov. I am—"

"You are the director of the FSB."

"I am, indeed."

"Is this just a changing of the guard, then?" Clark asked.

The FSB man shook his head emphatically. "*Nyet.* No, of course not. I am not here to continue with this madness."

Clark just looked at him.

Biryukov said, "My country has a serious problem and we find ourselves needing to call on your expertise. At the same moment, we realize that you are here, right here in Russia, and you seem to have a bit of a problem yourself. It is fate that brings us together today, John Clark. I am hoping the two of us can come to a quick and mutually beneficial agreement."

Clark wiped sweat from his forehead with the back of his hand. "Keep talking."

"There has been a terrorist incident in Kazakhstan involving our space launch facility at Baikonur."

Clark had no idea what was going on beyond his field of view. "A terrorist incident?"

"Yes. A terrible thing. Two rockets tipped with nuclear bombs are in the hands of terrorists from the Caucasus, and they have the manpower and know-how to launch the rockets. We have asked for assistance from your former organization. I am not speaking of the CIA, I am speaking of Rainbow. Unfortunately, the men leading Rainbow at the moment find themselves unprepared for the magnitude of this problem."

"Call the White House."

Biryukov shrugged. "We did. Edward Kealty sent four men with laptop computers to save us. They are at the Kremlin. They did not even go to Kazakhstan."

"So what are you doing here?"

"Rainbow is positioned there right now. Forty men."

Clark just repeated himself: "What are you doing here?"

"I have asked my president to appeal to Rainbow to let you take temporary command of the organization for the Baikonur operation. Russian Spetsnaz forces would assist you in any way you wish. The Air Force, as well. In fact, you will have the entire Russian military at your disposal." He paused, then said, "We will need to take action by tomorrow evening."

"You are asking *me* to help you?"

Stanislav Biryukov shook his head slowly. "I am begging you, Mr. Clark."

Clark raised an eyebrow as he looked up at the head of the FSB. "If you are appealing to my love of all things

644

Russian in order to stop the attack on Moscow, well, sorry, comrade, but you've caught me on a bad day. My first inclination is to root for the guy with his finger on the button over there in Kazakhstan."

"I understand, in light of present circumstances. But I also know that you will do this. You will want to save millions of lives. That is all that you will require to accept this role, but I have been authorized by President Rychcov to offer you whatever you want. Anything."

John Clark stared at the Russian. "Right now I could use a goddamn bag of ice."

Biryukov acted as if he had just noticed the swollen, broken hand. He called out to the men behind him, and soon a Spetsnaz sergeant with a medical kit came over and began unwrapping the towel. He placed cold gel packs on the horrific injuries, and he slowly moved the two twisted fingers back into place. He then began to wrap the entire hand and ice packs with compression bandages.

While he did this, Clark spoke through winces of pain. "Here are my demands. Your people talk to the press about how Kovalenko conspired with Paul Laska to bring down the Ryan administration with fabrications about me. The Russian government distances themselves from the allegations completely, and hands over any evidence they have on Laska and his associates."

"Of course. Kovalenko has brought shame and embarrassment on us all."

The two men looked at each other in silence for a moment before Clark said, "I'm not going to take your assurances. There's a guy at *The Washington Post*. Bob Holtzman. He's tough but fair. You can have your ambassador meet with him, or you can call him yourself. But this needs to happen before I do anything to help you out of that little fix you are in at the spaceport."

Stanislav Biryukov nodded. "I will contact President Rychcov's office and see that it happens today." He then looked around at the torture implements on the table. "Between you and me, between two old men who have seen a lot more than many of the young people who have risen to the top ranks today . . . I would like to apologize for what the SVR has done. This was not an FSB operation at all. I hope you will tell your new president that personally."

Clark responded to this request with a question: "What will happen to Valentin Kovalenko?"

Biryukov shrugged. "Moscow is a dangerous place, even for an SVR leader. His operation, his rogue operation, I will say, has been an embarrassment for my country. He will make important people angry when it is found out what he has done. Who's to say he might not meet with an accident?"

"I am not asking you to kill Kovalenko on my behalf. I am just suggesting that he will have a problem when he finds out I've been freed by the FSB."

Biryukov smiled. Clark could tell the man was not in the least bit concerned about Valentin Kovalenko. "Mr. Clark. Someone has to shoulder Russia's responsibility in this unfortunate affair."

John shrugged it away. He wasn't going to worry about saving Kovalenko's ass right now. There were innocent people out there who actually deserved his help.

John Clark and Stanislav Biryukov climbed into a helicopter five minutes later. Heavily armed commandos helped John walk, and the medic applied cold packs and compression bandages around his broken ribs. As the helo lifted off into the night sky the American leaned over to the head of the FSB. "I need the fastest plane to Baikonur, and a satellite phone. I need to call a former colleague from Rainbow and get him here. If you can speed up his visa and passport process, it would be very helpful."

"Just tell your man to get himself on the way to Baikonur. I will contact the head of customs authority of Kazakhstan personally. There will be no delays getting him in the country, I can promise you. You and I will meet him there. By the time we land, Rychcov will have negotiated authority for you to lead Rainbow once again."

76

Chavez, Ryan, and Caruso met with Mohammed al Darkur shortly after touchdown at Allama Iqbal International Airport in Lahore, the capital of the state of Punjab. The Americans were pleased to see that the ISI major had recovered from his shoulder wound for the most part, though it was evident from his stiff movements that he was still dealing with some issues.

"How is Sam?" Mohammed asked Chavez as they all climbed into an ISI van.

"He's going to be okay. The infection is clearing up, wounds are healing, he says he's a hundred percent good to go, but our bosses wouldn't hear of him coming back to Pakistan just yet."

"It is not a good time for anyone to come to Pakistan. Especially Lahore."

"What's the situation?"

The van headed toward the airport exit. In addition to the driver, Mohammed had one other man in front, and he passed loaded Beretta 9-millimeter pistols out to the Americans as he talked. "It is getting worse by the hour. There are nearly ten million people here, and anyone who can get out of town is doing just that. We are only ten miles from the border, and the public fully expects an invasion by India. There are reports already of artillery crossing in both directions.

"The PDF has moved armor into the town, you will see for yourselves. There are police and military checkpoints going up even now amid rumors of foreign agents in the city, but we will not have any problems passing."

"Anything to those rumors about Indian spies?"

"Maybe so. India is agitated. Understandably in this case. Joint Intelligence Miscellaneous has fomented a real international crisis, and I do not know if we can be pulled back from the brink."

Caruso asked, "Is your government going to fall, especially now, after your bombs turned up in the hands of Dagestani terrorists?"

"The short answer, Dominic, is yes. Maybe not today or this week, but certainly very soon. Our prime minister was not strong to begin with. I expect the Army will depose him in order, they will say, to 'save Pakistan.'"

Chavez asked, "Where is Rehan now?"

"He is in a flat in the old section of Lahore called the Walled City, near the Sunchri Mosque. He does not have a lot of men with him. We think just his assistant, Colonel Saddiq Khan, and a couple of guards."

"Any idea what he's up to?"

"None, unless it is to meet with Lashkar terrorists. This is an LeT stronghold, and he has been using them in operations over the border. But, honestly, Lahore seems like the last place for Rehan to be right now. The city is not a fundamentalist stronghold like Quetta or Karachi or Peshawar. I have a pair of men near his flat, so if he leaves for any reason we can try to follow him."

Al Darkur took the Americans to a nearby apartment. They had just settled in when Chavez's mobile phone rang.

"Go for Ding," he said.

"Hey." It was John Clark.

"John! Are you okay?"

"Makin' it. Remember when you said that if I needed you, you'd come running?"

"Hell, yes."

"Then get your ass on a plane, pronto."

Chavez looked across the room at the two younger operators. He'd have to leave them on their own, but there was no way he wouldn't be there for Clark. "Where am I heading?"

"Center stage."

Fuck, thought Chavez. He just said, "The Cosmodrome?"

"'Fraid so."

John Clark had changed into Russian camo fatigues and a heavy coat by the time he climbed out of the helicopter in the parking lot of the Sputnik Hotel. The bandaging on his hand and his head was of a professional grade, Biryukov had seen to it that an orthopedic surgeon had flown along with them from Moscow to attend to the American's wounds.

It hurt like a bitch. John was pretty certain his hand would bother him as long as he lived, even after the God knows how many surgeries he'd require to have the bones put back together, but that was a worry for another day.

The snow fell heavily during his arrival. It was eight a.m. local time, and the Sputnik looked to Clark to be in near chaos. Different organizations of men, both uniformed and in civilian dress, had staked out tiny kingdoms both outside and inside, and there seemed to be no one in charge.

While John walked from the chopper to the hotel everyone in his path stopped and stared. Some knew he was the former commander of Rainbow, here to take control of the situation. Others knew he was John Clark, the international fugitive wanted by the United States for multiple murders. Many simply recognized the presence of the man, who walked with purpose and authority.

But everyone saw the bruised face, a dark purple jaw and black eyes, and a right hand encased in fresh white dressing.

Stanislav Biryukov was by his side and a dozen more FSB and Alpha Group men followed them as they entered the hotel and marched through the lobby. In the hallway leading to the main conference room military officers and diplomats and rocket scientists alike all stepped aside for the procession.

Biryukov did not knock before entering the command center. He had spoken with President Rychcov moments before landing at Yubileinaya and, as far as Biryukov was concerned, he had all the authority he needed to do whatever he goddamn well pleased around here.

The command center had been notified of the arrival of the American and the FSB director, so those working there were seated and ready for a conversation. Clark and Biryukov were asked to sit at the table, but both men remained standing.

The director of the Russian intelligence agency was first to talk. "I have spoken with the president directly. He has had conversations with the commanders of NATO regarding Rainbow."

The Russian Ambassador to Kazakhstan nodded. "I have spoken with the president myself, Stanislav Dmitrievich. Let me assure you, and let me tell Mr. Clark, that we understand the situation and we are at your service."

"As am I." General Lars Gummesson entered the room. Clark had met Gummesson when he was a colonel in the Swedish Special Forces, but he did not know the man, other than the fact he was the current head of Rainbow. He'd expected friction from the officer, it would be only natural for someone relinquishing command, but the tall Swede saluted Clark smartly, even while looking curiously at the older man's beaten face and wounded hand. He recovered and said, "I've talked to the leadership at NATO, and they have explained that you will be commanding Rainbow for this operation."

Clark nodded. "If you have no objections."

"None at all, sir. I serve at the pleasure of my government and at the pleasure of NATO leadership. They have made the decision to replace me. Your reputation precedes you, and I expect to learn much in the next twenty-four hours. Back when Rainbow was actually used in direct action, that is to say, back when you were in charge, I am sure you learned many things that will be helpful in the coming hours. I hope to see action tonight in any way you can use me." Gummesson finished with, "Mr. Clark, until this crisis has passed, Rainbow is yours."

Clark nodded, not as happy about taking on this responsibility as the Swedish general seemed to think he would be. But he had no time to worry about his own circumstances. He immediately began working on the operation. "I need plans of the launch control center and the missile silos."

"You will get them immediately."

"I will need to send recon units out to get an accurate impression of the target areas."

"I anticipated this. Before dawn we inserted two teams of two men each to within one thousand yards of each of the three locations. We have reliable comms and real-time video."

"Excellent. How many Jamaat Shariat men at each site?"

"Since the launch from 109, they have consolidated their men. There seem to be about eight to ten tangos around each launch silo. There are four more at a bunker near the access road that leads to the Dnepr area. We have no idea how many are in launch control. From a distance we've seen one man on the roof, but that doesn't really help. The facility is essentially a bunker, and we cannot get our eyes in there. If we attack, we will have to attack blind."

"Why can't we use surface-to-air missiles to take out the rockets if they launch?"

Gummesson shook his head. "When they are still very low to the ground that is possible, but we are unable to move the equipment close enough to take them out before they are moving too fast for SAMs. Missiles fired from aircraft cannot reach them, either."

Clark nodded. "Figured it wouldn't be that easy. Okay. We also need our own operations center. Where are the rest of the men?"

"We have a large tent outside for CCC." Communication, command, and control would be the Rainbow operations center. "There is another tent for equipment and a third where the men are billeted."

Clark nodded. "Let's go there now."

Clark and Gummesson talked as they walked with Biryukov and several Alpha Group officers toward the parking lot. They had made it into the lobby of the Sputnik when Domingo Chavez entered through the front door. Ding wore a brown cotton shirt and blue jeans, no coat or hat, though it was well below freezing.

Chavez noticed his father-in-law from across the lobby and he approached. As he neared, his smile faded. He gave the older man a gentle hug, and when he pulled away Ding's face showed unbridled fury. "Jesus Christ, John! What the fuck did they do to you?"

"I'm okay."

"The hell you are!" Chavez looked around at Biryukov and the other Russians, but he continued to address John. "What do you say we tell these Russians to fuck themselves, then we can go home, find a couch and a TV, then sit back and watch Moscow burn to the goddamned ground?"

One of the big Russian Spetsnaz men, an English speaker obviously, moved on Chavez, but the smaller, older Mexican-American stood up to him. "Fuck you."

Clark found himself having to play peacemaker. "Ding. It's okay. These guys didn't do this to me. It was a rogue SVR guy and his crew."

Chavez did not back down from the big Slav standing over him, but finally he gave a half-nod. "Okay, then. What the fuck? Let's go save their asses, I guess."

77

Mohammed al Darkur knocked on the door of Ryan and Dominic's flat at nine a.m. The Americans were up and drinking coffee, and they poured a cup for the Pakistani major while he talked.

"There have been developments overnight. Artillery shells from India have struck the village of Wahga, just east of Lahore, killing thirty civilians. PDF returned fire into India. We don't know about damage there. Another shelling, just a few miles further north, damaged a mosque."

Ryan cocked his head. "How strange that Rehan, the guy who's orchestrating this entire conflict, happens to be in the area."

The major said, "We can't discount his involvement in these acts. Rogue Pakistani forces could be firing on their own country in order to escalate Pakistan's response."

"What's the plan today?" asked Caruso.

"If Rehan leaves his flat, we follow him. If anyone comes to Rehan's flat, we follow them."

"Simple enough," replied Dom.

Georgi Safronov sat alone in the third-floor cafeteria of the LCC and finished his breakfast: coffee, a reconstituted bowl of potato soup from the cafeteria, and a cigarette. He was bone-tired, but he knew he would get his energy back. He had spent most of the early morning conducting phone interviews with news stations from Al Jazeera to Radio Havana, spreading the word of the plight of the people of Dagestan. It was necessary work, he needed to leverage this event in any way possible to help his cause, but he had never worked so hard in his life as he had in the past few months.

While he smoked he watched the television on the wall. It was a news report showing Russian armored forces moving north near the Caspian Sea in northern Dagestan. The commentator said Russian government sources were denying this had anything to do with the situation at the Cosmodrome, but Safronov knew that, like much of Russian television, it was a bare-faced lie.

Several of his men had seen a television in a ground-floor office, and they rushed in to the cafeteria to embrace their leader. Tears welled in his eyes as the emotion of his men brought his own nationalistic pride to the forefront of his consciousness. He had wanted this all his life, long before he knew what that feeling inside him was, the sense of purpose, of untapped power.

A need to belong to something greater.

Today was the greatest day in Georgi Safronov's life.

A call came over the radio that Magomed Dagestani—Georgi's *nom de guerre*—was wanted in the launch control room for a call. He assumed it was his awaited conversation with Commander Nabiyev, and he hurried out of the cafeteria. He was anxious to talk to the prisoner and to make arrangements for his arrival. He took the back steps down to the second floor, then entered the LCC through the south stairwell entrance. He put on his headset and took the call.

It was the Kremlin crisis center. Vladimir Gamov, the director of the Russian Federal Space Agency, was on the line. Georgi thought his own family relationship with Gamov was the only reason the old gasbag was the one communicating with him, as if it made any difference. "Georgi?"

"Gamov, I have asked to be called by another name."

"I am sorry, Magomed Dagestani, it's just that I have known you as Georgi since the 1970s."

"Then we both were misled. Are you going to connect me with Nabiyev?"

"Yes, I will patch him through in a moment. First I wanted to let you know the status of the troop movements in the Caucasus. I want to be clear. We have begun but there are over fifteen thousand troops in Dagestan alone. Twice that in Chechnya and more in Ingushetia. Many are on leave, many are on patrols or multiday exercises and away from their bases. We simply cannot move them in a day. We are pushing everyone north we can. We are flying people out via the airport and the air base, but we will not have everyone out by your deadline. If you can give us one more day and one more night you will see our full commitment."

Safronov did not commit to anything. "I will check with my own sources to make sure this is not a propaganda trick. If you are really moving units north, then I will consider extending the deadline for one day. No promises, Gamov. Now, let me speak with Commander Nabiyev."

Georgi was put through and soon he found himself speaking with the young leader of the military wing of his troops. Nabiyev informed Safronov that he was told by his captors that he would be delivered to Baikonur that evening.

Georgi wept with joy.

Clark, Chavez, Gummesson, and Rainbow planners spent the entire day in their heated tent in the parking lot of the

Sputnik Hotel, going over schematics and maps and photographs and other materials to help them prepare for an attack on the Cosmodrome.

By noon Clark had come up with ideas that Spetsnaz had not thought of for their hit, and by three Chavez and Clark had an attack plan that was marveled at by the Rainbow officers, men who had been forced into a risk-aversion mentality in the past year and a half. They took a short break, and then the various assault teams broke off for unit planning while Clark and Chavez briefed Russian Air Force pilots.

At seven p.m. Chavez lay down on a bunk for ninety minutes of rest. He was tired, but he was already amped up about the evening ahead.

Georgi Safronov was told that Israpil Nabiyev would arrive in a Russian Air Force transport helicopter around 10:30 p.m. The Dagestani rocket entrepreneur and terrorist, after conferring with some of the thirty-four remaining rebels, told Gamov how the transfer would be made. His stipulations were specific to ensure that there were no tricks on the part of the Russians. He wanted Commander Nabiyev's chopper to land on the far side of the parking lot at the LCC, and Nabiyev alone to walk the seventy meters to the front entrance. The entire time he would be under bright spotlights mounted on the roof of the LCC. There would be gunmen on the roof as well as gunmen at the front entrance of the LCC to ensure no one else got out of the chopper.

Gamov wrote everything down, conferred with the crisis center, who agreed to all Safronov's requests. They did have one caveat. They demanded that all the foreign prisoners be released from the LCC at the same time Nabiyev was released from the helicopter.

Safronov smelled a trap. "Director, please, no tricks. I will require simultaneous video feed from inside the helicopter linked to us here in launch control. I will also require direct radio comms with Commander Nabiyev for the journey from the airport to the LCC. If you stock the helicopter with your troops, I will know it." Gamov again left the call to confer with others, but when he returned he agreed that an audio/video link with Nabiyev inside the helicopter could be established en route from the airport so Safronov and his people at the LCC could see that the Dagestani military commander was in the helicopter with only a few crewmen and minimal security watching over him.

Georgi was satisfied, and he ended the call to notify his men of the arrangement.

The streets of Lahore were still chaotic at nine p.m. Jack and Dominic were alone at the time, sitting in a fast food restaurant a quarter-mile from where Rehan and his entourage had gone into a mosque. Al Darkur had sent one of his own men into the mosque to keep an eye on the general, and al Darkur himself had gone to a nearby police station to requisition body armor and rifles. He had also contacted a friend in an SSG unit stationed nearby, asking the captain to send men to assist him on an intelligence operation in the city, but the SSG had been inexplicably ordered to remain in their base.

Ryan and Dom watched the news on a TV set up on the counter of the restaurant. They were hoping for news of events in Kazakhstan, but in Lahore, Pakistan, at the moment at least, all news was local.

They had just finished their fried chicken and were sipping their Cokes when a booming explosion rocked the street outside. The glass panes in the windows shook, but they did not break.

The two Americans ran out of the restaurant to see what had happened, but just as they made it onto the sidewalk, another explosion, this one closer, nearly knocked them down.

They assumed a pair of bombs had gone off, but then they heard a hellish sound like ripping paper broadcast through an amplifier. This sound ended with another explosion, this one even closer than the first two.

"That's incoming, cuz!" Dominic said, and both men joined the crowd on the sidewalk running in the other direction.

Another ripping-fabric noise and another crash, this one a block away to the east, turned much of the crowd to the south.

Jack and Dom stopped running. Ryan said, "Let's get inside. Not much else we can do." They ran into a bank building and got far from the windows. There were another half-dozen explosions, some barely audible in the distance. The sounds of sirens filled the air, and then distant chattering of automatic gunfire.

"Shit. Did the war just start?" Dom asked, but Jack thought it likely that Pakistani forces in the city were getting jumpy.

"Like Darkur said, this could be some Rehan-allied PDF artillery battery swinging their own guns around on orders from their leader."

Dom shook his head. "Fucking beards."

Outside the bank, PDF armored cars raced by, civilian vehicles swerved out of their way.

Jack's phone chirped, and he answered it.

It was al Darkur. "Rehan is on the move!"

Rehan finally left his flat near the Sunehri Mosque at nine p.m., during the height of rush hour in the congested city. In addition to the commuters, the rush out of town continued, clogging streets that were filling up quickly with Pakistani Defense Force armor and troops.

Ryan, Caruso, al Darkur, and two of the major's subordinates had trouble tailing the general and his entourage at first, but when Rehan and his small team pulled into a parking lot on Canal Bank Road, where they met up with three carloads of young bearded men in civilian dress, the van following them found them easier to keep an eye on.

Ryan said, "There must be a dozen guys in those cars, plus Rehan and his crew makes sixteen."

The major nodded. "And these new men do not look like ISI or PDF. They are LeT, I would swear it."

Ryan said, "Mohammed, if we have to go up against sixteen bad guys, I could use a little more firepower."

"I'll arrange for that, do not worry." And with that the major grabbed his mobile phone.

78

Clark and Chavez stood outside a Russian Air Force Antonov An-72 transport airplane parked on the tarmac at Krayniy airport near the town of Baikonur, twenty-five miles south of the Dnepr facility at the Cosmodrome and forty miles south of Yubileinaya Airport. The Antonov's engines roared, even at idle.

Also parked there on the tarmac were four Mi-17 helicopters, a smaller Mi-8 helicopter, and a gargantuan Mi-26 helicopter. A flurry of men and women moved around the machines, fueling them and loading them under the artificial lights of auxiliary power units and portable spotlights.

A light blowing snow whipped around the only two Americans on the airfield.

"Has Nabiyev arrived yet?" Ding asked John.

"Yep, he's up at Yubileinaya. He'll be ferried over at 22:30."

"Good." Chavez was head to toe in black Nomex. He wore a helmet on his head, and an oxygen mask dangled from it. On his chest an HK UMP submachine gun, .40 caliber, hung over a chest rig full of magazines. Even with the silencer on the SMG's barrel it was barely wider than Ding's shoulders with the shoulder stock folded closed.

Domingo Chavez was kitted up just like he had been for many years back in Rainbow, although he did not use his old call sign. The man leading his former team was here and active on this mission, so his Rainbow

Two call sign was not available. Instead he was handed the moniker Romeo Two by the Rainbow comms men. Someone joked that the R designation was due to the fact that Domingo was retired, but it didn't matter to him. The men of the Rainbow teams could call him Domingo Chavez, for all he cared. He had so much else to worry about.

"You need help getting into your chute?" Clark asked.

Ding said, "Not from you, lefty." Both men smiled dryly. The attempt at gallows humor fell short. Chavez said, "The loadmaster on board will get me set up." He hesitated a moment and then said, "You've done damn fine work on this op, John. But still . . . we're going to lose a lot of guys."

Clark nodded, looked off at the choppers full of Rainbow men loading up. "I'm afraid you're right. It's all down to speed, surprise, and violence of action."

"And any luck we can make along the way."

John nodded again, then reached out to shake his son-in-law's hand. He stopped midway, recognizing that the bandages were going to make a normal handshake impossible, so then he switched to his left.

Ding asked, "How bad are you hurting?"

Clark shrugged. "Broken ribs mask the broken hand. Broken hand masks the broken ribs."

"So you're golden, then?"

"Never better."

The two men embraced warmly.

"See you when it's over, Domingo."

"You bet, John."

A minute later, Chavez was on the An-72, and five minutes later Clark was on board one of the Mi-17s.

*

Al Darkur, Ryan, and Caruso followed Rehan and his entourage of ISI men and LeT operatives to the Lahore main railway station. The city was in a state of alert, which should have meant organized checkpoints and enforced curfews and the like, but Lahore was a city of ten million, and virtually all of them were certain tonight would be the beginning of a shooting war in their city, so there was much more chaos than order on the streets.

Ryan and Dominic rode in the back of the Volvo van with the major. Al Darkur had passed out police body armor and big G3 rifles to everyone in the truck, and he donned the same gear.

Fires burned in the city from the earlier artillery barrage, but no more shelling had occurred. The panicked citizenry would cause more casualties, Jack was certain, as he had seen dozens of car wrecks and fistfights and pushing and shoving at the rail station.

Rehan and his four-vehicle convoy pulled into the streets inside the station property, but then the rear car stopped suddenly, blocking the path of traffic. The other cars raced forward, the heavy crowds in the street scrambled out of the way.

"Shit!" said Ryan. He worried they would lose their man. They were a half-dozen vehicles behind the parked car, and they could just make out the top of the convoy vehicles as they turned east, remaining inside the grounds of the train station.

Al Darkur said, "We are dressed as police. We will dismount, but remember to act as police."

And with that, Mohammed al Darkur and his two men climbed out of the Volvo, and the Americans followed. They left the car there in the road, a cacophony of horns honked in anger behind it.

They ran on between the cars, pushed their way onto the sidewalk, and sprinted after the convoy that was, again, bogged down in the thick pedestrian traffic around the train station.

Rehan and his men got through the scrum in the street, and then they turned and headed up a railway access road that crossed the fifteen tracks of the station as it headed to a large cluster of metal-roofed warehouses on the northern side. This was a quarter-mile away from the station and all of the passenger traffic.

With al Darkur and his two men in the lead and the two Americans behind, the five men on foot sprinted onto a public railway-crossing path above the employee road. Below them, the four vehicles pulled between several links of rusted rail cars sitting alone on the far side of the yard. The cars had no engines, they were just positioned there in front of a storage building alongside the tracks.

The five men on the crossing path stopped and watched the sixteen men get out of the vehicles and walk into the warehouse.

The sounds of another artillery barrage on the city came from far to the south.

Ryan was panting from the run, but he said, "We need to get out of the open and get a better vantage point to watch that building."

Al Darkur led them the rest of the way across the path, where they took over the second floor of a small boardinghouse.

While al Darkur assigned his two officers to guard the stairs, Caruso, Ryan, and the major entered the large dorm room that faced the train station. Ryan pulled his infrared binoculars from his backpack and scanned the area. Ghostly shapes moved between the parked rail cars, walking or running to and from the roads, climbing fences to get nearer to the active tracks.

These were civilians, people desperate to get out of the city.

He looked at the warehouse through his optics and he saw the glow of a man in an upstairs window. The man just stood there, looking out. To Ryan, the form looked like that of a sentry.

Another white glow appeared on the opposite corner window of the building a minute later.

He passed the binoculars to his cousin.

Al Darkur borrowed a scoped rifle and checked himself. He also looked over the space between his position and Rehan's new location. "What's that? One hundred fifty yards away?"

"Closer to two," said Dominic.

"I'd like to get closer," Ryan said, "but we'd have to cross a lot of open ground, go over about five sets of tracks, and then climb that cyclone fence on the other side."

Al Darkur replied, "I can try and get more men here, but it won't be anytime soon."

Dom said, "What I'd give to know that fucker's plan."

Chavez jumped alone from the rear ramp of the Antonov An-72 at twenty-four thousand feet. He pulled his ripcord within seconds of exiting the aircraft, and within a minute of leaving the plane he was checking the GPS and altimeter on his wrist.

The winds immediately became a problem; he fought hard to stay on course, and he realized he was having trouble bleeding off the altitude fast enough. The op called for him on target right as the Mi-8 helicopter landed in front of the LCC, which meant he needed to time it just right. As it stood, he planned to be under canopy for just over twenty-two minutes.

He looked below—somewhere down there would be his target—but he could see nothing around him except for an impenetrable soupy blackness.

He'd executed dozens of these high-altitude, high-opening jumps in his Rainbow days, but the men currently assigned to Rainbow, while competent jumpers, did not have enough nighttime HAHO experience as far as Clark and Chavez were concerned. They would still be parachuting into the target in these swirling winds. Their role in this op was no picnic, but Clark's mission called for someone to land on the roof of the LCC covertly, which meant a different type of jump.

There was another reason Chavez decided to jump alone. The sniper/spotter team watching the LCC had reported movement on the roof of the building—sentries scanning the sky for parachutes.

With the bad weather, Clark and Chavez were banking that one man could make it undetected, at least until he was in position to engage targets on the roof. But the chance of success for a covert jump onto the target declined with each additional chute in the air.

So Ding flew his ram jet chute through the snow alone.

The video feed showing Nabiyev in the back of the Mi-8 came online when a crewman boarded the chopper at the airport, shortly before takeoff. Nabiyev could speak directly with Safronov in the launch control room, though the video and audio were understandably a little choppy. Still, the camera served its function. It scanned around the helicopter to show just four men on board other than Israpil himself, who had been taken out of his handcuffs and dressed in a heavy coat and hat. Georgi asked him to look out the window and confirm when he could see the lights of the LCC, and the Dagestani prisoner positioned himself to do that.

The Rainbow sniper recon team that had been watching the LCC all day had moved from one thousand yards' distance to only four hundred under cover of night. Now they were positioned deep in the grass with eyes on the rear of the LCC. They watched the building through their scopes. The intermittent lighting and the snowfall made the view through their glass confusing, but the spotter noticed a pair of long shadows moving against a steel heat exhaust unit on the north side of the roof. After tracking the movement for a long time, he saw the head of a man come into view for just a few seconds before it moved below his sight line. The spotter confirmed this with his sniper, then fingered the send button on his radio.

"Romeo Two, this is Charlie Two, over."

"Romeo Two, go."

"Be advised, we have two sentries on the roof."

Nine hundred and fifty feet above the LCC roof, Ding Chavez wanted to reply to the German-accented spotter that he couldn't see shit. Only the GPS on his arm was directing him toward his target. It was down there somewhere, and he'd deal with any shitheads on the roof when he got there. Unless . . . "Charlie Two, Romeo Two. I'm not going to see those guys till I land on them. Are you in position to engage?"

Back on the ground, the sniper shook his head, and the spotter replied on his behalf, "Not at this point, Romeo, but we're trying to get a target."

"Roger that."

Chavez felt for the UMP on his chest. It was there, in position, right over his body armor. He'd have to use it as soon as his feet touched the roof.

If his feet touched the roof. If he missed the roof, if some miscalculation took him off course or if some low-level gust pushed him away at the last second, then the entire mission would be in serious jeopardy.

And if a gust came at the wrong time, pushing Ding to the eastern parking lot, where the big chopping rotor blades of the Mi-8 were spinning, Chavez would not stand a chance.

He checked his altimeter and his GPS and then pulled his toggles, adjusting the canopy of his ram-air chute above him to turn him slightly to the south.

At 10:30 on the nose, the Mi-8 approached the LCC. Safronov was still watching the video comm link to the helicopter, and Nabiyev saw the big bunker-looking building with the large bright lights on the roof. He took the camera from the cameraman and positioned it against the window so that Safronov himself could see. Georgi told Israpil that he would meet him inside the front door in minutes, and then Georgi ran out of the launch control center with several of his men. They descended the stairs, crossed the dark entry hall, and opened the blast-proof iron doors.

Four Jamaat Shariat gunmen took positions in the open doorway, but Georgi himself stood to the side; he only looked around the iron door, lest someone lurking out in the snow try and take a shot at him.

Behind them the foreign prisoners were led into the hall, then huddled against the wall by two guards.

The Russian helicopter landed at the far end of the

parking lot, seventy yards from the blast-proof doors of the LCC, directly in the spotlight beams from the roof.

Safronov looked out the door into the swirling snow illuminated by the lights. He radioed his men on the roof and told them to be ready for anything, and not to forget to keep an eye out toward the back of the building as well.

The small side door of the chopper opened, and a bearded man in a hat and coat appeared. He covered his eyes against the light and slowly began walking across the hard-packed snow in the parking lot.

Georgi was already thinking about what he would say to the military commander of Jamaat Shariat. He would need to make certain the man had not been brainwashed, even though he had noticed no evidence of that in their previous conversations.

Chavez watched the chopper land, then turned his focus back to the roof of the LCC, two hundred feet below his boots. He would make his landing, thank God, though he would land faster and harder than he wanted. As he descended with a sharp bank to the south he made out one . . . two sentries posted there.

One hundred and fifty feet down.

Just then the roof access door opened below him, sending more light across the roof. A third terrorist came through the door.

Fuck, thought Chavez. Three tangos, each on a different compass point from his landing site. He'd have to take them in rapid succession, nearly impossible when dealing with a rough landing, spotty lighting, and a weapon that he could not even bring to bear until he cut away from his canopy before it pulled him over the side of the roof.

One hundred feet.

Just then, Ding's headset came to life.

"Romeo Two, Charlie Two. Have one target in sight on northwestern roof. Will engage on your command."

"Waste him."

"Repeat last command?"

Fucking Germans. "Engage."

"Roger, engaging."

Chavez turned all focus away from the man on the northwestern portion of the roof. That was no longer his responsibility. If the sniper missed, well, then Ding was fucked, but he couldn't think about that now.

Twenty feet.

Chavez flared his chute and landed at a sprint. He kept running, pulled the disconnect ring on his chute and felt it drop free from his body. He grabbed his suppressed HK and spun toward the man at the access door. The terrorist had already lifted his Kalashnikov in Ding's direction. Chavez dropped to the roof, rolled over his left shoulder, and came out of his roll on his knees.

He fired a three-round burst, catching the bearded terrorist in the throat. The AK flipped into the air, and the tango fell back into the doorway.

The suppressed gunfire, while certainly not silent, would not be heard over the sound of the Mi-8's rotors.

Ding had already shifted focus to the right. As his eyes spun, he caught a distant unfocused image of a sentry on the northwest corner as his weapon rose, and then the left side of the sentry's head exploded and the man dropped where he stood.

Chavez focused, though, on the man at the eastern portion of the roof now, just twenty-five feet or so from where the American knelt. The terrorist did not have a weapon up, though he was looking right into Ding's eyes. As the

Dagestani struggled to bring his sights to this new target who had just dropped out of the night sky, he shouted in fear.

Domingo Chavez, Romeo Two, double-tapped the man with two .45-caliber rounds to the forehead. The man backpedaled a few steps as he fell.

Ding stood, relaxed just slightly now that the last threat had been dealt with, and he reached for a fresh magazine for his UMP. While doing so he watched the stumbling sentry, waiting for him to fall onto the cold concrete roof.

But the dead man's body had other plans. His rearward momentum continued to carry him back, and Chavez recognized in an instant of horror that the body would fall off the roof. He would land in a heap right in front of the door below, right in the lights illuminating the man walking from the chopper.

"Shit!" Chavez sprinted across the roof, desperate to catch the sentry before he tumbled off and gave away the entire operation right at its most vulnerable point.

Ding let go of his HK, launched off the ground, and in the air he reached at full extension for the dead man's uniform.

The Jamaat Shariat gunman fell backward over the edge of the roof.

79

Israpil Nabiyev climbed out of the helicopter and stepped into the light. Before him the huge building sat in the snow. The thirty-two-year-old Jamaat Shariat leader squinted and took a step on the hard snow, then another, each step bringing him closer to the freedom that he had sought for these many long months he'd been held prisoner.

The butt of a rifle struck Nabiyev in the back of the head, sending him tumbling onto the snow. The blow dazed him, but he climbed back up to his knees, tried to get up and walk again, but two of the guards from the helicopter grabbed him from behind and secured his wrists with metal cuffs. They turned him around and pushed him back onto the chopper.

"Not today, Nabiyev," one of the men said over the whine of the helicopter engines. "The LCC for the Rokot system looks a lot like the LCC for the Dnepr system, doesn't it?"

Israpil Nabiyev did not understand what was happening. He did not know that he was fifteen miles west of the Dnepr facility, and had been duped into thinking he was being handed over to Safronov and Jamaat Shariat. The helicopter lifted off again, it turned around at a hover, and then it flew off, away from the bright lights.

Georgi Safronov holstered his Makarov and motioned for the prisoners to be sent out to the waiting Russian Air

Force helicopter. The American, British, and Japanese men and women, all bundled in heavy coats, filed past him and out into the light. In front of them, the bearded man came closer; he was just thirty meters away now. Georgi could make out a smile on the man's face, and this made Georgi himself smile.

The prisoners moved faster than Nabiyev, Safronov noticed, and he motioned for his countryman to pick up his pace. Georgi wanted to shout to him but the chopper engine was too loud, even here.

He waved his hand forward one more time, but Nabiyev did not comply. He did not look injured—Georgi could not understand what was wrong.

Suddenly the man stopped in the parking lot. He just stood there, facing the building.

In a heartbeat Safronov went from elation to suspicion. He sensed danger. His eyes scanned the lot, the helicopter behind, the prisoners rushing to it.

He saw nothing, but he did not know what danger lurked in the dark out past the lights. He took a step back deeper into the hallway, tucking himself behind the door.

He looked to Nabiyev, noticed the man had begun to move forward again. Safronov was still suspicious. He squinted into the light, stared at the man's face for a long moment.

No.

This was not Israpil Nabiyev.

Georgi Safronov screamed in rage as he unholstered his Makarov and held it low behind his back.

Chavez's gloved left hand grasped the iron post holding the spotlight. The fingers ached and burned, because Ding's body hung off the building, and his right hand held

674

the pants of a dead terrorist just above the ankle. One hundred and forty pounds of dead weight wrenched Ding's shoulder nearly out of its socket.

He knew he could not pull himself back up onto the roof and continue his mission without tossing the body, and he could not toss the body without exposing the mission.

He could not imagine his situation getting much worse, but when he saw that the Russian FSB operator disguised as Nabiyev had stopped dead in his tracks to stare at the spectacle twenty feet above Safronov and his gunmen at the front door, Chavez just shook his head over and over, hoping to get the man moving again. The man did move again, fortunately, so Ding went back to concentrating on not dropping the body or losing his own grip.

Just then, above him in the snowy sky, he saw the movement of several shapes.

Rainbow operators under their chutes.

And below him, twenty feet from the tips of his swinging boots, he heard gunfire.

Safronov ordered one of his men to go out to Nabiyev and check him for explosives. The Dagestani gunman complied without question; he ran out into the lights and the snowfall with his rifle in his hand.

He made it ten feet before he spun on the soles of his boots and fell dead to the pavement. Georgi had seen the flash of a sniper's shot in the darkness on the far side of the helicopter.

"It's a trap!" Georgi shouted as he raised his Makarov and fired it at the imposter standing alone in the center of the parking lot. Safronov emptied the gun of its seven rounds in under two seconds.

The bearded man in the snow himself pulled a gun, but he was hit over and over in the chest and stomach and legs by the .380 rounds from the Makarov, and he staggered and fell.

Georgi turned away from the door. He began running toward the LCC, his pistol still in his hand.

Two gunmen Safronov left at the doorway raised their AKs to finish the writhing man off, but just as they readied to fire, a body fell across their line of sight. It was one of their comrades from the roof. He slammed into the steps in front of the door, right in front of them, and it took their eyes out of the sights of their rifles at a critical moment. Both men looked at the body quickly, then resighted their weapons on the injured imposter twenty-five yards away.

A sniper's round took the gunman on the right in the upper chest, knocking him back into the entry hall of the LCC. A quarter-second later another bullet fired from a second sniper took the other man in the neck, spinning him on top of his comrade.

Chavez pulled himself back onto the flat roof and rolled up onto his kneepads. He did not have time to assess himself for injuries, he only had time to heft his weapon and run toward the stairwell. His original plan, devised by him and Clark, was to breach the LCC's bunkerlike ventilation shaft. It was nearly forty inches wide and accessible here on the roof. From here he could descend directly to a vent over the LCC, climb out in the auxiliary generator room, shut down the backup power generator to the entire building, stopping the launch cold.

But that plan, like a lot of plans in a military and intelligence career as long as Ding Chavez's, had failed before it even began. Now he could only breach the LCC all by himself, make his way down, and hope for the best.

Twenty Rainbow operators had parachuted from a massive Mi-26 helicopter at a height of five thousand feet, their drop zone was the rear parking lot of the LCC. Their jump was timed so that Chavez would have the opportunity to remove the sentries from the roof of the building, but they were cutting it so close they could not be certain he would succeed. For this reason they all carried their MP-7s on their chests with the suppressors attached and the weapons ready to bring to bear on any threats, even if they had to fight while still on the way down.

Of the twenty jumpers battling the winds and poor visibility, eighteen hit the rear drop zone, a respectable feat. The other two had equipment problems on the way down and ended up far from the LCC and out of the fight.

The eighteen Rainbow men split into two teams and hit the side loading dock and the back door, blowing open both sets of steel doors with shaped charges. They fired smoke grenades up the hallways and then fragmentation grenades farther on, killing and wounding Dagestanis at both entry points.

The former hostages entered the side door of the helicopter but then were immediately rushed out the door on the opposite side. They were confused, some did not want to go back outside, they shouted at the pilot to get them the fuck out of there, but the Spetsnaz and Rainbow operators there kept them moving, sometimes by force. They ran past soldiers who had already filed out of the far side door of the helo when it landed and had now taken up prone firing positions in the dark on the far edge of the parking lot.

The civilians were directed with soft red flashlights to run out into the snowy steppes, and as they ran men ran with them, passing out heavy body armor. The soldiers helped them put it on as they continued out into the desolate landscape.

A hundred yards from the rear of the chopper was a small depression in the ground. Here the civilians were told to lie in the snow and keep their heads down. A few Spetsnaz men with rifles guarded them there and, as the gunfire at the LCC picked up, they continued to order the civilians to tuck tighter together and to remain as still as possible.

Safronov had made it back to the control room. He heard explosions and gunfire all around the lower level of the LCC. He kept two gunmen with him; the others he'd sent up to augment the security on the roof and down to the three entrances to the building.

He ordered the two men to stand at the front of the room, alongside the monitors, and point their weapons at the staff. He himself moved between the tables so he could see the work the men were doing. The twenty Russian engineers and technicians looked at him.

"Launch sequence for immediate launch!"

"Which silo?"

"Both silos!"

There was no system to send two Dneprs simultaneously, so it would all have to be done manually. They had the launch link to 104 in place at present, so Georgi ordered that silo to deploy first. He then ordered a second team of men to finalize launch prep on the second silo, so he could send that missile skyward close behind the first.

He pointed his Makarov at the assistant launch director, the highest-ranking engineer in the room.

"One-oh-four clears its silo in sixty seconds or Maxim dies!"

No one argued with him. Those with nothing left to do sat there, panicked that they would be shot because they had outlived their usefulness. Those with last-second duties to prepare the launch worked furiously, arming the power pressure generator and checking each of the three fuel stages of the LV for the correct readings. Georgi and his pistol were right behind them through the entire sequence, and all the launch engineers knew that Safronov could have been sitting in any one of their places doing their job. No one dared attempt to do anything to thwart the launch.

Georgi would see through any trickery.

"How long?" Safronov screamed as he rushed to the control panel with the two launch keys. He turned one, then put his left hand on the other.

"Twenty-five seconds more!" screamed the assistant launch director, nearly hyperventilating from panic.

A large explosion boomed in the hallway just outside. Over the radio one of the Dagestanis said, "They are in the building!"

Georgi removed his hand from the key and took his walkie-talkie from his belt. "Everyone come back to the control room. Hold the hallway and the rear stairs! We only need to keep them back for a few moments more!"

80

Chavez was halfway down the rear stairwell, turning at the landing, when the door to the LCC opened below him. He leapt back, out of view. He could hear gunfire throughout the lower floors of the building, and he was also receiving the Rainbow teams' transmissions in the comms set in his ear. Two of the three teams were in the hallway on the other side of the LCC, but they were being kept at bay by over a dozen terrorists who held fortified positions in the hall.

Ding knew that the president of the Russian rocket company—he hadn't bothered to learn the son of a bitch's name—could launch the missiles with little preparation.

Clark's operation orders to all the men on the mission were cold. Even though there would be a dozen unwilling participants in the launch control room, Clark had stressed that they were not innocents. Chavez and Rainbow were to assume that these men would launch the missiles that could kill millions—under duress, maybe, but they could launch them nonetheless.

Chavez knew that it was up to him.

For that reason Ding had been outfitted with six fragmentation grenades, an unusual load-out for a mission involving hostages. He was authorized to kill everything that moved in launch control to assure that the Dnepr rockets did not leave those silos five miles to the east.

But instead of reaching for a frag, he quickly took off

his sub-gun, placed it silently on the stairs, then quickly climbed out of his chest gear, only taking his radio set from it and hooking it to his belt. Removing his vest made him lighter and faster and, he sure hoped, quieter. He drew his Glock 19 pistol from his right hip and quickly spun the long suppressor onto the barrel.

He carried special Fiocchi 9-millimeter subsonic ammunition for his handgun; he and Clark had discovered it when training in Rainbow and he knew that, when fired through a good suppressor, it made his Glock as close to whisper-quiet as a firearm could ever be.

Clark had stressed that the entire operation hinged on speed, surprise, and violence of action—Ding knew he needed all three of these factors in spades in the next sixty seconds.

He lifted the Glock to eye level and took one calming breath.

And then he kicked his legs over the railing, spun one hundred eighty degrees, and dropped through the air toward the men in the stairwell below.

"Fifteen seconds to launch of 104!" shouted Maxim. Even though Safronov was only five feet away, Georgi could barely hear over the gun battle raging in the hallway.

Safronov stepped to the remaining launch key and put his hand on it. While doing so he turned and looked over his shoulder, across the dozen Russian engineers, and at the two exits across the room. On the right, two Jamaat Shariat stood inside the doorway to the rear stairs; two more men were out in the stairwell guarding access from the first and third floors.

And on his left was the door to the hall. Two men were positioned just inside the doorway here, and whatever remained of Jamaat Shariat was outside, martyring themselves in the fight to give Safronov every second he needed to get at least one of the nukes in the air.

Georgi shouted to his four brothers in the room with him. *"Allahu Akbar!"* He looked quickly to Maxim seated below him for confirmation that the pressure cap had been charged for launch. The Russian just nodded blankly while looking at his monitor.

Georgi heard a grunt and then a scream, his head swiveled back to the stairwell, and he saw one of his two men there falling backward, a spray of blood squirting from the back of his head. The other man was down already.

The two Jamaat Shariat men across the room saw this, and they had already spun their weapons toward the threat.

Safronov turned the key and then reached for the button, his eyes on the doorway. Suddenly a man in a black tunic spun through the doorway in a blur, his long black pistol high and swinging toward Georgi without hesitation. Georgi saw a flash of light as he began pressing the button to launch the Dnepr, and he felt a tug in his chest. And then a second tugging on his right biceps.

His arm flew back, his finger left the launch button, and he fell back onto the table. Quickly he reached for the button again, but Maxim, still seated at the control panel, quickly reached up and turned both keys up into the disarm position.

Georgi Safronov felt strength pouring from his body in a flood; he half leaned, half sat, on the table by the control panel, and he watched the man in black, the infidel, as he moved along the wall in some sort of run-crouch, like a rat hunting for a meal in an alley. But the man in black fired his gun as he moved; it flashed and smoked, but a fresh ringing in Georgi's ears drowned out any noise.

The man in black killed both of the Jamaat Shariat men guarding the hallway door. Just killed them like they were nothing, not men, not sons of Dagestan, not brave mujahideen.

All the Russian engineers at tables dove for the ground. Georgi was the only man standing now, and he realized he was still standing, still alive, and he still controlled the fate of Moscow and he could still destroy millions of infidels and cripple the government that enslaved his people.

With renewed strength Safronov used his left hand now, and reached back to turn the keys to rearm the silo.

But as he put his fingers on the first key, a movement in front of him caught his eye. It was Maxim, he was standing from his chair, he was swinging his fist, and he hit Georgi Safronov square on the nose, knocking him over the top of the table and onto the floor.

Domingo Chavez helped the Russian technicians secure and barricade the door between the LCC and the hallway, which would help to keep all the terrorists in the hallway.

In Russian, Ding shouted to the dozen men there, "Who has served in the military?" All but two raised their hands quickly. "Not in the rocket forces," Ding clarified. "Who is good with an AK?" Only two kept their hands up, and Chavez gave them each a rifle and instructed them to watch the door.

He then rushed over to the guy he came to kill; he still didn't know the motherfucker's name. He saw a big Russian sitting on top of the wounded man. "What's your name?" Ding asked in Russian.

"Maxim Ezhov."

"And his name?"

"Georgi Safronov," the man said. "He is still alive."

Ding shrugged; he had meant to kill him, but he would not kill him now that he was no threat. He searched the man quickly, found a Makarov and a few extra magazines and a phone.

A moment later, Chavez activated his radio headset. "Romeo Two for Rainbow Six. Launch keys secured. Repeat, launch keys secured."

The Mi-17 helicopters moved low and fast over the flat landscape. A unit of eight Rainbow operators took Launch Silo 103, along with the sniper/recon team that had been in place for a day and a half. Five miles to the south, another unit of eight, again with covering fire from two men in the snowy grass, killed the Jamaat Shariat forces there.

Once Rainbow secured the rockets, specially briefed munitions experts climbed down into the silo and stepped onto the equipment deck to access the third stage. Headlamps illuminated their work while they opened an access hatch to expose the Space Head Module.

A third helo, a Russian Army KA-52 Alligator gunship, flew to within a kilometer of the bunker near the turnoff to the Dnepr facility. Inside were four Dagestani rebels. No one asked them if they wished to surrender. No, their position was rocketed and auto-cannoned until the four men's bodies were so thoroughly mixed with the rubble that only the insects, carrion, and wild dogs that would populate the steppes in the springtime would ever recover them.

And a fourth helo, an Mi-17, landed at the LCC. John Clark stepped off the aircraft and was led inside by Colonel Gummesson.

"Rainbow casualties?" asked Clark.

"We have five dead, seven wounded."

Shit, thought John. *Too fucking many.*

They took the stairs out of the lobby to the second floor, moved through the carnage of the hallway, where fourteen Dagestanis died in a futile attempt to buy their leader enough time to launch the nukes. Bodies and body parts and blood and scorched metal were everywhere. Bloody medical dressings lay in wads and Clark could not walk without kicking spent brass or empty rifle magazines.

In the LCC he found Chavez, sitting in a chair in the corner. He'd hurt his ankle in an awkward landing after leaping over the stair rail. His adrenaline had dulled the pain for those critical few seconds afterward, but now the joint swelled and the pain grew. Still, he was in decent spirits. The men shook hands, left hand to left hand, and then they hugged. Ding then motioned to a man in a camouflage uniform in the corner. A Rainbow medic from Ireland was treating him. Georgi Safronov was white and covered in sweat, but he was definitely alive.

Clark and Chavez stood in the launch control room while the launch engineers, until ten minutes ago hostages here in this room, powered down and reset all of the systems. The Irish medic continued to work on the wounded terrorist, but Clark had not checked on him.

Over Clark's headset a call came through: "Delta team to Rainbow Six."

"Go for Rainbow Six."

"We are at site 104. We have opened the payload container and have accessed the nuclear device. We have removed the fuses and rendered the weapon safe."

"Very well. Losses to your men?"

"Two injured, both noncritical. Eight enemy killed."

"Understood. Well done."

Chavez looked to Clark; he'd heard the exchange in his headset as well. "I guess he wasn't bluffing."

"Guess not. One down, one to go."

A full minute later, a second transmission came over the net. "Zulu team to Rainbow Six."

Clark grabbed the radio. "Go for Six."

A Canadian nuclear munitions expert said, "Sir, we've breached the Space Head Module and opened the payload container."

"Roger that. How long until the weapon is rendered safe?"

A pause. "Um, sir. There *is* no weapon."

"What do you mean? Are you saying there is no device at 106?"

"There is a device, but it's definitely not a nuke. There is a tag on this thing, let me clean this so I can read it. Wait one . . . Okay, it's in English. From the markings on this device, I do believe that what I'm looking at here is a 1984 Wayne Industries, S-1700 school bus engine."

At launch control, Clark turned to Chavez, their eyes met. A moment of panic.

Ding stated the obvious in a breathless whisper. "Fuck me. We've lost a twenty-kiloton nuke."

Clark's head swiveled over to the injured man on the floor. The Rainbow medic was tending to him still. The Dagestani had a bullet wound in his chest that, Clark could tell from having been around others with such an injury, would be excruciatingly painful. He had a second hole in his upper arm. Georgi's breath was shallow, and his face dripped sweat. He just stared up at the older man standing above him.

The American put his hand on the shoulder of the medic. "I need a minute."

"Sorry, sir. I am just about to sedate him," the Irishman said as he swabbed Safronov's forearm.

"No, Sergeant, you are not."

Both the medic and Safronov looked up at John Clark with wide eyes.

The Irishman said, "Aye. He's all yours, Rainbow Six." And with that he stood and walked off.

Now Clark knelt over Georgi Safronov. "Where is the bomb?"

Georgi Safronov cocked his head. Through his short wheezes he said, "What do you mean?"

Clark drew the SIG in his coat with his left hand and shouted, "Goin' hot!" to the men in the launch control room. He then fired four rounds into the concrete under the large wall displays, just past where Safronov lay. The injured man shuddered with new fear.

But Clark wasn't shooting at Safronov. He was, instead, rendering the tip of his pistol's barrel nearly red-hot from the expulsion of explosive gases.

He took the hot barrel, grabbed Safronov by his right arm, and jammed the barrel into the jagged bullet wound in his biceps.

Safronov screamed like a banshee.

"No time to fuck around, Georgi! Two rockets! One nuke! Where is the other fucking bomb?"

Safronov finally stopped screaming. "No! Both Dnepr-1s were armed. What are you talking about?"

"We aren't idiots, Georgi. One of them was armed with

687

a goddamned bus engine. You didn't think we'd have armament experts here to—"

Clark stopped talking. He could see it on Safronov's bloodstained face. A look of confusion. Then a look like . . . like what? *Yes.* Like a man who just realized that he had been betrayed.

"Where is it, you son of a bitch? Who took it?"

Safronov did not answer; he seemed overcome with anger, his pale face speckled with this fury.

But he did not answer.

"Going hot!" Clark shouted again, and pointed his pistol at the wall so he could turn it once again into a searing torture device.

"Please, no!"

"Who has the bomb?"

81

Jack Ryan Jr. looked through the thermal binoculars at the warehouse a hundred fifty yards away. He'd just gotten off the phone with Sam Granger, who told him Clark and Chavez, along with Rainbow, had ended the terrorist incident at the spaceport in Kazakhstan. He'd relayed this to Mohammed and Dom, who were both elated. Now they were concentrating on making sure whatever Rehan had in store here did not come to pass.

"What is your plan, you son of a bitch?" he whispered softly.

His phone vibrated in his pocket and he grabbed it. "Go for Ryan."

"It's Clark."

"John! I just heard from Granger. Great work!"

"Listen to me. You have problems."

"We're okay. We've tracked Rehan and his men to a warehouse at the Lahore Central Railway Station. They are in there now and we are waiting on more SSG soldiers to arrive so we can take him down."

"Jack. Listen! He's got a nuke!"

Jack opened his mouth to speak, but nothing came out. Finally, softly, he said, "Oh, shit."

"He switched out a bomb with Safronov. It must be with him right now."

"Do you think he's about to—" Jack could not even say it.

"Kid, you've got to work on that assumption. When he

learns the Baikonur attack failed, he may reason that the Pakistani government might hold onto power. He will be desperate to start a bigger war so the Army can take control. If a nuke flattens Lahore, Pakistan will retaliate immediately with their own weapons. Both countries will be devastated. Rehan must have a place he can go wait it out."

Again Ryan tried to speak, but there were no words. "What can we . . . What do we . . . None of us know how to deactivate a bomb, even if we could get past the ISI and LeT men holding it. What the hell are we going to do?"

"Son, there is no time for you guys to get out of there. You *have* to go after the bomb. Just gain control of the weapon and our experts here will talk you through removing the detonators."

Jack Ryan Jr. just muttered, "Understood. I'll call you back."

Just then, Ryan heard the low thumping of helicopter rotors approaching from the west.

Caruso was by his side. "I only heard one half of that conversation, but it sounded bad."

Jack nodded, then called out to al Darkur, "Mohammed. We need the best nuclear munitions expert we can find in the area to get their ass here right now."

Al Darkur had heard enough of the conversation to put it together. "I will call Islamabad and get my office to work on that, but I don't know if we have time."

Riaz Rehan stood behind Drs. Noon and Nishtar from the Pakistan Atomic Energy Commission. The two scientists leaned over the bomb; it was still housed in the wooden crate marked "Textile Manufacturing, Ltd." The bearded men made final adjustments to the detonator. They had bypassed the fuses, and now, with the press of a button, a countdown clock would begin running backward from thirty minutes.

When the clock reached zero, the northern half of the city of Lahore would cease to exist.

Rehan had devised Operation Saker's fallback plan some months back. From the very beginning he had known that there were only two ways to ensure that the government of Pakistan would fall. If a stolen Pakistani nuclear device was detonated, anywhere on earth, there was no question that the prime minister and his cabinet would be forced from power in disgrace.

And if a shooting war with India broke out, there was no question that the Army would declare martial law, push out the prime minister and his cabinet, and then quietly sue for peace.

The first event, that Safronov and his militants blew up a bomb, was, of course, preferable, but the second event meant war, nuclear war. It would leave Rehan and the Army in power, but facing the possibility that they would rule only over nuclear ash.

Safronov had failed, so Operation Saker was possible now only with war. Detonating a nuke in Lahore in the midst of the current crisis would start this war. It was a pity, but Rehan knew that Allah would forgive him. Those good Muslims who died here would die a martyr's death, as they had helped to create the Islamic caliphate.

That said, Rehan himself wasn't planning on going out in a mushroom cloud. He looked at his watch as the thumping of the helicopter rotors filled the sky. His Mi-8 was here to pick him and his men up. He, Saddiq Khan, and the four other JIM men with him would leave via air, they would race to the north, and they would be safe from the blast in plenty of time. From there they would continue on to Islamabad, where Army units were already amassing in the streets.

The general thought it likely a military coup could be under way by daybreak tomorrow.

The helicopter landed outside, and Rehan ordered the PAEC doctors to initiate the detonation sequence.

Nishtar and Noon were honored to be the ones who cleared the pathway to the caliphate.

With a press of a button Noon said, "It is done, General."

The twelve LeT men knew their role, as well. They would remain behind to guard the weapon, and in so doing they would be *shahideen*. Martyrs. Rehan embraced each man quickly with the charisma that had been getting men like these to do his bidding for more than thirty years.

The ISI men walked quickly toward the door, with Rehan the nucleus of the entourage. The thumping of the rotors just outside was nearly deafening as the Mi-8 landed in the parking lot. Colonel Khan pulled the metal door open and stepped out into the night. He beckoned the rest of the group forward, but his eyes shifted up quickly at the shouting of an alarm from one of the Lashkar operatives in the second-floor window. He spun back toward the rail yard in front of him, and he saw what had drawn the guard's attention. Two dark green pickup trucks bearing the logo of Pakistan Railways raced across the access road of the tracks, approaching the helicopters.

Khan turned to Rehan. "Get in the helicopter. I will get rid of them."

The trucks stopped just twenty-five yards shy of the chopper and fifty yards from the front loading dock of the warehouse. They parked next to a pair of full coal carrier cars left parked on a spur of track at the edge of the access road, and several men climbed out of the trucks. Khan could not see how many, since their bright lights were in his eyes. He just waved to the men, motioned for them to turn around and go away, and he pulled his ISI credentials out and held them up to the light.

A man stepped in front of the beams and walked closer. Khan squinted, tried to make him out. He gave up, just reached out his hand with his ISI credentials, and told the man to turn around and forget what he saw here.

He never did see the man's face, and he never did recognize Mohammed al Darkur, and he never did see the pistol in the major's hand.

He saw a flash, he felt the ripping in his chest, and he knew he'd been shot. He fell backward, and as he fell, al Darkur's second shot caught him under the chin and blew out his brains from below.

As soon as al Darkur killed Colonel Khan, Caruso and Ryan, both having just climbed onto the coal carrier next to the trucks, opened fire on the windscreen of the helicopter with their booming G3 rifles.

While they fired at the helo, Mohammed's two officers flanked to the right. They ran to the corner of a small switching station on the edge of the tracks. Here they opened fire on the men in the windows of the warehouse.

The LeT gunman quickly had al Darkur's men sighted, and one of the two officers was killed with an AK blast across his legs and pelvis. But the second officer took out the sentries, and when al Darkur made it over to his position and picked up his fallen comrade's G3, they suppressed the men firing at the loading door to the warehouse.

Ryan and Caruso's heavy gunfire killed the pilot and copilot of the Mi-8 almost immediately. Their bullets—each man fired a full thirty-round magazine through the aircraft—also tore through the cabin, killing and injuring several of the ISI guards who had already boarded. Rehan himself was at the chopper's door, and the gunfire, just barely heard above the sounds of the Mi-8's engine and rotors, made him dive to the parking lot, and then roll away from the helo. His men returned fire on the gunmen on the coal carrier, five ISI men against two attackers, but the ISI men were armed only with pistols, and Jack and Dom picked them off one at a time.

Rehan climbed to his feet, ran behind the helicopter, and raced down an alleyway to the west of the warehouse. A surviving member of his protection detail ran behind him.

Caruso and Ryan dropped from the coal container. Jack said, "You and the others go for the warehouse. I'm going after Rehan!" The two Americans ran off in separate directions.

82

Jack turned down three darkened alleyways before he caught sight of the fleeing general and his bodyguard. Rehan was in good condition, as evidenced by the way he ran, and the way he knocked others to the ground as he did so. Sporadic groups of civilians, laden with family possessions, rushed through all parts of the railway station, looking for conveyance out of the embattled city. Rehan and his younger goon pushed past them or barreled over them.

Jack dumped the big cumbersome rifle in favor of the Beretta pistol, and he sprinted with it, alternately finding and then losing and then finding Rehan in a warren of outbuildings and warehouses and disconnected rail cars across the tracks from the busy train station.

Jack turned back to the west; other than the light of a sliver of moon it was completely dark here, and he jogged between two sets of parked and dormant passenger trains. He'd made it no more than fifty feet between the trains when he sensed movement ahead. In the dark a lone man leaned out from between two cars.

Jack knew what was coming; he dove headfirst to the ground and rolled on his shoulder just as the crack of a pistol shot filled the air. Ryan continued his roll, came out of it on his knees, and he returned fire twice. He heard a grunt and a thud, and the darkened figure fell to the ground.

Jack shot the still man a third time before moving forward, warily, to check the body.

Only when he got close enough to roll the man over on his back was he able to tell that this was the bodyguard and not General Rehan.

"Shit," Jack said. And then he ran on.

Ryan saw Rehan in the distance a moment later, then he lost him again as a long passenger train lumbered past, but when it continued on he saw the big general moving one hundred yards on, toward the crowded train station.

Jack stopped, raised the Beretta, and aimed it at the distant figure in the dark.

With his finger on the trigger, he stopped. A hundred-yard shot for a pistol was optimistic, especially now that Jack was breathing heavy from the run. And a miss could send a round right into a building chock-full of hundreds of civilians.

Ryan lowered the handgun and sprinted on as trains approached in both directions.

Dominic Caruso and the surviving ISI captain kicked in a boarded window on the south side of the warehouse. The boards crashed onto the floor, and immediately the two men dove out of the way of gunfire. The captain reached around with his rifle and fired several semiauto shots inside the building, but Dom gave up on this entry point and ran around the warehouse, finding a disused side door. He shouldered in the door, it broke at the hinges, and he fell to a dusty floor.

Immediately heavy gunfire from the center of the warehouse erupted, and sparks and dust kicked up all around Dom. He leapt to his feet and scrambled back out of the doorway, but not before a bullet fragment from a ricochet off the wall tore through his right butt cheek.

He stumbled to the concrete outside, grabbing onto his burning wound. "Motherfucker!"

He stood again slowly, and then looked around for some other way to get into this building.

Mohammed al Darkur grabbed a Kalashnikov dropped by a dead LeT militant near the front door to the warehouse. With it he fired a full magazine at a cluster of men crouched behind a large crane and a large wooden container near the center of the room. Several of his rounds tore into the box; splinters flew in all directions.

Al Darkur spun the dead man over and took a rifle magazine out of his pocket and reloaded, then leaned around and started firing more selectively. He thought it possible the box contained the nuclear device, and he did not feel great about shooting the contraption with an assault rifle.

He'd killed two of the Lashkar terrorists, but he saw at least three more close to the box. They returned fire on Mohammed's position, but only sporadically because they were also taking fire from two other directions.

The major worried that they were all in for a protracted gunfight. He had no idea how much time he had until the bomb went off, but he figured that if he was going to be crouched here much longer he, and much of Lahore city, was going to be incinerated.

General Riaz Rehan climbed onto the first occupied platform of the Lahore Central Railway Station that he reached after his long run. Crowds of passengers were boarding an express train to Multan in the south of Pakistan. The general pulled his ISI credentials and pushed his way into the masses; as he gasped for breath, he shouted that he was on official business and everyone needed to get out of his way.

He knew he had only twenty minutes to get out of town and clear of the blast. He needed to be on this train when it moved, and when it moved, he needed to make sure the conductor kept the train going through Lahore without stopping at any other stations.

Whoever the hell had just attacked him was still fighting it out with the Lashkar-e-Taiba cell back at the warehouse; Rehan could hear the persistent gunfire. He'd seen only a couple of shooters, and they looked like local police. Even if they did overrun his cell, he was sure that no gang of street cops was going to disarm his bomb.

He made it onto the train, still pushing and wheezing, and he shoved his way through the phalanx of passengers standing in the aisles. He needed to get up to the front car, to wave his credentials or his fist or his gun in the conductor's face to get the train out of here.

The train did begin to move, but it rolled painfully slow; Rehan himself moved faster than the wheels beneath him as he made it closer to the front. He punched a man who would not step aside and shoved the man's wife back down into her chair when she tried to grab his arm.

In the passenger car nearest the locomotive, he found a little space to run, then he made his way forward to the vestibule with the door to the outside and the door to the next car. He passed the open door on his right and saw the platform pass by. Just as he looked a young white man in a police utility vest leapt onto the moving car, crashing his shoulder against the wall of the tiny hallway between the cars. He looked right at Rehan, and the Pakistani general swung his pistol toward the man, but the big white man grabbed the general and knocked him against the wall.

The pistol fell to the floor of the car.

Rehan recovered quickly, then launched himself at his attacker, and the two of them slammed their bodies hard against the surfaces in the small confines of the vestibule for thirty seconds before they fell back through the door, into the crowded coach car. Civilians scrambled out of the way as best they could. Many screamed, and some men shouted and shoved the fighting pair back toward the vestibule.

Here they continued to fight. Ryan was faster, fitter, and better trained in hand-to-hand combat, but Rehan had more brute strength, and the Pakistani used this, and the tight quarters, to render his opponent unable to get the upper hand.

Jack saw he wasn't going to win anytime soon against the bigger man while pressed into the tiny tin can of the vestibule between the cars, and he did not want to leave the area, since he knew his friends were fighting to the death for control of the nuclear weapon, so he did the only thing he could think of. With a scream to muster all of his strength, he wrapped his arms around the big general, kicked his feet up on the wall of the vestibule, and pushed back with all his might.

Rehan and Ryan tumbled together out of the train. Their bodies separated as they hit the hard ground and rolled alongside the track.

Major Mohammed al Darkur had given up at the front entrance of the warehouse; the gunfire was just too heavy. Instead he moved around to the side, where he found his ISI captain still firing through an open window.

From the sound of it, there were no more than three or four men remaining prone behind the crane, but they had good cover.

And then the rear wall of the warehouse, behind the LeT gunmen, exploded inward. Wood and mortar and brick blew into the room behind a large truck that continued rolling through the wall, only to crash into the crate and stop. While al Darkur watched from the open window he saw the militants stand and open fire on the vehicle, pouring jacketed lead through the windshield.

Dominic appeared at the new opening in the rear wall. Mohammed had to hold his fire immediately, as the American was directly downrange from him. The major held his hand up so that his captain would check his own fire.

While they watched, Dominic fired over and over from his G3 police rifle into the men. There were four, and they bucked and spun and fell to the ground as he moved on them in a crouch, his big weapon firing during his approach.

"Mohammed?" Dominic shouted after the shooting stopped.

"I am here!" he replied, and al Darkur and his captain ran into the large open room, up to Dominic. The American looked into the long wooden crate, and then down at a wounded militant lying next to it. "Ask him if he knows how to turn off the bomb," Caruso said.

Mohammed did, and the man answered. Immediately al Darkur shot the terrorist in the forehead with his rifle. By way of explanation, al Darkur shrugged. "He said no."

The portion of track where Ryan and Rehan found themselves was still in the grounds of the Lahore Central

Railway Station, and the ground around them was full of the detritus one would find in any urban rail yard; stones and trash and portions of discarded track were strewn all around the two men as they both climbed to their feet after their rough landing from the train that passed alongside them. Jack Ryan knelt for a big rock, but the general kicked at him before he could get it. Ryan ducked the blow and then rammed Rehan in the chest with his shoulder, knocking him back to the ground. As the two men fought in the dirt and rocks and trash alongside the moving train, the Pakistani took hold of a small segment of iron rebar, and it whipped through the darkness and missed Ryan's face by just a few inches.

Jack took a few steps back, away from Rehan, turned to find something to use as a weapon, but Rehan barreled into him from behind. Both men crashed back into the ground. Jack grunted with the impact, his Kevlar vest saving him from a broken jar that would have sliced him open.

Rehan climbed up to his knees, Jack still facedown below him, and the general grabbed a large brick from the trash around him. He lifted it up into the air, over Ryan's head, and prepared to crush his skull.

Jack bucked hard, throwing the larger man to the ground next to him.

Ryan reached out, ready to grab *anything* to use as a weapon, and his right hand wrapped around a heavy and rusty railroad spike. He took the spike, leapt to his knees, and then leapt again, diving toward Rehan, who was trying to climb back up off the ground.

In the air, Jack positioned the spike in front of his Kevlar vest, pressing the head of the iron point against the rigid vest, and he held it there with his hand as he landed on his enemy. He slammed down on him with all his weight.

His body and his vest hammered the rusty spike into General Riaz Rehan's chest.

Jack rolled off the big man and climbed slowly back to his feet.

Rehan sat up, looked down at the iron barb sticking into him, bewilderment on his face.

Weakly, he put a hand on it. He tried to pull it out of him, but he realized he could not, so his hand fell back to his side.

Ryan, his face covered in dirt and smeared blood from the encounter, said, "Nigel Embling sends his regards."

"American? You are American?" Rehan asked in English as he sat there.

"Yes."

Rehan's look of surprise did not waver. Still, he said, "Whatever you think you just did . . . you failed. In minutes the caliph will reign in Pakistan. . . ." Rehan touched his hand to his lips and then looked at it; it was covered with blood. He coughed out a thick wad of blood now while the young American stood over him. "And you will die."

"I'll outlive you, asshole," Jack replied.

Rehan shrugged, then slumped over on his right shoulder; his eyelids remained open but his pupils rolled back in his head.

Ryan heard police sirens that seemed to come from the railway station, a few hundred yards back. He left the general's body right where it lay and began running across a dozen sets of train tracks and toward the warehouse.

*

Ryan ran back into the warehouse with his pistol raised, but he holstered it when he saw his cousin and al Darkur looking into a large packing crate. Dom was talking on his phone with one hand, and shining a flashlight with his other.

Ryan got al Darkur's attention. "Listen. There are about to be fifty cops pulling up in a minute. Can you and your man go out and talk to them, ask them to give us a minute?"

"Of course." Mohammed and his captain left the warehouse.

Jack shouldered up to Dom. "What's the word?" As he said this, he saw the red countdown clock on the detonator switch from 7:50 to 7:49.

"I took a picture of the device and sent it to Clark. He's got experts with him that will take a look and then let me know if we're about to glow in the dark."

"Not funny."

"Who's joking?"

"Are you okay?" Ryan saw blood on the back of Caruso's pants.

"I think I got shot in the ass. What about Rehan?"

"Dead."

Both men nodded. Just then the Canadian Rainbow munitions expert came on the satellite phone and told Caruso how to reset the altimeter trigger, which would stop the manual countdown.

Dom finished with two minutes and four seconds remaining. The clock stopped, and the two men sighed in relief and shook hands.

Ryan helped Caruso down to the floor, Dom lay on his hip to keep his wound from getting any filthier than it already was, and Ryan sat down next to him.

Within another twenty minutes al Darkur's unit of SSG had arrived along with PAEC engineers to render the weapon safe.

By then Ryan and Caruso were gone.

Epilogue

It was five p.m. in Baltimore and President-elect Jack Ryan flipped off the TV in his study. He had been watching the news reports from the Baikonur Cosmodrome, and he'd had two conference calls with his aides, members of his cabinet-to-be, during which the matter was discussed at length.

Also discussed in the meeting was the worsening situation between Pakistan and India. Skirmishes had been reported along the border, but some reports suggested the shelling in Lahore and the areas around there were not by Indian forces, but rather PDF units allied with rogue ISI officers.

Ryan would take office in less than a month. Officially this was Ed Kealty's problem, but Ryan was hearing grumblings from Kealty's people—most of whom were reaching out to the Ryan camp in hopes of grabbing some sort of employment in the D.C. area—that the lame-duck President had already flipped the lights off in the Oval Office. Figuratively speaking, of course.

His phone rang, and he grabbed it without thinking. "Hello?"

"Hey, Dad."

"Where are you?"

"In a plane, heading home."

"Home from where?"

"That's what I called to talk to you about. I've got a story to tell you. I need your help with the crisis in Pakistan."

Ryan Sr. cocked his head. "How's that?"

Junior spent the next twenty minutes telling his father about Rehan and the ISI and the theft of the nukes, about the Haqqani network and the Dagestani militants. It was a hell of a story, and the father interrupted the son only to ask him what kind of encryption his phone was using.

Jack Junior explained that he was on The Campus's own aircraft, and Hendley had seen to it that the equipment was state of the art.

When he was finished, Ryan Sr. asked his son again: "Are you okay?"

"I'm fine, Dad. Cuts and bruises. Dom took a bullet in the ass, but he'll be fine."

"Oh my God."

"Really, he was joking about it twenty minutes later."

Jack Sr. rubbed his temples under the arms of his eyeglasses. "Okay."

"Look, Dad. I know we have to keep The Campus away from you, but I thought you could talk to the players over there in India, persuade them to back off a bit. We do think the man in charge of this entire operation is dead, so it will fizzle out fast if no one does anything stupid."

"I'm glad you called. I'm going to get on it right now."

The call ended a few minutes later, but the phone immediately rang again. Ryan Sr. thought it was his son calling back. "Yeah, Jack?"

"Uh, I'm sorry, Mr. President. Bob Holtzman from the *Post.*"

Ryan fumed. "How the hell did you get this number, Holtzman? This is a private line."

"John Clark gave it to me, sir. I just spoke with him after having an interesting meeting with a Russian intelligence officer."

Ryan calmed down but remained on guard. "A meeting about what?"

"Mr. Clark did not want to speak with you directly. He thought that might put you in a compromised situation. Therefore, I am in the odd position, Mr. President, of having to explain some things to you. Mr. Clark told me you had no knowledge whatsoever about the Russian intelligence—Paul Laska plot against you."

If Jack Ryan Sr. had learned one thing in his many years working with Arnie van Damm, it was this: When dealing with a journalist, never *ever* admit that you don't know what he is talking about.

But Arnie was not here right now, and Jack dropped his veil of self-assuredness.

"What the *fuck* are you talking about, Holtzman?"

"If you have a minute, I think I can enlighten you, sir."

Jack Ryan Sr. grabbed a notepad and a pen, and he leaned back in his chair. "I always have time for a respected member of the press, Bob."

One week later, Charles Alden slammed the phone down in the office of his Georgetown row house just after eight a.m. This would be his first of several calls to Rhode Island, he had resigned himself to that fact. He'd been trying to get in touch with Laska for the past three fucking days, and the old bastard would not answer or return his calls.

Alden decided to pester the man. As far as he was concerned, Laska owed him for the risks he had taken in the past few months.

The DD/CIA fumed as he left his office and headed downstairs to his kitchen for another cup of coffee. He had not bothered to put on a suit this morning, a rarity for a Tuesday. Instead he would sit in his warm-ups and drink coffee and call Paul goddamned Laska until the son of a bitch answered his phone.

A knock at the front door diverted Alden from his route to the kitchen.

He looked through the peephole. A couple of suits in trench coats stood on his stoop. Behind them, a government Chrysler was double-parked on the snowy street.

He pegged the men for CIA security officers. He could not imagine what these guys wanted.

Charles opened the door.

The men entered quickly without waiting for an invitation. "Mr. Alden, I am Special Agent Caruthers, and this is Special Agent Delacort with the FBI. I'm going to have to ask you to turn around and face the wall, please."

"Wha . . . What the hell is going on?"

"I'll explain everything shortly. For your and my safety, please face the wall, sir."

Alden turned slowly on legs that suddenly felt weak and slack. Handcuffs were placed on his wrists and then the pockets of his warm-up pants were professionally gone through by Delacort. Caruthers stood back in the doorway, watching the street.

"What the hell do you think you are doing?"

Alden was turned toward his front door and walked back out into the cold. "You are under arrest, Mr. Alden," said Caruthers as they headed down the icy steps to the street.

"What the fuck? What is the charge?"

"Four counts of unauthorized disclosure of national defense information and four counts of unauthorized retention of national defense information."

Alden added it up in his head quickly. He was facing more than thirty years behind bars.

"Bullshit! This is bullshit!"

"Yes, sir," said Caruthers as he put his hand on Alden's head and guided him into the back of the Chrysler. Delacort had already slid behind the wheel.

Charles Alden said, "Ryan! This is Ryan's doing! I get it. The witch hunt has begun, right?"

"I wouldn't know, sir," said Caruthers, and the Chrysler drove off toward downtown.

The same day, Judith Cochrane left her Pueblo, Colorado, hotel at nine-thirty in the morning, and she began her familiar drive to ADX Florence.

Her client would finally be removed from the Special Administrative Measures and transferred to a better facility on the East Coast; they had not told her where yet for security reasons, but she knew it would be somewhere in the D.C. area, so it would be close to her home.

Without the SAMs, Saif Rahman Yasin would be able to sit in a room with her while they worked together on his case, close over a table. Sometimes there would be other attorneys present, and the guards would be ever present, but there would be a modicum of privacy, and Judith Cochrane had thought of little else for some time.

Too bad that conjugal visits would not be allowed. Judy smiled as that thought came to her.

Well, a girl can dream, can't she?

The rental car began making an odd noise that she hadn't heard before. "Damn it," she said, as it got louder and louder. It was a thumping, and she did not know cars at all, other than where to put the gas.

As it grew even louder, she slowed her vehicle. She had the entire road to herself, and there was nothing but flat country around her and huge mountains far to the west.

She decided to pull over to the side of the road, but just as she started to do so, she was startled by a huge shadow passing over her car.

Then she saw it, a big black helicopter streaked just overhead, flew up the road another hundred yards, and then turned sideways, blocking her path.

She stopped the rental car in the middle of the road.

The helicopter landed, and men with guns jumped out, ran up to her with their guns pointed at her, and when they got close she could hear their screaming.

She was pulled out of her car, turned around, and pushed up on the hood. Her legs were kicked open, and she was frisked.

"What do you want?"

"Judith Cochrane. You are under arrest."

"On what goddamned charge?"

"Espionage, Ms. Cochrane."

"Oh, that's ridiculous! I'll drag every last one of you before a judge tomorrow morning and your shitty careers will be over!"

"Yes, ma'am."

Judith screamed at the officers and demanded their badge numbers, but they ignored her. They handcuffed her, and she called them fascists and robots and vermin, and she called them sons of bitches as they led her to the helicopter and helped her on board.

She was still screaming when the helicopter took off, turned to the east, and flew away.

She would not know it for some time, but she had been sold out by Paul Laska in an attempt to save himself.

The Emir sucked fresh air into his lungs for the first time in months. It was dark when he was led out of ADX

Florence and into the back of a Bureau of Prisons van, and the heavy snow further obstructed his view.

He had been looking forward to this day for months, since Judy Cochrane had promised him she would get him out of his tiny cell and into a federal prison near Washington. A prison where he could exercise and watch television and have more books and access to other members of his defense who would help him fight the Ryan administration.

As the van rolled through the entrance of a small airport, the Emir fought a smile. The next stage in his captivity would be the next stage in his quest to damage the infidels. He would get time in court, Judy had told him, and he would have a chance to say whatever he wanted to say. At first he had been instructed not to say a word about his capture, but now Judy encouraged him to talk as loudly and as often as possible about the circumstances of his kidnapping at the hands of Americans. Although he had been captured in the United States, he intended to continue his story—he'd told it so many times to Judy that he himself almost believed it now—that he had been yanked off a street in Riyadh.

Judy believed it; that fat fool would believe anything.

The van lurched to a stop, and the FBI men helped him out and into a blinding snowstorm. They led him forward, and in seconds Yasin could smell jet fuel as he approached a large aircraft. He'd expected some sort of corporate jet, but instead it was a large cargo craft.

He began walking up the ramp with the men on either side of him. At the top of the ramp there was no snow, only several men who stood at attention.

They were wearing camouflage uniforms.

They were soldiers. American military.

The FBI man tapped Yasin on the shoulder. "Have fun at Gitmo, asshole."

What? Yasin tried to back up, but men held him. "No! I will not go. I am to go to Washington for my trial. This is incorrect. Where is Judith?"

The FBI man smiled. "Right now she's in custody in Denver."

They gave him one more try to walk forward, but when he refused, four muscular young men grabbed his arms and legs. He was lifted into the air and carried inside the aircraft. Seconds later the ramp lifted, and it closed on the Colorado snowstorm, stifling his screams of protest.

Jack and Melanie enjoyed their dinner, their wine, and their conversation. They had not seen each other in weeks, and although their last parting had been awkward, the chemistry between them seemed undamaged.

Ryan was glad Melanie had not asked too many questions about the cuts on his face. He told her he was back into his MMA classes and a new student had gotten a little overzealous in training. She seemed to believe him, and the conversation had drifted off his face and onto all the news about his dad's upcoming inauguration and the near disaster in Russia and the averted war between India and Pakistan.

Melanie told Jack about Rehan. He had been on the news to some degree, and the CIA/NCTC analyst was careful to keep her detail in the realm of open-source information. Ryan pled ignorance and showed his fascination with her work, but he was, himself, careful to avoid conveying anything that might make her suspicious that he knew more than he was saying.

But then she said something that made him lose his polite but only mildly interested gaze.

"Too bad they let his number-two guy slip away."

"What's that?" Jack said.

"I think it's been on the news, in Pakistan, at least. Yes, I'm sure I read it in *Dawn* today, their paper. A colonel who worked for him, Saddiq Khan. He survived and is missing. You never really know in these situations if that is significant or not."

Jack nodded, then said, "How about some dessert?"

They ordered dessert, and Jack excused himself to go to the bathroom. When he was out of view, Melanie stood quickly and stepped outside the restaurant; her mobile phone was already to her ear when the door shut behind her.

She waited for a moment for an answer on the other end, her eyes fixed on the lobby of the restaurant, careful for any signs that Jack was on his way back to the table.

"It's me. He was there, in Pakistan. . . . Yes. There is no doubt in my mind. When I told him Khan was still alive he looked like he'd been poleaxed. No, of course it's not true, but right now he's in a bathroom stall, no doubt calling someone in a panic, trying to get confirmation."

The young woman listened to her instructions, acknowledged them, then ended the call and rushed back inside to wait for her date to return to the table.

He just wanted a decent book to read ...

Not too much to ask, is it? It was in 1935 when Allen Lane, Managing Director of Bodley Head Publishers, stood on a platform at Exeter railway station looking for something good to read on his journey back to London. His choice was limited to popular magazines and poor-quality paperbacks – the same choice faced every day by the vast majority of readers, few of whom could afford hardbacks. Lane's disappointment and subsequent anger at the range of books generally available led him to found a company – and change the world.

'We believed in the existence in this country of a vast reading public for intelligent books at a low price, and staked everything on it'
Sir Allen Lane, 1902–1970, founder of Penguin Books

The quality paperback had arrived – and not just in bookshops. Lane was adamant that his Penguins should appear in chain stores and tobacconists, and should cost no more than a packet of cigarettes.

Reading habits (and cigarette prices) have changed since 1935, but Penguin still believes in publishing the best books for everybody to enjoy. We still believe that good design costs no more than bad design, and we still believe that quality books published passionately and responsibly make the world a better place.

So wherever you see the little bird – whether it's on a piece of prize-winning literary fiction or a celebrity autobiography, political tour de force or historical masterpiece, a serial-killer thriller, reference book, world classic or a piece of pure escapism – you can bet that it represents the very best that the genre has to offer.

Whatever you like to read – trust Penguin.